THE STOCKHOLM SYNDICATE

and

THE PALERMO AMBUSH

By the same author

SINISTER TIDE
THIS UNITED STATE
THE SISTERHOOD
THE CAULDRON
PRECIPICE
FURY
THE POWER
BY STEALTH
CROSS OF FIRE
WHIRLPOOL
SHOCKWAVE
THE GREEK KEY
THE JANUS MAN
COVER STORY
TERMINAL
THE LEADER AND THE DAMNED
DOUBLE JEOPARDY
THE STOCKHOLM SYNDICATE
AVALANCHE EXPRESS
THE STONE LEOPARD
YEAR OF THE GOLDEN APE
TARGET 5
THE HEIGHTS OF ZERVOS
TRAMP IN ARMOUR

Colin Forbes, born in Hampstead, London, writes a novel every year. For the past twenty-plus years he has earned his living solely as a full-time writer.

An international bestseller, each book has been published worldwide. He is translated into thirty languages.

He has explored most of Western Europe, the East and West coasts of America, and has visited Africa and Asia. He lives in the countryside well south of London.

Surveys have shown that his readership is divided almost equally between men and women.

THE STOCKHOLM SYNDICATE

and

THE PALERMO AMBUSH

COLIN FORBES

PAN BOOKS

The Stockholm Syndicate first published 1981 by William Collins & Co. Ltd
The Palermo Ambush first published 1972 by William Collins & Co. Ltd

This omnibus edition published 2002 by Pan Books
an imprint of Pan Macmillan Ltd
Pan Macmillan, 20 New Wharf Road, London N1 9RR
Basingstoke and Oxford
Associated companies throughout the world
www.panmacmillan.com

ISBN 0 330 41508 5

1 3 5 7 9 8 6 4 2

A CIP catalogue record for this book is available from the British Library.

Typeset by CentraCet Limited, Cambridge
Printed and bound in Great Britain by
Mackays of Chatham plc, Chatham, Kent

THE STOCKHOLM SYNDICATE

For Jane

Author's Note

I would like to record my appreciation for the help and time the following provided in my research, and to emphasize that they are in no way responsible for any errors of fact,

Henry Augustsson (goldsmith), Iwan Hedman (the Swedish Army), Otto Holm (the Swedish police), Marie-Louise Telegin, and two others who must remain nameless.

Chapter One

The deadly game had begun. It was close to midnight, and Jules Beaurain started across the *Grande Place*. His manner apparently relaxed, his eyes were everywhere as he scanned windows, rooftops, doorways for any sign of the slightest movement.

'I don't like the idea. You'll be a sitting duck for their best marksman,' Sergeant Henderson had warned him.

'A *mobile* duck,' Beaurain had replied. 'And your men will be all along the route.'

'I can't guarantee they see him before he sees you,' the Scot had persisted. 'It only takes one bullet . . .'

'That's enough talk, Jock,' Beaurain had said. 'We're going to do it. Warn all the gunners I want him taken alive.'

So now they were doing it, and Brussels was almost deserted on this warm June night. A few tourists stood on the edges of the square, reluctant to go to bed but unsure of what to do next. Beaurain continued towards the far, dark side. Forty years old, five feet ten, thick hair and eyebrows dark, the hair brushed back over a high forehead, he had a military touch in the way he held himself, an impression reinforced by a trim moustache and strong jaw.

Born in Liège of an English mother and a Belgian father he had by the age of thirty-seven risen to the rank of Chief Superintendent in the Belgian police in command of the anti-terrorist division. A year later he had resigned from the police when Julie, his English wife, was caught in terrorist crossfire during a hijack at Athens airport, and died. Since then he had built up Telescope.

A curtain moved in a high window. It was at third-floor level, an excellent firing-point. The curtain parted. A man in a vest leaned on the window ledge, peering down into the *place*. Beaurain ignored him. The window was well lit, silhouetting the watcher. A professional wouldn't make that mistake.

This was the third time he had followed this route at the same hour. Always before he had varied both route and timing. It was the only way to stay alive once you were the Syndicate's target. He paused at the entrance to the rue des Bouchers, a cobbled road which led uphill away from the great open space of the *place*. He wished to God he could smoke a cigarette.

'No cigarettes,' Henderson said. 'It would help pick you out from a distance. Make it difficult – make him come to you . . .'

Beaurain took one last glance over his shoulder into the *place*. He shrugged, confident that the tourists were innocent enough, and started up the cobbles. Instinct told him the attack would come in this narrow street. Leading off it were half-a-dozen possible escape routes, alleys, side streets.

'Keep to the shadows,' Henderson said. 'It will upset his aim . . .'

Maintaining an even pace, Beaurain climbed the street. Henderson had twenty armed men at strategic positions along his route. Some would be at street level; others at upper floor windows overlooking the route. Some would be on the rooftops, he felt sure. And somewhere Henderson would have his command post, linked with every man by walkie-talkie. That was the moment the drunk appeared, staggering down the street towards him. He was singing softly to himself. Then he stopped, leaned against a wall and upended a bottle with his left hand. It was Stig Palme, one of Henderson's gunners. He was keeping his right hand free for his pistol. He stood against the wall as the Belgian passed. A pattern was beginning to emerge. Palme was the back-up man, the gunner who would change direction and reel up behind Beaurain covering his rear. Now there was a fresh problem – more light.

Through windows open to the warm night he heard the babble of diners' voices, the laughter of women and the clink of glasses. He had no option but to walk through the shafts of light, a slow-moving silhouette.

Beaurain was dressed casually, in a dark polo-necked sweater, dark blue slacks and rubber-soled shoes. He carried a jacket over his right arm. And then he saw something which really worried him.

Ahead on his route he saw a van parked at an intersection with a side street. *Boucher* was inscribed in large white letters across the rear doors. Each door had a window high up, like portholes. Why had he assumed that the Syndicate would send only one man? Supposing they had surrounded his route with a team to guide the killer to his objective. Above all, who would be taking delivery of meat at this hour of the night? Something brushed against his leg.

He didn't jump. He didn't pause. He glanced swiftly down. A fat tabby brushed against him again and then padded ahead, tail waving like a pennant, stopping at intervals to make sure Beaurain was still with him. As he passed a side street on his right he saw two lovers entwined in an embrace. Good cover for a gunman, Beaurain realised. If only Palme, whose voice he could just hear, were nearer. But the couple hadn't moved before he lost sight of them. And it was too late now to do anything about it. Palme would have to cope with them if they were trouble. Beaurain's eyes were now glued on the two windows at the rear of the parked van. The enemy could be watching his approach, and he had to watch several ways at once – the van, the various branches of the intersection and the windows above the restaurants.

And then it happened in the one way they had felt sure it would not happen. The assassin chose the direct approach. He appeared out of nowhere at the corner close to the parked van, a short, heavily-built man wearing a light raincoat, lifting with both hands a large Luger pistol, the muzzle obscenely enlarged with the attached silencer.

Beaurain had a brief impression – a plump face, cold eyes – then he flung away his jacket as he dropped to the cobbles, rolling sideways with great agility. The gunman had two choices – swing the gun in an arc and lower it to the target, or lower the gun and then swing it in an arc. He chose the latter. The wrong one. It gave Beaurain two extra seconds.

Raising the gas-pistol he had been holding beneath his jacket Beaurain aimed and fired in one movement. The tear-gas missile hit the gunman in the chest, exploded, smothered his face. The van doors were thrown open and Henderson had leapt from his command post. Using both hands he grabbed the assassin's gun arm, wrenched it upwards and backwards in one violent movement. Something cracked. The man opened his mouth to scream.

Palme had covered an astonishing distance uphill. His clenched fist hit the open mouth, stifling the scream, then his knee drove into the gunman's stomach. The man would have jack-knifed forward under the impetus of the blow, but he was held in Henderson's fierce grip. Henderson was wearing a gas-mask, but the tear-gas was affecting Palme and he was forced to retreat.

Others, also in gas-masks, had appeared from inside

the van and they crowded round Henderson and his prisoner, helping to haul and lift their captive into the vehicle. The rear doors closed. Henderson tore off his gas-mask, handed it to the driver and told him to get moving. Palme picked up the gunman's Luger, gave it to Henderson and climbed in beside the driver.

Beaurain had retrieved his jacket and hidden his pistol. 'I have a car down this side street,' Henderson said; but Beaurain was momentarily distracted. Framed in the nearest restaurant window he saw a woman's head appear as she allowed a waiter to light her cigarette. The woman had dark hair; she was dining alone.

'We'd better move, sir,' Henderson urged.

Only when he was settled in the passenger seat, and Beaurain behind the wheel, was the Scot able to relax a little, to relay his information. Beaurain started up the Mercedes 280E and began to follow a circuitous route which would take them out of the city to the south.

'Chap we grabbed was Serge Litov. I tailed him once in Paris.'

'They sent a Russian? It doesn't make sense,' Beaurain said. 'Although we did hear he'd defected. Do we know who to?'

'I'd expected they might send Baum. He's even more dangerous.'

'Odd, isn't it?' Beaurain agreed. 'And how did your command post happen to be just at the right place?'

'Partly luck, partly reconnaissance. The gunners

scoured the area and came up with a concealed Suzuki near that intersection. A powerful job – and I guessed it might be the getaway machine. So I told Peters to shift the machine. Then we parked the van at the intersection. Seemed the obvious place. Are you all right, sir?'

'You know something, Henderson? For some reason I seem to be sweating.'

'That'll be the warm night, sir.'

'We may have left a little early.'

'I thought the plan was to get clear of the area and back to base as soon as we had the fish in the net.'

'No, I don't mean the van – I mean you and I. Supposing Litov had succeeded, had killed me. And then you in turn killed him, which could easily have happened. The Syndicate must have foreseen that possibility. So, what would they do?'

'Leave someone in a position to observe what happened and report back. But was there anywhere they could safely have placed a watcher?'

'In that restaurant opposite the side street.'

To let in more cool air Beaurain pressed the switch which slid back the sun-roof of his beloved 280E. 'Probably I'm wrong,' Beaurain concluded, and speeded up to overtake the van transporting Litov somewhere ahead of them. But he still couldn't forget the slim white arm of the girl extending her cigarette-holder towards a waiter. It bothered him that he hadn't seen her full face.

Chapter Two

Sitting by herself at the window table in the Auberge des Roses, Sonia Karnell had witnessed the violent events in the rue des Bouchers with the aid of her compact mirror. Constructed of the finest glass and always kept highly polished, the mirror was one of the tools of her trade. While all the other diners were enjoying their meal and noticing nothing, Sonia was giving an imitation of a vain thirty-year-old who could not stop looking at herself.

She watched the swift and decisive assault on Serge Litov. The murderous efficiency of Telescope's operation impressed Sonia and she decided she must include this in her report. She waited ten minutes and called for her bill.

As she left the restaurant, she ignored the admiring glances of several males. She walked rapidly to the hired Peugeot she had parked a quarter of a mile away. With the roads almost clear of traffic once outside the city, she reached her destination in under two hours.

Entering Bruges was like travelling back through a time machine five hundred years. The old city was a labyrinth of waterways and medieval streets and squares. Her nerves started to play up as she approached the Hoogste van Brugge. It was the man she had come to see who worried her. He did not take kindly to the bearers of bad tidings.

It was two in the morning when she parked the car and walked a short distance down a side street and then turned into the confined and cobbled alley which was the Hoogste van Brugge. Dr Otto Berlin resided at No. 285 during his rare visits to Bruges.

As she used the key to open the heavy door of No. 285 Sonia Karnell never gave a thought to the building opposite.

The cine-camera equipped with an infra-red telephoto lens was operated by a patient Fleming. He started up the camera as soon as she approached the building although he then had no idea whether the dark-haired woman had any connection with No. 285. He kept it running until she had closed the door behind her. The windows opposite were masked by heavy curtains.

'It didn't work – Litov failed. Worse still, Telescope captured him alive and took him away in a van they had ready waiting.'

Sonia was anxious to get over the worst at once, not knowing how her chief would react. Dr Berlin sat behind a baize-covered table in a tiny room on the first floor. The only light came from a milky globe on the table, shaded with dark red cloth. She faced him across the table, her chair drawn up close to support her back. As he said nothing she went on talking, to appease him. Although a native of Stockholm, she was speaking in fluent French.

'Telescope had men everywhere. I saw it all from the restaurant Litov told me to go to. Beaurain came up the street on foot again . . . it all seemed so innocent and natural . . . the van I hadn't taken any notice of, but that was where some of them were hidden . . . they poured out of it when Litov was about to shoot at point-blank range. Litov of all people! How could he walk into such a trap?'

'He didn't.'

Berlin was a fat man, no longer forty certainly but probably not sixty. His greasy black hair hung across his forehead. He wore a dark moustache curved down to the sides of his mouth and his glasses had heavy rims and thick pebble lenses. He wore a pair of pigskin gloves. He had replied to Karnell in the language she had been speaking. She stared in amazement at the reply.

'He didn't?' she repeated. 'But I'm sure it was Litov!'

'It was Litov,' Berlin agreed.

'Then if it was Litov I don't understand,' she burst out. 'His job was to kill Beaurain and escape.'

'No. His job was to infiltrate Telescope and locate its main base. Only then can we mount a plan to destroy Telescope and all its works.'

'And Litov,' Karnell protested, 'having been taken to this base, simply has to observe its location, escape and come running back to us with the information? Litov, of course, will have no trouble escaping . . .'

Berlin leaned across the table. By the glow of the lamp his huge shadow loomed across the ceiling. He hit the side of her face with the back of his hand. 'Never speak to me in that tone again,' he said.

'It was just the shock of what you said,' she stammered. 'The fact that you had not trusted me.'

'You know how we work, my dear Sonia.' His voice was a soothing purr now, but still with the guttural accent which could not disguise completely the harsh menace he conveyed. 'Each knows only what is necessary to know to do his or her job at the time. I think we will leave now. You have parked the car in the T'Zand? Good. On the way we will warn the entire network to keep alert for Beaurain's next move.'

The blow to the side of her face had not really hurt her; it had been little more than a rather bear-like caress. Had Berlin really struck out, she would have ended up sprawled on the floor against the wall, possibly with her neck broken. He stood up and she wrinkled her nose at his soiled and crumpled suit. Berlin took two hand grenades from a cupboard, each of which he examined with care before depositing one in either jacket pocket. They were primed ready for use.

He led the way down the staircase, squeezing between banister rail and the peeling wall-plaster.

Sonia Karnell checked the time. 2.30 a.m. Berlin was a man who preferred to conduct his business and to travel by night. 'Who lives during the dark hours?' was one of his favourite sayings.

She turned on the pocket torch always kept in her handbag and followed Berlin into the street. The houses in the Hoogste van Brugge, all joined together and all built centuries ago, were like up-ended matchboxes – the thin side facing the street. Berlin had taken a beret from somewhere and crammed it on his head.

'You're sure you mean the word is to go out at all levels?' she said. 'Right up to the top?'

'Right up to the top,' he assured her.

There was no change of expression behind the thick pebble glasses as her torch caught the lenses for a second, but Berlin knew the reason for her checking, for her surprise. The word would now go out which was rarely invoked, the word which would alert a whole army of watchers to observe and report on the activities, movements and conversations of Jules Beaurain, head of Telescope. The code-word was *Zenith.*

It would go out to hotel receptionists, airport personnel, railway staff, petrol station attendants, Customs and Immigration officials at ports. Theoretically it would be impossible for Jules Beaurain to move in western Europe without his movement immediately being reported to Berlin.

But the word would also go out to a much more exalted level. Most important of all – and this was what had so shaken Sonia Karnell when she had fully grasped this was a *Zenith* call – the word would go out to men controlling banks and industries who, with the same urgency and motivated by the same fear as the lowliest baggage handler, would report on all and any contact they might have from now on with Jules Beaurain. It would become known throughout western Europe that the Belgian was a marked man. The next codeword would be the one sent out to kill him.

From the first-floor window of the house opposite, Fritz Dewulf had busily operated his cine-camera. The pictures of the woman would be good. The results on the man should be even better – Dewulf was confident. He had him on film full-face as he had stared up and down the street. He hoped it was the man Dr Goldschmidt was most interested in because the doctor paid according to value – the market value.

And I wonder who Goldschmidt hopes to sell these pretty pictures to in due course, Dewulf mused as he settled down to wait out the rest of the night vigil. It was just possible the owner of No. 285 would return later, although Dewulf doubted it; there had been an air of finality about the way the fat man had shuffled off down the street. For the next few hours at any rate. A sudden thought crossed the photographer's mind and he grinned. Maybe Goldschmidt would sell the film to the fat man who starred on the reel! It had happened before. It was not a conclusion Dewulf would have drawn had he known anything about the personalities involved.

Berlin sat silent and motionless in the passenger seat of the Peugeot as Sonia Karnell headed towards Ghent and Brussels. Sonia, who could drive almost any car with the expertise and panache of a professional racing driver – just one of her many talents which Berlin appreciated – was careful not to break the silence. Experience had taught her to be sensitive to her chief's moods; the slightest misjudgement could provoke a vicious outburst. When taking a decision he might not speak for an hour.

'The darkness helps my concentration,' he had once explained. 'I am a natural creature of the night, I suppose. Most people fear it – I like it.'

They were passing open fields on both sides with no sign of human habitation visible in the dark when she turned off the main road, slowing as she negotiated a sharp downward incline and proceeded cautiously along a cinder track with her headlights full on. Berlin stirred as though emerging from a coma.

'We are there already?' he demanded in some surprise.

'Yes, you have been thinking.' She said it in the way someone might say, *You have been sleeping*.

'Turn the car round so if there is an emergency . . .'

Only with a considerable effort of will was she able to stop herself bursting out in irritation. Unlike Berlin, who never seemed fatigued, she was tired and edgy and the prospect of bed seemed infinitely desirable. *Of course* she would have turned round. And what Berlin meant was that if she ran into trouble where she was going he must be in a position to drive away from the danger, leaving her to fend for herself. Sonia did not resent this; she understood the necessity for it. But the fact that he thought she needed reminding infuriated her.

She dipped the headlights, switched off the engine and left the key in the ignition. Next, without a word, she reached under her seat for the Luger. She placed the weapon in his lap and turned away, opening her door.

'Be careful to check that Frans and that bitch are alone before you go on board.'

The warning astonished her. Something momentous was imminent, or he wouldn't treat her like this. They must be close to the climax of the operation against Telescope, she decided. Gripping a torch she made her way down the little-used track. The stench of the canal was in her nostrils. Now she had to climb again, to mount the embankment to where Frans Darras' barge was moored. As she reached the top of the track her thin torchbeam shone on the large bulk of the barge. Then a searchlight – so it seemed to her – blazed on and glared into her eyes. She could see nothing at all, for Christ's sake. Was it the police? And inside her bag was a Walther automatic with a spare magazine. She raised one hand to fend off the fierce glare. From nearby she heard Frans' voice speak in French.

'It is her, Rosa. You can put out the light.'

Sonia, blinded still, gave full vent to her feelings.

'You stupid bitch! You could have called out instead of lighting up the whole world with that bloody lamp.'

It was Frans who came out of the darkness, holding a shotgun, and with her own torch pointed the way onto the barge.

'We've got a *Zenith*, Frans. That's why I'm here.'

'*Zenith*!'

'Keep your voice down, man.'

Frans took the lamp from Rosa and handed her the shotgun. 'Keep a lookout on deck,' he said. He continued in hushed tones to Sonia, gesturing to where the car was parked. 'He is here?'

'He is here. He won't be pleased with that idiocy with the searchlight.' They went below-deck.

'It was my fault – I told her to aim the lamp while I stayed in the dark with the shotgun. We heard the car – how could we be sure it was you and not the police or the other people?'

'What other people?'

Sonia forced herself to speak casually, but could not meet his eyes for fear of revealing her shock at what he had just suggested he knew.

'I mean Telescope, of course . . .' He stopped in mid-sentence. 'I will transmit the signal,' he mumbled, opening a cupboard. 'What is the complete message? I'll write it down.'

'Yes, you had better do just that,' she said coldly, watching his every movement now. 'Transmit over the whole network, "Jules Beaurain ex-Chief Superintendent Belgian police lives apartment off Boulevard Waterloo Brussels Zenith repeat Zenith".'

Removing a bundle of screwed-up clothing from the lower shelf of the cupboard, Darras fiddled with a corner of the roof and the apparently solid back slid aside, exposing a high-powered transceiver. He pressed another button and a power-operated aerial emerged on deck and climbed into the night alongside the TV mast. Now he was ready to transmit and the signal he would send out was so strong it could reach any part of western Europe. He also set a clock-timer for three minutes, which must be the duration of the transmission. Police radio-detector vans normally needed five minutes to get a fix on any transmission their listening posts picked up.

'I will leave you,' Sonia said in the same cold voice. 'You will get the barge moving before you actually transmit?' she demanded of Darras.

'I was just waiting for you to leave.'

'Then hurry.'

Climbing the greasy steps to the deck, she felt the planks under her feet vibrate gently as Darras started up his ancient engine. Rosa was nowhere to be seen. Sonia scrambled back down the path and then up the nettle-bordered cinder track. Berlin had put out the side-lights. He was clasping the Luger which he handed to her without a word. His hand closed over hers as she reached for the ignition.

'You were longer than usual. And what was that with the light?'

Being careful to keep her story concise – he couldn't stand long-windedness – she told him what had happened. With shoulders hunched forward he listened with great concentration.

'What do you think?' he asked eventually.

'I'm worried. I don't like the Rosa woman, but that's not relevant – but I think she has influence over Frans.'

'And Frans himself?'

'He worried me even more. I think he's losing his grip. I'm sure he was going to operate his transmitter while the barge was stationary.'

'That was the point which struck me,' Berlin said thoughtfully. 'Turn on the engine now.'

'You think we should cut the Darrases out of the network?' she asked as she started the car up the track towards the road.

'It is more serious than that,' Berlin decided. 'I think we shall have to send a visitor.'

Chapter Three

When Serge Litov was manhandled into the butcher's van and the doors slammed shut, he was already in pain from the arm Henderson had broken. But in his grim life one of the qualities he had been trained in was to endure pain and his mind was still clear as the van moved off.

He had been placed on a stretcher on a flat leather couch bolted to the floor on the left side of the van which was equipped rather like a crude ambulance inside. A man wearing a doctor's face-mask loomed over Litov and by the aid of an overhead light examined the arm and then spoke in English.

'I am going to inject you with morphine to relieve the pain. Do you understand me?'

Litov glanced at the two other men in the van, sitting against the other side. They wore Balaclava masks, dark blue open-necked shirts and blue denim trousers. One of them held a machine-pistol across his lap. Two pairs of eyes stared coldly at Litov, who spoke English fluently, as he considered whether to reply in the same language – a decision which might influence his future vitally. It would conceal his true nationality.

'How do I know there is morphine in that hypodermic?' he asked.

'You are worried it is sodium penthotal – to make you talk? As a professional man I would not do that – not to a man in your condition.' The Englishman's voice was gentle and there was something in the steady eyes watching him above the mask which made Litov – against all his training – trust the man. 'Also,' the doctor continued, 'you have a flight ahead of you. Why not travel in comfort?'

As soon as he had been flopped onto the stretcher Litov's undamaged left arm had been handcuffed at the wrist to one of the lifting poles. Both ankles were similarly manacled and a leather strap bound his chest. He was quite helpless and waves of pain were threatening to send him under.

'I'll take the needle,' Litov agreed, exaggerating the hoarseness in his voice. The doctor waited until the van paused, presumably at traffic lights, then swiftly dabbed the broken arm with antiseptic and inserted the hypodermic. When the van moved on again he waited for a smooth stretch of road and then set Litov's arm and affixed splints.

Time went by, the van continued on its journey, speeding up now as though it had left the outskirts of the city behind. Litov was trying to estimate two factors as accurately as he could: the general direction the van was taking and its speed, which would allow him roughly to calculate the distance it covered.

Earlier there had been several stops, traffic light

stops, but now they kept moving as along a major highway. He chose his moment carefully – when the van paused and the trio on the opposite couch looked towards the front of the van as though there might be trouble. He glanced quickly down at his wrist-watch; something they had overlooked. Two o'clock.

As the vehicle started up again and his three captors relaxed, Litov half-closed his eyes and calculated they had roughly travelled two hundred kilometres, allowing for the van's speed and twelve pauses. They had to be a long way outside Brussels. West towards the coast? They would have reached it long ago. South towards France? They would have crossed the border long before now – which would have meant passing through a frontier control post and there had been nothing like that. North towards Holland? The same objection. The frontier was too close for the distance travelled. Same applied to Germany – which left only one direction and one area to account for the distance covered. South-east: deep into the Ardennes.

Following the same route, Beaurain had long since overtaken the van. He had by now passed through Namur where vertical cliffs fell to the banks of the river Meuse. At this hour there was hardly any other traffic and they seemed to glide through the darkness. Beyond Namur he drove through Marche-en-Famenne and Bastogne where the Germans and Americans had fought an epic battle during World

War Two. The country they were travelling through now was remote, an area of high limestone ridges, gorges and dense forests.

'Jock,' Beaurain said as he slowed down to negotiate the winding road, 'on the surface I was lucky back there in Brussels. Had Litov been just a second or two faster it would have been me you'd have carried inside that van.'

'We had it well-organised. You were quick yourself.'

'That motor-cycle, was it difficult to locate?'

'Not really, although we were looking for something like that. It was propped against an alley wall very close to that intersection.'

'I see.' Beaurain glanced at Henderson's profile. His sandy hair was trimmed short, he was clean-shaven and his bone structure was strong. A firm mouth, a strong jaw and watchful eyes which took nothing for granted. Beaurain thought he had been lucky to recruit him when he had resigned from the SAS – although really it was the other way round since Henderson had left the Special Air Service to join Telescope. The bomb in Belfast which had killed the Scot's fiancée had decided him to change the course of his life. He was by background, by training, the perfect man to control the key section they called The Gunners.

The radio-telephone buzzed and Beaurain picked up the receiver, driving with one hand. The telephone crackled and cleared. 'Alex Carder here,' a soft deliberate voice reported in French. 'Any news re delivery?'

'Benedict speaking,' Beaurain replied. 'Expect the cargo in thirty minutes. Have you the manifests ready?'

'Yes, sir,' Carder replied. 'We can despatch the cargo immediately on arrival. Especially now we have the time schedule. Goodbye.'

Beaurain replaced the receiver. 'The chopper's ready as soon as Litov arrives. To make it work we need a swift, continuous movement.'

'I have been thinking about what you said in the rue des Bouchers. I think you're right – the Syndicate *would* leave someone close by.'

'Which means that by now they know we have Litov, so we have to work out how they will react to that news.'

'Something else worries me.' The Scot stirred restlessly in his seat. 'I didn't mention it to you at the time because everything was happening so fast.'

'What is it?'

'The safety catch was still on when we took the Luger away from Litov.'

They were now well inside the Ardennes forest. The full moon oscillated like a giant torch between the palisade of pines lining the road. They hadn't met another vehicle in twenty kilometres. Ahead, at a bend, the headlights shone on stone pillars, huge wrought-iron gates were thrown open. The scrolled lettering on a metal plaque attached to the left hand pillar read *Château Wardin*.

The Château Wardin – this was where it had all started, Beaurain reflected, as he drove up the winding drive. The formation of Telescope. For three days after the burial of his wife he had remained inside his Brussels apartment, refusing to answer the doorbell or the phone, eating nothing, drinking only mineral water. At the end of the three days he had emerged, handed in his resignation as chief of the anti-terrorist squad and asked the owner of the Château Wardin for financial backing.

The Baron de Graer, president of the Banque du Nord and one of the richest men in Europe, had provided Beaurain with the equivalent of one million pounds. His late wife's father, a London merchant banker, supplied the second million. But it was de Graer's gift of the Château Wardin as well, which had provided the training ground for the gunners whom Henderson trained as Europe's deadliest fighters.

Recruitment had been carried out with far greater care than by most so-called professional secret services seeking personnel. The motive had to be there: men and women who had suffered loss in the same way as Beaurain. Wives who had lost husbands in the twentieth-century carnage laughingly known as peacetime. Henderson had brought with him several

Special Air Service men – taking care the motive was never money. The Scot despised mercenaries.

Telescope had been involved in three major operations. At Rome airport it had shot four terrorists who had hijacked an Air France plane. No one had spotted Henderson's snipers who escaped dressed as hospital orderlies in an ambulance. And Düsseldorf: a bank siege involving hostages. No one ever worked out how unidentified men wearing Balaclava-type helmets reached the first floor and then descended one flight to destroy the heavily-armed robbers with stun-grenades and machine-pistols. Vienna: a hijack with Armenian terrorists – unidentified snipers operating at night had killed every Armenian and then disappeared like ghosts. But in each episode – and many others – the local police had found the same object left as a trademark. A telescope.

Most West European governments were hostile to this private organisation which achieved what they were unable to. But rather than risk the general public knowing of Telescope's existence, they compromised – allowing their own security forces to take responsibility for the events in Rome, Düsseldorf and Vienna.

'It would make the politicians look so stupid, Jules,' René Latour, head of French counter-espionage, had explained when he was dining with his old friend Beaurain during a visit to Brussels. 'Do you remember that remark I once made to you about three years ago,' he continued. 'That the President regards me as his telescope because I take the long view?'

'No, I don't remember,' Beaurain had lied.

'It came back to me when all our security services were holding a meeting about Telescope – and wondering who could be the boss of such an outfit.'

'Really,' Beaurain had replied, ignoring Latour's searching glance and changing the subject.

Information. The Belgian had foreseen from the very beginning that the transmission of swift and secret information to his organisation was essential if it was to be able to act with the necessary speed and ruthlessness. And in this direction only, money was used; large fees were paid to an elaborate network of spies in all branches of the media, in many branches of government, in many countries. And always they operated through two watertight cut-outs, phoning a telephone number where someone else called another number.

But it was the Château Wardin with its seclusion, its variety of terrain, its hidden airstrip and helipad, which was the key to Telescope. This was Beaurain's main base.

As soon as the van drove in, the gates of Château Wardin were closed behind it. Litov was still awake. He was concentrating furiously, trying to make out what was happening, why there had been a slowing down in speed. Before the sudden almost right-angled swing at a sedate pace they had been travelling fairly fast along a road which had many bends. They had to be somewhere out in the country because he had not heard the sound of one other vehicle for a long time.

Also there were other indications that they might be nearing their destination – a restless stirring among the guards; one of them came over to check his handcuffs and the strap; the doctor was putting his equipment away in a bag. The van was moving very slowly, turning round curves all the time, first this way and then that. Litov began to worry about the English doctor's remark. 'You have a flight ahead of you, a trip by air . . .'

The directive given to Litov by Dr Berlin personally had been clear and straightforward. 'You will be taken prisoner by the Telescope organisation who will then take you to their base for interrogation. It is the precise location of the base I need to know. Once you have discovered it, you use your many talents to escape. It does not matter how many of their people are killed. And when you are taken in Brussels they will definitely not kill you – or injure you more than necessary . . .'

It was this last prediction which had not ceased to puzzle Litov, which had almost caused him to ask Berlin how he could possibly know that for sure; except that you did not ask Dr Berlin questions. How could Berlin have known they would take trouble to preserve his life?

The van negotiated the bends of the sweeping drive lined with trees and dense shrubberies. Half a mile from the gates it swung round another bend, the drive straightened and the moon illuminated a large Burgundian-style château with a grey slate roof. The windows were long and crescent-shaped at the top and a flight of stone steps led up to a vast terrace.

The driver swung onto a track round the side of the château and continued through dense woodland. Well out of sight of the château, he pulled up in a huge clearing.

Litov tensed. The rear doors were thrown open and a hellish sound beat against his ear-drums, the sound of the starting-up of a helicopter's rotors.

Litov had the powerful scent of pinewood in his nostrils. The guards, taking one end of his stretcher each, lifted him out. Litov, out in the open, saw above him a half-circle of dense pine trees, the halo of a moon behind cloud.

He had guessed right: he was somewhere in the Ardennes. As they carried him away from the van he saw Beaurain standing by a ladder leading into a chopper. What type he couldn't identify.

Knowing this would be his last chance, Litov opened his eyes wide before they carried him up the ramp. The chopper, throbbing like some huge insect eager to fly away, stood in the centre of a pine-encircled clearing. No sign of a road or house anywhere. It would be impossible to pinpoint it later, even from the air. A long straight main road, a winding smaller one, presumably a house, probably a big one, and a clearing among pines nearby. There must be scores of such places in the Ardennes.

They carried him up a ramp into the rear of the machine and laid his stretcher on another leather couch with an iron rail running alongside it. Litov couldn't hear the purr of the ramp closing above the roar of the rotors, but he was aware of sudden total darkness. One of the guards produced handcuffs and linked the stretcher with the iron rail. They were very thorough, these bastards. As if on cue, the machine began its climb into the night.

In the front cabin, which was isolated from the flying crew and from the cargo hold where Litov and his guards were, Beaurain and Henderson sat drinking the coffee made for them by Louise Hamilton, Beaurain's personal assistant. A dark-haired English girl of twenty-seven, dressed in slacks and a blouse which did not entirely conceal her excellent figure. The strong bone structure of her face showed character. The tools of her trade were not those of what the business world knows as a personal assistant. She carried a 9mm. pistol made at Herstal in her handbag and she faced Beaurain across the table. For the whole of the journey, while he was forced to be in one place, she would brief him on what had happened through the day and take his dictation. She began by reporting, 'Alex says it's a straightforward fracture. It will hurt for several days, but it will mend as good as new if he doesn't mess about with it.' Beaurain was momentarily too tired to answer her. Henderson said nothing.

'I've read his file, Jules,' Louise persisted. 'He's got a record that makes me shudder. You think he'll break?'

Beaurain studied her across the table before replying. They had now climbed to two thousand feet and were flying smoothly. The pilot had his instructions and would carry them out to the letter. Through the window on his right the early streaks of dawn, the start of another glorious day. He sipped his coffee.

'Litov doesn't have to break,' he said.

'He doesn't? Then what the hell is all this about?'

'Chief's right,' Henderson said. 'Litov doesn't have to get the thumbscrew treatment, although we may have to drop him down a few flights of stairs so he doesn't catch on. He just has to be tricked.'

The helicopter spent three hours in the air as far as Litov could reckon it, though he could no longer see his watch. He had no way of telling the direction the chopper was taking. All the windows had been blacked out so he hadn't even the moon or the dawn light to go by. At one point Beaurain and the man he took to be his chief of staff came to look at him and to talk briefly with the doctor and the guards.

Fatigue was taking its toll of his powers of endurance and he was having trouble staying awake, when he felt the chopper lose altitude. Three hours. They could be in England, Italy, Spain, anywhere. The doctor left his chair and came over to Litov.

'I'm going to blindfold you,' he said. 'Don't feel too helpless – I'll take this off as soon as we have arrived.'

Litov kept his eyes closed as he felt the band of cloth tied round his head. The chopper was descending at speed, dropping vertically. The doctor inserted ear-plugs so he heard nothing except the faint roar of the rotors. With a bump the machine landed. Within minutes he was being lifted and carried and he knew he was in the open.

They had not, however, deprived Litov of his sense of smell, and the first thing he noticed on leaving the helicopter was the acrid stench of a bonfire. An English bonfire. How could he forget it? He had once been attached to the Soviet Embassy in London. There were, of course, bonfires in other parts of Europe, but . . . The men carrying the stretcher paused and the doctor removed the ear-plugs. He assumed it was the doctor. The men transporting him began walking again. Complete silence for several minutes. They had switched off the engines of the helicopter. No sound of traffic anywhere. Then the silence was broken by the roar in the sky of a large jet lumbering upwards. Litov made a mental note. Only a crumb of information, but Berlin gathered in every crumb available.

'Careful up the steps,' a voice said, in German.

Germany? Yes, or even Austria. Telescope's base could be in either of these countries. Feet scrunched on gravel, the first time he had heard their feet since leaving the chopper. The smell of the bonfire had disappeared. Litov strained every faculty to gather clues.

The stretcher tilted; his head was lower than his feet. He thought there were six steps and then the stretcher levelled out. Footsteps on stone, another slight lift, the footsteps became a padding sound – presumably they were now inside a house moving over carpet. A door being unlocked, the stretcher set down on a hard surface, a heavy door closing, a key in a lock. His blindfold was removed.

The same precise routine had continued for a week. So precise, Litov was now almost convinced he was somewhere in Germany, that Telescope was mainly controlled by Germans – something no-one had even guessed at so far as he knew. There was the bus, for example. The room he was imprisoned inside measured sixteen feet by twelve, the walls were stone as was the floor, and the window facing his single bed was high in the wall and made of armoured glass, he suspected. But it was louvred and kept open.

It was through this high window that he heard the sound of the bus stopping each day, always precisely at 3.50 p.m. He could hear passengers alighting and getting aboard; at least he assumed that was what was happening, but he could never catch the language they spoke in. Then there was something else which he couldn't work out.

At 3.55 p.m. each day another vehicle stopped, smaller, it seemed from the engine sound. There would be a pause of about twenty-five seconds followed by the slam of a metal door. Then the vehicle would drive off.

The daily incident puzzled Litov. His frustration was all the greater because he stood five feet six tall and the window was six feet above floor level. Without something to stand on he was never going to see through the window. And there was nothing to stand on. The only furniture in the cell-like room was his single bed against the opposite wall whose leg-irons were screwed into the stonework. And there was nothing he could use in the small, spotless toilet leading off the cell.

One thing Litov felt sure of: the building where he was imprisoned must be in the country and the window must overlook a country road. A bus only once a day suggested a remote spot. Nor was there any chance of his taking the risk and shouting while the bus was stopped – his interrogator infuriatingly always chose this time of day to visit him and he had with him an armed guard. Each day he arrived sharp on 3.30, bringing his own chair which he later took away.

Beaurain himself introduced the interrogator on the day he arrived at nowhere. 'This is Dr Carder. We need the answers to certain questions he will ask. Until we get those answers your diet will be restricted.'

This was a blow to Litov, predictable but still a blow. A non-smoker and a man who never touched alcohol, he did like his food and generally ate three cooked meals a day. Perched on the edge of his bed, he regarded the men Beaurain had left with him. One was a guard and, because he now always wore the Balaclava, Litov would not recognise Stig Palme, the man who had attacked him in the rue des Bouchers. The other, the doctor, puzzled him.

'I believe you smoke?'

The Englishman, who had used his own language, extended a packet of Silk Cut cigarettes. Litov shook his head, secretly a little triumphant. They had no idea who he was, no dossier on him – otherwise his non-smoking habits would have been recorded.

Dr Carder wore no mask. He sat on his wooden chair with his legs crossed and began to light an ancient pipe. Litov guessed he was in his early sixties. He wore a tweed jacket with leather patches on the elbows, grey trousers, a pale check shirt and a dark green tie. His thick hair and moustache were brown, his weatherbeaten face lined, his grey eyes mild and slow-moving.

'Shall we begin with your real name?' Carder enquired.

'James Lacey.'

'That's what your passport says. We can come back

to that and try again, if you'd rather. Where were you born?'

'I've forgotten . . .'

The guard standing by and holding a machine-pistol made a menacing gesture but Carder restrained him. 'Our guest has every right to make any reply he wishes – after all, we are in no hurry. All the time in the world, if need be.'

Carder reminded him of a man who spins out his job to fill the day, not caring whether he completes a task or not. It was all so different from what he had expected. No threats, not a sign that they would resort to torture. Carder went on asking his questions, relighting his pipe every few minutes, showing no reaction to Litov's answers or when he gave no reply at all. At the end of half an hour Carder stood up, yawned and stared down at Litov.

'It's going to take time, I can see that. You know something, Mr Lacey? I once had a man in this room for two years before he came to his senses. I'll see you tomorrow. Same time.'

Then the door had opened and closed, the key turned in the lock on the outside, and Litov was alone with his thoughts. *Two years!* To stop himself thinking about it he concentrated on working out how to get a sight of the bus which stopped outside.

Carder's wooden chair. After several days of the afternoon interrogation routine Litov decided he needed the chair to stand on if he was ever to see out of the louvred window. That posed two problems. Carder had to forget to take the chair away after one of his visits, and he had to leave the cell soon after he arrived. He came at 3.30; the bus stopped at 3.50 p.m.

There was also the spy-hole above his bed, a small glass brick in the stone work. Litov had stood on his bed and examined the small square, but he could see nothing. Presumably they stationed guards there on a roster basis and he would be seen if he ever did get the chance to see out of the louvred window. But after one week, when the opportunity presented itself, he grabbed it.

It was his seventh day in the cell. Suffering from the steady pain of his arm and a diet of orange juice and water Litov felt it was more like seven months since his capture in Brussels. Carder arrived precisely at 3.30 and began with the irritating ritual of lighting his pipe. When he had it going nicely he looked at Litov without speaking for a minute, which again was what he had done each day.

'Changed your mind?' he asked at last.

'About what?' Litov glanced at the guard, wondering whether he could knee him in the groin and snatch the machine-pistol. But they had it all worked out. The guard stood well back, his weapon held across him so he could point the muzzle in half a second.

Carder, as always, had placed his chair six feet from the bed, so Litov could not snatch him as hostage and threaten to break his neck. The Telescope people seemed to know their business. Then they made their first mistake.

'About your name,' Carder said.

'John Smith.'

'Ah yes, of course. It's a good job we have all the time in the world,' Carder mused and peered into the bowl of his pipe. 'Can't make out what's wrong with this thing today. It's been playing up ever since I first . . .'

The cell door swung open and another masked guard stood in the entrance. 'Telephone for you, Doctor. Sorry for the interruption, but they said it can't wait.'

Carder got slowly to his feet. 'Well, if you'll excuse us just for a minute, Mr Smith,' he said, and left the cell, followed by the guards. The door was slammed shut and locked from the outside. Litov sat very still, expecting someone to come back at any moment, but they didn't. The chair was still there. *They had forgotten the chair.*

He checked his watch. 3.47. The bus was due in three minutes. He waited for two everlasting minutes. He stared at the square of glass brick above his bed. If anyone was watching they would be back soon enough, but it was a risk he had to take. He wanted his first look at the outside world in seven long days.

He needed to see the bus. He moved swiftly, marked in his mind where the chair stood and then lifted it to the window and climbed onto it.

As he had guessed, it was a country road, a narrow tarred road with a grass verge and trees. The bus came round the corner almost at once, a red single-decker. It stopped, the doors opened automatically and three people got off, two women carrying shopping baskets and a man with a labrador on a leash. The bus was there only a few seconds, and then was driving off out of sight. But Litov had seen its destination in the window at the front above the driver.

Fascinated, he watched the passengers walk away off down the road. Another vehicle came round the corner, and pulled up almost underneath the window. Leaving the engine running, the uniformed driver attended to the emptying of the pillar-box while Litov studied the legend embossed on the side of the van which was also painted bright red. *E II R*. Her Majesty's mail-van was collecting the post. He watched the van until it too had disappeared, got down off the chair and put it back in exactly the position Carder had left it. Then he lay down on the bed and closed his eyes.

Guildford. That had been the destination on the front of the bus. Telescope's base was in Surrey, England. And now he came to recall his earlier calculations of time spent aboard the chopper, everything fitted. He was being held at some house out in the country on a bus route to Guildford.

'He certainly took his first opportunity,' Henderson observed, clearly pleased.

'Not a man to underestimate,' Beaurain agreed.

'And the dossier says . . .' Carder was reading from a folder. '. . . Litov was attached to the Russian Embassy in London between July 1975 and December 1977 when he was returned to etc., etc.'

'Which suggests he is reasonably familiar with southern England,' Henderson pointed out. 'He was followed by Special Branch to Woking, which is just north of Guildford, several times. They lost him every time, of course, the stupid buggers.'

Beaurain, Henderson and the doctor were finishing their cold drinks. It was another ferociously hot day.

'We'll keep him here a few more days,' Beaurain said. 'Let him have a few more sessions with the doctor. Then he can go.' He stared hard at Henderson. 'You had better start making arrangements at once to organise the biggest underground dragnet you possibly can. Litov will head back for the Syndicate's base, but he will expect to be followed.'

'He's an expert at losing tails,' Henderson said.

'Exactly. So you'll need to use the leapfrog technique. Whatever happens he mustn't succeed in shaking loose from that dragnet.'

'I'm on my way, sir.'

'And I,' suggested Carder, 'had better get back to Litov. You'll be about, sir?'

'Not for the rest of the day – I have a meeting in the city and won't be back until late.'

Beaurain made his way to the front of the house, nodded as a guard opened the door for him and ran down the steps from the terrace to his Mercedes. Louise was waiting in the passenger seat. From a track into the woods walked a man wearing an English bus driver's uniform.

Beaurain acknowledged his salute and drove away. At the bottom of the drive he turned right and speeded up as he passed a signpost. *Bruxelles 240 km.* 'Well, Louise, we've won the second round. I think we may have shared round one, but round two is ours.'

The imposing double doors of the Banque du Nord on the Boulevard Waterloo in Brussels were closed. Beaurain left Louise in the car and pressed the bell, giving the pre-arranged signal. The left-hand door was opened a few inches. The uniformed guard recognised Beaurain and then swiftly closed the door again when he was inside.

'Monsieur le Baron is expecting you,' the guard said, and escorted him to a small, gilt-framed door. He unhooked a phone and spoke into it while the lift descended. Beaurain approved of all this security: the people upstairs were being informed he was on his way.

'You will be met at the top,' the guard said, and stood aside to let him step into the lift. The lift stopped on the second floor and a second uniformed guard waited for him, a man Beaurain did not know. The guard checked a photograph after a searching glance at Beaurain's face, then led him along a marble-floored corridor to a heavy panelled wooden door at the end. The guard ushered Beaurain in; it was one of those locks you could open by turning the handle from the inside but not from the outside. The door was closed behind him.

'My dear Jules, it is good to see you. And again my apologies for phoning you at the château and asking you to travel all this way at this hour.' The Baron shook his hand and gestured towards the telephone. 'You know I do not trust that instrument for important conversations.'

Something was amiss. Beaurain sensed the atmosphere as the Baron de Graer, president of the Banque du Nord, ushered him to a leather armchair and then mixed two double Scotches and soda without saying anything. The Baron was small and slim, his hair still dark, his eyes had the sparkle of a man of forty though he was a good deal older than that, his nose like the beak of an owl. Then his guest spotted what had alerted him to the tension. The Baron's usually smiling mouth was compressed tight, like that of a man struggling for self-control – or of one who was terrified. The latter was surely out of the question.

'Cheers! As the English say!'

The Baron managed the pleasantry with an effort and sat down next to Beaurain in another armchair. Beaurain studied him closely, remaining silent.

'I am so sorry for dragging you all this way at such short notice . . .'

He was finding excuses to delay saying what he had called Beaurain to tell him. Extraordinary: de Graer was a man of immense character. 'It made no difference,' Beaurain replied, watching his host very carefully. 'I had to come in anyway for a meeting with Voisin.'

'The Police Commissioner?'

What the devil was going on? The Baron's tone was sharp and anxious. Beaurain had the strange sensation that his world was being shaken all round him, a feeling of instability and of menace such as he had never known. Was he growing too sensitive to people, to atmospheres? Perhaps Louise was right when she said he badly needed a holiday?

'Yes,' Beaurain replied as evenly as he could. 'The subject is how to co-ordinate efforts to eradicate terrorism and there should be top people there from the States and from all over Europe. Is something wrong, Baron?'

'You may well be refused admission to the conference.' The Baron swallowed his drink in one gulp and stared at the far wall.

'I have a specific invitation to sit in on the meeting, I don't anticipate any difficulty when I arrive there. What on earth has caused you to make such a suggestion?'

This time the banker looked directly at Beaurain. His grey eyes had a haunted look and, yes, there *was* fear in his expression. He used a finger to ease the stiffness of his starched collar. 'There are things you do not know, Jules. Power so enormous it is like a vast octopus which has spread its tentacles into every branch and level of western society. This morning the Syndicate sent out world-wide a signal naming ex-Chief Superintendent Jules Beaurain formerly of the Brussels police. It was a *Zenith* signal.'

He stood up and walked quickly to the cocktail cabinet. He refilled his glass, adding only a nominal dash of soda. Then he did something else out of character. He went behind his huge desk and sat in his chair, as though conducting a formal interview. Beaurain stood up, put his glass carefully on the desk, and began strolling slowly round the room, very erect. The Baron recognised the stance as the one Beaurain used when on duty in charge of the police anti-terrorist squad.

'Do you mind telling me,' he began, 'how you know about a signal sent by the Syndicate which, so far as I know, has not yet been proved to exist? And,' he ended with deliberate coarseness, 'what is this crap about *Zenith*'?

'*Zenith* means that the person named is to be kept under constant surveillance, that every move they make, everything they say, everyone they meet – all their activities down to the smallest detail, so far as is possible – must be reported to the Syndicate.'

Beaurain stopped in front of the desk and took his time lighting a cigarette, standing quite still, studying de Graer as though he were a suspect.

'I'm sorry, Jules, but I felt I must warn you . . .'

'Shut up! Shut up and answer my questions.'

'You cannot speak to me like that!' de Graer protested. He was standing up, his right hand close to the buzzer under his desk that would summon his secretary.

'If you press that buzzer I'll throw whoever comes in down your marble stairs. Then I'll probably break your wrist. For God's sake, are you telling me you're one of them – the Syndicate?'

'No! How could you believe . . .'

'Then tell me how you know about this *Zenith* signal? Who transmitted it to you?'

'A woman phoned me. I have no idea who she is or where she is when she phones. No clue as to . . .'

'And why, de Graer,' Beaurain interrupted, 'do the Syndicate phone you if you're not one of them?'

'You're not going to like this . . .'

'I haven't liked any of it so far.'

'The Banque is a very minor shareholder in the

Syndicate. That is how I have been able to pass information about them and their possible future activities to you from time to time. You know, surely, that after what I have been through I would never help them in a major way.'

After what I have been through. Beaurain had trouble not allowing his manner to soften at the banker's use of the phrase. Just over two years earlier his wife and daughter had been held hostage in the Château Wardin by Iraqi terrorists seeking to bargain for the release of two of their comrades held in a Belgian prison. It was just before Beaurain had given up command of the anti-terrorist squad. The negotiations had been botched, a clumsy attempt at rescuing the hostages from the château had led to the death of the Baron's wife and daughter.

Soon after the brutal killings the Baron had made over the Château Wardin and its ten thousand hectares of wild forest and hills and cliffs to Telescope's gunners and other staff. The Baron would no longer go near the place.

'It is because of what you went through,' Beaurain told him in the same distant tone, 'that I cannot understand your having anything to do with this diabolical Syndicate. You said the Banque was a very minor shareholder – what does that mean, for God's sake?'

'It has contributed only a very small amount of money.'

'To the Syndicate?'

'Yes – now please hear me out, Jules . . . When I was approached it seemed a good idea to accept their offer because it gave me a pipeline into their system, a pipeline I could use to feed back data to you. And this I have done.'

'That's true. It is also true that you would never reveal the source of your information.'

'I felt you would not approve.'

'In what form was the offer made?'

The banker was beginning to sweat; tiny beads of perspiration were showing on his forehead. The atmosphere inside the luxurious office was electric and to de Graer it seemed it was becoming impossibly overheated. He made a move in the direction of the drinks cabinet, changed his mind, stood irresolutely behind his desk. Beaurain thought, he's on the edge of a breakdown. He kept his tone distant, repeating the question.

'In what form was the offer from the Syndicate made to the Banque?'

'Over my private phone – God knows how they got the number. They have people everywhere.'

'Who made the offer?'

'The woman I am supposed to phone about you. Yes, Jules, for God's sake – about you! I'm supposed to relay every word we have exchanged in this room.'

'The woman has a name?'

'Originally she just told me to call her Madame.'

'Her accent?'

'Flemish is the language she uses.'

'And the offer she made?'

'A shareholding in the Syndicate which would yield enormous profits for the sum we invested. Three hundred per cent annually was mentioned.'

'How do you conceal this criminal act from the other directors?'

'I paid the money in cash out of my private account.'

'You are lying, de Graer.'

The accusation was like a blow in the face to the old baron. Beaurain actually saw him flinch, his face drained of blood. He seemed to age before the ex-chief superintendent's eyes. Beaurain felt sorry for his friend, but he refused to allow it to affect his judgement. He had to break through the barrier he sensed was there.

'You dare to speak to me like that, Beaurain . . .'

'I know when you are lying. I've spent a lifetime training myself to know things like that. You're lying now – or not telling me everything. What really happened?'

'She threatened Yvette.'

'Who?'

'My niece, my sister's daughter. After what happened to my own child. For God's sake, have a little pity, Jules . . .'

'I'm going to smash these people into the ground if it takes me the rest of my life. I just have to know where I stand with you – who I can trust.'

'Hardly anyone now, I fear. And you are in great danger.'

'And the nature of the threat?' Beaurain still kept his voice a distant monotone, hoping to defuse the terror which had penetrated the heart of one of the most powerful banks in Brussels. De Graer did not reply in words. Taking a chain linked to his waistcoat he produced a ring of keys, chose one, inserted it in a desk drawer, opened it and produced an envelope which he handed to Beaurain. Beaurain took out the card inside, which at first sight seemed like a greeting card until he looked at the picture. It was primitive, crude, quite horrible and fiendishly effective. It was a drawing of a child's doll sitting up in bed. Minus a head. Blood dripped from the truncated neck. At the foot of the bed a photograph of a child's head had been pasted onto the card. Beaurain looked up at the banker. 'That's her?'

'Yes, that's Yvette.' De Graer couldn't keep still. He kept glancing towards the drinks cabinet and then forcing himself to remain behind his desk. 'Can you imagine how I felt when that arrived?'

'You have warned your sister?'

'She mustn't know anything about it.' The banker was close to panic now. 'Her husband is a prominent lawyer, as you know. He would create a great fuss – which might lead back to the Banque. I have complied with their demands – supplied them with funds – so Yvette is safe.'

'You hope.'

'Damn you, Jules! Don't say things like that! I have done my best, but the Syndicate has agents everywhere. No doubt there is someone inside this building who watches me.'

'Have you told this Madame who calls you about Telescope?' Beaurain asked slowly.

'For God's sake, do you think I would betray the organisation I helped to build? What a question.' De Graer mopped his forehead with his handkerchief, beyond caring. Then he made a supreme effort and got a grip on himself. 'I am relying on Telescope to destroy the Syndicate. The police and security services are helpless – they are not even convinced this new octopus exists. You would have found that out if you had been able to attend the Commissioner's international conference.'

'But I am attending it.'

'You will be stopped at the door. Someone influential at that meeting has also received a *Zenith* message to exclude you. Do not ask me who it is – I don't know. Don't ask me how I know.'

'This is the end of your connection with Telescope then?'

De Graer smiled bleakly for the first time. Producing the ring of keys at the end of the gold chain again he opened a much deeper drawer and brought out a briefcase which he placed on the desk. The key was in the lock. When Beaurain opened it he was staring at stacks of banknotes which filled the case. Swiss francs; a quick glance told him the serial numbers were not consecutive. Laundered money and quite untraceable. He shut and locked the case and looked at the banker.

'Another contribution to Telescope, Jules. The equivalent of half a million pounds in sterling.'

'Thank you, Baron. Thank you, very sincerely. Now, the telephone number Madame gave you to contact her?'

'She will know – Yvette, my niece . . .'

'She will not know, but we might decide to trace her and put her out of action. Permanently.'

De Graer hesitated only a moment before he riffled through a card index on his desk, extracted a card and handed it to Beaurain. The banker had invented the name Pauline for Madame and he watched unhappily while Beaurain noted the number in his book. 'This is getting almost like wartime,' de Graer commented. 'Your use of the word "permanently".'

'She threatened a little girl's life, didn't she? And you presumably have to report something to Madame about my visit – since you're convinced there is a spy inside the Banque? Agreed, then. You tell her I came to you as an old friend in some agitation because an attempt was made to assassinate me near the *Grand Place*. Tell her the assassin was able to make his escape. Tell her I looked shaken.' He picked up the brief-case. 'Thank you again for the contribution. Before I go, is there anything else you can tell me about the Syndicate?'

De Graer hesitated, then stiffened himself. 'All the members – shareholders . . .'

'Contributors to this criminal international organisation . . .'

He saw the banker flinch before he continued. 'There will be a full meeting in about a fortnight's time. I have been told I shall have to travel to Scandinavia, although where exactly I don't know.'

'Let me know when you get more details,' Beaurain told him as he walked towards the door. 'And from now on use a payphone in the street for calling the Château Wardin.'

The guard on the second floor accompanied him down in the lift. Was there an aura of hostility about the man? Beaurain was looking at everything with fresh eyes. And the guard was carrying a gun in a shoulder holster, an innovation for the Banque du Nord.

As he left the lift the guard did not look at him, remaining behind as the ground floor man took over – again in silence – and escorted him to the main doors. Beaurain paused before stepping out. A phone call could have been made, men could have been summoned. Louise Hamilton was sitting in the passenger seat and her expression was grim.

'Something wrong?' Beaurain enquired as he got behind the wheel.

'That creep in the blue Renault in front is what's wrong. He's given you a ticket. I told him who you were, but it made no difference.'

'I'll have a word with him. Something odd is going on. I'll explain later.'

Beaurain noticed that the policeman was in plain

clothes. The man, lean-faced and swarthy, wound down the window at his approach. 'I was just considering having you towed away.'

'You know who I am?'

'Yes, but that . . .'

'I don't know who you are – and only uniformed branch concerns itself with traffic offences. Your action is harassment. Show me your warrant card.'

'I don't have to show you anything.'

'So now I don't think you're in the police and I'm going to drag you out of that car and find some identity on you.'

Worried by Beaurain's expression, the man produced his police card. Beaurain nodded, tucked the traffic ticket into the man's top pocket and walked away, angry and puzzled. Since his resignation he had received the same courtesies as when he had been chief of the anti-terrorist squad. Was this development the result of the *Zenith* signal de Graer had received? Behind the wheel of the 280E, he said nothing to Louise but switched on the ignition and drove off.

'We're being followed,' she said. 'A cream Fiat with two men inside. It was parked behind me. When that man was giving me a ticket I saw him signal the couple behind us.'

In the mirror Beaurain saw the car. Three men in plain clothes had been detailed to watch him. The terror had started.

Chapter Four

Arriving at police headquarters, Beaurain parked by the kerb and took Louise into the waiting room. Normally he would have told her to take the car to his apartment and wait there. Now he thought she would be safer inside.

'Keep an eye on Miss Hamilton for me, Pierre,' he told the duty sergeant.

He was late for the conference called by Commissioner Voisin so he ran up the stairs, leaving Louise alone in the cheerless waiting room.

Outside in the street one of the two men who had followed the Mercedes emerged from a payphone and Pierre, the duty sergeant inside the police station, replaced his receiver. He glanced across to where Louise was sitting with her back to the window and left his post. The reception desk was now unmanned and there was no-one else in sight.

The two men from the Fiat walked into the station, glanced across at the reception desk and entered the waiting room. One stayed by the door to keep an eye on the corridor. Louise, reading a paperback she had taken from her shoulder-bag, glanced up and froze.

'You are Louise Hamilton?'

The man addressing her was tall and bony-faced. He wore a light trench coat, a soft-brimmed hat and dark glasses. Louise stood up quickly and looked towards the reception desk which she saw was unoccupied. That struck her as off-key, as did the manner and appearance of the two men. The man outside the waiting-room was shorter and bulkier than his companion, and chewed gum as he kept glancing along the empty corridor.

'May I see your identity card?' she asked.

She was already moving. The bony-faced man was not in her way and she kept edging steadily towards the doorway.

'I don't have to identify myself in here. Hey! Where are you going . . . André!'

Louise slipped into the corridor and headed for the main exit.

André was the next barrier to be eluded. He moved back towards the doorway and she didn't think she could get into the street before he caught up with her. She turned as he came forward, raised her steel-tipped heel and ground it deliberately down his shin. André choked off a scream with his hand.

Louise ran, threw open one of the outer doors and fled into the warmth and freedom of the open air. There was no-one about in the early evening, and the Mercedes was still parked by the kerb. She had the key in her hand as she reached it but froze as she heard André shout. 'I'm shooting – she resisted arrest.'

She thrust the key into the lock, swung the door open and ducked down behind the wheel, slamming the door behind her. Only then did she look back at the police headquarters and while she did so she was slipping the key into the ignition lock and firing the motor.

The short, bulky André, hobbling with pain, was outside the entrance door endeavouring to aim a pistol with a bulging muzzle. The tall man was struggling with him, forcing the gun up into the air.

'No shooting, André. Pietr will stop her.'

Pietr? He had to be the man who had given her the parking ticket outside the Banque du Nord – because now he was parked in his Renault a short distance behind her. The Fiat was parked immediately in front of the Mercedes, blocking her in. Except that behind her Pietr had left a gap – to make things look less obvious? – and was now starting up his own engine to drive forward and sandwich her.

She backed the car. Behind her Pietr saw the Mercedes ram towards him and panicked. He backed out of her way at speed and hit a stationary truck. André and his companion were half-way across the sidewalk. She drove out into the street and slammed her foot down on the accelerator. She had to get away before they could start their pursuit. As she came up to the first intersection the lights were in her favour. She turned left into heavy traffic as the lights changed. Neither car could find or catch up with her now. But would Jules' apartment be safe?

*

'I'm afraid you can't go in, sir.'

Beaurain took a tighter grip on the case the Baron de Graer had given him. His smile concealed his dismay at the uniformed policeman's reply. He had not really believed what de Graer had said. *You may well be refused admission to the conference.* He considered shouldering the gendarme aside, but the latter unbuttoned the flap of his holster, exposing the butt of his pistol. Beaurain had known the man for fifteen years, a reliable plodder with neither initiative nor imagination.

'You value your retirement pension, Georges?' he asked casually, and watched the man, whose eyes could no longer meet his, shuffle his feet uncomfortably as though his shoes were too small.

'I have my orders.'

'Whose orders were they?'

'Commissioner Voisin himself posted me at these doors.' Beaurain snatched the pistol from his holster with his left hand and pushed the guard aside with his right, bursting into the large room beyond and slamming the door closed behind him.

The conference room was furnished with a long, wooden table seating about a dozen people. Commissioner Camille Voisin, large in body with a wide thin mouth and small eyes which moved restlessly like his plump hands, was in the chair. Beaurain glanced round at the others, all of whom he had known for years, high-ranking security officials from Western Europe, and Ed Cottel of the CIA.

'My apologies for arriving late,' Beaurain began smoothly, noting there was no place for him, 'but I got held up.'

'You are not included in this meeting, Beaurain.'

It was Voisin who had spoken, rising from his chair to show his displeasure and more of his gross figure. He stared at Beaurain and made one of the obvious comments he was notorious for.

'You have a pistol in your hand.'

'Brilliant! It belongs to the idiot outside who tried to refuse me admission.'

'Exactly as ordered.'

'My invitation came direct from the Minister, Voisin. Do you wish to contact him?'

Voisin's pudgy hands fluttered aimlessly, conveying to his colleagues how impossible life was. There was a phone on the table but he made no attempt to call the Minister.

'Jules, come and sit next to me.' His old friend Ed Cottel had collected a seat from by the wall and placed it next to his own. Beaurain opened the door and shoved the pistol back into the holster of the guard standing disconsolately outside. 'Do be careful not to lose this again,' Beaurain said severely. As he sat down next to the American he exchanged salutations with the others.

René Latour of French counter-espionage, an odd note in a gathering of policemen. Harry Fondberg from Stockholm, chief of Säpo, the Swedish secret police. Peter Hausen, the shrewd chief of Kriminalpolizei from Wiesbaden, sat in another chair. Voisin stared at him, and he decided to go on the offensive.

'I appreciate being asked to attend this meeting, but perhaps I could be briefly informed of its subject?'

'Voisin couldn't be brief if the doubling of his salary depended on it,' Cottel commented loudly.

'There are two subjects on the agenda,' Voisin snapped. 'The first is the location and destruction of Telescope, the private army of terrorists operating inside Western Europe and the United States. We have been instructed by my Minister to identify the top man in this subversive organisation, to locate their base and their sources of finance.'

'*You* may have been instructed to do this by *your* Minister,' Cottel interrupted, 'but his instructions hardly apply to Washington or, I should have thought, to any representative of any other country present. Furthermore . . .' Cottel rolled on as Voisin opened and closed his mouth, 'furthermore I have to challenge your description of Telescope.'

'I was not, of course, suggesting that anyone else is bound by my Minister's instructions . . .' Voisin began hastily.

'I have to challenge your description,' Cottel continued, 'because during the past two years the Telescope people, as they call themselves – perhaps because they see further than some of us – have been responsible for knocking out at least forty-five top terrorists, during airport hijacks, embassy sieges and kidnap rescues. There are colleagues of mine who unofficially approve of Telescope for what it has achieved.'

'You suggest nothing be done about these pirates?' Voisin was angry at the murmurings of approval which had greeted Cottel's opinion. The American ignored the question.

'Commissioner, shouldn't you tell Jules Beaurain the second item on our agenda?'

'It is a co-ordinated discussion on whether another criminal organisation known as the Syndicate exists.'

'Of course it exists. We all know it,' Cottel said with disgust, 'but we don't like admitting it. We do know that millions of dollars have moved to Western Europe to help finance it. We suspect that several American multi-national corporations have transferred vast sums to the Syndicate. Furthermore . . .' He raised his voice at Voisin again, who closed his mouth. 'Furthermore,' he repeated, 'the sums of money at the Syndicate's disposal are so enormous that whoever controls it wields power almost without precedent. Gentlemen, I suggest the first priority of this meeting is not Telescope – it is to co-operate in tracking down and destroying the Syndicate.' He looked at the Commissioner. 'I have finished, M. Voisin – for the moment at any rate.'

'I agree with Mr Cottel,' said Peter Hausen.

'Commissioner Voisin, I agree with my colleague, Peter Hausen, and, therefore, with Mr Cottel,' the French counter-espionage representative added crisply.

'Shall we have a show of hands?' enquired Beaurain gently.

'That will not be necessary,' Voisin snapped, anxious to avoid any further demonstration of the united front against him. 'The first requirement, surely, is to prove the Syndicate exists.'

'Assume it exists and go on from there,' growled Cottel and lit a cigarette.

'Who is behind it then?' demanded Voisin.

'The Kremlin,' replied Cottel.

It was 7.30 p.m. when Louise Hamilton arrived at Beaurain's apartment off the Boulevard Waterloo. Confident she had not been followed, she parked the Mercedes in the ancient garage and let herself inside the first-floor apartment.

The living-room was expensively furnished, the kind of place you would expect a widower to live in – except that it was tidy and organised. After her experience at police headquarters she didn't feel hungry, so she slipped off her shoes and flopped onto a couch. The reaction was setting in. She could hear the voice of the detective in her mind: *I'm shooting – she resisted arrest!*

The entire Brussels police force knew Jules Beaurain. He had always been popular because he treated his men fairly and was incorruptible. Since his resignation many of them – especially at headquarters where he was a frequent visitor – had come to know Louise as 'Jules' friend'. They knew nothing about her work for Telescope. The phone rang. She lifted the receiver and said, '*Oui?*'

'Louise Hamilton, *n'est-ce pas*? You had better get back to your own country by the first plane.'

'Who is this? I love callers without the guts to identify themselves,' Louise said coolly.

The voice was a woman's, probably in her early thirties. Her command of English was good but there was an accent Louise couldn't place. Let the little bitch chatter on a while longer, she thought.

'If you hang around we have people expert in breaking legs. Then they go on to the hands. You are left-handed, *n'est-ce pas*?'

'Why not come and deliver the message yourself?' Louise suggested. 'I'd love to meet you face to face.'

'When your face has been ruined you will not talk in this way, I am sure of that!' The voice ended with a note of venom, and the connection was broken.

Louise replaced the receiver slowly, automatically noting the time the call had ended. Beaurain had an unlisted number – how had the woman managed to obtain it?

The second – more alarming – thought was how the caller had known that she would find Louise in the apartment. It was the first time for over a week she had entered the place. She might have been trailed from police headquarters – but she had taken great pains to see that she was *not* followed. That left only one other – equally unsettling – solution. The apartment was being watched on a round-the-clock basis.

She went over to the window and peered through the net curtain. Below she saw the narrow, deserted road. She stared at the first-floor windows opposite but they were also masked. Were there watchers behind the net curtains?

Louise went into the kitchen to calm herself by preparing dinner. Somewhere in the same city another woman was probably sitting down to her meal after making a phone call.

'Did she sound scared?' enquired Dr Berlin as he scooped a generous helping of melon.

'No!' Sonia Karnell had paused before reluctantly deciding that – as always – it was much safer to tell the truth to Berlin. He always knew when you shaded a meaning. Outright lying she would not have considered. 'She sounded like a woman who was expecting just such a warning and had worked out what her reply would be.'

'Like you, she is tough, ruthless – and well-trained. A pity she has to be the sacrificial goat.'

Sonia Karnell, dark-haired, five feet six tall, and thirty-two years old, was Swedish by birth, a native of Stockholm and fluent in six languages, including English. Despite the heat of the evening, Berlin wore his normal black suit across his ample form. As he spoke he looked frequently at Karnell across the table to gauge her reactions. He was always watching the people around him, especially those closest – and none was closer than Sonia Karnell – like a man whose greatest fear in life is betrayal.

'We flew here today just so I could phone her?' she asked.

'Eat your melon – it helps replace moisture. Yes, we flew here partly to make a phone call. Had Beaurain answered, you would have made the same menacing noises about Hamilton – but this may be more effective. When he hears what happened.'

'A sacrificial goat. What does that mean, Otto?'

'Let me eat. The plan is based on the fact that the first complete meeting of the Syndicate takes place near Sweden in two weeks' time. We have a problem because Telescope has as its objective our destruction.'

'How does my phone call fit in? I don't understand.'

'Patience!' The eyes behind the thick pebble glasses studied her. 'I have contacts inside the European police – high-level informers. There is a discreet understanding between Beaurain and certain of his old colleagues who agree with his methods. It was a police contact who informed me Beaurain is Telescope's chief, and determined to wipe out the Stockholm Syndicate. So we must destroy them first before the meeting, otherwise there could be a catastrophe. Beaurain is getting too close.'

Sonia Karnell, her white face framed by her close-cut hair, started eating her melon to please Berlin. The heat was appalling! 'Why threaten Beaurain's tart?'

'To distract him. One thing is needed before our soldiers can attack – we must know the location of Telescope's main base, which we should learn soon from Serge Litov.'

'What's going to happen to her?'

'Gunther Baum will deal with her. That will shake Beaurain's nerve.'

She stopped eating, unable to swallow. 'You are going to use that animal on her?'

'He will produce the necessary effect – fury on the part of Beaurain. This may well cause him to make a mistake. Terrify those you can. Those you can't: upset their balance.'

'And are we going back to Bruges?'

'For a short time, yes. Until Litov returns with the location of Telescope's base. After all, I have to attend to my rare book business if we are to make a living!'

'So this woman threatened you?' Beaurain said as he paced round his living-room. It was ten o'clock: as usual, Voisin's meeting had gone on for hours. Beaurain was very disturbed by the fact that the caller had been able to obtain his phone number; by the fact that it was Louise who had been threatened; above all by the bizarre incident at police headquarters.

'She gabbled on about having my legs and hands broken,' Louise said calmly, 'as well as cutting my face. A regular little madam. I'd like five minutes alone with her. Oh, and none of this would take place if I caught the first plane back to England. She was trying to rattle *you*, Jules.'

'I wonder who the hell it was,' he said.

'The Syndicate, of course. They're stepping up the pressure.'

'They're certainly doing that – to get into the meeting this evening I had to push aside a guard who had been put on the door to keep me out. That can only have come from the Syndicate.'

She sat up straight. 'Surely you don't think Commissioner Voisin could have been got at?'

'That does seem unlikely – but someone at that meeting must have asked to keep me away. As you can imagine, Voisin would be glad to oblige – he's too lazy to take any initiative himself. I don't know. It should have been impossible for the Syndicate to penetrate Brussels police headquarters – but they managed. Those two men were certainly not detectives. What's getting me is how they ensured the reception desk was unmanned.'

'Just before they came in I heard the policeman on duty take a call. When they arrived he had disappeared.'

Beaurain crashed his fist into his palm. 'That was Pierre Florin behind the counter when I arrived.'

'Has he been with the force for some time?'

'Only twenty bloody years. I'll have a few questions to ask him!'

'That woman is succeeding in rattling you.'

'What's rattling me,' he snapped, 'is the penetration this criminal organisation has apparently achieved. We shall have to release Serge Litov immediately – and see where he leads us.'

'You were going to keep him longer,' she objected, gripping his arms tightly. 'Now they are making you react to their timing.'

'Don't forget what Henderson noticed the night Litov tried to shoot me – the safety catch still on his Luger. With a professional like that! They took the opportunity I gave them in order to exploit it themselves. We are using Litov to find the source of the Syndicate. They're hoping Litov will escape and tell them where we're based. Litov is in the middle and probably knows it. After today's happenings I'm going to speed up the process and release Litov.'

Beaurain broke off as the doorbell rang repeatedly. Louise tensed and let go of his arms. 'Who could that be?' she asked quietly.

'It's the special ring I arranged with Ed Cottel. He said he'd call round.'

'You hope it's Ed,' she said, extracting her pistol from her handbag.

'You're right – from now on we don't make any assumptions. And, by the way, he's here on a double mission – to help track down the Syndicate, which he is convinced exists – and also to wipe out Telescope.'

It was indeed Ed Cottel outside and when Beaurain had re-locked the door, the American, who knew Louise Hamilton well, hugged her, nodding his acceptance of a large Scotch.

'This new Syndicate scares the guts out of me,' he said. 'I've been talking to Washington – someone I can trust – since that for-ever-and-a-day meeting. The fragments we keep picking up frighten me more each time.'

'Why did you say at the meeting you thought the Kremlin were behind the Syndicate?'

'Because I can tap a computer.'

Ed Cottel was a slim man in his early fifties. His most outstanding characteristics were his hooked nose, his West Coast accent and his restrained manner reflected in the Brooks Brothers suits he invariably wore. He reminded Beaurain more of an Englishman than an American. He was so independent-minded that the Belgian was surprised Washington had chosen him to come to Europe to collaborate with its security services.

'Tap a computer, Ed? What are you driving at?'

'It's just about the biggest computer in the world, and it contains records on every person of prominence in politics and industry, including the top Russians. You've heard of Viktor Rashkin?'

'The Kissinger of the Kremlin – but so much quieter

that the international press doesn't know he exists,' Beaurain replied.

'At the moment he is First Secretary at the Russian Embassy in Stockholm.' Cottel peered at the bottom of his glass. 'First Secretary – that's a laugh. Leonid Brezhnev's wonder boy and top trouble-shooter – and trouble-maker – and he's only a First Secretary. It's the usual cover, of course. Moves about a lot, does our Viktor,' he said thoughtfully.

'You said you can tap a computer,' Beaurain reminded him. 'How does this link up with Rashkin?'

'At Voisin's comic meeting I mentioned the money transferred from the States to finance Syndicate operations over here. I got a tip while I was in Washington, and I went to the computer and found out about a recent transfer of five million dollars from an Arizona bank to one here in Brussels. The recipient at this end, I'm pretty sure, was Viktor Rashkin. Did you know,' he enquired casually, 'that Rashkin is in Brussels right now? Flew in with some other people aboard his private jet from Stockholm. It's now under observation at Brussels airport.'

'And where did he go in Brussels? You seem to know more about my own back yard than I do.'

'Only because of the computer. We lost Rashkin the moment he left the airport with his friends.'

'Friends?'

'A man and a woman – and before you ask, we don't know who they are and we have no description. So we're not always that smart, Jules.' He stared up at the ceiling, carefully not looking at them. 'One thing you might find interesting. Voisin kept me back after the meeting had closed. I had said in a written report on Telescope that we might just be able to identify its personnel – or at least the leaders. Want to hear the damnfool mistake I made?'

'Up to you, Ed,' Beaurain said, with a show of indifference. Curled up again on the sofa Louise looked tense. 'I could do with some more coffee if you have the strength.'

'Of course.'

She walked to the kitchen, able to hear the conversation through the door. Cottel's reference to identifying the people in Telescope had shaken her. How the hell could he possibly do that?

'Have another drink, Ed.' Beaurain sat in Louise's place on the sofa where he could study the American without appearing too interested. He folded his arms. 'You stayed behind with Voisin. That must have been entertaining.'

'In my report I suggested that the key men and women running Telescope might have suffered personal losses from terrorism. Wives, sisters, husbands, girlfriends. I suggested we made a list of all those who had recently suffered personal loss through criminal and terrorist action. Among that list we may spot likely candidates – because I'm sure that was the motive for starting up Telescope. Disgust with the incompetence of governments. Dammit, Jules, the motive is one of mankind's most powerful – revenge.'

'That list would take years to build up.'

'Not using that computer I have access to.'

'Oh, I see. And you told Voisin?'

'No. Voisin asked me to use the computer to build up the list. If I don't do it, he'll ask someone else. And now I must get going – I'm catching the night flight to the States.' Cottel stood up. 'I'll be back soon. And don't forget about Viktor Rashkin.'

'You think he's a member of the Syndicate, for God's sake?'

'Not a member – but I think he funnels funds through to whoever is running that outfit.' He scratched his head. 'Don't know if it means anything,' he remarked casually, 'but have you ever heard of the *Kometa*?'

'No, but it sounds Russian.'

'It is. One of our satellites has been following its progress down the coast of the Baltic. It's a huge hydrofoil. Normally the Soviets only use them on rivers like the Volga – but this one is now off Poland. Not so far from Sweden. Where is it headed for and why? No-one can work it out – which is what makes it worrying. See you both . . .'

After Cottel had left, Beaurain dialled a number. He settled himself into a chair and perched the phone amid the crockery Louise had laid. 'Is that you, Jock? Jules here. The mobile cargo we picked up recently is to be put on a train early tomorrow morning at

Brussels Midi. Yes, that's right – *Midi.*' Midi was one of the three main-line stations in Brussels. 'Organise an all-round escort to supervise proper handling of the cargo. Understood? Next, stock up the floating fuel store with supplies and await instructions. Got it? And take care – someone might be starting a fire and there's plenty of tinder about.'

He put down the phone, shifted the receiver off the table and looked up, suddenly aware that all sounds from the kitchen had ceased. Louise was standing close to him, holding an empty scoop. He threw up his hands as though in self-defence.

'I know you've laid the table – but I haven't disturbed your beautiful setting.'

'I want to know what's going on – and quickly or the food will be ruined.'

'You heard the conversation.'

'Which was in code. First of all, where is Jock now? It sounds as though things are moving.'

'Jock was at our sub-base near the station, although by now I expect he'll be on his way to the Château Wardin.'

She glanced at her watch to check the cooking time and perched herself on his lap. 'For "mobile cargo" I read Litov – who's going to be dropped at Brussels Midi and allowed to run. I'm worried we'll lose him.'

'Hence my reference to "an all-round escort", the full-scale dragnet I want Jock to throw round all Litov's possible escape routes – because elude us he will try to do. And, since he will assume we're tracking him, we must trick him into thinking that he's succeeded. Then see where he leads us. Tomorrow will be a big day. Satisfied?'

'Not yet.' She caressed the side of his face with her scoop as she continued. 'What about your reference to "the floating fuel store"? Is that the steam yacht, *Firestorm*? It is? And where is she now?'

'Midway between Scotland and the mouth of the Baltic. I've kept her ready there since I first heard the phrase "Stockholm Syndicate". Jock will radio her to take on board provisions, check weapons and ammunition, above all equip her with a team of gunners. He's going to have a busy night is Jock. And now I'm hungry.'

'You always are. It's chicken – cooked the way you like it. I suppose tomorrow we'll watch them plotting Litov's movements on the map.'

'More than that. Later tomorrow we're visiting the Fixer in Bruges. He may be able to tell us who is the real power behind the Stockholm Syndicate.'

Chapter Five

The Fixer. Dr Henri Goldschmidt, dealer in rare coins, was one of Bruges' most eminent citizens. Beaurain estimated his present age at about sixty but could only guess – the doctor guarded his private life jealously and you dared not ask him the wrong question. The penalty was to be instantly crossed off his list of social acquaintances.

'They are excluded from my *milieu,*' he once explained. 'And, of course, once excluded they can never be re-admitted.'

He spoke eight languages fluently, including French, English and German; he also used his finely-shaped hands to aid his flow of conversation, gesturing with controlled deliberation to emphasize a point. He was the confidant of royalty, American millionaires and French industrialists. Less well-known was the fact that he was on good terms with some of Europe's top gangsters. This was the man Beaurain was going to meet.

One hour before dawn the huge Sikorsky helicopter took off from the Château Wardin. Litov – who had endured his last 'interrogation' at the hands of Dr Alex Carder – was lying on a stretcher, as on the 'outward' journey, his damaged arm expertly protected with a splint and bandages and his left wrist and ankle handcuffed to the stretcher. His right ankle was also manacled.

There were two guards in the gunners' normal battle uniform – denim trousers, crêpe-soled shoes, windcheaters and Balaclava helmets which completely masked their appearance. One was Stig Palme. The second was a twenty-nine year old German, Max Kellerman. A year earlier he had been looking forward to a brilliant career as a lawyer. Then his fiancée had been caught in terrorist crossfire when the police had been tipped off about a bank raid in Bonn. They were still unaware that the tip-off had come from Jules Beaurain. It was something he had also concealed from Kellerman, as he had once explained to Louise.

'If Kellerman knew I started the whole thing off he *might* blame me for the death of his fiancée.'

Litov had been blindfolded before he left the large cell he had occupied for over a week. Once again he was relying on sound and his sense of smell to double-check what he had learned about Telescope's main base. The same bonfire smoke had hit his nostrils when they carried him from the building to the ramp at the rear of the chopper. They took him the same way out – he felt and heard the change from carpet to stone; then the stone steps followed by an absence of sound suggesting grass. The bonfire stench didn't seem strange:

from his tour of duty in London he recalled that the British kept foul-smelling fires smoking all summer.

'Don't forget to light that bonfire in good time,' Beaurain had reminded Stig Palme. 'Litov is bright – he must not get a whiff of the Ardennes pines while he's being carried aboard'.

It had been 3 a.m. when they had come to collect Litov. Still wearing his wrist-watch, he had managed to check the time before one of the masked guards applied the blindfold. If he was being returned to the same starting-point the flight from England should take about three hours.

When the Sikorsky landed, Litov, still imprisoned on the stretcher in the cargo hold, found himself re-living his earlier experience in reverse. There was a bump as the chopper came to earth, a pause while the rotors stopped spinning, followed by the purr of the hydraulics as the automatic ramp at the rear of the cargo hold was lowered.

His blindfold was removed by a guard with a Balaclava concealing his face. These people didn't miss many tricks, Litov thought smugly – and then he was being lifted down into broad daylight. The strong scent of Ardennes pines entered his nostrils and above he saw the tops of the trees encircling the secret helipad. The two guards carried him to the familiar van with *Boucher* across the rear doors. They dumped him on the same leather couch alongside the left-hand wall, the doors were closed and Kellerman and Palme sat facing their captive with machine-pistols across their laps.

'We are driving you to Brussels Midi station,' Kellerman told Litov in English as the van began to move. 'Here are your papers, Mr James Lacey or whatever your name is.'

Litov could hardly believe it. Kellerman bent over him and returned his wallet to his inside pocket. Was this a trick to throw him off balance, to make him relax before they subjected him to torture or a trial of endurance?

But he half-believed the guard who returned to his seat as the van gathered speed. Why should they let him go at all? The guard gestured towards the wallet he had returned.

'You will find all your money intact. Belgian francs, deutschmarks, Dutch guilders. Telescope does not steal like the Syndicate.'

Litov stiffened, tried to keep his face expressionless. What the hell was going on? This was the first admission that these men belonged to Telescope. And why the casual mention of the Syndicate? To test his reaction? Of one thing Litov was now certain – he was being freed in the hope that he would lead them to the Syndicate's headquarters. He had trouble concealing his satisfaction. They were in for a surprise, a very nasty surprise indeed.

*

Pierre Florin, desk sergeant at Brussels police headquarters, requested a week's leave soon after the two men had accosted Louise in the reception room. It was the sight of Beaurain running up the stairs to attend the meeting and the realisation that the girl knew Beaurain which had scared Florin. Because of his long years of service his request was immediately granted.

He spent most of the seven days in his bachelor's apartment in south Brussels. One of the fake detectives visited him one evening.

'Why have you taken this leave, Florin?' he demanded. 'It draws attention to you at just the wrong moment.'

'I am worried. Beaurain . . .'

'You are a fool. Beaurain is no longer on the force.'

'He carries enormous influence.' Florin could not keep still, and kept moving restlessly about, fussily moving cheap mementoes of holidays in Ostend. 'I would not like to be grilled by Beaurain,' Florin continued, confirming the other man's opinion that he would crack under interrogation. 'I want my money.' The lean-faced man extracted a sealed envelope and dropped it on the floor, making Florin stoop to retrieve it. Then he left and reported his doubts to Dr Otto Berlin.

It took Dr Berlin several days to locate Gunther Baum, the East German whose speciality was the removal of people. Baum and his companion, a nondescript individual who carried a brief-case, arrived unannounced at Florin's apartment. Wearing dark glasses, Baum was smartly dressed in American clothes. Outside Florin's apartment he took the silenced Luger from the brief-case and held it behind his back as he pressed the bell.

Gunther Baum was medium built and deliberate in his movements. 'Never hurry,' he often warned his assistant. 'It draws attention to you.' He was wearing a straw hat which, with his tinted glasses, masked his whole upper face, revealing only a pug nose, a small thin mouth and a fleshy jaw. Cupped in his left hand he carried a photo of Pierre Florin. It was best to proceed in a methodical manner.

Florin opened the door and glanced nervously at the strangers before starting to close it again. 'We are the Criminal Division. A message from headquarters. Concerning the incident there about one week ago. We may come in, yes?'

'Of course . . .'

Baum spoke in a sing-song French. He spoke in short sentences as though he expected everyone to accept him at face value. It never occurred to Florin to ask for some form of identification. They proceeded into the apartment, first Florin, then Baum and his companion, who carried the empty brief-case and closed the door.

'You are alone?' Baum asked.

'Yes, I seldom . . .'

'Keep walking, please. We have been asked to look at your bedroom. Statements have been made that a woman visits you who keeps bad company.'

'That's ridiculous.'

'This we are sure of. Keep walking. Open that cupboard – I must be sure we are alone.'

They were inside the cramped bedroom and Florin reacted like a robot to Baum's instructions. He opened up the cupboard at his visitor's request. Baum pressed the tip of the silencer against the base of Florin's neck. The Belgian stiffened at the pressure of the cold metal. 'Step into the cupboard slowly,' Baum commanded in the same sing-song French. 'You stay there out of the way while we search for evidence.' Terrified, Florin stepped inside the cupboard, his face buried among his clothes. Baum pressed the trigger once.

He slammed the door against Florin's toppling body and turned the catch. Without saying a word he handed the Luger to his companion who immediately hid it inside his brief-case as Baum removed his gloves and shoved them inside his pocket. 'Time to go,' Baum said.

It was his normal routine when working on a close-up job. Baum never kept the gun a second longer than necessary. It was his companion's task to transport the incriminating weapon so that Baum could never be compromised; it was a risk Baum's companion was paid good money to take.

'Now for the bargee Dr Berlin is worried about. We want to keep our employer happy, don't we?'

At 9.30 a.m. a butcher's van pulled into the kerb at Brussels Midi station. Serge Litov had been released from the handcuffs and was sitting facing Max Kellerman who was pointing his machine-pistol at the Russian's belly. Litov could still not fully believe he was about to be freed; the one thing which reassured him was the sound of heavy traffic outside.

'When you get out don't look back,' Kellerman warned, 'or this van will be the last thing you'll ever see. One quick burst and we'd be away. And there is a whole team of our people outside to make sure you board a train – any train.'

Stig Palme, still masked like Kellerman, unbolted the rear doors, opened one a few inches and peered out. He opened it wider, Litov stepped down into the street and the door was closed. Kellerman now moved very fast.

Stripping off the boiler suit he had been wearing, he stepped out of it. Pulling off the Balaclava helmet, he lifted the top of the couch Litov had been seated on, took out a trilby hat and jammed it on his head. He grabbed a suitcase and a fawn raincoat from inside the couch. The suitcase's corners were tipped with steel to serve as an improvised weapon. Sliding back a plate at the front of the van he spoke to the driver.

'Well?'

'He behaved – went straight into the station booking-hall.' Kellerman ran to the back of the van and dropped into the street. No-one noticed. Kellerman walked across to one of the swing doors and entered the booking-hall. Litov was standing at the ticket counter by the first-class window with only one man in front of him. While he waited he glanced behind and saw a Belgian woman with a poodle on a lead joining his queue. She was muttering away to herself as she burrowed in her handbag for fare money. Expensively dressed, which fitted her presence in the first-class queue. Litov noticed things like that.

'Stupid old cow,' he thought. 'Women never have their money ready.'

The man in front of him moved away and with a quick glance at the station clock Litov asked for his ticket in a low tone. The ticket clerk asked him to speak up. Litov did so, anxious not to draw attention to himself.

'One seat on the *Ile-de-France* Trans-Europ Express to Amsterdam. One-way and a non-smoker. I shall have time to catch it?'

'Plenty of time.' The clerk was writing out the car and seat number. 'Arrives here 9.43, reaches Amsterdam 12.28.'

Behind Litov the woman with the poodle was still investigating her handbag and muttering away to herself in French. She irked Litov: people like that ought to be locked up. He paid for his ticket and moved towards the platforms, glancing round at the milling crowd, trying to locate the hidden watchers he knew must be there.

Everything seemed normal. The bustle of passengers criss-crossing the large booking-hall, the general air of frustration and anxiety, the constant background voice over the speakers relaying an endless list of train arrivals and departures all over Europe.

At the first-class counter the woman apologised to the clerk. She couldn't find her purse. Would he serve the next passenger while she . . . She glanced across to see Litov walk out of sight onto the platforms. She hurried over the concourse, her poodle trotting briskly by her side, to Max Kellerman who stood reading a newspaper. Stopping abruptly, she let the poodle walk on and contrived to let the leash wrap itself round the German's legs.

'So sorry,' she burbled in French, her voice low as she untwined the leash, 'Colette does like men. The 9.43 T.E.E. to Amsterdam,' she went on. 'Five stops – Brussels Nord, Antwerp East, Roosendaal, Rotterdam, The Hague, then Amsterdam . . .'

'Get the news to Henderson,' murmured Kellerman. 'Tell him I'm on my way.'

Kellerman quickly joined the short queue which had formed at the first-class window. Behind him the fussy lady in her sixties had made her way to a telephone kiosk.

*

It was not long until the *Ile-de-France* de-luxe express would be arriving en route for Amsterdam. The T.E.E.s stopped for precisely three minutes. Nevertheless Serge Litov, after walking up and down the platform, suddenly returned to the booking-hall.

Left behind on the platform, Max Kellerman, wearing his raincoat and hat and carrying his suitcase, waited where he was in case Litov reappeared at the last moment and boarded the express. Litov might be standing watching the exit doors to see if anyone followed him. Or buying the ticket for Amsterdam might be the first of his tricks to throw off the shadows he knew were watching.

In the booking-hall Litov hurried to a phone box, shut the door and called a Bruges number. He watched to see if anyone appeared to be dogging his movements. What he didn't notice was a woman with a poodle who was perched on a nearby seat ostentatiously eating a sandwich. If Litov had happened to spot her, the sandwich would have explained her presence – having booked her ticket she had a long wait for her train and preferred to spend it in the booking-hall.

'If he leaves the station, you follow him, Alphonse,' she said quietly to the man sharing her seat.

'It doesn't look as though he is catching the Amsterdam express.'

'He still has time,' Monique replied equably.

'I'd like to know what he's saying,' muttered Alphonse.

Inside the phone box Litov's Bruges number had connected and he identified himself quickly. 'Serge speaking, your friend from the Stampen. They let me out – just like that.'

'Berlin here. Keep this call brief, I'm expecting another. Where are you?'

'Brussels Midi station. I've bought a ticket for Amsterdam. Which route – and can you get me a back-up? They're bound . . .'

'It was our friends?' Berlin interjected sharply. 'And you know their home town?'

'Yes and yes. I'm short of time. I have to catch that express. Or don't I?'

'Of course. Then continue on by air, if you understand me. Help will meet you at Copenhagen – to deal with any difficulty you may encounter. Goodbye.'

In the tiny terraced house at Bruges, Berlin replaced the receiver and looked across the table at Sonia Karnell pouring out coffee. He waited for the cup before satisfying her curiosity.

'Serge Litov is starting his run. He is at Brussels Midi. Telescope has let him go and he says he knows the location of their main base.'

'But that's marvellous.'

'Is it?' Berlin looked round the drab walls, the gilt-framed pictures you couldn't see in the gloominess caused by the looming houses on the other side of the narrow street. 'We shan't know whether he has succeeded until I have questioned him. The thing now is to sever the link between Litov and Telescope's trackers. He will catch the first plane. Find out when it reaches Copenhagen and have someone waiting there – someone capable of eliminating any tracker. Today is going to be dangerous – for everyone. Including the esteemed Dr Henri Goldschmidt – The Fixer.'

The lookout in the first-floor window saw the 280E coming, wending its way through the traffic towards the heavy wooden doors at the entrance to the sub-base near Brussels Midi station. He phoned down to the guards and the doors swung smoothly inwards for Beaurain to drive into the yard. Beside him Louise Hamilton looked back and saw the doors closing off the view of the traffic beyond.

'I wonder where Litov is now?' she said.

'Let's go upstairs and find out.'

The cobbled yard was small. It was entirely enclosed by old six-storey buildings. The rooms overlooking the courtyard were the property of Telescope, held in a dummy name by the Baron de Graer. The only other vehicle in the yard was the butcher's van, already refuelled from the petrol pump in the corner and turned round so it could leave immediately.

Henderson was sitting in a functional first-floor room. In one corner a wireless operator wearing his earphones sat in front of a high-powered transceiver.

The Scot, who stood up as they entered, had been sitting at a table facing a large wall map of northern Europe. On the map he had marked all the possible air, road and rail routes from Brussels Midi with a red felt-tipped pen.

'What are the little blue pins?' Louise asked.

'Each one shows a gunner I can contact by radio or phone inside three minutes.'

'There are scores of them!'

'Only wish I had more,' the Scot replied laconically. He looked at Beaurain. 'The moment of truth has arrived. Litov, code-named Leper, is at Brussels Midi. He has made one two-minute phone call. He bought a T.E.E. ticket for Amsterdam. Train leaves 9.43.' He looked at a large wall-clock. 'That's about now.'

Serge Litov played it cagey from the moment he returned to the platform. Carrying his ticket, he went up to the special T.E.E. board which illustrated the sequence of the carriages. Voiture 3 was immediately behind the engine.

From behind his newspaper Max Kellerman – who was leaving Litov to do the moving about while he remained in one place – watched him carefully study the ticket and then the board. It was a pantomime for the benefit of watchers.

In his mind Kellerman went over the stops the express made before arriving at Amsterdam. Brussels Nord, Antwerp East, Roosendaal, Rotterdam and The

Hague. At all these stops Henderson would already have arranged to have a gunner stationed in case he got off. Kellerman's job was to stay on board until Amsterdam. The T.E.E. glided in, five de-luxe coaches preceded by its streamlined locomotive. The express stopped.

Litov climbed aboard Voiture 3 the moment the automatic doors had opened, pushing rudely past a woman waiting to alight. It was the old trick: wait until just before the automatic doors closed and then jump back onto the platform – leaving your shadow on board, carried away by the train. But Litov reappeared, descended the steps and stood on the platform. What the hell was he up to? Kellerman had one eye on Litov, the other on the red second-hand on the platform clock.

Behind him Alphonse strolled into view and took up a position on the opposite platform. Kellerman climbed aboard, joining a woman who was a late arrival, so they looked like a couple. Once inside the coach he sat down in a seat near the entrance to the next coach, Voiture 3.

There is no warning when a T.E.E. express is due to depart; no call from the guard, no whistle blowing. The doors close, the train draws out of the station. Litov, watching the second-hand on the clock, timed it perfectly. He ran up the steps into the coach a second before the doors met.

'Triple bluff,' said Kellerman to himself as the train pulled out.

The next stop, Brussels Nord, was only a few

minutes away. Would Litov get off after only one station, despite booking all the way to Amsterdam? Because from Brussels Nord he could catch a train or a cab to the airport. Kellerman could have relaxed now. His assignment was to stay on board all the way to Amsterdam. Instead he sat tensely, trying to put himself inside Litov's mind, to predict how he would react at Brussels Nord.

Inside the temporary headquarters for Operation Leper the tension was rising. Louise kept pacing up and down in the small room. Beaurain sat down next to Henderson, the picture of relaxation as he lit a cigarette. They had done all they could. It was up to the men in the field.

'Who have you got aboard the train?' he asked.

'Max Kellerman. He can be a bit insubordinate.'

'He's among the best we've got. Uses his brain.' He stopped as the phone rang. Henderson picked up the receiver and spoke briefly in French.

'That was Louis. The Leper boarded at Midi. So he has started to run. All we can do now is wait – for the next message.'

At 9.53 the T.E.E. slid into Brussels Nord station and the doors hissed open. This was a two-minute stop. Max Kellerman had made up his mind. He was standing at the exit of his coach furthest away from Voiture 3.

Kellerman was not recognisable as the man who had boarded at Midi. He had taken off his hat and light raincoat and put them inside his suitcase. He had donned a pair of glasses. His thick thatch of dark hair, previously hidden beneath the hat, was now visible.

Alighting from the express he glanced to his left, saw no sign of Litov and swung round to give the impression of a passenger about to board the train. In his mouth he had a cigarette and he was deliberately making the gas lighter misfire: it gave a reason for pausing at the foot of the steps.

'He's going to get off at Nord and head for the airport,' Kellerman had decided during his few minutes on the train. 'After his confinement he'll be impatient, anxious to reach home base. I would be.'

He was disobeying his orders. On no account was he to leave the train before Amsterdam. Kellerman was relying on his observation of how Litov had handled his problem at Midi. And if he was continuing to Amsterdam he would surely have pretended to be leaving the express here – by getting off and loitering near the exit doors.

The German found himself watching the platform clock. In ten seconds the doors would close. Nine–eight–seven–six . . . Litov had fooled him. He was staying aboard. At the last moment Litov rushed down the train steps, onto the platform and hurried towards the station exit. No-one could have got out in time to follow him. Kellerman smiled grimly and strode towards the exit.

There he saw Joel Wilde, the ex-SAS gunner Henderson had sent to Nord for just this contingency. Kellerman outranked him. 'He's mine,' he said as he walked past.

He was through the doors in time to see Litov leaving the station on the far side of the booking-hall. He came up behind him as the Russian waited for the next cab. 'The airport. Move it,' Litov informed the driver and climbed into the back.

He was so confident he had overlooked the obvious precaution of waiting until he was inside the cab to give his destination. It was out of character. Or was it? They had been careful to keep Litov without food for the past twenty-four hours, giving him only fruit juice. He could be light-headed and over-confident. Or that phone call from Brussels Midi could have arranged back-up to any shadow who attached himself to Litov when he left the express. If so, Joel would sort that one out.

Kellerman glanced over his shoulder before climbing inside the next cab which drew up. Joel Wilde was close behind him. You never heard the bastard – until it was too late. Kellerman lowered the window and looked up at him.

'Thanks for everything. I'm going to make the airport in good time.'

'You're welcome. Our love to Sharon. A smooth flight.'

Joel watched the cab pull away and turned round to face the station exits. No-one else was coming for a cab. No-one was heading for a private car. But during the next few hours the Syndicate would send someone to take out any man they detected following Litov.

'I'll chew his balls off.'

At the headquarters of Operation Leper, Henderson put down the phone, caught Louise Hamilton's amused eye and clapped a hand over his mouth.

'That was Joel Wilde from Nord station. The Leper left the express – as you thought he might – and has taken a cab to the airport. More to the point, Max Kellerman is running his own railway again. He got off too – and he's followed the Leper in another cab to the airport.'

'Max is a good man, one of our best,' Beaurain commented.

'Where is the Leper heading for?'

Henderson stood up and went over to study the air routes marked on his wall-map. He moved a blue pin – Max Kellerman – to a position on the road to the airport. Just ahead of this he placed the red pin representing Serge Litov.

Beaurain joined him and checked his watch against the wall-clock. 'You'll hear soon enough. Get someone to look up all the airline flights taking off within the next two hours. I don't think the Leper will linger longer than he need. You mind the shop till we get back, Jock. We're going to take a train to Bruges and have a word with my old friend, Dr Goldschmidt. It's just conceivable he can tell us the name of the man who is running the Syndicate.'

Chapter Six

Gunther Baum sat perfectly still in the passenger seat of the Renault, which had been driven by the lean-faced man beside him. On his companion's lap lay the brief-case containing the loaded Luger. Baum had not yet requested the weapon.

As during his visit to Pierre Florin he was proceeding with caution. Again he wore a straw hat and tinted glasses. In his left hand he held a photo of Frans Darras and his wife, Rosa. It was best to proceed in a methodical manner.

'I trust they are both on board,' Baum said. 'And at least we have found the barge where it was supposed to be – you can see the aerial.'

He held out his gloved hand. His companion had not replied, knowing Baum often thought aloud to make sure there was nothing he had overlooked before he completed a job. When it involved two people at once it always required a little more finesse.

Baum took the gun, made sure the silencer was screwed on tight and opened the door with his other gloved hand. 'You follow with your tool-kit in three minutes counting from now.' His companion checked his own watch quickly. In Baum's world seconds counted.

Baum climbed deliberately and slowly. Reaching the towpath he held the Luger behind his back and looked around. The barge was moored and its deck was deserted but he heard voices from the cabin below. There was no-one on the tow-path. The one feature Baum missed was a small boy perched in the branches of an apple tree. Baum stepped aboard and pocketed the photo.

Frans and Rosa Darras were arguing so loudly they did not hear Baum descend the steps into the cabin. They would not have heard him anyway. Coming out of the daylight it was difficult to see clearly in the cabin and behind his tinted glasses Baum blinked.

'I have a message and some money for Frans and Rosa Darras,' he said.

Startled, the bargee turned quickly. 'That's us. Who are you?'

'Both of you will turn and face the wall.'

Baum had produced the Luger from behind his back and aimed it at a position between them. 'I have come to remove your transceiver,' he continued in his sing-song French. 'Face the wall until we have completed the work. Behave yourselves in an orderly manner and you can rest assured no harm . . .'

They had both turned together to face the wall. Instinctively Frans grasped Rosa's hand to reassure her. Baum was still talking when he pressed the muzzle against the base of Frans Darras' neck and fired once. Darras was falling when the muzzle pressed into the neck of Rosa who, frozen with terror, was unable to move. Baum pressed the trigger a second time.

His companion appeared with his brief-case and tool-kit. Baum handed the Luger to him at once and the weapon was returned to the brief-case. He stood quite still while his companion swiftly removed the transceiver and its power-operated aerial. On the canal bank above them the little boy in the apple tree had remained in its branches. He was sucking an orange as Baum reappeared at the top of the steps, and it slipped from his fingers, hitting the tow-path with a clunk. Baum turned and scanned the area.

Hidden amid the branches no more than twenty feet away, the boy watched the sunlight flashing off the tinted lenses as Baum continued searching while his companion also reappeared on deck, the brief-case in one hand, the transceiver and aerial awkwardly held under his arm. He was sweating with the effort.

'You heard something?' he asked.

'Time to get back to the car,' said Baum.

They were driving along the main highway, heading for Brussels, when a train passed in the opposite direction. Inside a first-class compartment Beaurain and Louise sat facing each other, gazing out of the window. They had a glimpse of a canal, of several barges moored close to a lock, barges with clothes-lines hung along the decks, TV masts and radio aerials projecting into the sunlight.

'Those people must lead a life of their own – they even have TV,' Louise remarked.

Beaurain was staring out without seeing anything, his mind on Goldschmidt. He nodded automatically, but registered what she had said to him.

'Shot in the back of the neck? Pierre Florin?'

Chief Inspector Flamen of Homicide sighed inwardly. Voisin had a habit of repeating statements you made.

'Chief Superintendent Beaurain had requested to see him as soon as he returned from sick leave,' Flamen continued and then waited for the expected reaction.

'*Ex*-Chief Superintendent Beaurain, you mean. Is it not peculiar that the policeman Beaurain wished to see should be murdered before he saw him?' demanded Voisin.

'It could have significance,' Flamen agreed.

'Had I better see Beaurain?'

'As you wish, sir – but it might be better if I saw him first. That way you won't find yourself in any embarrassing situation, if I may so phrase it.'

'You may indeed, Flamen.' Voisin smirked. Clearly Willy Flamen understood the delicacy of his position, the political importance of never having to take a decision that might backfire.

'Found in his apartment,' Flamen continued. 'No sign of a break-in.'

'So he knew his murderer,' Voisin jumped in.

'It would seem so,' Flamen agreed tactfully, although he knew it didn't necessarily follow. 'Shot in the back of the neck,' he repeated. 'Reminds me of something nasty – but I just can't recall what it is.'

'You had better leave for Brussels now, before Bruges is flooded with police,' Dr Berlin told Sonia Karnell inside the tiny house in the Hoogste van Brugge.

'Something is going to happen?'

'A couple of loose ends are being tidied up by Gunther Baum – Frans and Rosa Darras aboard the barge. They were getting slack – it was you who warned me when you delivered the *Zenith* signal about Beaurain.'

Karnell had stood up to leave. Her brow was crinkled with apprehension. 'What have I been responsible for? I thought you were only going to warn them.'

'It is a warning!' Berlin raised his voice and used the fingers of one hand to stroke the curved ends of his moustache. 'A warning to the other people running our communications. But that's why there may be police activity round this area soon. Also because I have decided to teach Dr Goldschmidt a lesson for spying on me with that photographer in the house opposite.'

'Not Baum again?' she asked quietly.

'You are too soft-hearted.'

'You are getting more brutal and I don't really like it.'

He relented and decided to tell her. 'Dirk is going to deliver one of his toys. He is a gentle soul. Now run along and I'll meet you later at the Brussels apartment before we go to the airport together.'

She nodded and left to find a cab for the station. Dirk Mondy ran the Bruges office when Berlin was not there. What toy could he be presenting to Goldschmidt?

As she left the house and headed down the narrow cobbled street she was relieved that it was not Baum who was calling. Even the mention of Baum, whom she had never met, terrified her. *I wouldn't know him if he came up my own stairs in Stockholm*, she thought.

At Bruges station Louise and Beaurain had to wait several minutes until a cab arrived, bringing a passenger to the station. The door opened, a girl wearing a windcheater stepped out, reached into her handbag for her purse and caught sight of Beaurain. For a fraction of a second she froze, then recovered, paid the fare and hurried into the station.

'Holiday Inn,' Beaurain told the driver. It was easier than explaining how to get to Dr Goldschmidt's address in a nearby side street. 'This is one of the most beautiful towns in Europe,' Beaurain remarked as the cab moved off. 'There's an area with canals and ancient bridges with willows dripping branches in the water. It is just the sort of place I'd hide up in if I were running some shady outfit.'

'You noticed that girl who got out of this cab at the station?' Louise asked in a low voice.

'Vaguely. Quite a looker.' Beaurain lit a cigarette.

'She was staring at you as though you scared her stiff. Have you ever seen her before?'

'Never in my life. Ah, here we are. I'm looking forward to seeing my old friend.'

The Holiday Inn was on the corner of an ancient square – the T'Zand. Down the side street where Dr Goldschmidt lived were old houses, steep-roofed and white. The atmosphere was so peaceful Louise felt ridiculous carrying a pistol.

'Here we are.'

Beaurain stopped outside one of the houses which carried an engraved plate on the wall by the door. *Avocat*. Lawyer. No name. He pressed the bell and glanced down the street. Forty yards away a Volkswagen was parked. A man sat behind the wheel. Impossible to see his face at that distance. The door opened on a chain.

'Your card, please.'

'Here, Henri. It is Jules.'

'Cautious, isn't he?' Louise whispered.

A slim-fingered hand took the card, the chain was removed and they stepped into a hallway. The door closed and Dr Goldschmidt regarded them both, a tall, stooped man with a silver mane of hair and a hawk-like nose. He wore a business suit which could only have been cut in Savile Row and peered at them through a pair of gold-rimmed glasses.

He said mildly: 'You are both carrying guns. Correct, Miss Hamilton? No, don't look at Jules for your cue. Am I right?'

'Yes – but how . . .?'

'Because he's a good bluffer,' Beaurain put in. 'When we entered the doorway we passed through a metal detector set into the door-frame and the bulb down here in the wall lights up faintly when metal is detected on a visitor. The bluff is he had no way of knowing the metal was a gun so he challenged you with an accusation which threw you off balance. He used to be one of Belgium's most eminent lawyers before he took up . . . the collection of rare coins.'

'Any more of my secrets you wish to reveal?' Goldschmidt asked with mock waspishness.

'Not at the moment – but please don't play games with my best girl.'

'Mamsele, a thousand apologies. And such a beautiful assistant.'

He ushered them through a doorway into a small but comfortably furnished room overlooking the street. The walls were lined with bookcases, a blue deep-pile carpet covered the floor. Goldschmidt pulled forward a leather armchair for Louise and fussed about her courteously. She looked straight at his penetrating grey eyes and decided she must establish herself or be dismissed as second-rate.

'You are afraid someone is coming to kill you, Dr Goldschmidt?'

'All the time – in my business.' He turned to Beaurain who was staring through the window at the parked Volkswagen. 'You said on the phone I could speak to Miss Hamilton as though I were talking to you.'

'That's true.' Beaurain sat down in a second armchair and Goldschmidt took a high-backed chair behind a large antique desk – which meant he was looking down at them. He used the technique of intimidation with so many people he even continued it with his friends.

'First things first,' said Beaurain in a business-like manner, and took out a long, fat envelope containing £20,000 in Deutschmarks of high-denomination notes. He dropped it on the desk. 'My contribution towards your favourite charity.'

Goldschmidt picked up the envelope, locked it in a desk drawer without opening it and inclined his head. 'Thank you. How can I help you?'

'I want to know who is running the Syndicate, some idea of the size of its operations, and where its headquarters are.'

'Terror.' Goldschmidt plunged straight into his subject. 'Terror is the weapon this Syndicate is using on a scale never before seen in Europe – or in the States, not that Washington will admit its existence. I have never in all my experience,' he continued, 'known such a situation.' He stared hard at Beaurain. 'The Syndicate controls men and women at the summit of power in this country. If you become its target you cannot save yourself.'

'I've never heard you talk like this before,' Beaurain said grimly. 'How have they managed this in such a short time?' He was thinking of the fear on the face of the Baron de Graer.

'They vary their method to suit the victim. Sometimes money is employed – very large sums, some of which originate in the United States. In other cases they employ terroristic blackmail. You remember the killing of the Baron de Graer's wife and daughter during the so-called kidnap attempt at the Château Wardin?'

'So-called?'

'Yes. It was planned from the outset that the wife and daughter would be killed. You look very grim, Jules.'

'I happen to know the Baron de Graer. Also I was in charge of the anti-terrorist squad at the time. Brussels stopped me using my normal method of going in with heavy fire-power. Brussels insisted on negotiations.' There was an undertone of bitterness in the Belgian's voice.

'It would have been too late anyway, Jules, had you done so,' Goldschmidt said gently.

'What the hell does that mean?'

'De Graer's wife and daughter were brutally murdered as soon as the kidnap took place. The rest was window-dressing.'

'*Window-dressing?*' There was an ominous note in Beaurain's quiet voice.

'I only learned several months later.' Their host turned in his chair to look out of the open windows. 'The killings at the Château Wardin were a demonstration of the Syndicate's power. A number of prominent citizens – up to Cabinet level – were phoned and told what was going to happen, that the same thing could happen to their own loved ones if they refused to co-operate. You see, the conspiracy started early.' He turned and looked at Beaurain's frozen expression. 'As I said, it is the uninhibited use of terror, intimidation and bribery. I suspect that soon whole countries will be practically run by this evil organisation. You are powerless to do anything about it, Jules. Or are you? By the way, I wondered whether your visit was to ask me about Telescope?'

'What do you know about it?' Beaurain asked.

'Very little. It is organised like the wartime escape routes for Allied fliers from Brussels to the Spanish border.'

'And its leadership?'

Goldschmidt did not reply at once. He took off his gold-rimmed spectacles and studied Beaurain as he polished them with a blue silk handkerchief. He glanced at Louise whose expression was deliberately blank; she hoped not too blank. He replaced his glasses.

'I know nothing of its leadership.'

'Getting back to the Syndicate . . .'

'It is controlled by three rarely-seen men. One of them is a dealer in rare books who, when he comes to Bruges, has a house in the Hoogste van Brugge – only five minutes' walk from where we are now. I find that a trifle insulting. Let me show you on the street map.'

Beaurain and Louise studied the map briefly. The address was, as Goldschmidt had said, surprisingly close. 'These three men have names?' Beaurain asked.

'The one in Bruges is a Dr Otto Berlin.' Goldschmidt extracted a card from a drawer and wrote on it. 'The second is a Dr Benny Horn, a Dane who operates a rare bookshop in the Nyhavn waterfront area in Copenhagen.'

'I know the area,' Louise said.

'Good, good. Do not go there alone, my dear, I beg of you. The third is a Swede, a Dr Theodor Norling, and he too is in the rare book trade. He has an address in Gamla Stan, the Old City district of Stockholm. You know that, I believe, Jules?'

'Yes.' Beaurain took the card and glanced at the address. 'I don't follow why they are all in the rare book trade. It's some kind of cover?'

'They can travel about – officially purchasing some rare volume for a valued customer. Rare books! They are cold-blooded killers.'

Goldschmidt spoke with abnormal vehemence. 'Trust no-one, Jules. There is treachery everywhere. Unless the Stockholm Syndicate is destroyed quickly it will have the whole western world in its grip.'

'Surely that's rather an overstatement,' Louise suggested gently.

'You think so?' The rare coin dealer gazed hard at the English girl. 'It operates like some international protection racket. Clearly you have no idea who they already have.'

'Where does the money come from?' asked Beaurain.

'That's the trouble,' Goldschmidt said. 'We know that billions of dollars have been transferred to Europe by certain American multi-nationals to support the Syndicate. In secrecy, of course, but the funds have been so huge they have moved the value of currencies and that you cannot hide. So, again, it *seems* like the Americans . . .'

'But you think not?' Beaurain asked. 'Who then?'

'If only I knew which of Berlin, Horn or Norling was the chief executive. The top controller goes under the code-name Hugo. That is a name you whisper. Find Hugo and you have the Syndicate by the throat.'

'Why do you call it the Stockholm Syndicate? Why Stockholm?'

Beaurain had deliberately returned to his old role of Chief Superintendent grilling a suspect, hurling question after question with such speed that the recipient answered without thinking.

'Because that is how it is known. My enquiries have traced funds through many channels – and always the end of the line is Stockholm.'

'How do the men who run this Syndicate extract billions of dollars from the States? By the same methods – intimidation?'

'Sometimes – many successful men leave skeletons behind as they climb. There is an American who has built up what he calls "a blackmail bank". That could be used by the Syndicate. That, plus the lure of huge, invisible – and so non-taxable – profits when the money is invested in European crime – the drug traffic and so on.'

'Are the Soviets involved?' Beaurain demanded.

'Viktor Rashkin, the protégé of Brezhnev, is at the Russian Embassy in Stockholm,' Goldschmidt observed. Unlocking the drawer which contained the envelope of money Beaurain had handed him, the dealer handed it back. 'Keep this. Use the funds for your investigation. As you know, my dear Jules, I am a supplier of information. May I just for once enter the prediction business?'

'Go ahead.' Beaurain pocketed the envelope. 'And thank you.'

'I have heard there is to be a meeting of all key members and "shareholders" in the Stockholm Syndicate within the next two weeks. The Americans are flying to Europe – the conference will take place somewhere in Scandinavia. I predict that within the next fourteen days there will be a frightful collision between Telescope and the Stockholm Syndicate. Only one organisation will survive.'

At that moment the grenade came through the window and landed on Goldschmidt's desk.

Beaurain reacted with great speed. If he lobbed it back into the street he might cause hideous casualties to passers-by. His hand grasped the obscene object, he rushed to the door, hauled it open and hurled the grenade as far as he could down the narrow hallway. Slamming the heavy door shut he waited for the explosion.

'Superb reflexes, my friend – as always,' Goldschmidt commented drily. The emergency had drained the tension out of his system.

'I think it's a dud.'

Beaurain was looking at the second-hand of his watch. He waited a little longer. Louise, white-faced but controlled, nodded towards the window. 'Just before it happened I heard a car start up and approach. There was a Volkswagen parked further up the road when we arrived. It had one man behind the wheel.'

'I noticed it. I'm going to check.'

'Be careful.'

Beaurain returned tossing the grenade in the air like a tennis ball. 'It's a fake,' he assured them. 'No primer.

Who wants to scare the living daylights out of Dr Goldschmidt? There's a note on this spill of paper. It says, "Get out of Belgium by nightfall."'

'Undoubtedly a message from Dr Otto Berlin. He objects to my compiling a dossier on his activities.'

'That address,' Beaurain said quickly. 'In Hoogste van Brugge. I think we'll go there immediately. What does Berlin look like?'

Goldschmidt was unlocking a drawer in his desk. 'My photographer who took these pictures – I was going to get them when the grenade interrupted us – says Berlin is about five feet ten tall, very fat, hair black and greasy, with a moustache curling down the sides of his mouth. Walks with a waddle like a duck. Short-sighted – wears horn-rimmed pebble glasses, sounds repulsive.'

'That's a very precise description.'

'Sounds most conspicuous for someone who wants to avoid the limelight,' added Louise.

'Here are the photos – you can keep them. They're very good, considering they were taken under poor conditions. Berlin has a girl assistant. Very distinctive hair-style as you'll see – very dark, cut close to the head like a helmet.'

Beaurain and Louise looked quickly at the prints but neither of them said anything. Berlin's assistant was the girl whose taxi they had taken. Beaurain shoved the prints in his pocket with the envelope containing the Deutschmarks.

'Thank you, Henri. You have been more helpful

than you may ever realise. From now on, be very careful.'

At the far side of the T'Zand Square they entered the Zuidzandstraat, a narrow street which was almost deserted. 'Prepare for trouble,' Beaurain said as they arrived at the entrance to the gloomy Hoogste van Brugge. It was empty, little more than a cobbled alley hemmed in between two walls of old terrace houses. Beaurain paused, checking house numbers on both sides of the corridor of stone. At the far end was parked a Volkswagen taking up most of the width of the alley.

'I reckon No. 285 is by that car,' Beaurain said.

'Which could be the car from which the dummy grenade came?'

'Just might be. Again, be ready for trouble.'

They started walking down the alley side by side, their rubber-soled shoes making no sound on the ancient cobbles. The walls of the lifeless houses seemed to be closing in on them. Although only a minute's walk from the bustling T'Zand Square they were in a different world.

They were half-way to the Volkswagen when Beaurain made a swift gesture. He pressed himself in the recess of a doorway on the left and Louise chose a doorway in the right-hand wall. Beaurain's acute hearing had caught the sound of a door being unbolted. They waited.

A man came out of a house on the right-hand side, glanced down the alley, then turned away and hurried to the Volkswagen. A tall, thin man with a springy step, he bore no resemblance to the description of Otto Berlin. They waited until he got inside the car and drove round the corner. Beaurain nodded and they started up the street again.

Another man, carrying a suitcase, emerged from the same house. A fat man with greasy black hair and a moustache whose ends curved down round the corners of his mouth. A man who waddled like a duck. He saw them, stopped, took something from his pocket, made a quick pulling movement and hoisted his right hand like a bowler throwing a cricket ball.

'My God! That's Otto Berlin!' Louise called out.

'Drop flat!'

Louise reacted instantly, sprawling on the cobbles. Beaurain fell on top of her, protecting her body. The missile Berlin had hurled fell on the cobbles about forty feet from where they lay. The silence lasted four seconds. It was followed by an ear-splitting blast as the grenade exploded. Chips of stone flew all over the place. As Beaurain and Louise remained prone the shock wave passed over their heads. Beaurain felt a stone sliver whipping through his hair, but Berlin had miscalculated the distance and dropped the grenade too far away to hurt them. Provided they had luck on their side. They had.

'Are you all right?'

Beaurain was on his feet, tugging the Smith & Wesson from its holster. He was too late. Otto Berlin had sprinted round the corner. Beaurain turned to Louise who was brushing dirt off her clothes. Her voice was shaky.

'I'm OK.'

'The station . . .'

Beaurain shoved the revolver out of sight. Not a soul had appeared so far. The Hoogste van Brugge seemed accustomed to grenades. Or perhaps the unseen inhabitants had found it paid to mind their own business.

'Why the station?' Louise asked as Beaurain grabbed her arm and hustled her back the way they had come.

'Because I think he could be heading there – to get the hell out of Bruges. And I saw a cab rank in the T'Zand Square.'

'Why didn't the Volkswagen driver take him?'

'How the devil do I know? Maybe Berlin wanted him out of town fast in case the car had been recognised.' They entered the T'Zand Square. 'We'll take this cab,' Beaurain said.

He only relaxed when the cab was moving. 'If only we could get hold of one of the three men Goldschmidt gave us we could crack this thing. Otto Berlin would be perfect. You're sure you're all right?'

'I seem to be in one piece.' She said nothing more until they arrived at the station. Beaurain was taking money out of his wallet when she grabbed his sleeve. 'Look! There's Berlin – just going into the station. He's still carrying his case.'

Running from the cab, they were able to pass straight through the barrier with their return tickets. An express to Brussels was just about to depart. Among the last-minute passengers scrambling aboard they saw the fat figure of Otto Berlin entering a compartment near the front of the train. They just managed to get aboard as the express started moving. Beaurain peered out of the window to make sure Berlin had not jumped off again. The platform was empty. He looked at Louise as they stood in the deserted corridor.

'This is an express. One stop before Brussels – Ghent, which is half an hour away. We've got him – he can't leave a train moving at seventy miles an hour.'

Chapter Seven

'We search the whole express – but I want to find Berlin without him seeing us. So we can track him. We start at the front of the train and work our way back. You go first, I'll trail behind you. That way he's less likely to spot us.'

The express was about half full. They walked rapidly to the front of the train but neither of them saw Berlin. They began working their way back towards the rear of the express checking every passenger.

'I'll check each lavatory as we go through,' Beaurain told her. 'If one is occupied we wait at a discreet distance and see who comes out.'

They had over fifteen minutes to go when they reached the end of the train. No Berlin. Standing in the corridor Beaurain lit them both cigarettes and they looked at each other. Outside the windows the sunlit countryside flashed past – and again they saw a canal and barges with T.V. masts and washing-lines.

'I can't understand it,' Louise said. 'You checked every lavatory. We've both seen every passenger aboard – so what the devil has happened to him? He can't have just vanished into thin air.'

'Except that he appears to have done just that.'

The stop at Ghent gave no help in solving the mystery. People got off. More passengers boarded the express. No-one even remotely resembling Dr Otto Berlin appeared. As the train left Ghent they made their way to the front, found an empty compartment in the coach behind the engine, sat down and stared at each other.

'Do we search all over again?' Louise suggested. 'We must have missed something.'

'We stay here until the train reaches Brussels,' Beaurain said firmly. 'At Nord we get out pretty sharp, wait by the barrier and check everyone off. No-one can board a train and disappear in a puff of smoke.'

At Nord the express emptied itself. Standing a short distance away from Beaurain, Louise watched the passengers trailing past, many of them with luggage and obviously travellers from Ostend and the ferry from England. A squabbling family already tired from their journey and the heat; a crowd of locals wearing berets and chattering away in French; the inevitable priest with his suitcase.

They watched the last person off the express and then joined each other and walked towards the exit. Beaurain spoke as they came outside the station into brilliant sunshine. 'We'll take a cab to Henderson's sub-base and see how the tracking of Litov is proceeding. Better than our efforts I hope.'

He arranged for the cab to drop them a few minutes

from the sub-base and they continued on foot. When they arrived in the first-floor room with the wall-map Beaurain only had to take one look at Henderson's face to know a disaster had occurred.

'Pierre Florin, the sergeant you wanted to interview, has been found murdered at his apartment,' Henderson informed them. 'Commissioner Voisin is anxious to see you as soon as possible.'

'How do you know about Florin?' Beaurain enquired.

'I phoned your apartment to see if you had arrived back – and Chief Inspector Willy Flamen of Homicide answered the phone.'

'And what the hell was he doing inside my apartment?'

'I wondered that too,' said Henderson, 'until he told me the place had been broken into. He called there to give you Voisin's message. And Flamen wants to see you – but he'll be waiting at his own apartment. I told him I was a friend and got off the line.'

Beaurain had hoped for so much from his interview with Florin: above all, who had paid him to be absent from the reception desk at the vital moment. Or should the question be who had frightened him so much that he had risked his whole career? *Terror*, Goldschmidt had said vehemently, terror was one of the Syndicate's main weapons.

'How are you getting on with Litov?' he asked the Scot.

'He's boarded a flight for Scandinavia – he bought a ticket to Helsinki. Max was right behind him and is now aboard the same flight – a Scandinavian Airlines plane flying to Stockholm via Copenhagen.' Henderson nodded towards the wall-map. 'It's marked there with the red line.'

'So his final destination could be Copenhagen, Stockholm or Helsinki,' Beaurain suggested.

'That's the way I see it,' the Scot agreed. 'Unless he's being clever and gets off at Kastrup or Arlanda and switches to another destination. If he does that, I have gunners at both airports to track him. And we always have Max Kellerman travelling in the same first-class cabin as him.'

'Where are they now?'

Henderson checked the clock. 'En route to Kastrup Airport, Copenhagen. Within half an hour of landing.'

'We'd better get over and see Willy Flamen.' Beaurain stood up, uneasy about something. How the devil had they let Otto Berlin slip off the Ostend Express? Henderson swung round in his chair.

'Maybe I didn't make myself clear, sir. It is Commissioner Voisin who is anxious to see you. Asked particularly would you give him some idea of your arrival time.'

'You made yourself quite clear. We're still going to call on Willy Flamen first. I'll contact you later to find out what's happening to Litov. Come on, Louise.'

Beaurain had reached the door when he turned and gave a final order. 'One more thing, put all our people inside Brussels on a red alert immediately.'

Louise waited until they were sitting in the Mercedes before she asked the question. The Belgian had a brooding look and had not yet signalled to the guard to open the gate.

'Jules, what was that about a red alert? That means everyone has to expect an emergency at any moment, doesn't it?'

'The request from Commissioner Voisin to go and see him immediately . . .' Beaurain signalled the guard, gunned the motor and drove out of the archway into heavy traffic. Louise noticed his eyes were everywhere: checking the mirror; glancing at both sidewalks; checking the mirror again. 'Plus the fact that Voisin wants me to warn him in advance when I'm going to arrive. It fits in with that *Zenith* signal.'

'But he's a Commissioner of Police! Jules, you aren't serious. You don't think Voisin is one of the Syndicate's men?' Her tone of voice expressed her incredulity. 'You may not like the fat creep but you're letting your prejudices cloud your judgement. Hey, where are we going? You've missed the turning to Flamen's place.'

'We're going to take a look at police headquarters. Flamen we visit later.' He eased into the kerb and parked. 'And I'd like us to switch places – you drive and I'll be the passenger. Be prepared to drive like hell.'

Louise walked round the car and got in behind the wheel. Beaurain had no qualms about giving her the order to drive this way: Louise Hamilton had been a crack racing driver at Brands Hatch in England. Without a word he extracted his .38 Smith & Wesson from his shoulder holster and rested the weapon in his lap.

There wouldn't be much traffic at this hour around the police headquarters, which meant the 280E would be conspicuous to watchers. And Beaurain had no doubt that the Stockholm Syndicate would know the model and the number of his car. It was a crazy idea about Voisin: he hardly believed it possible himself. But he kept hearing Goldschmidt's voice. *Trust no-one, Jules. There is treachery everywhere.*

'If you're so suspicious,' Louise said with a hint of sarcasm, 'you should have sent a team of gunners to check out police headquarters.'

'You're probably right. But to tell you the truth, that didn't occur to me until we'd left Jock.'

'Well, here we are. We'll soon know now.'

Oh my God! Louise's exceptional self-control prevented her swerving. For a moment she couldn't speak to warn Jules – then she saw he had grasped his revolver with one hand and with the other had lowered his window.

'Jules – on both sides – two cars . . .'

'The one with a single man inside too?'

'Yes – they called him Pietr. He was the policeman in the blue Renault. He tried to block me in when I was getting away.'

'Proceed as slowly as you're going now, as though we haven't seen anything. Be ready to accelerate like a rocket when I say "go".'

'They'll have us in a crossfire if they see us.'

'They've already seen us. Hold down the speed. They're waiting for the moment when they have us sandwiched.'

'That couple in the car on the right – the short bulky man's called André and he's a killer.'

She continued cruising forward, her eyes whipping from side to side. Both cars were parked facing the oncoming Mercedes. Both could drive out and create a barrier she'd never pass. Was Jules really more tired than she had realised? The Fiat stationed on the right began to move from where it was parked outside the entrance to police headquarters.

As Louise had warned, they were going to be trapped in a crossfire. The cars had been waiting for them, had known that sooner or later Beaurain would arrive to keep his appointment with Commissioner Voisin!

'Go!'

Beaurain shouted the command and her reaction was a reflex, her foot ramming down hard on the accelerator which responded with instant action and power. The Fiat containing the two men was heading on a course which would take it across her bows, forcing her to stop, while they poured a hail of gunfire into it.

On his side Beaurain had already seen the thin man beside the driver lifting a sub-machine gun. Out of the corner of his eye he saw what he had foreseen – that the Renault was still parked at the kerb. No man can drive and aim a weapon accurately at the same time, and Pietr was aiming his silenced weapon through the open window.

Beaurain fired four times at the oncoming Fiat. The 280E was surging forward like a torpedo under Louise's expert control. Three of Beaurain's bullets hit the man with the sub-machine gun. Blood splashed the shattered glass of the Fiat's windscreen. The car began to swerve wildly as Beaurain fired again and hit the driver.

'Don't move your head!'

Beaurain turned to his left, laid his arm along the back of Louise's seat and fired two more shots. One hit the target. Blood spurted from Pietr's head and he slumped over his wheel. Beaurain saw it all in a blur as the 280E screamed past police headquarters where no-one had appeared despite the cannonade and the screech of tyres.

Louise's skilful manoeuvring took them past the moving Fiat and then they had left behind the carnage and Beaurain, looking back, saw no sign of pursuit. It was as though police headquarters had been stripped of patrol cars and personnel while the Syndicate killers tried to complete their job.

'You certainly handled that,' Louise commented as she changed direction again in case of pursuit. 'I wouldn't have known which car to tackle first.'

'The Fiat – because it carried a sub-machine gun and it was moving. Now, head for Willy Flamen's apartment.'

'Get out of Brussels, Jules: better still, out of Belgium. Both of you. Preferably tonight. The cold-blooded killing of Pierre Florin should be enough warning.'

Willy Flamen stared over the rim of his cup at Beaurain and Louise as they drank the coffee and ate the sandwiches provided by his wife. The policeman was a man who spoke his mind and possessed great courage. Which made his advice all the more disturbing.

'You're telling us to run? That's not like you, Willy. Anyway it was agreed at Voisin's meeting that I should investigate the Syndicate.' He smiled wrily. 'The brief was to confirm its existence, for God's sake.'

'Well recent events should have convinced you of that,' Flamen commented, pausing to light his pipe. Beaurain recalled that he used it at moments of crisis. 'And there is worse to come – if you can believe that's possible.'

'Do cheer us up,' Louise joked.

He pointed his pipe-stem at her. 'Enjoy this, then. Jules let it be known he wanted to interview Florin, the sergeant who was on desk duty just before he took sick leave. As you know, Florin was found murdered at his apartment. When I made a search there, I found a notebook belonging to you, Jules – it had your name in the front. A small black notebook – easily dropped when someone is in a hurry.' He sat back in his chair and went on puffing his pipe. Louise stared at him, the muscles of her jaw tight.

'And I believe my own apartment has been broken into and ransacked,' Beaurain said quietly.

'That is so,' Flamen agreed. 'Ransacked to cover the stealing of the notebook later left in Florin's apartment. Voisin wants me to hold you for questioning,' he added casually.

'In what connection?' Beaurain asked tightly.

'In connection with the investigation of the murder of Pierre Florin – because you were going to question Florin and also on the evidence of your notebook being found there.' Flamen produced a small black notebook from his pocket and pushed it across the table. 'That is yours, I take it, Jules?'

'You know it is.'

'By the way, Florin was shot in the back of the neck. One shot.'

'The old Nazi method of execution.'

'Of course!' He snapped his fingers. 'That's what it reminded me of. It could be the signature of the executioner – a German trained by the Nazis. By the way, have either of you visited Bruges recently?' Flamen enquired placidly. His pipe was smoking furiously and he was staring out of the window.

'Yes,' Beaurain answered shortly. 'Today.'

He kept his answers as brief as possible and avoided mentioning that Louise had accompanied him. Willy Flamen could be clever and devious. 'Why?'

'Because this morning a bargee called Frans Darras and his wife, Rosa, were brutally murdered aboard their barge. The same technique was used – both were shot in the back of the neck. One bullet apiece. Voisin has dived in head first, linked the three killings together because of the *modus operandi* – and linked them all with you because of Florin. The fact that you were in Bruges today won't help when he hears.'

Flamen broke off to answer the telephone. He listened and then asked a number of questions rapidly. The topic of the phone call was obvious. Flamen broke the connection, excused himself, and used the phone to despatch a team of investigators and forensic experts. Replacing the receiver, he gave a grunt and then looked at both of them with a grim smile.

'Where have you parked your Mercedes, Jules?'

'In a side street out of sight.'

'Good.' He stared at the ceiling. 'There was a bloodbath outside police headquarters not fifteen minutes ago. Voisin is going mad – as if that were news. Three men attacked a vehicle passing headquarters. All three are dead, and one was armed with a sub-machine-gun. Some fool of a woman peering out after it was nearly over says that four men who were attacked were travelling in a Mercedes. She didn't specify a 280E.' He waited for comment.

'So?' asked Beaurain.

'I'm glad to see you both looking so well.' His manner became very serious as he leaned forward over the table. 'More than ever I think you should leave Belgium tonight. Surely you can continue your investigation from a safer country.'

'Name one,' said Beaurain. 'But thanks, Willy.' He left it at that. 'One thing which puzzles me is how the Syndicate operates its communications – because you can bet your pension it will have a system and a good one. Is anyone working on that?'

Flamen stood up and brought a map of Belgium from a side-cabinet which he spread out over his desk. 'There has been an unusual amount of illegal radio traffic during the past six months.'

'In these ringed areas?' Beaurain asked, studying the map.

'Yes. A colleague of mine compiled this and I borrowed it – I thought it might interest you. I can't make head or tail of the thing.'

'But you think it has some significance?' Louise enquired.

'That's what I'm not sure about,' Flamen admitted. 'We have a fleet of radio-detector vans scattered throughout Belgium. Some are under the control of counter-espionage.'

'And these ringed areas show the areas of the most intense activity during the past six months?' Louise asked. While she and Flamen were talking Beaurain was staring at the map with a scowl of concentration.

'That's right,' Flamen agreed. 'The trouble is the Syndicate's transmitters keep moving while transmitting. That increases the difficulty of location enormously. They must have the transmitters inside tradesmen's vans – something innocent-looking which wouldn't look out of place travelling along a highway.'

'How do you know these are Syndicate transmissions? Has someone broken the code?' Beaurain asked.

Flamen hesitated. 'That's top secret information from another department. Frankly, until today I wasn't sure myself, and no-one else is, so this is between the three of us. One of our men did crack one code. Two days later he was killed. Shot in the back of the neck. One bullet.'

'Order Captain Buckminster to take *Firestorm* into the Kattegat and then proceed full steam ahead until he's anchored off Elsinore.'

Immediately after their meeting with Chief Inspector Willy Flamen, Beaurain and Louise had driven back to Henderson's control headquarters. On arriving Beaurain had begun to issue a stream of instructions to Henderson. Within minutes the atmosphere inside the room – which had been tense before they returned – became electric. At one stage Henderson swung briefly in his swivel chair to ask a question.

'All this means, sir, that Telescope is temporarily evacuating Belgium – including the Château Wardin? Is it really essential to go that far?'

'If we are to fool the Stockholm Syndicate we have to put into action what you have rehearsed time and again, Jock. We withdraw so swiftly we're gone before they suspect what's happening.'

'May I know the reason?'

'I'm just coming to it. I'm gambling everything on two people being right – Goldschmidt in Bruges and Ed Cottel of the CIA. They both state that a full meeting of the Stockholm Syndicate is taking place somewhere in Scandinavia in less than two weeks' time. Telescope must be there in force to confront them.'

'Why should Goldschmidt and Cottel be right?' Louise objected.

'They don't have to be,' Beaurain said, 'but we have to take a decision and it's bound to be a gamble. The point is they have entirely different sources – literally in different continents. But they both say the same thing. About two weeks away – a meeting. Locale – Scandinavia.'

'Hence you're moving *Firestorm* towards the Baltic?'

'It's so packed with men and equipment it has become a mobile version of Telescope. We now have a force at sea we can land almost anywhere in the

Scandinavian zone. My huge gamble,' Beaurain admitted, 'is that this will be the scene of Goldschmidt's predicted collision between Telescope and the Stockholm Syndicate. Our next move,' he told Louise, 'is to pay a brief visit to Ed Cottel who is now back at the Hilton.'

'If you can reach it alive,' commented Henderson.

'It's the Baltic – just as I suspected,' said Captain 'Bucky' Buckminster, Captain of the steam yacht *Firestorm*, to his First Mate as he read the decoded signal. 'At the moment we sail through the Kattegat and wait at the entrance to the Øresund . . .' His wiry hand traced the course on the chart spread out on the chart-table. 'On arrival we anchor off Elsinore – unless we're ordered to proceed at full speed into the Baltic, which wouldn't surprise me.'

Buckminster was a tall, restless man of fifty who had commanded a destroyer in the Royal Navy before retiring at his own request.

'We do realise the murder of your daughter in Beirut must have come as a great shock, Bucky,' one of his superiors had told him. 'But why don't you give your decision more time? You'll lose your pension, you love the sea, and who's going to give you another command like the one you're resigning?'

'No-one, sir,' Buckminster had lied, meeting the Admiral's eyes without flinching. It would not have done to reveal that he would be taking over command of a vessel which carried at least as heavy a punch as the destroyer whose command he was relinquishing, even if it was concealed under the guise of a powerful steam-ship built and operated for the Baron de Graer.

Seen from the air, the impression of idle luxury was confirmed by the blue swimming pool. It would have taken a very keen pilot's eye to notice the size of the helipad aft, capable of landing the largest type of Sikorsky in the world, the chopper which the Americans in Vietnam had called a gunship.

The same keen pilot's eye might also have wondered about why so formidable a winch was needed aboard a Belgian millionaire's floating plaything. And had he happened to be flying over when the giant hatch had been open, something else might well have caused him to lift his eyebrows the size of the hold and the fact that it contained a small float-plane, a very large launch complete with wheelhouse and several power-boats.

Before agreeing to join Telescope, Buckminster had gone secretly to Brussels to discuss what had been presented to him as 'an interesting proposition in view of the brutal and tragic murder of your daughter'. On his arrival in Brussels he had learned to his dismay that he was meeting a Belgian. Impossible for him to imagine himself taking orders from someone who wasn't British. He received a further shock when he was introduced to Jules Beaurain, who, dressed casually in a polo-necked sweater and slacks, became the image of an Englishman when he opened his mouth. Buckminster agreed to take command of *Firestorm* even before he had seen the vessel.

Now he stuffed the signal from Henderson in his pocket. The powerful rotors of the giant helicopter could be heard in the sky.

'Dead on time, sir, as always,' First Mate Adams observed, checking his watch.

'Has she brought everything we need?' demanded Buckminster.

'The earlier signal – didn't feel it was necessary to report that to you – confirmed that Anderson airlifted from the Scottish coast two bazookas, extra submachine guns, extra ammunition, a supply of hand-grenades and various small-arms. No alcohol was included in the consignment,' Adams said with a grin.

Buckminster shaded his eyes as he watched the incoming chopper whose sheer size never ceased to surprise him. His reprimand was the more devastating for being delivered as he stared upwards.

'Adams, I decide what is and is not necessary. In future you will show me all – repeat all – signals reaching this vessel.'

'Of course, sir. Fully understood, sir.'

'Another point. I run a dry ship, therefore your presumably humorous reference to alcohol is not appreciated.'

'Really am very sorry indeed, sir.'

In his best quarterdeck manner Buckminster lowered his hand and glared at his First Mate.

'Just so long as it doesn't happen again. Now, I

leave you to see to it that Anderson and that bloody great chopper of his land safely on the helipad.'

Turning his back on Adams, he studied the chart again and taking a pencil from his pocket drew his projected course. The Sikorsky lowered its great bulk onto the helipad. The sea was calm, a sheet of rippling blue which sparkled and glittered in the reflection from the sun shining out of a clear sky. All this was lost on Buckminster as he studied the chart. Nor was he dwelling on the fact that below deck he was carrying some of the most deadly killers in the world a large nucleus of ex-Special Air Service men, and men from various nations who all had their own reasons for hating terrorism.

'Who and where is our opponent?' was the question he was asking as *Firestorm* increased speed and headed for Elsinore.

At precisely the same hour – and also in the glare of a blazing sun – the 2,000-ton Soviet hydrofoil MV *Kometa* was proceeding at twenty knots off the Polish coast near Gdansk. Captain Andrei Livanov turned as Sobieski came onto the bridge and concealed his dislike of the newcomer with an effort. Livanov was a Muscovite and proud of it. Having to consort with such people as Poles did not suit his temperament.

'Is there some problem, Sobieski?' he asked.

'None whatsoever, Comrade.'

'Then you had better return to your control headquarters to make sure no problem does arise.'

Peter Sobieski, a well-built man of forty with a cheerful and extrovert personality, glanced at his temporary – and nominal – captain and then lit a cigarette.

'If a problem arises you will not be able to eat. If an emergency occurs you will have a nervous breakdown,' thought Sobieski, who disliked Russians as much as Livanov disliked Poles. He did not say the words out loud. Instead he blew smoke across the bridge, an action which touched off Livanov's edgy nerves. 'You will not smoke on my bridge!'

Sobieski added insult to injury by grinding the cigarette under his heel. At that moment a radio signal received from the shore station was handed to Livanov. It did not improve his temper. The signal asked why *Kometa* was cruising like an ordinary vessel and not using her surface-piercing foils.

Captain Livanov concealed his anger. First the man in charge of the sonar room had been replaced by Sobieski. The Pole undoubtedly knew his job; Livanov had to admit that he was at least as good as the regular man. But Sobieski was Viktor Rashkin's creature. And Viktor Rashkin, the wonder boy of the Soviet political world, was Leonid Brezhnev's creature.

It was Rashkin, the second most powerful man in the Soviet Union, who had ordered *Kometa* to proceed along the Baltic shore on its way to Germany. And it was the brilliant Rashkin who had come aboard briefly before *Kometa* departed from Leningrad, bringing with him Peter Sobieski.

'He will take control of the sonar during this voyage of your remarkable ship,' he had informed Livanov.

Livanov was on the verge of asking *Is he qualified?* before he realised the danger of the question. He hoped he was. He dared not cast doubt on Rashkin's judgement.

'He is my assistant,' Rashkin had said. 'He is also a Pole. Do not look surprised, Comrade Livanov. We and our European allies are one big happy family – so why should we not co-operate?'

Had there been a note of cynical irony in Rashkin's remark? The captain of *Kometa* had glanced quickly at him and a pair of shrewd eyes had met his own. Livanov did not understand this man whose expression changed with alarming suddenness. They said he had been an actor before he served his apprenticeship with the KGB.

Livanov was thinking of this conversation as he cruised off Gdansk and read the signal from shore control. Very well, he would show them. Sending Sobieski back to his sonar room, Livanov issued his instructions and the huge vessel began to pick up speed. He himself operated the lever which transformed *Kometa* from a normal vessel with her hull deep in the water to a streak of power elevated above the sea on massive steel blades like giant skis.

Onshore several pairs of eyes watched the spectacle through field-glasses. Some of the watchers had never seen a hydrofoil. There were expressions of sheer astonishment as *Kometa* flew across the vast bay. Fresh signals were despatched to the captain – this time of congratulation. Livanov chose to ignore them. He was thinking now of the passengers he would be taking on board at his next port of call. A detachment of MfS – members of the dreaded state security from East Germany.

Chapter Eight

Beaurain and Louise found Ed Cottel finishing a meal in an elegant café on the Hilton's ground floor. Overlooking a glassed-in veranda with a dense wall of trees and shrubberies, the Café d'Egmont had the atmosphere of somewhere in the country. It was safe to talk – Cottel was almost the only diner.

'Can I get you something?' he asked without ceremony.

'Just coffee, thank you,' Louise said. Beaurain also asked for coffee and declined anything to eat. They were short of time; the Belgian was anxious to return to Henderson's headquarters to check on the progress of Serge Litov.

'I hear, Jules, they're thinking of charging you with multiple murder, rape and God knows what other mayhem. I must say you've been busy while I was away.'

'Who told you these interesting titbits? Voisin?'

'Who else? He spent the whole time I was with him telling me what an outrage it was that you should control the investigation into the Syndicate. I think what particularly infuriated him is my insistence that he report this fact to all West European police chiefs and heads of counter-espionage. Now, he's trying to unseat you.'

'Was he . . . nervous?' Beaurain enquired casually.

Cottel crinkled his brow and rubbed his crooked nose, which Louise always found attractive. 'Now that you mention it,' the American decided, 'I guess the answer is "yes". Like a man who felt threatened.' He sipped at his coffee. 'Sounds pretty goddam ridiculous.'

'Maybe. Have you dug up any more information about the Syndicate, Ed?'

He waited until their coffee had been served and then started talking.

'First thing is that our latest satellite pictures taken over the Baltic show that big hydrofoil – the Soviet job, *Kometa* – creeping along the coast of Poland and heading for East Germany. It looks as though its ultimate destination could be the port of Sassnitz. And from there it's only a short distance to Trelleborg, a small port in Sweden. There also happens to be a ferry service between Sassnitz and Trelleborg.'

'What about that list of people for Voisin – the list you thought might lead to the personnel of Telescope?'

'Dammit! Never did get round to that – you've no idea how these transatlantic trips disappear – you get back and wonder what the hell you accomplished.' Cottel drank more coffee. 'I told Voisin that as soon as I hit his office – got in first before he asked.'

'You always were a good tactician, Ed,' murmured Beaurain. 'Do you now have Washington's backing to track down the Stockholm Syndicate?'

'In a word, no.' The American looked grim and wiped his mouth with his napkin. 'Queer atmosphere back home – especially close to the President. No-one wants to know. They all say wait till after the election – concentrate on exposing Telescope. One reason is they're upstaged by Telescope. But more important is the election. The man in the Oval Office isn't exactly the president of the century and there are people who would like to dump him before the Convention. If news of the Stockholm Syndicate ever leaked to the press – the fact that a huge piece of its finance is coming from American conglomerates looking for huge tax-free profits . . .' Cottel made a gesture with his napkin and then crushed it. 'Out of the window would go any chance of the President being re-elected. You can trace a line from the Stockholm Syndicate almost up to the Oval Office.'

'You mean that?' Beaurain asked sharply. 'You're not guessing?'

'Do I ever guess?' asked Cottel. 'I have more news.'

'Less unnerving than what you've told us so far, I hope,' said Louise.

'Viktor Rashkin fits into this thing somewhere,' Cottel said, keeping his voice low. 'We keep a close eye on Viktor, who is not a nice person. I can tell you he has just left Brussels Airport this evening aboard his Lear jet.'

'Alone?' Beaurain queried.

'No, not alone. He was accompanied by a fat man very muffled so you couldn't see his features – and also a girl, likewise with her features concealed.' He finished his coffee. 'I wondered whether anyone was interested in the flight plan Rashkin's pilot filed. His destination.'

'You're going to tell us anyway,' Louise said.

'Copenhagen – and then Stockholm. Which is why I'm catching the first plane out of here for Stockholm in the morning,' Cottel informed them. 'When you need me, you can find me at the Grand Hotel.'

'We're going to need your help?' Louise asked innocently.

'We're all going to need each other's help before this develops much further,' the American predicted.

The jet taxied to a halt at Copenhagen's Kastrup Airport. Inside the passenger cabin Viktor Rashkin lit a cigarette and gazed at his companion.

'What is your next move, Viktor?' she enquired. 'Isn't the opposition beginning to show some teeth?'

'The opposition – Beaurain in particular – is reacting just as I expected.' His dark eyes examined the tip of his cigarette. 'The important thing is to keep him away from Denmark for the next few days. The big consignment is on its way and nothing can – must – stop it.'

'How much is it worth?'

'On the streets something in the region of forty million Swedish kronor. I think we should leave the plane, my dear.'

'To go where?' Sonia Karnell asked.

'To pay a discreet call on our friend, Dr Benny Horn.'

'Max here, Jock. Speaking from Kastrup Airport. The subject left the flight here instead of proceeding on to Stockholm.'

'How can you be sure?' Henderson interjected tersely.

'Because you wait on the plane if you're going on – and the flight is now airborne for Stockholm. Because at this moment I'm watching Serge Litov . . .'

The large and heavily-built man – he was over six feet tall but like other men conscious of their excessive stature he stooped – had entered the booking-hall and now stood holding a short telescopic umbrella. His gross form was topped by a large head and a tan-coloured hat which partially concealed his strong-boned face. English was the language he used when he conversed with Serge Litov. He appeared unconnected with the Russian.

'Where is the man requiring my attention, sir?'

His jowls were heavy and fleshy; he was about sixty years old and the personification of a successful stockbroker. Litov could hardly believe this was the intermediary sent to cut out any intervention he might have spotted.

'Do I know you?' Litov asked sharply, covering his mouth with his hand as he lit a cigarette. The fool had not used the code. Had he himself walked into a trap? But in that case why had the Telescope people released him in the first place?

'I am, of course, sir, George Land. Coming from London you must know and appreciate as I do the beauties of St. James's Park at this time of the year.'

His mouth hardly moved – and yet Litov had heard every word quite clearly. *St James's Park* – that was Land's identification.

'The lake is what I like in St James's Park,' Litov responded, and the word 'lake' completed the code check. 'How did you know someone was following me?' George Land gave him the creeps, though he was not easily disturbed. Like a perfect English butler – and he was just about to despatch a fellow human being permanently.

'I knew someone was following you because I watched from outside the entrance doors. I observed your furtive glances in a certain direction. Also, I see now there is perspiration on your brow, if I may make mention of the fact, sir.'

The constant use of 'sir' did not help. Land was so cool and collected; his restrained courtesy was beginning to get on Litov's nerves. 'You see that man in the payphone?'

'I can see the gentleman quite clearly.'

'Get rid of him – permanently. As soon as I've got out of this place.'

'It would be helpful if you would remain where you are until I have reached the phone box. In that way he will notice no change in what interests him – yourself.'

Land briefly grasped the dangling umbrella with his left hand. And then Serge Litov understood as though he had been trained to use the weapon all his life. The umbrella was a camouflaged dagger, spring-loaded and designed so the blade projected from the tip at the touch of a button.

'I'll wait here,' he said reluctantly.

'It has been a most profitable conversation, sir,' said Land discreetly and proceeded across the almost deserted booking-hall as though bent on making a phone call.

'I said I was watching Litov,' repeated Kellerman to Jock Henderson from inside the payphone. 'He appears to be waiting for someone to collect him.'

'Or he could be playing a game,' the Scot pointed out. 'He'll still have that ticket to Stockholm.'

A large English-looking man was wandering across the hall towards the payphones. He was close enough for Kellerman to see his fleshy cheeks. As he walked with a slow deliberate tread he swung a telescopic umbrella back and forth from his right wrist. Otherwise, the booking-hall was empty. The other passengers had departed for Copenhagen via the airport bus or taxis and no other flight was due to land or take off.

'He's waiting here,' Kellerman repeated, 'and . . .'

'You keep repeating yourself, Max,' Henderson said sharply. 'Is anything wrong?'

'No. From Litov's behaviour I'm sure he's going into Copenhagen – maybe just for the night. I anticipate an attempt to evade surveillance while he's here – then he moves on to his next destination, which may not be Stockholm.'

'You think he's spotted you, then?'

'I didn't say that . . .' Kellerman's brow was wrinkled as he tried to talk to Henderson and think at the same time. 'But with a man of Litov's experience I'm assuming he'll *expect* surveillance.'

Kellerman suddenly grasped what had been worrying him outside the payphone. It was the huge English-looking man advancing on the bank of payphones. *He hadn't once looked at the booth occupied by Kellerman.* Which simply wasn't natural behaviour. In fact he was deliberately *not* looking at Kellerman's payphone even as he continued his steady, doomsday-like tread towards it. Beaurain came on the line, crisp, decisive.

'Beaurain. Trouble at your end?'

'Yes . . .'

'Louise books into the Royal Hotel later this evening. Goodbye.'

Kellerman carefully did nothing untoward. The large man was close to the door of his box, staring fixedly at an empty booth as his outsize feet continued their purposeful advance. By now Kellerman had noticed the telescopic umbrella swinging back and forth. The man wasn't a poof, he was certain.

He maintained his stance until the last moment: phone held to ear, head half-turned away, suitcase propped against side of payphone with one leg. George Land, jowls shaking, took one final glance round the booking-hall, a sweeping gaze which told him it was empty and that Litov was leaving without looking back. He pressed the button and the spring-loaded stiletto blade shot out of his umbrella which he held like a fencer about to make a savage lunge.

His thick lips slightly parted, he turned back to use his left hand to pull open the door of the booth occupied by Max Kellerman. The door was open.

Kellerman was inside the box, stooping to pick up the suitcase. Land stared at the side of the German's neck. He moved in closer, and took a strong grip on the umbrella ready for the lunge.

Everything moved rapidly out of focus for Land as Kellerman straightened up and slammed the steel-tipped edge of his suitcase into the giant's right kneecap. Land gulped with pain but did not cry out. His large face convulsed in fury. Like a handcuff Kellerman's right hand closed over the wrist which held the umbrella. The handcuff twisted and jerked upward in one violent arc of ninety degrees. The vertical stiletto-like blade entered Land's throat and his eyes bulged.

Kellerman had already transferred his grip to the two lapels of the Englishman's jacket and he spun him round before he could fall and heaved him inside the payphone. The receiver was still swinging from its cord as the Englishman's body began to slide down the rear wall, its feet projecting into the booking-hall over the umbrella on the floor.

Kellerman pulled a soft cap from his pocket and rammed it on his head as he moved swiftly across the still deserted booking-hall with only one idea in mind. To catch up with Serge Litov. The cab carrying Litov was just leaving the kerb as he came into the open air. Kellerman climbed into the next cab and closed the door before giving his instructions.

'Please follow that cab. Do not lose it – the passenger inside is responsible for an incident in the airport hall.'

The driver was quick-witted. While he checked on the identity of his passenger he was driving away from the airport, making sure he did not lose the vehicle ahead. He could take his passenger back to the airport if the replies were unsatisfactory. His passenger over-rode his questions by volunteering information.

'You will read about the airport incident in the morning papers. I am *Kriminalpolizei* working in liaison with the Belgians and your own people. Here is my card.' Kellerman flashed an identity paper which the driver hardly saw. To build up confidence and dispel all doubts, keep talking fluently, confidently . . .

'Do not crowd that cab, please. It is vital the passenger does not know he is being followed. There will, of course, be a large tip for your co-operation. Please, also, be careful when the cab approaches its destination. I must not be just behind when it stops. I appreciate it will not be easy.'

'I will manage it. No problem,' the Dane replied. Kellerman sank back into his seat and kept quiet. It had worked. Near the end of the conversation give them a problem to occupy their minds, then shut up!

'Serge Litov should be here by now. I cannot imagine what is detaining him. One thing I insist on is punctuality.'

The Danish antiquarian book dealer, known by the few Danes who met him as Dr Benny Horn, sat in the darkened room polishing his rimless spectacles and fidgeting as he checked the illuminated hands of his watch. His companion, a girl, smiled in the dark and listened to the gentle lapping of the water which came through the open window from the basin of the Nyhavn harbour outside.

'There could have been trouble at the airport,' he

fussed. 'Let us suppose Litov was followed – it is to be expected . . .'

'Then George Land will have dealt with the follower. And that might explain the delay.'

'Unless Litov involved himself in the fracas.'

'He has his instructions which he won't disobey.' The girl was amused by his exhibition of an irritable and pedantic dealer in rare books. Outside the open window headlights appeared, an engine stopped. Sonia Karnell saw a cab had arrived. 'Make sure he has not been followed,' Horn called to her.

'We are very close to Nyhavn,' Kellerman's driver said.

They had driven through a maze of streets and squares lined with ancient buildings and the German would have been hard put to it to trace the route on a map. He was fairly sure they were moving in a northerly direction. What the hell was Nyhavn? He waited, hoping the driver would elaborate, and the Dane obliged.

'Nyhavn is the old port area – seamen's bars to the left of the water and tourist trap shops to the right. That's our friend's likely destination.'

The cab ahead was the only vehicle in sight now. If they kept on driving much further it was only a matter of time before Litov spotted that he had a tail. The cab in front turned sharp right and the German guessed they had reached Nyhavn.

The middle of the street was occupied by a long, straight basin of water with its level well below that of the street, like a canal in Amsterdam. A forest of masts projected into the night sky. On either side of the brightly-lit street overlooking the waterway was a wall of seventeenth-century houses.

Kellerman's driver earned his tip. Instead of turning right alongside the basin he drove straight on past the end of the water, round a corner, and stopped. The brilliant lighting vanished. There were shadows everywhere.

'He would have seen us. I'm sure he's stopping somewhere down Nyhavn and it's a short distance before you're on the waterfront.'

'Thank you.' Kellerman gave him money. 'Would you wait? I shan't be long.'

The problem was that he would be conspicuous walking along Nyhavn carrying a suitcase. It also restricted his movements if he were attacked – and he had not forgotten the assault with the umbrella. That weapon was reminiscent of Bulgarian techniques.

Free of his suitcase, he strolled round the corner back into the lights. Litov was climbing a short flight of steps to a house at the far end. 'Tourist trap shops on the right . . .' his driver had said. The Russian was entering one of the houses on the right – easy to pinpoint even from a distance because each house was painted a different colour. A most helpful arrangement.

It was also helpful that there were people about.

Kellerman strolled a short distance down the left-hand side and saw the flights of steps leading down to the basement bars. Returning the way he had come, he walked round the end of the harbour basin and continued down the tourist-trap side until he drew level with the house Litov had disappeared into. At the top of a short flight of steps in the blaze of street lights Kellerman could make out a name engraved in large letters on a plate. *Dr Benny Horn*. He had located the base of another of the three-man directorate running the Stockholm Syndicate.

It was time to meet Louise at the Royal Hotel.

When Serge Litov climbed the steps at the Nyhavn address he was relieved to see the name engraved on a plate to the right of the heavy door. *Dr Benny Horn*. Litov pressed the bell.

'Come in quickly.'

The door closed behind him and he stood in darkness. There was the sound of a lock being turned, of bolts being shot home. Then a blaze of light illuminated the narrow hallway, so strong it made Litov blink. He looked quickly behind him. A slim, dark-haired girl, her hair cut close like a helmet, stood aiming a Walther pistol. It was Sonia Karnell.

Litov had expected to meet Dr Otto Berlin, the man who had issued him with his instructions to penetrate Telescope's headquarters. Instead, facing him in the hallway, stood a man wearing a skullcap, a bow-tie and a neat suit which was in considerable contrast to Berlin's careless dress. He was also clean-shaven and stood with his hands clasped across his slim stomach while he contemplated Litov in a manner which irritated the Russian.

'Who the hell are you?' he demanded brusquely. 'I've come a long way and I'm damned tired.'

He stopped as he felt the muzzle of Sonia's Walther press against the back of his neck.

'You are also damned impolite,' the man facing him remarked in a cold distant voice. 'I am Benny Horn, the man Dr Berlin ordered you to report to when you had completed your mission, as I believe the phrase goes in your circles.'

Litov flinched at the sneer in Horn's voice; he flinched also as he felt the gun barrel jabbing into his neck.

'Come into this room and report at once what you have discovered,' Horn ordered and led the way into a room overlooking Nyhavn. Litov sat down in an armchair indicated by Horn, who himself occupied a stiff-backed chair behind an antique desk. Unlike Berlin, who slouched all over the place, Horn sat erect and again clasped his hands as he stared at the new arrival.

'Coffee, Litov?'

Sonia did not wait for a reply as she poured a cup of black coffee from a percolator and added a generous spoonful of sugar. She knew his tastes, Litov observed. The Walther pistol had disappeared. Unlike the hallway, where he had been so dazzled by the glare he had hardly been able to focus on Horn, here in the book-lined room the lighting was dim, but Horn sat in one of the shaded areas. He waited until Litov had drunk half the cup of coffee and then began to fire a barrage of questions at him.

'You located Telescope's base?'

'It is in southern England – near Guildford in the county of Surrey.'

'How do you know that?'

Litov explained how he had seen the red bus with the destination *Guildford* on the front. Horn seemed more interested in the pillar box where letters had been collected. What time of day had the postman collected? Had he seen anyone *post* a letter in the box? The barrage of questions went on and on – almost as though Horn were hoping to catch him out in a lie. Litov couldn't understand the ferocity of the cross-examination.

'How were you able to time the flight of the helicopter in both directions?' Horn demanded at one stage.

'Fortunately they let me keep my watch.'

'They *let* you keep your watch? You had it with you all the time? The watch you are wearing at this moment?'

Litov barely concealed his irritation, but remembered the cold, detached look in Horn's eyes and the cold pressure of the pistol against the back of his neck. 'Yes,' he said. 'While I was at the house near Guildford the interrogator, Carder, even mentioned the watch once. He said it would stop me becoming completely disorientated if I knew the time.'

Horn went on asking Litov again and again to repeat the story of his experiences since his capture in Brussels. Then it ended abruptly. Horn stood up and came round to the front of his desk, staring down at Litov as he polished his rimless spectacles.

'Wait here,' he said suddenly. 'On no account attempt to leave this room.'

Horn hurried out into the hall followed by the girl who shut the sound-proof door. They went into a room at the back and sat facing each other across a table. 'What do you think?' Horn asked, removing his skull-cap.

'The bus convinces me.'

'We must send a heavy detachment of specialized troops by air to locate and destroy that base.' He stopped speaking as the front door-bell rang. Sonia Karnell slipped into the hall and returned shortly. 'It is Danny.'

Waiting in the hall was the cab-driver who had transported Kellerman from Kastrup to Nyhavn when they followed Serge Litov.

Max Kellerman had settled himself into Room 1014 at the Royal Hotel – but he was ready for an emergency departure. He chose the quick-service restaurant –

where the service lived up to its name and the food was on a par with the service – for several reasons. It was part of the shopping and reception hall complex, which meant that as he ate he was able to observe the reception counter from a discreet distance. This could pay life-saving dividends – as Kellerman had discovered in the past. It enabled you to observe who booked in at the hotel after your own arrival. A method of assassination employed all over the world was for the hired killer to take a room in the same hostelry as his victim.

If – as Kellerman had done – you left your room key with reception while you ate and watched – you could sometimes spot a caller making an enquiry about you. The receptionist would swivel his head to see whether your key was on the hook. It was impossible to be sure the receptionist had checked your key – but if you were already suspicious it was added confirmation.

Kellerman lingered over his meal, savouring the Scandinavian food. He was already beginning to enjoy the relaxed atmosphere he sensed in the Danes who inhabited Copenhagen, which was refreshingly free of the normal multitude of high-rise blocks. The multistorey Royal Hotel, oddly enough, was an exception. Jules Beaurain and Louise Hamilton arrived at the reception desk at precisely 10.30 p.m.

*

'Louise, I've been to the scene of the murder aboard the barge near Bruges – there was *a witness,* a boy who spends half his time in a tree-house he's built.'

'Hold on a minute, Willy, here is Jules.'

The call came through at the Royal Hotel in response to an earlier call from Beaurain to Willy Flamen at his home address. Flamen had been on his way home and his wife had promised that he would call back the moment he arrived. Beaurain emerged steamily from the bathroom where he had just taken a shower.

'It's Willy Flamen,' Louise told him. 'About that bargee and his wife. He says he's found a witness.'

'I'll take it. You go downstairs and keep Max from feeling lonely. He's still drinking coffee in that restaurant, watching reception.'

'Time you gave up,' she said to the German when she had joined him and had ordered coffee. Only one man on duty now and a general atmosphere of boredom and closing-down for the night.

'It comes when you least expect it,' he replied.

'What does?'

'The breakthrough. The incident which means nothing at the time and everything later on. Waiting is the key to success. Any policeman will tell you that.'

'And when you were a lawyer in Munich did you meet a lot of police?'

A flicker of pain crossed his face. He responded in a slightly grating voice behind which she detected a hint of menace – not for herself, but for some unknown killer. She really had blown it. 'I'm sorry, Max. It was in the Munich shoot-out that your wife was killed. What was she like?'

'Irreplaceable.'

'Sorry again. I'll keep my big mouth shut.'

'You don't have to,' he assured her. 'And I'm sitting here for a reason – I don't understand why the Syndicate mob didn't have more back-up at Kastrup Airport when I arrived with Serge Litov.'

'Where is Louise?' asked Beaurain, slipping into the chair alongside Kellerman in the ground floor restaurant.

'She took off after someone.'

'What the hell are you talking about?' asked Beaurain, his face devoid of expression.

'It's strange,' the German commented. 'I was just saying – it comes when you least expect it. A breakthrough. I was just coming up to your room to tell you. We were sitting here when a girl went up to the reception counter and we saw the clerk turn round and look towards where my key was hanging. She rolled his pen onto the floor behind the counter to keep him busy while she checked the register of guests. She could have been anything European. She had a distinctive hairdo – very black hair cut short and close to her head – like a helmet. What's wrong, Jules?'

Beaurain's eyes were hard. 'I'm waiting for you to get to the point,' he said with an unnerving quietness.

'After she had gone outside, Louise followed her and waited at the door for my signal.'

'Why not the other way round? Why didn't *you* take the tail job?'

'For a reason I'll give you in a minute.' The German met Beaurain's gaze levelly. 'I went up to the receptionist and spun him a story about thinking I'd recognised the girl as a friend of my wife's. He opened up immediately – strange coincidence and all that. The girl was looking for a man who had dropped a wallet her husband had picked up. She described me perfectly and said her husband thought I'd come into this hotel. He – the fictitious huband – had been rushing to a business appointment and would come back in the morning.'

'So she got your name?'

'She got that – and my room number.'

'And Louise?' asked Beaurain.

'I gave her the go-ahead. The "black helmet" girl got into a car and Louise followed her in the car you hired. I couldn't – just in case I was recognised from the incident at Kastrup.'

'I've just heard someone else call the girl Black Helmet, and since it was an intelligent child's description it is likely to be accurate. She was visiting a couple on a barge near Bruges just before they were murdered.'

Chapter Nine

Kellerman was shaken by Beaurain's news. He sat staring at the reception counter where the girl they had christened Black Helmet had played her tricks on the receptionist.

'Who is this intelligent child?' he asked in a toneless voice.

'I was talking on the phone to Willy Flamen when Louise came down to join you. A boy he interviewed had built a makeshift cabin in the branches of a tree overlooking the Darras' barge.'

'How does this tie up with Black Helmet?'

'If you'll keep quiet until I've finished, I'll explain,' Beaurain told Kellerman coldly. 'This boy lives nearby and he sounds a loner. He makes a habit of creeping out of his bedroom after dark and spending half the night in his hidey-hole. The Darras' barge has been moored to the same place on the towpath for quite some time.'

'Perhaps their role was to act as a link for the Stockholm Syndicate.'

'That was my thought too. Now, this boy – who impressed Willy, I gather – was hiding in his cabin, probably snooping on what the Darras' were up to, when a car arrives long after dark. He saw a girl visit the Darras', someone shone a lamp full on her face. The description fits Black Helmet perfectly.'

'It's a long way from Bruges to Copenhagen.'

'Well, Louise and I made the trip. Why not Black Helmet? The kid was also there when Darras and his wife were murdered – although he didn't realise what happened at the time. He probably saw the killer and his companion arrive at the barge: an odd-sounding couple from his description.'

'This precocious child is a veritable mine of information,' Kellerman said cynically, not fully convinced of the danger to Louise.

'The killer,' Beaurain continued, ignoring the interruption, 'was dressed like an American according to the kid. Also he wears a straw hat and dark glasses and is of average height and build. His companion is thin – that was all Flamen could get on him. They operate in a strange way. The kid actually saw the thin man take from a brief-case what he called "a big gun with a bulging nozzle" and hand it to the "American" as they stepped onto the barge. My own theory – and Flamen is inclined to agree – is that Black Helmet called on them a few days earlier, gave them some final instructions, and they then became a liability to Dr Otto Berlin who ordered the two killers in to deal with them.'

Kellerman pushed away his cup which a Filipino waitress had refilled with coffee. 'It's all speculation, though. You still haven't conclusively linked them – or the girl – with the Syndicate.'

'Black Helmet's description fits perfectly the pictures Dr Henri Goldschmidt showed us of the two people leaving a house in Bruges. One was Dr Berlin. With him was a girl. Black Helmet.'

'Forty million Swedish kronor worth of heroin,' said Benny Horn. 'Intriguing how much money you can carry in one suitcase.'

He was facing Sonia Karnell in the narrow hallway and carried the case in his right hand. On her return she had locked the door behind her and was eager to make her announcement. Horn had been waiting for over an hour, however, and his impatience overrode her sense of the dramatic.

'I have news.'

'Tell me quickly. The van for Elsinore is waiting outside. This consignment is so huge I won't be happy till it's outside Copenhagen.'

'Armed with Danny's description of the man who followed Litov here from Kastrup, I checked the King Frederik Hotel where Danny left him. His passenger played it clever – obviously a professional. He didn't book in at the King Frederik. I had to start hunting, hoping to God he'd chosen a large place and not some fleapit.'

'I have understood you so far,' Horn said quietly.

'I tried the Palace. Told my story and gave them

Danny's description of the man. All I had going for me was that few people book in as late as this. No luck at the Palace. But 1 struck gold at the Royal Hotel.'

'Yes?'

The excitement in her manner made Horn contain his impatience. She must have uncovered something important. Which was a blasted nuisance when he wanted to leave Copenhagen fast. The consignment of heroin had arrived by a small boat, which had briefly docked at the end of Nyhavn while Sonia was out searching for the mysterious shadow.

'He's staying at the Royal,' Karnell continued. 'Description fits Danny's. But I got a chance to read the register upside down and two more people arrived even later. One is Jules Beaurain, the other Louise Hamilton.' Dr Benny Horn slowly put the suitcase down on the carpet and stared at the girl.

'You have interesting company in town with you tonight, Jules,' Ed Cottel of the CIA told him over the phone. 'Viktor Rashkin landed at Copenhagen in his Lear jet after flying from Brussels.'

Beaurain sat on the edge of the bed in his room at the Royal Hotel, listening closely to his American friend. He had phoned the Grand Hotel in Stockholm on the off-chance that Ed might have arrived. It occurred to him that Cottel didn't seem to worry much about the security of an open telephone line.

Max Kellerman, perched on the edge of a wooden chair, looked stiff and serious, and Beaurain knew he was worried sick about what was happening to Louise. There had been no word from her since she had followed Black Helmet out into the night.

'Ed,' Beaurain replied into the mouthpiece, 'was there anyone with Rashkin when he left the Lear jet at Kastrup?'

'Yes, a girl. Difficult to see at a distance – just as it was with the big R, apparently. She had dark hair, cut short. End of description.'

'So where did they go when they left the plane? And is it still at Kastrup, waiting to take him on somewhere tomorrow maybe?'

'My man lost them again when they left the airport. They had two cars waiting – one for passengers, one to set up interference if anyone tried to tail them. The girl left with the big R. And the man I hoped to contact here isn't at home in his apartment in Gamla Stan – that's Swedish for the Old City. He's a book dealer. Rare editions.'

'Has he a name?'

'Dr Theodor Norling. Keep in touch. Bye, Jules.'

It was 10.30 p.m. when Beaurain broke his phone connection with Ed Cottel in Stockholm. In Washington, DC, it was only 4.30 p.m. and the atmosphere in the Oval Office at the White House was tense. The President, who faced an election in less than six months' time, had long become accustomed to seeing the world entirely through electoral glasses. His every action was judged by one criterion: would it gain or lose him votes in November?

The fact that he was already being called 'one of the worst presidents in the history of the United States' had only bolstered his determination to see that his country – and the world – was subjected to four more years of the mixture as before. Seated behind his desk, his legs raised, his ankles crossed and resting on it, he looked at the only two other people with him.

His wife, Bess, sat upright in an easy chair, leaning slightly forward in a characteristic manner which an unkind columnist once described as 'Bess rampant and ready for blood'. The second person, equally unpopular with the press, was his chief aide, Joel Cody from Texas. The subject of the conversation, which – like so many White House conversations – had been initiated by the President's wife, was Ed Cottel.

'You're sure this Ed Cottel was checked out before he was sent to Europe, Joel?' the President demanded.

'Right down to his underpants. He's West Coast – not Ivy League, thank God – and he has a leaning towards this private organisation, Telescope, and its objectives, although he tries to conceal it. He also believes the real menace is the Stockholm Syndicate and that we should concentrate all our fire on that.'

'For Christ's sake, Joel!' Tieless, his shirt front open, the most powerful man in the western world sat up straight, whipping his feet off the desk together with a sheaf of papers which fluttered to the floor. 'Until we've won the election we don't want to know about that Stockholm Syndicate. There are rumours that some of the top contributors to our campaign chest may have dabbled their fingers in that thing.'

'So when the crunch comes we want Telescope to be the target, not the Syndicate?' Cody suggested. 'And this way that's what we get.'

'You wouldn't care to explain that, Joel, would you?'

'I think you'll find Joel knows what he's doing,' Bess reassured her husband and then subsided, for the moment.

'Cottel is sympathetic to these Telescope people, whoever they may be,' Cody explained. 'We do know further that he is a personal friend of this Belgian, Beaurain – rumoured to be one of the chiefs of this Telescope outfit. So, while officially Cottel is locating the key personnel of Telescope – ready for the western security services to swoop when the time comes – he will really be trying to help the Telescope organisation all he can. We're having him watched – that way he leads us to the whole outfit pretty soon now.'

'Why don't we send this Harvey Sholto you keep recommending – you said Sholto hates the guts of Telescope.'

'Which is well known,' Cody assured the President smoothly, 'so Sholto wouldn't get anywhere near them. Ed Cottel only took this assignment so he could secretly keep the heat off Telescope – and he'll end up leading us to the capture and exposure of the whole goddam underground organisation.'

'I like it, Joel, I like it.' The well-known smile suddenly left his face. 'Haven't you overlooked something? Supposing Cottel digs up information we'd just as soon he didn't – such as names of some of the big companies whose chairmen have contributed money to the Syndicate?'

'That's all taken care of,' Joel assured him confidently. 'If Cottel gets out of line we send over Sholto to take care of him. I may even send him in any case.'

'Don't give me those sort of details,' the President said hastily. 'In fact, I don't know anything about this Harvey Sholto. And I don't really understand what you've just said, so let's change the subject.'

Louise Hamilton felt sure she would lose the dark-haired girl. The same girl she and Beaurain had seen outside Bruges station when they took her vacated taxi. Leaving Kellerman with hardly a word, she walked out the back way and got behind the wheel of the hired Citroën.

'I want hired cars waiting for me at Copenhagen, Stockholm, Helsinki and Oslo,' Beaurain had instructed Henderson. Thankful for his foresight, Louise drove round near the main entrance and stopped. Seconds later the dark-haired girl came out, summoned a passing cab and got inside. As Louise followed the cab, keeping a rough check on its route with the aid of the Copenhagen street map open on the seat beside her, she soon began to suspect the girl's destination. The house on Nyhavn Kellerman had described.

Within minutes she knew she had guessed correctly. The cab ahead turned right, the basin of water was there in the middle of the street, the forest of masts above fishing boats tied up to the quays. Louise took a quick decision. Tooting her horn, she speeded up and overtook the cab with inches to spare. It was not the act of someone who wished the cab's passenger to be unaware of her presence – and inside the cab Sonia Karnell hadn't even noticed the Citroën as she felt inside her handbag for the front door key. Coming close to the main waterfront, where the wall of houses ended, Louise pulled in at the kerb and watched the cab coming up behind her in the rear-view mirror.

'If you have guessed wrong, my girl,' she told herself, 'you've had it.' The cab stopped a dozen yards behind where she was parked. She watched while the short-haired girl paid off the cab, went up the steps, inserted a key and went inside, closing the door behind her. The cab drove past her and was turning right along the waterfront on its way back into the centre of Copenhagen.

Louise didn't hesitate. The moment to check on a place is when someone has just arrived. Nobody expects a shadow to have the audacity to approach so close when the person they have followed has just entered a building.

She was walking along the pavement within less than twenty seconds of the door closing. She reached the bottom of the short flight of steps, the smell of brine in her nostrils, saw the engraved plate to the right of the heavy door and tiptoed swiftly up the steps.

Dr Benny Horn. The same name Max Kellerman had mentioned. This was the house which had swallowed up Serge Litov after his dash from Brussels. Was this journey's end for the Russian? She doubted it very much. Glancing down she saw a squalid-looking basement area, the glass of the windows murky with grime, the steps streaked with dirt. It was in great contrast to the freshly-painted front door and surrounding walls of the house.

She returned to the Citroën at once, climbed behind the wheel, locked all the doors from the inside, took out a peaked cloth cap and rammed it loosely over her head. With her strong jaw-line the cap gave her a masculine appearance; in the bad light – she was midway between two street lamps – she could easily be mistaken for a man. She slumped down behind the wheel as though asleep and waited, her eyes fixed on the rear-view mirror.

Beaurain felt one satisfaction which offset the considerable anxiety he felt about Louise. He sat on his bed and drank more coffee, watching Max Kellerman pace back and forth with the restlessness caused by enforced inaction. Beaurain voiced his satisfaction to try and cheer up the German.

'At least I guessed right when I sent *Firestorm* into the Kattegat. Serge Litov headed for Copenhagen as soon as he thought he'd shaken himself loose.'

'Where will *Firestorm* be at this moment?'

Beaurain checked his watch. 'Just after midnight. She'll be just about off Elsinore. It's the narrowest passage between Denmark and Sweden.'

'And Henderson?'

'He and his men from Brussels should by now be aboard her. They caught the flight before us as soon as I heard Litov had alighted from the Stockholm flight here.'

'And how did they get from here to *Firestorm*?'

'By courtesy of Danish State Railways. They came from Kastrup straight into Copenhagen. From the main station just across the way from this hotel – they caught an express to Elsinore, which is less than an hour's journey due north of the city and straight up the coast. I'd told Buckminster by radio what to expect and when. At a remote point on the coast just north of Elsinore, Henderson's party onshore exchanged signals by lamp with *Firestorm,* which promptly sent a small fleet of inflatable dinghies powered with outboards to pick them up.'

'How do you manage it?' Kellerman had stopped pacing and was sitting in a chair as he poured them both more coffee.

'I'm lucky,' Beaurain smiled grimly. 'It helps if you

have the pieces on the board in the right squares at the right time. In this case particularly *Firestorm*. Goldschmidt in Bruges was emphatic that a meeting of the Stockholm Syndicate is due to take place in Scandinavia. There was mention of it at Voisin's meeting, the one I had to fight my way into.' He frowned. 'That was the first time they tried to grab Louise. What the hell can have happened to that girl?'

'I'm sorry.' Max spread his hands.

'Shut up! I've already told you it's not your fault. And you both took the right decision.'

They were waiting for the van. Dr Benny Horn, wearing a dark-coloured raincoat and a soft, wide-brimmed hat, stood once again in the hallway holding the suitcase which contained heroin to the value of forty million Swedish kronor. He had just completed making several phone calls.

'Have you fixed up anything for Beaurain and Co.?' asked Sonia Karnell, who had changed into a different trouser suit.

'Gunther Baum is now in Copenhagen. He will pay them a visit at the appropriate moment.'

She shuddered as always at the mention of Baum. 'I thought he was in Brussels.'

'He was. Guessing that Beaurain would follow Litov to Copenhagen, I instructed him to make himself available here. I have just talked with Baum on the phone. The great thing is to have one's servants available at the right time,' Horn remarked.

'Is it sensible to have our destination – Helsingør – painted in large letters across the side of the van?'

'Yes, it merges into the background at Helsingør which,' Horn continued in a contemptuous tone, 'is a provincial town, always feeling that cosmopolitan Copenhagen looks down on it.'

He stopped speaking as the doorbell rang in a particular way, a succession of rings. Karnell had extracted the automatic from her handbag, switched off the hall light and opened the door. The van had arrived – she could see the bloody great name she objected to: *Helsingør*.

The driver, a short bulky man wearing a blue boiler suit and a beret, handed her the ignition keys and went inside. Out of the corner of her eye Karnell saw Dr Horn make a brief gesture with his head in the direction of the shuttered room where Litov was still waiting for fresh instructions.

Helsingør. Shakespeare's Elsinore where Kronborg Castle was linked with Hamlet's name. No historical foundation for the myth, but it was very good for Elsinore's tourist industry. Louise saw the van out of the corner of her eye as it passed down Nyhavn, heading for the waterfront where it would turn right or left.

Back into the centre of Copenhagen? In her rear-view mirror Louise had seen the couple, the man with the suitcase and the dark-haired girl, come out of the house and climb into the front of the van delivered by the man in the boiler suit.

She had observed that the girl climbed in behind the wheel, that the man clutched the suitcase, casting a quick glance up and down the street and a final look over his shoulder before climbing into the cab as passenger. The final look over his shoulder had been in the direction of the nearest fishing vessel moored to the quay. On the deck stood a seaman looping a cable for no very obvious reason.

Was he a guard who watched the house for the occupants? Who would look twice at a seaman? Louise felt sure there *had* been a signal exchanged between the girl's companion and the sailor. To her relief the seaman immediately went below deck as the van was leaving. He would not be there to see her own departure.

She set off as soon as the van had disappeared round the corner. The word *Helsingør* was obviously a blind: wherever she tracked the van to it would not be Elsinore. There was very little traffic about at this late hour so she was able to follow the red lights of the van at a distance. Was the passenger who had clutched the case so possessively Dr Benny Horn? She shrugged; Jules had taught her the futility of wasting energy speculating to no purpose.

After driving through a district of wealthy suburbs they came out onto the coast road. On her right the dark waters of the Øresund rippled placidly by the light of the moon. There were the coloured navigation lights of an occasional vessel passing up or down the Sound.

The van and the shadowing Citroën were travelling north. Louise knew that with the sea on her right there was only one route they could be taking – and that route took them to Elsinore! Could the name on the van be a piece of double bluff? Or was Dr Benny Horn running an apparently legitimate business which had offices in Copenhagen and Elsinore? Jules had repeatedly said idle speculation was a waste of time.

My God! Jules – he would be doing his nut back at the Royal Hotel! She hadn't managed to inform him where she was or what she was doing. It couldn't be helped; the van ahead was almost the only link Telescope had left with the Stockholm Syndicate.

'Have it out with Jules later,' she told herself. 'And just hope to God following this van turns out to be worthwhile. Then he can't say one damned thing.'

It was one o'clock in the morning when the phone rang in Beaurain's bedroom. Kellerman had fallen asleep in a chair instead of returning to his own room. Beaurain had just checked the empty coffee pot with an expression of disgust. He grabbed for the receiver, almost knocking the instrument on the floor in his haste. It was Louise.

'I'm going to talk fast, Jules.' He understood her

meaning: at night, hotel operators, bored and idle, had been known to listen in on calls. 'I'm in Elsinore – you've got that?'

'Yes,' he said tersely.

'The girl at the reception counter took me to the place where Max was a few hours ago. On Nyhavn.'

'Understood.'

'She drove a man in a van with the word *Helsingør* on the side – nothing else, just the name – to Elsinore. He's hugging a suitcase like a gold-brick. Just south of the town they have stopped at a house which backs onto the rail track. There are shunting yards and loaded freight cars. Two have a large consignment of what looks like compressed paper – packing materials.'

'Got you.'

She was gabbling on, throwing all sorts of details at him irrespective of whether they seemed significant to her. He understood what she was doing exactly; they had used the same technique before.

'My position is a bit exposed. I'm actually inside Elsinore and no-one's about at this hour. The only hotel I've seen is closed.'

Position exposed. She was signalling danger to him. Beaurain recalled the chairman of the Banque du Nord who had warned him about the *Zenith* signal. He told her to hold the line for a second. Checking a map of Denmark, he picked up the receiver.

'Still there? Can you drive north out of the place a few miles?'

'Yes, I'd drive back to Copenhagen but I'm short of petrol.'

He gave her the name of a tiny place on the coast, instructed her how to get there by road. 'You drive down to the beach, Louise, and wait there with your headlights pointed out to sea. At fifteen minute intervals precisely – commencing on the hour – you flash your lights six times at five second intervals. Henderson will be coming to collect you himself.'

'From the sea?'

'From *Firestorm* in a small motor-boat. Now, have you got it?'

'I'm leaving at once.'

She broke the connection. No prolonged conversation, no asking of a dozen questions which flooded into her tired mind. Just obey orders. And something in Jules' tone had said, *get the hell out of there fast*.

Inside his bedroom, high up in the Royal Hotel, Beaurain replaced the receiver and looked at Kellerman who still sat upright in his chair.

'She's followed two people to Elsinore – one is the girl, Black Helmet, the other could be Benny Horn – who, incidentally, was carrying a suitcase. I'm guessing because there was no time to ask her for descriptions. I think she's in danger. I just hope Henderson reaches her in time.'

He put in another call to the address near Brussels Midi station from where, earlier, Henderson had directed the watching operation on Serge Litov. As he had anticipated, it was Monique who answered the phone. She had taken over control of the command centre in Brussels. In as few words as possible he told her the signal to be sent to Jock Henderson aboard *Firestorm*, now somewhere just north of Elsinore. He replaced the receiver again and yawned loudly.

'Time you caught up on your sleep,' Kellerman suggested. 'You take my room and I'll wait here for Monique to phone back.'

'Thanks, but I can't sleep until I know Louise is safe aboard *Firestorm*. You go get some sleep.'

'You think I'll sleep until *I* know she's safe?' the German demanded.

Beaurain grunted tiredly and grinned. Then he sighed.

'It's just that I'm not sure how far the tentacles of this octopus, the Stockholm Syndicate, spread. De Graer shook me: they've threatened his niece now so how far can we really trust him? How far can we trust anyone? That's why our first call in the morning will be on an old friend of mine, Superintendent Bodel Marker of Danish police Intelligence. He runs his outfit from police headquarters. That's only ten minutes away. He's dependable.'

'Of course, they do know we're here – I'm sure that girl spotted your name in the hotel register.'

'So, we look out for two men – one dressed like an American, the other carrying a brief-case, the brief-case containing the killer's gun.'

*

Inside the house on the outskirts of Elsinore, Dr Benny Horn sat polishing his glasses as he watched Sonia Karnell making up her face. The room was smartly furnished with modern pieces, the walls freshly painted in white; the heavy drapes masking the windows were pulled closed.

'Do you have to keep fiddling with those glasses?' Karnell asked irritably. 'What about that girl in the Citroën?'

'I'm thinking about her,' Horn replied mildly. 'Carl is watching her, and since he hasn't returned yet she must still be inside that phone booth.'

'But isn't it madness?' Karnell became more vehement the more she saw how calm Horn was. 'She is phoning the Telescope people to tell them where we are.'

'I sincerely hope so. My whole plan for destroying them is based on the knowledge that they followed Serge Litov to Copenhagen. You located our primary target, Beaurain, who will be destroyed when he leaves the Royal Hotel. Litov discovered the main Telescope base in England near Guildford – and we have people already searching the area. Now the girl may lead us to the remainder of Telescope's force on the European mainland.'

He broke off as a lean-faced man dressed inconspicuously in dark blue came silently into the room. 'Developments, Carl?'

'The girl finished phoning. She's on her way back to the car.'

Horn turned to Sonia Karnell. 'So now you follow her. And use the Porsche parked at the back – she will not recognise it. Carl has placed the explosive device in a box in the boot.'

'Why not kill her here?' Karnell snuggled coaxingly against his velvet jacket.

'Because we don't want blood all over the place here. It is our respectable house. I've been known here for many years.'

'That's a laugh,' she said quickly in French, the language they invariably used together, although it was neither's mother tongue. He pushed her away roughly. The eyes behind the rimless lens had lost their placidity, were cold and darkly intense. Eyes which had frightened countless men in their time.

'You will not joke about such things. You will not argue when I give you an order.' She struggled into her duffel jacket, shaken by his reaction. 'You will follow her because she may well lead you to another Telescope base in Denmark. Find out all you can, then use the device. Return here as soon as you can. There is much to do tomorrow. Understood?'

'Of course.'

'Good luck. Be quick – you must not lose her.'

Unlocking the car, Louise Hamilton glanced round in the darkness, listened for five minutes, which is too long for anyone to keep perfectly quiet. Her next precaution was to take her small torch from her shoulder-bag and shine it on the hood. The hardly visible match was where she had left it; no-one had raised the bonnet in her absence.

As she started the engine and drove slowly out of Elsinore she had the route map of Denmark open on the seat beside her. It took her two minutes to realise she was being followed. She was not surprised. Never underestimate the enemy – one of Jock Henderson's favourite maxims. Louise Hamilton had assumed only a short time after leaving Copenhagen that the couple *must* suspect that her car was a tail.

To escape any risk of detection she could have hung well back and almost certainly lost the van. The other option was to subordinate every other consideration – including personal safety – to making sure she did not lose the van. She had chosen the second option, and must have been spotted within ten minutes of leaving Copenhagen.

Now the roles were reversed. Heading north from Elsinore towards the remote rendezvous on the shore-line with Henderson, Louise was aware of the Porsche following at a discreet distance – but not so discreet that there was any danger of the sports car losing her.

Karnell concentrated on the red lights ahead, flicking her eyes away from them at intervals to maintain night vision. The Citroën puzzled her – because of the direction it was taking. The girl behind the wheel then disconcerted her more severely because of a sudden change in her way of driving. The car accelerated and disappeared round a bend in the road. Karnell pressed her foot down, tore round the corner and then jammed on her brakes.

'You stupid little cunning tart.'

The contradictions of her insult didn't bother the Swedish girl. Coming round the bend she had found the red lights immediately ahead, the Citroën cruising very slowly like someone looking for a turning.

It wasn't that at all, and Karnell knew it. The girl had speeded up and then braked as soon as she was out of sight beyond the bend. Just far enough from the bend to ensure that the Porsche wouldn't ram her – although it might have skidded off the road.

'Bitch! Bitch! Bitch!' Karnell snarled.

The Citroën was picking up speed again. Karnell glanced at the device on the seat beside her, a device which was protected with foam-rubber inside a cardboard box bearing the name of a well-known Copenhagen florist. Much as she disliked handling explosive, Karnell was beginning to look forward to attaching some extra equipment to the car ahead.

She kept the speed of the Porsche down as the Citroën vanished round another bend at speed. Sure enough, rounding the bend herself she saw the car was only a short distance ahead. Once again the driver had jammed on the brakes as soon as the Citroën was out of sight.

'You caught me once. Twice never, you whore,' Karnell said triumphantly.

It happened about two kilometres after these two incidents. It happened without warning. Karnell saw the red lights suddenly leap away and vanish round a fresh bend in the road. It was again impossible for Karnell to see beyond the bend, which was lined with trees and undergrowth. She reduced speed and approached with great caution. Crawling round the bend she gazed stupefied ahead and in her state of shock pulled into the side of the road.

The road ahead was deserted. No red lights. No traffic at all. The Citroën had vanished into thin air.

Chapter Ten

Henderson himself was in command of the dinghy crossing the calm sea under the moonlight to the remote beach where *Firestorm* had seen the flash of Louise Hamilton's headlights from the Citroën. Two other men were aboard and all three were armed with sub-machine guns and hand grenades.

Louise's manoeuvre for losing the Porsche seemed to have worked – for a time. That depended on the determination and ingenuity of the other driver. Everything had hinged on conditioning the Porsche's driver to approaching bends with great caution and *at low speed*. On the third occasion Louise had accelerated as she came up to the bend, swung round the curve, saw the road immediately ahead clear to the next bend and had rammed her foot through the floor. As she roared through the dark she counted the right-hand turnings which were little more than tracks.

Approaching the third, she checked again in her mirror, saw no sign of headlights coming up behind her, slowed and veered sharply off the highway down a tree-lined track which crunched under her wheels. She kept up the maximum possible speed until she had turned a sharp bend in the track, out of sight of the highway. Now she only hoped to God she had chosen the track which led to the remote beach and the sea where *Firestorm* was waiting for her. Five minutes later, standing by the Citroën and watching the incoming outboard, she knew she had chosen well.

Stealthy footsteps in the night – behind her and coming down the track. Above the mutter of the outboard Louise was sure she had heard the hard crunch of slow-moving footsteps, the steps of someone who is careful where they place their feet – but is forced by the thick undergrowth on both sides of the track to make their way along the gravel.

She looked out to sea again and saw the outboard already cutting its motor. Henderson climbed out over the side. Another man disembarked, took hold of the side of the craft and held it in the shallows ready for swift departure. Louise moved along the water's edge towards the Scot who ran to meet her, crouched low and grasping a sub-machine gun in both hands.

'Anything wrong?' were his first words. As he spoke his eyes were scanning the woods and the entrance to the track.

'I thought I heard footsteps – I must be jittery.'

'Anyone follow you from Elsinore?'

'One person – in a Porsche.'

'Get into the outboard. Tell Adams to start it up.'

Stealthy footsteps. Henderson distinctly heard them before the outboard flared into power. The crunch of footsteps on gravel as someone came closer to the parked Citroën. He ran back, keeping a low profile, giving the order as he scrambled aboard in his half-length rubber boots.

'Masks on. Assume we're observed.'

Louise looked back briefly to the hired Citroën which looked sad and abandoned on the lonely beach. But she would be returning soon: to pick up that car and drive back to Elsinore.

Sonia Karnell was irked by the crunching sound of the gravel as she moved forward with her gun held out before her. She could normally move as silently as a cat – but confined to the gravel track she made a noise.

But the fact that the track had been made up of pebbles had been of enormous help. When she had lost the girl in the Citroën, Sonia Karnell's stupefaction had been quickly overtaken by the realisation she had been tricked.

There was a series of turnings off to the right – towards the nearby sea. The problem had been to locate which track the bitch had used. Karnell was convinced she had not driven much further along the highway – since she could see too far for the Citroën to have vanished to the north. No, it had been swallowed up by one of the tracks cut through the woods to the sea. The only question: which track?

Crawling along, losing valuable time, but knowing she had to proceed in a systematic manner, the Swedish girl stopped at the entrance to each track, got out of the car and examined it with her torch. At the third track she found skidmarks where a car had turned sharply off the highway. She followed her torchbeam only a few yards checking the very clear indentations of a car's tyres. When she returned to the Porsche she even saw stones and dirt scattered over the highway.

She drove the Porsche down the track far enough to conceal it from the highway. The last thing she needed at this stage was a Danish patrol-car – and the discovery of the bomb, which would be rather difficult to explain. Then she crunched her way cautiously down towards the beach, her Walther at the ready.

'Oh, I should have bloody known!'

Through the gap in the trees at the end of the track she saw what was responsible for the sudden burst of engine sound – an outboard rapidly growing smaller as it headed for the tip of a headland to the north. Whipping a pair of night glasses from her shoulder-bag, she focused them with expert fingers.

'You clever Telescope bastards! Bastards!'

In the twin lenses the four people crouched in the dinghy came up clearly, but they were all wearing

Balaclava helmets which concealed their features. Even with the field glasses, only the eyes showed through slits in the woollen helmets.

There was no vessel in sight they could be making for. What she did not know was that immediately after the outboard had been winched over the side in response to the flash of Louise's headlights, Captain Buckminster – on Henderson's orders – had withdrawn *Firestorm* out of sight behind the tip of the headland.

'Just in case Louise has been followed,' Henderson had observed to the ex-naval captain, 'I suggest you pull north behind the headland when we head for the shore.'

'Then you lack my support,' Buckminster had objected.

'At this stage I think it may be more important to conceal from the Syndicate our main and most deadly weapon *Firestorm*.'

And so Sonia Karnell was left swearing on the foreshore as the dinghy disappeared. She vented her fury by taking great care over her actions during the next few minutes.

She would have taken great care in any case: you do not fool about with bombs. The extra care she took was to plant the device underneath the Citroën without leaving any clue to its existence. Once the job was complete, she wriggled herself from under the car and shoved the torch back inside her pocket. She had activated all the systems and she walked round the vehicle before leaving it, to make sure there were no tell-tale traces.

The bomb was controlled by a trembler. If the Citroën were driven at reasonable speed and had to pull up sharply for any reason: *Bang!* If the Citroën were taken up or down an incline at an angle exceeding twenty degrees, no matter how slowly: *Bang!* Before leaving the booby-trapped car she took one last look out to sea where Louise Hamilton had vanished on the outboard.

'Don't forget to come back for your car, darling. I just wish I could be here.'

On the sidewalk outside the Royal Hotel two men stood studying a street map of Copenhagen. It was 8.30, a glorious morning on the following day, the sun shining brilliantly out of a clear blue sky with a salty breeze in the air.

Rush hour had begun, streets were crowded with traffic, sidewalks crowded with pedestrians, and the two men merged with the background. They were patient men and they had stood in different positions for over an hour – but each position always gave them a clear view of the main exit from the Royal Hotel.

An observer could have concluded that they were used to working together: they rarely exchanged a word. One man was dressed like an American. His companion carried a brief-case.

On the same morning Dr Henri Goldschmidt of Bruges arrived in Copenhagen aboard a flight from Brussels. A car was waiting for him and the chauffeur transported him to the Hotel d'Angleterre.

He always stayed at the Angleterre when he visited the Danish capital and the manager was waiting to greet his distinguished guest and accompany him to his suite. After seeing that he was satisfied, the manager informed the reception desk that the normal instructions applied: in case of enquiry from the outside world Dr Goldschmidt was not staying at the hotel.

Up in his suite, the coin dealer was well aware that Jules Beaurain and Louise Hamilton were in the same city. Immediately the couple had left his house in Bruges he had summoned Fritz Dewulf, the Fleming who had operated the camera in the house facing No. 285 Hoogste van Brugge.

'Fritz,' he had said, 'I want you to proceed immediately to Brussels Airport and take up residence, so to speak.'

'Who am I waiting for?'

'Jules Beaurain and, possibly Louise Hamilton. You can obtain their photos from our files.'

Among the most important tools of his trade, The Fixer counted his very considerable collection of photographs, many of people who believed no photographs of them existed. Armed with the prints, Dewulf departed for Brussels Airport.

He had to wait for many hours, snatching bites at the buffet, and by evening his eyes were prickling from the strain of checking people's faces. Then he saw both of them – Beaurain and Louise boarding a flight for Copenhagen.

'Copenhagen?' Goldschmidt repeated when Dewulf phoned him. 'It really is a beautiful city. I think it is time I visited it again.'

Jules Beaurain ordered a large breakfast for two and then called Max Kellerman to his bedroom. The sun shone in through the wide picture windows high above the city as they wolfed down the food and consumed cup after cup of steaming coffee. The Tivoli Gardens seemed to be almost below them, although several streets away.

'I've talked to Monique,' Beaurain had informed Kellerman when he arrived, 'and she confirmed that Henderson radioed her from *Firestorm*. Louise was picked up and taken aboard. They are landing her again later this morning after I have contacted them again. First, we see Superintendent Bodel Marker at police HQ.'

'I don't see the connection,' Kellerman said through a mouthful of bacon and eggs.

'I can't decide whether Louise should wait for us in

Elsinore or drive all the way to Copenhagen and link up with us here. Elsinore could be a diversion, something to distract us from the real action elsewhere.'

'I don't see it,' said Kellerman. 'Louise said when she called us last night that she had followed the girl we saw at the reception counter downstairs. She also mentioned a passenger who could well be Dr Benny Horn, the Dane your friend Goldschmidt named as one of the three men controlling the Syndicate. They're enough to go after, surely.'

Beaurain wiped his mouth with a napkin, dropped it on the trolley and went over to stare out across the city. 'The van, Max. The van which prominently carries the legend *Helsingør* – and nothing else on the outside. It's too obvious – like a finger pointing us. In the wrong direction.'

'Louise did follow it to Elsinore, though.'

'Yes, I suppose so. Now, time for us to keep our appointment with my old friend Bodel Marker at police headquarters.'

'I thought he was in Intelligence,' said Kellerman as he swallowed the rest of his coffee.

'Deliberate camouflage. There he has plenty of protection. No-one is going to notice him coming and going. And he has his own set-up, including his own system of communications.'

The phone rang just before they left. It was the American CIA man, who had arrived in Stockholm. His conversation with Beaurain was short.

'Jules, I still can't track down Norling. I'm convinced he's not in Stockholm, but he's expected. I don't think Viktor Rashkin is here either. I gather from certain sources I've screwed the hell out of, that both are expected soon.'

'Something wrong, Ed?'

'A funny atmosphere in this city. Noticed it as soon as I began looking up old contacts. Don't think I've gone over the top, but the atmosphere smells of naked and total fear as soon as the Stockholm Syndicate is mentioned. And I've had a weird warning from a Swede I've known for years and whose life I once saved. Oh, I don't know.'

'Go on, Ed,' Beaurain said quietly, gripping the receiver tightly.

'I was told a signal had been sent naming me. The word *Zenith* was mentioned. Does it mean anything?'

'It means you're on the Syndicate's list. It means you'll be spied upon and your every move reported. It means you're in grave danger. Ed, you need to be armed. There's a place in Stockholm where you can buy . . .'

'Teach your grandmother to suck eggs,' Cottel said quickly. 'What the hell is this *Zenith* thing? People make it sound like I have the plague.'

'That's how you'll be treated unless you use every ounce of clout when you want something from the authorities. I'm about to find out whether there's a *Zenith* signal out for me in Copenhagen. So, from now on, trust no-one. And the higher you go the more dangerous it could get.'

'Great. Just great. Anything else before you tell me to have a nice day?' enquired Cottel.

'Yes. Any idea where the *Zenith* signal originated?'

'Washington, DC.'

There was a glazed look in Beaurain's eyes as he replaced the receiver. A thought occurred to him. Kellerman was gazing out of the window down the street where crowds of cyclists had joined the cars, and the pedestrians were hurrying along the side-walks. In Denmark people seemed anxious to get to work. Beaurain picked up the receiver again and was put through to Monique in Brussels almost immediately.

'Monique. Check something for me, please. Contact Goldschmidt in Bruges and ask him whether he knows if Dr Otto Berlin has been seen there – or in Brussels, for that matter – since Louise and I were last there. Call you back later.'

He put on his jacket and turned to Kellerman. 'We'll leave the second car I hired in the parking lot and walk out the main entrance. It's only a few minutes on foot and I could do with the exercise.'

The front entrance to the Royal Hotel debouches onto a side street. Leaving by this entrance, Beaurain and Kellerman turned right and began walking towards the main street leading to the nearby Radhuspladsen, the main square in the centre of Copenhagen. On the opposite side of the street from the Royal Hotel which rises into the sky on a corner site, is the main railway station. The station building stands back a short distance from the street and in front is a large well about thirty feet deep through which the rail tracks pass.

It was this curious local layout Kellerman had been studying as he looked out of the bedroom window while the Belgian had been phoning. Reaching the street, they paused at a pedestrian crossing.

'We cross over here,' Beaurain explained. 'Go down that street over there and the police headquarters complex is ten minutes walk, if that. What's wrong, Max?'

The lights were still against them. Other pedestrians were waiting for the lights to change. Kellerman had his hand in his jacket pocket and now his face was tense. Beaurain followed his gaze and saw only the crowd waiting on the other side of the crossing.

'Two men,' Kellerman said. 'One with a brief-case which contains the weapon. Wasn't that how a little boy described the men who murdered the bargee, Frans Darras, and his wife Rosa?'

Gunther Baum had come to the conclusion that both the Belgian, Beaurain, and the German, Kellerman, were professionals. Their maximum alertness would be when they were in deserted alleys, lonely country lanes – conversely their minimum alertness would be in a crowded street at rush hour first thing in the morning after a good breakfast with the sun shining down and the promise of another glorious day opening out before them . . .

Baum was an exceptional psychologist – but he had not grasped that in confronting Telescope he was dealing with exceptional men. He would have been appalled to know that his fellow-countryman had already observed a false note in the manner of the two men constantly studying the large street plan of Copenhagen. The oddity in their stance he had seen from the tenth floor bedroom of the Royal Hotel. At the time, waiting for Beaurain to complete his phone call, Kellerman merely noted the position of the couple.

One with a brief-case which contains the weapon . . .

The lights had changed, the pedestrians were swarming over the crossing. Beaurain and Kellerman were caught up in the swirl. Beaurain grasped who Kellerman meant at once and scanned the oncoming crowd. *Zenith!* Desperately Beaurain went on scanning faces, with Kellerman a step or two ahead as though he had some urgent purpose. Beaurain did not distract the German in any way. He had learned to give his trained gunners their heads in an emergency situation. He had almost reached the sidewalk, the crowd had thinned out, when he saw . . .

One man of medium height and build dressed in a suit of American cut, wearing a straw hat – apt in this weather – and dark, shell-shaped glasses. He already had his hand inside the brief-case his companion held towards him. They had emerged from behind the map, which was mounted on two high wooden posts with an open gap below. It was through this gap that Kellerman had first noticed the two pairs of legs, had remembered the odd couple he had seen from the tenth floor. The German had watched and seen them come into view seconds before he began to move over the crossing. He'd just had time to make his remark to Beaurain.

As always, Baum had timed his move perfectly; he had been known to plan executions with a stop-watch. Appear from behind the street plan just as the lights changed. Be ready for the targets as they stepped onto the sidewalk. Two shots with the silenced Luger in the confusion of the morning traffic and minutes could pass before people realised what had happened.

Beaurain was not armed. He knew Kellerman was not carrying a gun. He saw Baum, who wore thin brown gloves, withdraw his right hand from the brief-case gripping the butt of a silenced Luger. Baum and his companion were about thirty feet away from their twin targets.

Kellerman was still several paces ahead, striding forward now the crowd had cleared out of his way. His long legs covered the ground at astonishing speed, although he did not appear to be hurrying. And he was striding straight towards Baum, who was taking aim with his left arm extended at right angles to act as a perch for the weapon. Max was going to be shot down in cold blood and there was nothing Beaurain could do to save him.

Suddenly Kellerman's right hand whipped out of his pocket holding the knife he had been nursing. In a blur of movement Beaurain saw Kellerman hoist his arm backwards then the knife was sailing through the air with the thrust of all the German's considerable strength behind it. The missile struck Baum's right shoulder, jerked his elbow and arm upwards and caused him involuntarily to press the trigger. *Phut!*

A bull's-eye! The silenced bullet hit a street light suspended high over the crossing. Sprays of shattered glass fell on pedestrians and there were shouts of surprise and annoyance. Baum still held on to the Luger and snapped off one more shot. His bullet missed Kellerman by a mile and shattered the windscreen of a passing Volvo. The car swerved across the line of oncoming traffic and ended up inside the window of a jewellery shop. Then the screaming began in earnest.

Pulling the knife from his shoulder, Baum dropped the Luger inside the brief-case which his companion still held open and they turned and ran. Kellerman sprinted forward to stop them, crashed into a French tourist who appeared from nowhere and both men fell sprawling. Kellerman dispensed with apologies and was on his feet again as Beaurain reached him.

'Where have they gone?'

'Towards the railway station,' Beaurain replied and

they both ran – in time to see Baum and his companion, who still carried the brief-case, vanish inside the main entrance to the old station building. Behind them they left traffic blocked in both directions, several cars which had crashed together when the Volvo swerved across their lane, and a growing crowd of tourists and locals forming a mob of sightseers, none of whom had the slightest idea of what had happened.

'We can't miss that American bastard in that garb. Bloody great checks.'

'So noticeable you never think he could be anything but normal. Now, watch it – you haven't got your knife now.'

They walked casually into a large reception area with places to eat, bookstalls, banks of phone booths, rows of ticket counters. After a swift glance round, Beaurain headed straight for some steps which led down onto the platforms. The flight of steps was crowded with people.

'There they are, Max!'

'Let's get to hell after the bastards!'

'Too late.'

The couple had just boarded a red train which started to move into the well-like area they had looked down on from the Royal Hotel. Kellerman was in a rage of frustration increased by the Belgian's outward coolness and resignation.

'Your friend, Bodel Marker, we're going to see. Call him, for God's sake, and get police to check that train.'

'Let's see if that's practical, Max.'

'How can we see?'

'By checking the timetable here.'

Beaurain led the German to a series of wall timetables. He ran his eyes down one timetable after checking his watch and shook his head, pointing with his finger.

'They'll be getting off any second now. That's the train they boarded and it's a local. You can see for yourself where the next stop is – just the other side of the Royal Hotel. We'd never get there in time and I don't think we wish to talk to the local police after what happened back there in the street.'

'And I think I can hear police sirens.'

'So we walk quietly towards the exit,' Beaurain suggested, 'trying to look as though we've just arrived in Copenhagen. Someone may have seen us run in here.'

And as they calmly walked out, the jackets they had removed during the short walk folded over their arms, two patrol cars screamed to a halt by the kerb and uniformed men went briskly inside.

Police headquarters in Copenhagen is known as Politigarden. A grim, triangular building constructed of grey cement, it faces a square called Polititorvet. Beaurain and Kellerman surveyed it from a distance before they went inside.

'Looks like a prison,' Kellerman commented. 'Most inviting.'

'They're not in the holiday camp business,' replied Beaurain.

'And I see they have a wireless mast on the roof.'

'It's that wireless mast I'm counting on – on that and Superintendent Marker of the Intelligence Department. He sounded friendly enough on the phone – but he didn't know then what I was going to ask him.'

They approached the five arched entrances beneath the flat-topped roof. A patrol car pulled in at the kerb as they were crossing the square and a uniformed policeman carrying a small package dashed inside, leaving his companion behind the wheel.

Beaurain led the way to a side-door which carried the legend *Kriminal Politiet*. He pushed open the door and entered an austere office where a policeman in shirt-sleeves sat behind a desk.

'My identity . . . Jules Beaurain . . . Superintendent Bodel Marker . . .'

He kept his voice low because there was another man in shirt-sleeves who had slipped into the room just ahead of them. The policeman behind the desk seemed to grasp the need for discretion.

'And the person with you?' he mouthed silently.

'My assistant – in charge of an undercover section. Marker will particularly wish to hear from him personally certain events he has witnessed. Name Foxbel.'

There followed a brief conversation on the policeman's internal phone. Beaurain could not understand a word he said because he was speaking in Danish.

The German nudged him in the back as the policeman stared at his desk. When Beaurain glanced round, Kellerman's eyes pinpointed the man who had entered the room before them: he was studying a notice on the wall. The policeman behind the desk finished his conversation, replaced the receiver and proceeded to fill in a form.

'He is waiting to see you,' he informed Beaurain. The man who had been looking at the notice moved towards the door. Kellerman timed it perfectly. One foot projected at the last moment, the man tripped and fell, half-saving himself by grabbing the edge of the policeman's desk.

'I will come back later. I have an urgent call of nature – something I ate this morning.'

A small, weasel-faced man with a leathery complexion and the agility of a monkey. Before anyone could react he had left the office. Kellerman heaved open the door and ran into Polititorvet. He was in time to see the patrol-car which had just arrived driving away, but there was no sign of the weasel. The man had vanished. Kellerman glanced up the curving flight of steps which led to the various departments in the building. He met Beaurain coming out, holding the form.

'Disappeared into thin air, Jules. He couldn't have escaped over the square – I was out too quick. He must have gone up there.'

Kellerman pointed up a spiral staircase of stone steps which disappeared round a bend. From previous visits to Politigarden Beaurain knew the staircase led to all the main police departments. He also knew that before you could enter any of the departments, there was a police checkpoint you had to pass. The only conclusion left was that the weasel-faced man was a member of one of the many departments. Beaurain explained this briefly.

'Then he must have an official position here. Has the Syndicate penetrated here too?' Kellerman speculated.

'Why do we have to suspect him?' asked Beaurain.

'Because I deliberately tripped him up, he never protested and his reaction was to get to hell out of that room as fast as his legs could carry him.'

'You're quite right. Let's get up and see Marker.'

Mounting the spiral, they reached the first floor. There *was* a barrier and a uniformed policeman behind the desk. The form was essential: it was checked carefully and then they were told to continue up to the second floor and turn right along the inner corridor until they reached Room 78.

'What is worrying you?' Kellerman asked quietly as they went on up the second spiral which, like the first, was entirely enclosed by a curving stone wall.

'The Syndicate knew we were coming,' Beaurain said grimly. 'Their organisation and thoroughness is incredible – we've never been up against anything like this before. In some ways the extent of their reach is frightening. The only answer is to go over onto the offensive and hurl them off balance.'

Beaurain's reaction was characteristic. Kellerman was intrigued about the reasons for his comment.

'Why is the organisation and thoroughness incredible? Have I missed something?'

'First, as I've just said, they had a man waiting for us here. But we were never supposed to get here, Max. We were supposed to be dead – gunned down near the station by that couple with the brief-case. And that means the man downstairs was simply back-up – warned to keep a look-out purely on the off-chance that the assassination set-up misfired. Next point, how did they know we were on our way to see Marker? Only two possible answers – they have someone on the switchboard at the Royal Hotel or – worse still – they have someone on the central switchboard here at Politigarden. This bloody *Zenith* thing is encircling us with a stranglehold.'

They had arrived at the second floor. Beaurain pushed open another heavy door and they found themselves out in the open air on a terrace-like corridor with a railing on the inner side. Kellerman thought it a curious arrangement: on the outside the building had been triangular in shape; now the centre was hollowed out into a huge circular courtyard entirely cut off from the outside world and open to the sky.

The courtyard, resembling the interior of an amphitheatre, was eerily deserted. They turned to the right and along their right-hand side the wall of the building continued in a circular sweep with more heavy doors at intervals.

'Weird building,' Kellerman remarked.

'Unique in my experience,' Beaurain agreed.

'I'll be glad when we get off this bloody platform. Anyone could use us for target practice and we're both unarmed.'

'Room 78. Relax, Max. You'll like Marker.' Beaurain turned the door handle and walked into the large room beyond. Kellerman was behind him when they both glanced into the room next door through an open doorway at the single object on a large desk. *A knife.*

'Forty million Swedish kronor worth of heroin.'

The man who had spoken the words and then paused was in his mid-fifties, a man of medium height and rounded stomach whose hair and eyebrows were grey and bushy. His pink complexion and his chubby cheeks, with the brilliant sparkle in his very blue eyes, suggested the keen walker or cyclist. Amiability radiated from him. This was Superintendent Bodel Marker, Chief of Intelligence and the man responsible for some of the Copenhagen police force's greatest coups.

His guests, Beaurain and Kellerman, who had been introduced as 'Foxbel', were seated in comfortable chairs, smoking excellent cigars and drinking delicious coffee. Kellerman was forcing himself not to stare at the knife which still occupied the central position on Marker's desk, an object to which no-one had so far made any reference. The door to the outer office was closed and only the three men occupied the room.

'One of the largest consignments of heroin ever moved in this part of the world,' Marker continued in his excellent English. 'It is on the move now – at this very moment following the same route as always, I am informed.'

'Would forty million Swedish kronors' worth of heroin fit inside a suitcase measuring roughly something like this?' Kellerman's nimble hands described in air roughly the dimensions of the case Louise had described the man who had travelled by van from Nyhavn to Elsinore as carrying. Marker looked at Beaurain before replying.

'He is my close associate and friend and I would trust him with my life, Bodel,' Beaurain replied quietly.

'Just as you did this morning!'

'Bodel?' Beaurain managed to inject just the right note of enquiry into his voice.

'Yours, I believe, Mr Foxbel.'

Marker lifted the knife, threw it across the desk so it fell over the edge and Kellerman was compelled to pick it up. He looked at the knife with a blank expression, gazed at the Dane, and then at Beaurain. Marker's amiability disappeared and his voice was thunderous.

'Less than one hour ago! Before you two arrive we enjoy peace and quiet and . . .' He paused, his fist crashed on his desk. '. . . I hear that within less than twenty-four hours of your landing we have a murder at Kastrup Airport!'

'Who was killed, Bodel?' asked Beaurain, quite unperturbed.

'George Land. Professional assassin according to Interpol. A big man. Carrying a British passport. He was found lying half-inside a telephone booth killed by his own favourite weapon – an umbrella with a built-in trigger mechanism which operated a knife.' Marker leaned forward over his desk and stared hard at each of his visitors in turn, 'Mr Foxbel . . . that's right, isn't it? Did you see anything odd when you flew in?'

'No,' Kellerman replied shortly.

'It's upset you – happening on your own doorstep,' Beaurain said to the Dane sympathetically.

'There's more,' Marker told him grimly. 'Less than one hour ago – while you were on your way here from the Royal Hotel – two men were almost killed by a couple of professional assassins in the very centre of our beautiful Copenhagen, by God! How did the intended victims save themselves? One of them hurls this knife with great accuracy and destroys the gunman's aim.'

'And the descriptions of the two potential victims fit us with remarkable closeness?' Beaurain suggested.

'We have your descriptions,' Marker admitted.

'And so far no-one can give us a clear description of the would-be murderers.' He smiled broadly. 'I'm glad you survived the attack.' He picked up the knife Kellerman had put back on the desk and held it out. 'This, I believe, is your property, Mr Foxbel.'

'Take it,' Beaurain said quickly. 'I came here to ask what you know about a certain Dr Benny Horn who has a house on Nyhavn.'

'Highly respected dealer in rare books,' Marker said promptly. 'The house on Nyhavn is both his shop and his home. He travels the world searching out rare volumes, so we are told. I think, Jules, you should be careful – if you are investigating the Stockholm Syndicate.'

Chapter Eleven

The conversation which followed was so horrifying that Beaurain could in later years repeat it word for word from memory.

'Why bring up the Stockholm Syndicate?' Beaurain asked.

'Because you mentioned Dr Benny Horn. Nothing can be proved, but I am convinced he is a member of the directorate which controls this evil organisation. So far they have tried to kill me twice,' he added casually.

'What about your family?' Beaurain asked slowly, watching Marker for any flicker of expression.

'They threatened to gouge out the eyes of my wife and cut off the legs of my ten-year-old boy below the knees. I have sent them both out of the country to a destination I will not reveal even to you.'

Beaurain was shaken. He had known Marker since he had become a superintendent and he knew the man had courage, but this was appalling. He stood up, lit a cigarette and fetched himself an ash-tray to give himself time to think.

'Who are "they"?' he asked eventually.

'Voices on the phone – often a girl, for Christ's sake. She was the one who spelt out the details of what would happen to my family.'

Beaurain looked towards the closed inter-communicating door. 'It is safe to speak, I assume?'

'There has been an armed guard on the far side of that door ever since you both entered this room. At this moment I am wearing a bullet-proof vest which I put on before I leave my flat every morning. The new system employed by the Syndicate relies on secret intimidation of the most ferocious kind – take my own example.'

'The threat must have been combined with some request?'

'Of course!' Marker looked savage. 'Give me one of your cigarettes, for God's sake. Thank you.' He paused a moment, studying the Belgian as though taking a major decision. Then he spoke with great vehemence. 'I do not expect you to comment on my statement – but it is vital that Telescope smashes the Syndicate. No government agency I know of can or will – they are like tethered goats waiting for the tiger to strike.'

Beaurain looked bemused. Marker sat on the edge of his desk close to the two men as though he needed the reassurance of their proximity. 'No government agency at all?' Beaurain asked.

'This man fell ten storeys from a balcony one night.' Marker took a small notebook from his pocket, scribbled a name on it, tore the sheet from the pad and gave it to Beaurain, concealing it from Kellerman. 'For your eyes only,' he said with a mirthless smile, 'as the best spies are supposed to say. But this is for real, my friend.'

Beaurain glanced at the name, refolded the piece of paper and handed it to Marker who thrust it inside his pocket. It was the name of one of the most well-known political leaders in Europe, who had dominated the Common Market before his 'accident'.

'How do you know that was the Syndicate?'

'Because when they threatened me they said he was going to die within seven days. Most people would have laughed, found it ludicrous. I took them seriously. I phoned my opposite number in the capital concerned. He thought I was mad. At least that's what he said.'

'What does that mean?' Beaurain put in.

'I'll tell you in a minute.' Marker continued vehemently: 'I forced my way through on the phone to the man himself. I warned him to seek immediate protection. He thought I was mad. Forty-eight hours later they pushed him off the balcony and sent him ten storeys down to smash to a pulp on the concrete below. The bastards!' Marker's face was flushed and Beaurain had never known him display such emotion.

'The man he is referring to left behind a wife and several children,' Beaurain informed Kellerman.

'Only an invisible organisation like Telescope can smash the Stockholm Syndicate,' Marker said. It was the second time he had openly referred to Telescope.

'They rely on the threat alone?' Beaurain asked.

'The swine offered me a bloody fortune in cash if I co-operated. All the big drug runs from the Far East for Stockholm come through here. I would turn my back on that – just for one example.

'What is "the same route as always", which I believe is the phrase you used earlier,' Kellerman enquired, 'in connection with the big consignment?'

'Amsterdam through to Copenhagen,' Marker said promptly. 'On from Copenhagen by train, across the ferry at Elsinore over the Øresund to Sweden. Then the last lap by the same train until it reaches its final destination – Stockholm. The train ferries at Elsinore are a damned nuisance. If they had to take it by scheduled air flight – or by car or truck – sooner or later we would get lucky in our searches. But you can't search a whole train – and whole trains cross from Elsinore on the giant ferries.'

'Thank you,' said Kellerman, and withdrew from the conversation.

'You said your opposite number you phoned about the danger to a statesman's life thought you were mad. *At least he said that*, you added. What did you mean?'

'I am perfectly sure he had already sold out to the Stockholm Syndicate.' Marker stood up and paced slowly round his desk. 'It is so easy, is it not? You take the large bribe, salt it away in a numbered bank account, and remove whatever horrible threat has been made against your wife, family, mistress or whoever. They offer you heaven or hell. Is it so surprising that many in countless different countries accepted the former and became part of the Stockholm Syndicate system – if only as informants? Cabinet ministers have made deals. Oh, yes, Mr Foxbel, do not disbelieve me – I have seen it in their eyes when certain subjects are raised.'

'It's a kind of leprosy,' Beaurain murmured. 'It will have to be burned out with red-hot pokers.'

'Do not underestimate them,' Marker warned.

'Do something for me, please.' Beaurain's manner had changed suddenly as he recovered from the shock of sensing that Marker had been close to despair. 'Check back on Dr Benny Horn's background – where he came from, how he set up in that house on Nyhavn.'

'I can tell you now. He was born in Elsinore – or just outside the port. He built up his business as a dealer in rare editions and two years ago moved to Copenhagen.'

'I want more than that, Marker!' Beaurain was brusque. 'I want men – a whole team – sent to Elsinore to interview every person who ever knew him.'

'He was something of a recluse – and travelling a lot in his profession.'

'I want him *pinned down*! Like a butterfly in a collection! Do you have a photograph?'

'One – he is a difficult man to catch in the camera lens. The picture is not good – taken at a distance with a telephoto lens.' Marker unlocked a steel filing cabinet, took out an envelope from which he extracted a photo. Beaurain glanced at it and then showed it to Kellerman who handed it back without comment.

'Show that picture to everyone who ever knew Horn in Elsinore. Find out whether – since he arrived in Copenhagen two years ago – he has ever spoken to or been seen by anyone who knew him when he lived in Elsinore. I just have a funny feeling about Benny Horn. I can call you here?' Beaurain queried.

'Better to call my apartment after eight in the evening. Here is the number. When you call say you are Krantz and give me the number of the phone you are using. Always use a payphone. Then wait for me to call from the payphone in my street.'

Beaurain paused. *Zenith*. The terror was appalling and spread across a whole continent, the scale of the terror even greater than he had realised. How many men were there of the calibre of Bodel Marker? Men who would live alone in their own private fortress with their families sent maybe thousands of miles away for safety.

Power was being exploited quietly to enslave and manipulate whole nations. And the most horrible aspect of all – on the surface everyday life proceeded as though nothing abnormal were happening.

'Contact Henderson priority, Monique. Tell him Elsinore is the present objective. Within two hours I want the place flooded with his people searching for a man and a girl. Here are the descriptions.'

Speaking from a street payphone near the Royal Hotel, Beaurain reproduced in a few words the vague impression of Dr Benny Horn obtained from the photograph Marker had shown him. The other description was more precise and was based on Kellerman's word picture of Black Helmet. The instruction to Jock Henderson was to find the couple quickly, mount a round-the-clock surveillance on them, but above all not to let them know they were being watched.

'Next request, Monique, please call Dr Henri Goldschmidt of Bruges and ask him to provide urgently everything possible on the origins and background of Dr Otto Berlin. Then, on my behalf, using the code word Leuven, call Chief Inspector Willy Flamen of Homicide with the same request – everything he can dig up on where Otto Berlin came from, his whole history back to his childhood. OK? I'll call you back when I can. We're on the move so forget the Royal Hotel.'

Leaving the phone booth, he joined Kellerman who had been strolling up and down outside as though waiting to make his own call. He relayed the gist of his conversation to the German as they hurried back to the hotel.

'She'll get through to Henderson immediately by radio aboard *Firestorm*.'

'Which is still just north of Elsinore? It sounds as though you're launching an invasion of one of Denmark's key ports.'

'Almost comes to that,' Beaurain agreed briskly. All his previous irritation and frustration had vanished now that he was able to set the wheels of action in motion.

Two outboard-powered dinghies had reached the shore north of Elsinore where Louise had left the Citroën the previous night. In the lead boat were Louise, Henderson and two guards armed with sub-machine guns. In the second boat four men, equipped with the same weapons and various other devices, watched the car which stood parked in the same position Louise had left it, the headlamps pointing out to sea.

It was eleven o'clock on a beautiful morning, the sun shining out of a clear blue sky. It was already very warm and the reflection off the wavelets was a powerful glitter. Louise walked towards the Citroën, shoulder-bag over her arm, ignition key in her hand. Henderson followed close behind while two of the guards fanned out beyond towards the forest and the track with their weapons at the ready.

'You're driving straight into Elsinore to look for those two from Nyhavn?' Henderson asked as she reached the car door.

'Yes, Jock.' She turned and he was very close to her. 'But only after we have gone over the car with a fine-tooth comb for explosive devices.'

'Why?'

Marker completed for him. 'On the contrary, my first action will be to hand the cassette to a certain person with instructions that – in the event of a third attempt on my life being successful – it will be handed immediately to a journalist working for the German publication, *Der Spiegel*. I doubt whether the Stockholm Syndicate yet controls that particular magazine,' Marker added.

'I don't understand you, Marker. I must go now. As far as I am concerned this conversation never took place,' he ended stiffly and left the office.

Within seven minutes Marker had also left the office and was on his way to the car he had summoned. No tape existed; no machine had been activated. But Marker would never forget the look on his superior's face when he had bluffed him that such was the case.

Arriving by train, all passengers alight at Elsinore unless aboard an international express bound for Sweden – because there the rail line ends. Its only extension is to the water's edge – across a road and up an elevated ramp inside the bowels of one of the giant train ferries which constantly ply back and forth across the Øresund.

In June the channel neck of the Øresund – at this narrowest point no more than four miles across to the Swedish port of Hälsingborg – is alive with the monster train and car ferries which have several different landing points round Elsinore harbour. On the morning Beaurain and Kellerman arrived in the Mercedes, the channel was enlivened further by yachts nimbly sailing and turning to keep out of the passage of the lumbering ferries.

Beaurain's 280E, without which he always felt lost, had been driven from Brussels to Copenhagen by the English driver, Albert, who always arrived at his destination in the nick of time. He reached the Royal Hotel fifteen minutes before Beaurain was due to depart for Elsinore. 'Why Elsinore?' Albert had asked as he drank his third cup of tea supplied by room service in Beaurain's room. 'Isn't that Hamlet's castle?'

'Because,' Beaurain explained as he completed his packing, 'one of the key Danish police chiefs we have just seen has confirmed a huge Syndicate consignment of heroin is passing along the usual route on its way to Stockholm. The route? Amsterdam to Copenhagen to Elsinore – where it crosses the water to Sweden.'

'A vulnerable link in the chain,' Albert observed between gulps of the dark tea, 'that bit where it crosses water. Means it has to go on a boat, and where do they put the consignment aboard the train?'

'Albert has put his finger on the key factor as usual,' Beaurain observed. He told the Englishman briefly about the suitcase Louise Hamilton had seen driven through the night to a house in Elsinore which backed onto the railway line.

Albert Brown, a small, wiry man of forty-two with

a face permanently screwed up in an expression of concentration, was an ex-racing driver, a Londoner, and a man who never took anything at face value. He had joined Telescope when his wife had been killed brutally by a murderer released from Broadmoor lunatic asylum.

'So,' he concluded after listening to Beaurain, 'the Syndicate may still have to put this whopping great consignment aboard one of the international expresses crossing these straits to Sweden?'

'If the heroin really is in that suitcase,' Beaurain pointed out.

'And if it is and we can locate it, we deal the Syndicate a good jab in the jugular.'

'We do more than that,' Beaurain said as he prepared to leave the room. 'We create such havoc we'll provoke a major reaction against Telescope by the Syndicate – which is what I want. A head-on collision, as Goldschmidt phrased it. The aim is to wipe out this evil thing.'

'We may be the only ones who can do it,' Albert said soberly, so soberly that Beaurain stopped picking up his case and stared at him because he had never known Albert, normally chirpy, adopt such a grim tone. 'I had a word with Monique before I started my mad dash here,' Albert continued. 'She gave me a message she said she'd sooner not trust to a telephone conversation. The chap who she spoke to was a Dr Goldschmidt from Bruges. Chap who controls the Syndicate answers to name of Hugo.'

'Goldschmidt told me about Hugo – he's one of the three-man directorate running the Syndicate.'

'That seems to be the point. I gathered Goldschmidt has only just come up with this piece of information – Monique said he seemed to be working like a beaver trying to dig up data for you. This Hugo – nobody has a clue as to who he is – may, according to Goldschmidt's latest information, not be one of the three-man directorate at all. He thinks there could be *a fourth man*.'

With Beaurain behind the wheel, Kellerman by his side and Albert sleeping in the back, they overtook the police car containing Bodel Marker on the motorway to Elsinore.

Marker had heard about Beaurain's 280E and the way he drove it in an emergency; half the police chiefs of Europe had heard about it. Nervous about a third attempt on his life, he looked back at Beaurain who waved to him through the windscreen. Astounded, the Danish Chief of Intelligence relaxed back in his seat.

'What's Marker doing on the same road as us?' Kellerman asked.

'Something must have occurred to him later after he went back to his office – or something happened. This way we get to Elsinore much earlier. Just sit back and relax.'

It was the last attitude Kellerman felt like adopting.

The police car containing Marker surged ahead, its siren screaming non-stop. Beaurain pressed his foot down and followed in the wake of Marker's vehicle, using it as a trail-blazer.

They passed traffic which had pulled into the slow lane on hearing the approaching siren. Marker's car sailed along the cleared highway, far exceeding the speed limit, and behind him sailed Beaurain's Mercedes, forming a convoy of two vehicles, and when Marker kept glancing back through his rear window Beaurain met the glances with an expression of imperturbable confidence.

Both vehicles arrived at the open space in front of the entrance to Elsinore's railway station with a screech of tyres as their drivers jammed on the brakes. Beaurain had just switched off his engine when Marker jumped out of the rear of his car and strode back to the Mercedes with a grim expression. The Belgian pressed the button which automatically lowered his window and smiled up at Marker.

'What the hell do you think you're doing?' Marker demanded. 'I could have you booked for dangerous driving.'

'Along with your own driver?'

'Dammit! This is an emergency.'

'If it's the heroin, we may be able to help. Don't look behind you, Bodel. Not obviously, anyway. Standing at the entrance to the station is a dark-haired girl called Louise staring watching the ferry coming into the harbour. She's wearing blue and carrying a shoulder-bag. She might just know the present whereabouts of the heroin. Incidentally, while we're asking questions, what made you suddenly decide to take a lively interest in the beautiful old port of Elsinore?'

'Heroin,' Marker replied tersely, his lips scarcely moving. He leant both elbows on the edge of the Mercedes window and glanced casually at Louise Hamilton who stood watching the bucket chain of giant ferries plying back and forth across the Øresund with brightly-coloured yachts like toys sailing between the giants. Sweden was a distant stretch of flat coast, a row of miniature oil storage tanks and a plume of smoke.

'Why Elsinore?' Beaurain asked as he lit a cigarette. Marker took the cigarette off him before he could put it in his own mouth. 'Thought you'd given up,' the Belgian continued, taking out a fresh cigarette.

The Dane's chubby face was thin-lipped with tension, his eyes icy and hard. He smoked the cigarette while he watched Louise Hamilton and scanned the dock area. A Volvo estate wagon pulled into the kerb a dozen yards behind the Mercedes and Beaurain watched it in his mirror. Marker seemed to be gazing in the opposite direction when he spoke.

'Man behind the wheel of that Volvo is Dr Benny Horn, rare book dealer with a shop on Nyhavn in Copenhagen. And, as I told you, he's possibly one of the three most powerful men today in the whole of Western Europe. Why has he stopped behind you, I wonder? Sight of my police car or your Mercedes.'

'Black Helmet!'

Kellerman said the words almost involuntarily. He had started watching in the wing mirror on his side and she was framed perfectly, the girl he had first seen talking to the receptionist at the Royal Hotel while he watched from the quick-service restaurant.

Black Helmet. Now the description fitted her beautifully and it occurred to Kellerman she looked as sexy as hell – her helmet of black hair cut close to the head without any covering, and wearing a pair of black slacks and a black windcheater. The same outfit as Louise Hamilton's; she even carried a shoulder-bag and only the colour of the outfits was different.

'What was that, Foxbel?' Marker asked quickly. 'Black What? You know the lady?'

'We think she may be closely linked with Benny Horn,' he told Marker. 'We haven't seen them together but one of our people gave us descriptions of two people who drove north last night to Elsinore with a suitcase.'

'Suitcase the size you described in my office?' Marker interjected.

'The very same. The descriptions of the two people fit Benny Horn and the girl passing the Volvo behind us.'

'Horn signalled her to keep moving, not to stop by the Volvo,' the Dane observed. Not once since the Volvo had pulled in behind them had Marker turned in that direction. He seemed to have eyes in the back of his head. And he was right, Kellerman thought:

Black Helmet had been about to get into the Volvo when Horn had given her a warning signal – a brief movement of the hand – to keep moving.

Black Helmet had speeded up her pace, passing the parked Mercedes without a glance. Reaching the corner she was able to see the exit from the station, and noticed Louise Hamilton standing there. So, the girl she had followed in the early hours had returned to Elsinore. The obvious assumption was that she had used the booby-trapped Citroën. Louise Hamilton should have been dead. Black Helmet reacted instinctively, and walked rapidly across the front of the station as though on her way into the booking-hall. She swerved, changing direction suddenly, coming up silently behind the English girl.

Her right hand was now held motionless by her side, the hand stiff, the edge hard. Her intention was to brush against the English girl, move past her a few feet, swing round and scream, 'Thief! You took my purse!' In the ensuing struggle one swift blow to the side of the neck would render her target unconscious.

'*What the hell is happening*?' exclaimed Marker. He had seen the Volvo move away, gliding off so unexpectedly there was no time to stop it. Seconds later Black Helmet had swivelled towards the station and then changed direction to come up behind Beaurain's girl. Marker was thrown off-balance.

Everyone involved assumed Louise Hamilton was so intent on watching the arriving train ferry that she had not noticed Karnell, who moved with the speed of a cobra. They were wrong. At the very moment Karnell brushed against her side and turned to shout the word 'Thief!', Louise Hamilton spun on her heel. 'I want you, you bitch!' she hissed. Her right leg snapped forward like a piston, the point of her shoe aimed at Karnell's kneecap. Had the blow fully connected the Swedish girl would never have been able to move once she collapsed on the ground. But Karnell saw the thrust of the shoe and started to spin her own body. The shoe tip cut the side of her leg but she was only hurt, not eliminated.

Staggering back towards the kerb, her right hand scrabbled inside her shoulder-bag for her gun. There was a burst of sound as a motor-bike revved its powerful engine. The machine had been parked close to the ferry point by the kerb, the man sitting on it dressed in helmet, goggles and leather jacket, apparently watching the frenetic activity in the Øresund. Now he sped across the road, over the rail tracks, and towards Karnell.

Louise tried to reach them, to topple the machine over sideways, but Karnell was seconds too fast. Despite her injury she made it to the edge of the sidewalk, swung one leg over the pillion seat of the waiting machine, and grabbed the rider round the waist as he surged off with a roar of power in the direction the Volvo had taken.

Beaurain did not even reach to turn on the ignition: he was watching Louise's reaction. She was staring in a fresh direction – towards the rail line where international expresses waited to move along the lines over the road, up the ramp and inside a ferry which would take them to Sweden.

'Bodel, I think they tried a diversion – at least that girl who got away on the motor-bike did. Her reaction was based on alarm – alarm at seeing a colleague of mine, whom she recognised, watching the ferry terminal. We don't go chasing after high-powered motor-bikes – that may well be just what they would like.'

'Why?' Marker demanded irritably.

'Because,' Beaurain said grimly, spacing out his words with great deliberation, 'the attempt at a diversion suggests to me that what you're after is under your nose.' He got out of the Mercedes and closed the door with a hard clunk.

'They would have guards, watchers,' Marker protested.

'They had,' Beaurain pointed out. 'The big man himself was in the Volvo. His girl was about to patrol round the station. There was a third Syndicate member – the man on the motor-bike. There will be more.'

'I get the sensation that I'm already being watched,' said Marker, his hands plunged deep inside his jacket pockets.

'You are – I have at least a dozen men within shooting distance of where we're walking now.'

'I said earlier that Telescope was the only organisation capable of destroying the Stockholm Syndicate,'

Marker murmured in an undertone. They stopped as they reached Louise.

'Can I talk?' she asked, covering her mouth with a cupped hand as she lit one of her rare cigarettes. She wasn't even looking at them. Curious, Marker glanced quickly along the axis of her observation. All he could see were two large open-sided goods wagons. Behind them an engine was moving along the line to link up with them. A railwayman with a flag guided the engine-driver. It all seemed perfectly normal to Marker.

'This is it,' said Louise, once Beaurain had confirmed that she could speak in front of Marker, who was still mystified. He glanced around more carefully, suddenly aware that the previously almost deserted area in front of the station had become populated. Several passengers had drifted out of the reception hall into the open. Tourists with knapsacks on their backs, two men holding fishing rods. At least Marker *thought* they were fishing rods.

Other men were now wandering across the road towards the ferry terminal. One of them, tall and sandy-haired, carrying a long sports bag, walked with a distinctly military carriage.

Crossing the road, he walked a short distance further on beyond the ferry terminal. Marker's eyes narrowed as he watched him put the bag down on the floor and raise a small compact object like a camera to his eyes while he scanned the harbour with the eagerness of a photographic buff always on the look-out for new subjects. It occurred to Marker that the camera could easily be a camouflaged walkie-talkie. Beaurain's face was expressionless as he also watched Jock Henderson take up the best strategic position for viewing the ferry terminal, its approaches, the railway station and the two wagons waiting to be put aboard the next ferry, which was entering the harbour and turning slightly to head for the landing. Everything so normal. The sun beating down, radiating warmth out of a perfectly clear sky. The steady thump of the wheels of the engine approaching the two wagons it would push across the road and up inside the bowels of the ferry once the vessel had berthed and was ready for its new cargo.

'You said "this is it". I see nothing out of the ordinary,' said Marker.

'You're not supposed to.'

'The man with the flag guiding the engine,' said Louise. 'He's been waiting there for fifteen minutes. He kept looking towards that man on the motor-bike who picked up the girl.'

Thunk! The slow-moving engine hit the rear of the two wagons and the railwayman dropped his flag to indicate contact. A shade late, Beaurain noted. The railwayman rolled up his flag. Behind them they could hear a massive gushing as the incoming train ferry displaced quantities of harbour water, the vessel's propellers already in reverse to slow her down and ensure a gentle contact with Danish soil. Customs officials and Immigration men holding brief-cases were moving restlessly in the vicinity of the landing point. All perfectly normal.

'Have you any men with you?' Beaurain asked suddenly.

'No,' Marker admitted reluctantly. 'I'm not supposed to be here, remember?' He glanced at Louise but she was staring in the direction of the shunting yards and apparently not listening. 'I couldn't bring a team – that would have alerted my chief. So, if the Syndicate is here in strength . . .'

'We'll deal with them – and you'll vanish,' Beaurain told him crisply. 'Officially you were never here.'

'I bloody well was – and am! You may need some official backing if it comes to a shoot-out. Where is the dope?'

'The first wagon full of packing materials,' said Louise quietly. 'Great sheets of it perched on end. That rail guard who flagged down the engine – before it arrived he was patrolling up and down beside the first wagon. During the night those two wagons were further down the track – behind the house I followed Horn to. Work it out for yourself.'

'Packing materials?' Marker repeated.

'Ideal for cutting out a secret compartment to take the suitcase with the heroin. And I saw Horn carry just such a suitcase out of his house on Nyhavn only last night – if that was Horn behind the wheel of the Volvo.'

'That was Horn,' Marker agreed. 'This suitcase . . .'

'It was driven to Elsinore by that black-haired girl who tried to chop me.'

They were running short of time. Already the train ferry from Sweden had stopped its engines, its ramp was being lowered to connect with the rail lines on the quay.

'She tried to chop me,' Louise continued tersely, 'because I was in the exact position to observe the heroin – for her to risk what she did I had to be in a most sensitive area.' She lost patience as Marker looked unconvinced. 'Dammit, do I have to draw you a picture? What the hell was Horn showing himself in this area for? Because it's his responsibility to see the consignment gets through. The money and effort they have invested in this load must be enormous. If we can take it away from them we'll have dealt them a savage blow.'

'And possibly just before the first full meeting of the entire Syndicate is held,' Beaurain murmured. Aloud he said, 'So what do we do as the first step, Louise?'

'Scare the guts out of that railwayman with the flag,' Louise replied instantly. 'I'm convinced he knows where the heroin is hidden, that he's been guarding it until it's safely on its way to Sweden. And we may have only minutes to do it. Any suggestions,

Max?' She looked at the German, who nodded and began to move.

Beaurain walked a few paces away and beckoned Louise over. They stopped and stared out at the regatta-like scene in the glittering Øresund.

'We are here in Elsinore for another reason – to meet our chief man in Stockholm, Peter Lindahl. For over a year his whole task has been to locate the head man behind the Stockholm Syndicate. Last night he phoned me at the Royal Hotel from somewhere between Stockholm and Hälsingborg. He has discovered the identity of Hugo.'

'Why didn't he tell you on the phone?'

'You must be tired,' Beaurain chided. 'You think that Lindahl is going to trust a hotel switchboard? Our conversation was well wrapped up, but that's what he meant. He's driving now to Hälsingborg and he'll soon be coming over. He told me he has a car space reserved on *Delfin II* for its midday crossing.'

'So within an hour we'll know the monster who is responsible for so much terror and cold-blooded killing.'

Chapter Twelve

'Bodel,' Beaurain began genially, putting an arm round the Dane's shoulder, 'you said that only Telescope had any chance of defeating the Stockholm Syndicate. I don't want you out of the way in some bar, just maybe standing over here by the kerb so you can help out if the local police arrive.'

'I'll stay.' Marker's chubby face was grim and hard as he remembered his superior invading his office back at Politigarden in Copenhagen, recalled how he had been told to drop this case, remembered what the Syndicate had threatened to do to his wife and son. 'And I'm armed,' he said.

'So are a lot of people round here,' Beaurain assured him.

Startled, Marker looked round the whole area. Before wandering round the back of the station to where the wagons were waiting, Kellerman had made a brief hand signal to Henderson. *Give me back-up*. The Scot had again raised the camera-like walkie-talkie and had given the order.

'Cover Max, surround entire action area immediately.'

Fascinated, Marker watched as some of the 'hikers' with packs on their backs drifted back inside the station. He guessed that there would be exits from inside the station into the shunting zone where Foxbel had disappeared. Other 'tourists' closed in round the front of the station between the ferry terminal and the shunting zone. Henderson himself picked up his sports bag and unzipped it. Now he could have his machine-gun in action in seconds. Henderson's main fear was that Syndicate men now concealed might appear in strength at any moment. Everything depended on Kellerman.

The Danish railwayman who had guided the engine with his flag was pacing up and down alongside the first wagon when Kellerman appeared. The German realised immediately that the main problem was the engine-driver waiting in his cab to shunt the two wagons aboard the ferry. He was relieved to see two of Henderson's back-up men dressed like hikers appear from the main station beyond the engine. With a swift gesture to them he indicated the engine-driver and continued walking towards the man with the flag, who shouted something in Danish.

'Don't understand the language!' Kellerman called back in English. He was still walking towards him, smiling broadly. It was amazing how a smile threw people off balance, even if only for a few vital seconds. The rail guard spoke again, this time in English.

'You are on private property and must leave at once. Go back! Go back the way you came or I will call the security police!'

'Good idea. You call them. Now! Before these wagons move!'

The back-up team had moved with their accustomed speed. Already one had engaged the engine-driver in conversation while the second man disappeared behind the locomotive, then silently reappeared climbing up into the engine cab behind the driver whose attention was distracted. A hand holding a choloroform-soaked cloth was clasped over the driver's mouth; in less than thirty seconds he was unconscious on the floor of his cab.

'You will get out of this area now!' The thin-faced rail guard slipped his hand inside his jacket and Kellerman leapt forward two paces. His right hand closed over the Dane's wrist, dragging the hand out, a hand which held a pistol. 'Danish State Railways issue?' the German enquired. As he spoke he twisted the wrist, broke it and the pistol fell to the ground. The guard's mouth opened to scream and the scream was stifled by Kellerman's other hand. The German was bending the Dane backwards and suddenly he kicked the man's feet from under him. The guard fell backwards and only Kellerman's grip saved him splitting his skull open on the rail. The German lowered him gently until his neck was resting on the rail. He tried to lift his head and something sharp pricked his throat, the tip of Kellerman's knife.

'Try shouting and I'll slit your throat,' Kellerman hissed.

'The wagon . . .'

'Will move any moment now,' Kellerman assured him. 'It will neatly slice off your head like a guillotine. Straight across the neck, leaving your head between the tracks, the rest of your body on this side,' he elaborated brutally.

'You wouldn't!'

'I would – and will. And if you lift your head to get it off the rail I'll stick you. Comes to the same thing, really, doesn't it? Where's the heroin?'

'What heroin?'

The words were cut off by the prick of Kellerman's knife against his throat. He lay sprawled with the pressure of the iron rail against the back of his neck, and when he looked to the left – the direction from which death would come – he saw the wheel's rim which was now assuming enormous dimensions in his mind.

'The heroin stashed for Sweden,' Kellerman said wearily, 'I really believe you're stupid enough not to tell me – in which case any second now: crunch!'

'They'll kill me if I speak.'

'The Stockholm Syndicate?'

'For Jesus Christ's sake have mercy!'

'And let all that heroin flood the streets? I'd sooner behead you.'

Despite the freezing of his emotions after the murder of his wife, Kellerman was impressed by the man's terror – terror of the Stockholm Syndicate even caught in this dreadful position. His gaunt face had almost aged since Kellerman had threatened him; there was the stench of the man's own sweat in the air, the sweat of fear which coursed down his face in rivulets and streamed over his neck, already dirty with rust from the rail. Still he didn't speak and the German was not sure what to do next. A bell began ringing, a steady ding-dong in slow time somewhere in the direction of the ferry terminal.

'The heroin . . . just above you . . . inside the second wadge . . . let me up, the train is moving!'

He jerked his head up violently, staring at the rim of the wheel to his left in gibbering terror. Kellerman withdrew the knife a second before the Dane could impale himself on its point. '. . . *the train is moving!*' Kellerman's reflex action was to grab the man's tie, swing his head to the side away from the wheel and clear of the line. Then, streaming with his own sweat, he realised what had happened.

The steady tolling of the bell continued, warning approaching traffic that a train was on the way. But this train wouldn't be moving because the engine-driver had been knocked out with chloroform, a fact which for a terrible split second Kellerman had forgotten when the bell started its racket. It was no surprise that the Dane had fainted and was lying inert by the track. He heard a rush of feet and hoped they were the feet of friends.

'Did he talk?'

Henderson's voice. Kellerman, his face showing strain, looked up. To his right the two 'hikers' who had dealt with the engine-driver were quietly slipping away to the main station. Gunners disguised as tourists blocked off the approach from the ferry terminal.

'Stop the bell – the train isn't going?' he said.

'The heroin?'

Marker's voice. A mixture of eagerness and anxiety. Kellerman used his sleeve to mop the sweat dripping off his forehead. He'd been shaken and he didn't mind admitting it. For a few seconds he'd had a vision of the head rolling free between the rails.

'We've got it,' he told them, 'if he told me the truth – and I think he did. I would have. In this wagon just above me the second slat back – "wadge" I think he called it.'

He stood up and stiffened his legs to stop himself swaying. Only Louise saw him surreptitiously wipe the damp palms of his hands on his trousers. He winked at her and she smiled sympathetically. It was at the most unexpected moments that the terrible strain of their work hit them like a sledgehammer, often when they were least prepared for it.

It was being handled with typical Telescope efficiency. Henderson had gone quickly back up the track directing the gunners to form a defensive cordon.

Beaurain had climbed up into the wagon with Marker and called down for the loan of Kellerman's knife which was handed up.

'The guard is in it up to his neck.' He paused as the potentially unfortunate phrasing occurred to him, then continued, looking at Louise. 'The engine-driver may be in it or he could be completely innocent. At the moment he's . . .' He made a gesture placing his hand over his mouth indicating he was out of action. Then, in the near distance, growing louder every second they heard the one sound Beaurain did not wish to hear, the sound of a patrol-car's siren screaming.

It was a potentially dangerous situation. Jumping down from the wagon, leaving Beaurain to wrestle with the compressed paper, Marker advanced to meet three uniformed policemen running down by the side of the wagon, waving his identification card in their faces and gesturing for them to get back. The chubby-faced Dane was magnificent in the emergency, talking non-stop in Danish, ushering the three men back towards the ferry terminal like a shepherd driving sheep.

'Get back out of this area! I have the whole place infiltrated with undercover men! Coming in here with your bloody siren wailing – you may have ruined an international operation planned for months! What the hell brought you here in the first place?'

'We received a message that there was terrorist activity in the region of this ferry terminal.'

'And the caller gave you his name and address, of course?' Marker demanded with bitter sarcasm.

'Well . . . no, sir,' the driver of the car admitted as he continued backing away with his two companions. They had almost reached the road now. 'It was the inspector on duty – said we had to get here as fast as we could – we were on patrol when he radioed us.'

'The inspector on duty!' Sometimes a stray shot hit the bull's eye, Marker thought with a tingle of excitement. No such order would normally be transmitted by the station inspector. The Stockholm Syndicate was here in Elsinore, its corrupt fingers reaching into the local police station. Because of one thing Marker was certain: the patrol car had been sent to disperse and interfere with Telescope's search for the huge heroin haul.

'Have you ever received a direct order personally from the inspector before – over the radio?' he asked, sure that he was right in his incredible long shot.

'First time it's ever happened in my experience,' the man told him, 'and I've been driving a patrol car for five years. I said to my mate it was odd.'

'I'm now going to tell you exactly what to do,' Marker told the driver, his expression grim. 'You will carry out my order to the letter or forget about any further career with the police. Wait in your vehicle. If you receive any further orders or questions from this inspector, tell him your car has broken down, that you have found nothing happening at the ferry terminal after a thorough search. And then, in a few minutes, you will drive me to your station.' He looked back to where Beaurain was still inside the rail wagon and saw nothing. God he was taking a gamble!

'What is the name of this inspector?' he asked.

The man gave him a name and then the trio of policemen returned to their car. It now all depended on Beaurain finding the heroin. He made his way back to the wagon where the man he knew as Foxbel stood on guard with the girl. At the foot of the wagon he stared up at the Belgian whose head was just visible above a huge sheet of packing material.

'Get up here fast, Bodel,' Beaurain called down.

'You haven't . . . not already?' Marker began.

'I said get up here, for Christ's sake. The timing is everything.'

It was so simple Marker was overwhelmed with a mixture of disbelief and relief. In the darkened confines of the rail wagon he stared at what Beaurain's torchbeam showed him. Then he was filled with sheer fury when he remembered that less than three hours earlier he had been ordered not to carry his investigations any further by one of the most powerful figures in the Danish police service.

Beaurain had used a nail file borrowed from Louise to pick the locks of the suitcase. Inside the case, which lay in a narrow defile between walls of the packing material, was a collection of transparent bags containing powder. The case was full, the haul enormous.

'Inside there? As simple as that?'

'As simple as that. I was careful not to break the seals.'

The hole had been carefully hollowed out of the second wadge of packing material – just where the rail guard had told Kellerman he would find it. Propped against the wadge was the thick panel of the same material which slotted into grooves and was then held firmly in place with transparent sealing material.

'Simple but effective,' Beaurain continued. 'The sealing material coincides with the labels designating its alleged destination. We have to take a very quick decision, Bodel, my friend. Only you and I and the two people standing guard outside this wagon yet know we *have* discovered the consignment.'

'Which is on its way to Stockholm apparently. If we let it go through, can your people really watch it closely enough?'

'We'll need help from Harry Fondberg, head of Säpo in Stockholm.'

Säpo was the Swedish secret police, a department which operated quite apart from the normal law-enforcement agencies. It was becoming stifling inside the wagon and there was a growing stench of something unpleasant like powerful glue. Beaurain assumed it was resin inside the material.

'Who contacts Fondberg – you or me?' Marker asked simply.

It took Beaurain a moment to grasp the significance

of what Marker had said. Then he was carefully closing the suitcase, re-locking it and calling for Louise to come up inside the wagon so he could instruct her.

'I'd better not hear you for the next few minutes,' Bodel said. 'Then if anything goes wrong you'll know I didn't betray you – it has become a way of life you know – betrayal.'

'You're actually leaving this enormous haul?' Louise asked when the Intelligence chief had gone. Having closed the case, the Belgian was easing it back inside its secret compartment, prior to replacing the panel and the self-adhering sealer he had taken so much trouble to preserve. 'How do you know you can trust Marker?' she whispered.

'I don't – we have to gamble.'

'He kept those policemen from the patrol-car away – perhaps it was to protect the consignment.'

'So we don't tell him everything we plan. Now, relay all these instructions to Henderson as soon as you can.' As he spoke he was continuing the delicate task of replacing the suitcase in its original hiding-place so there would be no signs it had been tampered with.

'Henderson must radio a signal to *Firestorm*. I want Anderson to use his Sikorsky to shadow the express hauling these two wagons all the way to Stockholm. He's to have two men on board he can land if necessary. Anderson is to be warned that the suitcase is likely to be dropped somewhere en route between here and Stockholm.'

'And how's Anderson going to see all that in the dark?'

'Because it's likely to be some place out in the wilds, which means they'll need some kind of signal exchanged between the man inside the wagon and those waiting close to the track – a flare, the flashing lights of a parked car, something Anderson will be able to spot from the air.'

'Anything else?'

'Plenty. Anderson must have a method of communication with Fondberg of Säpo. I'll phone Fondberg myself as soon as we get clear of this damned wagon. He has a radio outfit and we can send a second message to Anderson letting him know how to radio signals to Stockholm. There, I really don't think anyone could tell we had tampered with their secret compartment. What is it, Max?'

'A suggestion. I travel inside this wagon.' Kellerman, who had been standing just below them and listening to the conversation, had shinned up to join them. 'Plenty of places to hide,' he said, looking round the gloomy interior, 'and that way the consignment is under close Telescope observation. Henderson gave me this water bottle.'

'One man alone? It could be dangerous,' Beaurain commented dubiously.

'I never thought I'd joined a kindergarten,' the German said drily.

'You're right,' Beaurain murmured. 'And this is something we don't let Marker know about,' he said firmly.

'Weapon, Max?' Louise offered the pistol she had collected while on board *Firestorm*. Kellerman shook his head, pulled up his right trouser leg and showed them a knife sheathed inside his sock. 'If I need something it has to be quiet, I suspect. What's the priority?' he asked Beaurain. 'Risking letting the consignment go or trying to track the Syndicate at all cost?'

'The priority, Max,' Beaurain said quietly, 'is preserving your own life. You'll be working without back-up.'

'Any more instructions for Henderson?' Louise asked.

'Find out the exact route of this train from the map inside the station – I think it's Hassleholm, Nassjö, Mjolby, Norrköping and then Stockholm. Transmit to Anderson not only route but also the timetable. And now we have one or two loose ends to tie up.'

'But not Max.'

Beaurain had turned to wish the German good luck but already he had vanished into the cavernous depths of the wagon without a trace. How he was going to stick the stench of resin Beaurain couldn't imagine. He leapt down to the ground beside the track. Marker was returning from the patrol-car which was still parked in the distance close to the ferry terminal.

'Everything is organised?' the Dane enquired.

'Your heroin is still aboard.'

The ding-dong of the bell warning traffic to steer clear of the road crossing was continuing and the turn-round of the train ferries was very swift. He was asking a very great deal of Marker. Not twenty feet from where they stood was the biggest haul of heroin ever to pass through Denmark. If Marker confiscated it his stock in Copenhagen would rocket; it would solve any problems he might have in fighting his superior; it would quite likely end with his taking over from that same superior.

'We could lose it en route,' Marker suggested tentatively, studying the Belgian's reaction closely.

'I have taken certain precautions.'

'Which I don't want to know about.'

'Which I have no intention of telling you about,' Beaurain assured him.

'You think you have a good chance of getting away with it?'

'Providing you personally arrest and hold incommunicado for three days this rail guard and the driver. Can you hold them somewhere in Copenhagen – not here in Elsinore? And you'll need another driver.'

'Certainly,' Marker agreed with enthusiasm. 'Those men in the patrol-car can help. They will handcuff both men and transport them to the police station. From there they will simply disappear for the required three days. You will let me know the ultimate destination of the heroin? I need as soon as possible an official report from Säpo chief Fondberg in Stockholm.'

Beaurain and Louise were waiting in the Mercedes, watching the rail wagon being attached to the Stockholm Express. In a matter of minutes it would be aboard the ferry, en route for Hälsingborg – where the express would move on to Swedish soil and begin its journey towards distant Stockholm.

'Do you think Max is going to be all right?' Louise asked as she accepted a few puffs from Beaurain's cigarette. 'That wagon looks very tightly sealed to me.'

'It is a huge gamble,' the Belgian admitted, 'but it is our only definite link with the Stockholm Syndicate. Max has to follow whoever collects the heroin and see where it leads him. It may well even lead to Hugo himself – if Max is lucky.'

'Is there no way to protect Max?'

'We are doing everything we can,' Beaurain replied with a note of irritation. 'I admit I'm worried that he is sealed up on his own in that wagon. And there is a chance that it will be handled by Horn in an uncharacteristic way. It was at Elsinore.'

'I don't get your reasoning,' she said, 'because there was Syndicate surveillance at Elsinore, so what different way are you referring to?'

'Horn did not have a platoon of men to back up and watch over the transshipment. If he uses the same method – and it *is* the more effective method – he will use the minimum number of people to take the consignment off the express when the time comes. Maybe only one man. What he loses in strength of numbers he gains by reducing almost to zero the danger that anything will be seen. And it is the normal technique for handling large dope consignments. Few men, much organisation.'

'What back-up does Max really have? I heard you talking to Jock Henderson before he drove back with his team.'

Beaurain's face, unusually lined with fatigue, became grim as he checked his watch. 'Every hour that passes, while Max is inside that wagon alone and nothing happens, increases his chances. Henderson is bringing men down by car from Stockholm to board the express at every stop. Anderson's Sikorsky will be watching the train from the air as far as he can. The point is both Harry Fondberg and I expect the consignment to be off-loaded from the express somewhere before it reaches Stockholm.'

'But isn't Stockholm the objective? Won't the centre of the spider's web of the distribution system be there?'

'Yes. But international expresses arriving in the Swedish capital – especially those passing through Denmark – are carefully watched and checked by the Customs and Drug Squad people. Much easier to take off that suitcase at an intermediary stop and transport it the rest of the way by air or road.'

> Signal from Harry Fondberg, SÄPO, to all units in Southern Zone. Sikorsky helicopter hence designated as DRAGONFLY proceeding very roughly on axis Hälsingborg–Stockholm to be allowed free access and under no circumstances repeat no circumstances intercepted. Regular reports of progress of DRAGONFLY to be sent to this office for personal attention Fondberg and in grade one security code. Any attempt by outside agencies to interfere with progress of DRAGONFLY to be reported personally and instantly to Fondberg. In case of emergency all SÄPO units will use all resources at their command to protect and preserve DRAGONFLY. Fondberg. SÄPO HQ Stockholm. 1640 hours.

The signal caused a sensation when received by local Säpo commanders in southern Sweden – which was roughly bisected by the rail route followed by the express carrying the consignment of heroin. Later, when shown a copy of the signal alerting the Säpo apparatus in the designated area, Beaurain considered it a typical Harry Fondberg ploy – clever, ingenious and misleading. It was what was omitted from the signal rather than what was included which was significant.

Chief Inspector Harry Fondberg of Säpo was one of the best friends Jules Beaurain had made during his years in the Brussels police force – and he personally knew every key police and security chief in Western

Europe, to say nothing of the counter-espionage people and his contacts inside the United States.

Fondberg was exactly forty years old. Undoubtedly he would have won the prize for the Most Unpopular Man of the Year had a poll been taken of leading Swedish politicians. In a country which prided itself on its tradition of neutrality in all things, Fondberg was the least neutral of men.

'I am not dealing with gentlemen,' he once said. 'So my methods have to be adapted to my customers.'

'Tell me no more,' his Minister of Justice had replied. Before he left the Säpo chief's office he added, 'But get results.'

Now, at the very moment when Beaurain and Louise were expecting the imminent arrival from Stockholm of Peter Lindahl, Fondberg was starting his long wait inside his office. He was prepared to stay up all night until something developed. A methodical man, he faced a wall-map of southern Sweden which showed with a system of pins and string the exact course the train would follow – and, consequently, roughly the route the Sikorsky, *Dragonfly*, would take. The phone rang. It was Erik Lebert, his assistant.

'The American entered Gamla Stan again. Same address. Still no-one there. He watched for a while and then returned to his hotel. I'm speaking from the lobby. Will I continue surveillance?'

'Yes. You will be relieved later.'

Fondberg replaced the receiver and squeezed his

chin with his hand as he gazed into the distance, a typical gesture when concentrating. The carefully-worded message told him that Ed Cottel, the American CIA man had once more surveyed an apartment near St. Gertrud Church in Gamla Stan, the Old City on an island joined to the main part of Stockholm by a bridge near the Grand Hotel.

Cottel was trying to locate Dr Theodor Norling, antique book dealer and a member of the three-man directorate which controlled the ever-expanding criminal organisation, the Stockholm Syndicate.

'Washington on the line, sir,' the operator informed Fondberg.

He was about to ask her to find out exactly who was calling, when it occurred to him that someone might have got round to informing him of Ed Cottel's arrival. He told the girl he would take the call and announced his identity when the connection was made.

'Joel Cody calling, Mr Fondberg. You know who I am?'

His caller was the President of the United States' closest aide! There was a trailing off at the end of the question. Was he supposed to stand to attention while he took the call, showing by his tone how flattered he was that such a man would use a few minutes of his precious time calling someone so far beneath him?

'What do you want, Cody?' Fondberg asked in a blank voice, using his other hand to switch on the recorder.

There was a brief pause, no doubt while Cody patted his dignity back into shape. He recovered quickly, keeping his tone of voice amiable and hail-fellow as though they had known each other for years. It was, in fact, the first time they had spoken to each other.

'First, I want to thank you sincerely for your truly whole-hearted co-operation with DC, which is greatly appreciated. I may say that appreciation is also felt by the most eminent personages in the United States, if you follow me.'

The stupid bastard meant the President. He used twenty words where five would do. There was an irritating trailing off at the end of every sentence, presumably to give Fondberg time to register due humility.

'Mr Cody, what is the precise purpose of your call?' asked Fondberg bluntly.

'We always like to maintain normal diplomatic courtesies, and in spite of what the press of certain countries says about our playing it close to the chest and not informing our Allies of what we are doing on their territory . . .'

'Yes, Mr Cody?'

Fondberg could stand it no longer. With his free hand he opened the bottom drawer, took out a pack of cigarettes, fiddled one into his mouth and used the lighter also secreted in the drawer to get it going.

'We feel you ought to know in advance . . .' The voice in Washington went hard. '. . . and not after the event, that one of our people will shortly be visiting your country.'

Fondberg knew something was wrong. He gave the conversation his full attention, listening to every nuance in the words being spoken by the President's sidekick.

'The person to whom I'm referring is highly regarded by us, and we sure would appreciate it if you could extend to him all your normal facilities and co-operation. His name is Harvey Sholto and his sphere of activity is security.'

'Which department?'

'Now, Mr Fondberg, I'm sure you have found that unfortunately the telephone is not, in the world we live in, the safe instrument we all wish that it might be. May I suggest that Harvey calls you up on arrival and arranges a mutually advantageous meeting, say at the American Embassy in Stockholm?'

'He can phone and make an appointment to see me here. Please let me have the flight number and ETA of this Mr Sholto.'

'All I can say is that he will be landing in Stockholm during the course of the next three days and I will pass on to him your message to call you as soon as he has settled in. Now, if you'll excuse me, Mr Fondberg, a certain light is flashing on my desk and I'm sure you'll understand when I say it's the one light I cannot ignore.'

Fondberg thought for several minutes before he asked for an urgent call to be put through to the man he knew best at Interpol. While waiting for the call he alerted security at Arlanda Airport to be on the lookout for a passenger travelling on an American passport in the name of Harvey Sholto. When asked how quickly to activate the surveillance Fondberg replied, 'At once.' It was just like the Codys of this world to play it clever, to inform him only an hour or so before Sholto landed.

When the Interpol call came through he gave his contact the name Sholto, Harvey, and was promised any data before the day ended: Fondberg stared at the wall-map showing the progress of the express carrying the heroin consignment. He suddenly wondered if there could be a link between the train and the unsettling news about Harvey Sholto.

Harry Fondberg's Interpol contact phoned back from Paris at ten that night. The Swedish chief of Säpo was still waiting in his office, convinced that something was bound to happen, that it would happen soon and, pray to God, it would give him the lever he had been desperately searching for to break into the Stockholm Syndicate.

'Harvey Sholto,' the Frenchman informed the Swede laconically, 'is a highly-trained killer. The Americans give him an X-l rating. It means I personally would not like to be in the sights of his high-powered rifle.'

'If you have a description ... just a moment, I will

take this down.' Fondberg deliberately had not activated the recording machine because it was understood that each would ask the other before any mechanical record was made. In this case Fondberg did not want any record existing which someone else might get hold of and play back. He scribbled down Sholto's description in a scrawl legible only to himself.

'There is more about this Sholto,' the Frenchman continued. 'Washington has used him for assassination in Vietnam, Africa and Central America, but we have not been able to discover that he is assigned to any particular agency. He carries very great influence in high places in Washington which has helped him carry out his assassinations.'

'Thank you,' said Fondberg. He exchanged the normal pleasantries automatically, then replaced the receiver and cuddled his chin in his hand, gazing into the distance with a grim expression. It was always the same problem: too much was happening at once. But what worried Fondberg most of all was a question which kept hammering away at his brain.

Who was Harvey Sholto's new target?

Chapter Thirteen

'Send an immediate *Nadir* signal on the police inspector and the railway guard.'

Nadir. Even more than *Zenith,* this signal caused sweating palms among the men who transmitted the message. They could not get out of their minds the thought that one day the Syndicate might send out a *Nadir* signal which included their own personal details. And once the word went out there was nowhere to flee to, nowhere safe from the octopus-like reach of Stockholm.

The order had been given by Benny Horn to Sonia Karnell as they sat side by side in a BMW saloon. They had changed cars within minutes of driving away from Elsinore station in the Volvo. It was a policy of Horn's never to stay inside the same vehicle for more than two hours. The BMW was parked by the waterfront in an area quite remote from the ferry terminal and the railway station. She walked across the plank linking the quay to a large fishing boat. For a vessel which could hardly be described as modern it carried some surprisingly up-to-date equipment.

The latest radar device was poised on the bridge,

and concealed inside the cabin to which she was descending by a flight of wooden steps was a powerful transceiver. The manner of concealment behind a panel was very similar to the one which Frans Darras had used aboard his barge outside Bruges.

'You want something, lady? This is private property.'

Arnold Barfred, the Danish owner of the vessel, deliberately spoke in a loud voice, using the English language, in case a passer-by was listening.

His eyes went blank as Sonia passed on the signal to him in a low voice and told him to hurry. 'It is a *Nadir* signal. None of us wastes a minute transmitting a *Nadir*. We just wish to get rid of it – and forget it.'

She didn't reply and hurried ashore. Behind her she heard the hatch cover close, sealing off entry into the cabin, the bolt snap home. Barfred was doing exactly what he said he would.

And in another way he had obeyed orders precisely. He had waited below deck for the car to arrive – so that just as the Darras' on their barge had never seen Dr Otto Berlin in Bruges, so Barfred had no idea of the appearance of Dr Benny Horn.

Sonia Karnell settled into the BMW and switched on the ignition, anxious to get away as soon as possible. Beside her Horn looked back at the fishing vessel, doubtless to make sure Barfred did not appear until after they had gone.

'We will just make sure that Beaurain's man from Stockholm is dealt with and then you can drive me back to Nyhavn. We will pick up a few things and fly straight to Stockholm.'

'Lindahl? He is coming here?'

'Yes, my dear, he is coming to Elsinore and hopes to arrive here shortly. He is fleeing Sweden by fast car as though all the hounds of hell were behind him. What he doesn't know is that they are in *front* of him.'

The huge motor ferry hardly moved in the gentle swell of the Øresund as it lay moored to the Swedish shore at Hälsingborg. A steady stream of cars bound for Elsinore drove up the ramp and vanished inside *Delfin II*'s open maw.

Aboard, the passengers were already taking up position on the upper deck which gave them a good view of Denmark only a short distance miles across the sea channel. Through a pair of high-powered glasses a Swedish tourist gazed at Kronborg Castle which rose up on the far shore, and children clung to the ship's rail.

It was difficult to imagine a more peaceful scene, an atmosphere more removed from violence. Dancing across the sparkling crests of the blue, sunlit waves were innumerable yachts, their coloured sails twinkling triangles flapping in the mid-channel breeze.

A grey Volvo disappeared inside the vast loading deck, and Beaurain's agent guided his vehicle to the position indicated by the ferry loader. Switching off the ignition, Lindahl sank back in his seat and automatically reached for a cigarette until he saw the *No Smoking* notice staring straight at him.

He didn't really mind. For the first time in days he could relax. Within minutes he would have left Sweden. In less than an hour he would be talking to Jules Beaurain in Elsinore.

Lindahl climbed out of his car, locked it carefully, made sure all the windows were closed, and then began to climb the staircases leading to the higher decks. Yes, thank God, it would soon all be over – once the deadly information he carried inside his memory was transmitted to Beaurain. He would be safe again.

Underneath the keel of the motor-ferry *Delfin II* Karl Woltz and his team of three frogmen worked swiftly and skilfully. They had left the large steam-launch, rocking at anchor a few hundred yards away from the ferry, ten minutes earlier. As Woltz had impressed on his three subordinates, 'Timing is vital, the crossing is short and the action must occur shortly before landfall.'

'Why then?' one man had asked.

'I don't know and I don't care!' Woltz had snarled impatiently. 'All I know is we are being paid a small fortune.'

Prior to slipping over the side of the steam-launch they had, as instructed, waited while *Delfin II* arrived from Elsinore, disgorged its human and wheeled cargo from Denmark, and started to take on board the cars and passengers waiting at Hälsingborg. Woltz himself had watched through field glasses, seeing only the driver of the blue Mercedes who, in his turn, was watching the cavalcade of vehicles crawling up the ramp inside *Delfin II*.

Woltz had no idea who this man was or what he was looking for. Nor would he recognise him again. The man standing by the Mercedes wore a light trench coat with the collar turned up and a soft hat pulled well down over his face. Then he gave the signal. Using a tightly-rolled newspaper like a baton, he rapped the bonnet of the car five times in an absent-minded manner. Woltz counted the rises and falls of the newspaper, then dropped his glasses, turning to the others waiting in the launch.

'We go! For God's sake handle the equipment carefully.'

Woltz had no way of knowing – nor would he have been interested – that the driver of the Mercedes had only given the go-ahead signal once he had seen Peter Lindahl drive his grey Volvo up the ramp and inside *Delfin II*.

'We want the entire ferry to sink within five minutes. There must be no survivors.'

This chilling instruction had been given to Woltz inside an empty two-storey house outside the Swedish town of Malmö. The organisation of whoever he was dealing with had stimulated Woltz's sneaking admiration. They had even gone to the trouble of fixing up a field telephone inside the house. As previously instructed, he had answered the instrument in a downstairs room, knowing that the man speaking was above him on the first floor. And nothing in the world would have tempted Woltz to creep up the staircase.

'Why not sink her in the middle of the Øresund? Why wait until she is close to the Danish shore?' Woltz had objected.

'That is not your problem. Just do as we tell you. You will be watched, of course. If you wish to get the balance of the money instead of a bullet in the back of the neck, start doing things our way.'

It had been eerie – the voice, the atmosphere inside the abandoned house. Woltz had been relieved to get out of the place. Now, hidden under the ferry's keel, watching his team through the perspex window of his face-mask, Woltz had no occasion to feel anything but professional satisfaction at a job well done.

Six explosive limpet mines were attached to various parts of *Delfin*'s hull. 'Do not forget that three of the mines must be attached under the car deck,' the voice in the house near Malmö had told him. Underneath the blurry silhouette of *Delfin*'s hull, Woltz was trying to concentrate on what he was doing rather than on the consequences of his act which would be swift and horrendous.

The limpet mines had magnetic clamps – so attaching them to the hull was a simple job. You held the mine in the correct position, pressed the switch and the magnetic feet sprang up and affixed themselves like suckers. The last thing was to wait until all six mines were attached like obscene metallic boils and then Woltz himself swam along beneath the hull, pausing at each mine to press another switch which activated the radio mechanism.

As soon as the last man was safely back aboard the steam launch Woltz ordered a crewman to send the signal – the signal confirming that the mines were in position, that the radio mechanisms had been activated, that it now only needed whoever was holding the control device to press a button and detonate all six mines.

The signal was a dipping of the Danish flag at the stern. Borrowing a pair of field glasses, Woltz focused them on the blue Saab which had appeared and was parked where the Mercedes had stationed itself earlier. To his disappointment, the driver behind the wheel wore a helmet and goggles.

Woltz had no way of knowing that he was looking in the wrong direction – that the Saab was simply being used to divert his attention from a very powerful white motor-cruiser behind him. This vessel was proceeding south – away from the car ferry – drifting with the tide at such a slow speed it was barely moving. On the bridge a bearded man wearing a nautical cap lowered the field glasses he had trained on Woltz's launch.

'That is the signal,' he said.

'Now we know Lindahl is aboard – and that the *Delfin* is a floating bomb,' replied Dr Benny Horn, who stood beside the captain.

Delfin II was two-thirds of the way across the Øresund. Three more ferries were on the move; two crossing to Sweden, the third approaching the ferry terminal outside the railway station at Elsinore.

Deep inside the bowels of the ferry Peter Lindahl was now sitting behind the wheel of his Volvo impatient to disembark. Lindahl, despite his relief at getting clear of Sweden, studied the other drivers carefully. No-one seemed to be taking any undue interest in him.

At the car ferry terminal Beaurain was watching a sleek white motor-cruiser drifting well south of the harbour. It was the drift which had first attracted his attention; you didn't normally just let a vessel like that float about. He handed the field glasses to Louise.

'Take a look at that white boat. There are two men on the bridge. Look at them, too.'

She adjusted the focus slightly and stared hard. Then she moved the glasses a fraction and Beaurain heard her intake of breath.

'What is it?'

'The second man – the one with the cap – looks like the man I saw climb into the van carrying the suitcase from the house on Nyhavn. He looks like Dr Benny Horn.'

On the bridge of the motor-cruiser Horn was staring fixedly at the progress of the ferry carrying Peter Lindahl to Denmark. He was gauging its distance from the Danish shore.

'*Now!*'

The bearded captain holding the radio-control device pressed one button and at the same second opened up the throttle. Pocketing the device, he opened up the throttle more. The prow of the cruiser lifted like the snout of a shark and the vessel leapt across the waves. 'You bloody fool, you'll draw attention to us,' cursed Horn, but his words were blotted out by the roar of explosions.

As the bearded captain pressed the button the radio impulse it released travelled in a fraction of a second to the receivers built into each of the six limpet mines attached to the hull of *Delfin II*. Along with the multitude of other victims, Peter Lindahl heard nothing. Sitting on top of one of the mines, it had been instant oblivion.

'Oh, God, Jules!'

Louise grabbed his arm and put a hand over her mouth. The giant ferry had been blown to pieces. A battering shock wave carried the sea in a minor tidal wave into the harbour, sinking countless small moored vessels during its passage before it smashed against the harbour wall.

Louise was frozen with horror. She had the awful impression she could see pieces of cars – wheels and chassis – spinning among the vast cloud of black smoke spreading rapidly into the sky. She looked behind her and saw everyone else frozen like statues. The only movement was the approach of Bodel Marker's car. In the distance sirens were starting to scream, boats were starting to put out to sea.

'What in hell has happened out there?'

Beaurain was facing Marker, watching his expression closely when he replied, his voice hard and clipped and, Louise noticed, very public school.

'The Syndicate has just blown up a car ferry. The number of casualties will be appalling. I doubt whether any man, woman or child aboard has survived. It will probably become known as "The Elsinore Massacre" and it will hit the headlines of every newspaper in the world tomorrow. And all to eliminate one, just *one* man.'

Louise knew that underneath the dipped, neutral manner was concealed a terrible, raging fury. Beaurain's eyes, always compelling, had an almost hypnotic quality as they watched Marker. The reaction of the Dane took her completely aback.

'And I thought I had bad news. The Syndicate has simply used the necessity for liquidating one of your own people and for that person I express my sincere condolences – to stage another demonstration.'

And now a breeze was wafting in from the sea – and the scene of the 'Massacre' – the faint whiff of petrol and something extremely unpleasant. Instinctively the trio walked a short distance away from the waterfront. Marker continued: 'A demonstration of the immense power and *ruthlessness* of the Stockholm Syndicate. A demonstration which will yield them at least as much as the murder of the Chief Commissioner of the Common Market.'

'If you're just saying that to ease the situation . . .'

'No, old friend,' Marker interjected firmly. 'I am not trying to ease the pain that you feel for what you erroneously believe is your fault. I did not tell you earlier because I was still not sure of you – that is how insidious and undermining of trust the actions of the Syndicate make all those who are touched by it. But only this morning I received a phone call.'

'From a girl?' Louise asked quietly.

'Yes, my dear, as before, from a girl. Again she warned me that sooner or later they would track down where I was hiding my wife and child, that they were already very close. That last bit was, of course, in the hope of scaring me into communicating with them in some way which would be detected by the Syndicate. She closed by saying a fresh demonstration of her organisation's power was imminent – that I would know what she was talking about when

I read about the disaster in the world's press tomorrow.'

Beaurain thrust both hands into the pockets of his jacket, one of his characteristic stances when he was undergoing deep emotion. 'And I presume other people in high places were also phoned the same message?'

'I know they were. Before Miss Hamilton and yourself arrived at my office I had just completed making a number of discreet calls.'

'A white cabin-cruiser,' Beaurain began in a blank monotone, 'flying the Danish flag when last seen, moving at speed on a southerly course about a mile off the Danish shore in the direction of Copenhagen. We believe we saw Benny Horn aboard. It took off like a bat out of hell almost at the moment of the explosion.'

'So,' Marker replied, 'by now he will have been put ashore at any of a dozen landing-stages along the coast where a waiting car will have picked him up – unless he has crossed the Sound to Sweden once out of sight of Elsinore. Still, I will put out an alert. Excuse me a moment.'

Marker went over to his car parked nearby, took the microphone from inside and leant against the car while he radioed his report. The driver was staring at the crowds of people who had appeared from nowhere and were growing denser as they gazed seaward where futile rescue activity was going on.

'You think it was definitely Benny Horn?' Louise asked after a silence lasting several minutes.

'I think he was probably the instrument. Whether he was the prime mover is another question,' he told her abruptly and turned to Marker who had now returned. 'Bodel, when you arrived here you said you thought you had bad news as though you were going to tell us something else before the ferry was blown up.'

'It seemed horrific . . . before this.' Marker waved a resigned hand towards the debris out at sea as Beaurain watched him closely. 'I told you I was going to have a word with the inspector who radioed that patrol-car to go to the ferry terminal by the railway station. I found I was just too late. There had been an accident.'

'What kind of accident?'

'He received a call purporting to come from his wife. After taking it he left the police station alone by car. They have just dragged the car out of the sea – the inspector was inside it. He was murdered. I know he was murdered because something has also happened to the two Danish railwaymen you asked me to keep out of circulation for three days. They never reached the police station.'

'What happened?' asked Louise. She felt her hair standing on end. Beaurain continued to study his old associate as the Dane went on with his story.

'They were in the patrol-car with the policemen. On

their way to the station they were flagged down by a man in front of a garage. A woman happened to be watching from about five hundred metres away – fortunately for her. The man who flagged down the car went inside the garage to fetch someone and then there was an almighty explosion. The car just disintegrated – rather like that . . .' Again the resigned hand made a gesture towards the sea.

In a deceptively detached tone, Beaurain said, 'They are killing everyone who has knowledge of the heroin. First the inspector they bought – or intimidated. Then the two railwaymen, both of whom must have known the approximate location of the suitcase. That is the Syndicate's method of protecting its investment. Effective, you must admit.'

'It's overkill.'

'Face it, Marker – the Syndicate runs one of the most efficient killing machines known in history – and each death is exploited to terrorise the maximum number of people who can be of service to the Syndicate in the future. Someone has thought up a foolproof system. Louise and I must go now,' he ended coldly.

'I will give you a lift to the railway station.'

During the journey Beaurain only spoke once, seated in the back of the car with Louise. She was looking out to sea when he asked for a cigarette: bits of bodies were beginning to float through the harbour entrance and he didn't want her subjected to any more harrowing experiences. During the ride to the railway station Marker relapsed into a sombre silence, staring through the windscreen without seeing anything. Beaurain was relieved when the Dane told his driver to drop them a distance from the station and wait for him. The three of them walked slowly towards where it had all started – the exit from Elsinore railway station.

'It's such an attractive town,' Louise said. 'All the houses old but freshly painted . . .'

She ended in mid-sentence and Beaurain gave her elbow a reassuring hug. She had been going to add something like, 'for such a ghastly horror to be perpetrated here.' Beaurain noticed that both his companions studiously avoided looking to their left over the harbour to the sea beyond. There was also an unnaturally quiet atmosphere among the people walking about who *were* staring seaward. Probably a number of them were in the habit of crossing over to Sweden from time to time. Using the car-ferries.

'While at the police station I asked about the enquiries I made about Dr Benny Horn,' Marker said in a dull voice. 'About his background and history, what he was like when he lived here in Elsinore. I must say they had responded to my request quickly. And they had showed around the photo I had taken of Horn in Copenhagen – I sent that out by despatch rider before I left the city.'

'And what did you find?'

'A few people who knew him when he lived here recognised the photo, others didn't.'

'What proportion?' There was an eager alertness in Beaurain's voice and manner.

'Fifty-fifty. The normal proportion,' Marker replied in the same dull tone. He was, Louise realised, still in a state of semi-shock, overwhelmed by the power and ruthlessness of the Stockholm Syndicate. 'Horn lived the same sort of hermit-like existence in Elsinore that he does in Copenhagen,' Marker continued. 'He was unmarried, had no relatives and spent a lot of time away from the place travelling – presumably to sell and buy rare editions.'

'How long had he lived in Elsinore?' Beaurain persisted.

'About twenty years. And he had his place a short distance outside the town in a very quiet area. That's all I could find out.' He stopped suddenly on the sidewalk and turned to Beaurain, his brow crinkled in perplexity and frustration. 'It doesn't make sense at all, does it?' he burst out.

'No, it doesn't.'

'What doesn't? Am I being dim?' Louise enquired.

'No,' Beaurain replied, 'but I think Bodel means this. For at least twenty years we have a man leading an apparently respectable and sober existence. All right, he keeps himself to himself, a bit like Silas Marner. Then this same man moves to Copenhagen – when would you say, Bodel?'

'About two years ago.'

'He moves to Copenhagen two years ago,' Beaurain went on, 'and what happens – almost overnight? He becomes one of the three men we think control the Stockholm Syndicate.'

'I see what you mean,' Louise said slowly. 'No, it doesn't make any sense.'

They had reached the concourse in front of the station where they had left the 280E parked, and Marker forced himself to speak with false exuberance. 'Well, what are you going to do now, Jules? Is there any way in which I can help you?'

'Drive back to Copenhagen after we've had lunch and think things over a bit. Thanks for your help and I know where to find you. I suppose you'll be staying on here for a while.'

Beaurain nodded in the direction of where a fleet of rescue and police craft were beyond the harbour poking around among the rapidly dispersing wreckage. Marker said yes, he would be staying on in Elsinore, shook them both solemnly by the hand and walked away slowly back to where his car was waiting.

'What are we actually going to do?' Louise asked. 'I know you didn't tell Marker the truth. And where are Henderson and his team of gunners?'

'Back on board *Firestorm* by now. I told him to leave once we had seen the ferry carrying the heroin depart. And Captain Buckminster has fresh instructions – to sail through the Øresund and wait at anchorage off Copenhagen. As for us, you are right, of course. I wasn't at all frank with Marker and not because I don't trust him. But suppose the Syndicate did locate where he has hidden his family. How long do you think he would resist their pressure for information?'

'How long could you expect him to?' Louise shuddered and compelled herself to look out to sea where the flock of boats was milling round aimlessly. One large launch was trawling over the side what looked to Louise like a shallow net. 'What is that thing, Jules? The boat with a loud-hailer keeping other craft away?'

'That will be Forensic. They will be gathering specimens of the debris for later analysis in the laboratory. That way they hope to discover what explosive was used.'

'Let's get back to Copenhagen – and then?'

'Stockholm.'

Beaurain paused as he took one last look at the confused armada beyond the harbour as if he wanted to imprint the scene on his memory. There was a set look to his expression; in some odd way he seemed to have grown younger rather than older, a youthfulness tinged with a merciless ferocity.

Beaurain made one more phone call before he left the Royal Hotel while Louise obtained flight reservations from the SAS airline counter in the hall adjoining the ground floor of the hotel. The call was to Chief Inspector Willy Flamen of Homicide in Brussels.

As he expected, Flamen was ready with the information he needed; in a very short time he had thoroughly investigated the early history and background of Dr Otto Berlin, dealer in rare books.

Berlin came from Liège, one of Belgium's largest cities, where he had built up a small but apparently lucrative business as a dealer in rare stamps. Part of his success lay in the fact that, unlike some of his European competitors, he was willing to travel any distance to conclude a worthwhile deal.

'You did say *stamp* dealer, Willy,' Beaurain queried. 'He's in rare books now surely?'

'Quite correct. He switched from stamps to books immediately on his arrival in Bruges about two years ago.'

Goldschmidt's photograph of Otto Berlin had been shown to the few people who had known Berlin in Liège. Flamen explained that Berlin was a bachelor, apparently totally absorbed in developing his business and with no close friends. Shown the photograph, the few people who had known him by sight had roughly divided into two sections – those who firmly said the picture was of Otto Berlin and those who said they didn't recognise it.

Flamen went on to explain that Otto Berlin had lived for about fifteen years in Liège before moving to Bruges. That was all Flamen had been able to come up with so far. There was an apologetic note in his voice but also, behind that, Beaurain thought he detected some other unspoken doubt. He tackled Flamen directly on the point.

The only other fact was something Flamen had obtained by phoning an acquaintance of Otto Berlin. Apparently Berlin had been excited just before he moved to Bruges, and he had conveyed this excitement over the phone without explaining the reason for it. And no, the man he had phoned had never seen Berlin again from that day to this.

Beaurain thanked Flamen, who then expressed the horror which was being felt all over the western world at 'The Elsinore Massacre'. The fact that there had been not a single survivor increased the dramatic impact, which TV stations and the radio everywhere were exploiting to the full. Louise returned, holding the folder with their air tickets, just as he replaced the receiver. He told her in a few words what Flamen had found.

'Nothing, then,' Louise decided after listening to Beaurain's account of the call.

'You don't notice a pattern?' the Belgian queried.

'It's almost a replica of Benny Horn's early days in Elsinore. No close friends. No family. Not at home very often because they spent so much time travelling on business. Jules, it's almost as though these people never actually existed!'

'Exactly!' Beaurain paused. 'But they did – do – exist. We have the evidence of two of the shrewdest police investigators in Europe – Marker here, Willy Flamen back in Brussels. In Liège one of these men, Otto Berlin, lived for fifteen years. In Elsinore there are people who confirm without a doubt that Dr Horn lived there for twenty years. Then they both suddenly change their addresses and pop up in Copenhagen and Bruges.'

'And almost at the same time,' Louise pointed out. 'Both men apparently appeared in their new lives only two years ago. Is it significant that there's a break in the pattern? Willy Flamen said Berlin was a stamp dealer in Liège and then switched to rare books as soon as he appeared in Bruges.'

'Possibly.'

'Who do you think is behind this monster?' Louise asked as she perched on the bed to fix her nylons. 'You have the feeling there is no-one you can confide in any more – in case he or she may be a member of the Syndicate, willingly or because they're under pressure.'

'Which I suspect is also part of their technique. The terror spreads ever wider, sucking more and more key figures in the West into its web. As to who is behind the monster, the answer appears to be Hugo, whoever he may be.' He looked up and handed back the airline folder. 'I'm convinced there's only one way to find out – to do what we're going to do. Fly to Stockholm and track down the location of the coming conference of the entire Syndicate. And we have Harry Fondberg of Säpo on our side, who may make all the difference.'

'Can we trust him?' she asked.

He was careful to keep control of his expression: not to let her see that she had just asked what he considered could be a leading question with a sinister answer.

Chapter Fourteen

The express had been stationary for over an hour. Kellerman had no doubt that the wagon was standing in a siding at Stockholm Central: there had been shunting after the express had stopped and he'd heard the distant sound of passengers' feet clumping along a stone platform. So far no-one had come for the heroin.

Kellerman was cramped in every muscle, parched with thirst. Taking the cap off his water-bottle he swallowed a modest portion of the water still remaining, recapped the bottle and then froze. There was a strange hissing sound which he couldn't immediately identify. Then he smelt a faint aroma and saw a whitish cloud drifting from the crack between the doors. The bastards were filling the wagon with some kind of gas.

Hauling his handkerchief out of his pocket he uncapped the water-bottle again and soaked the handkerchief. He was already feeling dizzy when he clamped the damp cloth over his nostrils to minimise the effect of the gas. They couldn't *know* someone was inside: it was another example of the Syndicate's meticulous attention to detail, a precaution *in case* someone was inside waiting for them.

Everything began to blur. Wedged against sheets of compressed paper at the end of the wagon he was out of sight when they opened the doors and two men climbed inside wearing gas-masks. He could just make out the silhouette of the masks through a blurred haze and they looked hideous. Kellerman leaned against the wagon wall, incapable of any action except struggling to keep quiet.

There was a ripping sound and he guessed they were using a knife to open up the compartment secreting the suitcase of heroin. And not a damned thing he could do to stop them. At any second he knew that he might lose consciousness. If he did that he would fall down, make a noise. They would see to it that he never woke up again.

One of the men appeared briefly holding the suitcase, stood in the opening and tore off his gas-mask. Kellerman saw it all as though in a dream. The man with the heroin jumped out of the wagon, there was a brief lack of sound except for the muffled murmur of nearby traffic, then the vrooming roar of a powerful motor-bike's engine, which cut off suddenly, as though the machine had turned a corner. Kellerman eased the handkerchief away from his nostrils and found he could breathe. The gas had drifted out through the open doors. He began to feel better, able to cope, then he froze again as he realised something was not right. *The second man was still inside the wagon.*

Kellerman stuffed his handkerchief back in his pocket and began to ease his way forward down the narrow passageway between the walls of compressed sheet paper. The air was bearable, but the German was horribly aware he was making noises as he moved forward. His sleeve scraped against the sides of the paper – only a slight sound, but more than enough to alert the man still in the wagon, who would be a professional. Why the hell was he still waiting?

Kellerman found him crumpled in a heap at the edge of the open doors, a short, heavily-built man still wearing the gas-mask and with a reddish stain spreading ever more widely over the uniform jacket across his chest. What the uniform might be Kellerman was not sure – it looked like a policeman's – but he jerked off the gas-mask and looked into a plump face with the eyes open. A familiar face, for God's sake, the face of Serge Litov. And someone had used a gun with a silencer to shoot him, although he was still just alive.

'Heroin . . . Norling . . . traitor,' were his dying words.

Passenger who landed Arlanda Airport Flight SK407 from Copenhagen as per attached photo identified as Gunther Baum. Originates from East Germany. Poses as business executive but is independent professional assassin charging extortionate fees due to reputation for always completing assignment. Present whereabouts unknown.

Chief Inspector Harry Fondberg of Säpo studied the signal which had just arrived from Interpol. He was fuming about the incident at Stockholm Central – where someone disguised as a police despatch rider had seized the haul of heroin from under his nose and murdered his own accomplice as a bonus. Then the phone rang and he heard Jules Beaurain had arrived.

The Belgian was ushered into his office and shown to a chair. The Swede was studied by Beaurain as they shook hands: no outward sign of nerves here in Stockholm. And his host's appearance was exactly as the Belgian remembered him from their previous meeting.

Thinning hair was brushed over a well-shaped skull. He had the blue eyes of the Scandinavian which, in Fondberg's case, held a hypnotic quality. His nose was strong, his mouth firm and he had a jaw of character. The Chief of Säpo, who worked under a Director solely responsible to the Minister of Justice, showed his guest the signal from Interpol. Attached was a glossy print.

'That's a copy of the picture we radioed to them,' Fondberg explained.

There were several people the photographer had caught in his lens and it was obvious they were completely unaware that their arrival was being recorded. Beaurain passed the photograph back to Fondberg.

'He tried to kill me in Copenhagen – in broad

daylight close to the Tivoli Gardens. His accomplice is with him.'

'Accomplice!' Fondberg grabbed the picture off the desk, glaring at it. 'Those damned fools at Interpol never said anything – and we radioed the complete picture. It was taken at Arlanda. The accomplice is . . .?'

'The ordinary-looking man behind Gunther Baum's right shoulder. You can just see he is carrying a brief-case. That is where the gun would normally be – he is Baum's gun-carrier and, I suspect, only hands him the weapon at the last moment. Baum is extremely well-organised. When did he come in here?'

'On the first flight this morning from Copenhagen – what we call the businessman's flight. The distance is so short, many spend the day in Stockholm, conclude their business, and are back in Copenhagen for the night.'

'Stockholm has more attractions than that, Harry.'

Fondberg smiled. 'Yes, indeed. But you see, the businessmen's wives also know that. So, if they are not back in their cosy little Danish houses before midnight, chop!'

'How did you happen to take that picture?' Beau-rain indicated the radio-transmitted photo of Baum and his companion.

'As you know, we have men watching Arlanda all the time for known criminals. If the watcher on duty is keen, sometimes he takes a picture of a passenger who strikes him as not quite right. Baum's was taken for that reason, I sent it to Interpol, and you see their reply.'

'You have his address?'

The Swede winced and lit a cigar before replying. 'The shot was random, as I have explained. Since the signal came in I have had people checking at all the hotels, but it is too early for anything yet.'

'You won't get anything anyway. He'll register with false papers wherever he stays. As you know, he is a top professional. So that is the man who has travelled here for the express purpose of killing me – or so you suspect?'

'I don't know,' Fondberg replied blandly. 'There are other potential candidates for the job. This man, for example.'

It was like the old days when they had co-operated together – with or without the agreement of their respective superiors. Beaurain stared at the glossy photo pushed across the desk at him. Again taken at an airport, doubtless Arlanda. An excellent print, this one, taken with a first-rate camera operated by a top-class photographer. The man was obviously totally unaware that his arrival had been recorded.

A big man, probably six feet one, broad-shouldered and with a large round head and cold eyes. Like Fondberg, the few streaks of thin hair were carefully brushed over the polished skull – but unlike Fondberg he was almost bald. Even caught unawares his demeanour was aggressive; the total lack of feeling in the blank eyes was reflected in the thin-lipped, tight mouth. The way he held himself told Beaurain that this man, in his early fifties, was in the peak of physical condition. He probably played an hour's squash before breakfast every morning – and his mood would be mean for the rest of the day if he didn't win.

'Who is the candidate and when did he get in and from where?' Beaurain enquired, his eyes still imprinting the man's features and general stance on his memory.

'American, of course. The dress tells you that. He is known as Harvey Sholto. He got in at Arlanda on the overnight flight from Washington. I was informed by no less a person than Joel Cody of his imminent arrival – person-to-person call. And the bastard tried to trick me.'

'Cody? The President's aide? The man who thinks that *finesse* is a French pastry? And how did he *try* to trick you?'

'By officially informing me that Sholto would be coming here within the next few days, when he had already arrived in Stockholm. He didn't allow for the closeness with which we watch all incoming passengers at Arlanda. Sholto's appearance rang a bell in the mind of one of the watchers with a camera so he took his picture. The people who are checking hotel registers for Gunther Baum are also checking for Harvey Sholto, the second killer to arrive just ahead of you.'

Fondberg added the final remark casually and puffed at his cigar while he gazed at the ceiling. It was the same game they had so often played in the past and was one of the many reasons Jules Beaurain liked Fondberg as much as any of the host of international colleagues he had come to know over the years.

'You're sure this is Harvey Sholto?' Beaurain queried, tapping the glossy print. 'So he's a killer too.'

'One of the deadliest. Our agent in Bangkok could have vouched for that. Except that he's dead now. He was very experienced and very good.' Some of the toughness briefly evaporated from Fondberg's exterior. 'He left a nice Swedish wife and three children. They found him floating in one of the *klongs* – canals. His throat had been cut from ear to ear. The Stockholm Syndicate never does a second-rate job, my friend.'

It was the first time Harry Fondberg had linked the Syndicate with the Swedish capital. Smoking his cigar, teeth clenched, he stared hard at his visitor. 'Are you going to do something about it?' he asked softly.

'Yes. Kill it.'

'You haven't the knowledge, resources or power. Above all you haven't the knowledge. How do they run their communications system? Tell me that. An organisation which has wrapped up a good part of Scandinavia and the Low Countries and is now rapidly penetrating Germany has to have a first-rate communications system.'

'Water.'

'I beg your pardon.'

'Water,' Beaurain repeated. 'It came to me finally when I was on the terrace of the Grand Hotel looking out over the Strommen. Harry, has there been an increase in illegal radio activity in recent months?'

'Here in Stockholm? Yes.' Fondberg's eyes were watchful. 'I also know we have been unable to track down a single one of the transmitters – which we suspect are very highpowered.'

'Over how long a period?'

'I'm told it started about two years ago.'

'Foundation date of the setting up of the Stockholm Syndicate,' Beaurain said grimly. 'Has anyone kept a record of the general areas of these illegal transmissions?'

'Yes, although I don't see how that will help.' Fondberg broke off to speak in Swedish into his intercom, then switched off. 'Our radio-detector vans have never been able to get a fix on a transmission. We think whoever is sending the signals uses a van and keeps on the move during the period of transmission.'

The Swede stopped speaking as a girl came into the room with a rolled sheet, placed it on the Säpo chief's desk, and left them. Beaurain got up and stood behind Fondberg as the latter unrolled a large-scale map of Stockholm inscribed with red circles. He snorted his disgust.

'Doesn't tell you a bloody thing!'

'Doesn't tell *you* a bloody thing,' Beaurain corrected

him. 'But for me it's the final confirmation that I'm right. Look at all the circles.'

'In so many different districts? No pattern.'

'You're losing your grip. The pattern is screaming at you. All the roads and districts circled include waterways.' Beaurain's tone became emphatic. 'Willy Flamen in Brussels showed me a similar record of heavy illegal radio traffic – and he couldn't see a pattern. Neither could I at the time – but all his marked districts throughout Belgium were close to canals. Same thing in Copenhagen when Marker of Intelligence showed me his records. The activity is always close to the Øresund.'

'You mean . . .'

'The bastards have their transmitters *afloat*. Aboard barges in Belgium which will move down the canal while they transmit. This is why they've never been caught. In Denmark they're on board fishing vessels or power-cruisers, again on the move just offshore while sending a signal. Here they're on the Strommen, on the . . .' Beaurain's hand hammered the city map as Fondberg studied it afresh.

'I believe you could be right,' Fondberg said slowly. 'If we can crack their communications system we sever the jugular of the Syndicate.'

'Let's get the timing right,' Beaurain suggested. 'I want one smashing Europe-wide hammerblow delivered at the same hour when the transmissions are going full-blast. Everywhere taken out at once including the barges in Belgium, where, incidentally, two Syndicate operators, a man and his wife, were recently executed. Each took a bullet in the back of the neck.'

'What?' Fondberg sat very upright and his intelligent eyes gleamed. 'That's an old Nazi technique. It raises a hideous new possibility – that the men behind this foul organisation are the Neo-Nazis! God, have we been blind!'

Harry Norsten sat behind the controls of his Cessna, ready to land in the centre of Stockholm. He had just received clearance and in the two passenger seats the man and the girl stirred as travellers do when approaching their destination. Norsten was not coming in at Arlanda, the great international airport many miles outside the city. The Swedish pilot was dropping his tiny aircraft into Bromma Airport, a short drive from the Grand Hotel.

The male passenger glanced out of the window, hardly interested in the familiar view. Of medium height, his hair blond with side-burns and a thick mane extending down his neck, the passenger wore large horn-rimmed spectacles. Dr Theodor Norling squeezed the hand of his companion, speaking to her in French. 'You are glad to be back home? You have had a busy time.'

A busy time. The girl whose jet-black hair was cropped close to her skull shuddered at the words. She was recalling what she had read in the morning paper about what was rapidly becoming known across the world as 'The Elsinore Massacre'. Then she was frightened because she realised her shudder had communicated itself to Norling who was still gripping her hand.

The blond head turned slowly. Staring straight ahead at Stockholm coming up to meet them, Sonia Karnell fought to regain her composure. Whatever she did, however she reacted, she must never show alarm, fear or repulsion. *He* disapproved of such emotions, regarded them as irrelevant in the task they were engaged on.

'Do I wait for you at Bromma or go home?' Norsten asked as he skilfully manipulated the controls for a perfect descent. He also spoke in French. The silent Dr Theodor Norling had once told him he liked to practise the language.

'You go home and wait for my call. I may need you again at very short notice.'

That was all. A typical Norling command. Clear to the point of abruptness and not a wasted word. Who the hell was he anyway? After acting as his pilot for over a year Norsten knew as little about him as the first day he had been hired except that Norling expected him to be available at all hours for a sudden trip and paid incredibly generous fees for the service – and his silence. The fact was that Dr Norling scared Norsten ice-cold.

'And one more thing, Mr Norsten,' the Swede had told him when they first met at Bromma and concluded their arrangement. 'It would be most ill-advised of you to broadcast my activities – or even to mention my existence as a client of yours.'

He had paused, his blond head motionless, the eyes behind the tinted glasses equally motionless as they gazed with concentrated intent at the pilot.

'You must realise that success in my business, Mr Norsten, often depends on my competitors being unaware of my movements – unaware even of when I am present in Stockholm. Indeed, it is a cut-throat trade I ply.'

Cut-throat . . . Norling had been staring at the pilot's throat when he used the phrase and Norsten was aware of an unpleasant prickling sensation in that region. Ridiculous! But that had been his reaction when he first agreed to do business with the book dealer. *Fear.*

They were a couple of bloody commuters, he reflected as he continued his descent – the sun glittering on the maze of waterways. Commuters between Stockholm and Copenhagen! And often at odd hours – flying through the night and landing before dawn.

He was pretty confident that at times they flew from Copenhagen to the United States. Once Norling had dropped an airline folder on the floor of the Cessna as they were descending to Kastrup. Norsten had caught a glimpse of the tickets which fell out before the girl grabbed for them. Destination: New York. So why not fly direct from Stockholm by ordinary scheduled flight instead of using the Cessna to cover the first lap to Copenhagen?

It didn't make sense. But Norsten, a prudent man, had long since decided not to question any of the book dealer's actions, or to probe into his background in any way.

As he landed he saw the beige-coloured estate car was waiting for them, empty. As usual. A most methodical man, Dr Theodor Norling. Who brought the Volvo to the airfield Norsten had no idea, but whoever it was always took good care to be well away from the scene before he landed his passengers. It was almost as though no-one was permitted to see what Dr Theodor Norling looked like unless it was essential. The fact that he possessed that knowledge sometimes woke up Norsten during the night in a cold sweat.

'The pilot, Harry Norsten, is developing a dangerous sense of curiosity about my identity and my life-style.'

Dr Theodor Norling made the remark to Sonia Karnell as she drove away from Bromma Airport behind the wheel of the Volvo and headed into the city. Removing his tinted glasses, he replaced them with a pair of gold-rimmed spectacles. From his suitcase he extracted a dark trilby hat and settled it on his head despite the blazing sun which was causing Karnell to drive with narrowed eyes. It gave him a professional air, this slight change in his appearance. Taking a pipe from his pocket he gripped it between his teeth, completing the transformation.

'Do we have to take any action?' Karnell asked.

'I have already made all the necessary arrangements to take him out at the appropriate time.'

The watchers stationed at Bromma Airport followed the Volvo with great skill, employing the leapfrog technique. Norling, an expert in surveillance, constantly checked in his wing mirror but was unable to detect any signs that they were being followed.

Ironically enough, it was Harry Norsten the Swede was checking for. Although well aware of the leapfrog technique, Norling noticed nothing. It was, in fact, ideal for the watchers in their vehicles – in heavy city traffic it was most unlikely they could ever be spotted since they were using as many as three cars and one delivery van.

There was a second factor which made it impossible for the ever-suspicious Norling to detect what was happening – the distance involved from Bromma to their destination was comparatively short. Even in heavy traffic, over a greater run Norling might well have eventually spotted what was happening as the four shadow vehicles continued their 'musical chairs' act.

'I drop you this side of the apartment?' Karnell queried.

'Of course. The usual precaution.'

They had entered Rådmansgatan, a good-class residential street consisting of old four- or five-storey buildings, all of which had been converted into flats. The street was also quiet and deserted as Sonia Karnell pulled in at the kerb, a good two minutes' walking distance to her apartment at Rådmansgatan 490. Norling slipped out of the car holding his case and within seconds she was driving away to park it. A Saab drove sedately by.

Without moving his head Norling registered every detail. Registration number; the two men sitting in the front, one of whom was yawning while the other stared straight ahead, concentrating on his driving. Both were dressed in casual Swedish clothes and Norling could see nothing odd about the car which vanished round a corner.

'Sonia will be able to confirm whether they followed her to the garage,' he murmured to himself, then crossed the street and walked at strolling pace towards the entrance.

'I'll drop you off here, Louise,' Stig Palme said. 'God we got lucky at Bromma.'

Louise Hamilton was most uncomfortably doubled up on the back seat and out of sight of anyone studying the passing car from the street. She sat up and eased the ache out of her legs as Palme pulled in at the kerb.

'Not lucky, Stig,' she remarked, checking her hair quickly in a hand mirror. 'Jules is just a superb organiser. And I can recognise Black Helmet – I should be able to spot the bitch by now.'

'Take care,' Palme warned.

Then she was gone, walking back down Rådmansgatan, carrying a shopping-bag with *NK*, the name of a leading Stockholm department store, printed on the side. She also carried, looped over her shoulder, the bag which contained the automatic supplied to her after her arrival by air at Arlanda. God, what a rush to reach Bromma! She turned a corner which hid the rest of the street – and the blond man with gold-rimmed spectacles who had left the Volvo was facing her.

This was the risk they had foreseen – that she *would* come face-to-face with him. Which was why Louise had done her best to change her appearance. She had discarded her trousers and windcheater and was wearing a bright yellow summer dress. Her hair was concealed under a silk scarf. Half her face was masked with enormous goggle-like sunglasses. Norling was only feet away from her, standing in front of the entrance to an apartment building. In his free hand he held a bunch of keys, one of them ready to insert into the lock. From behind gold-rimmed glasses distant eyes stared straight at her.

On her side of the apartment entrance there was a

shop door. Praying it was open for business, she grasped the handle, turned it and walked inside, closing the door without a glance back.

Norling opened the front door leading into the apartment block and then glanced swiftly into the shop. The girl with the absurdly huge glasses was standing with her back to him ordering something from the woman behind the counter. He frowned, moved out of sight quickly, went into the apartment block and closed the front door. Inside, a flight of stone steps led upwards. It was very quiet and apparently deserted. Norling paused, one foot on the lowest step, his blond head cocked to one side. He was listening for the slightest sound.

Satisfied, he ran lightly up the steps, making scarcely a sound. Arriving on the silent first floor he paused again, this time to look out through a pair of double windows giving onto a curious enclosed roof-like area. There existed, he knew, access to that roof from another staircase.

Again satisfied, he unlocked the door, which involved two separate keys for two separate locks. Norling walked into a pleasant, roomy apartment and closed the door behind him.

The living-room – which overlooked Rådmansgatan – had a polished wood-block floor covered with colourful rugs. A curious Oriental lantern hung from the ceiling for night-time illumination. Norling sat in a chair, picked up the phone and dialled a Stockholm number.

He had just replaced the receiver when Sonia Karnell's keys rattled in the locks. Norling made no assumptions: when she pushed the door open he was facing her directly, both hands raised and clasping the Luger pistol. 'What's wrong?' she asked.

'Arlanda has reported the arrival of Jules Beaurain and his mistress in Stockholm.'

In the *patisserie* Louise Hamilton had slipped inside to avoid recognition by the blond man, she was now ordering slowly a range of cakes and pastries. It was a quality shop and the woman behind the counter clearly expected her customers to choose carefully. Louise wanted to give the blond man plenty of time to get off the street before she emerged.

Then it happened. Sonia Karnell appeared on the pavement outside the window and stopped to search in her handbag for her door keys. As she had seen the blond man peer in earlier, Louise now had an excellent view of the dark-haired girl – in the mirror lining the wall behind the counter.

But the girl outside had only to glance into the shop and she might recognise the single shopper: Louise instinctively knew she would be recognised. She stopped herself moving in time. The slightest movement would be caught out of the corner of the dark-haired girl's eye. Was all this frenetic search inside the handbag a cover for the fact that she had already recognised Louise? The English girl became aware that the woman behind the counter was staring at her strangely. She hadn't spoken for half a minute.

'I'll have some of the chocolate gâteau, the one with cherries. About a quarter of the cake – I see it's cut . . .'

A clear and direct look at the mirror image of Black Helmet would have told Louise exactly what the situation was – and that was the one thing she knew she must not do. Her head was bent over the counter, examining the display while the woman packed what she had ordered into a carrier. Black Helmet disappeared, moved past the window to the apartment block entrance. Louise pretended to have trouble with the currency, to give the girl time to get well inside the building, then left the shop.

Before she left she was careful to pick up the carrier full of the food she had purchased with her left hand. Her right hand hovered over the unbuttoned flap of her shoulder bag – over the compartment holding the 9-mm. gun. She stepped into the street.

It was empty. Quite empty.

She hurried to the door to the apartment block. Swiftly she ran her eye down the small metal plates with the occupants' names. Only one woman. *Apartment 2. Sonia Karnell.* She walked back up the street to where the Saab was parked with Stig Palme behind the wheel.

'Get me back to the Grand Hotel,' she told him as she climbed stiff-legged into the back and slammed the door shut. Stiff-legged with tension, God damn it.

Without being told, Palme chose a different route,

one which would not take them past the apartment block – so anyone watching from a window overlooking the street would not see the Saab pass the building a second time. In the mirror Louise caught Palme's eyes and the Swede winked. He had detected the tension she was struggling to control. She began speaking to Palme and his companion as though delivering a report.

'If anything happens to me the address is Rådmansgatan 490. I'm pretty sure the hideaway is Apartment Two – occupied by a Sonia Karnell. Only woman shown as occupying an apartment. Not conclusive – it could be in a man's name.'

'She parked the Volvo,' Stig pointed out. 'Again, not conclusive, but I think you're right. We're moving in on them.'

'Or they're moving in on us.' Bloody hell, she was still talking through clenched teeth. That episode in the *patisserie* had been murder. She went on giving her 'report' for Beaurain in the same clipped tone. 'Male passenger, fair-haired, sideburns, hair thick on neck, wears gold-rimmed spectacles. A little taller than Dr Benny Horn or Otto Berlin. He could just be Theodor Norling, but I'm guessing. That apartment wants a round-the-clock stake-out.'

While Louise Hamilton and her two companions were following the Volvo from Bromma Airport, Beaurain was still at police headquarters with the Säpo chief,

Harry Fondberg. The Belgian had just called London and was talking to Detective Chief Inspector Swift of Special Branch.

Swift had known Beaurain for years and, like many of his international colleagues, still treated the Belgian as though he were in charge of the Brussels anti-terrorist squad. His news was a tonic to Beaurain – at whose suggestion Swift had sent a special team to the Woking–Guildford area of Surrey. Their task seemed strange – they had travelled backwards and forwards on single-decker buses in the hope of detecting suspicious foreign visitors.

'The score so far, Jules, is fifteen – all with false passports and all carrying concealed weapons. Some very tough characters.'

The trick played on Litov had been two-edged. Primarily planned to lead Beaurain to the Syndicate's base, it had also been hoped it would syphon off to England a number of the Syndicate's top soldiers – who would not be avaitable if and when the main clash took place. Special Branch had scooped the pool.

'It's all the wrong way round!' Fondberg poured more coffee as he shook his head. 'I get this oily bastard of a presidential aide, Joel Cody, on the phone like he's admitting me to some exclusive club. He says Harvey Sholto is *on his way* to Stockholm when he has already arrived – I told you, my people at Arlanda saw him.'

'What is really worrying you, Harry?'

'Normally we have good relations with the CIA.

But Ed Cottel arrives without a word from Washington. I repeat it's the wrong way round. They tell me about Sholto, a very dangerous and suspect character. Why focus attention on Sholto and hide Cottel?'

'You're assuming they know Cottel is here,' Beaurain commented.

'You mean . . .?'

'I'm not sure what I mean, Harry. Do you have a photo of Sholto? An earlier one from his Far East days I mean.'

Fondberg reached into a drawer, took out a folder and produced two photographs. One of them was the picture of Sholto taken arriving at Arlanda. The big, broad-shouldered man with the large, round, almost bald skull and the cold eyes.

It was the second photo which interested Beaurain, a photo with crinkled edges and creases which showed a man taken against a background of a hut in a jungle. The build was the same, as was the shape of the head, but it was difficult to believe it was the same man. For one thing he had a thatch of thick hair and a moustache.

'How long ago was this taken and who took it, Harry?'

'Two years ago. A clandestine shot taken by our man in Bangkok. He could have been one of the top European contact men in the drug-smuggling circuit originating in the Golden Triangle. Drugs which eventually end up on the streets of Stockholm, Malmö, Gothenburg and so on.'

'This Far Eastern shot is definitely Sholto?'

'That's the name our man in Bangkok attached to it. And there's something else which makes me worry about having Harvey Sholto free on the streets. I told you that our man in Bangkok was found floating in one of the *klongs*?'

'Well, I phoned someone else in Bangkok who hears all the rumours. Remember,' Fondberg warned, 'I used the word *rumours*. The word out there is that the man who killed our agent flew in from Manila. He used to be one of Harvey Sholto's contacts when he was out there.'

'You're not suggesting the Americans . . .'

'I'm not sure. But the one who is blanketing this city with eyes is Ed Cottel.'

'May I take these photos of Sholto? You have copies? Good.' Beaurain took the envelope the Swede had slipped the prints inside and pocketed it before Fondberg could have second thoughts. Only now did he raise the subject which he knew would embarrass the Säpo chief enormously. 'Thank you for releasing my man so quickly at Stockholm Central. The drug consignment from Elsinore was . . .'

'Boy, did we balls that one up!' Fondberg slapped the top of his desk to emphasize his chagrin. 'I surround the whole area with police. I play it clever and tell them to keep well back from the wagon containing the drug haul. The Syndicate sends in two men wearing Swedish police uniforms. Jules, I let it slip through my fingers – forty million kronor. And what is there to show for it?'

'A great deal, Harry,' Beaurain said soothingly. 'A direct link between Norling and the drugs – and therefore with the Stockholm Syndicate. Remember Serge Litov's last cryptic words – *Heroin . . . Norling . . . traitor*. At long last Norling is tied in with the whole infamous business.'

'Except that's not evidence,' Fondberg pointed out with unusual bitterness. 'The last words of a now-dead Russian. Why a Russian? And on top of that the drug haul is gone.'

'Harry, have you *any* information on Norling?'

'Yes. He poses as a dealer in rare editions.'

'Poses?'

'May well, indeed, be a genuine book dealer to cover his real activities. It would explain his long absences away from Stockholm, since an international dealer travels a lot. He has an apartment in Gamla Stan – the Old City. Very close to the Church of St Gertrud.' The Swede took a street plan of Stockholm from another drawer. 'Here, I'll show you.' He drew a cross on the plan. 'I have also heard that the real power behind this organisation is a shadowy figure called Hugo.'

'Hugo?'

'Yes, identity completely unknown. The word is he terrifies even the members of the Syndicate.'

The phone rang. Fondberg, normally slow-moving

and deliberate, grabbed for the instrument. He listened, spoke several times in Swedish, then slammed it down as he stood up behind his desk.

'Norling has been seen in Stockholm. He's in a Renault heading for what we call Embassy Row – where all the foreign embassies are. Not far away is a large marina with a whole fleet of boats. A car is waiting for us.'

In the living-room of Sonia Karnell's first-floor apartment in Rådmansgatan the blond man was checking the mechanism of a Walther .765 automatic. The girl watched him: ironically, the weapon was a police issue pistol. For the third time he rammed home the magazine into the gun and then slipped it inside his shoulder holster.

'As I told you, my dear, Beaurain and Hamilton are in Stockholm – just as the first of our distinguished visitors from the States are beginning to fly in for the conference.'

'What are you going to do about it?'

'Ensure that within a few hours no matter where they go they will be paid a visit.'

'So much blood.'

'Your favourite play is *Macbeth?*' Norling asked genially. He lifted a hand as he saw her preparing to leave with him. 'This time I go alone. We must not be seen together any more than can be helped while we are in Stockholm. San Francisco will be a different matter, but I am a little nervous while I have this in my possession.' He hoisted the suitcase which had been waiting for him at the apartment. 'After all, my dear, forty million kronors' worth is not to be treated lightly.'

'And you are going where?'

'First to collect the Renault. It *is* in the garage with the Volvo? Good. The time has come – and this I will handle personally – to send out a *Nadir* signal on Louise Hamilton and Jules Beaurain. They are to be executed on sight.'

Sonia Karnell folded her arms quickly and forced herself to relax, to show no sign of the mounting tension she felt. Tension to Norling meant a person's nerve could be cracking – as he had suggested might be the case with the pilot, Harry Norsten. And to safeguard the Syndicate's security he would not hesitate to send out a *Nadir*. The person named could then never survive – often his worst move would be to seek police protection.

'The Renault has a full petrol tank,' she assured him as his left hand rested on the door latch. 'You still haven't told me where you're going.'

'To the marina, of course. The one near Embassy Row.'

Chapter Fifteen

At the moment when the sighting of Dr Theodor Norling behind the wheel of a Renault was reported to Harry Fondberg, activity in Stockholm was building up a steadily increasing momentum in many districts.

Unmarked cars carrying Beaurain, Fondberg and other officers left police headquarters and sped through the city, weaving in and out of the traffic and causing drivers to jam on brakes and curse. The cars were heading for the Royal Motorboat Club, the marina in the Djurgardsbron district. In the front car, which he was personally driving, Fondberg explained to Beaurain: 'We have a written description of Norling and one photo taken with a telephoto lens. Both have wide distribution among officers I hope I can trust.'

'You can't trust everyone inside the police?' asked Beaurain quietly.

'What do you think?' replied Fondberg. 'My department, of course, comes under the ultimate control of the Minister of Justice. I had to go over the head of my superior to get some freedom of action. Can you guess what the Minister asked me to do if he agreed to let me quietly probe into the Stockholm Syndicate?'

'I'd rather not.'

'Mount a twenty-four hour guard on his home with Säpo men. And these days he travels everywhere in a bullet-proof limousine with Säpo outriders on motor-bikes. That was the price for keeping me in business.'

'It is happening in other countries.'

Fondberg's normally controlled voice rose to a pitch of fury. 'I don't care. It's time it was stopped!'

'That's why I'm here. Be ready to look the other way. Aren't we close to the Grand Hotel? Good. Can we stop there for a couple of minutes? There may be someone I want to pick up if they've returned to the hotel.'

Behind the wheel of his Renault, Dr Theodor Norling was making slower progress than he had hoped, but he was driving more carefully than Fondberg's caval-cade surging through the city. He had no desire to be stopped by a *Polis* car for a traffic offence – bearing in mind the contents of the suitcase by his side.

Even so, he was close to Diplomatstaden, the foreign embassy area which was very close to his ultimate destination – the boat marina where a whole cluster of vessels would be bobbing at anchorage. He checked his watch. He should be there in about ten minutes with a little luck.

*

Sitting in the rear of the Saab which Stig Palme was driving back to the Grand Hotel, Louise eyed the cloth-covered weapon at her feet. It was Stig Palme's favourite gun and in standard use in the Swedish Army. A model 45 9-mm. machine-pistol, it was equipped with a movable shoulder-grip, could be used for single shots with a gentle pressure on the trigger – or fire a lethal continuous burst of thirty-six bullets in six seconds.

Telescope had gradually built up secret caches of arms and ammunition all over Europe. It was too dangerous to move across borders with weapons – although the steam yacht, *Firestorm*, purchased from a Greek millionaire, had been cunningly re-designed to provide so many hiding-places it was a floating armoury. In Sweden, Stig Palme's weapons cache was in the cellar of a house out in the country – just off the E3 highway leading to Strängnäs.

'Here we are,' Palme called out cheerfully. 'The Grand Hotel.'

'Stop here!'

The Swede reacted instantly and smoothly, pulling in at the kerb before he reached the main entrance. To the right there was the usual row of Mercedes and Citroëns parked, their well-waxed surfaces gleaming. To the left the windowboxes of geraniums gave a splash of brilliant red, and a gardener was trimming them ruthlessly.

'Beaurain is waiting for us,' said Louise.

She had just spoken when the Belgian opened the rear door, pushed his head inside and spoke quickly. 'The hotel said you were out – I had a feeling you might be back any minute. We're on an emergency – Theodor Norling has been spotted by himself in a Renault.'

'He came in to Bromma Airport in a Cessna – with Black Helmet! She seems to turn up everywhere. Her name could be Sonia Karnell. Address of apartment is Rådmansgatan 490. Norling was carrying a suitcase, *hugging* it.'

'Christ! Has he fooled us? Was it about the same size as . . .'

'The one which was hidden aboard the express for Stockholm? Yes, it was.'

'You see that Saab over there, with the man behind the wheel carefully not taking any notice of us? That's Harry Fondberg. Don't lose him, Stig. We think Norling's destination could be the boat marina near Embassy Row.'

'I know it.'

Beaurain forced himself to stroll casually the short distance back to Fondberg's car although his legs were screaming at him to run. He got inside, closed the door and lit a cigarette. 'Norling has a suitcase which sounds exactly like the one snatched from the wagon you surrounded at Stockholm Central station. He flew into Bromma from somewhere.'

'God Almighty!' Fondberg had started up his car which was the signal for the other two cars parked further back to prepare to move. 'You mean he could be carrying the big consignment, the one for which my man in Bangkok died? Hold on to your seat-belt!'

The American behind the wheel of the hired Citroën wore a Swedish-style nautical cap. In his mirrors he had observed everything – Beaurain waiting inconspicuously on the sidewalk after a brief dash into the hotel; the arrival of the Saab which contained Louise Hamilton in the back and two unknown men in the front. He had noted the urgent conversation between Beaurain and Louise; the Belgian's careful stroll back to another Saab, with Harry Fondberg waiting behind the wheel. He waited until the convoy departed with the second Saab carrying Louise bringing up the rear – then he drove out from the row and followed. Ed Cottel of the CIA knew a crisis when he saw one.

From the moment they left police headquarters they preserved radio silence. Fondberg had taken the precaution of sending a message to the man who had spotted Norling that only if the target was *not* heading for the marina was he to send a brief message over the radio.

There had been no signal by the time the 'convoy' left the Grand Hotel, a convoy consisting of two unmarked police cars, followed by Stig Palme and Louise Hamilton who, in their turn, were closely followed by Ed Cottel's Citroën – equipped with a radio that had been skilfully attached after the hiring of the vehicle. It kept Cottel in touch with what Fondberg had called his 'eyes'. Remaining one vehicle behind Stig Palme's Saab he was using his radio link.

'Carmel calling. You read me? Good. Any sign of Ozark?'

'Monterey here, Carmel. No, repeat, no sign of Ozark. Am continuing surveillance pending further instructions.'

'OK, you do that.'

With an expression of resignation the hooked-nosed American replaced the microphone and concentrated on not losing the Saab. It had been going on for days and the only thing to do was to persist; sooner or later something had to break.

Ozark was the code-name for Viktor Rashkin, First Secretary at the Soviet Embassy in Stockholm. The odd thing was he seemed to have vanished off the face of the earth.

'Pass me the gun – lay it on the seat beside me.'

Stig Palme made the request to Louise as they continued in the wake of two unmarked police cars. Palme knew that they were close to Embassy Row, which meant they were close to the marina. Without asking why, Louise lifted the weapon wrapped in oil-cloth and gently laid it on the empty seat in front.

'I may need Christine,' he remarked. It was typical

that Palme should confer a girl's name on his favourite weapon. When using her in action he was accustomed to use some pretty racy language. 'We're being followed. *Don't* look round. He's driving a cream-coloured Citroën.'

'Any idea since when?'

'He was parked with his back to us outside the Grand Hotel. And he's been using the usual technique of keeping one vehicle between us all the way. The Syndicate obviously has a team watching the Grand Hotel.'

'Just one man, you said?'

'With a highly-trained killer they only need one man. Better for getting away after he's done the job. Beaurain could be the target,' he said, and relapsed into silence.

Fascinated she watched while Palme drove with one hand and used the other to unwrap the oil-cloth and expose Christine. The machine-pistol was already fully-loaded. 'We're on top of the possible target area,' Palme warned and then stopped the car.

Dr Theodor Norling pulled in at the kerb by the landing stage. The marina was vast. There was a breeze coming off the water which freshened the air and countered the blaze of the high sun glaring down out of a cloudless sky. For a few seconds he paused after locking the car, standing quite still with the the suitcase in his hand.

Arne, reliable as usual, was walking towards him. Norling was trying to sense anything unusual in the scene before committing himself to water. A whole fleet of craft of varying sizes and types bobbed at anchor, a galaxy of vibrating colour in the intensity of the sun. Already Norling could feel its heat on the back of his neck. There were expensive cruisers equipped with all the latest electronic devices, small power-boats, larger launches, a whole diversity of yachts, some with coloured sails.

'The power-boat is ready to take you out to the *Ramsö*,' Arne informed his employer.

'I'm in a hurry,' Norling replied curtly.

Behind him, beyond a screen of shrubs and trees and across the unseen road rose the buildings of the American Embassy with a flight of steps leading up to them. From a flagpole the Stars and Stripes fluttered in the breeze. Before getting into the power-boat Arne held waiting for him, Norling turned and gave the flag a brief salute. An onlooker would have found it impossible to decide whether the gesture was ironic or serious.

'God, that's him – and he's getting away!'

Three cars had arrived alongside the marina. It was Louise, jumping from the third car and running up to where Beaurain and Fondberg stood, who confirmed the worst. Before leaving Stig Palme, who had pulled up a cautious distance from the police vehicles, she had snatched a pair of field glasses from the glove compartment, nearly dislocating herself leaning over the seat. Focused on the receding powerboat, the lenses brought up the two figures on board only too clearly.

She had not recognised the man steering the craft towards the powerful cruiser riding at anchor. The second man, nursing a suitcase, was only too horribly familiar. The encounter outside the shop on Rådmansgatan when he had stared at her through his gold-rimmed glasses. In the lenses the sun – for a brief second – flashed a hint of gold off those same glasses.

'It's him,' she told Palme, and ran to Beaurain to repeat the warning.

'Are you quite sure?' asked Beaurain, glancing uncertainly towards Palme.

'Bloody hell, do you think I'm blind!' she screamed at him. 'I was as close to him as I am to you!'

'Harry, can you have that cruiser intercepted – if that's what he is headed for?'

Fondberg shook his head dubiously and there was a grim look on his face. 'Point One, I have no authority or reason to intervene. I could always argue I didn't know it was Norling, but . . . Point Two, that vessel can really move – and the river police are never where you want them.'

'Then this, Harry, is where you look the other way.'

The power-boat carrying Dr Norling had now arrived alongside the cruiser. Through her binoculars Louise watched the Swede move nimbly aboard, holding the suitcase in his left hand. Crewmen had appeared on the bridge of the vessel which was clearly about to depart.

'Forty million kronors' worth of heroin in that suitcase,' the Belgian hammered home. 'Soon it will be flooding the streets of Stockholm, creating more untold misery.'

'For Christ's sake!' protested the exasperated Swede. 'Don't you think I feel helpless enough?'

Louise studied the so-called dealer in rare books through her field glasses. Beaurain was standing next to her and behind Fondberg's back. She lowered the glasses and saw him make a brief gesture describing the outline of a suitcase. Suddenly she looked behind her and over to the right where Stig Palme had parked the Saab.

Palme was leaning against the car to steady himself. He was holding at shoulder level the machine-pistol. The muzzle was aimed out across the water towards the cruiser which was still motionless. Then the silence of the peaceful morning was splintered.

It lasted six seconds – the time it took for Stig to empty thirty-six 9-mm. bullets. And Palme was a crack shot. Louise had the lenses of her field glasses screwed into her eyes. Norling was still clutching the suitcase when the hail of bullets ripped into it, shredding the casing and the contents. The suitcase was literally blasted over the side of the cruiser and into the water, scattered in a multitude of fragments which littered the surface of the water and began drifting away. And so accurate was the Swede's fire that – so far as Louise could see – not one bullet had touched Norling.

'What the hell . . .!'

Fondberg was sliding his hand inside his jacket and under his shoulder when he felt Beaurain's hand grip his arm: 'I said, Harry, this is where you look the other way, God damn it!'

'Sorry. Instinctive reaction. I hope your man moves fast.'

He called out a brief command to his men, who froze, and then turned back to watch the white cruiser. Palme was already behind the wheel of his car. The weapon had vanished. Without haste he backed the Saab and drove quietly away. A flock of birds, disturbed by the fusillade, had risen with a beating of wings and headed out over the water. In the sudden silence the noise of their ascent could be heard clearly. Then it was drowned by a distant, muted rumble as the white cruiser began to move.

'He must be mad as hell, wouldn't you say?' Beaurain observed.

Aboard the *Ramsö* Norling had given the order to *move*! Again he looked at the hand which had been holding the suitcase, still unable to believe he was completely unscathed. When the bullets started coming he had felt a hard tug, the case had been wrenched from his grasp as though by supernatural forces, then came the cascade of fragments, a cloud of precious powder. All gone! As the cruiser started moving he could actually *see* a white scum on the water. He hastily went below decks into his cabin and sank into a chair. He was shaking with uncontrollable rage. Alone in his luxuriously-furnished cabin he sat with both hands gripping the arms of his chair.

'Beaurain! First in Brussels, then Copenhagen and Elsinore – now here in Stockholm itself!'

He was talking to himself, a habit of which he was fully aware and of which he occasionally made use as a safety valve. It had started long ago with another life, so far away from Sweden. Behind the lenses of his gold-rimmed spectacles his eyes were remote and cruel. He looked up as a man descended the steps and came into the cabin, Olof Konvall, the wireless operator.

'I'm sorry, sir.' Konvall, a small, highly-strung man with a grizzled face, took a step back when he met Norling's gaze. The venom in the stare was scaring. 'I didn't intend to intrude – but normally when you come on board you have a signal you wish to send.'

'Stay where you are, for God's sake!' Norling's show of rage was most unusual; his normal manner was an icy calm. 'Tell the captain I wish to switch to another vessel at the earliest possible moment.'

'I will tell him at once.'

'Don't go! I haven't finished yet.' Norling paused, forced himself to loosen his clenched grip on the wooden arms of the chair, to let his fury dissipate itself. Now he had himself under perfect control. His voice became remote, detached, like a chess-player who has decided on the next move.

'You are to send out immediate *Nadir* signals on Jules Beaurain. The other recipient is his mistress, Louise Hamilton. Let the word go forth. And first Hamilton alone is to be subjected to a demonstration at grade three level. Now you may go.'

'Oh my God, how horrible!'

Louise froze with shock and revulsion, the key to her bedroom door still in her hand. Like most people in a hotel she had walked in and closed the door behind her under the odd delusion that this was – temporarily at least – a safe refuge.

'Christ! I think I'm going to be sick!'

She leant back against the door and forced herself to recover. Her stomach obeyed her and then she caught sight of herself in the mirror and was shocked by her appearance: her lips were drawn back over her teeth in an expression of murderous fury – and she knew in that second that if the person responsible for the outrage had still been in the room she would have killed them. Someone rapped on the self-locking door.

She stood to one side and turned the door handle. Palme walked into the room and stared at the gun aimed point-blank, then his gaze swivelled. He closed the door.

'Isn't it sickening,' she said as lightly as she could,

but she didn't fool the Swede as she slipped the gun back inside her shoulder-bag. He said the one thing which could have lightened the atmosphere.

'I think the management will agree to changing your room.'

There was a second knocking on the door. Stig Palme motioned her to slip into the bathroom, which was a mistake because it was even more hideous there than in the bedroom. She gritted her teeth, then thankfully heard Beaurain's voice, a sharp tone. 'Where's Louise? Has she seen . . .?'

'She's in the bathroom. I sent her in there when . . .'

He found her sitting on the bathroom stool with her legs crossed, one arm supporting the other as she gazed directly at him and calmly smoked the cigarette she had just lit, her only concession to the experience she had just undergone.

'Only a sick mind . . .' she began.

It *was* – if possible – even worse in the bathroom. An aerosol paint spray had been the weapon used – used with such diabolical skill that Beaurain suspected the perpetrator must be a trained artist. Sprayed over every surface in the bathroom were obscene pictures involving a woman indulging in every type of perversion imaginable. And in every instance the face depicted was a caricature – but immediately recognisable – of Louise Hamilton.

The bedroom walls and every other available surface had been similarly treated. Beaurain watched her smoking her cigarette and then reacted in just the right way.

'We must at once reserve another bedroom on a different floor and with an entirely different layout. In actual fact, as long as we stay at this place I suggest you spend each night in my room. God knows the bed is big enough.'

'Thank you,' she said gratefully.

'Can I have a word with you in a minute?' Palme asked Beaurain.

'After we've got the room business sorted out.'

'What are you going to tell the manager?' Louise enquired.

Beaurain knew instantly what was worrying her – that the manager was bound to wonder what sort of people she knew who could act in this way. She felt besmirched by such vile obscenity. Again he knew exactly the right reply. 'That my ex-wife is insanely jealous and has already in another country been charged with the same type of offence. Also,' he paused to smile, 'that she will by now have left Sweden to escape the attention of the police.'

Fifteen minutes later they had ensconced Louise in an entirely different room, this time on the second floor. It overlooked the street up which marched the mounted horse troops after the changing of the guard at the Royal Palace, explained an assistant manager who was obviously going out of his way to make her forget her recent experience. At the door he paused before leaving.

'May I take it that Madame had not propped her door open for a short time while she left the room?'

Louise smiled, her face still bloodless: 'No, I certainly had not propped the door open in any way.'

'Of course! Madame does not, I trust, mind my asking? Thank you. Ah, here is a bottle of champagne. Please accept it as a small present from the management.'

Stig Palme was conferring with Beaurain as they sat in the Swede's Saab parked outside the hotel. The choice of locale for their conversation had been Palme's.

'This way we know we are not being recorded. You have seen how the bedroom doors lock, how from the outside you must turn the key before you can enter the room? I think,' Palme continued, 'it is possible the Stockholm Syndicate have committed their first major blunder – opening up a trail I can follow which just might blast their organisation wide open.'

'It's going to be a race against time,' Beaurain warned. 'I have the strongest feeling Hugo is going to launch an all-out offensive to wipe *us* out.'

'Because we've just lost him his major heroin delivery?'

'Partly – but maybe even more because of this.' Beaurain nodded towards a large Mercedes which had just glided to a halt outside the Grand Hotel. Out of the rear door a short stout man holding a brief-case had emerged while two other men, who had left the car seconds earlier, took up positions near the foot of the steps and were staring in all directions.

'Who is the little fat man who needs armed guards?' Stig asked.

'That is Leo Gehn, president of the International Telecommunications and Electronics Corporation of America. One of the richest and most powerful industrialists inside the States – they say he contributed a million dollars to the President's electoral campaign. Maybe he contributes even larger sums to the Stockholm Syndicate.'

'I don't follow, Jules.'

'After leaving the marina we returned to police headquarters – to see if Fondberg's Säpo people had any further information. They had. A whole list of European and American power élite are arriving aboard a stream of aircraft – some aboard scheduled flights, some in their private jets – putting down at Arlanda. They seem to be staying at two hotels – the Saltsjöbaden Hotel and here at the Grand. So far, apart from Leo Gehn, the presidents or chairmen of five of America's biggest corporations have flown in – to say nothing of men like Eugène Pascal from Paris and a score of others. Fondberg suspects they are here for the secret meeting of the Stockholm Syndicate – that they're all men who have either voluntarily contributed money in return for the vast profits they'll gain from international crime – or they have been subjected to the most hideous intimidation. I need just one I can crack, Stig – just one.'

Taking the cigarette out of his mouth, he stared through the windscreen at the person alighting from another chauffeur-driven limousine at the entrance to the Grand Hotel. Out of the rear door stepped one of the most elegant and striking women Palme had ever seen, her jet-black hair piled up on top of her head.

'I said I needed just *one*! That, Stig, is the Countess d'Arlezzo.'

'But surely her husband is the man who will run their affairs?'

'Her husband, Luigi, was bought by Erika for his aristocratic connections. She personally runs the banking empire she inherited from her father. Wait here.'

The Countess lingered on the sidewalk at the foot of the flight of steps, dismissing all attempts to hurry her inside with a casual wave of her slim hand while she drank in the view of the Royal Palace and the Houses of Parliament. Beaurain grinned to himself as he saw the gesture; how like Erika. He was within a few feet of her when a heavily-built man in a dark suit stood in his way.

'Stay back an' 'old da position,' he ordered.

'Out of my way or I'll break your arm,' Beaurain said politely and smiled.

'Jules!' The woman, in her early forties, had swung round at the sound of his voice and stepped forward.

Impetuously she embraced him while the guard stared in confusion.

'You must come up to my suite,' she continued, linking her arm in his. 'Luigi? I expect he's somewhere with a bottle – didn't you know? These days he's hardly ever sober.'

When her cases had been brought up and they were alone she took him by the hand and was about to lead him into the bedroom. He shook his head, turned on the radio loud to counter any possible concealed microphones and faced her as he threw the question in her teeth.

'I take it that your banking consortium has contributed money to the coffers of the Stockholm Syndicate?'

'The equivalent of several million pounds,' she replied without the slightest hesitation. 'It is supposed to be a loan but I don't regard Hugo as a particularly good risk.'

He studied her for a moment. She stood very erect and, while she spoke, inserted a cigarette in a long holder. He lit it for her. Of all the people caught up in the labyrinth of the Syndicate, she was possibly the only one with the nerve to tell him the truth without a second's hesitation. So why had she given in to them in the first place?

'I was one of the people who was told over the phone about the death of the Chief Commissioner to the Common Market – one week before he died in his so-called "accident". That was how it began.'

'And how did it go on?' he pressed.

'I was told what would happen to me if I refused to transfer funds to Stockholm. The murder of the Chief Commissioner convinced me they meant what they said. I am a coward, so I gave in.'

'What did they threaten you with?' the Belgian demanded.

'That I would be found – I can remember the exact phrase – hung and twisting like a side of meat turning in the wind. I didn't fancy that too much, Jules.'

'Why are you here?'

'To attend the meeting, of course. The conference of the Syndicate, if you like. I gather Hugo – or his representative – will carve up the loot, allocate territories to different groups, and then the profits from these will be shared among investors in proportion to the funds supplied. That is what he calls us,' she remarked, her expression bitter. 'Investors – as though we were engaged in a legitimate enterprise.'

'And you are engaged in?'

'Prostitution, gambling, drug-trafficking, blackmail, extortion, you name it, we're in it – up to our lousy necks.' The bitterness in her manner increased as she stubbed out her cigarette, inserted a fresh one in the holder and again waited while Beaurain lit it for her. They were still standing close together in the beautifully-furnished room and the tension of their discussion seemed to preclude any thought of sitting down.

'Thank you,' she said after he had lit her cigarette and continued, her voice low and vehement, which was unlike Erika: in the past he had always admired her sense of detachment. 'And one crime is cleverly dovetailed in to aid another.'

'How do you mean?' he asked sharply.

'Oh, the high-class prostitutes – and they are among the classiest and most expensive in Europe – are used to compromise leading political figures, who then have to do the Syndicate's bidding or be publicly ruined. You remember there was a man in Milan.'

'I know who you mean, Erika. You were rather fond of him.'

'Not as much as of you, but yes, I was fond of him, Jules. A week before the scandal broke I was phoned and told that he was about to be ruined. I called him to warn him but there was nothing he could do – the photos had already been taken, the pictures which were then sent to the newspapers and TV. He shot himself – so it appeared.'

'And what does that mean?' Beaurain was startled. It had always been his understanding that the Milanese politician concerned had committed suicide.

'He was murdered by the Syndicate and his death faked to look like suicide. In ruling circles in Rome it was clearly understood this was simply another "demonstration" organised by the Syndicate – like the fatal fall of the Chief Commissioner. Can you imagine the horror of it? Even we who have so much money and once controlled international businesses are now puppets of this foul thing, the Stockholm Syndicate.'

'Who do you deal with? Hugo?'

'No. I have no idea who Hugo is. On the rare occasions when I am contacted, it is by the member of the directorate who is in charge of the Mediterranean Sector – a Dr Otto Berlin.'

'And, finally, where is this so-called summit meeting to be held?'

'We have not been informed yet – but I have been told to be ready to fly to the south coast of Sweden as soon as the instruction comes.' Again the bitter note. 'Yes, that is what they give us – instructions. At least I *tried* in Rome.'

'You must not reproach yourself. Does Luigi . . .?'

'Know anything about it? Of course not! Can you imagine what sort of help I'd get from that broken reed? Within a day of being told anything he would probably be blabbing it to the world in a drunken stupor. Jules . . .' She came very close to him, so close he could savour to the full the very faint aroma of the scent she was using. 'Jules, can you do anything?'

'Yes, and first I want you under my protection. You will put on a coat and walk straight out of this hotel with me. Leave everything else and come with me this instant. I have people outside and we'll hide you until this is all over.'

'I can't, Jules.'

'Why the hell not!' The exasperation was genuine. This was not like Erika.

'Because of Luigi. If I disappear they will kill him. He is in Rome.'

'One phone call and I can have him scooped up and flown out of Italy.'

'No, Jules!' She put her index finger over his mouth, removed it as he relapsed into silence and kissed him full on the lips. He found he could even remember her taste. 'I must act normally, go to the meeting – but if you give me a phone number I will call you and tell you where the meeting is being held as soon as I know.'

Beaurain didn't like it. He felt uneasy but he couldn't budge her. Eventually he gave her Harry Fondberg's private phone number and the code-word *champagne* which she must use if she found it was impossible to reach Beaurain; then she could leave a message. As he walked out of her room and closed the self-locking door, he passed a man who was slowly pushing a service trolley along the corridor. The trolley's contents were concealed under a large white cloth. It was only later that he remembered the man. Too late.

Stig Palme drove his compact car up the steep road alongside the Royal Palace and turned into Stortoret, the main square where an ancient stone pump stood protected by stone bollards. A few minutes later he parked the Saab close to the entrance to one of the maze of alleyways in this medieval quarter of Stockholm.

The tiny shop he was visiting was situated half-way along the deserted alley, cobbled underfoot and so narrow he could have easily reached out his arms and touched both sides. He entered without ceremony, noted that the place was empty except for the owner and shut the door. He then turned the card hanging against the glass to indicate Closed.

Outside the shop over the door hung a huge key symbol. And the man who supplied master keys in Stockholm was its owner, Tobias Seiger. The price varied according to the status of the hotel and Seiger's estimate of how much he could screw out of the buyer. In return, complete secrecy was guaranteed. It was this wall of secrecy Stig Palme had to break down.

His mission was not helped by the fact that Seiger knew and disliked Palme. A short, bull-headed man, Seiger had a jeweller's glass in his right eye when Palme entered. Observing Palme's action in closing his shop Seiger carefully removed the jeweller's glass and placed it in an open drawer below Palme's eye level. Palme moved. His left hand whipped over the counter, gripped the pistol Seiger had been feeling for and pocketed it. Seiger found himself staring into the barrel of Palme's own gun.

'I have very little money on the premises,' he began.

'We're going to talk, Tobias.' The locksmith stood in a permanent stoop, brought on by years of cutting keys. His manner was a mixture of aggressiveness and oily persuasion. He had the morals of a brothel-keeper. 'The Grand Hotel . . .'

'Did you say the Grand?'

The shop was cluttered with cupboards and there was dust and grime everywhere, including a film of dirt on the outside windows – so it was very dark. Even so Palme's sharp eyes caught the brief flicker of expression which vanished off Seiger's slack-lipped face almost before it appeared. *Alarm. Terror?* This was going to be more difficult than he had anticipated.

To overcome Seiger's fear he was going to have to produce an atmosphere of hideous terror to prise open the oily bastard's mouth. Palme pressed the muzzle of his gun into Seiger's left ear.

'I can make you a key – the master key,' Seiger babbled.

'Don't get naughty with me, Tobias. You know exactly what I'm after – I saw it in your eyes. The identity of the person who has recently asked you to do just that – supply him with a master key for the Grand Hotel.'

When discussing the horrific vandalisation of Louise's room, both Beaurain and Palme had realised only one explanation was possible. The culprit had obtained a copy of the master key and probably from a nearby source. And, Palme thought to himself, where could be nearer than the establishment of Tobias Seiger in Gamla Stan just across the water from the hotel itself?

'I cannot tell you! It would cost me my life. The people involved are ruthless, totally ruthless.'

The terror was in Seiger's eyes, in his tone of voice, in the way he physically cringed away from Palme until the wall prevented him retreating any further. Palme's left hand caught hold of Seiger's necktie and tightened it, his knuckle pressed against the locksmith's Adam's apple.

Seiger would have screamed with the pain but the pressure of the knuckles made it impossible for him to utter a sound. The gun muzzle was pressed lightly against his right eye and the large Swede loomed over the stoop-shouldered shopkeeper.

'You can always leave Stockholm until the trouble is ended,' he said with an engaging smile. 'When did you last have a real holiday? Ages, I expect. An honest man like yourself, plying his trade, *deserves* a holiday.'

He released his grip on the necktie suddenly and Seiger collapsed in a heap against the wall, his legs spread out at an absurd angle across the stone-paved floor. He used one hand to massage his bruised throat, glaring up at the intruder, then when he saw what Stig Palme was doing his expression changed, he tried to climb to his feet, found he hadn't the strength and held up a hand as though to ward off a blow. What words had not managed a gesture was achieving. Terror!

Stig Palme stood over the collapsed figure, doing what he was doing with great deliberation and without a glance down at the locksmith. He was screwing a silencer onto the muzzle of his Luger.

The atmosphere in the tiny shop was nauseating. On entering the place Palme had been aware of a musty, damp odour – a smell associated with a place which never sees the sun and where the ventilation leaves much to be desired. Added to this now was the stink of sweat streaming down Seiger's body, staining his armpits, moistening his face, the smell Palme had encountered more than once before, the stench of terror.

'These people kill!'

'We are aware it is the Stockholm Syndicate. I need a name, an address,' said Palme matter-of-factly.

The latter he had no hope of – the most was a name, the least a description he could circulate in the Stockholm underworld and hope to come up with something.

'The alternative is I blow you away.'

And Tobias Seiger, who spent most of his life in this pit of semi-darkness, came up with pure gold.

'A blond-haired man – I can't give you a name. It was strictly a cash transaction, of course ... fair-haired with sideburns ... The hair was thick on the back of his neck ... and he wore gold-rimmed spectacles. A little shorter than yourself – but not small ... about five foot eleven. We conversed in French.

I have seen him twice before ... I know where he lives.'

Stig Palme was careful to maintain a perfectly blank expression. It increased the pressure, keeping a sense of detachment when he was screwing on the silencer. Christ Almighty, Seiger was actually describing Dr Theodor Norling, one of the three men controlling the directorate of the Stockholm Syndicate. Why had he not sent some minion to get the master key? Then he recalled Beaurain telling him that Norling had an apartment not far away in the posh area near St Gertrud's Church. When Seiger came to *I know where he lives* Palme forced himself to keep silent. In interrogation the art was so often to know when to keep your mouth shut.

'... it was a strange coincidence,' the locksmith babbled on, 'I could hardly believe it myself when I saw him on my way to work ... I often spend the night with my sister who lives in Strängnäs ... Driving in on the E3 highway I had an urgent call of nature. I stopped by the roadside ... can I have a drink?'

'No!'

It was such a delicately poised thing: any pause could stop the flow of words if Seiger thought better of what he was doing. And what the hell was all this about the E3 and out in the country? Norling's apartment was in Gamla Stan. Denied a drink, the voice, now cracked, railed on.

'As I was behind a tree I saw this man come out of

a house in the distance . . . I always carry a small pair of field glasses in my pocket . . . my hobby is bird-watching. It was him! I waited as he got out his car and drove off in the direction of Stockholm, the way I was going. I followed in my own car until the traffic was heavier and caught him up. He did not see me! The Volvo he was driving carried American diplomatic plates.'

It was coming at Palme fast but he kept his head. In a monotone he asked about the location of the house. This involved some detailed explanation even though Palme knew the route to Strängnäs well. He had to pinpoint the location of the house which, apparently, stood back off the highway but in view of it and was quite isolated.

'One of those old-fashioned houses,' Seiger ran on. 'Gables and bulging windows like they used to build. It must be at least fifty years old.'

'Stay where you are!'

Palme gave the order in a cold voice and Seiger remained on the floor behind the counter. Palme walked slowly towards the door, turned the key quietly and stepped out. As he did so he moved to his left, sliding along the glass of the shop window – the last thing someone waiting for him would expect. And someone was waiting for him. Two of them. Medium height. Heavily-built. Wearing sunglasses. Something wrong with their shoes. Definitely not Swedish.

The man on the left darted forward, his knife

extended from his hand. They'd made only two mistakes. They hadn't realised he'd seen the silhouette of one man from inside the shop as he glided slowly past the window. And the other man had gently tried the locked door, making the slightest of sounds.

Their second mistake was in not noticing Palme's right hand down by his side as he emerged from the shop, the hand still holding the Luger with the silencer. As the killer darted towards him he whipped up the Luger and fired. *Phut!* A small hole appeared in the assassin's head between his eyes. The second man had seized his chance to dash inside the shop, confident his companion would eliminate Palme. The Swede followed him inside the open door just in time to see him lean over the counter.

Had Seiger not compelled Palme to relieve the locksmith of his Walther automatic he could have saved himself. Palme had hardly re-entered the shop when the assassin rammed home the knife deep into Seiger's chest. There was a choking cry, a slithering sound as Seiger sank to the floor again out of sight. Palme pressed the muzzle of his silenced Luger into the back of the neck of the killer. It seemed rough justice: these bastards were fond of using the old Nazi method of execution.

The man froze, began to say something in *German*. Palme pressed the trigger once. *Phut!* In the silence of the unsavoury-smelling shop it sounded like no more than the expelling of a breath of air. The assassin sprawled his arms across the counter as though trying to hold himself up. Palme stood back as the man folded up and fell in a heap on the floor. Taking Seiger's automatic out of his pocket he quickly cleaned all fingerprints off it and dropped it inside the drawer which was still open.

He left the shop cautiously, using the handkerchief to wipe the handle. The gloomy alley was still deserted – except for the crumpled form of the first assassin at the foot of the window. Palme concealed his Luger inside his belt and behind his jacket. Moving swiftly back up the alley to the road where he had parked his Saab, he climbed in behind the wheel and drove slowly away.

Chapter Sixteen

A modern complex of buildings painted in yellow and ochre, the Russian Embassy in Stockholm is cut off from all contact with the outside world by walls and wire fences which are patrolled round the clock by guards supplied, curiously enough, by A.B.A.B., one of the two leading security services in Stockholm. On the inside it is different. All entrances are controlled by the KGB. The walls of the complex are festooned with the lenses of TV cameras which watch all who approach, lenses which project towards the outside world like hostile guns.

Only a privileged élite are allowed ever to leave the confines of the embassy. From outside you may see a Russian woman with her hair in a bun walking behind the wire – one of the wives of the personnel staffing the embassy. She will serve her term there and return to Russia without ever having seen anything of the beautiful Swedish capital. None of these restrictions, of course, applied to Viktor Rashkin.

'Welcome back, Comrade Secretary,' greeted his assistant, Gregori Semeonov, as his chief entered his office.

'Anything to report?' Rashkin asked curtly as he sat down in his large leather-backed swivel chair behind his outsize desk. He had not given even a glance to the stunning view through the bullet-proof picture windows behind him. Heavy net curtains masked them, making it impossible for anyone in a block of nearby flats to see into the room. The view looked out across a trim area of well-kept lawn and beyond, the waters of the Riddarfjärden glittered in the noon-day sun. Rashkin was tense. Semeonov sensed it.

'There is a signal requesting your urgent presence in Leningrad. You have arrived back in Stockholm just in time – the First Secretary is visiting the city tomorrow and wishes to confer with you while he is there.'

Semeonov handed his chief the decoded signal. He watched while the Russian studied it with half-closed eyes.

Only forty years old, Rashkin was of medium height, average in build and his dark hair was cut very short. Clean-shaven, his eyes were penetrating and had an almost hypnotic quality. As a young man he had spent two years training to be an actor before a senior KGB talent-spotter observed his intensely analytical mind. He was recruited immediately into the élite section of the KGB where he quickly learned the wisdom of suppressing his gift for mimicry.

Despite the fact that his first-class mind swiftly assimilated the flood of information and training directed at him, Viktor Rashkin was not at home inside the KGB. But he had also become fluent in six languages by the time he met Leonid Brezhnev at a Kremlin party. The meeting of the two men was a decisive moment for Viktor Rashkin, a moment which, if mishandled, would never occur again.

Most men would have played it safe, striving to impress the master of Soviet Russia, and being careful to agree with everything he said. Rashkin gambled all on one throw of the dice. He released himself from the mental straitjacket imposed on him by the KGB and for the first time in three years became his natural self. Those nearby who witnessed his conduct were appalled.

Rashkin let his natural gift for mimicry re-assert itself, imitating members of the Politburo who were actually present in the room under the glittering chandeliers. Gradually a hush fell over the great hall in the Kremlin where the party was being held. Only two sounds could be heard – the sound of Rashkin brilliantly imitating world-famous figures on both sides of the Iron Curtain, and the roar of Leonid Brezhnev's laughter as he shook with amusement at such a wonderful contrast to the sombre expressions of the Politburo members.

From that night Viktor Rashkin's future was assured – from being an obscure but promising recruit of the KGB, he became Brezhnev's trusted and secret trouble-shooter. The fact that he was a natural linguist – and that his flair for acting made him a brilliant diplomat – helped to rocket him to the dizzy heights.

The Washington dossier on Viktor Rashkin grew thicker and thicker, but the few privileged to read it complained that despite the quantity of the data, the quality left a great deal to be desired. 'It's so damn vague,' the US President grumbled. 'Now you see him, now you don't.'

April ... Believed to have spent three days in Addis Ababa. Purpose of visit: presumed discusssion of further military aid to present Ethiopian regime.

May ... Reported to have made lightning visit to Angola. Dates of visit uncertain. Rumoured agreement concluded with Angolan regime.

July ... Presence reported in Havana. No positive confirmation of visit. Previously reliable Cuban woman agent code-named Dora signalled arrival of important personality in Cuban capital. Strong suspicion visitor to Castro was Viktor Rashkin.

December ... Presence of Viktor Rashkin positively confirmed in Stockholm where he holds position First Secretary at Soviet Embassy. This official position believed to mask his real activities. Was observed attending royal reception at Palace in Stockholm. Next day believed he left Sweden for unknown destination.

For the CIA and National Security Agency analysts it was infuriating. As one of them had expressed it after reading the above extracts from agents' reports and a host of other material, 'I'm not even sure Viktor Rashkin exists. *Believed to ... presumed ... Reported to have ... Rumoured agreement ... No positive confirmation of visit ... Strong suspicion* ... What kind of dossier is this?'

The man was a will o' the wisp, a shadow flitting in the night. To his assistant, Gregori Semeonov, a senior officer of the KGB, his chief existed but he was almost as elusive as the Washington analyst had suggested. As they conferred in Rashkin's office at the Soviet Embassy in Stockholm the short, burly Ukrainian had no idea where his chief had arrived from.

'I have made your reservation on Flight SK 732 departing from Arlanda for Leningrad at 13.30 tomorrow. Normally this flight is from Gate Six,' Semeonov continued pedantically. 'The ticket is in your right-hand top drawer.'

'A return ticket, I hope?'

Rashkin was studying the contents of a folder from another drawer to which he alone held the keys. As he expected, the stupid, peasant-like Semeonov completely missed the irony of his question.

'What is the exact location of the hydrofoil, *Kometa*?'

'Captain Livanov is waiting at Sassnitz until you give the order for him to proceed to the agreed position off the Swedish port of Trelleborg. I gather he has again complained that we are risking his vessel in asking him to cross the Baltic.'

'I have ordered him – not asked him – to proceed to Trelleborg when I give the signal. We must remember to tell him to keep his hull below the horizon so he cannot be seen from the shore. And the Swedish liner, *Silvia*, is in position?'

'Yes, Comrade Secretary.' Semeonov paused and Rashkin waited for the next piece of bureaucratic idiocy. He was not disappointed. 'I cannot understand why we have hired the *Silvia* and put aboard only a skeleton crew. She is in no position to make a long voyage.'

'Just so long as you have carried out my instructions. You may go now.'

Rashkin had no intention of revealing his strategy to this man who was, after all, only the creature of Yuri Andropov, head of the KGB and a powerful member of the Soviet Politburo. And he was perfectly aware that it was Semeonov's chief task to report back to Andropov all Viktor Rashkin's activities, a task Rashkin was at great pains to frustrate by never revealing to the Ukrainian anything of the least importance.

Semeonov, his hair cut so short that Rashkin secretly termed him 'Bristle-Brush', was not able even to leave the room without further comment. At the door he turned and spoke in his measured, deliberate manner.

'I will confirm that you may be expected in Leningrad aboard SK 732 from Arlanda tomorrow.'

As the door closed Rashkin shut the folder embossed with a small gold star indicating its extreme level of secrecy, pushed back his chair and swore aloud. 'Five minutes in this place and I'm screaming to get out again. Bristle-Brush is becoming impossible to live with.'

*

'I can do nothing more, Jules. I have received specific orders that our distinguished guests are not to be interfered with in any way – on the contrary, while visiting this country they are to be granted every courtesy and consideration. The trouble is, Sweden stands to gain a considerable amount of international business while hosting this conference.'

'They admit a conference is taking place?'

Harry Fondberg and Beaurain were again in the Swedish security chief's office at police headquarters. But on this second occasion the atmosphere was quite different. To Beaurain's astonishment, Fondberg's manner was formal, as though he were covering up a deep sense of embarrassment.

'There has been a reference to a conference, yes,' Fondberg admitted.

Beaurain stood up. 'I presume this means I can no longer rely on you for any assistance? That is the situation, is it not?'

The plump-faced, capable Swede paused, clearly reluctant to let his old friend leave. 'There was a message for you, by the way,' he said. 'It was phoned through to me just before you arrived. I was not able to persuade her to leave her real name.'

'Her?'

'Yes, it was a woman. The message for you was simply, *Offshore from the port of Trelleborg. A hydrofoil. Champagne.*' Fondberg excused himself as the phone rang. He listened, spoke a few words and then replaced the receiver, his expression sombre. 'There has been a death at the Grand Hotel. An important lady.'

'The Countess d'Arlezzo.'

Beaurain made it a statement and Fondberg's sensitive ear did not miss the inflection. He stood up behind his desk, his eyes alert, his mouth hard as he met the Belgian's grim gaze. Beaurain continued, 'Earlier today I was talking with Erika – the Countess – in her suite at the Grand. I have known her for a long time. She told me she had been threatened by the Stockholm Syndicate. That phone call tells me roughly where the conference of the Syndicate will take place. We had arranged she should use the code-word *champagne* to identify herself. I believe I passed the person who must have been keeping an eye on her for the Syndicate, a waiter pushing a trolley.'

'One of the Grand Hotel's regular staff – a waiter – has been found trussed up and stuffed inside a broom cupboard.'

'How did she die?'

Beaurain walked over to the window with hands clasped behind his back while he waited for the reply, and stared out at the sunlight which Erika would never see again. His eyes were quite still.

Fondberg was beginning to feel very uneasy. He cleared his voice before he spoke. 'She was found hanging from the shower in the bathroom. She used her bath-robe cord, a common . . .'

'I would be found . . . hung and twisting like a side of meat turning in the wind.' Beaurain repeated for

Fondberg's benefit the words Erika had used. The Swede sank into the chair behind his desk and stared dully into the distance, tapping the stubby fingers of his right hand on the desk top, a sure sign that he was deeply disturbed. He listened while Beaurain related the whole of his conversation with the woman who had been one of the most powerful figures in Western Europe.

The Belgian's voice grew harsher as he concluded his version of his last meeting with Erika. 'So these are the people to whom you are extending every courtesy and consideration – that was the phrase, was it not? And they – all these members of the Stockholm Syndicate – are as guilty of Erika d'Arlezzo's murder as if they personally had tied round her neck the cord of her own bath-robe and strung her up to that shower.'

'I said nothing about a murder.' Fondberg wriggled uncomfortably behind his desk and, for the first time in their long friendship, he was unable to meet Beaurain's gaze.

'Christ Al-bloody-mighty!' Beaurain's fist smashed down on the desk-top. 'You are not going to stoop so low that you will allow them to get away with this faked suicide?'

'*No!*' Fondberg came out of his mental daze and stared straight at Beaurain. 'Of course I know it wasn't suicide! Had you understood Swedish you would have known I was speaking to the forensic expert who has already arrived at the Grand. I told him to send his report to me personally at the earliest possible moment. No-one else will be permitted to see it. I shall myself announce its findings to the international press now gathering here hoping for news of the "business" conference. It will cause a bombshell!'

'The Syndicate will come after you,' Beaurain warned his old friend, but, he admitted privately to himself, he was also testing him. Such was the quick-sand atmosphere of treachery and fear the unseen organisation had generated. Fondberg's reaction made him feel a little ashamed.

'Wrong, my friend. I am going after the Stockholm Syndicate! In committing this murder they have made a big mistake. They hoped their influence was strong enough to squash any attempt at a legitimate investigation. They overlooked the fact that I might intervene.'

Events moved at bewildering speed during the next few days. On receipt of Beaurain's urgent signal sent by Stig Palme from a transceiver hidden in the basement of a house in the town of Strängnäs, Captain 'Bucky' Buckminster left his anchorage off Copenhagen and proceeded south and east into the Baltic.

'We have to wait off the coast near Trelleborg,' he told Anderson, the chief pilot of the giant Sikorsky which they carried on the helipad. 'Just below the horizon so we cannot easily be seen from the Swedish shore.'

'Any exercises once we get there?' Anderson enquired.

'Yes. Intensive training with the power-boats and dinghies equipped with outboards – in fact all the fleet of craft in the hold. Another activity Beaurain wants toned up is the training of frogmen in underwater warfare.'

'The Countess d'Arlezzo, president of the well-known group of banks, who was discovered hanging from the shower in the bathroom of her suite in the Grand Hotel was, in the opinion of the well-known pathologist, Professor Edwin Jacoby . . .'

Harry Fondberg, who was addressing a press conference called at very short notice – other reporters were still arriving, pushing their way into the crowded room – was possessed of a certain dramatic sense which he now used to the full. Beaurain watched him from a position at the back of the room. Heads craned as the pause was stretched out. Most of the western world's leading newspapers, TV stations and magazines were represented.

'. . . was MURDERED!'

Pandemonium! The small plump chief of Säpo waited as men and women milled in the room – some already rushing for phones to catch editions about to go to press with the staggering announcement. The Countess d'Arlezzo's beauty had been compared with that of Sophia Loren; her business influence with that of Onassis. As the initial reaction subsided, Fondberg ruthlessly piled on the drama. Now it was too late for anyone to try and hold down the lid on the case. It was his first promised blow at the Stockholm Syndicate.

'In a moment Professor Jacoby will tell you his reasons for stating that in his opinion the alleged suicide was faked, could not have taken place in the way meant to fool the police. Or, shall we say, certain powerful criminal groups with international connections believed their influence was so great that no-one would ever dare reveal the truth?'

Louise whispered to Beaurain. 'God! That's really blasted the case wide open. Whoever Hugo is, he's going to go crazy!'

'That's Harry's tactic,' Beaurain murmured. 'He hopes that by throwing him off balance he'll provoke him into making yet another blunder. And listen to this!'

The questions were now coming like bullets as reporters fought to catch Fondberg's eye. High up on a platform, he selected his questioners for their influence. Someone ran onto the platform with a note – doubtless from some Minister. Fondberg waved the messenger away and stuffed the message unread inside his pocket.

'Are you saying the Countess was mixed up in criminal activities?' asked someone from *Der Spiegel*.

'I am saying she was being blackmailed and intimidated in a way which would only be used by animals.

I have the most reliable of witnesses that she was actually threatened with death in the form her murder took.'

'Your witness?'

'Would ex-Chief Superintendent Jules Beaurain of the Brussels anti-terrorist squad, previously in charge of Homicide, satisfy you?'

'Thank you. Yes!' said *Der Spiegel*.

'Christ!' Louise whispered. 'He's blowing the whole works.'

'And the one thing the Syndicate can't stand is publicity,' Beaurain whispered back. 'It's a dark evil creature which operates in the darkness.'

'Would you care to elaborate on the structure of these powerful criminal groups you refer to?' *The Times* – of London.

'Check up on likely personalities at present in Stockholm.'

'Names, we need names!' *The New York Times*.

'You are here! Do some of your own investigative work, may I suggest!'

'Leo Gehn has just arrived in the capital, I hear.' *The New York Times*.

'I have heard that also,' Fondberg replied blandly. 'Next question, please.'

'Who controls the international criminal groups you referred to in reply to an earlier question?' *Le Monde* of Paris.

There was a prolonged pause. Tension built up in the packed room as Fondberg, one arm supporting another, a hand under his chin, seemed to be considering whether to answer the question. One thing was clear and heightened the tension until the atmosphere became electric: the chief of Säpo *did* know the answer . . .

'A directorate of three men.' Fondberg spoke slowly and with great deliberation. As he paused again, the door next to Beaurain was pulled open. A man took three paces forward and stopped, holding a Smith & Wesson with both hands, the muzzle raised and aimed point-blank at Harry Fondberg.

Louise had a blurred impression of a short, burly figure wearing a boiler suit. Beaurain grabbed the man's wrist and elbow. There was a single explosion. The bullet fired in the tussle – which would have blown Fondberg off his feet – embedded itself in the ceiling. There was a shocked, incredulous hush which lasted several seconds, during which the only sound was the scuffle of feet as Beaurain overpowered the gunman. Uniformed guards were appearing in the hall beyond the open door. Beaurain hurled the would-be assassin with all his strength backwards into their arms.

'Check him for other weapons!' he snapped. 'Or do I have to do the whole damned job for you? He came within an ace of killing your boss.'

Chaos broke loose. The room erupted into movement as the mob of reporters stormed towards the doorways. Beaurain hauled Louise back out of the path of the turbulent crowd and pressed her back against the wall. In thirty seconds the room was occupied by only three people: Beaurain, Louise and Harry Fondberg.

The Swede jumped agilely from the platform and ran towards the Belgian, holding out his hand. 'For saving my life I can only say thank you.'

'We stage-managed that rather well. Maybe we should go into the theatrical business,' Beaurain whispered.

'I have the information you asked me to dig up on Dr Theodor Norling's background before he came to Stockholm. It tells us nothing,' Fondberg informed his listeners.

Beaurain and Louise were sitting at a round table in the Säpo chief's office, eating hungrily from a selection of dishes which Fondberg had ordered from a nearby restaurant. Beaurain nodded at Fondberg's remark as the Swede studied the report without enthusiasm.

'It is the same with all these provincial police forces – they think we live the high life here and they can't even answer a civil request without grumbling at how busy they are.'

'Tell us what there is to know about Norling,' Beaurain suggested.

'Born in Gothenburg, his parents moved when he was seven years old to Ystad.' He looked at Louise. 'That is an old medieval port on the southern coast in the province of Skåne. The people in Skåne are very different.'

He might have been talking about the end of the world, as certain New Yorkers refer to the Deep South. Perhaps this was the Deep South of Sweden, Louise reflected. Fondberg continued reading from his folder.

'When I say Ystad I mean a small place close to it. The first thing Theodor Norling's parents did when they arrived from Gothenburg was to separate. His mother ran off with a ship's engineer while the father managed to get himself killed in a traffic accident a few weeks later. Young Norling was taken in by some aunt who had money and he was partly educated abroad. He returned to Skåne when he was twenty, attended the funeral of his aunt who had just died, and promptly used the legacy she had left him to set up in business as a collector.'

'Let me guess,' interjected Beaurain. 'A collector of editions of rare books?'

'Wrong!' Fondberg chuckled delightedly at having scored a point when he saw Beaurain's expression. 'As a collector and dealer in old coins.'

'And he travelled a lot,' Beaurain persisted, 'during the course of his business.'

'Yes,' Fondberg admitted.

'And most of his business was done abroad and locally he was known as a bit of a hermit and he never got married?'

'Yes,' Fondberg agreed, almost reluctantly. 'It is a waste of time my reading this folder since you seem to know the contents. It is true he was a hermit – and disliked on that account since he gave the impression he felt himself superior to the locals.' The Swede chuckled again. 'The truth of the matter probably is that he was very superior! Any more predictions?'

'Only one. He arrived suddenly in Stockholm to set up business as a dealer in rare books about two years ago.'

'Ten out of ten!' Fondberg did not even bother to refer to the folder.

'So,' Beaurain suggested, 'to sum up, Theodor Norling has now no known living relatives. Correct? And have your people down there in darkest Skåne found any close friends he left behind who could identify a picture taken of him?'

'Yes – and no. As you suggested I sent the picture we have of Norling, a picture which had to be taken secretly because of a directive from higher up. The Ystad police showed it to the very few people who knew Theodor Norling when he was in business down there. Some immediately identified him from the photo. Others said they didn't think that was the man they had known as Dr Theodor Norling.'

'The man they had known as Dr Theodor Norling.' Beaurain repeated the words slowly as though relishing every syllable. The chief of Säpo was now looking thoroughly piqued. Louise did nothing to enlighten him.

'It's bloody uncanny,' was her unladylike remark.

'What is?' Fondberg pounced.

'How we've heard this story before. Twice to be precise.' She looked at Beaurain who nodded giving her permission to go ahead. 'What you have told us about the background and origins of Dr Theodor Norling is an almost exact replica – with a few minor variations – of the background histories of the other two members of the so-called directorate controlling the Stockholm Syndicate.'

'You mean these men are sleepers who are now activated?'

'No, oddly enough, the other way round.' It was Beaurain who spoke.

'You mean someone has invented dummy men?' Fondberg suggested.

'Not even that, Harry. Dr Berlin certainly existed, was quite definitely brought up in Liège in his early days and started his business as a book dealer there. There are still people who remember him. Vaguely.'

Fondberg shook his head and lit a cigar. 'I am lost. Which, I suspect, is your intention, you bastard.' He turned to Louise and bowed formally. 'Please excuse my language, but you work with him, so . . .'

'I agree with you,' Louise assured him.

'Let's try to find you – since you're lost, Harry,' Beaurain continued imperturbably. 'Dr Theodor Norling's background is vague because his parents vanished from his life early on, because his life-style was that of a hermit, because he travelled a lot on business and was seen very little before he came to live permanently in Stockholm. *Two years ago.*'

'All that is in the goddam folder,' Fondberg pointed out.

'Dr Otto Berlin's background is vague because Liège is a large city, because he had no relatives and few acquaintances, because he also travelled a lot owing to the nature of his business. His character, too, was hermit-like. Perhaps it goes with the trade. So again, as with Norling, old acquaintances shown a photograph say "Yes, that's him," or "No, doesn't look much like him." Only one photograph is available of Berlin. These men seem to be very camera-shy.'

'I am still lost,' Fondberg growled.

'The third man was – note the past tense – Dr Benny Horn who now lives in Copenhagen but originally came from Elsinore. And while I remember it, when do you think Dr Otto Berlin moved himself from Liège to Bruges? *About two years ago!*'

'It is getting interesting,' Fondberg was compelled to admit. He glanced at Louise. 'This dishonest and devious man you choose to work for plays these games with me whenever he gets the opportunity. In England I think they call it dangling you on a string.'

'Benny Horn's background antecedents are equally vague when you go into them with a sceptical eye,' Beaurain continued. 'He was in the book dealer business for fifteen years in Elsinore before he moved suddenly to Copenhagen. Since then, no-one in Elsinore has seen him – not that there are many who would be interested.'

'Another hermit?' Fondberg enquired.

'As I said, it seems to go with the trade. So, although he has a solid background of fifteen years' residence on the outskirts of Elsinore you can't track down many who actually knew him – and then only vaguely. The local police produce his photograph and we get a repeat performance. Some say "yes" and some say "no" when asked to identify Horn. It's quite normal, as you know.'

'I still don't understand it,' complained Fondberg. 'They're not sleepers, they're not dummy men.'

'Someone went to a lot of trouble in Belgium, in Denmark, and here in Sweden searching out these men, Harry. The whole thing is quite horribly sinister – worked out by a brilliant mind and manipulated in a diabolical manner. What we are actually looking for is the fourth man.'

'The fourth man?'

'The one they call Hugo, the man whose very name evokes terror, sheer terror.'

Chapter Seventeen

The temperature was a comparatively pleasant 42°F., an east wind sweeping over the airport chilled the face, the expressions of the airport staff were sombre; a prejudiced observer might even have used the word 'sour'. As far as the eye could see the landscape and buildings were depressing. Scandinavian Airlines Flight SK 732 from Stockholm had just touched down at Leningrad.

Ignoring the stewardesses waiting by the exit, Viktor Rashkin left the plane and walked briskly to the waiting black Zil limousine. The KGB guard saluted, held open the rear door while Rashkin stepped inside, closed it and motioned to the chauffeur who started the machine moving at once. Rashkin was known for his impatience.

The cavalcade – a Volga car full of KGB agents preceded the Zil limousine while another followed in the rear – sped away from the airport and Rashkin glanced outside unenthusiastically. Why the hell did Brezhnev need to have personal reports on progress of Operation Snowbird? Rashkin suspected the old boy, surrounded by old-age pensioners, simply wanted a few hours of his company. He always asked for impersonations and roared his head off while Rashkin mimicked his victims.

Relaxing back against the amply-cushioned seat he gazed out through the amber-coloured curtains masking the windows. In the streets the people were curious – and resentful. Apparatchiki were on their way to some unknown destination and, ahead of the cavalcade, police were stopping all traffic to allow Viktor Rashkin swift passage. The driver of one car forced to halt by the kerb carefully waited until the second car-load of KGB men had passed and then spat out of the window.

'Arrogant sods – living off our backs.'

It was a common sentiment Rashkin would have seen in the eyes of the staring pedestrians – had he looked up. He didn't bother. He knew what he would see. One day the lid would come off. There had to be a limit to the patience of even these stupid serfs.

Earlier at the Europe Hotel situated off the Nevsky Prospekt there had been more dissatisfaction as all visitors had been moved out of their rooms to other hotels at a moment's notice. No explanation had been given as squads of KGB agents moved in to replace the normal staff.

Now the Europe resembled more a fortress than a hotel with special squads of agents checking the identity of everyone who approached the entrance. Guards patrolled all the corridors and armed men displayed their presence aggressively. First Secretary

Brezhnev was in town. His announced purpose was to visit Leningrad. His real purpose was to confer with his protégé, Viktor Rashkin.

'So,' Leonid Brezhnev continued, 'the Stockholm Syndicate can be said to be flourishing?'

'We can say more than that,' Rashkin announced confidently, his manner totally lacking in the usual servility shown to the master of the Soviet Union. 'We can say that we have now placed puppets under our control in most of the key positions in Western Europe – chairmen of huge industrial concerns, heads of transport systems, controllers of some of the great banks and – above all – certain cabinet ministers. By involving them – through one method or another – in the Syndicate, we have compromised them so all they can do is to obey our instructions.'

'A takeover without war, a takeover which is invisible and not even seen by the masses to have taken place!' Brezhnev's tone expressed his immense satisfaction with what he obviously regarded as a great victory.

'It is like Hitler's Fifth Column practised on a far vaster scale,' Rashkin commented.

'These three men you found who form the directorate – Berlin in Bruges, Horn in Copenhagen and Norling in Stockholm. Why are they needed?'

Rashkin prevented a sigh of exasperation escaping. This was caused by the First Secretary's advancing years – his infuriating habit of changing the subject for no apparent reason. Yet oddly it was combined with a flair for remembering an extraordinary amount of detail over a vast range of projects. You had to watch the old boy – underestimate him and he'd catch you out in the flick of a horse's tail. And that, Rashkin reminded himself grimly, only happened once. He explained crisply, careful not to appear patronising.

'These three men are essential. Each controls a certain geographical sector – Berlin, the Mediterranean up to the mouth of the Rhine, Horn the United States . . .'

'Yes, yes, I remember that bit.'

'So any member of the Syndicate in that sector co-operates with the sector commander, who is a West European. This camouflages totally the fact that real control is in our hands.

'How do you explain to them why the conference is taking place aboard a Soviet vessel – the hydrofoil, *Kometa?*'

A shrewd point. *But oh God, we have gone all through this before!* Rashkin smiled to relax himself. 'They already believe that much of the Syndicate's profits will come from surreptitious dealings in the proceeds from crime inside the Soviet Union, that there are *Soviet* members of the Syndicate!'

'Good, good, Comrade!' Brezhnev smiled slyly, leaned forward and squeezed Rashkin's shoulder. The younger man guessed what was coming next and was not disappointed. 'Now, what about a few of your impersonations to cheer up an old Bolshevik who has to sit all day long staring at sourfaces? For a start, why not our esteemed Minister of Defence, Dimitri Ustinov?'

A moment later he began to laugh out loud: in that short space of time Rashkin's acting genius had transformed him into a different human being. He had become Marshal Dimitri Ustinov.

Attempt on Life of Security Chief Fails.

'God damn it, what crazy maniac acted without my orders and committed this supreme idiocy? And if ever there was a time we do not want anything like this it is now! Now! Now! Now! Do you hear me? Well, why don't you say something instead of standing there like a whore on a street corner?' Rashkin demanded. Karnell grabbed a decorative plate from the wall and hurled it at him. It shattered on the side of his head – and when he put his hand up it came away streaked with blood.

Rashkin looked at Sonia Karnell and took a handkerchief from his pocket with the other hand. He wiped the blood from his fingers, his manner suddenly frigidly calm. While talking he had been raving like a madman, shouting at the Swedish girl as though it were all her fault.

'It was a bumpy ride back from Leningrad,' he told her. 'The turbulence was most unusual.'

'The turbulence since you arrived has not only been

unusual,' she said viciously. *'It has been unbearable. Do you hear me, Viktor Rashkin?'* she suddenly screamed at the top of her voice. 'And the plate I broke over your stupid head was your present to me.'

'I know.'

'I just wanted to make sure you know – because I'm glad. Do you hear me, you pimp? I'm glad.'

Her well-defined bosom was heaving with passion and her white face was a mask of rage. His reaction, as always, was unexpected and disarming. He sat down on a sofa, lit two cigarettes and offered her one.

'The newspaper story disturbed me,' he remarked mildly. 'Coming on the eve of the conference when we want everything peaceful with nothing to disturb our influential guests. Such men and women like to live without any publicity. There is only one solution, Sonia.'

Karnell played with the large diamond ring he had given her and waited for his next pronouncement. She had asserted her independence; Viktor despised and mistrusted all those who played up to him. She had by now learned how to handle this brilliant and strange man.

'We quietly wipe out Beaurain's organisation, starting at once,' he decided. 'We now have plenty of troops in Stockholm, including Gunther Baum.'

'But how are you going to find them? We know Beaurain and his tart are at the Grand but the rest?'

'Our people will call discreetly at all major hotels in the city. They will check on any new arrivals during the past week. They should not be difficult to identify – we are looking for Commando-style men, a number of whom we suspect previously belonged to the British terrorist SAS.'

'Who, of course,' she interjected sarcastically, 'are far worse than the KGB execution squads.'

'I must leave now. You can alert our people and get the search under way at once. Gunther Baum is to be put in charge of both search and subsequent liquidations – as many of them as possible to look like accidents. I am going to the house to collect all the folders before the conference commences aboard *Kometa*.'

One of those old-fashioned houses . . . Gables and bulging windows like they used to build . . . must be at least fifty years old . . .

Stig Palme recalled the description the murdered locksmith had given him of the house in the country where he had seen Dr Theodor Norling.

'At least I assume it was Norling,' Palme continued while Beaurain, Harry Fondberg and Louise Hamilton listened to him as they sat eating lunch in the Opera House restaurant. It was a convenient meeting-place because it was close to the Grand Hotel and was quiet. No-one occupied a table anywhere near them.

'It's all right, Stig,' Beaurain assured the Swede, 'I'm damned sure it was Norling. He was personally attending to organising another of the Syndicate's "demonstrations". Don't forget – poor Erika was supposed to have committed suicide – but other members of the Syndicate would have known better. Now, Harry, this raid on the house in the country, which Stig can locate for us. Can it be soon? And a combined operation between my people and Säpo. Unofficially, of course?'

'It can be today!' Fondberg announced and took a deep puff on his cigar to show his satisfaction at the prospect of action.

Six cars were moving along the E3 highway beyond the outskirts of Stockholm and out in open country. Palme had been chosen to lead the assault convoy because he was Swedish, and because he knew the location of the house which the dead locksmith, Tobias Seiger, had described. In the second vehicle Jules Beaurain sat behind the wheel of his Mercedes which Albert had driven to Stockholm.

'You really think this house could be the HQ of the Stockholm Syndicate?' Louise asked as she peered eagerly out of the window.

'I'm guessing – but it would fit the basic requirements of a headquarters from Stig's own recollection of the place. Hugo won't want anywhere in Stockholm. It's OK for Theodor Norling to have his apartment in Gamla Stan – I think Norling just meets people there, just like Otto Berlin meets people in Bruges.'

'In mobility they find safety?'

Beaurain paused. 'Something like that. But an old house right out in the country, well back off the road so it attracts no attention, and yet close to a highway which gives swift access to Stockholm. As I said, I'm gambling, but it fits the basic requirements.'

'Some gamble!'

Louise twisted in her seat and looked back down the curving highway through the rear window. She could see at least two of the four cars following them – and inside each car Henderson had installed a team of four men accustomed to working together as a group. And – the thought occurred to her – had Harry Fondberg known the arms concealed aboard these vehicles he would have had a fit. Sergeant Jock Henderson, riding in the third car, was organised for a small war. And he was in radio contact with all the other vehicles, using a pre-arranged code which would have meant nothing to any outside listeners.

'Of course it could all be for nothing,' Louise remarked. 'And where is Harry Fondberg? Incidentally, I presume you know there's a traffic helicopter flying along the highway?'

'I had noticed the chopper,' Beaurain informed her solemnly. 'I happen to know Harry Fondberg is aboard it. And, as you so cheerfully predict, it could all be for nothing.'

*

The Cessna was waiting for Viktor Rashkin – he could see it in the distance! Throwing his peaked cap onto the rear seat, he grabbed the pilot's helmet by his side and confidently climbed out of the car, locked it in the parking zone and strode across the airfield.

In the control tower a man picked up a pair of field glasses, focused them on the figure striding towards the Cessna with a springy step and asked to be excused. Instead of heading towards the lavatories he stepped inside the nearest payphone and dialled Ed Cottel's number. In his room at the Grand the American answered with his room number.

'Westerberg here,' his caller identified himself. 'Ozark is just leaving. Official destination Kjula, as usual.'

'Understood,' Cottel replied laconically. 'Goodbye. And let's hope we win a bundle.'

Kjula was a small military and civil airfield about fifteen kilometres from the town of Strängnäs which you reached by travelling along Highway E3 – the route Beaurain and his gunners were now moving along.

Before leaving the Grand to join the convoy Beaurain had slipped into the CIA man's room to tell him what he planned and the location of the strange old house where the locksmith had seen a blond man with sideburns leaving. The only fact Beaurain had omitted to mention to Ed Cottel was that the locksmith had reported the fair-haired man as leaving the house for Stockholm in a Volvo estate wagon carrying American diplomatic plates.

Two minutes later Cottel was behind the wheel of his hired Renault parked outside the hotel. He was going to have to make speed to catch up with Beaurain's convoy.

They were travelling through the province of Södermanland along the E3 highway and Louise was fascinated by the beauty of the scenery. 'I had no idea the countryside just outside Stockholm was so lovely.'

'Yes, it's attractive,' Beaurain agreed.

Louise sat entranced as the sun blazed down once again out of an immaculate sky and the highway spread ahead, passing through tiny gorges where granite crags closed in on the road, then opened out again to reveal rolling green hills covered with fir trees, fields of yellow rape, the occasional wooden farmhouse painted a strong rust-red standing out in stark contrast to the surrounding green. She glanced in her wing mirror and stiffened.

Taking the field glasses from the glove compartment she swung in her seat and aimed the glasses through the rear window at the Renault roaring up behind them. Behind tinted glasses the face of Ed Cottel came rushing towards her.

'We're being followed,' she said tensely. 'Ed Cottel's right behind us. Any second he'll drive through our rear window.'

'I know.'

The Renault was too damned close for Louise's comfort. Beaurain waved Cottel to move ahead of the Mercedes. Within minutes, moving round a curve, Beaurain spotted a roadsign, a large white letter 'M' on a blue ground. He pointed it out to Louise.

'That indicates a lay-by coming up. We can pull in there and see what Ed is getting so excited about. I told him where we were going.'

Beaurain hooted and signalled that he was pulling into the lay-by. When he had stopped he remained seated behind the wheel of his car and waited while Cottel, who had parked further along the lay-by, climbed out of his Renault and began walking back towards them.

'Wouldn't it be nice to get out and greet him?' Louise suggested.

'Not until we find out what he's up to,' Beaurain replied.

They were now well out in the country and there was very little traffic on the E3. More rolling green hills capped with dark smudges of fir forest, a landscape which seemed to go on forever. The warmth of the sun beat down on the Mercedes as Cottel approached them on foot.

For his normal sober and well-cut suit he had substituted a pair of old jeans, sneakers and a shabby anorak. The American leaned on the edge of the open window, greeted Louise politely and then said, 'My people tell me Viktor Rashkin – piloting his own

Cessna – took off from Bromma some time ago with a flight plan giving his destination as Kjula airfield.'

'Which leads you to think, Ed?'

'That if you wanted to fool someone you might fly to Kjula and then drive back from the Strängnäs direction as though heading *into* Stockholm. Just a thought. Mind if I continue tagging on behind?'

'Suit yourself, Ed.'

While Cottel walked back to his Renault, Beaurain pulled out of the lay-by and sped past the American to catch up with Palme's Saab. In his rear-view mirror he saw the car with Henderson at the wheel approaching. The other three car-loads of gunners would not be far behind.

'You were pretty rude to Ed,' Louise observed.

'I merely used as few words as possible in the conversation. We are, in case you've forgotten, working to a time-table with Harry Fondberg.'

'Now give me the real reason.'

'Supposing you wanted to divert someone's attention from a certain direction what would be the most effective way of doing it?'

'Point them in another direction. You can't mean Cottel keeps drawing your attention to Viktor Rashkin's movements to divert your attention from Washington, for God's sake?'

Harvey Sholto, the man from Vietnam, the man whose past and present were clouded in vagueness, and the man about whom presidential aide, Joel Cody, had taken the trouble to phone Harry Fondberg to tell him of his imminent arrival, was staying at the Hotel Reisen.

He had chosen the hotel with care. It was located on the island which contained Gamla Stan. Its front overlooked the Strommen belt of water. With a pair of field glasses used from his bedroom window the tall, heavily-built, bald-headed American could see across the water clearly to the front entrance of the Grand Hotel, the cars parked outside and anyone who entered or left the hotel. He had been sitting astride a chair watching through his field glasses when he saw Beaurain and Louise leave the hotel and climb into the Mercedes.

Hurrying downstairs, he got in behind the wheel of the Volvo he had hired and drove swiftly along the river front and over the bridge to the mainland. He arrived in time to insert his vehicle into the traffic within tracking distance of the Mercedes.

Wearing a straw hat – which completely concealed his bald head – and a large pair of shaped tinted glasses, he had changed his appearance so that only a face-to-face encounter would make him recognisable to someone he knew. Glancing to his left he saw a Renault driving briefly alongside him. The two cars were parallel for only a few seconds, but long enough for Sholto to recognise the hooked-nosed profile of CIA agent Ed Cottel.

Sensing that he was following Beaurain, Sholto

changed to shadowing the CIA man. He observed the forming-up of the convoy of cars which followed a Saab being followed by Beaurain's Mercedes as they changed direction and, in a matter of minutes, were moving out in the direction of Strängnäs on Highway E3.

It was Sholto who formed the invisible tail of the convoy, careful to keep the last car in sight while he lit cigarette after cigarette and his button-like eyes gleamed with concentration. As he continued driving, staring through the tinted glasses at the unrolling highway, he felt under his armpit the comforting bulge of the Colt .45 in its sprung holster. On the seat beside him an Armalite rifle was wrapped in a blanket. It was beginning to look as though his urgent mission decided on in Washington was almost completed.

For long stretches in the open country the E3 has no barrier protecting the flat farmland alongside – the road simply merges with the level grassland. Palme had hidden his Saab by driving straight off the deserted highway over the grass and parking his vehicle behind a copse of trees. When Beaurain appeared he waved to him to follow suit and waited to guide the other vehicles in the convoy off the highway.

'What's Ed doing?' Louise asked as Beaurain skilfully and slowly manoeuvred the ton-and-a-half of metal along the same route and behind the same copse.

'Doing his own thing – as usual,' Beaurain observed laconically.

The American continued along the highway and was soon out of sight beyond a curve. Overhead the traffic helicopter had appeared again, the machine carrying Harry Fondberg.

'Lose altitude,' Fondberg ordered, sitting in the seat alongside the pilot. He rested his elbows on the arms of his seat to give stability and focused his high-powered binoculars on the Renault which had earlier stopped for a brief consultation with Jules Beaurain.

'Got you.' Fondberg made a note of the registration number and then told the pilot to regain height. His next focus of interest was the convoy of vehicles leaving the road, ploughing over the grass and assembling behind a copse of trees to form a *laager*. It seemed to the chief of Säpo that interesting developments were about to take place.

Concerned with the movement of the convoy out of sight behind the trees, Fondberg missed the passage of a beige Volvo driven by a man wearing a straw hat. Having noted where the vehicles had left the road – and also aware of the traffic helicopter overhead – Harvey Sholto proceeded at a sedate pace along E3 until he was out of sight beyond the bend.

One of those old-fashioned houses . . . Gables and bulging windows like they used to build . . . must be at least fifty years old . . .

Concealed with the others behind a second copse of trees, Palme used his left hand to scratch at his crew-cut. The murdered locksmith had been incredibly accurate when he described both place and location. The house was just where he had expected to find it. It looked like the house in *Psycho*.

Even Palme, who was not overly sensitive to atmosphere, felt there was something distinctly wrong with the place.

'I don't like it,' he told Beaurain who stood alongside him with Jock Henderson just beyond. The Belgian was scanning the place with his own field glasses. He was inclined to agree. It looked a little too damned quiet. Curtains at all the windows, half-drawn to keep out the strong sunlight the way people do to protect rugs and carpets – or when they are away.

The steps up to the open veranda had a rickety look and the paint was peeling, but the rest of the house looked in good condition. The tarred drive ran straight up to the base of the steps and then curved round the right-hand side of the house. On the same side there was the silhouette, partially masked by the trees, of an ancient outhouse.

'Any sign of occupation?' Louise whispered.

There was something about the atmosphere of the place which encouraged whispering, something about the heavy, hot silence which hung like a cloud over the strange building.

'Can't see a damned thing,' Beaurain said as he

lowered his glasses, but there was a lack of conviction in his voice. 'What do you think?' he asked.

'I don't like it,' Palme repeated and again scratched his head with his left hand; his right was holding a loaded machine-pistol.

'I suggest we surround it first, sir,' Henderson suggested crisply. 'Then move in from all sides at an agreed moment. There's a drainage ditch just behind us with grass grown up all round it – a perfect conduit if we wriggle on our bellies and head for the rear of the house and then circle round.'

'There's a lake not far away,' Palme observed. 'A lot of them in this area. This one's reasonably large.' He showed the map to Beaurain, who made a remark he was later to regret.

'Can't be of any significance. I agree, Jock, we approach with extreme caution. Surround the place and then move in from all sides. Jock, get it organised – and *get it moving!*'

The 'traffic' helicopter with Harry Fondberg aboard had flown away some distance and when Louise shaded her eyes against the glare of the sun she saw it as little more than a speck. Fondberg was deliberately moving out of the battle area so as not to alert the opposition. Louise stood behind the trees which concealed them from the highway, staring again at the house through her field glasses.

Henderson and his team of twelve armed gunners, equipped with walkie-talkies, had already disappeared along the drainage ditch. Watching the grasses above the ditch Beaurain could not see the slightest sign of movement. He just hoped that from an upper window in the house it was not possible to see down into the ditch. He heard an exclamation from Louise, who had moved a few yards away and was still surveying the general area of the house. He joined her.

'What is it?'

'When Stig was interviewing that locksmith in his shop didn't he say he'd seen a Volvo station wagon with American diplomatic plates?'

'Yes, he tried to follow the car on its way into Stockholm and lost it. Why?' There was a note of impatience in Beaurain's tone.

'Because parked behind the house there is a Volvo station wagon – the only thing is the diplomatic plates are Russian, not American.'

'Seiger must have been so terrified he tried to hold back some of the truth. And that car means someone is inside that house!'

Chapter Eighteen

Dr Theodor Norling stared from behind the curtain of the first-floor window. There were gaps in the sea of grass alongside the drainage ditch and there he had seen the approaching men slithering along like snakes on their bellies.

He had just collected what he had come for – a sheaf of red folders which had been concealed beneath a trap-door on the ground floor. Now they were safely inside his brief-case, and he had to get away. The upper part of his body was clad in a loose-fitting hunting jacket with capacious pockets. He was holding the brief-case in his left hand; his right hand dug into one of the pockets and felt the hard metal pineapples – grenades.

Swiftly he left the room and darted down the curving staircase. The place was almost empty, barely furnished, and the heels of his shoes echoed throughout the house as he descended.

The furniture which did exist was of a curious nature. Under each window stood a large box which might have been mistaken for an old-fashioned radiator. They were nothing of the sort. Before leaving the ghostly house Norling was careful to collect a compact device with a red button and a slide. He raised the miniature aerial and moved the slide across into the 'active' position. He now had to be very careful not to depress the red button too early.

Outside he ducked behind the parked Volvo and ran under cover of some trees to cross the ditch where it turned and continued behind the house. As he had hoped the ditch was empty; the first man had not yet reached the corner. Behind him he was leaving a powder keg.

Crouched low, he was now moving directly away from the house and the highway, taking advantage of every piece of natural cover: a patch of undergrowth, a group of trees, an outcrop of granite rearing up out of the earth. When he reached the outcrop he stopped, climbing up a small ravine and peering cautiously over the rim.

Some distance behind him the blue waters of a lake rippled and glittered in the sun like mercury. This was the lake which Beaurain had thought couldn't be of any significance. From the summit of the granite crag Norling could just make out, among the reeds lining the shore, where his float-plane was hidden.

He turned his attention back to the house which he could see clearly from his position – the house, the parked estate car, and the line of men who, having encircled the house, were rising up from the ditch and staring at their objective without advancing. Norling clutched the radio-detonation device firmly in his right hand, his index finger close to the red button. One push would detonate the vast quantity of high-explosive installed inside the house.

Ed Cottel drove only a short distance beyond the drive to the house, which reminded him of the old houses still preserved in faraway San Francisco.

'Probably built about the same period,' he speculated aloud – and knew immediately that the fact that he was talking to himself was a sign of tension. Wanting to use his transceiver, he drove the Renault off the highway and pulled up behind a clump of undergrowth.

He lowered the flap, exposing the dials, fiddled with them and then called his man at Kjula, the military and civil airfield fifteen kilometres from Strängnäs. 'Sandpiper calling ... Sandpiper calling ...'

'I read you, Sandpiper. I read you. Ozark has landed. Repeat Ozark has landed.'

Cottel signed out and glared at the shimmering haze dancing over the fields. For Sweden it was getting pretty goddam hot. So – Viktor Rashkin had made his usual landfall at Kjula. The pattern was repeating itself.

It had been clearly established by the watchers at Bromma and at Kjula that the Russian made regular flights along this route. He left the Cessna – piloted by himself – at Kjula, climbed behind the wheel of a waiting Volvo 245 station wagon, and eventually drove along Highway E3 as though heading back to Stockholm – the place he had just flown from. It hadn't made sense.

The trouble was Cottel had always lost the Volvo long before it reached the turn-off to the old house where Beaurain appeared to be about to start his own private war.

The Cessna left behind at Kjula was always flown back to its home base of Bromma by a hired pilot, presumably waiting for Rashkin's next outward flight.

Cottel caught a flash where there shouldn't be a flash. He flung open the door, ducked his head, rolled out bodily over the rough ground.

The first high-velocity bullet shattered the Renault's windscreen, punching a hole through the glass behind where Cottel's head had been. *The second and third bullets hit their targets, destroying both front tyres.* Under shelter of the Renault Cottel loosed off three shots in rapid succession as near as he could manage to where sunlight had flashed off the lens of a telescopic sight. He waited and heard the sound of a car engine starting up. By the time he reached the highway the vehicle and the would-be assassin had gone.

Harvey Sholto was furious with himself for missing the target – something almost unique in his experience. There was a traffic control chopper floating about somewhere – he'd seen it earlier and the one thing he could do without was interference from the local pigs. Covered in the rear of the Volvo lay the

Armalite rifle, its barrel still warm from the three shots he had fired. As soon as he'd realised he'd missed Cottel with the first shot he had switched his aim to the tyres.

Using one hand to drive, he removed the straw hat and mopped sweat off his bald head. This was cleaning-up time – knocking off all the loose ends. It had worked well at Stockholm Central. Wearing Swedish police uniform and equipped with the powerful motor-bike, Sholto had slipped through the cordon with the suitcase of heroin strapped to the pillion and delivered the consignment to the apartment in Rådmansgatan.

It was also Sholto who had used the silenced gun to kill Serge Litov after they had retrieved the heroin. Litov was an important part of the cleaning-up process. He rammed the wide-brimmed hat back on his head and pursed his thick lips. So, Cottel was still on his list. He would get a second chance.

'There's someone on that granite crag, Jules,' said Louise urgently.

'Where?'

'That bloody great rock sticking up behind the house.'

Beaurain had to take an instant decision. He had to assume that Louise *had* seen something. Instinctively he sensed there were only seconds left before something happened . . . a man or men on the crag overlooking the house ... a clear view of Henderson's men surrounding the house ... a clear field of fire for automatic weapons to mow down everyone ...

'Withdraw! Withdraw! Henderson withdraw for God's sake now!'

To make his voice carry Beaurain had cupped his hands into a man-made megaphone. He was risking blowing the whole operation. He was risking getting half his men killed if he had guessed wrong – if Louise had imagined something. His desperate shout would have given the whole game away, wiped out Henderson's most important weapon – the element of surprise.

Henderson reacted instantly, but used his own judgment.

'Take cover! Take immediate cover! Attack imminent ...'

Beaurain and Louise saw the horror from their distant vantage point by the copse of trees.

The bay windows burst outwards, disintegrating into a hail of debris which cascaded over a huge area. The steps leading up to the front door took off like a rocket: a huge amount of explosive must have been placed underneath them to catch anyone trying to reach the veranda. The walls of the house were hurtling like shrapnel through the air, shards of wood with jagged ends. The roof rose up as though clawed skyward by a giant hand. And all this was accompanied by an ear-battering roar which temporarily deafened Beaurain.

Harry Fondberg, returning to the house area in the

helicopter, stared in sheer stunned horror at the aerial view. The chopper shuddered briefly as the shock wave hit the machine. Fondberg recovered his wits swiftly, and gave the pilot a natural and humanitarian order.

'Put down on the highway at the entrance to the drive,' he said into the mike. 'And fast!'

And now the fire came. Like so many Swedish dwellings the house was built of wood. A fierce tongue of yellow flame speared its way up through the spreading black smoke, a tongue which danced and grew. The sinister crackle of flames spread fast, devouring the remnants of the house which had stood alone for so many years.

Dr Theodor Norling had not waited at the top of the crag to see the result of pressing his red button. He had scrambled down the side of the crag furthest away from the house and by doing so had saved himself. At the back of the house had stood a large log-pile, ready for the coming winter. The explosion had taken these ready-made missiles and hurled them away from the house with the force of an artillery barrage. Norling heard the thunderous clatter of the logs bombarding the far side of the rock. Then he began moving towards his objective, half-running and half-crouching to escape detection.

*

The helicopter had been damaged on landing. It had been a chance in a thousand, possibly compounded by the pilot's shock at seeing a whole house fly into pieces – but when he landed at the entrance to the drive the rear of his machine was a shade too close to Beaurain's parked Mercedes. It caught the car only a glancing blow, taking out no more than a sliver from the roof – but it was the small tail rotor whose tip had struck the car. The rotor spun off the chopper and skittered across the highway.

'We can't fly again,' Fondberg was informed. 'I'm sorry – but without the tail rotor we've lost our rudder.'

'Not to worry.' The Säpo chief was preparing to leave the helicopter. 'Be ready to radio for medical help – but not, repeat not – until I have checked the situation.'

He met Beaurain returning down the drive while Louise remained near the wreckage, scanning the countryside with her field glasses. Beaurain was running and his expression was grim. He waved Fondberg back and the Swede stood where he was until Beaurain had reached him.

'Harry, get that chopper into the air and start looking.'

'Rotor tail's gone. Pilot chipped your Mercedes when we were on the ground. What's happened up there?'

'Place was one gigantic boobytrap,' Beaurain told Fondberg. 'Suggest anything to you, Harry?'

'Should it?'

Beaurain was talking fast, filling Fondberg in on the position as swiftly as possible. 'How long ago since the Elsinore Massacre? Another case of a large quantity of explosives detonated by remote control. The same hand pressed the button here to turn this house into a pile of rubble. I wanted your chopper in the air looking for the mass-killer – the maniac – who seems to be getting madder.'

'Your men . . .' Fondberg spoke quietly and looked up the drive to where there was a scene like the smoke of battle. 'How are they? I can call a fleet of ambulances.'

'Not necessary, but many thanks. Henderson reacted a split second too early for the killer, radioed everyone to take cover – so they dropped flat. Result – the blast-wave and the shrapnel-effect passed right over them. One or two have cuts and bruises, but nothing they can't fix up themselves. Otherwise you wouldn't see Louise back there doing her birdwatching act.'

'I think she may have found an interesting specimen,' Fondberg observed. 'I'll stay here with the chopper to cover for you if a patrol-car arrives. They do creep about on the E3.'

Beaurain turned and saw Louise beckoning him. He ran back up the drive and now the stench of charred wood was increasing. Black smoke billowed, the fire inside the smoke-filled nest was a searing, crackling inferno. As he came close to Louise who was standing where she could see behind the house, he saw the familiar figure of Henderson in the distance running towards a granite crag rearing up out of the ground.

'What is it, Louise?' Beaurain demanded.

'Norling.'

'Where?'

'I'll tell you if you'll shut up for ten seconds, for Christ's sake!'

'I'm mute,' he told her.

'To the right of that large crag Henderson is heading for with some of his men.' She handed him her field glasses. 'I thought I saw movement in the grass, then I thought I was wrong – then I saw it again. The trouble is his blond hair merges with the landscape. And Stig is puzzled.'

Palme was standing a few yards away, his face smoke-blackened, his stubble of hair singed with the heat which had flared out from the house, holding his machine-pistol ready for action. Now Henderson had reached the base of the crag while Beaurain continued scanning the field of yellow rape Louise had indicated. Surely there was nowhere there a man could hide, let alone keep moving. Then Beaurain saw what she was driving at. And at almost the same moment something else happened. Palme began receiving a message on his walkie-talkie.

There was a deep gulley running across the field of rape and along it a fair-haired man was moving at a steady trot – not so fast that he could easily be picked out, but fast enough to be putting plenty of ground between himself and the house he had just annihilated.

'Why is Stig puzzled?' he asked Louise.

'Stig says the fair-haired man – Oh, hell, it must be Norling – is heading straight for a lake which bars his way.'

'Message from Sergeant Henderson, sir,' Palme put in, proffering his walkie-talkie. 'He says he can see a blond man running towards a lake which he will reach in about two minutes. He has a good view of the target from the top of the crag but the range is too great for opening fire. He proposes sending a cordon across country to surround the fugitive – but would like a word with you.'

'Beaurain here,' the Belgian said into the instrument. 'I want that man at all costs – preferably alive, but dead rather than let him escape.'

'We're moving now, sir,' Henderson's voice confirmed. 'And at the base of this crag I found something odd – show you later.'

Palme took a firmer grip on his machine-pistol and spoke with great conviction. 'We can get him. He has kept to the gulley to make himself invisible, but that gulley winds – it's marked on the map. An old stream-bed. We go straight across country. OK?'

'OK,' Beaurain agreed. He had hardly spoken when Palme was moving at a steady trot away from the blackened ruin, his weapon held diagonally across his body ready for immediate use. Behind the sturdy Swede followed Beaurain and Louise.

They soon saw that Palme knew what he was talking about. Because of their starting point and Norling's present position they had a good head start on Henderson and his circling cordon. The trio led by Palme would reach the blond-haired man first. Arriving at the deep gulley, they went down one side, crossed it, climbed the other side, and Louise gasped when she saw the view.

Without her realising it they had been climbing gently since leaving the area of the house and now they were on a low ridge with the ground ahead falling away from them. The boomerang shape of a lake spread out below, unruffled by even a whisper of breeze, the sun blazing down on the startling blue surrounded by the yellow of the rape. Norling was only a few hundred metres ahead. They had got him!

'The plane – the float-plane – concealed in those reeds!'

It was Beaurain who first grasped Norling's plan of escape and – because of the accident to Fondberg's chopper – how close he was to succeeding. Away to their left and behind them Henderson's men were spread out, in correct military fashion, in a fan-shaped cordon. It was Beaurain who detected the terrible danger.

'Get down! Drop flat for God's sake!'

The fair-haired man had turned, seen the trio and his reaction was immediate. Standing quite still he fumbled inside one of his pockets, fiddled briefly with something between both hands, hoisted his right arm up and bowled the missile overarm. His hand returned to his pocket for a second object. The first grenade was sailing though the air heading straight for where Beaurain and his companions had been standing.

They sprawled flat among the rape, hugging the ground. There was an ear-splitting explosion. Debris rained down on their reclining figures. Norling had their range. Beaurain shouted a second warning. 'Lie still, don't move, don't show him where we are.' He had just finished his warning when the second grenade burst. Again debris was scattered all round them.

Beaurain did not have to shout a third warning. Both Louise and Palme remained perfectly still. Seconds later a third grenade detonated. Then a fourth . . . a fifth . . . a sixth . . .

The grenades were landing further and further away from where they lay. Norling was running to the lake, stopping briefly to hurl another grenade, then running again. Beaurain stood up cautiously. His caution was wasted.

Norling had already reached the float-plane and was inside the cabin, and the engine burst into action. As Louise and Palme climbed to their feet, Beaurain aimed his Smith & Wesson and fired twice. It was quite hopeless. Out of range. 'Use the machine-pistol!' he shouted to Palme.

Palme was already cuddling the stock against his shoulder, but as he did so the float-plane streaked out across the lake and he didn't even bother to press the trigger. As Henderson came running up followed by two of his men Beaurain shrugged his shoulders and lit a cigarette. He watched as the float-plane lifted off and continued its flight at a low altitude, vanishing over the fold of a hill.

'Fondberg's chopper,' Henderson suggested. 'If we get him in the air fast . . .'

'Which we can't – because in landing he lost his tail rotor.' Smoking his cigarette, Beaurain looked down towards the lake where the float-plane had been half hidden inside the belt of reeds. 'Stig, he took off in one hell of a hurry. Go down to where that float-plane was and see if you can find anything. We'll meet you back at the drive.'

When they arrived back on the highway Beaurain told Fondberg the bad news and the Säpo chief put out a call for the float-plane on his radio. 'Not that you can expect much,' he warned Beaurain. 'The trouble is we have plenty of those machines buzzing about in this part of the world – and especially further south where the country is littered with lakes. So what have we discovered?'

'You tell me,' Beaurain suggested.

'The Syndicate's explosives dump – probably stock-piled for bank robberies – and their temporary head-quarters which is now a pile of smoking rubble. That's it.'

'Except look who's coming down the road.'

Ed Cottel had walked. Since the unknown gunman had shot out his two front tyres he had been walking back down the highway. And Cottel objected to walking, couldn't see the point of it when there were things called automobiles available. He gave Fondberg and Beaurain a terse account of his experiences while Louise listened; then he absorbed what Beaurain told him about what had happened to them.

'You say there was a Volvo 245 parked behind the house?' he checked when Beaurain had completed his story. 'None of this makes much sense. One of my watchers reported Viktor Rashkin had left in a Cessna – piloting himself – taking off from Bromma with a flight plan for Kjula. Then he gets in a Volvo 245 and drives in this direction. It turns out that there was a Volvo 245 parked out of sight behind this house. Now you tell me the guy who peppered you with grenades before he took off in his float-plane was Dr Theodor Norling. Are you sure?'

'There's nothing wrong with my eyesight,' Louise rapped back.

'Ed, I'm more interested,' Beaurain interjected, 'in who might be the killer who tried to wipe you out when you were sitting in that hired Renault off the highway.'

'No idea,' Cottel said brusquely.

'And who are all these watchers you keep occupied tracking the movements of Viktor Rashkin?' Beaurain persisted. 'You seem to have an obsession with the Russians.'

'Just with one Russian – because I'm convinced he fits in with the Stockholm Syndicate somewhere. I'll provide you with my record of those movements and see whether you can spot any pattern. As to my watchers – it's taken me God knows how long to build up a network of people throughout Scandinavia at all the airfields and seaports, people who've no idea who is employing them but like the money they get.' A dry smile wrinkled his tanned face. 'I guess Harvey Sholto would blow his top if he knew how I was using the funds I get from Washington. You've no idea how adept I've become at what we call creative accountancy.'

'What we call fiddling expenses,' Louise remarked.

'So now perhaps you understand,' the American continued, directing his remark to Beaurain with a hint of sarcasm, 'my obsession with the Russians.'

'No, frankly I don't. You seem to have forgotten that one of the Syndicate's own people deliberately murdered Serge Litov at Stockholm Central after he had served his purpose. *Touché* – you said the Russians fitted in with the Syndicate somewhere.'

'To hell with you,' Cottel replied amiably.

'How much power does Harvey Sholto have in Washington?' Beaurain asked out of the blue.

'You don't mention his name – even favourably – if you want to keep your job on the government payroll. Officially he doesn't even exist.'

'I see,' the Belgian replied, and Louise wondered what he saw.

*

Harry Fondberg suggested that the entire Telescope force started back for Stockholm before the patrol-car he had summoned arrived. He was going to be the innocent bystander who had spotted the house exploding from the air while on another mission.

On the return journey Palme waited until they were well clear of Fondberg before producing something from inside his windcheater. 'You were right to ask me to check round where Norling took off in his float-plane,' he commented to Beaurain. 'He must have been climbing into the cockpit when he dropped this and there was no time to go back for it.' 'This' was a slim red folder.

'Norling carried a brief-case,' Beaurain recalled. 'It looks as though at the wrong moment the case came open and in his haste to get away he never noticed. The brief-case looked pretty heavy, probably crammed with these folders.'

'Anything interesting?' Louise enquired.

'Give me time – I've only just released the security device. One surprise: the language used is English – or American. The spelling is American – *labor* instead of *labour.*'

'It's a good thing Ed Cottel is travelling in one of the other cars,' Louise remarked. 'I think if he heard that remark he'd blow his top.'

'It might be a better thing than even you realise at this stage,' Beaurain replied cryptically, his eyebrows furrowed as he rapidly read through the sheets contained inside the folder. 'This is a little too damned convenient, isn't it? It could be a plant left behind deliberately. How come if it did drop out of his brief-case when he was climbing into a float-plane on the edge of a lake that the bloody thing isn't even wet?'

'Because,' Palme informed him smugly, 'I found it resting on the edge of an old bird's nest made of reeds and God knows what else – a big nest. And don't ask me what bird! I don't watch them.'

'OK, Stig. We can take it that this is genuine.'

'With Stig's discovery my own little contribution isn't going to rate very high in the history of Telescope discoveries,' Henderson said apologetically. 'I found it at the foot of the far side of the big crag behind the house from where Norling detonated all his explosive.'

Henderson handed his discovery to Beaurain who had turned in his seat and was staring fixedly at the object Henderson was holding. As though mesmer-ised he reached out a hand, took the object and held it in the open palm of his hand.

'What's so exciting about that?' Louise asked.

'Thank you, Jock,' Beaurain said slowly, balancing the object as though it were made of gold. 'You have just handed me the final key and proof I needed as to what the Stockholm Syndicate is really all about.'

'It's the broken-off heel of an elevated shoe,' Louise objected. 'That's all.'

'That's all,' Beaurain agreed sardonically.

*

From his room in the Hotel Reisen overlooking the Strommen and the Grand Hotel across the water Harvey Sholto had put in a call to the home of Joel Cody, the President's aide. It was an arrangement that had been made before he left Washington to fly to Stockholm. Any operator intercepting a call to the White House just had to listen in to *that* kind of call. This way Sholto could be phoning any ordinary individual.

'Appalachian calling,' he opened cautiously.

'Rushmore here.'

Joel Cody himself had answered, and he was alone, so Sholto could start talking. He kept his voice so low that twice Cody had to ask him to speak up.

'Cottel . . .' He said the name quickly and deliberately mispronounced it. '. . . is getting close. I persuaded him to keep his distance earlier today but he's breathing down our necks.'

'Real close?' enquired Cody. 'I mean, you're not panicking over nothing? This is a delicate situation and we wouldn't like it to blow up in our faces.'

'I'm telling you Cottel is within spitting distance of what you wouldn't like your best friend to tell you about. To say nothing of the guy you work for. And that's not all! You ever bought a telescope, one of those things you look through to see the girl taking off her bra in the window across the way? Well, they're also breathing down our necks. Correction – they're breathing down *your* neck. And you know something? I thought you had an election coming up.'

'OK, OK,' Cody replied hastily. 'You're the man on the spot, you decide. You have, of course, our complete backing.'

'With that I should start running. But Harvey Sholto stays in business while presidents come and go – so shove it. And I'll see what I can do.'

Sholto rammed down the receiver onto the cradle before the man in Washington had time to respond. High-powered rifle or revolver, the next time he would be shooting for real. And there were a lot of people to deal with in a short space of time. Just like the old times in Vietnam. He caught sight of his bald-headed reflection in the dressing-table mirror. Still, he had once killed twenty individual men in Saigon in different parts of the city in one day. And that had been to please Washington. Correction: to *save* Washington.

The news which determined Beaurain's final strategy came from an old friend just arrived at the Grand Hotel. The agitation Beaurain had detected when he had visited the Baron de Graer in his office in the Banque du Nord had disappeared. This time the Baron's expression was composed as he sat in an armchair close to the bathroom where Beaurain had turned on all the taps to scramble any possible listening device hidden in the room. But despite his placidity Beaurain saw in his eyes a steely determination.

'We – you – have to destroy the Syndicate, Jules,' he remarked as he trimmed off the tip of his cigar and then lit it slowly, puffing with evident pleasure. 'You might say I have recovered my nerve.'

'Did you ever lose it?'

'The last time I saw you in Brussels I was a trembling wreck – I have had time to think since. The information you need is this. I am, as a minor member of the Syndicate, invited to what they are pleased to call their summit conference. *The scum!*'

'We'll deal with them.'

'Meeting place is supposed to be the liner *Silvia,* now lying a few miles off the coast of southern Sweden near the port of Trelleborg. That's a blind. The real conference takes place aboard the Soviet hydrofoil, *Kometa*. All the leading European financiers, industrialists and politicians who have become members will be taken out aboard power-boats and cruisers from Trelleborg – to meet their American counterparts. They are moving out of Stockholm at this very moment.'

'By what route?'

'Mostly by air. Some aboard scheduled flights from Arlanda to Malmö and then on by car. Others will use smaller and private planes to get them to an airstrip close to their destination.' He began pacing restlessly round the room. 'This Hugo has to be identified and hunted down, Jules. He is the real leader and yet no-one has ever seen his face.'

'But we have heard of him,' Beaurain said soothingly. 'When is this summit due to take place?'

'Hugo – whoever he is – has chosen a curious time.

Once on board *Kometa* the visitors will be taken on a short voyage – it will take place between 20.50 hours and 2.43 the following morning, which coincides tomorrow precisely with the few hours of darkness at this time of the year. '

'And you have no idea at all – even remotely – who Hugo might be?' Beaurain pressed.

De Graer threw up his hands in a gesture of frustration. 'Do you think I have not asked myself that question a thousand times and more?'

'How long have you known these details of the summit conference?' asked Beaurain.

'A message came through on the telephone less than an hour ago. The short notice is obviously deliberate – to give no time to react.'

'Who phoned – a man or a woman?'

'I'm pretty sure it was that girl who phoned me when I was in Brussels. The one I called Madame.'

'Always it is a woman, a girl, who makes these phone calls,' Beaurain said reflectively. He looked at the Baron. 'I cannot thank you enough for the information you have provided. Can I take it that under no circumstances will you attend this meeting on board *Kometa*?'

De Graer stopped pacing and grasped Beaurain's arm. 'I only came here to see if I could help. I am now catching the first flight back from Arlanda to Brussels – but I am taking the precaution of booking my ticket only when I get to Arlanda. No-one except yourself will then know of my departure.'

'Very wise. Take care.' Beaurain shook the old warrior by the hand. 'Louise and I will be leaving for Trelleborg shortly. That is all I am going to tell you.'

Descending in the hotel's splendid lift with its red leather padding and gilt-framed mirrors – which seemed to go so well with the world of the Baron de Graer – Beaurain pondered on what the banker had said. Who, he wondered, really was Hugo?

Chapter Nineteen

The short time before Beaurain's departure for Trelleborg was packed with activity. Beaurain was preparing very carefully for the final clash between Telescope and the Stockholm Syndicate.

His temporary headquarters was the interior of a laundry van, a mobile headquarters Palme kept in reserve in a garage in Stockholm. Similar mobile headquarters inside a variety of vehicles were available in every country in Western Europe. The interior of the laundry van was fully equipped with a high-powered transceiver, a telescopic aerial, maps of every major province in Sweden, charts of the seas offshore, and long-life rations. The van was parked in a side street close to the Grand Hotel.

As Beaurain, sitting on a flap seat at the rear of the van, read signals which had come in from *Firestorm* at sea, Louise stood by his shoulder. Some time earlier, Palme had driven off in his Saab to Rådmansgatan 490. Beaurain's instructions had been simple and direct.

'If the place is empty, rip it apart. I don't know what we're looking for – something unusual, something you feel doesn't fit in with a normal middle-class Swedish girl's way of life, something Norling keeps in that apartment.'

'*Firestorm* is lying off Trelleborg,' Louise remarked.

'Bucky Buckminster is doing exactly what I told him to – keeping below the horizon and using his chopper to mount a series of recces.'

'Well, they've found both the liner *Silvia* and the Soviet hydrofoil *Kometa*.'

'Yes, and the significant thing is that *Kometa* is situated a few miles further out to sea and due south of *Silvia*. So any power-cruiser ferrying VIPs from Trelleborg to *Kometa* can make it appear from shore that it is *Silvia* they are heading for.'

'Will it be a savage encounter?' Louise asked quietly.

'I expect a most brutal and bloody clash with no quarter given on either side. This is an organisation with billions behind it, with men of enormous influence involved. They live in a world all their own where the only thing that counts is the maximum profit. Look at the horror of the Elsinore Massacre – and that was just to make sure one man – one man! – didn't reach us with information. I'm not too happy about any of it.'

'Why?' asked Louise. She watched him while he lit a cigarette and took only a few puffs before stubbing it out. One of the disadvantages of holding a meeting inside a stationary laundry van.

'I think Hugo may have gone over the edge,' Beaurain told her.

'You mean . . .'

'Hugo still, I'm convinced, has his first-class brain functioning perfectly. It's just that he no longer takes human life into account at all.'

'What's going to happen?'

As if on cue, there was a rapping on one of the rear doors, Palme's signal that he had returned from the apartment on Rådmansgatan. Checking through the one-way glass window in the door, Louise released the latch and the Swede scrambled inside. He was holding a blue cloth bag.

'Something very peculiar,' were his first words.

'Which is?' Beaurain prompted him.

'This bag – hidden where women always think no-one will ever look,' Palme said laconically. 'In a recess on top of a wardrobe well above eye level. Contents are interesting.'

Beaurain took the bag and burrowed inside. Two items were neatly stored inside plastic envelopes. They were American passports and when Beaurain showed them to Louise they saw that the photographs and details of the holders were still to be added. 'Final proof – and the mystery deepens,' was his tantalising observation.

'Very illuminating . . .' Louise began.

'We have to make one more visit to Harry Fondberg, another to Ed Cottel, then we all make our way to Trelleborg by different routes and modes of transport. Scheduled air flights, cars – this laundry van must go as our mobile headquarters – and some can go direct to *Firestorm* by boat. Inform Jock to organise the move south *fast*,' he told Palme.

From Harry Fondberg's office at police headquarters, Beaurain used the phone to call both Willy Flamen and Bodel Marker. Fondberg and Louise sat listening to his conversations and Fondberg smoked another of his cigars as he listened and nodded his approval. Eventually Beaurain put down the phone after making his last call.

'You'll all have to collaborate very closely and get the timing synchronised right across Western Europe,' he warned Harry Fondberg. 'You heard me arrange with Willy to co-ordinate with Wiesbaden for Germany and with Paris – and Bodel Marker links up with Amsterdam. God knows they have enough water in Holland.'

'It will be the biggest mass-arrest Europe has ever seen,' Fondberg promised Beaurain. 'And it will happen everywhere at the same time, as soon as the next set of signals start transmitting – you predict tomorrow about midnight.'

Beaurain stood up. 'And now Louise and I must get moving.' He hesitated before he continued. 'We have an appointment which concerns the American connection.'

'The American connection?' Fondberg was puzzled.

'Yes. It's the key to the whole evil system.'

*

The rendezvous with Ed Cottel took place late in the evening at a remote spot off Highway E3 which leads towards Strängnäs. Beaurain had chosen a location on a side road on the way to an old iron mine which had ceased working. The mine was called Skottvångs Gruva, and the meeting point was deep inside a fir forest which closed in on either side of the road like a wall.

The location had been suggested by Palme and marked on a map delivered to Cottel in his room at the Grand so that on receipt he barely had enough time to drive to the rendezvous. The dramatic atmosphere, heightened by the time of the meeting – 10 p.m. – was all part of Beaurain's plan, as he explained to Louise while they were driving along the E3. In the back of the Mercedes Palme sat in silence, his machine-pistol concealed in an oil-cloth sheath.

'I'm playing on Ed's nerves,' Beaurain told her, 'screwing them up to the maximum pressure point, hoping he'll blow.'

'I thought he was your friend,' Louise observed.

'And who is in the best position to fool you? Read history – it always turns out to be the one closest to you. Julius Caesar could have told you – Brutus.'

'But you've known him for decades.'

'Don't forget that house that damned near blew up in our faces – and Ed Cottel kept well clear of it. Another thing, he keeps pointing me at Rashkin and away from Washington. It could even be that Harvey

Sholto is in Stockholm to find out who Ed really is. I'm just not sure – I hope to be after this meeting.'

On this cryptic note Beaurain fell silent, turning off the main highway onto a forest-lined road which had no traffic at all, a road which Louise found creepy in the gathering dusk.

'Sorry about that mistake I made in the lobby of the Grand Hotel,' Palme called out from the rear seat.

Beaurain shook his head dismissively. In a rush when delivering the rendezvous message to Cottel, Palme had used a hotel pad to scribble brief written instructions on the route to reinforce the marked map. On his way back from Cottel's room he had hurried down to the lobby to rescue the pad in case the impression of his writing was imprinted on it. *The pad had disappeared.*

The Mercedes was moving at no more than thirty miles an hour, its headlight beams lancing across the enclosing palisade of tree trunks. Palme leaned over frequently to check the odometer, checking the distance from where they had turned onto the road leading to Skottvångs Gruva. Beaurain was still cruising, watching the dashboard clock which registered 9.50 p.m. 'We're ten minutes early – deliberately,' he remarked. Louise didn't like the atmosphere: Beaurain had not told her what was going to happen. And now there were only three of them left in Stockholm.

The main movement south towards the port of Trelleborg had started and was well under way.

Commanded by Jock Henderson, all the gunners were being withdrawn from the Swedish capital and sent by various routes and differing forms of transport to reinforce the heavy contingent of troops already aboard the fast and heavily-armed steam yacht, *Firestorm*.

'Drop me off here, Jules.'

It was Palme who had spoken after leaning forward again and checking the odometer for the last time. Beaurain dipped his lights, cruised a few more yards, hardly moving, then switched off all the lights and stopped the car.

'Don't worry, Jules, I'll be close enough,' Palme whispered as he opened the door.

'Happy to rely on you. But watch it, Stig. We can't be sure.'

Can't be sure of what? Louise bit her knuckles to stop herself asking questions. Sitting rigidly in the dark with only the illumination from the dashboard she noticed something else. As Palme left the car he did not close the heavy door with his normal *clunk*! He went to considerable trouble to close it as silently as he could.

Then they were moving again, Beaurain switched on all the lights and they were turning a bend and the headlight beams illuminated another stretch of highway hemmed in by dense forest. Here and there tracks led away through the wall of trees, tracks for timber wagons by the look of the deep ruts bored into the ground. They had moved only a very short distance beyond the bend when two headlights came on and glared at them, stayed on for three seconds – Beaurain was checking by his wrist-watch – and went out.

Beaurain stopped the car and Louise sensed the tension although there was no physical contact between them. The twin headlights repeated the process twice – switching on for three seconds and then going out again. So far as Louise could gauge, the car beaming its lights at them was parked at an angle just off the road on one of the tracks. It was ridiculous and yet eerie. In her nervousness she giggled.

'It's like Checkpoint Charlie – you know, an exchange between East and West.'

'Except that this time it's an exchange between West and West.'

'What does that mean, for Christ's sake?'

'An exchange of views. That should be Ed Cottel in his new car.'

'Then it's all right – if it's Ed?'

'If you say so.'

Louise felt a tremble of fury. 'Why the hell do we have to meet him in this godforsaken spot?'

'I told you earlier.'

'To put pressure on Ed? That's crazy.'

'His idea,' Beaurain told her. 'We're here at his request – a meeting between me and him well outside Stockholm.'

'I don't like being out here. I feel something is desperately wrong.'

'Something is desperately wrong. We have to try

and find out what it is, who Hugo is, who really is running the Stockholm Syndicate before we move down to Trelleborg.'

'These signals – car lights flashing on and off.'

'Were agreed when we arranged this rendezvous. They're supposed to identify us to each other.'

'Supposed to?'

'And now the exchange of signals has taken place we head straight for Cottel's car, then stop. So, we will do just that.'

Beaurain, who had kept the engine idling during the exchange of signals, released the brake and drove forward at very slow speed. The Mercedes was hardly moving as he swung off from the road onto the springy grass at the edge of the forest. And as he approached the stationary Renault the vehicle remained dark and without any sign of life.

Beaurain turned the wheel slightly, swinging Louise's side of the Mercedes away from the Renault. He stopped and whispered in her ear before switching off the engine. 'Open your door, slip out and back onto the road. Don't close the door – just push it to. If you hear shots take cover and wait for me to call out to you.'

She hated obeying the order, leaving Beaurain on his own, but her training at the Château Wardin asserted itself. Without a word she did as she had been told, using the Mercedes to hide her from the Renault as she slipped back through the forest to the road.

Left alone, Beaurain took his Smith & Wesson from its shoulder holster, held it by his side and quietly slid out of the car.

'I have a machine-pistol trained on you! Drop the gun, Hugo!'

Hugo!

Two things jolted Beaurain – the use of the name *Hugo* and the fact that the voice was definitely the gravelly tones of Ed Cottel. Also the American had switched on a powerful torch which almost blinded Beaurain – but let him see the barrel of the machine-pistol. Beaurain estimated the muzzle was just about aimed at his gut. At that range and with that weapon the worst shot in the world couldn't miss. And Cottel had taken medals on the firing ranges at Langley. Beaurain dropped his revolver.

'That's better, Hugo. Now let's place our hands on the top of our head, shall we? That's better.' The torch light was doused, which again affected Beaurain's vision. But the American didn't need it – not with a blaster of a gun at such close range.

Beaurain's excellent night vision was now reasserting itself. He could make out clearly the American's silhouette – and the silhouette of the machine-pistol which never wavered as it remained aimed point-blank at its target. He asked another question, enunciating his words with great clarity so they echoed among the dusk descending on the forest. There was a strong smell of pine in Beaurain's nostrils.

'Who fooled you, Ed? Who took you for a ride in a

big way? I have a feeling you've been manipulated like a puppet.'

The gravelly voice sank to a monotone as Ed Cottel began reciting a list of events like a litany, his tone remote and cold. 'You were in Bruges at the same time as Dr Otto Berlin, director of the Syndicate's southern sector. Department of Coincidence? You were in Copenhagen when Dr Benny Horn, director of the Syndicate's central sector, was in the city on one of his rare visits. Department of Coincidence? To say nothing of your presence in Elsinore when God knows how many innocent souls were massacred aboard that ferry to shut the mouth of one man.'

'Watch it, Ed,' Beaurain said very quietly. 'Before I smash your teeth in.'

'No! You watch it, you bastard! I arrive in Stockholm and try to locate the elusive Dr Theodor Norling, director of the Syndicate's Scandinavian sector. He can't be found anywhere. Then he arrives. And hell, who do you think also arrives at the same moment? Ex-Chief Superintendent Jules Beaurain.'

'If you say "Department of Coincidence" again I'll kick your kneecap off,' Beaurain told the American. 'Who's been feeding you this poison?'

'Very clever, Jules. You pretend to be tracking down this Hugo, so who is the last person in the world anyone is going to suspect just could be Hugo? Yourself. And now I'm going to feed you on a platter to Washington – unless I have to press this trigger.'

'Which would be a very convenient conclusion to the whole complex case – from your point of view.'

'What do you mean?' Cottel demanded.

Beaurain's voice had hardened when he made his statement and the American detected a subtle change in the Belgian's personality. He noticed there was also a physical change: Beaurain suddenly stopped wriggling his shoulders as though trying to ease the cramp out of his muscles. Cottel was sensitive to personality changes and an interrogator of many years' experience. He was still trying to work it out when a cold hard rim of metal was pressed against the base of his neck.

'You have three seconds to drop the machine-pistol before I blow your head off your shoulders,' Palme told him. 'My orders are to pull the trigger even if you open fire on Jules Beaurain. I have started counting.'

The shock tactic approach had been worked out by Beaurain in advance and was based on his knowledge of the American's psychology. Cottel was a realist and had long ago learned never to buck the odds if there was another option, a chance to live and fight again another day. He didn't hesitate. He dropped the machine-pistol.

'Walk two paces forward,' Palme ordered.

The American obeyed and behind him Palme

quietly stepped to one side before he scooped up the weapon – in case Cottel had kicked out behind him seeking a vulnerable part of the Swede's anatomy.

'So now, at long last, we get to meet Hugo,' Beaurain said, 'and we have penetrated the American connection.'

'What the hell are you talking about?' Cottel blazed.

'Shut your trap, Ed, for ten seconds. Louise,' Beaurain called out, 'come here and listen to this rubbish.' He waited until she had arrived. 'Meet Hugo,' he invited.

'*Hugo*?'

'To cover his tracks he was going to offer me up to his chiefs in Washington – on a platter was the phrase, I believe. Who is the big man in Washington, Ed? The one you really report to? I offer Joel Cody as a suggestion.'

'I don't report to anyone back in the States any more than I can,' Cottel replied quietly. 'And when I do send anything it amounts to no more than meaningless words.'

'Why?' Beaurain pounced.

'You should know – because I don't know who I can trust. Your Syndicate has penetrated the highest echelons.'

'Someone did tell you I was Hugo.' Beaurain was suddenly convinced the American was not lying. And yet there had to be an American connection. He had proof. 'Who told you?' Beaurain persisted.

'One of my watchers. No, you don't get his name.

Tell your thug to pull the trigger now, but you still don't get his name.'

'Even though he was bought?' Beaurain asked softly. 'Bought to twist the existing facts in a way only Hugo could have done to make everything seem exactly the opposite to what it is? Have you a transceiver in that Renault? You have? Then get through now to the contact who pointed the finger at me.'

'Why?' Cottel asked.

'Because you'll find he's not available. By now he will be dead. He's served his purpose and when a man has served Hugo's purpose he's eliminated. Go on, Ed, get back into that car and use the transceiver to call your contact. He should be available?'

'Round the clock.' The American sounded doubtful. 'Every one of my watchers is now holding himself available round the clock. I'd expected to clean up the whole business within the next twenty-four hours.'

'Starting with me? You were fooled, Ed! *Fooled!*'

'Give me a couple of minutes. Get your man to check me for extra weapons.' He waited while Palme obliged. 'He can hold me in the sights of his machine-pistol.'

Cottel didn't wait for a reply. Slipping behind the wheel of the car he fumbled in the dark, attached a head-set and reached for the microphone. It seemed to Beaurain it was a one-way conversation. Only two minutes later the American climbed slowly out of the car and accepted the cigarette Beaurain offered.

'There are things you should know, Jules,' he said

dully. 'And there is an American connection. Stupid Ed Cottel was chosen to come to Europe because Washington thought he was more concerned with tracking down the Telescope organisation. Making enquiries, quote, as to whether the Stockholm Syndicate existed, close quote, was supposed to be a sideline. I think Washington found out I was directing all my resources and firepower on locating the Syndicate after I came over. I've had trouble making contact back home.'

'You just tried to call up your contact who said I was Hugo, who *convinced* you I was Hugo. Any reply?'

'None at all. And he was supposed to be waiting for a signal from me, staying up all night if necessary.'

'He's probably floating down the Riddarfjärden by now. You see, Ed, he'd served his purpose, so Hugo has disposed of him. You're supposed to have served your purpose now . . .'

'Which is?'

'You should have shot me as Hugo. Then sat down and written out your highly confidential report for Washington. End of any rumours about a Stockholm Syndicate, end of any speculation starting in the American press about who was financing it, end of any horrendous scandal which might break and lose the President the coming election.'

'I think I got most of it wrong.' Ed was deliberately looking at Louise when he made the statement. 'I was conned, but good. Jules, you have any information on the financing of the Syndicate?'

'One of the big contributors is Leo Gehn, chairman of the I.T.E. combine, who is also a generous contributor to the President's campaign war chest. Just imagine those two facts hitting the headlines.'

'You think this definitely goes all the way up to the White House?' Cottel asked tersely.

'Harvey Sholto arrived in Stockholm direct from Washington a few days ago,' Beaurain threw at him. 'Joel Cody phoned the Säpo chief to let him know of Sholto's imminent visit – but didn't let him know Sholto was already in the city. Luckily Fondberg's men at Arlanda spotted him coming in, but didn't follow him. Why should they? And Sholto hasn't surfaced. No contact with Fondberg or anyone. He just went to ground.'

'Sholto! Jesus Christ!'

'And,' Beaurain pressed on, 'neither Cody nor anyone else reported you were coming into Stockholm.'

'They didn't?' There was sheer incredulity in Cottel's voice. 'I kept a low profile to do a better job but I assumed the Säpo people would know I was in town. I don't like this, Jules. Who's next?'

'You are.'

Beaurain raised the .38 Smith & Wesson he had picked up from the ground and fired.

*

Further along the road towards the old iron ore mine at Skottvångs Gruva, a large man wearing a wide-brimmed straw hat and outsize tinted glasses sat behind the wheel of his hired Audi. He had not been able to get any closer for fear of being seen. He heard the sound of three distinct shots being fired.

He waited twenty minutes. Earlier that day he had taken up a position behind a pillar in the lobby of the Grand Hotel. He had seen the Swedish peasant with a head like a melon writing on a notepad. As soon as the man had disappeared inside the elevator he had palmed the pad and walked out. Back at the Hotel Reisen the careful scraping of a pencil had brought up the impression on the next sheet of the pad, showing clearly the words *Skottvångs Gruva.* Now the plan had worked. Cottel's watcher at Bromma had been bought, the information passed to Sholto, who had directed him in turn to pass the misinformation to Cottel, implying that Beaurain was Hugo.

After twenty minutes he drove away towards the mine. In due course he would swing round in a loop which would bring him back onto the E3. A cautious man, Sholto had no desire to encounter any survivors of the forest shooting on his way back to Stockholm – and then on to Trelleborg.

Chapter Twenty

The following morning it was a main item on the news. The mystery lay in the identity and – more precisely – the occupation of the two foreigners who had shot each other. Jules Beaurain had fired the first shot with a .38 Smith & Wesson revolver, so the theory went. A Belgian, he had at one time been in the Brussels police and had risen to the rank of Chief Superintendent. This detail alone was enough to give the item major billing in a news editor's eyes.

The American, a visitor to Stockholm identified as Edward Cottel, had fired one shot at Beaurain from a .765 Walther which, oddly enough, was the hand-gun carried by the police. There had been a second bullet from the Smith & Wesson found in Cottel's body and presumably Jules Beaurain had transported him from the scene of the shooting in a hired Renault.

The macabre location of the American's body was the bottom of a deep hole close to the mine. A wire railing which normally protected visitors from any risk of falling into the hole had been flattened, again presumably when Beaurain man-handled the body out of the car and into the pit.

The Belgian's own corpse had been found a short distance away, collapsed as he tried to reach the Renault. End of story. The detective interviewed had been very firm on this last point. 'The investigation is proceeding . . . no further information available at this stage.'

Harvey Sholto used a payphone on his way to Bromma Airport, dialled the Trelleborg number, and identified himself as soon as the familiar voice came on the line. 'It worked,' he said, hardly able to conceal his satisfaction. 'You've seen the news bulletins?'

'Several times. A classic case of the mirror image technique. You show a man what he's waiting to see and he reacts logically.'

'Except that the logic isn't there.'

'But has it ever been there since we started?' the voice enquired. 'I will see you in Trelleborg. The sea is most pleasantly calm.'

They watched them flying into the airstrip outside Trelleborg. Using the laundry van which had been Telescope's temporary and mobile headquarters in Stockholm, they sat in a concealed position behind a clump of trees. And they recorded in a notebook the identities of some of the most powerful and wealthy figures in the western world.

'That's Leo Gehn,' said Palme, staring through his

binoculars from the front passenger seat. 'He's chairman of . . .'

'International Telecommunications and Electronics – I.T.E. for short,' Albert said crisply as he noted the details – name, time of arrival, type of aircraft and whether guards accompanied the newcomers.

'He's brought someone with him as a passenger – Count Luigi d'Arlezzo, the husband of that poor woman who was strung up at the Grand.'

'Does he look very upset?' Albert enquired.

'He looks relaxed and relieved, the bastard. I suppose now his wife is conveniently out of the way he's playing at running his own banking empire. Hence Gehn taking an interest in someone he wouldn't normally give the time of day to – bet you anything Gehn is making a play to take over the controlling interest.'

'Look at this one who's just arrived aboard a Cessna all by himself,' Palme said. 'Funny thing is he's landed on a quite different part of the airstrip as though he isn't with the main party. Dr Henri Goldschmidt of Bruges.'

A car was waiting for the coin dealer. It was only later that they learned Goldschmidt had been driven straight to a hotel, that he had stayed in Trelleborg after strolling round the harbour area as though interested to see who was attending the conference. He did not even stay at the hotel overnight; very late in the day he proceeded on to Copenhagen.

And on the sea-front at Trelleborg another Telescope team was similarly checking the passengers arriving from the airstrip in a steady flow of limousines. The two-man team, sitting in a Peugeot equipped with a transceiver which kept them in direct touch with Henderson, were compiling their own record as the passengers transferred to waiting powerboats which immediately put to sea.

Henderson, who had returned from his second visit of the day to *Firestorm*, took a cab to within a hundred yards of the Savoy Hotel. There he paid off the vehicle, waited until he was sure he was not being followed, and walked the rest of the way to the hotel.

Room 12 was his destination. He had a brief word with the receptionist who phoned Room 12 and then informed Henderson that M. Chavet would be glad if he would go up immediately. The Scot ignored the lift and ran lightly up the stairs. He paused outside Room 12 and then rapped on the door with an irregular tattoo. The door opened almost at once.

'Come in, Jock,' said Beaurain. 'Louise and I thought you'd have news for us soon.'

'And this is Ed Cottel,' Beaurain said to Henderson, introducing the American. 'He's officially in Room 14, registered under the name Waldo Kramer. You can talk freely in front of him.'

The trio – Beaurain, Louise and Cottel – listened in concentrated silence while Henderson reported on the intense activity at the airstrip and then on the waterfront. He handed Beaurain a list of names of all the people who had arrived for the Syndicate's summit conference. Cottel looked over Beaurain's shoulder, ran his eye down the list and whistled.

'God Almighty, there are men there I'd have sworn were completely above suspicion.'

'Which is what makes the Syndicate so dangerous,' Beaurain murmured.

There were two lists – the one recorded by Stig and Albert and the check list compiled by the two men sitting on the sea-front watching the VIPs transferring from their limousines to the power-boats.

It was the second list Beaurain was studying with a frown; where the watchers had been unable to identify someone – and there were very few such cases – they had written a brief description of the unknown arrivals. One description read, *Two men. One dressed like an American with a straw hat. His companion carried a brief-case.* With his thumb underlining the comment, he showed the sheet to Henderson.

'That has to be Gunther Baum and his companion, the one who carries the Luger in the brief-case until Baum is ready for it.'

'Gunther Baum?' Ed Cottel was interested. 'He's reputed to be one of the most professional assassins in the world. From East Germany but nothing to do with the Commie régime according to our information. Not something to be added to the asset side.'

'He's in charge of security aboard *Kometa*. I'm convinced of it.' Beaurain looked at Henderson.

'When you hit the hydrofoil don't underestimate Baum.'

'What are we going to do now we know where they're meeting?'

Henderson looked at Beaurain who opened a drawer in the dressing-table, took out a ship's chart and unrolled it on the double bed while Louise held the other end. 'This was obtained from a Polish member of *Kometa*'s crew, a man who needs help to get his wife out of East Germany. Remember, Captain Buckminster has stood off Trelleborg for several days. During that time various gunners have been sent ashore in the guise of tourists and made it their business to frequent the waterfront bars. That is how the Pole was found. He is just the man we need secretly working on board that vessel – he controls and watches over the radar defences. I'm not even giving you his name, Ed.'

'My question was, what are we going to do?' Cottel repeated.

'Destroy them.'

'Just like that?'

'Yes – and with the aid of this chart which clearly shows the course planned for *Kometa* during the four hours of darkness when the actual conference takes place.' Cottel was now alongside the Belgian, studying the chart. Beaurain's index finger traced the course of a dotted line drawn on the chart.

*

They met Harry Fondberg at a pre-arranged rendezvous on the outskirts of Trelleborg. Beaurain was behind the wheel of the Mercedes when he picked up the Säpo chief at a bend in the country road. Fondberg's vehicle was nowhere to be seen and the only other occupant of the car was Louise who sat by herself in the rear. Fondberg settled into the front passenger seat alongside Beaurain, and the Mercedes moved off, heading away from Trelleborg.

'East German MfS – state security men – have been coming in on the ferry from Sassnitz both yesterday and today,' the Swede told Beaurain. 'It has almost assumed the proportions of an invasion. A handful linger in the town, trying to look like tourists, which is laughable.'

'Why?' asked Louise.

'You know what the weather is like. This marvellous heatwave during the day and it's still warm at ten o'clock at night. These cretins from Sassnitz are all walking around in short leather jackets and trilby hats! My men tell me they have to be careful not to burst out laughing when they see them. But the majority have gone out by power-boat to *Kometa*, presumably – to act as security.'

'Under the command of Gunther Baum,' Beaurain informed him.

'That homicidal maniac? What does it all mean? He's not MfS.'

'Intriguing, isn't it? I think Hugo has waved his wand again. And you did a marvellous promotion job on the "double murder" yesterday night out at the old iron mine of Skottvångs Gruva. Hugo will be bound to be just that little over-confident now he thinks Ed and I are dead.'

'Just so long as the media never learn the truth,' Fondberg said gloomily. 'They'd crucify me. If you're going to launch an all-out assault on *Kometa* from *Firestorm* tonight and officially I've never even heard of either vessel – why is it so important you appear to be dead? To make Hugo less cautious – I can see that, but . . .'

'To throw him right off-balance when I eventually come face to face with him,' Beaurain said grimly. 'And that might well not be tonight. I have a funny idea. Hugo could be holding a party and not attending it himself although he's supposed to be the host.'

'No, I don't see,' Fondberg said. 'I don't see at all. And you might like to know that at this moment I'm in Gothenburg – and have witnesses to prove it.'

On the June evening of Beaurain's final attack on the Stockholm Syndicate sunset was at precisely 20.50 hours. Over the Baltic darkness fell, concealing the presence of the 2,500-ton motor ship *Firestorm*. Against all international regulations Captain 'Bucky' Buckminster, the ship's captain, was showing no navigation lights. If any vessel approached him on a collision course the radar screens would warn him in good time. Beaurain was going over the details of the assault plan for the last time in the main cabin.

'I trust that everyone fully understands the complex nature of the deception operation we shall be practising?'

Twenty gunners clad in underwater gear, oxygen cylinders on their backs and an assortment of arms and explosives in their possession, stared back at Beaurain and said nothing. Beaurain sensed the usual tension which was inevitable before a major operation.

'I can now tell you we have an ally on board *Kometa.*' Beaurain turned to the outline drawings showing the composition of the various decks of the Soviet hydrofoil. 'It is thanks to this ally that we have this diagram which should make all the difference to the success of our attack.'

'Don't we help the poor bugger?' muttered Albert rebelliously. 'If he's left aboard he'll . . .'

'I was just coming to that.' Beaurain placed his wooden pointer on a particular cabin. 'That is where you will find him waiting, sitting in front of his apparatus. He is a Pole; he is the sonar controller; his name is Peter Sobieski; he speaks English and the password he will repeat to you to ensure identification is *Waterloo, Waterloo.*'

'Pretty bloody appropriate,' Albert commented, 'considering we're trying to wipe out the whole lousy outfit with one blow.'

'Then don't forget that Wellington said afterwards it was a pretty damn close run thing – and I come from Belgium. Now, any questions?'

'Sobieski's sonar is the one thing which could give us away,' Palme observed. 'He will see us coming.'

'So aren't you pleased we have an ally who will be the only person checking the sonar screens. Next question.'

It was important to defuse the tension as much as possible – and yet not let any feeling of complacency or over-confidence arise. A difficult combination. Beaurain tackled the over-confidence problem now.

'But even though we have Sobieski watching those screens don't forget the opposition is – what would you call it, Henderson?'

'Formidable!' Jock Henderson stood up quickly on cue, swung round and addressed the assembled men. 'Sobieski reckons the conference will be guarded by thirty heavily-armed state security types from a special unit in East Germany. For some reason not one of them speaks a word of English.'

'That,' Beaurain interjected, 'I suspect is so they don't overhear or understand a word said at the conference which obviously will be conducted in English. Leo Gehn, the boss of I.T.E., for example, has no other language than American.'

'I had the funny idea,' interjected Ed Cottel who was sitting next to Louise at the back, 'that both languages were the same.'

'We all dwell under our illusions,' chirped the irrepressible Albert.

There was a burst of over-loud laughter. At least, Beaurain reflected, that had eased the atmosphere a bit. He nodded to Henderson to continue.

'These MfS people have been well-trained, may have been warned to expect an intrusion, and Sobieski – again has warned they are armed with percussion grenades for dropping over the side.'

There was a general groan, which was only half-facetious, and Beaurain decided any complacency was rapidly disappearing. In the front row Palme shrugged his shoulders without making a sound. He was one of the most formidable fighters in the room.

'They are also armed with automatic weapons,' Henderson went on. 'We expect them to be patrolling the decks – and yet the object of the exercise is to seize control of the vessel without any undue noise until the last possible moment.'

'Knives in the dark and this,' Albert said laconically. He held up his hand, the edge stiff and hardened ready for a lethal chop.

'On the plus side,' Henderson told them briskly, 'we have the complex and confusing deception operation worked out by Jules Beaurain. With a bit of luck the man controlling *Kometa*'s defences won't know what the hell is going on until it's too late.'

A crew member slipped into the room, made his way to Beaurain and handed him a message. Beaurain looked at it, handed it to Henderson, who glanced at the few words and stood up again.

'Gentlemen! *Kometa* has started to move on her prescribed easterly course. Our own plan now starts to move – phase by phase as arranged.'

Chapter Twenty-One

'Put *Regula* over the side.'

This had been Beaurain's first order and was the opening phase. The large launch, flying the Danish flag, had been lowered into the sea and released. Her engines – far more powerful than anyone would expect inside such a vessel – started up and she disappeared into the distance, heading after *Kometa* at a speed and on a course which would soon bring her up on the port side of the Soviet hydrofoil. And it was no coincidence that *Regula*'s size, shape and colour was very similar to that of a Danish coastguard vessel.

'Launch Smithy.'

Beaurain had given this command when *Firestorm*'s radar scanner showed that the 'coastguard' vessel *Regula* would shortly overhaul *Kometa*. The float-plane, hauled out of the same cavernous hold which had carried *Regula*, was winched over the side and gently lowered onto the calm black Baltic. From the bridge Beaurain watched with field glasses as Smithy took off on a course which would take him precisely between the stern of *Kometa* and the bow of *Firestorm*.

Beaurain had worked out the whole plan on the back of an old envelope. He now gave his third order.

'Launch Anderson.'

Captain Buckminster gave his own order, briefly slowing down the speed of *Firestorm* while Anderson, the pilot of the giant Sikorsky, lifted off from the helipad aft of the bridge. Alongside him sat his co-pilot, a Frenchman from Rheims, Pierre Cartier. Thirty-one years old, small, lightly-built with a pencil moustache, Cartier nursed a sub-machine gun in his lap as the chopper climbed vertically and flew on an easterly course. Like Smithy in his float-plane, their course was aimed for the stern of *Kometa*.

'You think I get a chance to use my weapon?' Cartier asked.

'Don't be so bloodthirsty,' Anderson replied, his eyes on the controls. 'That's just for emergencies.'

'Then I must hope for emergencies!'

On the bridge of the motor vessel Captain Buckminster watched his radar screen as Beaurain walked a few paces to the huge bridge window and peered into the night. They had picked up speed as soon as Anderson had taken off and he thought he could just discern the lights of the Soviet hydrofoil.

'You think it's going to work?' Buckminster enquired.

'If I was in command of *Kometa* I would be as confused as hell within the next fifteen minutes. And we need only about ten minutes for Henderson and his underwater team to hit *Kometa*.'

'Let's hope to God it doesn't start moving and rear up on its foils. Henderson will never board her if that happens.'

'Which is why Phase One concerns a convincing-looking Danish coastguard launch,' Beaurain replied.

Captain Andrei Livanov swore silently as Viktor Rashkin appeared. The latter wore a dark blue naval blazer ornamented with gold buttons and pale grey slacks. His step was springy, his manner brisk. He established a sense of his supreme authority with his opening words.

'Our guests are now comfortable in the main dining-room, so our meeting is about to start. Please proceed at full speed round Bornholm as planned. Get this thing up onto its skis or whatever you call them.'

'Surface piercing foils.'

Livanov, a thin-faced man of fifty who hated having so many Germans aboard, was staring out to the port side where his First Officer, Glasov, was making notes on a pad. Rashkin glanced in the same direction and then his look riveted on what he saw in the distance. The lights of another vessel, and the flashing of a signal lamp.

'What the hell is that?' he demanded.

'Danish coastguard vessel,' Livanov replied, keeping his words to a minimum. It was one safe way he could express his intense dislike.

'Tell it to go away.'

'You do not tell coastguard vessels to go away.'

'Why Danish?' rasped Rashkin irritably.

'Because the island of Bornholm, which we are approaching, happens to belong to Denmark. What is the signal, Glasov?'

'We are to heave to and identify ourselves.'

Without referring to Rashkin, the captain gave the order and the former only realised what was happening when he felt the vessel slowing down, noticed the absence of vibrations beneath his feet and realised *Kometa* was now stationary. Glasov was using a lamp to signal their reply when Viktor Rashkin blew his top.

'Who gave the order to stop the engines? I shall report this act of sabotage to Moscow.'

'Report away!' Livanov snapped. 'If you want our brief voyage to attract no attention we must adhere to international law, we are already in Danish territorial waters, we must comply with the coastguard's requests.'

He broke off and walked rapidly to the window on the port side. Out of nowhere a float-plane had appeared, had *landed* on the calm black sea between the Soviet vessel and the coastguard ship. With its navigation lights on it had the appearance of a firefly and its actions were extraordinary. And now that Glasov had completed his reply to the Danish coastguard, the lamp was flashing again, sending *Kometa* a new signal.

'What's that thing out there?' Rashkin asked.

'A sea-plane. I think the pilot must be drunk. Let's just hope he doesn't head our way.'

The tiny plane did indeed appear to be in the control – if that was the word – of someone who had imbibed too generously. The machine, scudding over the dark sheet of water, was now zig-zagging. It was crazy, quite crazy. And so many things were beginning to happen at once.

That was the moment when Anderson lowered his Sikorsky over the bridge of *Kometa*. His arrival was heralded by a steadily increasing roar. Livanov pressed his face against the glass and stared up into the night. What he saw astounded him.

'Look above us, for God's sake!' he shouted at Rashkin.

The belly of the chopper, which seemed enormous in the night, was almost touching the top of the bridge. Livanov couldn't see any sign of how many men might be aboard the machine. Livanov could only see that if the pilot came down a few feet more there was going to be a holocaust on his bridge. To add to his agitation the din churned up by the Sikorsky's rotors was deafening. A hand grasped his arm; his First Officer, Glasov, was pulling him gently towards the rear of the bridge so he could get a better view of the Danish coastguard vessel. A searchlight slowly began to sweep the sea from aboard the coastguard ship. Glasov shouted in his captain's ear.

'That searchlight from the coastguard vessel is searching for a floating mine.'

'Oh, my God!'

Another voice shouted in his other ear, the voice of Viktor Rashkin, but Livanov detected for the first time a note of uncertainty in the Russian's voice. 'Start up the engines! Immediately!'

'You have seen what is happening just ahead of us and directly in our way?'

Rashkin followed the line of Livanov's stabbing finger. For the first time he noticed the fresh tactics of the drunken pilot with his bloody float-plane. The machine was criss-crossing over the course *Kometa* would be taking if the ship did start moving, moving at right-angles to the Soviet hydrofoil.

'And,' Livanov took great delight in informing this swine of a party boss, 'that searchlight is looking for a floating mine. You wish us to move before they have located it? You look forward to the outcome? *BOOM!'*

Rashkin was suspicious. Too much was happening at once. But he found the appalling din of the chopper's rotors made it hard to think straight. What was happening? He watched the probing finger of light, fighting to detach himself from his present surroundings, from the noise and the activity which was overwhelming his brain. *Never permit the enemy to disorientate you.* During the time when he had trained with the KGB his mentor, a veteran, had drilled the advice into his brain. But where was the enemy?

*

On the 'coastguard' vessel *Regula* there were very few lights – no more than the orthodox navigation lights. Harry Johnson, who had monitored the arrival of the KGB security squads in Trelleborg aboard the ferries from Sassnitz in East Germany, commanded *Regula*.

A lean, tense man of thirty, his face had a scowl of concentration as he stood close to the helmsman inside the wheelhouse and held his wrist-watch in his right hand. The chronometer on the bridge of *Regula* was accurate, God knew – but it was his wrist-watch he had used to synchronise with all the other timepieces before he had left *Firestorm*.

Alongside him stood Jock Henderson clad in his wet suit, oxygen cylinder on his back, face-mask pulled up on his forehead, his automatic weapon clasped in its waterproof sheath. The explosives were inside a separate container strapped to his lower back.

'You'll be leaving soon, Jock,' Johnson said.

'I know.' Henderson was watching the sweep hand of his waterproof watch. He glanced up and checked again: the lights of the Sikorsky which appeared to be sitting on *Kometa*'s bridge; the flitting back and forth of Smithy in his float-plane across the path of the Soviet vessel to discourage any movement. Then the searchlight beam shone out from *Regula*'s stern.

'*Go!*' said Johnson.

Henderson led the twenty-man team over the port side of *Regula*. Once in the water, his face-mask in position, he passed under the keel of *Regula* before swimming underwater direct for the hydrofoil. The magnetic compass attached to his left wrist showed him the precise course to follow – and this was very important considering what Johnson was going to activate in the near future. It was also the aspect of the assault that had most worried Johnson when discussing it with Henderson earlier.

'The underwater vibrations will be terrific,' he had warned.

'So we make sure we're far enough away, we get the timing right and we don't feel a thing – or very little,' Henderson had replied.

'Bloody tricky. I wouldn't like to be coming with you.'

'You'd manage.'

'Then there are the bubbles from your breathing apparatus – from the apparatus of twenty men. Those damned bubbles could easily be spotted by lookouts aboard that Soviet hydrofoil.'

'Which is where Jules Beaurain's scenario comes in – to make them look in the wrong place – or places – at the crucial moment of our approach.'

'There's always the unexpected factor,' the dour Johnson had replied. 'Like the sonar room on the Soviet vessel.'

Alone inside the sonar room aboard *Kometa* the Pole, Peter Sobieski, who had agreed to co-operate with

Telescope, was studying the screen which clearly showed the approach of Henderson's assault team. On such a calm night it was impossible that they should not show up on one of the screens.

Peter Sobieski, a thin, nervous but intelligent man in his early forties, was worried. He had taken all possible precautions. The door behind him was locked so no-one could walk in and surprise him. As he continued staring at the screen, one thing above all else preyed on his nerves. The presence of Gunther Baum aboard as head of security. Sobieski knew he could turn a dial which would fog the scanner, obliterating all tell-tale trace of what was moving steadily closer to the hydrofoil second by second. But, try as he might, he was unable to stifle his anxiety about Gunther Baum.

Gunther Baum was suspicious. As he patrolled the open deck on the port side he tried to work it out: the combination of that ridiculous float-plane, the Danish coastguard ship and the large helicopter hanging over the bridge like a time-bomb. He had suggested to Viktor Rashkin that six of his men riddled the machine with automatic fire.

'Very clever,' Rashkin had commented. 'Positively brilliant.'

Baum had basked in the glow of apparent approval. He was totally unprepared for Rashkin's next statement. 'Suppose the chopper is also Danish coastguard, which seems likely since there is an airfield on Bornholm. We don't want an international incident with the guests we have below! And if I had said, yes, where would the chopper have crashed? Right on top of our bridge! So could you please return to your duties of patrolling the ship and overseeing its defences?'

All this had been taken into account when Beaurain worked out his original plan: if the helicopter hovered low enough no-one aboard would dare open fire for fear of causing a conflagration to break out on *Kometa*. And Baum returned to the open deck fuming, with his companion at his heels, still carrying the brief-case holding the silenced Luger.

Checking that his men were on the alert, he wandered slowly along the port side staring at the inky blackness of the water. Standing by the rail he found First Officer Glasov, a mean-faced man whose every action was based on how it would advance potential promotion.

'Everything does not seem to go according to plan,' Baum said.

'If you had been at sea as long as I have that is what you would expect,' Glasov replied rudely.

Baum was under the distinct impression that the rudeness was calculated, that Glasov wished to get rid of him. Shrugging his shoulders he moved over to the starboard side to check the position there. Glasov watched him go and then turned back to stare at the sea. In the distance a searchlight aboard the coastguard ship was probing for something, but immediately underneath where he stood Glasov saw the light from a porthole reflecting on the water.

Glasov clenched the rail tight with both hands and stared again to make sure his eyes had not played him a trick. Then he saw it again. *A circle of bubbles . . .*

First Officer Glasov practically threw open the door into the sonar room – at least that was his intention. Unexpectedly the door, locked from the inside, refused to budge and he slammed into what felt like a brick wall. When he had recovered he began hammering his clenched fist against the upper panel. Sobieski took his time about unlocking the door quietly, turning the handle and opening it suddenly. He confronted Glasov, fist raised in mid-air for a fresh onslaught.

'Have you gone mad?' Sobieski enquired calmly.

Glasov stared at him in sheer disbelief. He outranked the controller of the sonar room and Sobieski was a Pole which, in Glasov's view, made him a member of an inferior race.

'You cannot speak to me like that!' Glasov snapped and pushed past the Pole who closed the door and quietly locked it again. Glasov swung round. 'Why was the door locked?'

'Security,' Sobieski replied with a wooden expression. 'On the instructions of Gunther Baum,' he lied.

'To hell with Baum. I think skin-divers are at this very moment approaching us and you should have detected them on the sonar by now.'

Sobieski had returned to his seat in front of his screens and controls and he folded his arms over a half-closed drawer. He had to play for time.

'These skin-divers,' the Pole replied in a flippant tone, 'you have seen them riding across the sea blowing trumpets?'

'I have seen the bubbles which rise to the surface from their breathing apparatus,' Glasov told him between clenched teeth. 'So you also must have seen them on your sonar.' He stared for the first time at the screen. 'What is wrong with the sonar screen?'

It was the question the Pole had been waiting for and had been dreading. Since he had deliberately fogged the reception with a turn of a switch nothing showed but static. The Russian walked a few paces further and stood in front of the equipment, the corners of his mouth turned down as he glared at the meaningless image. And Glasov knew enough to work the switches – Sobieski surreptitiously checked the time. This was the very moment when the screen must not be clear. And still the ship vibrated with the roar of the Sikorsky's rotors.

'It is interference,' Sobieski explained.

'We are being jammed? Enemy interference!'

'Nothing of the sort.' Sobieski sounded weary. 'No machine is perfect and they all develop bugs. It is likely that there is a . . .'

But then Glasov turned the switch, the static vanished and a clear image showed of an unknown number of swimmers approaching *Kometa*.

'You bloody traitor! You will be shot! And your family will be . . .'

Sobieski raised his right hand out of the half-open drawer holding a Walther PPK and fired two shots at point-blank range. Glasov staggered, spun round in a semi-circle and crashed to the deck. The Pole dragged Glasov by the ankles across the planks and bundled him into a huddled heap which fitted the inside of the bottom of a cupboard. Fetching Glasov's cap, which had fallen off, he crammed it over his slumped head, closed both doors and locked the cupboard, then ran to the sonar screen and turned the switch again in case of fresh visitors. The invading force would be aboard within minutes or less – provided they were not spotted by Gunther Baum's security patrols.

In the large dining-room of *Kometa* many small tables had been brought together to create one huge and impressive table around which were seated the guests from so many nations. Even aboard the *Titanic* there was less power and influence than was gathered that night aboard the Soviet hydrofoil in the Baltic.

At the head of the table, as befitted his status, was the American industrialist, Leo Gehn, occasionally drinking mineral water, while the rest of the guests consumed ever larger quantities of champagne, encouraged by Viktor Rashkin who made frequent visits from the bridge to soothe his guests.

'A little local difficulty ... concerning some officious Danish coastguard. Doubtless he knows who we have aboard ... it is his brief hour of glory ... briefly to detain with his minor authority such a distinguished gathering ...'

Then the mine detonated.

From this moment on the terror started – terror for those who had themselves used their money and their power to terrorise so many in different countries to do their bidding.

'Explode the mine!'

Aboard the 'coastguard' vessel *Regula,* its captain, Johnson, was still holding his wrist-watch in his hand when he gave the order. He spoke into the small microphone slung round his neck – so the message reached not only the man who detonated the mine let loose to float with the current but was also transmitted to the members of the crew operating the mobile searchlight and the swivel-mounted machine-gun.

The trio receiving the order knew precisely the sequence of events they must bring about. First, the man with the searchlight swung its beam to light on the mine itself; not too difficult a feat since he was wearing infrared glasses.

The moment that happened the second man – controlling the swivel-mounted machine-gun – swung its muzzle, being careful not to aim his gunsight at the mine but only in its general direction, and opened fire. He was using tracer bullets and the Baltic was suddenly illuminated with a miniature fireworks display.

The man whose job was to set off the detonation by remote radio control waited for the first two events to take place. Only when the mine was visible in the searchlight beam, only when a curve of tracer bullets was streaming through the night did he operate the switch. The result was spectacular.

The mine exploded with a dull resounding boom suggesting enormous power. An eruption of water like the Yellowstone Park geyser was superbly illuminated in the searchlight beam. The machine-gun ceased firing. The searchlight went out. Aboard *Kometa* everyone was temporarily stunned. At that moment – on schedule – Sergeant Jock Henderson passed under the hull of the still-stationary hydrofoil.

Kometa was a 'surface-piercing hydrofoil' – a kind of craft invented in Messina, Sicily, a fact not advertised inside Soviet Russia. A large vessel of 2,000 tons, its top speed was thirty knots, which could only be achieved when it was skimming over the surface of the water so that no 'drag' factor any longer applied. Basically the entire vessel, at the pull of a single lever on the bridge, reared up out of the water on what were really massive steel wings.

By careful checking of his waterproof watch Henderson had timed the boarding of *Kometa* to coincide with Johnson's detonation of his mine – the moment of maximum distraction for those aboard the Soviet vessel. A large number of his underwater team were still in the sea, concealed now beneath *Kometa*'s hull, when the mine exploded. They felt a sharp push in the back as the shock wave of the blast reached them. By now Henderson was perched on the starboard surface-piercing foil at the stern.

Half out of the water and just behind him Palme stared upwards at the overhang of the ship's rail, holding a harpoon-gun in his right hand. Using the rope and drag-hook like a lasso, Henderson had swung it round his head until the momentum was strong enough, then hurled it upwards and heard the gentle *thunk* as the rubber-covered hooks took a firm hold on the rail.

It was very bad luck – but in Henderson's view they had used up their share of luck – that one of Gunther Baum's East German security men happened to be patrolling the stern as the ladder took hold. He was taken aback for a few seconds when the grapple appeared out of nowhere, then he unlooped his automatic weapon from his shoulder and peered over the rail. Henderson was a perfect target, silhouetted in his frogman's suit. The security man raised his weapon and took swift aim.

There was a hiss of compressed air, no other sound at all, as the spear released from Palme's harpoon-gun thudded into the German's chest. He slumped forward over the rail, dropping his weapon into the sea. Henderson climbed the ladder, reached the rail, glanced along the deserted deck. Using one hand, he tumbled the man over the side. Palme had already climbed the ladder and a file of men were appearing, their heads bobbing in the water like sea-monsters. Henderson, now over the rail and standing on the deck with Palme, glanced at his watch.

'Less than two minutes before Johnson signals the Russian captain he can get moving.'

'We have just made it.'

Before the engines of *Kometa* began throbbing underfoot, all the twenty men were aboard the hydrofoil. Advance scouts had been sent a short distance forward to deal with any fresh patrols. And Henderson had been very explicit in his instructions regarding this stage.

'According to Sobieski, the Polish sonar controller aboard, we'll be out-numbered by the East German security guards – and those johnnies are trained to prime condition. There are thirty of them. So for as long as possible we use the silent kill.'

The advance scouts – under Palme's command on the port side, under Max Kellerman's command to starboard – were armed with knives and wire garottes. Their instructions were to use firearms and grenades only as a last resort – and preferably not until one of the two section commanders gave permission.

On the port side a second security guard in a leather

jacket took a step forward and then stopped, staring in disbelief. He was still trying to decide whether he had seen the outline of men in frogsuits when one of them stepped out behind him from between two lifeboats and plunged a razor-edged stiletto with a savage upward thrust just below the left shoulder-blade. The East German grunted. He was dead before he hit the deck.

His executioner reported the incident and then cautiously moved again towards the bridge. The head count of guards eliminated was important: it told both Palme and Kellerman how many of the opposition were still alive. As the hydrofoil began to get under way Henderson's task was quite different and exceptionally hazardous.

Several times Jules Beaurain had emphasised the danger of the mission Henderson had suggested for himself. 'You could be very exposed,' the Belgian had warned, 'if they start the vessel up while you're still working on the main foil.'

'I have allowed for that,' Henderson had assured his chief. 'It is a chance I have to take. It is the only way I can attach timer-and-impact explosives to the most vulnerable part of *Kometa*.'

Timer-and-impact explosives were a new device which the mild-mannered boffins at Château Wardin had recently invented. The device worked initially like time-bombs. But the refinement covered the possibility that the timing mechanism might not work.

Independent of the timer, the explosive detonated

instantaneously on impact with another object, and the force of the impact needed for detonation could be varied by setting a meter which was an essential part of the device.

Henderson's objective was now to reach the bow of *Kometa* in the shortest possible time, attach the special explosives to the giant foils in the shortest possible time, and, assuming he survived what Beaurain had called 'a real Russian-roulette risk', he would then make himself available for the final assault against the bridge.

The Sikorsky had been lifted high into the night. In his float-plane the pilot, Smithy, had suddenly adopted more sober behaviour and was flying across the Baltic away from the Soviet ship prior to taking off – leaving the sea clear for Captain Livanov to resume his course. On the bridge the Russian had received the signal from the coastguard vessel informing him that the floating mine had been destroyed, that it was safe to proceed.

Both Livanov and Viktor Rashkin now felt confident that all was well – that the extraordinary behaviour of the helicopter pilot was simply the Danes taking every precaution to ensure *Kometa* obeyed instructions until the danger was past.

'After all,' Livanov pointed out, 'we did see the mine explode! I would not like the bow of this ship to have collided with that.'

'You are, of course, right,' Rashkin agreed. 'And now I suggest we proceed at top speed round Bornholm – which means demonstrating to our guests the thrill of skimming the wavetops. And I must now return to the dining-room.'

Livanov gave the order to increase speed and *Kometa* began to move, a dart of glowing light shooting towards the flashing lamp which was the lighthouse close to The Hammer on the island of Bornholm. *'Skimming the wavetops'* was not the phrase Livanov would have used but it did describe the sensation of travelling aboard the hydrofoil at full power. Reaching out a hand, Livanov personally pulled at the lever which operated the foils. The ship rose up until its whole length of hull was clear of the Baltic – supported only by its immense blades of steel.

As Rashkin left the bridge the two teams of invaders, one led by Palme, the other by Max Kellerman, had silently despatched five of the thirty East Germans guarding the ship. They were also putting into effect the second part of Beaurain's plan – which involved stationing men at the head of all companionways and exits leading to the main deck. Anyone attempting to mount the steps from a lower deck would immediately feel the impact of a harpoon. Both to port and starboard Stig and Max were now in control of the rear half of the ship. Only one man was facing problems: Henderson was in danger of losing his life.

*

The magnetic clamps Henderson had activated held him by the forearms and legs to the huge steel blade as he fought to complete his task. He was now lifted clear of the Baltic which was flashing past below at incredible speed. And the forward movement of the hydrofoil was creating a powerful wind which blew in his face, half-blinding his face-mask with spume and surf, tearing at his body in its attempt to rip him free from the blade and hurl him down into the water where the stern foils of *Kometa* would pass over him, cutting him to mince.

'God damn them!'

He had hoped to finish attaching the explosives and to have hauled himself over the rail and onto the ship's deck before the vessel continued its cruise. Cruise? This was more like a bloody race he thought, and when he wiped his face-mask free of surf smears he could see in the distance a flashing lamp. The lighthouse above The Hammer, the dreaded cliffs at the northern tip of the island of Bornholm which they were approaching fast.

As he positioned the second device underneath the foil – out of sight from anyone looking down from the deck above – the vibrations of the engines pounded his body as though he were operating half-a-dozen road drills. Henderson literally found he was shaking like a jelly. Only by making a supreme effort was he able to position the second device, activate first the magnetic clamps which attached it to the blade, then turn the switch which activated both timer and impact systems.

To negotiate the steep-angled support he had to repeat his earlier performance, switching off the magnetic clamps strapped round his left leg and arm, supported only by the other two holding his right forearm and leg. He then had to haul himself higher with his free left leg and arm. The process then had to be reversed so he could climb higher still up the prop, closer to the hull, this time employing his right leg and arm. His progress was not helped by the wind plucking furiously at him, by the roar of the hydrofoil thundering through the dark, by the engine vibrations which were rapidly weakening his remaining physical reserves.

Don't give up or you're finished!

It was the first time Henderson could remember having felt compelled to consider the possibility, and now he was realising it would be wiser never to look down. In his weakened state he was beginning to suffer from vertigo. The sight of the surf-edged water sheeting past below was dizzy-making. Every movement was a reflex of will-power. He didn't really care whether he made it or not – and the thought galvanised him with self-contempt.

A million years later he hauled himself over the rail and collapsed on the deck, lying still while he waited for his natural resilience to assert itself. That was when the machine-gun fire started, punctuated by the crack of stun and fragment grenades.

*

'Give me the gun, Oscar.'

Gunther Baum reached out a hand without looking and Oscar gave him the Luger immediately. The East German was standing on the port side and had no reason at all to suspect anything out of the ordinary. Ahead of him stretched the open deck. He could see dimly the sway of the lifeboats slung from their davits as *Kometa* showed her honoured guests what she was capable of, moving like a bird. Behind Gunther Baum his companion, Oscar, took a tighter grip on his own automatic weapon now he was no longer concerned with the brief-case.

'Is there something wrong?' Oscar shouted. It was the last sentence he ever uttered. The words were hardly out of his mouth when a missile hurtled towards him. He screamed and staggered back, Palme's harpoon protruding from his chest. Swiftly Baum, who was concealed in the darkness, aimed at a moving shadow and fired. The shadow dropped. Baum shouted in German at the top of his voice.

'Mass on the bridge! Withdraw from the deck!' Then he unscrewed his silencer and fired into the air twice.

Theoretically it was sound strategy, as Palme was the first to recognise. Baum was planning on assembling his men on the ship's equivalent of the high ground – the bridge from where they could pour a hail of gunfire down onto the intruders approaching from the deck below.

Baum reached the bridge because of the swiftness

of his movements, running crouched up the steps and pressing himself upright against the rear of the bridge. From here he could see exactly what was happening. He witnessed a massacre – of his own troops.

On the port side Palme projected the beam of a powerful lamp on his staircase; on the starboard side Kellerman employed the same tactic. Caught in the glare of the two lights, the MfS men jammed on the staircases were targets which could not be missed. There was a continuous rattle of automatic fire from the Telescope men and Baum saw his guards collapsing and tumbling over each other as they went back down the staircases. He raised his Luger and aimed it at the glaring lamp. As though anticipating he had pushed his luck far enough, Palme turned off the lamp at that moment and jumped to one side. Two bullets from Baum's Luger thudded harmlessly into the woodwork beside him.

It was Henderson, emerging on the rear of the bridge from the starboard side, who saw the almost invisible Gunther Baum pressed close to the woodwork. A brief glimpse, he pinpointed his position when the German fired his two bullets. Taking a grenade from his pocket, Henderson removed the pin, counted and then *rolled* it along the deck. The grenade stopped rolling a few inches from the feet of Gunther Baum. There was a flash which illuminated the whole of the rear of the bridge, showing Baum as its sole occupant, a thunder-crack as the grenade detonated.

Baum fell forward, arms out-stretched, slithered over the rail and hit the deck below.

It was time to storm the interior of the bridge, take complete control of the vessel – and destroy it.

Chapter Twenty-Two

'Slow down to five knots,' Rashkin ordered as he ran back onto the bridge. He had come up from below via a small stairwell which led to his cabin and the main dining-room.

'Slow down?' Livanov was confused.

'For Christ's sake give the order – we are under attack.'

He broke off as he heard a loud explosion beyond the rear of the bridge. He did not know that this had killed Baum but he immediately grasped that the opposition had won – they had reached bridge level. Without issuing further orders he disappeared down the small stairwell, paused cautiously at the bottom, a Walther automatic in his hand, saw that the passage-way was deserted and ran to his cabin.

He had already warned all his guests to remain in the dining-room, assuring them that they were in the safest place, that the intruders would be dealt with speedily. Rashkin had sensed that Baum's defences were being overwhelmed, that this would be followed by the destruction of *Kometa* and all aboard her. Someone was taking violent vengeance for the killing of Jules Beaurain. Telescope were in action.

The speed of *Kometa* had been considerably reduced by the time he reached the cabin. A man of great agility, it took him hardly any time to strip off his outer clothes and wriggle himself into the skin-diver's suit he had brought aboard secretly in a hold-all bag. Rashkin had only survived in his present position by always preparing for every contingency – and he never neglected his escape route.

As he unscrewed the porthole cover he was armed with two weapons – a sheath knife and the waterproof watch attached to his wrist. It was most fortunate that his cabin was on the starboard side. As he swung back the cover he could see clearly the warning flashes of the lighthouse above The Hammer on Bornholm. And he calculated the hydrofoil was no more than a couple of miles from the Danish island.

Climbing backwards through the porthole, he lowered himself until his body was hanging against the hull, supported only by his hands. He let go without hesitation or trepidation, knowing that at this position there was no risk of his hitting the submerged foil – the speed *had* dropped to five knots and the vessel was moving like an ordinary ship. There *was* a risk, however, in getting caught in the stern undertow, hurled into the wake and chopped to pieces by the propeller.

He felt his feet catch the slow-moving hull and kicked out with all his strength, lunging himself backwards and away from the hull which was gracefully sliding past him. Then, still lying on his back, he began to swim with strong purposeful strokes. Behind him the hull went on gliding past. Above he saw the lights of the dining-saloon. The ship seemed oddly deserted.

The interior of the bridge resembled a slaughterhouse. A few of Baum's surviving security guards had retreated there to join Livanov just before Henderson ordered the final attack to begin. He used one word.

'Grenades!'

Three minutes later, followed by Palme and several of his gunners, he entered the deathtrap. He first checked the steering gear. Someone – doubtless Livanov – had at the last moment turned the vessel onto automatic pilot. Like a robot – or a ghost ship – the huge hydrofoil *Kometa* was cruising slowly across the Baltic. He began organising the evacuation of his own men: three were dead, seventeen had survived due to the element of surprise and the co-operation of Peter Sobieski. Palme had personally found the Pole and brought him to the bridge. Henderson was talking to Max Kellerman who had just arrived on the bridge.

'What is the position with that international scum waiting in the dining saloon? The élite of the Stockholm Syndicate?'

'Trapped inside the saloon. The special section fought its way down, wiped out the guards and then welded up the doors with the equipment they brought. The passengers might get out if they try smashing the windows, but I don't think they will try it in time. The shooting rather discouraged exploration.'

'Fix the bombs to the doors, then leave – all of you – by the smashed windows,' said Henderson. 'I stay until I get this damned ship moving.'

'You'll have trouble leaving her,' Palme interjected. 'I mean when she's travelling at top speed. And the rescue boats are coming in.'

'I said fix those bombs,' Henderson repeated.

It was the green Verey light Henderson had fired into the night sky which had summoned the rescue boats. Coming up fast behind *Kometa,* the British motor vessel with Beaurain and Louise aboard and commanded by Captain Buckminster had paused after the green flare exploded like a firework.

'My God! Jock's done it!'

Louise was so relieved that she hugged Beaurain publicly as they stood on *Firestorm*'s bridge. Already power-boats lowered over the side were plunging through the night towards the slow-moving *Kometa,* their searchlights turned on full power to locate Telescope's gunners who would be diving into the sea.

Behind the wake of *Kometa,* which was still moving at five knots, a series of tiny lights were beginning to appear, all bobbing on the water. Power-boats despatched from *Firestorm* were already slowing down, each heading for a light.

The 'coastguard' vessel *Regula* had returned to its mother ship and was being winched aboard prior to being lowered, dripping with sea water, into the cavernous hold of *Firestorm*. And by now Henderson was alone on the bridge, leaning out of a smashed window as he watched the last gunners leaving. He was enclosed inside the bridge with the bodies of the dead East German security guards and attached to all entrances to the bridge were the special bombs – bombs which exploded outwards on detonation *away* from the interior of the bridge. The objective was to ensure that anyone who might escape from the dining-room could never reach the controls on the bridge alive.

It had been Viktor Rashkin's plan to swim the two miles to Bornholm's shoreline, taking his time, but as he saw a power-boat with one man aboard heading in his direction he took a swift decision. The power-boat was heading on a course which would take it past him by about twenty yards. He waited for the right moment, hoisted himself briefly out of the water and waved.

The crewman from *Firestorm* saw him and changed course, reducing speed. His orders were to pick up as many men as he could in the shortest possible time.

The fact that the man swimming in the sea carried no flashing light did not strike him as strange, nor did he notice that the colour of the frogman's suit was wrong. He hauled his first rescue aboard.

'How did it go?' he asked before he started up the engine to continue the night's work. He was gazing at the man he had picked up who was removing his face-mask with his left hand while his right hand tugged at some equipment behind his back. Both men were now seated and facing each other.

'It went well. All according to plan,' Rashkin replied.

'Beaurain will be pleased . . .'

The rescuer broke off in mid-sentence. He had seen Rashkin's face – which briefly expressed alarm at the reference to Beaurain – and knew that this was not one of Henderson's gunners. And then Rashkin's right hand swung round from behind his back and plunged the knife it held up to the hilt in the chest of his rescuer.

The man gurgled, his eyes stared, he slumped forward. Rashkin used both hands to heave him over the side and then gave all his attention to what was happening around him. Switching off the searchlight at the bow of his own power-boat, he turned on the throttle. Then he guided the power-boat towards the west coast of Bornholm. He had earlier taken the trouble to read about the island and he was heading for a quiet stretch of the Danish shore. It always paid to take every contingency into account. He was now trying to recall the flight times of the local aircraft which flew from Rønne airfield to Copenhagen.

Inside the huge dining-room of *Kometa* the members of the Stockholm Syndicate seemed to be gripped by paralytic fear, an emotion which froze all power of decision. At the head of the table Leo Gehn, one of the most powerful men in the western world, sat like a Buddha, apparently working out the potential profits from the region of the north European sector allocated to him earlier in the meeting. When Count d'Arlezzo, a slim Italian who, conversely, could not keep still, peered over the American's shoulder he saw to his horror that Gehn was repeating on his pad the same figures over and over again.

Most of the rest of the thirty people present stayed well away from the doors and pressed their faces against the windows. They were staring at the flashing lamp of the lighthouse above The Hammer of Bornholm. Ironically, the arbiters of blackmail, murder and wholesale intimidation were stricken with indecision.

On the bridge Henderson left the ship following the route the others had taken, but under rather different circumstances. The *Kometa* was now reared up on its giant foils. The vessel was moving at its top speed of thirty knots. The hydrofoil was on a fixed course plotted by the Scot and was working on automatic pilot. He climbed out of one of the smashed windows and made for the rail as the wind hit him. Holding on to an upright, he flexed both legs, waiting for the ship to ride on an even keel if only for a few seconds. *Now!*

He dived outwards and downwards, passing well clear of the foil and plunging vertically into the Baltic – far enough away, he hoped, and deep enough down to clear the lethal clawing suction from the propeller. As he surfaced he was amazed to see how far *Kometa* had travelled, a receding cluster of lights. He pressed down the switch which turned on the red light attached to his head-gear. Recovering from the impact of the deep dive he saw close by the power-boat despatched from *Firestorm* with the sole purpose of rescuing Henderson.

The vertical cliffs of The Hammer are protected by isolated pinnacles of rock which rise up out of the sea like immense rocky daggers. Round the base of these leviathans of nature the sea swirled gently, hardly moving, so still was the Baltic on that night and at that hour. *Kometa* hurtled on like a projectile, reared up on its foils, approaching The Hammer at right angles. The last moments must have been a terrifying experience for the men who had planned to weld all the evil in the West into one huge crime syndicate. Then *Kometa* struck.

The collision between flying metal hull and immovable rocky bastion was shattering and thunderous. But fractions of a second later it was followed by the detonation of the explosives Henderson had attached to the foil – explosives which were timed to go off within fifteen minutes, but which also detonated on any major impact. The meeting between *Kometa* and The Hammer was a major impact. The ship fragmented instantly. The explosion hurled one of the foils high in the air before it crashed back into the sea. The hull actually *telescoped*, squashing like a concertina before the bow sank, so, for a few moments, the stern hung in the air.

A plume of black smoke rose from the base of The Hammer, dispersed by a gentle breeze which was now blowing. Then there was nothing. No trace that *Kometa* had ever existed. And only the sound of the power-boat's engine as it sped back towards *Firestorm*.

Sitting motionless in the stern Beaurain was unusually silent. He pointed out to no-one what he had also seen – the cotton-thin wake of a power-boat proceeding south of them at a measured pace towards the west coast of Bornholm. When he later heard that one power-boat had mysteriously not returned he knew that Viktor Rashkin had escaped.

Chapter Twenty-Three

The signals went out from *Firestorm* at midnight. Beaurain sent them in prearranged codes to Fondberg waiting in Stockholm, to Marker waiting at the strangely-shaped police headquarters in Copenhagen, and also to Chief Inspector Willy Flamen in Brussels.

By ten minutes after midnight the biggest dragnet ever launched on the continent was under way as detector vans and fleets of patrol cars waited for a spate of Syndicate transmissions. They started at exactly three in the morning. Fondberg phoned Beaurain over the ship's radio-telephone shortly afterwards.

'What was the significance of your timing?' the Swede asked.

'Because someone must have reached Bornholm about midnight. His first task would be to send a message warning what is left of the Syndicate of the catastrophe.'

'What catastrophe?'

'Wait for news from Bornholm tomorrow morning.'

'Anyway you were right! It's working!'

Fondberg sounded excited. All over Europe the

detector vans were homing in on the sources of the mysterious transmissions – because for the first time they were not looking on the roads. They were concentrating on the *waterways*. And due to the emergency the transmissions were prolonged.

In Belgium, France and Holland, barges were being boarded as the Syndicate's radio operators were caught in the middle of transmitting. In Denmark, ships in the Øresund were being boarded. In Sweden, launches and cruisers on the waterways inside Stockholm were being raided. In Germany the barges were on the Rhine. And by launching synchronised attacks at precisely the same moment there was no opportunity for one section of the Syndicate to warn another. At one sweeping blow the entire communications system – without which the Syndicate could not operate – was wiped out.

'A fair-haired girl left the apartment at Rådmansgatan 490 and took the airline bus to Arlanda. She is expected to arrive in Copenhagen at . . .'

Fondberg called Beaurain again on *Firestorm* as the vessel raced westward away from Bornholm, heading for the Øresund and Copenhagen. As arranged with Beaurain earlier, Fondberg had mounted a round-the-clock surveillance on the Rådmansgatan apartment. Two of his men had followed her and, on arrival at Arlanda, they had watched her check in at the Scandinavian Airlines counter for the next flight to Copenhagen.

'. . . 08.30,' Fondberg continued. 'And the first Danair flight out of Rønne on Bornholm is Flight SK 262 departing Rønne at 08.10 and arriving Copenhagen at 08.40. Who do you expect to be aboard that aircraft?'

'Better you don't know, Harry,' Beaurain had replied. 'And thanks for the information on the blonde girl. Be in touch.'

He broke the connection on the radio-telephone and looked at Louise who had been listening in. She was frowning with perplexity.

'Blonde?' Louise queried. 'Can that be Sonia Karnell?'

'It can be – and it is,' Beaurain assured her as he rubbed his bloodshot eyes. When had he last slept? He couldn't be sure. 'A blonde wig,' he explained.

'Of course. God, I must be losing my grip. But I'm completely shattered. What did you mean by saying we must break the American connection before Harry Fondberg phoned? And who is flying into Copenhagen from Bornholm?'

'Answer both your questions when I'm sure.' Beaurain took one of his sudden decisions. 'I think we'll get to Kastrup Airport ahead of everyone – we'll get Anderson to fly us there in the Sikorsky. And we'll take some back-up, including Stig.'

He checked his watch. Four o'clock in the morning.

It had been daylight for over an hour and the sky had all the appearance of yet another glorious, cloudless day of mounting heat. They should be at Kastrup by five o'clock; there would be very little activity at that hour and – with a little luck – no-one to observe their arrival in the Danish capital.

They had passed perfunctorily through Customs and Immigration and were moving into the main reception hall when Louise stopped and gripped Beaurain's arm. Gently she pulled him back behind a pillar, then gestured with her head towards a closed bookstall. Beaurain peered cautiously round the pillar while Palme and the other three men froze behind them. Beaurain studied a man standing in profile by the bookstall, holding a magazine which he appeared to be reading.

'Ed Cottel,' he murmured.

'The American connection,' Louise said.

They retreated out of the reception hall and deeper inside the airport buildings. Palme conducted his reconnaissance and returned with the news.

'They have troops all round the airport,' he reported. 'All possible exits are covered and we're heavily outnumbered. Men in cars apparently waiting for passengers. Men in taxis. There are two men out on the highway pretending to deal with a defective street lamp.'

'Where did you get the boiler suit from, Stig?' Louise asked.

Palme looked apologetic. 'I found a cleaner in the toilets.'

'You knocked him out cold and hid him in a closet,' Louise told him.

'Yes. But in this I was able to wander everywhere – especially when I was carrying the pail. No-one *ever* notices a man in a boiler suit carrying a pail.'

Only Beaurain appeared unperturbed. Palme looked round to make sure they were unobserved, then produced from his jacket underneath the boiler suit three guns – a Colt .45, a Luger and a small 9-mm. pistol which Louise promptly grabbed as Beaurain took the Luger.

'The mechanic who handled the chopper when we landed here,' Palme explained, 'is a friend of mine and keeps weaponry for me so he can slip it to me after we've passed through what are pompously known as official channels.'

'Ed Cottel is going to take us out through his own troops,' said Louise. She took a firm grip on the pistol with her right hand and covered the weapon with her folded coat. 'Any objection?' she asked Beaurain.

'Go ahead.'

She walked briskly back into the main reception hall and Beaurain followed more casually. She made no attempt to conceal her presence and marched straight towards where Ed Cottel was still standing pretending to read his magazine. Not for the first time Beaurain admired her sheer nerve, her audacious tactics. She reached Cottel who looked up and spoke.

'Don't any of you leave the airport, Louise, for God's sake. It is surrounded by extremely professional killers.'

'Under this coat I have a gun aimed at you point-blank. Now, as a matter of academic interest, who are these killers?'

'They're the American connection,' said Cottel matter-of-factly. 'But that's not me. I guess I still have some explaining to do.'

Beaurain was behind her. He took Louise's arm and squeezed it.

'I'm going to use that payphone over there for a minute,' he said. 'While I'm doing it, why don't you two exchange experiences – and maybe it would be safer to walk back further inside the building complex and join Stig and the rest of them.'

They sat on a seat by themselves while Cottel explained it to Louise. A short distance away Palme kept watch. It had all started when Washington had asked Ed Cottel to come out of retirement and do one last job for them – track down the Telescope organisation. He had agreed and then at the last minute, when it was too late to substitute anyone else, had informed his superiors he was combining the Telescope mission with a personal investigation into the Stockholm Syndicate.

'When Harvey Sholto said "What's that?" in front

of certain top aides who are next to our President – and they all tried to look as though they didn't know what the hell I was talking about – I knew something was wrong. From that time on I was a marked target on a limited schedule.'

'What does that mean?' Louise asked.

'That I would be allowed to proceed to Europe in the hope that I'd expose Telescope.' He gave a lop-sided grin.

'Whatever that might be. Once I'd done that, I'd be liquidated – probably by Harvey Sholto himself. Luckily the Säpo chief's men in Sweden spotted the early arrival of Sholto so I took extra precautions to keep underground. Once they realised I was devoting all my energies – using all the network of informants and helpers I built up over twenty years – to crack the Stockholm Syndicate, my limited schedule, as they so nicely phrase it, ran out. They sent out a *Nadir* signal on me. To be terminated with extreme prejudice.'

'Why is Washington so worried?'

'Because most of the President's electoral campaign funds come from precisely those American industrial corporations who are members of the Syndicate.' Cottel's voice became briefly vehement. 'You know how our President avoids issues likely to embarrass him – he looks the other way, pretends they don't exist.'

'I still don't understand it fully, Ed. This Harvey Sholto – how much power has he? What is his official position?'

'No official position at all any longer. More power than anyone else in Washington below the rank of president because of what he knows. Christ, Louise, I've as good as told you – that's the guy who photocopied all Edgar J. Hoover's files! Those files had all the dirt on every influential figure in the country. He's built up dossiers so dangerous, no-one in Washington dare touch him. But what was the use of just scaring people? And then he thought up the idea of the Stockholm Syndicate. He contacted Viktor Rashkin in Stockholm – I suspect they must have met secretly in the Far East earlier.'

He broke off as Beaurain reappeared, his former fatigue no longer apparent, and he checked his watch as he came up to the seat. 'We'll be out of here in five minutes, maybe less.'

'How?' Cottel asked sceptically.

'By courtesy of Superintendent Marker of Danish police Intelligence. At the moment a fleet of police cars full of armed men is racing to Kastrup. I told him where Sholto has placed his troops – it is Sholto, isn't it, Ed? I thought so. Those two pretending to repair a street lamp are in for a shock.'

'There'll be shooting?' Cottel queried.

'Not a shot fired would be my guess. Viktor Rashkin is due here aboard a Danair flight from Rønne and they won't want the place swarming with police. I think I can hear police sirens now.'

'You can't touch Rashkin,' the American warned. 'The bastard can always claim diplomatic immunity.'

'So we wait a few hours and I think Rashkin will solve the problem for us. Yes, you can hear the sirens. Sound to be a hell of a lot of them.'

There was no shooting. Bodel Marker had sent an overwhelming force to Kastrup and none of the men waiting for Beaurain put up resistance. The fact that they carried firearms was more than sufficient reason for putting them behind bars. Beaurain then explained the final move in detail to Marker, one of the key men responsible for smashing the Syndicate's communications system. He obtained the Dane's full agreement to his plan, not all of which was strictly in accordance with the law. And it was Marker who provided transport in the form of unmarked police cars for Beaurain and his companions to move into the city.

'What was all that about?' Louise asked as they drove away from Kastrup.

Marker had provided them with three cars. In the lead vehicle, a Citroën, Beaurain was driving with Louise beside him while in the rear sat Palme and Anderson, the laconic Sikorsky pilot. The two cars following them, both Audis, contained Max Kellerman and five of Henderson's gunners. Henderson was driving the third car, guarding their rear.

'I will guide you to the arms depot,' Palme announced.

'Here in Copenhagen?' queried Louise.

'Over this bridge and turn right,' said Palme calmly.

'Into the Prinsesse Gade.' The three cars pulled into a drab side street and parked. Minutes later Palme had returned with his suitcase and they were on their way again, heading back to the main road.

'Where are we going now Stig has tooled up, as he would say?' Louise enquired.

'To the house on Nyhavn – which is where the whole horrendous series of events is going to end unless I've guessed wrong.'

'You wouldn't care to elaborate?' They drove over the Knippels Bro into the heart of Copenhagen.

'The American connection is Harvey Sholto – Ed explained about the Edgar Hoover dossiers. With those and his high-level connections Sholto organised the Syndicate membership in the States. He links up with Rashkin, who organises the European end; I suspect that Rashkin has been running a one-man band.'

'With the aid of a three-man directorate?'

'Let's see what happens at the house on Nyhavn,' Beaurain said.

Ed Cottel, who had stayed behind at Kastrup, watched through a pair of high-powered glasses the arrival of the DC-9 jet – Danair Flight SK 262 from Rønne. As he watched passengers filing off the plane he began to worry. He couldn't identify Viktor Rashkin. Then he had an idea. He hurried to the main exit where cabs waited for fares.

He was rewarded for his flash of inspiration – or so he thought, when he saw a Mercedes with Soviet diplomatic plates pull in at the kerb. A slim man carrying a Danair flight bag appeared, the rear door was opened by the chauffeur, closed, and the limousine glided away, followed by one of Superintendent Marker's 'plain-clothes' cars when Cottel gave the driver a signal. Sweating with the anxiety he had felt, Cottel waited a little longer, watching the departing passengers before he walked rapidly along the airport building front to a parked car which was Marker's control vehicle and equipped with a transceiver. He slid in beside the man behind the wheel.

'I'd like to report to Jules Beaurain.'

'Be my guest,' the Dane invited, handing him the microphone. 'If you can get through it will be a miracle – on a clear day like this the static is bloody murder – what with the high pressure area over Scandinavia.'

'Talking of high pressure . . .' Cottel mopped his damp forehead as he called Beaurain. The Belgian replied at once with great clarity.

'The big R.,' Cottel began, referring to Viktor Rashkin, 'had a Merc with C.D. plates waiting to pick him up. Our friends have followed. Funny thing, when I watched the passengers disembarking earlier I couldn't spot him through the glasses.'

It was just one of those throwaway observations you make, particularly when you have been keyed up, when you are short on sleep, when you thought you had blown it and then found you hadn't. The Belgian's reaction was tense, almost explosive.

'Listen to this description, Ed. A grey-haired man of medium build. Probably a snappy dresser, could even be wearing a velvet jacket with gold buttons. Rimless glasses. May be wearing a skull-cap like Orthodox Jews go in for.'

Cottel stared at the microphone open-mouthed, then got a grip on himself. 'A guy just like that got into a beat-up Volkswagen as the limousine took off. I didn't take much notice of him – and he wasn't carrying a Danair bag.'

'He wouldn't be,' Beaurain informed him. 'You wouldn't recognise him, but Dr Benny Horn has just arrived in Copenhagen. You're waiting now for the flight bringing in Sonia Karnell from Stockholm? Good. I think we're all going to meet up at the house on Nyhavn. And good luck – no-one has yet located Harvey Sholto.'

'You think he's in the city too?' Cottel asked grimly.

'He has to be.'

For the first time in weeks the weather changed as they approached Nyhavn. The sky clouded over, a faint hint of mist drifted in from the sea and, as they arrived at the familiar basin of water, the seamen's bars on the left and tourist shops on the right, it began to drizzle. A fine spray of moisture descended on the tangle of ship's masts in the basin. The stones in the street were moist. The convoy of three cars drove a short distance past the end of the basin, out of sight of Nyhavn, and then parked.

'They *may* have watchers observing Horn's house,' Beaurain warned, 'so our first task is to locate them and take them out.'

'*May*?' Louise queried. 'The Syndicate always has watchers.'

'That was before this morning.'

'But they still had Kastrup airport staked out with men,' she objected. 'You had to get Marker to send out a whole team to pick them up.'

'That was because Rashkin was coming in. He would have phoned Copenhagen from Bornholm and asked for protection – heavy protection – to be laid on after what happened to *Kometa*. But the Syndicate in Europe is coming to the end of its resources, its power is broken, the leaders went down with the Soviet hydrofoil.'

'Then who are we expecting to see at the house on Nyhavn?'

'Hugo.'

Palme opened the suitcase from the arms deposit flat in Prinsesse Gade, and handed out weapons and ammunition. All hand-guns were equipped with silencers. He conferred briefly with Max Kellerman.

'There is a man watching from the flat almost opposite – there. I'll take him. Then there is a man on the deck of a fishing vessel making too much of looping up coils of rope. He's moored outside Horn's place. You take him.'

It was very quiet in the drizzle as Palme and Kellerman moved off down different sides of the basin, both of them adopting a sailor's way of walking, merging with the odd man who even at that hour came staggering up the steps from one of the basement bars. Palme went into the building and up to the first floor flat where he had spotted his watcher. He kicked the flimsy door in and let the force of his own momentum carry him straight across the sparsely furnished room. In his right hand he held a Luger with a silencer. A man who had been staring out of the open window, sprawled on a sofa, grabbed for the automatic weapon by his side. Palme shot him twice and peered out of the window.

The seaman tending coils of rope had disappeared from the deck of the fishing vessel. In his place crouched Max Kellerman who was now doing the same job. It put him immediately facing the front door leading into Dr Benny Horn's house.

A few minutes later he signalled to Beaurain and Louise as they stood looking into the window of an antique shop. The area was clean. And, standing on the top step and close to the front door of Horn's house, Palme had found the right skeleton key to open the expensive security lock. He walked in ahead of Beaurain and Louise, Luger extended in front of his body, eyes flickering up the narrow staircase, along the narrow hallway, his acute hearing sensitive to the slightest sound. The place *smelt* empty to Palme; occupied not so long ago but empty for the moment.

The calm waters of the shipping basin were dappled with drops of fine rain – and Max Kellerman laboriously coiled rope on the deck of the fishing vessel. Louise stepped over the threshold of Dr Benny Horn's house and Beaurain closed the door.

'The place is clean.'

In an astonishingly short space of time Palme had checked the ground floor, run upstairs, checked the first floor, returned to the hallway, vanished down a flight of steps behind a door leading to the basement and reappeared to make his pronouncement. He was a big man, Louise thought, yet he could move with the grace and speed of a gazelle.

'A kind of library room at the front,' Palme explained, pointing to a door. 'Bookshelves from floor to ceiling, heavy lace curtains masking the window overlooking the front . . . Kitchen and dining-room at the back with rear door on the first floor opening onto a fire escape down into a small yard. There is an exit into a side street from the yard. One of the gunners found it and stationed himself there. No-one gets in here without us knowing.'

'Then the front room to await our guests?' Beaurain suggested.

Outside the drizzle continued to fall and Max

Kellerman ignored the fact that he was getting wetter and wetter.

Sonia Karnell was the first to arrive at Nyhavn. She arrived in a taxi from Kastrup Airport, paid off the driver and climbed the steps, the drizzle forming a web of moisture on her jet black hair. In her left hand she had the key ready; in her right she carried a suitcase and from a strap dangled a shoulder-bag.

It was the shoulder-bag Louise Hamilton was studying as she kept well back inside the library room and watched through the heavy lace curtains. Beaurain was also inside the room, standing pressed flat against the wall close to the opening edge of the closed door.

'She's suspicious of something,' Louise hissed.

The Swedish girl had looked back at the deck of the fishing vessel moored to the quay. She saw the wrong man coiling rope. *She saw Max Kellerman.*

Kellerman reacted instinctively. From under a fishing net he raised the barrel of his sub-machine gun, one of the weapons Palme had distributed from his arms deposit. No-one else was close enough to see it. Karnell saw it. She turned the key, dived into the hallway, slammed the door shut behind her and leant for a moment against the side wall. Louise walked out of the library room.

'Hello, Sonia. A long way from the Rådmansgatan.'

Louise was holding the pistol aimed point-blank,

but the Swedish girl was either a suicide case or guessed these people did not want the sound of shooting yet. She leapt at the English girl like a tigress, dropping the suitcase, her hands extended like the claws of an animal. She aimed for the eyes. Louise hit her with the barrel of the pistol across the side of the temple. Karnell felt the side of her face and blood oozed between her fingers, the colour matching the tint of her nail varnish.

'Drop the shoulder-bag, Sonia,' Louise ordered. 'Slowly – try and grab your weapon and I'll shoot you in the stomach.'

She watched while the shoulder-bag dropped on the hallway floor to join the suitcase. She was alone with the girl; Beaurain had remained invisible inside the library room and Palme had not shown himself at the top of the narrow staircase. It would be easier to scare the guts out of Karnell if the girl thought she was alone with Louise. Then Louise got it! Of course! A signal that the coast was clear, that it was safe for Horn to come inside when he arrived. Of course!

'What's the signal?' Louise asked viciously, advancing closer so that Karnell backed against the wall.

'Signal?'

'You stupid bitch!' Louise raised her pistol. 'And you had good bone structure! This gun should re-arrange it so no man will look at you, let alone . . .'

Louise's mouth was slightly open, her teeth clenched tight; her gun arm began to move, the gunsight aimed to rake over the bridge of Karnell's nose, which like the rest of her was perfectly shaped. Karnell screamed, 'The front room . . . a card in the window . . . it means everything OK. Come on in!'

'What card?'

'In the drawer . . .' In her terror she pushed past Louise, ran into the library and opened a drawer. Louise was close behind her but the only thing Karnell took out of the drawer was a postcard of old Copenhagen. Running to the window, she pulled aside the curtain, perched the card on the window and let the curtain fall into its original position.

Then she saw Beaurain for the first time. 'You *know* – don't you?' she said.

'I know,' Beaurain agreed, 'so now we just wait.'

Louise body-searched the Swedish girl but the only weapon she was carrying was a pair of nail-scissors. Presumably she would have found a weapon in the house, given time.

Harvey Sholto came to Nyhavn unseen and took up his position unnoticed. Flying in from Copenhagen on the same flight as Sonia Karnell, he mingled with the other travellers on arrival at Kastrup, selected a cab, gave the driver careful instructions and a generous tip, then settled in the back seat with the tennis bag he had collected from a locker at Kastrup.

His large bald head was concealed beneath a black beret and he was wearing a shabby raincoat he had taken from the suitcase he had left inside the locker.

Most people – asked to guess his nationality – would have said Dutch or French.

'I drop you here?' the cab driver checked.

'Yes. And don't forget where you pull up for a short time. I want to surprise my girlfriend as I explained.'

'Understood.'

The cab had stopped a few yards before Nyhavn came into view round the corner and Harvey Sholto stepped out and left the cab parked at the kerb. The drizzle suited him well; it linked up with his shabby raincoat. He paddled past the end of the basin and walked down the *left-hand* street, past numerous seamen's bars. He drooped his shoulders, which made him appear a shorter man.

He walked head down, like a man absorbed in his own thoughts, but his eyes were everywhere. The place had to be crawling with that bastard Beaurain's troops. Yes, he was pretty sure one of them was stationed on the fishing vessel moored to the quay outside Horn's house. The cab arrived just in time before the man looked up and saw him, crawling past Sholto as though unsure of its destination.

Aboard the fishing vessel Max Kellerman slipped one hand under the net concealing the sub-machine gun. There was something wrong about this cab. He watched it crawl past, reach the end of the basin, and then stop. No-one got out. It just stopped while the driver gazed up the basin. *The driver!*

Out of the corner of his eye Kellerman watched while the driver took his time over lighting a cigarette and flicked the match into the water. Kellerman revised his opinion. The man was due to pick up a fare and was early so he was enjoying a quiet puff and a few minutes' peace. The cab drove off out of sight.

It was during this charade that Harvey Sholto slipped into the doorway Palme had gone through himself before killing the watcher on the first floor. The sight of the dead body shook him, but only for a second.

He next dragged the sofa over to the window to act as a back support. From the tennis bag he took the Armalite rifle which was separated into its various components and assembled the weapon. At this range the telescopic sight he screwed on was superfluous, but Harvey Sholto was a careful man.

Checking that everything was arranged to his satisfaction he settled down to wait. They were all coming to the house on Nyhavn. As Cottel mounted the steps he would blow him away with one shot. Then he need only lower the firing angle a few degrees and he could blow away the man on the deck of the fishing vessel before he recovered from the shock. He lit a cigar and willed himself to stay still.

The Volkswagen also crawled alongside the Nyhavn basin, but this vehicle was moving down the tourist-trap side of the street. When Kellerman saw it coming he ducked out of sight. At the wheel Dr Benny Horn drove on past the entrance to his house and then parked at the kerb. Clambering out of his ancient vehicle, he adjusted his skull-cap, screwed up his face at the drizzle and walked back to the house with the plate bearing his name. Like Sonia Karnell he had the key in his hand when he reached the top step. Inserting it, he walked inside and closed the door. Beaurain appeared from the open doorway leading to the library, holding his Luger and aiming it point-blank the new arrival.

'Welcome at last, Viktor Rashkin.'

Ed Cottel, who had followed Sonia Karnell from the airport and then lost her in a traffic jam, was further delayed by a puncture in one of the busiest sections in the city. He was then delayed by traffic police until he persuaded them to use the transceiver in his car to call headquarters. Eventually he found himself a cab.

In the first floor flat on Nyhavn, Harvey Sholto was satisfied he could do the job. He had stood well back in the shadows of the small room and zeroed in the Armalite telescopic sight on the front door of Horn's house. It was like taking candy from a baby. Then he saw the cab approaching on the other side and took a firmer grip on his weapon.

The cab blocked off his view while Cottel was paying off the driver and Sholto took one final puff on his cigar and ground it under his large foot. The cab moved off, Cottel glanced round and then mounted the steps. Sholto zeroed in on the centre of his back and between Cottel's shoulder-blades, slightly to the left. His finger took the first pressure. He spoke under his breath without realising he was doing it.

'It's been a long time, bastard, well, here it comes.'

It hit Harvey Sholto in the middle of the chest, lifted him clear off his feet and jerked him ceilingwards like a manipulated marionette. In mid-air his large body jack-knifed. Gravity brought him back to the floor which he hit with a tremendous thud. He lay still, outstretched, like one of the chalk silhouettes police draw to show where the corpse was found.

It was the cigar smoke which had attracted Kellerman's attention to the open window originally. Little more than a wraith, dispelled by the drizzle as soon as it came into the open air, the movement of the smoke had been sufficient for him. Someone was waiting inside the room supposedly occupied only by a dead man. At the sight of the rifle aimed at Ed Cottel he had sprayed the window with one short burst from his sub-machine gun.

Beaurain pushed the man with the skull-cap against the wall of the passageway and stuck the barrel of his Luger into his prisoner's throat. Cottel slipped into the house, and at the head of the staircase Palme appeared. Louise closed the door and Beaurain ushered Horn into his own library, followed by Ed Cottel.

'Sharpshooter opposite,' Palme explained as he came down the stairs. 'His target was Mr Cottel. Max took him out.'

'Viktor Rashkin?'

They had entered the library and it was Louise who repeated the name Beaurain had used with incredulity in her voice. Beaurain used his left hand to remove the skull-cap, to tug free the wig of false grey hair. The rimless spectacles he unhooked and threw on the floor.

'It's not as though he needs them to see. Let me introduce Dr Benny Horn, better known as Viktor Rashkin, First Secretary at the Soviet Embassy in Stockholm. And we mustn't forget other people know him as Dr Otto Berlin of Bruges and Dr Theodor Norling of Stockholm. A trio of eminent and murderous dealers in rare books.'

The light in the library was dim. It would always be dim behind the heavy lace curtains, but the drizzly morning made it even more difficult to see. Louise had no trouble seeing what she still found almost incredible – stripped of his guise as Benny Horn, the man she was staring at was a young forty, eyes intensely observant, his prominent cheekbones Slavic, and even with Beaurain's gun at his throat he exuded an air of authority and confidence. He met her gaze boldly. Then Beaurain said something else and Louise thought she saw a flicker of fear for the first time on Rashkin's face.

'This is also Hugo, controller of the Stockholm Syndicate and the man who masterminds bloodbaths like the Elsinore Massacre.'

'Are you sure?' Louise began. 'Why the elaborate deception?'

'To give him three different "front" men for dealing with the members he was recruiting for the Stockholm Syndicate. No-one at the outset would be happy dealing with a Soviet Communist. But most important of all to fool the Kremlin – especially Comrade Leonid Brezhnev, his patron.'

This time Louise, who was studying Rashkin closely, saw all expression leave his face; it went completely blank. Beaurain was striking very close to home.

'And why would he do that?' Louise asked.

'Because he was going to defect from Russia once the Syndicate was set up!' The accusation came viciously from Sonia Karnell who had remained silent up to this moment. 'Billions of dollars you said we would have, and now look where we are!'

'Shut your trap,' he told her. It was the calm, detached manner in which he uttered the words which Louise found so frightening. And Rashkin did not look frightened. She noticed Palme had left the room with Ed Cottel after a whispered remark from Beaurain. They were alone with Rashkin and his Swedish mistress, Sonia Karnell. Why did the Russian still seem so confident?

'He was going to defect,' Sonia repeated. 'He knew

he'd never make the Politburo with all those old men standing in his way. He deceived the Politburo – and Brezhnev especially – into believing he had formed a directorate while he remained at a remote distance as Hugo. Once the Syndicate was organised we would leave for America and run it from there. *Yes* – he's Hugo. And *yes,* he secretly worked with Harvey Sholto who used the J. Edgar Hoover files brought up-to-date to persuade key Americans to join the Syndicate. Not that they were reluctant when they realised the enormous non-taxable profits they'd make.'

'But he didn't *invent* Berlin, Horn and Norling, did he?' Beaurain queried gently. 'They were murdered, weren't they?'

'I had nothing to do with that!' Karnell burst out. 'He looked for recluses, men who wouldn't be missed if they suddenly "moved away" – men he could disguise himself as reasonably well.'

'How did you find out, Beaurain?' Rashkin asked, again calm.

'All their backgrounds were similar, too similar. When you vanished off the Brussels express from Bruges I later realised you had disguised yourself. Litov's dying words at Stockholm Central – *"Heroin . . . Norling . . . traitor"* – pointed to a Russian. Otherwise why should he, a Russian, use the final word? As Norling, you blew up the house outside Stockholm and left behind *an elevated heel* – to vary your height from your other two "creations". Also your reported movements as Rashkin always coincided with the appearance of one of your three "inventions".' The Belgian moved as Rashkin aimed a blow at Karnell.

Rashkin gave a gulp and a grimace of pain. Beaurain had tapped his Adam's apple with the Luger. Then he smiled, a smile which was grotesque because it reflected the pain. But the will-power which had enabled him to come so far still showed. With an immense effort he spoke the words.

'You cannot touch me. I am Viktor Rashkin. I am First Secretary at the Soviet Embassy in Stockholm. I have diplomatic immunity.'

'He's carrying a French passport in the name of Louis Carnet,' Sonia Karnell screamed. 'I can testify against him. He's a mass murderer.'

'Oh, I agree,' Beaurain interrupted. He searched Rashkin carefully for weapons and extracted from an inner pocket a French passport. Karnell had been telling the truth. It was made out in the name of Louis Carnet. He returned it to the Russian's pocket.

'But I agree,' he said. 'Viktor Rashkin has diplomatic immunity and is, therefore, untouchable.' Keeping his Luger aimed at Rashkin he stared again through the window, and Louise saw he was looking across the basin to where Ed Cottel stood in front of the house where Harvey Sholto had positioned himself. Pulling back the curtain, Beaurain showed himself. Cottel gave a thumbs up gesture, which seemed to combine the signal for all's well with a gesture pointing towards the window of the room where

Sholto's body lay. Rashkin watched him like a cat but he did not see the American or his gesture.

'You know where the front door is,' Beaurain told him.

Rashkin did not hesitate. He gave Sonia Karnell a glance which terrified her, then left the room. They heard him open the front door, close it and run down the steps. Beaurain beckoned Louise to join him at the window. Karnell seized her chance to run out into the hallway and up the stairs. There was a rear exit from the building, a flight of iron steps which was the fire escape leading to the cobbled yard. In the library Beaurain gripped Louise's arm.

'Let her go.'

'But she'll get away. She tried to kill me.'

'No-one is going anywhere. The whole of Nyhavn is sealed off. And from the front window of the room above this one Stig – with a pair of binoculars – got a good view of the position in the room across the way.'

Outside Viktor Rashkin had run down the steps and walked rapidly to his parked Volkswagen. He was confident his reference to diplomatic immunity had checkmated the Belgian. Slipping behind the wheel of his car he switched on the engine, started the wipers to clear drizzle from the windscreen and backed to a bridge crossing over the basin.

At the far end of Nyhavn where he had planned to turn right for the city centre he had seen a cordon of cars blocking the route. He crossed the bridge and turned down the other side of Nyhavn.

He pulled up in front of the building where Harvey Sholto had settled himself in position to take out Ed Cottel. As the Russian left the car he saw again what he had spotted in his rear view mirror on entering his car – another cordon closing off the other end of the basin. What he overlooked was Ed Cottel concealed in a nearby basement area. He was Beaurain's back-up – in case the Belgian's basic plan didn't work out.

Beaurain and Louise continued watching from the library window. 'Rashkin saw that both ends of the street are blocked so now he's gone into his safe house to decide his next move,' Beaurain commented. He turned as Palme came into the room.

'There has been a tragedy,' the Swede said with a wooden face. 'The Karnell woman tried to get away via the fire escape. She was in a hurry – somehow she lost her balance on the top step and went all the way down. I am afraid she is dead. Her neck is broken. What is happening to Benny Horn?'

'I don't know.' The words were hardly out of Beaurain's mouth before he jerked his head round to stare at the house opposite.

Inside the house, Viktor Rashkin, whose whole success in life had hinged on his supreme self-confidence, his conviction that he was capable of out-manoeuvring any opponent on earth, had run up the stairs with his springy step. He reached the door leading into the room, pushed it wide open and stood framed in the doorway.

Harvey Sholto was not dead, although he had taken

terrible punishment from the fusillade of bullets Max Kellerman had fired up at the window. Since then, as more blood seeped onto the sofa onto which he dragged himself, he had been waiting with the Armalite rifle propped in readiness, the muzzle aimed at the door, his finger inside the trigger guard.

The door flew open, a man stood there, a blurred silhouette, the silhouette of the man on the fishing vessel who had emptied half a magazine into him. He pressed the trigger. The bullet struck Viktor Rashkin in the chest. He reeled backwards, broke through the flimsy banister rail and toppled all the way down to the hall below. He was dead before he was half-way down.

Later

The Baron de Graer, president of the Banque du Nord of Brussels, arrived in Copenhagen by plane the same afternoon as the events just described took place in Nyhavn. He met Jules Beaurain, Louise Hamilton and Ed Cottel in a suite at the Royal Hotel. At the request of Beaurain he handed to Cottel photocopies of a whole series of bank statements, many emanating from highly-respected establishments in the Bahamas, Brussels and Luxembourg City. They showed in detail the movements of millions of dollars transferred via complex routes from certain American conglomerates to the Stockholm Syndicate.

'I'll take these at once, if I may,' Cottel said, and left

for another part of the hotel. The reporter he had earlier contacted from the *Washington Post* had just arrived and wished to fly back to Washington the same night with the photocopies.

'People are impressed with documents, Jules,' the Baron said as he drank the black coffee Louise had poured. 'Documents can be concocted to say anything you want them to say. But print them in a newspaper and they are taken for gospel.'

'It's the end result that counts,' Beaurain agreed.

Ed Cottel also returned to Washington the same evening. In addition to the incriminating bank statements, he had handed the reporter photocopies of the contents of the red file Viktor Rashkin had dropped from his brief-case when – disguised as Norling – he had fled in his float-plane from the devastated house outside the Swedish capital. The file named names – the company executives of American and European conglomerates who had approved the contributions to the Stockholm Syndicate. Unfortunately many were financial supporters of the President of the United States.

In Copenhagen Superintendent Marker was spared any hint of an international incident since the dead body of Viktor Rashkin was in due course buried as that of an unknown Frenchman, Louis Carnet, identified by the passport found on him. The same neat solution also was applied to the man armed with the Armalite rifle. Marker did later hint to an exceptionally inquisitive reporter that information from Paris led him to believe the deaths of the two Frenchmen were a gangland killing, something to do with the Union Corse. The reporter filed his story but it never appeared; a plane crash with a high casualty rate took over the space instead.

On 4 November in the United States the incumbent president was defeated in a landslide victory by his opponent. Much of the credit for the victory was laid at the door of the *Post* reporter who had, after a relentless search, come up with evidence suggesting the holier-than-thou occupant of the White House had not lived up to his image.

THE PALERMO AMBUSH

For Jane

Author's Note

Certain events which form the background to this narrative are true; the characters are fictitious. In 1943 the American Government, searching for allies behind the enemy lines, took a bizarre decision – they called in the aid of the mafia.

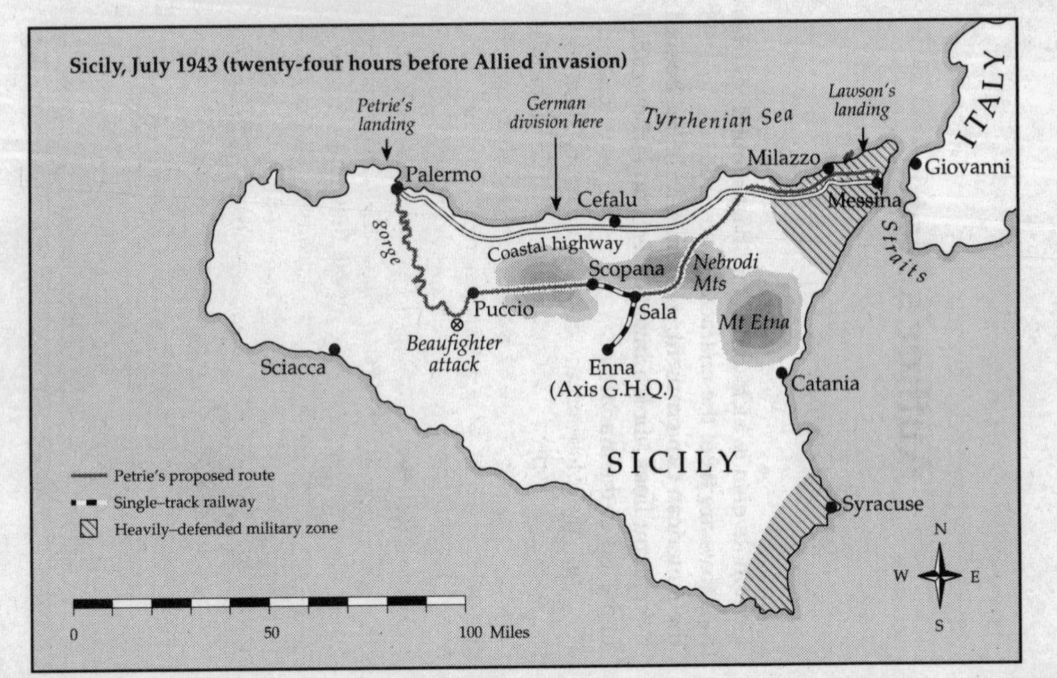
Sicily, July 1943 (twenty-four hours before Allied invasion)
Petrie's landing
German division here
Tyrrhenian Sea
Lawson's landing
ITALY
Giovanni
Milazzo
Palermo
Cefalu
Messina
Straits
gorge
Coastal highway
Scopana
Nebrodi Mts
Puccio
Sala
Mt Etna
Beaufighter attack
Sciacca
Enna
(Axis G.H.Q.)
Catania
SICILY
Petrie's proposed route
Single-track railway
Heavily-defended military zone
Syracuse
N
W
E
S
0
50
100 Miles

Chapter One

Monday. 5 July 1943

'The whole plan is a disaster – you'll be damned lucky to get back alive . . .'

The enemy coast was in sight, a blur of mountain in the night, and Major James Petrie's urgent warning echoed in Lawson's brain as the flying-boat touched down on the Mediterranean and its floats skimmed up bursts of spray. The machine lost momentum rapidly, cruising forward parallel to the shore half a mile away while Major Lawson clung to the door-frame behind the naval pilot and watched the black water rushing past below him. As the plane came to a halt, rocking gently on the swell, Lawson manhandled three dinghies over the side where they landed with a splash and then bobbed with the waves, still moored to the flying-boat. The moon came out from behind the clouds just when Lawson was praying it would remain hidden, flooding down and illuminating the eight men of the Allied landing party as they filed past Lawson and dropped into the unsteady craft while the twin props of the aircraft flickered to a halt. As he watched the coast, looped a Sten gun over his shoulder, automatically counted the shadowed figures, Lawson remembered other warning words Petrie had repeated when it was too late to alter the plan. 'Dawnay should never have approved this crazy idea. Eight men – nine with yourself – is too many for the jobs, Bill. They'll be falling over each other . . .' In his haste to leave the flying-boat one man stumbled over the legs of the man in front and only the quick grab of Lawson's hand saved him; it was a good job Petrie was still in Tunis waiting anxiously for news of the raiders' progress, Lawson thought grimly.

It was ten o'clock when the nine soldiers, disguised as peasants, pushed their dinghies clear of the flying-boat and began paddling towards Axis-occupied Sicily, began their nerve-racking journey over a horribly moonlit sea which eddied gently in saucer-shapes of shadow and illuminated water. Behind them the flying-boat, piloted by Lieutenant David Gilbey, rolled in the perpetual swell with its engines silent: it was part of the plan that Gilbey should give them time to get close inshore, should not risk arousing enemy attention until the heavily-armed raiders were almost on the beach.

Lawson sat in the lead dinghy, paddling mechanically as his tiny craft rose and dipped among the waves while he scanned the deserted shore, stared at the railway embankment beyond, and then looked back at the flying-boat which had brought them all the way from Tunis to the coast of Sicily. At least Petrie had been wrong about their mode of transport. 'A flying-boat is too noisy for this type of operation,' he had insisted at the briefing conference when all his objections had been overruled by Brigadier Dawnay and the planners. 'The enemy will hear it coming – because it will have to fly in close to Sicily to off-load the dinghies and the Messina coast is crawling with troops.' Yes, it looked as though Petrie had been wrong about that – so maybe he had been wrong about the other things, too. It was a hope which gave little comfort to Lawson: Petrie, the veteran of ten raids behind the enemy lines, was rarely wrong about these things, whereas Brigadier Dawnay, 'the iron man, iron from the neck up', as Petrie called him, had arrived from London barely six weeks ago.

As they came closer to the lonely beach the only sounds in the night were the slap of wave-tops against the dinghies, a low cough as someone nervously cleared his throat, the swish of paddles entering the sea as the nine men stroked their way in to the Sicilian shore. Lawson glanced over his shoulder and the silhouette of the flying-boat still rocked slowly from side to side, the silhouette where Gilbey was sitting in front of his controls waiting for the moment to leave. In the rear dinghy Corporal Carpenter was hunched forward more than the others as he supported the wireless transmitter on his back, a cumbersome object which reminded Lawson of a further comment Petrie had made. 'For God's sake, Bill, ditch that wireless transmitter. If you run into trouble, have to make a break for it, Carpenter will hold you up horribly carrying that thing. You can always use the underground transmitter Gambari's operating from inside Messina . . .' But Dawnay had insisted that the transmitter should be taken, as he had insisted on plenty of equipment, on using a flying-boat – 'standard procedure off the Dutch coast, you know . . .'

Suddenly they were almost on top of the beach, but this didn't surprise Lawson; it often happened when you came in over calm water. In less than a minute they'd be on firm ground, running over the thin belt of grey sand as they headed for the first cover, the rail embankment which reared up beyond the coastal highway linking Messina in the east with distant Palermo in the west. Resting his paddle, Lawson made a quick gesture and the dinghies spread out, one on either side of him, spreading out the target in case they met opposition as they landed. He gave an order in little more than a whisper to the stony-faced British sergeant behind him.

'When we hit the beach I want to reach that embankment ahead of the others, so show a bit of speed, Briggs. And you other two.'

'We'll be right behind you, sir.'

It was a detail but it could be a vital detail: Lawson wanted his crew first on the embankment so he could give the others covering fire if an enemy patrol appeared at the wrong moment. He looked back as the flying-boat's motors started up and the sputtering roar was unnervingly loud across the shot-silver sea. Then he was searching the rugged landscape in front of them for the slightest sign of movement. The mountain loomed above him and there was not a single house in sight; only the desolate beach hemmed in at either end by spillages of rock, a beach too small for any major landing, so there were no sinister wires which would indicate it was mined. The dinghy edged backwards, topped a crest, slithered through foaming surf over wet sand as Lawson jumped out and the others followed while the last man paused briefly to haul the craft well up the beach. Lawson crouched low as he sprinted over the sand, crossed the ribbon of empty highway, and scrambled up the earthen embankment. At the top he dropped flat while he scanned the mountain slope above, a slope littered with crags and boulders which could conceal any number of the enemy.

Then Lawson swore as a Messerschmitt streaked down out of nowhere, heading in a power-dive for a point behind him where the flying-boat was preparing to take off. Petrie had been right after all. It had taken them fifteen minutes to reach the beach from where Gilbey had waited; long enough for a wireless message to be sent to a nearby airfield to get the fighter plane aloft. He made another gesture as more men thudded flat on the embankment and three of them ran back to collect the dinghies and bring them inland. It seemed a useless precaution – hiding the dinghies now – but it was just possible that the fighter had been on a routine patrol when it observed the enemy plane lying on the sea. There was still a thread of hope that the enemy might not know of the landing, that the Messerschmitt pilot, intent on his target, sheering down from a great height, might not have seen the minute figures hauling the dinghies over the sand into the lee of the embankment. 'Better get inland fast, sir,' Sergeant Briggs suggested.

The motors of Gilbey's machine were swelling into a steady roar but the aircraft still hadn't sufficient power to start taxiing over the water as the Messerschmitt continued its murderous dive, heading down at an extreme angle, its engine rising to a screaming pitch. Lawson ignored what was happening out at sea as he stared up at the numerous crags and boulders on the mountain above. Between the embankment where they lay and the nearest crag was a zone of barren, open mountain slope without any kind of cover, an area about four hundred yards wide. If there were men concealed up there the landing party would be slaughtered as it crossed that open ground.

Corporal Carpenter, the wireless operator, had taken up his correct position on the extreme left flank of the line of men sprawled behind the embankment. It would be his job to bring up the rear, the least vulnerable position at present, so while he waited he looked over his shoulder out to sea. The flying-boat was moving, cruising forward as spray burst where the floats scudded over the sea, and the drumbeat of its engines quickened as it turned away from the coast prior to leaving the surface. Grimly, Carpenter saw the arrow-descent of the fighter change direction a fraction, heard the spit of its guns as it flashed down over the retreating flying-boat's tail, saw a puff of smoke and a tongue of flame flicker along the fuselage. The machine was gaining height when Gilbey lost control as the fighter pulled out of its dive and soared upwards. The flying-boat wobbled uncertainly, its right wing dipped, touched the sea, then the machine cartwheeled spectacularly, swinging over through an angle of a hundred and eighty degrees. Carpenter heard the hard smack as it smashed against the water upside down. There was a hollow explosion, a cloud of dark smoke, a little wreckage, then silence as the fighter climbed out of hearing.

Lawson heard the disaster without seeing it, heard again Petrie's prophetic words. 'A flying-boat is too noisy . . .' He pushed the memory out of his mind and without further hesitation gave the signal to advance. The eight men went up the mountain in a straggled line with their automatic weapons held in front of them, their coat pockets heavy with spare magazines and grenades, and two of the men bore an extra burden – thirty pounds of high-explosive apiece for the sabotage job they had come to do. They were well spaced out as they advanced up the open slope, spaced out to vary the range for any marksman who might be waiting for them up on the silent crags.

Carpenter, knowing what was expected of him, was still concealed behind the embankment, easing the load on his shoulders as he prepared to follow them, guessing Lawson's intention as he watched the receding figure of his commanding officer and waited for the uplifted hand. He heard instead the appalling rattle of small-arms fire, a mixture of rifle shots and automatic fire as a concentrated fusillade poured down from the crags and boulders above the line of advancing men. Lawson's men opened up briefly on targets they couldn't see; some darted forward, some ran back in a vain attempt to reach the shelter of the embankment, but the enemy commander on the heights had chosen his moment perfectly and the range was point-blank as men rolled in the dust and lay still while the fusillade continued. Lawson was hit almost at once, firing only a short burst from his Sten before he went down. Lying on his side, he tried to get up and knew it was impossible. More bullets struck him. In less than a minute nothing stirred on the slope as the enemy troops came cautiously out of their concealed positions.

In less than a minute – but in that brief period Carpenter had released the transmitter from his back, had opened the flap and extended the telescopic aerial. Carpenter was a London Cockney, a cab-driver in peacetime, and he attended to his duty phlegmatically in spite of what he had just seen. He didn't look over the embankment again as he methodically tapped out the vital message. 'Flying-boat alerted enemy. Orpheus landing party wiped out . . .' He was still tapping out the warning when a rifle butt descended with cruel force on the back of his head, ending the message in mid-sentence. Two hours later the signal was handed to Major Petrie.

Chapter Two

Wednesday Night. 7 July

Two uniformed figures hurried through the darkness of the African night towards a large square tent where the canvas whipped and billowed as the dust-storm battered it. At a distance of no closer to the tent walls than twenty yards, armed sentries stood guarding all the approaches to the meeting-place, stood twenty yards away so there could be no danger that a man might overhear a single word of what passed at the conference which had been urgently summoned for ten o'clock at night. Major James Petrie, DSO, led the way, reached the tent first and grabbed at the swaying flap to unfasten it by the time his superior, Colonel Arthur Parridge, came up behind him.

Parridge glanced up at the sky, decided the storm was worsening, then walked into the deserted interior which held a long trestle table lined with chairs. The map laid over the table was filmed with sand. He stood for a moment, brushing dust off his khaki-drill uniform as he looked round. The empty tent was illuminated by oil-lamps slung from a wire suspended over the table and the lamps were flickering uneasily, casting restless shadows across the walls as Petrie entered and Parridge spoke. 'This time, Jim, keep your damned mouth shut.'

'You're asking a lot, sir. Under the circumstances.' Petrie glanced at the colonel and the strain lines were showing at the corners of his mouth. Parridge, prematurely white-haired, but still only in his late forties, grunted. Under the circumstances. Yes, it had been a bloodbath, Lawson's raid, and he didn't feel he could convert the request into an order, so he said something else.

'Remember, you're going on leave to Algiers in the morning.'

'At least it will take me away from Dawnay. That raid was a bloody fiasco. Nine men lost the moment they arrive – and for nothing . . .'

'That's what I meant about keeping your mouth shut,' Parridge observed as he walked to the end of the tent and took a chair farthest from the head of the table where Brigadier Dawnay would sit when he arrived. 'Your place is here,' he went on and tapped the chair next to him, determined to keep Petrie as far away from the brigadier as possible.

James Petrie was twenty-nine years old, a mining engineer in peacetime, who had joined the army strictly for the duration. Since he had been attached to Parridge's Felucca Boat Squadron in the Mediterranean he had led ten raids behind the enemy lines, an activity where the casualty rate was so high that few officers survived more than a couple of months. Petrie had survived for more than two years, had become an expert at staying alive in enemy territory, had recently returned from serving as liaison officer with the Sicilian underground, as vicious a gang of cut-throats as could be found in the whole Mediterranean. Two months he had spent on the island ensuring that the Sicilians looked for the right military information, arranging for this invaluable data on which the invasion plans had been based to be wirelessed back to Allied Force Headquarters. On his return to Tunis his comment on the Sicilians had been brief and to the point. 'In Sicily it wasn't the Germans who worried me – it was our so-called allies who scared the guts out of me.'

Strange, Parridge was thinking, how some of these lads who hated the war, hated the years it was taking away from them, excelled in the craft of murderous combat. Perhaps it was because they came to it fresh, saw what was in front of them without minds warped by out-of-date military doctrine, minds like 'Thruster' Dawnay's . . . He put the image of the choleric brigadier firmly out of his mind; bad enough when the bastard actually walked into the tent without imagining his presence there beforehand. And the worst problem would be keeping Petrie quiet. Dark-haired and clean-shaven, his face tanned to mahogany by the African sun, Petrie was one of those rare individuals people noticed the moment he entered a room. They noticed the strong jaw-line, the firm mouth, the nose hooked at the bridge, the restless eyes which seemed to observe everything, and so arresting was the impression he made that they were inclined to overlook a turn of the mouth which suggested a sardonic sense of humour. 'Look, Jim,' Parridge said, 'I wasn't going to mention this until it came through – I've recommended you for further promotion. By the time you're back from Algiers you should have your half-colonelcy.'

'Thank you, sir.' Petrie didn't seem enormously impressed by the news.

A hand clapped him on the back as Captain Edward Johnson, US Army, who had just entered the tent, took the chair next to him. 'I thought you were hellbound for the fleshpots of Algiers.'

'Tomorrow morning, Ed. Six ack emma. On the dot. This is positively my last farewell appearance.'

'Good for you! Don't get lost in the casbah chasing after those girls with veils!' Captain Johnson, two years younger than Petrie, lit a cigarette, and Parridge smiled sourly to himself: Brigadier Dawnay was a non-smoker who preferred others to share his virtue, especially those of junior rank. It would be interesting to see how the brigadier handled this problem in Anglo-American relations. The room was filling up with people as more officers came into the tent and spread themselves round the table. Someone spotted the map and groaned audibly. 'Sicily! God, another Lawson raid coming up. I'd better get a chit from the MO right away . . .'

While Petrie and Johnson talked, Parridge studied the American and decided he liked what he saw.

Dark-haired, with a command of Italian as fluent as Petrie's, he seemed casual rather than formidable, a man who smiled easily and often, but as Petrie had discovered when Ed was sent to help him for a short while inside Sicily, Johnson knew what he was about. In peacetime the American had served with the US Border Patrol, a special government body which watched the frontiers of the United States to keep out smugglers and even less desirable characters. And he had served on the more dangerous frontier, along the border between the States and Mexico where a knife was commonly used for more than slicing bacon. In a few months' time Johnson would make a first-rate leader of landing parties.

The babble of voices stopped suddenly and Parridge stiffened at the warning silence which could mean only one thing: Brigadier Frederick Dawnay was arriving. Petrie finished what he was saying to Johnson, leaned back in his chair and stared at the inflated ceiling as the wind shook it with a fresh blast, an appropriate enough prelude to what was coming. Captain Stoneham, one of the British planners responsible for the Lawson raid, entered the tent and took a seat near the head of the table. For a second his eye caught Petrie's, then he looked away quickly. He was followed by Colonel Lemuel Benson, Johnson's superior, and the American joined several of his fellow-officers already spaced round the table. Like so many current operations, this was an Anglo-American affair, and at this conference Benson would have coequal status with Dawnay. Inside the tent it was becoming intolerably stuffy and several men were mopping their foreheads as the tent flap was pulled roughly aside and a short, stocky officer in a red-tabbed uniform strode in brandishing a stick which he slammed down on the table. It was immediately apparent that Brigadier Dawnay was not in the best of tempers. 'Sit down, gentlemen,' he growled. 'We haven't time for ceremony tonight!'

'But God help the man who didn't stand up,' Petrie thought cynically as he resumed his seat.

'For the benefit of those not present at the previous meeting I'll outline the situation quickly,' Dawnay went on. 'We are, of course, faced with a major emergency. The German–Italian forces have now been thrown out of Africa and we are about to launch our first attack on the European mainland . . .'

Pausing, he sniffed the air. 'There's a man smoking there.' Johnson stubbed out the cigarette as Benson put away his cigar-case with a long face. 'Lawson's raid was a failure,' the brigadier barked, 'but, in case any of you have forgotten, there's a war on and these things happen. The next thing is to put it right – and damned quick! The enemy had six enormous train-ferries plying the waters between the mainland of Italy and Sicily a few months ago. These vessels were able to carry vast quantities of men and munitions into the island. Five of them were sunk by air attack earlier, but since then the Germans have militarized the straits of Messina on a colossal scale – we know, in fact, that Jerry has placed over seven hundred guns to guard the straits – and it is the opinion of our air chiefs that they're unlikely to break through that barrage. The sixth and last train-ferry, the *Cariddi*, is still afloat, shielded by the umbrella of those guns, is still available to transport large numbers of men and guns swiftly into Sicily.' He paused again. 'Lawson went in to sink the *Cariddi*. He failed. If that vessel remains afloat it could lose us the war. And we have exactly forty-eight hours left in which to send her to the bottom.'

'Isn't that rather over-dramatizing the situation, sir?' Johnson inquired sceptically.

Dawnay glared at him, then dipped his short-cropped head to listen to Colonel Benson. Nodding, he looked at Johnson again. 'It's pretty important that you grasp the situation,' he said bluntly, 'because you may be asked to command the next team sent in to blow her up. Everything has been tried to sink that train-ferry – high-level bombers, motor-torpedo boats, and earlier this evening a flight of torpedo-bombers tried to get through to her. Like Lawson, they failed. Squadron Leader Weston was one of the casualties.'

Petrie stirred in his seat, ignored Parridge's frowning attempt to make him keep quiet. 'You mean Weston is dead, sir?' he inquired.

'It's reported that his machine blew up in mid-air. So the Navy can't get up the straits because they're too narrow, there are too many shore batteries and too many E-boats. The RAF can't get low enough through the hellish barrage to pinpoint the target when she's in Messina harbour where she ties up.' Dawnay looked grimly round the tanned faces lit by the murky oil-lamp glow. 'That leaves the Army to do the job.' His fist crashed on the table. 'We've got to send in another sabotage team and they must get there this time! Not only get to Messina – they must penetrate the dock area which is guarded by the Nazi élite, they must get aboard that train-ferry, they must plant explosive charges in her belly and send her to the bottom of the bloody straits!'

'You said we had forty-eight hours, sir,' Parridge queried. 'When is the deadline?'

'Midnight, Friday, July 9.'

There were gasps, then a hush as Dawnay stared round the table and Parridge leaned forward. His tone was crisp and demanding. 'In that case the sabotage team has only *twenty-four* hours to do their job – a day and a night will be needed to make preparations. At the very least!'

'I said it was an emergency.'

'Have we had any more news from our Italian agent inside Messina, Gambari?' There was a hint of desperation in Parridge's voice as he realized for the first time how impossible the situation was.

'Only that the *Cariddi* is still afloat,' Dawnay replied woodenly. 'And now I'll explain for Captain Johnson's benefit why I have not over-dramatized the situation. Allied Forces Headquarters calculate that if we invade Sicily our amphibious forces can defeat the enemy troops at present on the island. *At present,* I said. But our intelligence people report that the 29th Panzer Division has been brought down to the Naples area and could move south to the straits at any moment. If the 29th Panzer is moved on to the island by the *Cariddi* just after we have landed it could turn the battle against us . . .'

'But could that really lose us the war?' inquired the irrepressible Johnson.

'Ed,' Colonel Benson intervened, 'the brigadier is still telling us how it could do just that.'

'If our first attempt to return to Europe fails,' Dawnay continued, 'the Germans will withdraw large forces from the Mediterranean and send them back to Russia. If that happens the Red Army will be thrown back a vast distance. Taken to its logical extreme, it could mean the end of Russia – all because one large train-ferry was still afloat. The *Cariddi* is the only vessel left capable of moving German armour across the straits in time to defeat us.'

'I go along with that assessment,' Benson said laconically. 'The brigadier isn't exaggerating, Ed.'

'Just checking, sir,' Johnson replied, equally laconic. 'I gather you want that train-ferry sunk.'

'By midnight on Friday,' Dawnay repeated. And that, Petrie was thinking, gives us the invasion hour for Sicily – some time in the early morning of Saturday, July 10.

'The question is,' Benson remarked, 'how do we go about the job this time?'

'Captain Stoneham has drawn up a plan which I've personally approved,' Dawnay informed the meeting. There was no audible groan but the faces round the table became a little tauter and Parridge glanced hastily at Petrie. With his arms folded and his eyes fixed on Dawnay, Petrie waited while Stoneham began to explain the new plan. Drop in by parachute ... very close to Messina ... no time to come in farther away in a less heavily-defended area ... the men must be heavily-armed to blast their way through any opposition ... At this suggestion Dawnay nodded his strong approval; he saw war only in terms of a dog-fight. A large team would be sent to allow for casualties ... at least nine men, including a wireless transmitter ...

Jesus! Petrie just stopped himself intervening. This was worse, far worse than the Lawson raid plan, was an open invitation to disaster. Parridge must have sensed something of what was passing through Petrie's mind because he tapped him on the arm, warning him again not to intervene. Petrie nodded, an acknowledgement which might have meant anything as Stoneham went on. 'The north coast of Sicily swarms with Italian MAS patrol-boats ... no good thinking of coming ashore from the sea ... parachute drop essential ...' Might as well drop 'em without 'chutes, Petrie thought bitterly, that way the slaughter would be over quickly. There were twenty officers assembled round the table, and half of them were staff, but the other ten, whose expressions were grimmest, glanced frequently to the foot of the table where Petrie sat like a stone figure. They want him to speak, Parridge knew without a doubt, wanted someone to get up and tell the brigadier that what was proposed was suicidal, stark, raving madness. And Petrie, the senior raider present, was elected.

'And that concludes my outline of how I see the operation,' Stoneham ended.

'Any comments?' Dawnay demanded perfunctorily. 'They'd have to be brief. None? Then it only remains to select the team . . .'

Perhaps deliberately, he was looking down at a sheet of paper as he spoke, but something in the overheated atmosphere compelled him to look up again. Everyone was staring at the foot of the table where Petrie had risen slowly as he gave Parridge an apologetic grin and then stared along the tent with a less amiable expression. 'Permission to speak, sir,' he requested quietly.

'You'll have to be very brief,' Dawnay repeated. 'The deadline's too close for a lot of gab.'

'I submit, sir, that it's also too close for another foul-up. We have to . . .'

'What the hell do you mean by that remark?'

Petrie's tone was as innocent as his expression. 'I thought you'd already assessed the Lawson raid as a complete foul-up.'

'You said "another",' the brigadier accused.

'I did. I was referring to Captain Stoneham's new plan. Air-dropping a sabotage team almost on top of

Messina would be like dropping men on a porcupine with steel quills. It's the most heavily-defended area on the island . . .'

'We have to take that risk. The deadline is barely forty-eight hours away.'

'So we can't afford to make a mistake, can we, sir?' Petrie inquired genially. 'This second team has got to do the job or it will be too late – too late to send in another lot. This time we have to get it right. The air-drop idea is useless anyway – tantamount to failure . . .'

'Why?' Dawnay rasped.

'Because of the deadline you've mentioned, sir. First, they'll have to be dropped at night when the moon is up, so there's a chance they'd be spotted. And the first requirement is to get the team inside Sicily so the enemy doesn't even know they've arrived. Secondly, air-drop parties nearly always get scattered coming down and valuable time will be wasted while they try to form up again. In Sicily they could lose each other for good. A parachute drop is out.'

'Any other objections?' Dawnay made no attempt to conceal the biting sarcasm in his tone and then he looked at his watch as though timing the interruption.

'Plenty, sir. In fact, I'm afraid I can't find one thing I like about Captain Stoneham's plan. He suggested at least nine men should go in. That's far too many – even disguised as peasants such a large body is bound to be conspicuous; in an emergency they'll get in each other's way; you'll have trouble whipping up that number who speak fluent Italian at such short notice . . .'

'We have to allow for heavy casualties,' Dawnay snapped.

'If there are *any* casualties it means they've been seen and that means they've failed . . .'

'Why this mania for all of them speaking the lingo?'

'Because that way they can move about more confidently as civilians – so they'll move faster. It all comes back to the deadline you yourself laid down.'

'How many men do you propose then, Major Petrie?' Dawnay leaned well forward as he asked the question and the atmosphere inside the tent had become electric. No one else moved, partly to catch every word, partly to escape being caught up in the duel developing between the two men.

'I'd send in a couple of men from here . . .'

'A couple!' Dawnay exploded.

'No more, sir,' Petrie insisted. 'And another point – Captain Stoneham listed the equipment to be taken. Far too much of it – this is a sabotage team, not an assault party. It must slip secretly through the enemy lines, must get on board the *Cariddi* before the Germans have the remotest clue they're there . . .'

He stopped in mid-sentence as Dawnay swung round in his chair, stared at the man who had just come inside the tent, jumped to his feet and saluted. A second later every man inside the tent was also on his feet and the silence was so complete that the sound of sand rustling beyond the canvas walls was clearly heard. The new arrival, short, compact, wiry, long-nosed, carried the crossed swords of a lieutenant-general on his khaki-drill shoulder-straps and wore a tank corps beret on his head. 'I'll take over now, Dawnay,' he said crisply and went to the head of the table. 'Sit down, gentlemen, we've got to get on with this. Where have you got to, Dawnay?' The small figure under the oil-lamp dominated the meeting as much by personality as by rank, and he reminded Petrie of a coiled spring as he sat listening to the brigadier while his gaze was fixed on the foot of the table. General Sir Bernard Strickland had taken charge.

With an impatient gesture he reached out a bony hand towards Captain Stoneham and that officer surrendered a sheet of paper which contained the outline of the plan he had recently expounded. Strickland read the sheet while he listened to Dawnay and then he stared towards the foot of the table a second time. Parridge shifted uncomfortably in his chair; now he knew why Petrie had been summoned to this meeting. His name had been added to the list by General Strickland. The small figure stood up, crumpled the sheet of paper slowly in his fist, dropped it on the table.

'Another time, Captain Stoneham, bring a waste-paper basket – it's the only place for rubbish like this. Your plan is a complete dog's breakfast.'

'Yes, sir,' Stoneham replied nervously.

'And report to me at my caravan tomorrow morning at 0800 hours. Dawnay, you'd better be there as well. Now, Major Petrie, how would *you* sink the *Cariddi*?'

Petrie had explained the method of getting inside Sicily unseen; Strickland had approved it. The general had walked the full length of the tent to stand close to Petrie while he listened with his arms folded behind his back; during the explanation his eyes never once left the officer's face. 'How many men do you propose for the team?' he asked. He had a slight lisp but it seemed to add to the force of his delivery and Petrie, remembering Dawnay's reaction, hesitated.

'Come on,' said Strickland, 'when I arrive in Sicily I'm going to knock the enemy for six, but I need your help to do it. When I land, that train-ferry must be forty fathoms deep.'

'Three men will be enough,' Petrie said quietly. 'More would jeopardize the success of the whole enterprise.'

'You think that's enough?'

'I'm sure it is. One is the commanding officer of the show, and he must speak fluent Italian. Two is the explosives expert – and he's already inside Sicily. I'm referring to Sergeant Len Fielding, the wireless operator I worked with while I was over there. He also happens to be a specialist with explosives – and he speaks good Italian. The third member of the team will be the second-in-command, and he must know the lingo, too. One of the two officers must also know enough about explosives to plant the charges in case anything happens to Fielding.'

'Equipment?'

'A gun for each man – one easily concealed. Knives and sixty pounds of high-explosive. That's it. That team must be able to run like rabbits, hide at a moment's notice, and not get bogged down with a load of old scrap-iron.'

'A wireless transmitter would be scrap-iron?'

'Definitely. In any case, our Italian agent inside Messina, Gambari, has his own transmitter. If we need to send a message we can use that.'

'And the team lands where?'

'Palermo.'

There was a muted gasp inside the tent as Petrie's finger stabbed down at the map over the Sicilian city. For the first time Strickland frowned. 'That's well over a hundred miles west of Messina.'

'The enemy will never expect a landing there – that's part of the idea, but only part of it. There are two halves to this problem,' Petrie explained forcefully. 'The first half is to get ashore unseen in an area where they'll never expect us – Messina and the whole countryside round it bristles with the enemy, Italian and German. Lawson's raid has alerted them on the north coast for a good distance west of Messina, so that's out. I have contacts in Palermo, so that's the best place to slip ashore. More important still, we can get transport there to rush us across the island . . .'

'By the coastal highway direct from Palermo to Messina?'

'No, that's too dangerous. There's half a division reported to have moved in west of Cefalù. Look, sir, they'll have to drive over this devious inland route . . .' Petrie's finger indicated a route through the heart of Sicily. 'Enemy troops are very thin on the ground here so they'll be able to keep going. And I think Gambari should be brought out from Messina to meet them halfway – here at Scopana. Gambari is important to this plan – he knows the sailing schedules of the *Cariddi*.'

'Makes sense.' Strickland bent over the map to check the route as Parridge looked at his watch. It was 10.30 PM. The general normally imposed a strict routine on himself: always up at 6 AM, always in bed by 9.30 PM. The breaking of that routine underlined the supreme importance he attached to this operation. Strickland grunted his approval, stared at Petrie again. 'You mentioned getting hold of transport in Palermo. How do they manage that?'

'That's another major reason for going in at Palermo. We need help on this job.' Petrie paused. 'We're going to use the mafia.'

Strickland rubbed his chin thoughtfully. Petrie had given him a shock which he was careful not to show.

'Your Sicilian underground friends, you mean?' he commented.

'If they're your only friends, it might be wiser to collect a few enemies,' Petrie replied.

'But you think we can use them?'

'AFHQ have *used* them for months to collect information about enemy troop movements on the island. I spent eight weeks inside Sicily coordinating their activities – and the Americans have sent in their own agents to contact the mafia. They've even released top *mafiosi* inside the States from the penitentiary* to help them. I don't like the idea, but on that island they're the nearest thing there is to a resistance movement – mainly because Mussolini's police battered them underground before the war. The fact is, they're all we've got.'

Colonel Benson intervened and Strickland twisted his head to stare at the American. 'Petrie is right, sir – about our sending people over there. And we may have to use some of them in the Allied Military Government set-up we've planned for later. The *mafiosi* speak Sicilian and they can keep their people under control when we need the island for future operations.'

'I know all this!' The general made an impatient

* Lucky Luciano, a notorious criminal, was taken from a New York upstate prison and housed in a city apartment. From there he sent orders to New York waterfront mafias and within a month all German saboteurs had been eliminated from the area – by the mafia.

gesture. 'I asked you, Major Petrie, where we are going to find transport in Palermo.'

'The mafia supplies the transport – either a vegetable truck or a car. That will take our men fast from Palermo to Messina by the cross-country route. And the third reason why I favour Palermo as the landing-point is because they'll need a guide, a reliable Sicilian who can make sure they don't get lost.'

'Such a commodity exists?' Strickland demanded. 'A reliable Sicilian? They're a gang of ruffians. Or did you meet someone in Palermo you can even half-trust?'

'I think so. There's only one man who can do that job – one man who has the guts to get the sabotage team all the way in time.' Petrie paused, wondering again what the reaction would be. 'I'm talking about Vito Scelba.'

'That villain!' Strickland was not amused. 'He's the biggest cut-throat in the Mediterranean.'

'You underestimate Scelba, sir,' Petrie replied mildly. 'He's the biggest cut-throat north of the equator. Worse than any Communist guerrilla I ever met in Greece. But he's also my fourth reason for choosing Palermo. He's not only boss of the mafia underground; he also controls the waterfront *mafiosi* of every port in Sicily – including Messina.' Petrie paused to let his observation sink in.

'You're thinking of the dockside area?'

'That's exactly what I am thinking of, sir. Scelba can use his men on the waterfront to smuggle the sabotage team inside those docks – and I gather it's one of the most heavily-defended areas in Europe.'

'You're confident that Scelba will do all this for us?' Strickland rapped out.

'Perfectly confident – if you pay his price. That way you ensure his loyalty.'

'What price?'

'I know he wants an official position in the Allied set-up when we take over Sicily – wants it badly. He'll demand to be made prefect of Palermo province, but he'll settle for appointment as mayor of Palermo city.'

'The bowler hats would have to decide that. You're prepared to recommend him for such a position since you were over there?'

Petrie spread out his hands with an air of resignation. 'I wouldn't appoint him road-sweeper if I had my way. I think it's probably a major blunder having anything to do with the mafia – in the long run it may prove we'd have been far wiser to have done without them. But if you want this job done you'll have to use Scelba.'

'That's politics,' Strickland said with distaste. 'My job is to win the war. The team will have to go in tomorrow night and I can always promise him he'll be mayor and think about it later. Now! The only outstanding question is – who goes? I believe that for the commander of the sabotage team you specified these requirements.' Strickland ticked them off on his fingers. 'One, he speaks fluent Italian. Two, he's familiar with Sicily. Three, he knows something about explosives. And there's a fourth qualification you haven't mentioned – he must be able to persuade this ruffian, Scelba, to cooperate. Is that right?'

'Yes, sir.'

'Do you realize, Major Petrie, that the specification you laid down exactly describes yourself?'

'I rather thought it might,' Petrie replied without great enthusiasm.

Parridge leaned round Petrie so the general could see him as he spoke. 'You doubtless haven't been informed, sir, but Major Petrie is starting a long overdue leave first thing this morning.'

'I see!' Strickland looked at Petrie critically. 'In that case he'd better decide pretty quick whether he's going on leave or whether he's still fit enough to go in and sink the *Cariddi* for us!'

'I think I can do the job,' Petrie said quietly. 'I'll take Captain Johnson as my second-in-command.'

'*Think* isn't enough!' Strickland stood with his hands on his hips and stared hard at the officer. 'The success of my invasion could depend on the sinking of that vessel!'

'I can do the job – so long as I work to my own plan.'

'Already agreed! And now I'm off to bed.' He turned to leave but Petrie spoke again and the general swung on his heel to listen.

'The 29th Panzer Division, sir. What is the latest report on its whereabouts?'

'Good question! The most recent news was that it

was still laagered in the Naples area.' Strickland frowned. 'That was yesterday. Reconnaissance planes photographed the area regularly but it's been ten-tenths cloud over there for the past twenty-four hours. We assume it's still there.' As the general left the tent and a buzz of conversation sprang up behind him Petrie took particular care not to look round the crowded table; he knew, without glancing up, what their expressions would show. Sympathy, and relief – relief that they weren't going into the cauldron.

At the German GHQ, Southern Europe, a round-faced, well-built man sat on the balcony of a Naples *palazzo* waiting for the telephone in the room behind him to ring. Field-Marshal Albert Kesselring was one of the ablest Axis commanders – perhaps because he was also one of the most independent – and insofar as he could he ignored the more dogmatic orders which came to him from Supreme Headquarters in East Prussia. And once again he was about to take his own decision, a decision which he deemed necessary because of the Intelligence reports which had reached him. The North African ports were bursting at the seams with a frightening array of troopships and warships, and elements of the vast Allied amphibious force had already put to sea from Alexandria. It was even rumoured that a huge convoy was coming close to Gibraltar direct from the United States. It was time to act, to make his dispositions.

At ten o'clock at night he sat in the darkness. No moon showed through the heavy overcast and he prayed that it would stay that way for a little longer. Then the phone rang, its insistent summons mingling with the sound of a sentry tramping the paved courtyard below. Kesselring got up quickly, went inside and picked up the receiver. 'Is that you, Klaus? How are you?'

'Ready, sir.' General Rheinhardt, commanding general of the 29th Panzer Division, never used four words where two would suffice. From his tent he could see through the opening the silhouette of a Mark IV tank with the crew sitting on the ground beside it, fully dressed, fully equipped, fully alert. Ready.

'Klaus, you're to move south at once. I know bridges are down, that you will have to make a lot of detours, but I want as much speed as you can manage. Position B is where you're headed for.'

'They've landed?'

'Not yet. But they're coming – and soon. I've no doubt where the blow will fall, so I'll keep in touch. No panics?'

'Everything normal. Is that all, sir?'

'For the moment, yes. Goodbye, Klaus.'

The phone clicked at the other end before Kesselring could replace his own receiver, and he listened a little longer to the odd atmospherics sputtering on the line. Were the Gestapo phone-tappers at work again? It couldn't be helped: he had been careful not to give away what he had in mind, and Klaus would react swiftly. In this assumption Kesselring was absolutely correct. Within sixty seconds of ending the call Rheinhardt had issued the order. Within thirty minutes a controlled flood of armoured vehicles was moving south under cover of the night and the cloud bank, heading for Calabria, heading for the eastern shore of the straits of Messina.

Chapter Three

Thursday. 8 July – Before Midnight

The glass was falling rapidly, the sea was churning like a boiling cauldron as mountainous waves swept towards the Italian MAS patrol-boat proceeding through the darkness, waves which lifted it to a surf-fringed crest and then plunged it down and down into a vast trough which it seemed must engulf the vessel until, at the last moment, the bows of the large craft rose wearily again to ascend the glassy wall of another comber looming above the deck, a quivering, tumbling wall of water which threatened to submerge the patrol-boat before it could surmount the next obstacle. The wind howl disappeared inside the trough, muffled by the dancing walls of sea on all sides, but the moment they reached the next crest its menacing shriek battered at the eardrums of the men aboard who were already soaked to the skin, their bodies bruised by the frequent hammering they endured as the vessel changed direction without warning, hurling them against a bulkhead, straining at already over-strained muscles tense with the struggle to hold on, to retain some sort of balance in a world which was totally without equilibrium as the ship, powered by throbbing engines, headed in towards the north coast of Sicily.

'Bit of a pounder,' Petrie yelled at the top of his voice to make himself heard by Lieutenant-Commander Vosper, who was holding the wheel.

'It's getting worse – look at the glass,' Vosper shouted back.

'And to think we could have landed by parachute!' Johnson commented. The American, standing beside Petrie in the confined area of the wheelhouse, had never been over-enthusiastic about dangling from parachute cords with the ravines of Sicily below him, but now Stoneham's original plan seemed infinitely preferable to this turbulent sea. Petrie didn't bother to reply as he resisted the instinct to duck his head: a curtain of dark water burst over the bows, cascaded over the window as Vosper turned the wheel a fraction and stared ahead while they crested yet another roller.

Not a man aboard the enemy patrol-boat captured by the Allies at the end of the Tunisian campaign was dressed correctly. The British naval crew under Vosper's command wore Italian naval uniform while Petrie and Johnson, each with a day's growth of beard on his chin, were dressed in the most disreputable of peasant clothes; shabby jackets and trousers underneath even shabbier coats, and in their pockets were screwed up the peaked caps Sicilian peasants wore throughout the year, no matter what the weather might be. They might have been a little less sodden had they not made regular trips out to the exposed deck in their anxiety to catch their first sight of Sicily, a routine which Vosper had recently warned them against when the American had almost vanished overboard.

'This isn't the boat I'd have picked for this trip,' he commented dryly. The choice of transport had been Petrie's: the MAS boat was the exact model of the numerous Italian vessels which patrolled the north Sicilian coast, vessels which were the main defence of this shore calculated by the enemy command to be the least likely target for invasion because it lay farthest from the Allies' African bases. Beside him Petrie was searching for something he prayed wasn't there – another MAS boat, a genuine enemy vessel prowling the darkness for any sign of intruders. If they were seen they would instantly be challenged to give the recognition signal changed every twenty-four hours by the Italian naval commander of Palermo harbour. If they were seen . . .

'Tarpaulin's coming adrift . . .' Johnson shouted the warning and then left the safety of the wheelhouse before Petrie could stop him, slamming aside the door and stepping on to the slippery deck which had been awash seconds earlier. Lashed to the deck aft of the wheelhouse was a huge tarpaulin drawn over a small Sicilian fishing-craft, and one corner of the protective covering had been torn loose by the constant spillage of the sea. They were ascending towards another crest when water again surged over the boat. Then the deck was clear again, swilling sea over its side as Johnson reached the tarpaulin, grasped the loose cord, whipped it round a deck-ring and tied it while he wedged his back against the wheelhouse as once more the vessel dropped like a stone.

He had just finished his task when the ship began a fresh ascent out of the trough. He nearly went overboard, grabbed at the deck-ring just in time, felt Petrie's hand lock round his forearm, then they both held on grimly as the boat's stern fell away. Sprawled on the steel deck, tilted at an extreme angle, Johnson had a horrible conviction that this time Vosper had miscalculated, that the vessel was going to cartwheel, tipping over backwards, swinging over as the stern acted as a fulcrum to turn them upside down. Staring up he saw a gyrating funnel of sea swirling round, saw Petrie staring down at him, his face a drawn mask over the bones, and then he lost his grip on the slippery deck-ring and only Petrie's hand clawed round his arm held him on the vessel as it went on climbing and heeling prior to overturning. It was a nightmare: Petrie's left arm, bent at a cruel angle behind him where his hand still gripped the rail which was their only contact with the superstructure, felt numb, was gradually losing all feeling as it took the weight of two men. Then the boat was heaving up its stern, levelling out on a crest as Petrie hauled, dragged, twisted him round and inside the wheelhouse where the American collapsed on the floor and quietly choked until his breathing began to return to normal.

'Fishing craft . . . was going . . .' He couldn't say any more as Petrie wedged him into a corner with his own body, sitting on the floor beside Johnson while he fumbled in his coat pocket and brought out a bottle of cheap Italian brandy. Removing the cap, he handed it to the American, who swallowed a few drops, started spluttering again, then took a deeper draught. Pulling a wry face, he handed back the bottle. 'Thanks . . .' He managed a caricature of a grin as he wiped his mouth. 'Filthy muck . . . not exactly French cognac.' It was pretty deadly, Petrie agreed as he took a swig and then handed the bottle to Vosper who shook his head, shouted that he never drank on duty, and then took a long swallow.

'You did a nice job there, Ed,' Petrie remarked as he recapped the bottle. Like everything they carried, such as it was, the bottle of cheap Italian brandy could be obtained inside Sicily. In case they were stopped and searched once they landed – if they ever did reach the shore – they carried nothing which would identify them as Allied raiders. Certain items they carried would certainly mark them as suspicious characters, but as suspicious Sicilian characters in the habit of stealing anything they could lay their thieving hands on. Their guns were Italian or German weapons which could have been purloined from enemy dumps on the island, weapons which had been obtained from the huge quantities of German and Italian munitions seized when a whole Axis army surrendered in Tunisia. Even the sixty pounds of high-explosive secreted in a sack inside the wheelhouse were German explosives, and the four timer mechanisms were standard issue to the Wehrmacht.

Although the storm still battered at them with appalling violence, the waves driving at them from all directions, pitching and tossing them perpetually, the crests were becoming lower, the troughs shallower – and somewhere the moon was breaking through the clouds, casting a cold glow which made the sea seem even worse because now they saw its hideous movements more clearly. But the glass was rising. When they caught their first glimpse of Sicily, Johnson had climbed to his feet and was standing outside the wheelhouse alongside Petrie. It was Petrie who saw the coast first, no more than a nebulous shadow in the distance as he pointed and Vosper, checking the compass, swung the wheel a few degrees to starboard. 'Over there,' Petrie said. 'Looks like a low cloud but I think . . .'

'That's Sicily,' Vosper confirmed. 'We'll be there in less than an hour. On schedule to meet your friends – if they've come out on a night like this.'

'The met report said the storm would by-pass the Sicilian coast,' Johnson reminded him. 'Not that I can believe it at the moment.'

As the deck rose and fell, as the waves burst and sent up clouds of steam-like spray which drenched them again and again, Petrie scanned the unstable world for any sign of the enemy, but they had the Tyrrhenian Sea to themselves as they dipped inside shallower troughs, climbed out of them, wallowing from side to side while they headed in closer to the smudge of mountain. When Vosper handed over the wheel to a rating and came out to join Petrie, Johnson took refuge in the doorway to the wheelhouse. They were on the fringe of the storm zone now where the weather could be dangerously treacherous, seeming to calm itself and then renewing its onslaught without warning. 'That fishing fleet will never come out in this,' Johnson shouted to Petrie.

'Depends what it's like closer in,' Petrie shouted back. 'It could be quite calm just offshore.' He replied automatically as he continued scanning the sea with narrowed eyes and Vosper, who had just completed his own visual search, was turning to go back inside the wheelhouse when Petrie grasped his arm and pointed westwards. 'What's that over there?'

'Over where? Can't see a thing,' Vosper said crisply.

'Keep watching where I'm pointing. I saw a shadow, something anyway. It went down in a trough . . . No, there it is again!'

'MAS boat!' Balanced in the doorway, Vosper lifted his night glasses slung from his neck, focused them quickly, watched for a long moment, then dropped them. 'Yes, that's a MAS boat and she's heading this way. I think she's spotted us. Better get under cover with those togs of yours.' Going back inside the wheelhouse, he issued orders down the voice-pipe. 'MAS boat off starboard bow. Guns to be manned. Engines to be maintained at present speed . . .' The patrol-boat came alive as men in Italian uniform took up position to convey the impression that the ship was on routine patrol, manning the 13.2-mm machine-gun, taking up depth-charge stations, and from the rear of the wheelhouse Petrie and Johnson looked at the blurred silhouette of the enemy vessel bouncing over a wave and then dropping out of sight. The tension grew minute by minute as the real MAS boat approached them broadside on from starboard, a tension which Vosper seemed impervious to as he took a signalling lamp from a locker and waited by the open window with the instrument perched on its edge.

Petrie observed the signalling lamp with some anxiety. This was the crisis they had feared, had hoped they would never face, because in this situation there were too many things to go wrong. The ship's guns were loaded, the two 17.7-inch torpedo tubes were armed, the British naval personnel behind the weapons certainly knew how to use them, and under normal conditions Vosper would have given an excellent account of himself. But this was worse: they didn't want a scrap, they didn't want anything to happen which would cause the wireless operator on board the enemy vessel to start tapping out a warning to Palermo naval HQ. And even if the oncoming vessel was sunk swiftly – before any message had been transmitted – the noise of the battle would certainly be heard on shore just as though a radio message had been sent. The secret would be shattered, the operation ruined, and there could be no question of taking Petrie and Johnson to their rendezvous outside Palermo. Without any apparent sign of strain Vosper waited calmly, waited for the code signal to be flashed across the water.

'Think we'll get away with it?' Johnson inquired as he huddled down with Petrie out of sight.

'If Scelba has sent us the right answering signal for tonight we should do,' Petrie replied as he watched Vosper closely. 'His man inside the Italian naval HQ is pretty good and the Italians are supposed to use the same signal exchange for twenty-four hours.'

'Supposed to?' Johnson wasn't too happy about this somewhat qualified reply, but it was Vosper who explained the problem as he watched the real MAS boat heaving and tossing as she crossed a rougher patch of water.

'In normal times the signal does remain the same for twenty-four hours,' Vosper told Johnson. 'But at difficult moments the signal can be changed unexpectedly as an added precaution. We use the same system ourselves.'

'And this,' Petrie informed Johnson, 'might just qualify as a difficult moment – with the enemy knowing that large amphibious forces are already at sea and an invasion pending. So don't bet on anything.'

'I just put my money back in my pocket.'

Sitting huddled on the floor with their backs pressed into the rear of the wheelhouse, Petrie and Johnson were probably more tense than either Vosper or the helmsman because they could see what was happening. All they could do was to watch Vosper's face caught in the moonlight and the naval officer's expression gave nothing away as they sat in their cramped position, their clothes pasted to their bodies, the pounding throb of the engines vibrating under them, the horizon only appearing briefly when the patrol-boat slipped deep into a fresh trough. Vosper straightened up, told the helmsman to maintain a steady course: the low silhouette of the real MAS boat was less than a quarter of a mile away when a lamp on board began flashing the recognition signal, a signal he watched carefully as he held the lamp ready to reply. For Petrie and Johnson it was an agonizing moment when Vosper told them what was happening because they had no way of knowing whether this was the signal expected. Petrie suddenly noticed a small detail. Vosper's forehead was filmed with sweat as he stood with a frown of concentration, and this could mean only one thing: he didn't recognize the signal being flashed to him. Palermo naval HQ had changed it since Scelba's man had sent the information; now Vosper would have no idea of the signal he was supposed to flash back. Petrie glanced at Johnson and guessed from his expression that he was experiencing the same pessimistic reaction. Then Vosper started flashing his own reply. When he had finished he waited with the lamp still rested on the window edge.

'OK?' Johnson called out softly.

'It was what I expected, but they may have changed only the answering signal, in which case their next action will be a shot through this wheelhouse.'

'And a happy birthday to you, too,' the American murmured.

The waiting period when the signalling had ended was worst of all, but then the nearby engine sound changed. 'It's all right,' Vosper told them casually, 'she's pushing off.' His voice changed, took on an edge as he spoke to the helmsman. 'Full speed ahead for Palermo!'

The prediction of the met officer in Tunis came true as the MAS boat sped in close to the mountainous shore: the sea became calmer and soon was no more than a gentle swell in the moonlight which had broken through the clouds, calm enough for Petrie to stand with Johnson on deck without holding the rail as he stared at an isolated peak in the night. 'There's Monte Pellegrino,' he remarked. 'You'll remember it from when you were last here.'

'I reckon I'm getting my bearings – Palermo's just

east of it. Hey! What the hell are all those lights bobbing about over there?'

'The fishing fleet Scelba said would be outside Palermo harbour. They fish at night here and those lamps are fixed to the prows of the boats – they attract the fish into their nets. I only hope to God that Guido's somewhere out there.'

They didn't say anything else as Vosper reduced speed and every revolution of the patrol-boat's engines took them nearer the coast, so that gradually the silhouette of the mountain grew larger, the bobbing lights came closer, and the nerves of the two watchers on deck tautened. They were approaching the high-risk phase for any landing party, the time when they moved within one mile of an enemy coast, and the gap between ship and shore was narrowing minute by minute. To avoid silhouetting themselves in their peasant clothes they crouched on the deck, resting on their haunches with their backs against the wheelhouse as the bobbing lights of the fishing fleet drifted towards them, orange lights which looked strangely festive in the moonlight. 'So far, so good!' Johnson muttered the remark as he used his coat sleeve to wipe sweat from his forehead where it had begun to drip into his eyes. It was chilly on deck but the faces of both men were coated with perspiration as they waited, still no more than cargo to be delivered by Vosper to the appointed rendezvous with the mafia.

Petrie had made no reply to the hopeful comment;

his eyes were scanning the undulating sea for any sign of another MAS boat. If they were challenged a second time it might not go so well: the enemy vessel would be able to examine them more carefully in these calmer seas and the scope for further deception would be greatly diminished. This was the period he feared most of all, the interval between coming in close and losing themselves among the fishing fleet. The engine-throbs slowed to a steady tom-tom beat. Vosper edged the patrol-boat towards the vessels strung out across the sea, saw one boat, its task completed, heading back for Palermo. So far none of them had shown the least interest in the familiar torpedo-boat chugging in their direction as though on routine patrol, and Petrie was waiting for one of the orange lamps to flash on and off four times, Guido's signal which would locate the position of his own craft. The lamps remained obstinately unblinking as Vosper leaned out of the wheelhouse and called quietly to Petrie in Italian, 'No sign of a welcome yet.'

'Nothing ever happens exactly as you expect,' Petrie replied calmly. He made a gesture to Johnson as he started moving to the rear of the wheelhouse. 'We'll get round to the port side ready to go overboard.'

Petrie and Johnson worked quickly, unfastening the cords which had secured the tarpaulin over the small fishing craft underneath. Above the throb of their engines and the slap of the waves against the hull, they could hear the doleful sound of the fishermen intoning a sea shanty while they hauled in their catch. As far as was known all the fishermen belonged to Scelba's *cosca*, the mafia 'union' which secretly controlled the fishing rights off the Sicilian coast despite the efforts of the *carabinieri* to destroy it. Under the pre-war direction of Moro,* the *carabinieri* had driven the mafia underground, but like an octopus it was still holding on with its tentacles under the surface, fighting to retain its power over the local population. Vosper certainly didn't envy Petrie his job of dealing with these people.

The ropes for lowering the fishing craft over the side were already laid under the boat, and more men appeared as the craft was eased to the edge and then, under Petrie's guidance, lowered to the surface of the sea. It was a tricky operation because the MAS boat was still moving slowly in case a second enemy vessel appeared, observed what was happening and wirelessed Palermo. In that case the landing would have to be abandoned. The fishing craft slid gently into the sea, all ropes except one were released, and then Vosper changed course to take them close to the fleet. For a moment he left the wheel with a rating, stepping out to the port side to clap a hand on Petrie's shabby back as Johnson shouldered the sack containing the explosives and supplies. 'Good luck, Jim.

* Moro was the police chief sent with extraordinary powers to Sicily by Mussolini to curb the mafia.

There's been no signal from Guido, but I still think you'll make it.'

'This one we have to make,' Petrie replied quietly. 'And thanks for the ride . . .'

He followed the American down into the swaying fishing-boat where Johnson had dropped the sack and was fiddling with the motor controls. In less than a minute, still hauled along under the lee of the patrol-boat, their own motor ticked over gently and Vosper performed a delicate manoeuvre: he signalled to the rating crouched close to the wheelhouse and the man released the last rope. Petrie whipped the loose rope aboard, coiled it swiftly under the orange lamp he had lit at the prow while Johnson gripped the wheel as the crucial moment arrived. Moving slowly under their own power, they watched the protective hull of the MAS boat sliding past them like a wall, then they were exposed to full view.

The nearest Sicilian vessel was less than a score of yards away. Men were crouched over its side as they hauled in a net, and their orange lamp tilted dangerously as the vessel heeled over under the weight of their catch. Vosper had contrived his departure so that he appeared to have slipped between two vessels of the fishing fleet – Petrie's and another – as he increased speed and the wake from his boat glowed whitely in the moonlight. They were completely on their own, less than half a mile from the enemy shore, coming in on the eastern fringe of the fleet.

'Slow her a bit, Ed,' Petrie whispered in Italian. 'We don't want to get too close until Guido's contacted us.'

'If Guido's here.'

'He'll be here.'

Petrie fell silent as he watched the nearest vessel where the crew was apparently absorbed in its task. They were not the most desirable of neighbours, these swarthy fishermen with bony faces and the look of men who would put a knife in your back for the price of a meal, and Petrie was still disturbed by the thought that Guido might have been caught. A sound made him turn his head quickly. As he looked, Johnson stiffened. 'What's the matter?'

'We have company – at the wrong moment.'

It was the sudden surge of power from Vosper's patrol-boat which warned him; the naval officer's burst of speed indicated that he had decided it might be a good idea to get to hell out of here. The wake of the retreating vessel surged in the moonlight as Vosper continued his sweeping turn and then headed due north away from Palermo. The spur to this burst of speed was only too obvious: another MAS boat was rearing in from the east, heading directly for the fishing fleet. Petrie looked round quickly for any sign of one of the fishing craft approaching them; Guido, if he was there, had left the moment of contact too late. 'Ed, give me the Schnellfeur,' he snapped as he watched a fishing-boat edging towards them. Johnson held the wheel with one hand, dipped the other into the mouth of the sack, passed the gun to Petrie as the MAS boat thundered towards them.

The German Schnellfeur – fast-fire – Mauser 7.63-mm automatic is a deadly weapon which can be used either as a handgun or an automatic machine-pistol. It takes a twenty-round magazine and, when used as a handgun, is carried in a wooden holster. This curious choice of material for a holster is essential: for long-range employment the holster is clipped to the pistol butt and this provides a stock which is held against the shoulder so the user can lay down devastating fire over a considerable distance. With a little luck and a lot of skill it could decimate the crew aboard a patrol-boat. Praying that he wouldn't have to attempt that grim execution so close in to the coast, Petrie waited while the thunder of the MAS boat's engines grew louder and two fishing craft drifted towards them. At a word from Petrie, Johnson swung the wheel, slipped them between the fishing boats and inside the fleet. Something hard clanged down on their gunwale. Petrie gripped the weapon under his coat tightly as he stared at the boat-hook fastened to their side, then at the man holding it less than five feet away. The Sicilian's voice was throaty and urgent and he spoke in Italian. 'The catch is good tonight?' he asked.

'The catch is bad for July – enemy submarines

disturb the waters,' Petrie replied, completing the password.

'I am Guido. Say nothing when the patrol-boat comes . . .'

Some signal must have been passed which Petrie didn't see – because without warning they were surrounded with fishing craft, lost inside a chaos of vessels as two men aboard Guido's boat manhandled a fishing net across the gap. Johnson, his engine stopped, grasped the net without hesitation and Petrie helped him to haul it into their boat. Chugging slowly, the MAS boat was now unceremoniously nosing its way in among the craft until its hull loomed above Petrie's boat and the commander appeared on deck with a loudhailer. The fishermen were muttering angrily at the intrusion as Petrie slipped his hand inside his coat again. This didn't look too promising: the machine-gun aboard the MAS boat was manned and other men on the deck above were armed with rifles. What the hell had made the commander suspicious? The Italian raised the loudhailer, bawled down through the instrument. 'Have you seen any sign of a British torpedo-boat tonight?'

'No! Only the other MAS boat!' Guido shouted back 'You are fouling our nets!'

'And you are too far out! Palermo does not permit fishing so far from the shore at present.'

'We go where the fish are! You want to eat in your mess, don't you?' Guido replied insolently.

'I shall report your conduct to harbour control!' the Italian commander snapped.

The MAS boat reversed out of the fishing fleet, turned to the west and sped out to sea as Petrie relaxed a little. So Guido had come out beyond the permitted limits to meet them; well, that was a little cooperation from Scelba he appreciated. He turned as the engine fired in the Sicilian's boat and Guido made a beckoning gesture shoreward. They were going in to Palermo at once, so soon they would face the next dangerous hurdle – the passage inside the heavily-defended harbour. It wasn't a prospect he looked forward to as Johnson started their engine and followed the Sicilian craft into the night.

For some reason the craft Vosper had seen heading for the shore was waiting a short distance away, but when Guido's boat moved south the lead vessel began moving again and behind them a group of boats followed in a huddle. There was some kind of plan here, Petrie felt sure, a plan which had doubtless originated in the devious brain of Vito Scelba. The Sicilians were chanting again, the sound of their doleful voices floating over a sea like black oil, a sea now as calm as a village pond, and Johnson found it hard to credit that only a short time ago they had been fighting for their lives in the storm. Petrie sat in the bows of the craft as the jetty wall came closer, a long high mole extending eastwards, and soon they were close enough for him to make out a gun position protected by sandbags, the helmeted silhouettes of the gunners, a marching sentry with rifle sloped. It looked as though they were going to get through.

Following Guido's example, Johnson reduced speed drastically so that they barely drifted forward under the lee of the jetty looming high above them. He was gazing hard at the Sicilian standing in his own vessel a few yards ahead; if trouble was coming they'd have a few seconds' warning from Guido's reaction. Petrie left the bows, came to stand beside Johnson. To enter Palermo harbour they had to sail past the jetty until they reached the entrance where a second, shorter mole, farther in, projected out from the east, almost overlapping the outer jetty wall. It was very quiet as the vessels slid forward under the stone rampart. The engines chugged dully, water slapped against the stone Petrie could have reached out and touched, and the chanting had stopped abruptly. In front of them Guido was standing very stiffly, as though expecting something he didn't look forward to. 'Trouble with that chap,' Petrie whispered, 'is he hasn't learned to relax.'

'Relax! At a time like this . . .' Words failed Johnson who was gripping the wheel tightly, his body like drawn elastic at a faint creaking sound travelled over the water. The boom was being swung open to admit the fishing fleet inside Palermo harbour. As they passed the tip of the outer jetty Petrie glanced up and saw the long barrel of an ack-ack gun poked skywards above his head, then the end of the wall glided past and he saw inside the harbour, saw the ancient rooftops, the shadowed wharves below them. The tug which had swung open the boom was puffing smoke into the moonlight sky and they were turning to starboard, drifting in behind Guido and the craft just beyond him. To Johnson it all seemed a shade too easy, and he had reached the state where he dare not relax unless that should be the signal for disaster. The spotlight flashed on seconds later, a glaring light which lit up the entrance like day. Petrie swore inwardly, took a firm grip on the Mauser.

The spotlight was stationed at the tip of the inner mole, its beam projected downwards so every vessel would have to pass through its searching glow. And I'll bet these boys can count, Petrie thought grimly, count the same number of boats in as they let out. And we're one over. Probably they could even identify the occupants of the craft caught in that hideous glare they were drifting towards. The boat ahead of Guido was hardly moving as Petrie grasped the manoeuvre: the lead craft was waiting for Guido and their own vessel to come up behind them so they could move through the spotlight in a huddle. Glancing to the stern, he saw other craft almost on top of them. Johnson also understood what was being attempted. 'Shall I speed up a little?' he asked.

'Maintain present speed,' Petrie murmured automatically: an increase in speed would draw attention to them. He looked quickly round the familiar anchorage, searching for warships, for troops on the dockside, but the place seemed as quiet as he remembered it. As Johnson turned the wheel a fraction to take them alongside the *mafiosi* craft ahead Petrie murmured again. 'There's a machine-gun behind that lamp. If it opens up, swing hard to port and I'll deal with the spotlight . . .' They were creeping forward when two boats behind them speeded up, passed them to starboard, swung in ahead of Guido and into the spotlight flare. The men on board were clearly illuminated in the glare, Petrie noted grimly. Then they passed beyond it and something happened which only Scelba could have planned. The two boats collided with a heavy thud, there was a chorus of Sicilian oaths, a burst of angry shouting as though a fight had broken out.

The man behind the beam reacted instinctively, swivelled the light to his left to see what was going on, and while the spotlight centred on the collision Guido and Johnson drilled past the end of the mole with a huddle of other vessels close behind them. Realizing suddenly that he was missing the rest of the fleet, the Italian swivelled his beam back again. For seconds only it lingered on Petrie's boat and then switched to the craft behind, leaving them lit only by the glow of their own lamp. And I'll bet, Petrie told himself, that one of the fishing craft has been beached somewhere farther along the coast, so they'll count the same number in as they checked out. Scelba wouldn't forget a little detail like that. 'We're there,' he told Johnson as they cruised over the water in

Guido's wake towards a deserted wharf. Johnson grunted; they were still inside the heavily-guarded harbour area. As they approached the wharf scum was thick on the surface and spars of wood floated in the discoloured water. There was a smell of stale oil in the night, a smell which mingled with the odour of rank fish. Guessing the American's reservations, Petrie explained a little further. 'I know this wharf, Ed. There's a subterranean passage underneath it which leads outside the harbour area.'

A heavy thud warned them that Guido had reached the wharf and then Johnson cut the engine and let the natural motion take them forward until they thumped into the Sicilian's craft. They had arrived inside Sicily. The enemy had no hint of their presence. And within an hour they should have reached the underground headquarters of the mafia. Then, Petrie thought grimly, his battle with Vito Scelba would begin.

Chapter Four

Friday. 9 July – Before Dawn

Don Vito Scelba, the key man in the operation, the only man in Sicily in Petrie's view who could outwit the massive Italian–German forces, who could – if he would – take a sabotage team the breadth of the island and inside the fortress-like defences of Messina, knew within five minutes that the two Allied agents had landed at Palermo. The phone message from his *mafioso* stationed in a house overlooking the harbour was brief and cryptic. 'The grain has been delivered.'

'Thank you, Nicolo. Stay where you are.'

Scelba replaced the receiver, knowing that Nicolo would immediately leave the building as instructed. There must be no risk of anyone connected with this operation being seized by the *carabinieri* – and the *carabinieri* were tapping half the phones inside Palermo these days in their frantic efforts to hunt down the mafia underground. Cupping his hand, he lit a dark cigar and stood motionless in the vast unfurnished room; until three days ago the *palazzo* which was his new temporary headquarters had been the home of the Gonzagos, one of the wealthiest families in Sicily. But now like so many others of their class they were gone, fleeing to the Italian mainland away from the endless assault of the Allied air forces.

Scelba was not as alone in the vast chandeliered chamber as it appeared; crouched low behind each of the tall windows overlooking an inner courtyard, *mafiosi* watched the darkness with shotguns in their hands; short, swarthy-faced men armed with the most diabolical weapons available on the island – *lupara*. The word had three meanings – denoting the ammunition, the gun, the way of death. Even in Sicily it was strictly illegal to dice up lead, to feed it inside cartridges, to load the horrible cartridges into a gun – but this was the staple ammunition of the mafia underground. In Sicily many died of the dreaded *lupara* sickness, a disease for which there was no known cure. The motionless figures by the windows of the unlit room waited while Scelba waited, lost in thought. This could be the most decisive moment in his long career, the turning-point he had waited for so many long, bitter years. Petrie had come back.

Signor Scelba knew more about the military record of Major James Petrie, DSO, than the wartime soldier would ever have suspected; he knew that Petrie was normally sent in to destroy vital objectives, that his recent eight-week stay on the island had been unusual inasmuch as he had simply acted as liaison officer between AFHQ and the mafia, and he had guessed correctly that the return of Petrie was for quite a different purpose. For one thing there had been the urgent radioed request for a car – with a full petrol tank. That suggested a long journey from Palermo and two possible destinations and objectives – the naval guns of Syracuse or the train-ferry, *Cariddi*, at Messina. His network of *mafiosi* agents spread throughout the island kept Vito Scelba well informed and he had heard of the near-desperate attempts of the Allies to sink the sole surviving train-ferry plying the Messina straits. Yes, it was probably one of these two cities Petrie would be heading for – Syracuse or Messina. And the AFHQ message, signed by Petrie himself, had further asked that he should be personally present when the two men from Tunis arrived. It was an interesting situation which might be capable of enormous exploitation.

Barely literate, a shepherd boy in his youth, Scelba had hoisted, bludgeoned and schemed his way up the mafia ladder until at twenty-five he became a *capo*, a chief of the hideous organization which 'protected' the poor of Sicily while they exploited them. As steward to a great landowner he had controlled the labour supply, tightening his grip over the people who worked for his employer. For those who cooperated with the mafia there was protection when they were in trouble; for the few who rejected his advances another kind of payment was meted out – a knife in the back in a dark alley, a draught of poison in a man's wine, or a shotgun blast in the face as he was walking home one night. Then Mussolini had seized power, and because fascism couldn't tolerate any other source of power, things had gradually changed for the mafia. In the late nineteen-thirties Moro had come to the island with his incorruptible policemen, a force specially picked to deal with the Sicilian scourge. And Scelba had gone underground.

Scelba, who had no education, was a man of vision. He foresaw an Allied victory – because without that the fascist police would remain and there would be no future for the mafia – and in an Allied victory he saw a tremendous opportunity. For a re-birth of mafia power. For Vito Scelba. For a renewal of the mafia links with Naples and Marseilles – and with New York. Vito Scelba had a dream, a dream of a vast international system powerful enough to fight governments, even whole countries by organizing crime on a global scale; although the word 'crime' never entered his calculations. For Scelba everything was a matter of business. Strange to think that the one man who might help him to achieve his ambition was an Allied soldier who thoroughly mistrusted him. Scelba smiled grimly at the thought as he smoked his cigar behind his cupped hand. He would have to go down into the cellars soon, but it was claustrophobic below and there was still time.

He checked his watch. A little after eleven. Petrie, he calculated, would arrive at midnight. Stubbing out the cigar under his boot, he picked it up again and slipped it into his pocket; there must be no trace left of their presence in this room. Before he went downstairs he looked about him curiously at the dimly-seen frescoed ceiling, at the gilt mirrors which lined the walls, at the expensive marble floor. Its luxury meant nothing to him. In his personal habits he was a simple man who needed only a roof to sleep under. Issuing a sharp order in Sicilian, he went through the door which led towards the entrance to the cellars to wait for Petrie. The mafia boss who controlled the Palermo underground was already preparing his ambush – the ambush for the post-war world.

'He's inside there? Are you sure?'

Petrie gripped Guido's arm, half-dragged him into a dark doorway off the deserted street while Johnson took up a position in front of them. They had come from the harbour area by an indirect route, threading their way through the network of alleys which honeycombed the Albergheria district, and twice they had almost run into large *carabinieri* patrols, while in the distance they heard constantly the rumble of Army vehicles. They were now on the fringe of the Albergheria and Petrie was staring at a *palazzo*, one of the great homes of Palermo. Behind stone walls elegant staircases curved upwards, reached a terrace, then curved up to a second terrace. The top of the main *palazzo* wall was decorated with statues, vague silhouettes which Petrie had momentarily mistaken for sentries looking down at them. 'Guido,' he said sharply. 'Scelba can't be inside there.' The Sicilian looked frightened at the open mention of the name, then protested.

'He is, *signore*. This is the Villa Gonzago – the family left for Naples a few days ago and the villa is empty. Quickly, we must not stay here! This way, *signore*!'

Guido was impatient to get away from the street and Petrie didn't blame him as they followed the Sicilian across a paved yard, through a gateway in a second stone wall which took them to the rear of the *palazzo*. It was pitch-dark now and they hadn't yet adjusted their night vision as Guido fumbled in his pocket and walked more slowly over a cobbled area so they could keep up with him. Reaching the wall of the *palazzo*, he thrust a key into a small wooden door, turned it, pushed the door inward. A torch flashed from the interior and by its light Petrie saw the ugly barrel of a shotgun aimed at Guido's throat. There was a brief exchange in Sicilian, a language so different from Italian that Petrie caught only a word here and there, then they were ushered inside a long passage. The Sicilian with the shotgun took the key from Guido, re-locked and bolted the door by the light the second *mafioso* was holding, and then led the way down the passage to the head of a flight of steps leading below.

'Welcome again to Palermo, Major Petrie!'

'There's a lot of activity outside, Signor Scelba,' Petrie said quickly as they shook hands. 'What's happening?'

They were thirty feet under the city, in the catacomb-like atmosphere of a large wine cellar lit by oil-lamps suspended from vaulted arches. There was a pungent aroma of sour wine in Petrie's nostrils, a feeling of damp and coolness on his cheek as the mafia chief courteously guided him to a plain wooden table in the centre of the cellar. 'You have come at a dangerous time,' Scelba warned him. 'General Bergoni is conducting a night exercise and there is a curfew throughout the city – but that is only a pretext. Later there will be a military sweep through one district. Houses will be searched from top to bottom, people will be dragged out in the middle of the night. They are still looking for us, you see.'

'Which district?'

'San Pietro, so I am informed.'

'Not the Albergheria?' Petrie persisted.

'No – unless they change their minds at the last moment as a security precaution.' Scelba regarded his guest with some amusement and Petrie suspected that once again the *capo* was emphasizing how much he risked by collaborating with the Allies. 'We will have some wine in a moment,' Scelba went on. 'As you can imagine, supplies are plentiful here . . .' Johnson was introduced by Petrie and then he took his place at the table while the other two men continued talking. The American had never met the mafia boss on his previous visit because Scelba rarely showed himself to Allied agents, but for the moment Johnson was studying the other occupants of the cellar who hardly attracted him as drinking companions. The five Sicilians sitting on the stones round the edges of the cellar were only half-visible in the glow from the oil-lamps, which was probably just as well. From what he could see Johnson summed them up as the scum of Palermo, grim-faced men in peasant clothes like his own, men who had been carefully picked to guard the mafia chief in his hideout, so it was more than likely that each man had already committed several murders by some foul means or other. They sat silently in the shadows, shotguns rested in their laps, and one individual who appeared to have lost an eye whiled away the time by picking at his teeth with the point of a broad-bladed knife. In his pre-war days along the Mexican border the American had encountered some unsavoury characters, but they were saints compared with this mob.

'Your health – and success to your enterprise, Captain Johnson,' Scelba toasted.

'Your own health!' The American raised the glass poured for him and drank cautiously. Scelba had sat down at the head of the table and for the first time Johnson could see him clearly. In his late fifties, the Palermo *capo* was an impressive figure even though dressed in shirt-sleeves and braces, a strong-featured Sicilian with a heavy jaw and eyes difficult to see behind a pair of tinted tortoiseshell glasses. Broad shouldered, the mafia chief was heavily built, but when he had received them standing up he was half a foot shorter than Petrie. Wiping sweat surreptitiously from his forehead with the back of his hand, Johnson was struck by the *capo*'s impassive manner, by the impression he gave of being in complete control of a dangerous situation as he sat with hands clasped on the bare table and a cigar between his thick lips. The tinted glasses made his eyes almost invisible and the American had the uncomfortable feeling that behind the lenses the eyes were assessing him, looking for weak points. Petrie put down his glass, glanced significantly at the *mafiosi* spread round the cellar walls. 'We haven't time to waste and I want to talk.'

Scelba spoke quickly in Sicilian, the men clambered to their feet, left the cellar by a second staircase which ran up behind where the *capo* was sitting. He waited until the thud of a closing door reached them and then looked at Petrie inquiringly. 'It is something very important that brings you back to Sicily so soon?' he asked softly.

'What makes you think that?'

'Because of the vehicle your wireless message requested.'

'The car is ready for us?' Petrie asked the question to avoid answering the *capo*'s inquiry, to learn as much as he could before Scelba began his devious bargaining session.

'No, there has been an accident.'

'Good God! The arrangement was that you would have transport waiting for us. And with a full petrol tank.'

'The arrangement?' Scelba settled himself back in

his chair and spoke with the cigar in his mouth. 'There has been no arrangement yet! Your message requested a vehicle and I simply acknowledged receipt of that message. And a full petrol tank also?' There was a hint of irony in the Sicilian's tone which irritated Johnson, but Petrie seemed insensitive to the *capo*'s manner as their host continued. 'Has your military command not heard that there is severe petrol rationing here?'

'Get it on the black market then,' Petrie told him brusquely. 'We know who controls that in Palermo.'

Johnson intervened, feeling that Petrie was going too far. 'We really do need to leave Palermo at the earliest possible moment,' he explained. The Sicilian turned to him, as though suddenly aware that he was still there, and a mocking note crept into his voice.

'Captain Johnson, a vehicle was ready for you up to five hours ago, then the *carabinieri* raided the garage where it was waiting and confiscated it for their own use.'

'So you've found another for us,' Petrie assumed with deliberate confidence.

'You have great faith in me – considering the difficulties we work under here,' Scelba observed. I hope that AFHQ realize that we take our lives in our hands every hour we collaborate with you, that the authorities are intensifying their efforts to hunt us down, that our families are always at risk . . .'

Something in the Sicilian's tone alerted Petrie. 'How is Signora Scelba?' he inquired.

'She is no longer in Palermo. I have sent her away to Catania together with my son.' Scelba paused, emphasizing how critical the situation had become, but the information interested Petrie: had the Sicilian already guessed the service they might ask him to perform, sending away his family to ensure their safety during his absence? The next words were more encouraging. 'My own car will be at your disposal . . .'

'Now?'

'As soon as it has been repaired. Men are working through the night to get it ready . . .'

'Through the night? When the devil will it be ready?' Petrie demanded. 'We planned to leave Palermo within the next hour.'

'Impossible! It will not be ready until dawn. It will wait for us at a crossroads in the country outside the city – driving through Palermo at the moment is too risky.'

'Dawn is too late, far too late . . .'

'You will manage, Major Petrie! You will have to, I fear, because the car will not be ready earlier. You are going a long distance?'

'Why do you assume that?'

'Because of the full petrol tank you asked for.' Scelba spread his hands apologetically. 'And I have distressing news, I regret to say. Your wireless operator, Sergeant Fielding, was killed earlier this morning while trying to escape the *carabinieri* on his way to the transmitter.' Scelba saw the alarm in Johnson's face and understood it. 'He was wearing peasant clothes like yourselves and he carried nothing which would identify him.'

Petrie lit a cigarette while he assessed the situation. The news was not good. With poor Fielding gone he would have to plant the explosive charges inside the belly of the train-ferry himself, which left them one man short. And the delay in their departure until dawn was little short of catastrophic with the midnight deadline, which would give them only nineteen hours to drive from Palermo to Messina, to penetrate the waterfront defences and get on board the target. It meant that Scelba simply had to come with them, to get them there in record time. He decided to dispense with the verbal skirmishing and dive straight in. 'Signor Scelba, we're here to hit a major target in Messina. I want you to drive us there yourself – or at least act as guide. We're going by the inland route – via Scopana.'

'Impossible!' Scelba appeared astounded. 'Messina is at the other end of the island! The inland route is very difficult. I might just be able to provide one of my men as a guide . . .'

'No!' Petrie rapped his empty glass on the table. 'Not one of your men – you! You are the only man in Sicily I can rely on to get us through.'

'It is impossible,' Scelba repeated. 'I must remain here to perfect the organization for when you make the big landing.'

'You've done that already.' Petrie's tone was equally uncompromising. 'AFHQ think the greatest service you can render us now is to take us to Messina – we have to be inside the docks before midnight tomorrow.'

Scelba grunted with unconcealed sarcasm. 'That is the most heavily-defended area on the island.' He prodded his cigar at Petrie. 'And the Germans are there in force – you cannot bluff them. To get you inside the docks is not possible . . .'

'Not for a man who controls the waterfront mafia?' Petrie inquired quietly.

'You ask me to risk my life . . .'

'You've been doing that ever since you started gathering information on troop movements for us.'

'But not with a mad risk like this one! It is hundreds of kilometres to Messina by the inland route. Every kilometre could be our last, every corner a death-trap . . .'

'But you'll come with us?'

'No!' Scelba paused, looked at Petrie over the end of his cigar. Even if you promised to make me prefect of Palermo province after the Allies have landed.'

There it was; the bargaining counter was on the table. Petrie carefully said nothing as the Sicilian refilled their glasses. They had come to grips and the mafia boss had shown them a glimpse of his ace card: appoint him prefect and he would – reluctantly – take them to Messina. After a hell of a lot of haggling. Since AFHQ would never stand for it, the problem was to persuade him to settle for the lesser post of mayor of Palermo city. And despite what Petrie had asserted at the Tunis conference he couldn't be sure that the *capo* would agree. 'There's no question of my people offering you a prefecture,' he said brutally. 'If that's what you want, forget it.'

'Then you must forget your operation.'

'I'll get there without you, for Christ's sake!' Petrie blazed with assumed temper. 'Just give us the car and the petrol and we'll make it on our own.'

'Not by midnight! You do not know the way . . .'

'I have a map,' Petrie snapped. 'We came prepared for the chance that you'd be bloody-minded.'

'He has a map!' Scelba's broad shoulders shook with merriment. His knuckled hand tapped the table genially. 'You should try it on your own! Try to find the track they call a road in that country. You will be lost within two hours . . .' He stopped speaking and stared with the cigar in his mouth as Petrie pushed his chair back slowly from the table prior to standing up as he gazed grimly at the *capo*.

'When I get back to AFHQ I take it I'm to report that you refused to cooperate with us?'

'Perhaps you should say "if I get back",' Scelba observed ominously.

'I'm to report your absolute refusal to help us?' Petrie repeated.

'You can hardly do that if I supply the car and the petrol.'

'We need you as well – you've admitted that

yourself. As far as I can see, you've just lost any hope you had of getting an official position in the Allied administration of Sicily.'

Johnson winced inwardly at the assertion. From his previous experience with the mafia along the Mexican border he knew that the organization placed a high value on what they termed 'respect' when negotiating; so far Petrie had not shown the slightest consideration for this attribute; and Johnson was now wondering what their chances were of leaving the wine cellar alive. Scelba regarded them thoughtfully over his cigar, showing not the least trace of resentment at what had just been said. 'It is always possible that the Germans will throw you back into the sea,' he said with a faint sneer. 'Where am I then?'

'Nowhere!' Petrie didn't mince his words. 'The *carabinieri* are already intensifying their search for you – if we lose, you're dead, Scelba. If we win, you're on top of the world. From where I sit I can't see you have any choice – but that's for you to decide.'

'You make it sound good, but you have nothing specific to offer me.'

'I didn't say that!'

'Didn't you?' Scelba leaned his elbows on the table and his near-opaque glasses gave him a sinister look. They were close to the crunch now, Petrie realized, close to the point where he must make his firm offer, but it was important to get the timing right, to convince the Sicilian that he could not bid them up higher. Beyond the oil-lamp glow alcoves led off from the cellar, alcoves where other *mafiosi* could be hiding in case the *capo* decided to terminate the whole business with a blast from their shotguns. It was an unlikely outcome, but the mafia was completely unpredictable and Petrie felt he was sitting on a stick of gelignite.

'You are prepared to make a definite offer?' the *capo* asked after a long wait.

'Yes.'

'If I send someone else, someone very reliable . . .'

'No! In that case, forget it. And we'll attempt it on our own.'

'You are blackmailing me,' the Sicilian said softly. 'I have supplied vital information about troop movements on which you have based your invasion plans . . .'

'Other agents have supplied valuable data from other parts of the island.'

'I was under the impression that I was more than an agent . . .'

'That depends on how you react now.'

'You are a difficult man, Major Petrie. I can see why they sent you to Sicily . . .'

'They knew I had to deal with you!' Petrie smiled for the first time since he had entered the cellar and a wisp of a smile appeared on the *capo*'s face.

'I hear no offer yet,' he commented.

'You would be appointed mayor of Palermo the moment the Allies gain control of western Sicily.'

'That is nothing . . .'

Petrie exploded. 'You know damned well, Scelba, that it's a great deal! It gives you the top position of power in your home city. It gives you control of Palermo . . .'

'I am Palermo already.'

'Then drive us out of the city instead of sneaking your car to some obscure crossroads!'

Scelba stared hard at Petrie who again showed amusement; this was the moment for friendliness, for easing the tension out of the atmosphere, because pride is precious to the mafia, and Petrie sensed that he mustn't drive the old ruffian too far. Instead, he kept up the momentum of his attack in a different way. 'You've got what you've been after ever since we first came here,' he went on. 'You played for high stakes – and you've won. I'm damned if I'd have given you the job, Vito, however badly we needed you.'

'Ah! A reluctant emissary!' The *capo* allowed a little of his own rough humour to show. 'You have, of course, offered very little, but because of my fellow-feeling for the Allies, I will accept . . .'

'It's conditional on your taking us to Messina.'

'That I shall attempt to do.' Scelba became brisk and businesslike. 'We must leave here two hours before dawn to get to the crossroads by then. But first, you must eat. There will only be pasta and wine, but it fills the stomach . . .'

The food was brought by a peasant woman from another cellar and Petrie, schooled by long experience of interrupted meals, ate quickly, whereas Johnson took his time, possibly because he found the return of Scelba's *mafiosi* to join them didn't increase his appetite. The American was developing a shut-in feeling cooped up inside the cellars far below Palermo, a sensation of being caught in a trap, and the dark, evil faces round the table did nothing to raise his spirits as he ate stolidly at the pasta which wasn't properly cooked. He was only halfway through his meal when Carlo, Scelba's nephew, burst in on them with his urgent warning.

He came running into the cellar, a large, hungry-looking peasant whom Petrie instantly mistrusted, followed by the men who had earlier admitted the two soldiers. He began talking without ceremony, and Scelba frowned as the words tumbled out between gasps for breath. '*Signore,* the *carabinieri* are coming – hundreds of them. They have tanks and armoured cars and they have surrounded the Albergheria. They are searching everywhere . . .'

'When did the operation start?' the *capo* demanded calmly.

'Over an hour ago.'

'You took all that time to get here?' The mafia boss drank from his glass and something in his manner told Petrie that he intensely disliked his nephew. It was nothing obvious; outwardly Scelba retained his normal air of impassive self-control, and the dangerous news Carlo brought appeared not to have disturbed him at all, but during his earlier eight-week stay on the island Petrie had come to know the *capo* well, and now he even wondered whether the *capo* believed Carlo.

'It was difficult, Don Scelba,' the nephew rattled on. 'I was almost caught myself – there are so many of them. Never before have I seen this number of troops inside the city. They have thrown an iron ring round the Albergheria – no one can escape . . .'

'Then we shall not try. We will wait here until they have passed over our heads.'

Petrie had the impression that the reply hadn't satisfied the new arrival. Twisting his cap in his hands, Carlo hesitated as he darted another glance in the direction of the two strangers sitting close to Scelba. Petrie was watching Carlo closely, wondering why he was in such a nervous state. And his nervousness was infecting the other men in the cellar – several *mafiosi* were looking at Scelba as though hoping for an order to evacuate the place. If we're not careful, Petrie thought grimly, this nasty piece of work is going to start a panic. Standing more erect, the nephew began speaking again. 'They are searching everywhere. They will be here within half an hour, perhaps even sooner. They have sent men inside Count Lucillo's palace so they are bound to come here . . .'

'Calm yourself, my friend,' Scelba told him. 'It is most unusual to see you in this state.' He considered for a moment, staring at his nephew through his dark lenses as the man shifted his feet uncomfortably. 'In fact, I do not remember ever seeing you like this before. Is there something else worrying you, Carlo?' he inquired softly.

'What else could there be, *signore*?'

'That is what I am asking you.'

'I am frightened for your safety, Don Scelba. If you stay, I am sure they will find you . . .'

'So you brought your own friends to protect me?' In the passage which led back to the rear of the *palazzo* something stirred and Petrie stiffened as he noticed two things at once: Scelba's right hand was lolled over the edge of the table and below it in his lap rested a large revolver which had not been there earlier; and in the passage several new figures had appeared, Sicilians who carried guns. The situation was more serious than he had realized. Putting his hand over his mouth he whispered to Johnson, 'Under the table, Ed, if anything breaks . . .' The nephew screwed up his cap tighter.

'They came with me to make sure I reached you . . .'

'I find your concern for my welfare most touching. Are you staying with us, Carlo?' Scelba inquired pleasantly.

'I must go to my house. My wife . . . you understand?'

'Of course, Carlo. It was good of you to come and warn me.' Scelba was at his most amiable as he stood up to shake hands, slipping the revolver on to the chair, repeating that he would remain in the cellar until the alarm was over. Carlo cast another glance at the strangers, refused Scelba's offer of a glass of wine, and went back hurriedly down the passage with his men. The *mafiosi* still in the cellar relaxed, lowered the weapons they had casually turned in the direction of the passage, looked to Scelba for instructions.

'This nephew of yours,' Petrie asked quickly, 'he's a member of the organization?'

'Of course!' Scelba was imperturbable as he finished his wine. 'Now, we will leave at once for the crossroads! With this military sweep in progress we shall have to move more carefully. You are ready?' He was staring at Johnson's half-eaten pasta.

'Not very hungry tonight for some reason,' the American told him lightly. 'I'm ready.'

'We get out through the cellars?' Petrie inquired as he stood up and watched Scelba pocket his revolver without comment.

'No, the *carabinieri* will search them. But do not worry – we are going out over the rooftops of Palermo. We shall be at the crossroads by dawn.'

Chapter Five

Friday. 5 am – 9.30 am

The crossroads was rutted and gouged where carts had changed direction, a junction where roads little more than mule tracks dropped steeply between stone walls to the intersection and then sheered up again from the bowl buried among barren hill slopes. Petrie flashed his torch on an ancient signpost which leaned at a drunken angle. Southeast to Petralia and Scopana, the direction they were to have taken; northwest to Palermo, from where they had come; northeast to Cefalù, west of the point where Lawson had made his abortive landing; and southwest to Sciacca on the southern coast. What the devil had happened to Scelba's car? He switched off the torch and stood listening with his head on one side as Scelba came down the verge behind them. He heard only the enormous silence of early morning; no dawn birdsong, because in the wilderness of the Sicilian interior nothing grows so there is nothing to keep the creatures of the air alive. It was almost too quiet.

'The local cab service must be on strike,' Johnson commented.

'It must be here somewhere,' Scelba growled as he

stared into the half-light with the revolver in his hand. He's not showing it, but he's bothered, Petrie thought. The car should have been where he could see it. A dozen yards above them was a wide gap in the stone wall they had passed on their way down to the crossroads. It was the only possible place where the vehicle could have been hidden and Petrie told them he was going back to have another look at that gap. Scelba followed closely at his heels and now, as they walked on the road, their boots scuffed up dust from its appalling surface. Petrie approached the gap cautiously, the Mauser in his hand as he peered round the end of the wall. The dark silhouette of a small car, a Fiat, was parked close to the inner side of the wall a short distance away, and so far as Petrie could see it was empty. 'Take care,' Scelba whispered in his ear. 'One of my men should be waiting with it . . .'

'There's no one there.'

'Then be very careful!'

Twenty yards beyond the gap a hill slope climbed steeply up from a shadowed gash which Petrie guessed was a ravine. There was no sign of life anywhere but he wasn't relying on eyesight in this treacherous light to detect the presence of someone else, someone who might be waiting for them, using the parked car as bait. Motioning to the Sicilian to keep perfectly still, he listened again. There was something wrong here: he sensed it. 'Wait here,' he whispered and started moving along the inner side of the wall, crouched low to make as small a target as possible. He was walking on tufts of grass, shrivelled-up vegetation which had been burned to a whiskery texture by the sun of many weeks, and he was careful not to make a sound as he crept closer to the apparently empty vehicle.

Reaching the Fiat, he squeezed himself into the space between wall and car, peered in at the back and front. Empty. On the surface everything appeared to be fine: they had their transport and now all they had to do was to get inside, start the engine, back it out of the field and take the road for Scopana. Obvious. A shade too damned obvious. He went back the way he had come, found Scelba crouched behind the wall with the revolver held in front of him. 'Your car's a grey Fiat? Well, that's it, but the chap who was supposed to wait hasn't. Could he have taken fright, run off before we got here? It's not a very cheerful place to hang around.'

'Pietro would wait! There is something peculiar here.'

'You could be right, so we'd better find out what it is.'

With Scelba he searched quickly in the vicinity of the car and found nothing. Even in Sicily it was cold at this hour and the chill penetrated Petrie's coat as they went on searching and came close to the shadowed gash. The ravine was about ten yards wide and deeper than he had expected, at one point a sheer drop to a depth of close on thirty feet to a dried-up riverbed below. Moving along the brink of the drop,

Petrie stopped frequently to stare into its depths while distant peaks became clearer, sharp-edged with rugged summits as the dawn spread. The growing light also penetrated the ravine and Petrie had returned to the point where it dropped away vertically when he stopped, grasping Scelba's arm. 'Do you see that dark heap at the bottom? It could be a man.'

'We should leave soon,' Scelba warned. 'There has been a lot of army traffic recently along this road from Palermo to Cefalù.'

'Your last report mentioned it, but I don't like mysteries. We can get down into the defile a bit farther on here.'

They scrambled down a zig-zag path which might have worried a goat, but despite his heavy build the mafia boss again showed great agility, propelling himself from boulder to boulder like a man half his age. Earlier Petrie had been surprised at the *capo*'s athletic ability when he had led them over the crumbling rooftops of Palermo, an obstacle course which only a man with unusual reflexes could have managed. They reached the base of the defile together. At the bottom Petrie, still fearing a trap, hauled out the Mauser before he began walking along the ravine. He paused as he reached a corner of rock where the river turned, listened again, then went forward a few paces and stopped. Spread over a boulder lay the body of a man in peasant clothes, staring sightless at the sky. It was hardly surprising: no one could survive a fall from such a height, smashing straight down on to solid rock. Petrie stood aside to give the *capo* a better view; Scelba bent down with pursed lips, then glanced up. 'Yes, this is Pietro, the man who brought the car. He knew this area so he should not have fallen . . .' Bending down beside Scelba, Petrie levered the body gently over so it lay on its face. The haft of a broad-bladed knife protruded from the back just below the left shoulder.

'That's why he fell,' Petrie said softly. 'Or else he was pushed over the edge afterwards. Is your nephew, Carlo, handy with a knife?'

'Carlo?' Scelba looked sharply at Petrie. 'Why do you think of him?'

'Because I spent eight weeks over here and got to know something of Sicilian ways. How old is that son of yours you sent away to Catania?'

'Seventeen. But I do not see . . .'

'I do – and I think you do as well. Carlo looked about twenty-four, I reckon. And I also saw him arrive in that cellar with a bunch of his own bully-boys. I think, Scelba, he hoped to find you alone, and in that case there'd have been an accident – and you'd have been the accident. When he saw you were well guarded he tried to scare you out into the streets where you'd run slap into a *carabinieri* patrol. I think this is a typical mafia situation – Carlo thinks he's ready to take over your position, and he's trying to eliminate you. Personally, knowing you, I feel sorry for him. What are you waiting for, Scelba,' Petrie asked shrewdly, 'the right opportunity to eliminate him?'

'I may talk about this later.' The *capo* stood up, stared at the sky which was now a pearl-grey colour. 'But I think the time has come to leave here quickly.'

They went back along the silent ravine, climbed the zig-zag, and when they reached the top it was broad daylight. Johnson stood up from behind the wall as they arrived and when Petrie told him what they had found he gave a noiseless whistle. Hoisting the sack over his shoulder, he followed Petrie to the car while Scelba stayed by the gap to keep an eye on the road. 'So someone bumped off the guard but left the car conveniently parked for us to drive off in,' the American speculated. 'It doesn't make too much sense when you remember they could easily have tipped the Fiat into the ravine as well.'

'Which happens to be the same thought that occurred to me. I wouldn't start that engine if I were you, Ed.'

While Johnson dumped the sack in the back of the vehicle, Petrie examined the bonnet carefully for tell-tale wires, for any evidence of a booby-trap. Finding nothing, he dropped to the ground and wriggled his way under the chassis where he examined the under-parts of the Fiat with the aid of his torch. He had no time to waste on checking; they were already four vital hours behind schedule; and Brigadier Dawnay would undoubtedly have been foaming at the mouth could he have seen what was happening. But it was this kind of precaution which kept Petrie alive over the past three years and he wasn't changing his habits now. Crawling out from under the car, he shook his head at Johnson's unspoken question, went back to the bonnet, took hold of the handle and turned it slowly.

Checking for booby-traps was always a nerve-wracking business: the constant fear was that some joker had come up with something new, had hit on some fresh technique for blowing you sky-high, a technique you would only discover when the charge detonated. Lifting the bonnet cautiously he almost laughed; not that it was very funny. They had used the oldest trick in the book – a stick of gelignite was wired up to the ignition system. It would still have killed everyone inside the car had they started it without checking. 'Ed, get me a pair of pliers out of that toolkit under the driver's seat – then go and fetch Scelba. He's going to talk before we leave here.'

Johnson took a quick look at the obscene cylinder before he went back to find the *capo*. 'Cosy neighbours they have in these parts,' he commented. Petrie cut the connecting wires carefully, lifted out the stick and placed it in a gully some distance from the vehicle. The gelignite showed signs of 'sweating', which meant it was in an unstable condition. He pointed to it as Scelba walked across to him slowly and then looked down through his tinted glasses. 'A birthday present from Carlo? Or is there someone else who can't wait to see you six feet under? It's your car, remember, that was wired so it would go up like a bomb the moment the ignition fired.'

'Carlo, I regret,' the *capo* explained quietly, 'is collaborating with the *carabinieri*. He does not realize that I know this and I have permitted him to live because a known traitor can be useful – you can feed to him what you wish the enemy to know . . .'

He stopped talking as Petrie, grim-faced, strode quickly back to the Fiat. The old bastard was lying in his teeth, he wouldn't let an outsider hear of any domestic dispute; it was all part of the mafia code, *omertà*, the code of strict silence the Honoured Society preserved towards the outside world no matter what vendetta they might conduct among themselves. As he got behind the wheel Scelba clambered in beside him, as calm as if they were setting off for a peacetime drive in the country. At least the old villain didn't scare easily, Petrie thought, as he started the car and backed it towards the gap in the wall, but he would have liked to know how many men Carlo could muster in an emergency. Not that there was much danger of further trouble from that quarter; for one thing, when they'd passed the crossroads there were three alternative routes the Fiat could have taken. He stopped to let Johnson get in at the back, then drove down towards the crossroads.

Early morning mist was beginning to fade as the sun, still invisible behind the mountains, climbed higher and the lower flanks of rugged summits came into view through a gap in the hills. Petrie drove over the crossroads, changed gear, started up a steep, winding hill between high stone walls which would eventually lead them to Scopana. Blast the mafia! They were positively medieval; even close relatives were prepared to knife one another in the back in their greed for power. In the back of the car Johnson sat with his revolver in his lap and the sack of explosives on the seat next to him while he stared out of the window on his left. Climbing sharply, they were coming to another gap in a wall, a place where stones without mortar or sealing of any kind had collapsed inwards, and the American hoped that this would give him a view across country. As they passed the gap he twisted his head, had a glimpse of the lonely crossroads a long way down, then stiffened as he saw a peasant on horseback staring up from behind the wall which bordered the road to Cefalù. It was only a glimpse but he had time to see the mounted peasant turn away, start riding off at speed as the car went on uphill.

'We've been spotted,' he shouted. 'There was a peasant on horseback near the crossroads. I think he was watching for us – he started riding off like hell towards Cefalù!'

'That's helpful,' Petrie commented. He glanced at Scelba. 'Now they know which way we're going so you'd better talk – if you want to stay alive.'

'I think we must prepare ourselves for trouble,' the *capo* informed them calmly. 'Carlo has a few friends and somewhere ahead they may try to ambush us.' He took his revolver from his coat pocket and laid it in his ample lap. 'He wishes to kill me, of course, but since you are with me he will have to try and kill you also. It looks as though I may have to attend to my little domestic squabble before I get back to Palermo.'

'How many friends?' Petrie asked tersely.

'A few . . .' Scelba made a vague gesture with the cigar he had extracted from his case. 'Do you mind if I smoke, gentlemen?' Petrie said nothing as they came close to the crest of the long hill; he was recalling something the *capo* had said earlier about the journey across Sicily. *Every kilometre could be our last, every corner a death-trap . . .*

The sun had climbed well clear of the horizon as they came over the hill and beyond the crest the road forked – left to Scopana, right to Sciacca on the southern coast. Petrie took the left fork and the bright orb of the ascending sun caught him briefly in the eyes. The sun was an old enemy he respected and feared. In Crete, in the Greek islands, above all in the Libyan desert during his early infantry days he had come to know the sun as the deadliest enemy of all. Another day had started, another fifteen hours when the sun would slowly wheel higher, scorching the tortured landscape with its burning rays, drying up the already parched earth a little more until, with no moisture left, the baked ground began to crack open under the pitiless glare as it was cracking open on the hill slope ahead of them.

'If we run into a *carabinieri* patrol, Scelba,' Petrie began, 'do you think they'll recognize you?'

'After we have driven half an hour, I do not think so. We move away from Palermo province into a new military zone.'

'If we do run into one you'd better do the talking. How are you going to explain us?'

'It is simple.' Scelba waved his cigar. 'I am taking you to my cousin's place in Scopana for you to do a job. What papers are you carrying?'

'They show we're from Taranto in Italy – that will get over any difficulty about our not speaking Sicilian. The identity papers were produced by an expert and they'll pass inspection, so you don't have to worry about that. And we're stone-masons – the sack on the back seat contains our tools.'

'Let us hope they do not ask to look inside the sack! As stone-masons you are perfect. Since the bombing there has been a great demand for your profession over here.'

'That's why we chose it. This damned road isn't getting any better.'

'This is nothing,' Scelba assured him genially. 'Farther on it becomes really bad. You must both realize that we have a very long journey ahead of us . . .'

They drove on across a vast tableland hemmed in by distant hills like frozen waves, and gradually it became warmer and the warmth started to fill the interior of the car. Scelba was the only man who had foreseen the necessity for divesting himself of his jacket and soon the other two men were in their shirt-sleeves as the air inside the vehicle became stuffier and the sun wheeled higher. It was still not hot, but unlike North Africa the atmosphere here was humid and Petrie, his hands gripping the wheel tightly, found he was licking his lips. From a brief motion of Scelba's head he realized that the *capo* had seen him, and understood that the first ill-effects were beginning to show. They were in the heart of the tableland now. Ahead the land was scrub and rock and burnt-out moorland, a desolation which looked completely waterless. The track began turning and twisting among huge boulders, some of them almost crag-sized, so that Petrie was perpetually swinging the wheel this way and that when he wasn't struggling to extricate the vehicle from some deep rut.

But above all else it was the dust which made their lives a misery, and dust was an insoluble problem. It lay so densely upon the evil road – and they were compelled to move at such a low speed – that the front wheels churned up clouds of the grey powder and plastered a film over Petrie's windscreen, gradually obliterating his view so that his first intimation that a deep rut lay ahead was liable to be when his wheels met it. Half a mile away a fresh cloud of dust was rising as a group of horsemen galloped over the tableland in an easterly direction, the way they were going. The *capo* dropped his hand on the butt of his revolver as Petrie called out, 'See them, Ed?'

'There's another lot to the right,' Johnson replied bleakly.

To the south, again about half a mile away, more horsemen were racing forward on a parallel course with the other group, sending up great clouds of dust as they thundered eastward at far higher speed than Petrie could drive as he crawled round the boulders. The threat was obvious and unnerving: Petrie had no doubt that the horsemen were Carlo's friends, that they were riding ahead to organize an attack on the Fiat, that the attack could only be a matter of time, and it could be significant that they were coming to the end of the tableland. Less than half a mile ahead the ground was rising, climbing up past a series of fantastic crags which loomed enormously in the gathering heat haze, and beyond the crags huge yellowish cliffs stood against the glowing sky. The trap would be sprung somewhere there amid the wilderness. 'Ed, get the waterbottle out of the sack – we're rationing ourselves to one mouthful apiece. Those horsemen are Carlo's, I take it, Scelba?'

'It seems likely.' Scelba had taken off his glasses to wipe them with a soiled handkerchief. 'I am sure you will find a way of dealing with the problem.'

'A few, you said!' Johnson snapped from the back of the car. 'I counted nearly twenty of them!'

'You have that automatic German gun with you,

Major Petrie,' Scelba observed as he replaced his glasses. 'Those men will be armed only with shotguns, revolvers and knives.'

Petrie looked at him. 'So a little matter of being outnumbered by seven to one needn't worry us at all? Is there some particular place ahead where they're likely to wait for us?'

'I think there is, yes. When we come near those cliffs the road will climb, then drop inside a gorge. The far end of the gorge is where I would set a trap if I were in their shoes.'

'How long is that gorge?'

'Less than two kilometres.'

'About a mile. Any way round it?'

'No.'

Lovely, Petrie thought, just lovely. He'd come prepared to elude Italians and Germans and now the first enemy they had to confront head-on was a pack of dissident *mafiosi*. And there was irony in the situation: Scelba was supposed to help them, but now they were going to have to help Scelba if they wanted to escape with their lives and get the job done. He took the bottle Johnson handed him, drank a mouthful, passed it to Scelba. The water tasted stale, like mineral water gone flat. Through the growing heat, the drifting dust, he drove closer to the crags, and in a quarter of an hour the yellowish cliffs loomed above them as the track began to climb, leaving the boulders as it ascended the rocky slope. Through the open window the dust enveloped the interior, filming the seats, coating the backs of moist hands, clinging to sweat-stained faces. Johnson could even taste dust and his mouth was parched and gritty as he stared anxiously at the cliff-top. He saw the big horseman a few seconds later, the figure of a large Sicilian wearing a peasant cap and perched motionless on his horse at the cliff edge. 'Jim, there's someone up there!'

'It is Carlo,' Scelba said quietly. 'All right, Carlo, do not get impatient. We are coming.'

As they drove down into the gorge the cliff walls on both sides closed round them, shutting out the sun's glare as they moved into the shadow. Mounted Sicilians, armed with rifles or shotguns, lined both cliff-tops as they rode slowly along the rim over a hundred feet above where the Fiat was crawling among the rocks. With their straw hats and their weapons they looked like bandits, and there was something eroding to the nerves the way they rode on, deliberately keeping pace with the car, eight men on the northern cliff, over a dozen on the other. 'Carlo has a lot of friends,' Petrie observed.

'They are all up there.' The *capo*'s tone was contemptuous. 'I have more men than that along the Messina waterfront.'

'Glad to hear it. We'll be needing them later.'

'Nice to hear there's going to be a "later",' Johnson

said with mock pessimism, but inwardly he wondered as he stared up at the slow-moving files. 'Why the hell are they drifting on like a funeral procession?'

'It is Carlo's way of showing that an execution is planned,' Scelba explained. 'He is paying me his respects.' He lifted the revolver in his lap. 'If he comes close enough, I will pay him mine.'

They drove on and on as the gorge, no more than two hundred yards wide, curved one way and then the other through the shadows while above them the files of horsemen plodded forward at an even pace like an escort. The crisis, Petrie was convinced, would come near the end of the defile where, according to the map, the cliffs sloped downwards and the assault could be launched from both sides. For the moment they could only crawl on through the endless gorge, but now Petrie was staring ahead through the windscreen, watching for the wedge of sky between the rock walls which would warn him they were approaching the exit. He checked the milometer. They had travelled over a kilometre since entering the gorge, over two-thirds of a mile, so they were getting close to it. As he turned the wheel he saw the file of horsemen on the southern cliff, still plodding forward and evenly spaced out, but some of them were missing, must have ridden on ahead. He thrust his head out of the window, looked up at the northern face. Some missing there, too. 'Ed, in a minute I'm going to pull up and get out – you take over the wheel. I'm going ahead on foot to see what they've cooked up for us. We've got to know what they're planning before it happens.'

'They'll see you . . .'

'Maybe not.' Petrie pulled up, left the engine running. 'Ed, give me the Mauser – I'll leave you the Glisenti revolver. Some of those horsemen have disappeared, and I think I can persuade the rest of them to perform the same vanishing trick. When I've left the car I want you to drive on at the same speed. Ready?'

Stepping out of the car, he aimed the Mauser at the clifftop, heard a distant cry, and the horsemen vanished. When he swung round to stare up at the southern face that was also deserted. As Johnson jumped in behind the wheel Petrie ran towards the northern cliff, and when he was close to the rock wall he began running along underneath it. In the middle of the gorge Johnson was driving the Fiat at minimum speed, threading his way among the rocks, and Petrie was counting on the sound of the Fiat's engine to deceive the *mafiosi* into thinking that everyone was still inside the vehicle. He tried to run faster, hugging the cliff wall, but it was difficult ground to cross; spurts of rock protruded from the cliff-face, shoals of loose stones littered the precipice base.

Jesus! Ed was out-distancing him and probably didn't even know it, blinded by the dust. Scrambling over another rock spur, Petrie heard the gears change and the Fiat began backing over the way it had come. Johnson's manoeuvre worked; when he changed gear again and moved forward Petrie was ahead of him, still under the lee of the cliff, his heart pumping madly, the agony of a stitch cramping his side, but well in front of the vehicle. And he could see round the curve now, could see where the cliff walls lost height rapidly, sloping down on both sides in great ramps, converging in towards each other so that close to the exit the gorge became a funnel less than a hundred yards wide. The exit was scarcely four hundred yards away, a triangle of hard blue sky extending upwards from its apex between the cliff slopes. He saw the smoke seconds later, smelt the acrid aroma of something foul burning, and then the smoke was drifting across the exit as he reached a point where a large buttress of rock sloped down the cliff and extended halfway across the gorge, forming a bottleneck where the track passed through. He ran up the nearside of the buttress, and from its crest he had a view of what lay beyond the bottleneck where the smoke was spreading rapidly.

The oily black smokescreen now spread right across the track beyond the bottleneck, but from his elevated position Petrie could see behind the smoke where the track ran straight, ran out of the gorge into hill country. A hundred yards beyond the neck formed by the buttress, scattered close to the track on either side, were more of the boulders, mammoth-sized masses of rock, and behind them he could see men moving on foot with their horses tethered in a cluster close under the southern slope. Then the smoke spread farther and hid everything. It was a clever stratagem: the car would have to stop when it came to the smoke; the occupants would get out of the vehicle to see what was happening; then they would be picked off by concealed *mafiosi*. Except that now he knew what was planned the tactic might be turned against them. Jumping from the buttress Petrie met the Fiat only yards away from the bottleneck as Johnson pulled up and leaned out of the window. 'Jim, what's happening . . .'

'Get in the rear seat! I'm taking over the wheel – I've seen how we can get through . . .' He scrambled into the seat the American had vacated, went on talking breathlessly as he handed the Mauser over his shoulder. 'They've set up a trap ahead of us . . . they're burning something to fog the road, hoping it will stop us. It's not going to – we're going straight through them – but we've got to watch that smoke. Ed, give me that bottle of Chianti . . .' He had his handkerchief folded when the bottle came over his shoulder, soaked the cloth liberally, then tied the improvised mask over his face with only the eyes showing. 'Both of you do the same,' he mumbled. 'That smoke could choke us and we need the windows down for shooting. Are you ready for what's coming, Scelba?'

To show how ready he was, the mafia boss took a handful of ammunition out of his coat on the floor and dropped it in his lap. 'Which side of the road are they?' he asked quietly.

'Both sides. You concentrate on the right – Ed, you take the left with the Mauser . . .'

'With this I take both sides,' the American answered as he hauled out spare mags from the sack and spread them on the seat beside him. He had already fixed his own mask and passed the bottle to Scelba. 'There's nothing in the way of the car?' he inquired.

There's everything in the way – boulders the size of houses, but the track runs straight and I think I can drive between them . . .'

'Through the smoke?'

'That just makes it a shade harder.' Petrie glanced to make sure Scelba had fixed his mask. 'We're going through. Now!'

The Fiat crawled past the bottleneck as though its driver were uncertain whether to proceed, and since there was no one in sight the waiting *mafiosi* could only guess at what was happening by the sound of the car's engine. The black rolling screen of smoke came closer as the vehicle crept forward and now the dense cloud filled the width of the gorge and curled at the edges where it came up against the cliff walls. A hundred yards . . . Seventy-five yards . . . Petrie rammed down his foot, the engine revolutions quickened and the Fiat built up speed as it roared forward. In his mind's eye Petrie was trying to visualize the boulders, to imagine a dead straight course which would take them hurtling down the track with clearance on both sides. He pressed his foot down farther and they went into the smoke.

The attack began instantly. A Sicilian, his face

covered with cloth, appeared close to Scelba's window with a shotgun elevated. Scelba fired, emptied half the chambers as the man vanished, fired again at a shadow, fired blind until his gun was empty, reloaded swiftly, then shot a third soot-smeared *mafioso*. The car swept on through the black fog as Petrie gripped the wheel with both hands and Johnson emptied a magazine out of his own window. The smoke was inside the Fiat now, dung-laden, paraffin-tinged fumes which eddied in front of Petrie's eyes as he hunched well down and kept the wheel fixed in the same position, praying that he was holding to a straight course. If he smashed into one of those massive boulders which were nowhere to be seen because there was no vision, the car, travelling at this speed, would concertina. His eyes were already feeling the ill-effects of the turgid fumes as he drove on, elbows dug into his sides, back braced, shoulders stiffened as he fought to keep the wheel in exactly the same position despite the fact that they were speeding over uneven ground which pushed and tugged at the racing tyres as though determined to throw them off course. And it was a long stretch through the boulder avenue; it needed only a slight veering off course for them to angle away and rush headlong into a rock. Any second Petrie expected to see an ominous solid shape looming up in front of his bonnet and the confusion was appalling, enough to distract any man with the bursts from the Mauser rattling in his ears mingled with the sharp reports from Scelba's revolver, the high-pitched beat of the engine, the shouts from the *mafiosi* outside.

Scelba was continuing an astonishingly high rate of fire, emptying his gun, reloading, firing again as men appeared in the fog and vanished. The nerve-shattering jumble of noise was increased by the frantic efforts of the *mafiosi* to stop the car as they fired shotgun blasts blindly, and they didn't always miss: behind Johnson, crouched low on the rear seat as he fired alternately through one window and then the other, the Fiat was open to the world where a shotgun blast had shattered the rear window, scattering glass all over him, and the roof was riddled with bullet-holes. But so far Petrie's gamble was working and outside in the gorge the *mafiosi* had been taken horribly by surprise. Expecting easy victims, they were now faced with a car moving at frightening speed as a fusillade of bullets poured from it, catching any man who came in close. Once, Johnson was emptying his gun when he saw a Sicilian less than a foot from the running-board, a fat peasant lifting a rifle as the Mauser burst laced his throat. The peasant jerked horribly, half-jerked his hand towards his neck, then fell backwards as the Fiat rushed past. And now, as though perversely adding to the hellish chaos of sound, Petrie started pressing the horn non-stop so its blaring shriek cut through the other sounds as he pressed it, released it, and immediately pressed it again as they passed the position where he estimated the horses had been tethered.

Inside the car the smell, the choking fumes, were getting worse as Petrie rammed his foot down even farther knowing that they couldn't go on like this much longer without swerving fatally. Then something happened which made him lose speed as rapidly as he dared: a boulder showed to the left. He lost more speed, and changed direction a fraction, straightened up again when he calculated he was back on course, and for the first time a Sicilian reached them. Revolver in hand, a tall, lean-faced man jumped on the running-board on Scelba's side. Carlo. Scelba shot him twice in the face deliberately, then he was gone as Petrie increased speed and pressed the horn continuously. The mafia boss had just solved his little domestic problem. A figure came out of the smoke, the front mudguard struck him a pounding blow, and Petrie wondered when the hell they were going to emerge from the black pall. Behind him Johnson fired a long burst at a muddle of staggering figures and then without warning they had broken through the ambush and saw riderless horses stampeding in all directions as Petrie tore the mask from his face, threw it out of the window and accelerated up the road leading into the foothills. He glanced at his watch. 9.30 AM. Less than fifteen hours to reach Messina and they were not yet halfway across the island.

In northern Calabria on the mainland of Italy it was also 9.30 AM, was also very warm, but the mountain peaks were lost inside the heavy cloud bank which had persisted through the night. Thank God, thought General Rheinhardt, mindful of the Allied air forces. Perched on a mound overlooking the river, he held a field telephone in his hand while he watched the spans of an emergency bridge being thrown over a watercourse. It was a damned nuisance, but they'd be moving again soon. He looked behind him where a column of German tanks stretched along the road while the crews sat eating on the verge, then stiffened as Kesselring came on the line.

'What's wrong?' The field-marshal's tone was sharp.

'A bridge down. Allied saboteurs must have attached timebombs to it. We were lucky – it blew five minutes before the lead vehicles reached it.'

'How much delay?'

'Two hours from now, maybe less, we'll be across it.'

'I want the 29th Panzer on the straits shore by nine this evening.'

'That would be pushing it, sir.'

'By nine this evening. Not one minute later!' Kesselring rang off. Rheinhardt decided he would be there by nine.

Chapter Six

Friday. 9.30 am – 12.30 pm

Two hours later the wheeling sun was still glaring down on the car, slowly roasting its occupants as they drove along a high ridge crest with an immense view out over Sicily on all sides, and the sight of the terrible landscape which surrounded them had brought a hush inside the Fiat. It was as though long ago this part of the world had been convulsed by a titanic upheaval, a catastrophe which had driven up bizarre mountains whose peaks had been bent as they forced their way upwards – while in other areas the earth had collapsed, leaving behind gaping chasms which plunged down from grim yellow-stone bluffs. Wherever Petrie looked there was some rocky horror – a precipice, a landslip, a sterile pinnacle – and he thought he had never seen a wilder region in all his wanderings as a mining engineer. A whole army, dying from thirst, could be swallowed up here and who would ever find them? Driving with one hand on the wheel, he swatted irritably at a persistent fly and then, as they drove past the putrefying carcase of a mule, a swarm of flies invaded the car and they all began swatting the pests.

'Isn't it time we wet our beaks?' Scelba suggested.*

'Later. We had a drink an hour ago,' Petrie reminded him.

'How far have we come?' Johnson asked hoarsely.

Petrie glanced at the dashboard, made a quick calculation, but it was Scelba who answered first. 'We have travelled eighty kilometres from Palermo. I think I should warn you that the road between here and Scopana gets worse . . .'

'Any more encouraging comments?' the American interjected.

Scelba twisted his bulk round in his seat and stared at Johnson through his tortoiseshell glasses. 'I think it best that you should know what faces us. It is not even warm yet and today will be very hot – from midday onwards it will become like an inferno. You see, Sicily is unique in Europe. The sun shines down, the iron-hard ground and the rocks absorb the heat, then they release it so . . .'

'Very interesting!' Johnson snapped. 'But if you could defer the geography lesson until next week when I have an ice-cold beer in my hand . . .' He stopped speaking; a vision of that glass of ice-cold beer was vivid in his mind and he cursed Scelba for putting it there. The *capo* shrugged, turned to face the front as Petrie repeated his answer.

* A common mafia phrase meaning the quenching of thirst and implying friendship. At least of a temporary nature.

'About eighty kilometres it is, Ed. And we'll stop after a while and have a drink.' The brief conversation had reminded him that they were still a long distance from the rendezvous at Scopana with Gambari, the Italian agent who operated from inside Messina and whom he had never met, and Messina itself was over two hundred kilometres away. There were less than thirteen hours left in which to reach the straits city, and with every hour that passed they were falling farther behind schedule because they could only crawl along this diabolical track the Sicilians called a road. It was the delay in leaving Palermo which had upset everything, the mischance of a *carabiniere* patrol finding the first vehicle and confiscating it. Beyond Scopana, Petrie thought, we'll have to take a chance and strike up north for the direct coastal highway to make up for lost time. Beyond Scopana . . . But how many hours yet before they reached the rendezvous with Gambari?

Scelba stirred restlessly in his seat. 'If you wish to reach Messina before midnight we must hurry . . .'

'Along this track – in this heat!' Johnson exploded. Scelba regarded him passively through his tortoiseshell glasses, then turned to Petrie and explained. A long way ahead after they left the ridge the road forked south to make a detour round a cliff as it headed for Petralia and Scopana beyond. But at this point there was also a track which led off to the north to a small village called Puccio, and from this village a main road ran direct to Scopana.

'It would save many miles if we could take that more direct route,' he pointed out.

Petrie pulled a crumpled cloth map from his pocket with one hand, a map of Sicily printed on silk, and spread it over his lap. There was something in what Scelba was suggesting: a main road came down from the coast, ran close to Puccio, continued on direct to Scopana, bypassing Petralia. 'This track leading off where the road forks,' he said, 'you really think the Fiat could use it?' Johnson peered over Petrie's shoulder and inwardly shuddered: the so-called second-class road they were moving along was indicated by a continuous line, but the link-track broke down into a series of separate dashes. What the hell that might indicate in Sicily he scarcely dared contemplate.

'I have only been across it by mule,' Scelba conceded, 'but a driver like yourself might manage it.'

'We'll decide when we reach it,' Petrie replied.

They drove on a long distance over the burning ridge and the only sounds were the soporific throb of the engine, the irksome drone of the flies, the slap of hand against irritated skin and the creak of overheated leather when someone tried shifting into a less uncomfortable position; beyond the ridge the air became heavier with haze and shimmer and the brutal landscape danced gently where the heat was building up. They ate without stopping and without appetite, ate tasteless salami and cheese and dried raisins, and tried to wash it down with the remains of the Chianti because the brandy bottle had been smashed by a bullet during the attack in the gorge. At the end of the meal Petrie rationed them to two mouthfuls of water each and to his surprise Scelba swallowed only a single mouthful, handing back the bottle when he was told to take more. 'It is enough,' he explained. 'I am used to this climate and we may need that water badly later.' Petrie stared at him in surprise, remembering his earlier plea for a drink; the Sicilian had only made the suggestion because he thought his companions needed it. Not that the mafia boss was noted for his compassion – he was simply determined that they should get through to the straits city to make sure that one day he became mayor of Palermo. I was right about Scelba, Petrie thought grimly: he is the man to get us through, blast his eyes!

The first warning sign of danger ahead came within five minutes of finishing their meal. The ridge was narrowing, poising the track on little more than a knife edge with a sheer drop of hundreds of feet on either side, when Johnson screwed up his eyes and peered towards the south. The sun glare was so fierce he had to shade his gaze with his hand to make sure, then he called out urgently. 'Jim, there's someone out there! On horseback.'

Petrie resisted the impulse to take his eyes off the road, swore to himself, stopped the car and left the engine running as he twisted round in his seat. 'Over there – on top of that big rock,' the American said. Petrie couldn't see a damned thing. He climbed out of the car carefully; little more than a foot of level track was available for him to stand on before the ridge plunged into space. The American joined him, pointed over the car's bonnet. Yes, Ed hadn't imagined it: the shimmering silhouette of a horseman was perched on top of a massive crag hanging in the haze. How the hell had he taken a horse up there? Cupping both hands like primitive binoculars, Petrie stared at the horseman perched less than a quarter of a mile away, a man in army uniform. Then he was gone, vanished like a conjuring trick, but there was no doubt that the soldier must have seen the Fiat.

'Who the devil was he?' Johnson inquired as he mopped the back of his moist neck.

'An Italian soldier. And he saw us.'

'Just one of them – out here?'

'That's what worries me – that he won't be on his ownsome.'

The lone horseman had been on the south side of the track, and now Petrie was swivelling his gaze methodically through a three-sixty-degree circle. He saw the wilderness through the dazzle like an endless mirage, a wilderness bereft of water, bereft of trees, bereft of life itself. He was completing the circle, staring in a north-easterly direction where distant peaks wobbled against the sky, when he found them. A file of uniformed figures toiling over another ridge on foot with pack mules which carried cylinders that looked like mortar barrels. He pointed briefly. 'Couple of dozen of them. At least. I'd say they're part of an Italian mountain division.'

'Jesus! And we came through here because there were no troops!'

'Because there were very few troops,' Petrie corrected him. 'That division is on some kind of exercise and the last thing they'll be expecting up here is enemy saboteurs. What the hell is there to sabotage out here?'

'You think we'll run into them?'

'It's possible. The trouble is they're on both sides of us. We'll have to try and slip past between them.'

It was a slim hope: Petrie admitted it to himself as he got in behind the wheel. One horseman to the south, footsloggers to the north. All the indications were that the troops were spread out across country and somewhere ahead they were liable to be spread across the track itself. Releasing the brake, he began driving forward very slowly sitting up straight to gain as clear a view as he could of the track immediately ahead. It was climbing now, a steady incline, and as they ascended loose stones disturbed by the wheels went over the edge and disappeared from view. Several times Scelba peered out of the window on his side without enthusiasm as he looked down into a chasm which dropped almost vertically, and behind him Johnson was watching the track ahead where it appeared to narrow even further. As they reached a crest and went over it Petrie braked abruptly. A crude barrier, a pole perched on wooden tripods, barred their way.

'What the hell does that indicate?' he asked irritably. The *capo* said he had no idea, that it could hardly indicate road-mending operations. Johnson lit a cigarette while Petrie got out to investigate; there was something about the barrier he found disturbing. He saw Petrie staring down the brink on the northern side, then grab hold of pole and tripods and send them hurtling over the edge. 'There was some kind of noticeboard which has fallen halfway down,' he remarked as he came back to the car. 'I couldn't read the wording on it so we'll just keep moving . . .'

The disaster struck them a hundred yards beyond. They were bumping along over uneven ground, driving out of one pothole into another, when the explosion came, a muffled roar which echoed across the wilderness as Petrie braked and a shower of debris descended on the bonnet and roof of the Fiat. A cloud of yellowish dust, fog-thick, blinded their view for half a minute as they waited inside the car, tense with the uncertainty of not knowing what had happened. Then the dust settled, drifted away down into the abyss on either side, and the track ahead came into view again. What was left of it. A large portion had been sheered away to the left, dropping wholesale into the abyss, so that now barely half the original surface remained, remained with a sinister jagged edge where the landslip had gone over the edge.

'Christ! What was that?' Johnson called out.

'Land mine!' Petrie wiped dust off his damp hands as he surveyed the track remnant. The track had widened since they had left the barrier point behind, but the section which had survived the explosion was meagre. 'That mountain division must have mined this part of the track,' he said. 'That noticeboard probably carried a warning. This is a difficult one, gentlemen, in case you haven't noticed. We can't turn back and, theoretically, we can't go forward. We can just stay here and fry . . .'

Petrie walked with some care along the remnant of track, placing one foot carefully in front of the other, and as he walked the old, familiar sensation started, the tingling sensation on the soles of his feet which would take the first fearful impact of detonation as a mine exploded under him. To his left the edge was ragged and crumbling, but his eyes were fixed on the ground ahead, searching for any sign of metallic project which would warn him that the next section of track was also laced with mines. Already his legs felt like jelly, his nerves screaming at him to retrace his steps before he was horribly mutilated, if not killed outright, and the sweat streaming down his back had little to do with the sun beating down on him. He walked on for some distance, then turned back and the return journey was no more comfortable.

When he climbed into the car his two companions stared at him grimly. 'We'll have to risk it,' he said, reaching for the hand-brake.

'You know that walk of yours didn't prove anything?' Johnson said quietly.

'No sign of any more of them, Ed.'

'But it wasn't anti-personnel mines that shifted that load over the edge,' the American persisted.

'How about piping down and letting me concentrate?'

But Johnson had a point, a possibly lethal point: the weight of a man walking was hardly likely to detonate mines laid to destroy vehicles, mines which could tear the track off a heavy tank or pulverise a light vehicle such as the Fiat as though it had been through a stamping mill. But the only way was forward, forward over the crumbling section of track where mines had already been detonated merely by the vibrations of the approaching car being transmitted through rock. Petrie moved forward as slowly as he dared without stalling the engine, and as they came closer to the landslip area he estimated again the width of surviving track. It appeared to be just wide enough to permit the passage of their four wheels – unless another piece decided to crumble away while they were passing over it. The engine beats were slow as they crawled forward, as Scelba braced himself against the back of his seat, as Johnson sat in the exact centre of the car to help maintain the delicate balance, as Petrie moved the wheel to take them a few inches farther away from the collapsing brink, which took them nearer to the abyss on Scelba's side.

There was, in fact, rather a lot which could go wrong, Petrie was thinking. If they detonated a mine the vehicle would be hurled over the brink, but they would be dead before they left the ridge. Even without a fresh explosion a section of the track, already rendered horribly unstable by the previous detonation, could crumble away. And if they were spared these considerable hazards he could still misjudge the distance by an inch or two, simply driving them over the edge into oblivion. At this point oblivion was about a thousand feet down, he calculated. The engine stalled. It was terribly silent as leather creaked when someone stirred, then they heard the distant hum of aircraft engines. Petrie leaned out of the window, glanced down to see the running-board perched on the edge of the drop, glanced up to see aircraft flying low on a course parallel with the ridge. Beaufighters. Allied aircraft looking for something to shoot up, something which moved.

His hand moved away from the ignition, flopped on his knee while he waited. The aircraft flew on towards the east, vanishing in the haze. 'Our friends,' Petrie said over his shoulder. 'Beaufighters . . .'

'I'd sooner be up there than down here,' Johnson replied with feeling.

Petrie re-started the engine, began crawling forward again as the track ascended and the car wobbled. Then the right front wheel *dropped*. Petrie stiffened.

God, the car was going over . . . The chassis jarred, came to a halt. A deep pothole had stopped them. He reversed carefully, the wheels spun uselessly for a moment, then took them back out of the depression. He prepared to accelerate to take them across the pothole, to accelerate with only inches to spare on either side of the vehicle. The car went forward, dropped into the hole, lurched out and Petrie swung the wheel a fraction as they headed straight for the edge, turning again just in time to avoid taking them over the other brink. Scelba's thumb pressed deep into the unlit cigar he was holding and Johnson stared ahead to where the track was widening again, willing the Fiat to stay on the ridge until they reached that safer area. Then they were moving forward more evenly as the abyss moved away from them, the ridge expanded, and Petrie drove faster, knowing they must have passed beyond the mined zone.

'Those Beaufighters gave me the creeps,' Johnson called out. 'I thought for a moment they'd attack us.'

'More likely than maybe you thought,' Petrie replied. 'I noticed back in the gorge that this Fiat's smeared with dust in a way that makes it look camouflaged. They just didn't see us.'

They drove on a long distance and then Scelba reported that they were almost at the end of the ridge, that soon the track would go down to a lower level and across tableland. 'And there you will be able to drive faster,' he remarked with a wooden expression.

Petrie made no reply as he took the car up to a circle of huge boulders where the track ran between them. They drove past the rocks and the track dropped down a long slope into a bowl bisected by a waterless stream. But although water was absent the bowl was not entirely empty: a score or more of Italian mountain troops were halted on either side of the track while they lay on the ground and ate lunch, and behind them stood a mountain-gun, unlimbered and half-concealed under a canvas sheet. Petrie maintained an even speed as he drove down towards them with the sun glaring in his eyes and flashing repeatedly on the windscreen. He held up a hand to cut out the glare and saw several men running up the slope towards him as the sun went on flashing off the glass. At the head of the running men was an NCO who drew his revolver as he ran, waving it furiously at the car as Petrie slowed down and then stopped when he realized that bullets could be coming through the windscreen in a matter of seconds.

'You *bloody* fools!'

The NCO could hardly speak as he pulled up close to the car and aimed his gun at Petrie, then he recovered his breath. 'There are enemy planes about! Don't you realize that flashing windscreen can be seen for miles from the air! You could have killed all my men! By God, I'll have you in prison for the duration. You're under arrest! All of you!'

*

They stood outside the car in the heat of the sun while the NCO examined their papers. Three Italian soldiers with rifles aimed at them stood close to the sergeant who was clearly not satisfied with their identity documents. As he checked them a second time Scelba glanced towards the troops sprawled on the ground as though searching for a familiar face. The situation was dangerous, Petrie had no illusions on this score: the NCO was so furious that their windscreen reflecting the sun might have attracted the Allied planes he was determined to have them locked up.

'I still find it very strange that you continued along the ridge after the road had collapsed,' the sergeant repeated. 'And you drove past a military barrier – you admitted it. That in itself is an offence.'

'We would have roasted alive had we stayed on the ridge,' Petrie protested.

'Better that you had been blown up by the mines,' the NCO told him savagely.

'I do appreciate your attitude,' the *capo* said stiffly. 'You know my name and I have connections in Messina . . .'

'To hell with your connections! You say I know your name. I wonder! How do I know that these papers are not forged? Tell me that!' He waved the handful of papers under Scelba's nose. 'I do not like the look of any of you – and I do not like the look of your papers!'

'You could be making a bad mistake,' Scelba

assured him. 'As a Sicilian I have every right to drive across the island . . .'

'You have not heard the reports then, eh?' the NCO demanded viciously.

'What reports?'

'That British parachutists – saboteurs – were dropped in this area early this morning. I repeat, you are all under arrest until enquiries have been made about your identity! You will be taken by truck later today to Enna and interrogated there by Intelligence . . .'

Scelba dismissed the whole idea with a wave of his hand. 'I have heard this kind of report all over Sicily and it never amounts to anything. We are plagued with spy fever . . .'

'You are under arrest!' the NCO bawled in his face.

'Are there any Sicilians in your division?' Scelba asked.

'Yes, but we will waste no more time talking. Come!'

Petrie glanced at Johnson as they walked down the hill after the enraged sergeant while the three soldiers followed in the rear. It was pointless to argue any further and it was damned bad luck that these reports should be circulating, but they highlighted the extreme state of tension now gripping the island. He looked back as he heard the Fiat's engine start up: a fourth soldier had climbed in behind the wheel and the car was coming down the slope behind them. In his rage the NCO had so far overlooked the simple routine of searching the vehicle, but it was an oversight he was bound to remedy before long. And the sack of explosives was still on the floor in the rear of the vehicle.

As they tramped down into the bowl the troops on the ground stared at them hostilely and one man operated his rifle bolt, but the NCO rapped out an order and the man laid his weapon back on the earth. Clearly the episode of the flashing windscreen had not put them at the top of any popularity poll, Petrie thought. They were marching towards a cave under a large rock overhang where a soldier stood on guard when Scelba halted, staring at a man who had stopped eating as he looked up at the *capo*. One of the soldiers behind him prodded his hip lightly with his bayonet, but Scelba refused to move, glaring back with such ferocity that the soldier paused uncertainly. The *capo* called out to the sergeant who had swung round. 'This man here knows me, Sergeant. He has not seen my papers so ask him who I am – it may stop you making a very serious mistake.'

'We will check your identity at Enna . . .'

'Ask him, please!'

The sergeant hesitated, but there was something in the *capo*'s manner which intimidated him. Petrie held his breath: everything now depended on the NCO's reaction, on the strength of the doubt Scelba had planted in his mind. With an impatient gesture the sergeant spoke to the soldier, who jumped to his feet. 'You know who this man is? You recognize him?'

'He is Vito Scelba . . .'

'Who is he?'

'I knew him when I worked on the docks at Messina, Sergeant. He is an important man with shipping interests . . .'

'I am trying to save *you* trouble, Sergeant,' Scelba intervened, changing his tactics. 'You are doing your duty, which I applaud, but in my own way I also help the war effort. Now you have conclusive proof of my identity and I can personally vouch for these two men with me.'

'You are in a hurry . . . ?' The NCO was again uncertain, a man who disliked going back on his own orders, but also a man who feared people with influence. And Scelba had cleverly provided him with a line of retreat. 'Perhaps since we now do have proof of your identity this changes the position . . .'

'I merely wish to continue my urgent journey concerned with dock repairs,' the *capo* explained persuasively. 'And your corporal has considerately brought my car so, with your permission, we should like to drive on at once . . .'

Within two minutes they were driving up out of the bowl with their papers inside their pockets. In the rear seat Johnson sat with his feet planted on either side of the sack of explosives as the Fiat climbed higher, went over a crest, and the military detachment vanished behind them. 'There are many Sicilians in the Army on the island,' Scelba observed, 'but even so we were lucky. They were bringing the car down to have it searched.'

'The same suspicion had crossed my mind,' Petrie replied dryly and then he concentrated on his driving. A long way beyond the burning ridge they saw the great bluffs Scelba had spoken of when he described how a track led off to the village of Puccio. They drove on steadily over the foul road and again they were facing the sun at a certain angle so its rays were flashing off the windscreen. And again Petrie had to raise one hand to shield his eyes against the glare to see where he was going as he weighed up the alternatives. It would save a lot of mileage if they could take the Fiat along that mule track and join the direct route to Scopana. They were very close to the bluffs when Petrie heard the sound of another engine, a shrilling-pitched whine at high altitude, and there was something about the whine which alerted him. He looked out, jerked his head in fast, stopped the car and switched off the motor.

'Get out! Take cover! Ed, take the sack . . .'

Grabbing his jacket, he leaned over the back seat and hauled the Mauser off the floor as Johnson left the Fiat at speed with his own jacket and the sack. The door on Petrie's side jammed, so he scrambled over the seat Scelba had vacated and ran after the other two men, leaving the road and haring across country towards a straggle of boulders with the scream of the diving aircraft in his ears. Reaching the rocks, he skidded flat on his stomach, wriggled close to a boulder and lifted his head a few inches. The Beaufighter, flying at zero height, its RAF roundel clearly visible, opened up with all its armament – cannon and machine-guns. The noise was deafening. The scream of the engine, the rattle of the machine-guns, the blast of the cannon-shells bursting. Rock fragments showered down on the boulders and Petrie winced at the sound: the fragments had the impetus and instant killing power of shrapnel. The shells ripped along the track, hammered into the Fiat. Bullets riddled the roof, shattered the windscreen as the three men pressed themselves into the earth while the cannonade thundered at their eardrums. Then it was quiet, the engine sound receded rapidly as the Beaufighter climbed, and Petrie dragged himself to his knees. Johnson had a dazed look; Scelba wriggled, raised his head cautiously, stared at the blood on his left hand. 'Keep away from the car,' Petrie warned. 'It's on fire.'

'Bastard!' Johnson was beside himself with fury as he watched the retreating plane. 'You're supposed to be our pal!'

'It was the car,' Petrie reminded him. 'The dust smears made it look camouflaged. They thought they were attacking an enemy vehicle . . .' He stood upright, then frowned as he stared from under his hand at the ascending aircraft. The engine was coughing, cutting out. The silence was total and for a moment the plane hovered in space before it started moving again – downwards. 'What's wrong?' Johnson asked beside him.

'Engine failure.'

'You mean . . .'

'There they go.'

Two more dots appeared in the heated sky, plumed into cones as the parachutes flared and the two-man crew began drifting downwards. Petrie swore briefly and colourfully, then turned to Scelba who was brushing dust off his clothes. 'Scelba! Are those two airmen dropping anywhere near Puccio?' The *capo* shaded his eyes, gazed at the floating parachutes for some time as flames crackled over the Fiat.

'They will come down somewhere near Puccio, yes,' he said.

Petrie swore again. One expressive expletive, and Johnson looked at him in surprise. 'You didn't get steamed up when they blasted our Fiat – so what the hell's wrong now?'

'Those two dangling from their flaming parachutes could be real trouble,' Petrie explained very deliberately. 'Losing the car means we have to hoof it to Puccio because it's the nearest place.' He turned to Scelba. 'Is there a phone wire into the village? Good, that's something at least. The point is, Ed, we'll have to make for Puccio fast and I'll try and contact Gambari in Scopana at the phone number he radioed to Tunis – in the hope that he can drive to the village and collect us.'

'Makes sense . . .'

'But those two parachuting airmen can take away our ace card – secrecy – just as they took our transport. So far the enemy has no idea we're here . . .' He pointed towards the sky. 'But he'll soon know they're about and the *carabinieri* will be combing the country-side to find them.'

'I see. They've buggered us twice over then.'

'It begins to look like it.' Petrie turned to Scelba who was flicking blood from his injured hand. The wound was superficial, but he used an Italian dressing to stop the bleeding as he made his remark. 'You were damned lucky with this, it just grazed you. An inch lower and it would have sliced off your hand neatly at the wrist.' The *capo* stared at him without expression as he mopped his forehead with his other hand.

'I have friends in Puccio,' he said.

'From now on we're going to need all the friends we can muster.' Petrie checked his watch. 12.30 PM. The sun was at its zenith, burning Sicily with its scorching glow, and they were going to have to walk to Puccio under that sun. Behind him there was a dull detonation as the petrol tank went up, and when he swung round a column of dark smoke was rising like a signal, a marker for the enemy to locate their position. 'We'd better get moving,' he snapped. 'The area will be swarming with *carabinieri* shortly.'

Chapter Seven

Friday. 2 pm – 3.30 pm

At two o'clock – ten hours from the deadline – the three men staggered up a hill slope, reached its crest, and looked down on Puccio. The tiny village was about a quarter of a mile below them, a compact circle of grey dwellings on top of a small hill. A church tower rose like a monument from the ragged carpet of shallow roofs and farther down the track a black-garbed priest on a donkey rode away from them as he came close to the village. He was the only living human being in sight.

Temporarily exhausted, they sank on the ground, their eyes fixed on the diminishing figure of the priest because he was a moving object in an otherwise dead world. Beyond the village Sicily was a heat blur, an aching dazzle they preferred not to look at. They had come across country steadily for an hour and a half under the broiling sun, across a rock desert which radiated up the heat so they had received the sun's blessing twice once when it shone down on their sweat-drenched backs and a second time as it came up at them from the ground's impervious surface. Petrie had led the way along the meagre track and the other two men had followed, plodding mechanically forward, their steps dragging, their legs aching, their backs prickling with the heat trapped under their wet shirts. It was only willpower which had brought them to the hill crest and now they were dangerously close to a state of dehydration, their bodies drained of all moisture, their minds still filled with the endless thudding sensation of boots on rock. It must have been an ordeal because Scelba had thrown away his cigar.

'That must be the road to Scopana!' Johnson said after a few minutes. He was pointing at a pale ribbon running eastward about half a mile beyond Puccio. 'I don't like the look of that village – why don't we cut across to the road and try and hijack some transport?'

'Because there might not be any,' Petrie replied staring at the empty highway. 'I'm going down to the village,' he went on through cracked lips. 'On my own.'

'That's crazy . . .'

'On my own, Ed. It's the only way. That village is pretty deserted and three of us will stand out like a delegation from the League of Nations.'

'There could be *carabinieri* coming to look for those parachutists . . .'

'They could be there already,' Scelba warned. 'We can't see into the square from here.'

'Then one man has a better chance of evading them than three,' Petrie replied. 'You see that small hill over there just this side of the road? I'll meet you on that hilltop one hour from now. If I don't make it, don't wait – try and grab some transport at gunpoint and drive to Scopana. You've memorized Gambari's phone number so you can call him when you get there. It'll be up to you, Ed, to take over and see the job gets done.'

'Supposing you get to that hilltop after we're gone?'

Petrie smiled wearily. 'Then I'll try and grab my own transport and catch you up. Look, Ed, so far we've done what poor Lawson wasn't able to – we're well inside Sicily, we've still time to reach Messina, and no one knows we've arrived. The best thing is to keep it that way – and if I can get in touch with Gambari and he can bring transport to us we're still in business. Hijacking a truck can lead to complications.'

'This man, Gambari,' Scelba said thoughtfully, 'he is an Italian?'

'Italian–American,' Petrie lied quickly. 'And now I'm going down there. Who are these friends of yours in Puccio?'

The *capo* pulled a large signet ring off his finger. He had to work it off because the finger had swelled with the heat, and then he handed it to Petrie. 'Wear that. It may help you because my friends will recognize it, will know you are intimately connected with me. Who are my friends? The grocer, the saddler, the coffin-maker . . .' He trailed off vaguely and Johnson grinned sourly to himself. The coffin-maker. Well, that figured: Scelba, the producer of bodies, and the undertaker, the man who buried them. A perfect partnership. He wiped the back of his neck with a sodden handkerchief as Petrie stood up, handed him the Mauser and took the Glisenti revolver in exchange. He couldn't wear his jacket in this heat to conceal the German gun, and in any case it would have looked strange had he attempted it.

'Watch it, Jim,' Johnson warned. 'That place might not be as peaceful as it looks.'

'I'll be doing nothing else but that. See you in an hour.'

Starting down the track with his jacket looped over his arm, Petrie noticed that Puccio had the curiously blitzed look peculiar to so many Sicilian villages. Its shamble of decrepit rooftops sliding in all directions gave the impression it had recently been subjected to a severe air raid, though he doubted whether a single bomb had ever fallen on the place. Poverty was the national industry on this benighted island, and if you could arrange it almost anywhere was better to be born rather than in this mafia-ridden hell-hole. As he dropped closer, the village had a closed-in feeling, the atmosphere of a hamlet where you never see anyone but you cannot rid yourself of the certainty that you are being watched.

Had he been approaching Puccio in the darkness, Petrie would still have known he was near a Sicilian village: the smell would have warned him, a smell compounded of animal dung and household refuse, to put it no lower. And the flies came out to meet him.

Wearily, he batted at them with his left hand as he walked uphill now, along a dust-covered road while his right hand inside the jacket pocket gripped the revolver. Inside the village the street was of beaten earth, a narrow street with the houses close together and washing festooned along wires which spanned the narrow gap over his head. Climbing higher up the incline, he passed an open doorway where saddles and animal harness lay on a stone floor. The saddler, one of Scelba's friends. But there was no sign of a telephone wire yet, so he went on up the street past the saddler's.

'S-a-a-l-e!'

The salt-seller, a large pannier basket looped over his back, came round a corner as a woman in a black dress appeared on a balcony and lowered a small basket from a rope. She shouted her order in Sicilian and the street vendor dumped his pannier on the ground. As Petrie walked past slowly he scooped up a pinch of salt behind the man's back, slipped it in his mouth and swallowed some water from the bottle he took from his jacket pocket. That should take care of the dehydration problem for a while. Walking even more slowly, he studied the tiny square coming into view at the top of the hill, the heart of Puccio, such as it was. Like the rest of the village, at siesta hour the square was deserted except for some mules tethered in a strip of shade thrown by a wall. The animals turned their heads to watch him with the resignation bred of generations of servitude and their action irked him; anyone watching from behind the shuttered windows overlooking the square had only to follow the mules' stare to see him. The square seemed peaceful enough and Petrie stood gazing at a telephone wire which ran to a small bar on the left-hand side. The grocer's shop was shuttered and closed but the door to the bar was open. Releasing his grip on the revolver butt, he wiped his moist hand on his hip and then took a fresh grip on the weapon as he walked towards the bar entrance. *Mario's*. The faded writing could just be made out above an open window where soiled lace curtains hung motionless in the foetid air.

From inside the entrance to the bar came a clicking sound which echoed sharply in the sun-drenched silence of the tiny *piazza*. The sound stopped, was succeeded by a coarse chuckle and a murmur of voices. Petrie stepped into a tiled passage, walked through the open doorway on his left. The sight of the bottles behind the bar counter, a crude wooden plank partitioning off a deep alcove at the back, made his chronic state of thirst almost a craving. The room was small, low-ceilinged and stuffy despite the open window where he saw the patient mules watching him again. Hadn't the beasts anything better to do with their time? They seemed to be checking his every movement. A dozen bare wooden tables occupied the floor and at several of these Sicilians sat playing some kind of checkers game. Tanned swarthy faces looked up at him from under peaked caps and then went back to their games and their wine. Petrie walked confidently up to the bar, asked the dark-haired young girl behind it for wine. 'Bianco, and a bottle of unopened mineral water.' Long-jawed, the girl had quick intelligent eyes and within seconds they noticed Petrie's right hand on the counter, noticed the distinctive ring Scelba had loaned him.

She hesitated in the act of uncorking a bottle and her eyes met his briefly, then dropped as she poured wine into a glass. Without looking up again she called out sharply, 'Arturo!' One of the men playing checkers stood up, wandered across to the counter, shoved his hands in his trouser pockets as the girl banged the bottle on the counter close to where Petrie's hand still displayed the ring. The peasant showed no reaction as the girl poured a second glass and pushed it towards him. Controlling a rising feeling of impatience, Petrie waited as he lifted his glass. The telephone, an ancient instrument attached to the peeling wall, was close to where he stood, but he wanted to see what was going to happen before he got involved in the endless business of a Sicilian phone call. The peasant, short and squat, with an unpleasant, moon-shaped face, lifted his own glass at the same moment. '*Salute!*' The single word was his only acknowledgement that he had seen the ring and then he went back to his table. Glancing round the room again, Petrie handed the girl a fifty-lire note.

'I'd like a Scopana number,' he said, keeping his voice low as she refilled his glass. 'Keep the change till you know the cost of the call.' He gave her the number he had memorized and waited, sipping a second glass while she revolved the bell-handle and stood with her hand on her hip. Yes, it was going to be a long business. And one of the many things Petrie had learned during his service with the Felucca Boat Squadron was that you don't linger under strange roofs in enemy territory a moment longer than is necessary. For no solid reason the atmosphere inside the bar disturbed him. The click of the checkers, the peasants sitting drinking and placidly waving flies away seemed oddly unreal; but here was the real Sicily, living each day as it had done since time immemorial. Apart from rationing, these villagers probably hardly knew there was a war on. 'Not long now,' the girl assured him in Italian, then switched to her own language as she spoke to the exchange. Not long now could mean an eternity on the island, Petrie reflected grimly.

The spasmodic clicking of the checkers pieces went on, a sound which began to irritate Petrie in his keyed-up state. He suppressed the urge to get moving, to get out of this place fast, and when he glanced at the tables again something caught his attention. Arturo was absorbed in his game with three other peasants, apparently no longer aware of Petrie's presence, but at another table a lean, hard-faced Sicilian was staring in his direction. Their eyes met and the peasant's gaze shifted back to his game, but there had been something in his expression which alerted Petrie. Now I look like one of them, he thought calmly, so what attracted Hard-Face's attention to me? It must have been something in Arturo's manner when he stood next to me. Turning his head casually back to the bar, he rechecked an item he had looked for the moment he had entered the place. A second exit. At the back of the alcove a door was half-open. In an emergency he could slip round the end of the counter and make for that door. He swallowed more wine as the girl lifted a dark eyebrow. 'The exchange – pzut!' Revolving the bell-handle ferociously, she lifted a finger. 'Ah! Scopana!' With a nervous smile she handed him the receiver like a blessing. Petrie took a firm grip on the instrument and leaned against the wall so he could watch the room. This was going to be damned tricky.

'I'd like to speak to Signor Gambari, please,' he requested in a low voice. 'Urgently.'

'I'm sorry. He is not here. Who is that?'

It was a man's voice which had answered, a powerful, controlled voice, and it had given Petrie the worst possible news. One of the peasants at Arturo's table got up and left the bar while Petrie wondered whether there had been a brief hesitation before the man in Scopana had replied.

'Who is that?' the voice repeated sharply.

Petrie took a deep breath. He'd have to risk it and give the identification phrase. 'I've brought the consignment of oranges from Palermo.' There was a distinct hesitation this time before the man at the other end replied.

'The price cannot be high in season. How many oranges?'

Petrie kept the relief out of his voice. The voice had given the pre-arranged reply so he was talking to Gambari. 'Ninety kilos, *signore*. I am afraid there may be a little difficulty getting the consignment to Scopana.'

'Where is it now?'

'In Puccio. That's a village . . .'

'I know the place! I could drive there and collect them at once. The problem is transport, I take it?' Gambari's voice was quick and competent and Petrie felt a surge of relief as he replied.

'Yes, we haven't any. But you'd better pick up the three of us outside the village . . .'

'On the Scopana road?' Gambari inquired.

'Not too far away from here.'

'I will meet you in one hour, maybe sooner. My car is a grey Mercedes, licence number ML4820. I will be travelling alone and I will meet you at the Cefalù fork. Coming from Puccio, the left-hand turning goes to Cefalù, the one straight ahead to Scopana. Understand?'

'Yes. And thanks. How far out . . .'

'The fork is about one kilometre east of Puccio.' The voice became more casual. 'You are late with the delivery, *signore*.'

Cautious Signor Gambari, Petrie thought. Yes, they were damned late: they had planned to arrive in

Scopana at ten in the morning. 'Over four hours late, I fear,' he said.

'When I arrive at the fork I will stop there and wait for you . . .'

The phone went dead. No wasted salutations, just a terminal click at the other end. Petrie was handing back the instrument to the girl when three men came into the bar and sat down at the table nearest the door. One of them was the peasant who had left Arturo's table, another of them wore an apron smeared with white powder. The grocer. Scelba's friends were assembling to see the man who wore the mafia boss's ring. Accepting his change, Petrie started walking towards the exit and then stopped. A roar of truck and motorcycle engines shattered the quiet. There was a squeal of brakes in the *piazza*, a thud of boots, then, as he moved back to the bar to make for the rear exit, *carabinieri* burst into the room with fixed bayonets as a sergeant shouted in Italian for everyone to stay where they were. The girl poured Petrie a drink quickly and he raised it to his lips as he leaned against the counter and waited.

The uniformed troops lined up with their backs against the side wall as they faced the occupants of the bar with their rifles at the ready. The sergeant, seeing Petrie on his own at the bar, shouted and gesticulated. 'You! Sit down at a table! At once!' Petrie slouched over to the empty table next to Arturo and sat down, directly facing the hard-faced Sicilian two tables away. The sergeant, liking the sound of his own voice, bawled out more threatening instructions as to what would happen if anyone moved, then stiffened to attention and saluted as an elegantly-dressed officer walked into the bar. 'This is Captain Soldano,' the sergeant shouted. 'Keep quiet!'

Since no one had spoken, the injunction was a little superfluous. Petrie glanced from under his cap at the hard-faced Sicilian. The peasant appeared to be in a state of indecision; once he almost stood up as though to speak, then he caught Arturo staring at him and changed his mind as Captain Soldano began addressing them in Italian, which meant he was from the mainland.

'Two British spies have been seen near Puccio and they may be hiding in the village. Have any of you seen any strangers arrive here in the past two hours? Anyone you have never seen in Puccio before?'

Soldano looked round the room expectantly, adjusted his cap to a more jaunty angle, his gaze wandering from individual to individual. His eyes rested on the hard-faced Sicilian, paused, then resumed their search. The peasants at the tables stared at each other blankly, shrugged their shoulders, and Petrie noticed that none of them looked in his direction. He was the only man sitting at a table by himself and even though he had been directed there by the sergeant he felt conspicuous. The girl behind the bar polished a glass as she looked at the ceiling, out of the window, at the soldiers, anywhere except at Petrie.

'There might be a reward for their discovery.' Soldano flicked his fingers as though riffling banknotes, and again he waited for a reaction. Petrie cursed inwardly at the double misfortune which had resulted from the Beaufighter's appearance. 'Two British spies . . .' Soldano was undoubtedly referring to the two airmen who must have been seen coming down by parachute. The peasants were repeating their earlier reaction, glancing at each other and shrugging their shoulders. It was a little unnerving: every civilian in the place must know he was a stranger and the only man Petrie was uncertain of now was the hard-faced Sicilian. There had been a significance in the way Soldano's gaze had paused when he saw the man, and Petrie was almost sure the Sicilian was a paid informer, the type of man Scelba had wrongly accused Carlo of being. And he was also pretty sure that the only thing keeping the man's mouth temporarily shut was the presence of Arturo and his *mafioso*. With the armed *carabinieri* only feet away it was a fragile balance of terror and he wondered how long it would last.

'Well,' Soldano announced philosophically, 'obviously no one knows anything of the matter, so we had better make use of the bar.'

It was a popular decision. Soldiers crowded forward to the counter and then stood aside as Soldano himself walked up to the counter and doffed his cap with an exaggerated politeness to the girl who poured him a drink with a blank expression. The tension should have relaxed, but instead it increased under the surface. Sentries were still posted at the door and no one seemed inclined to leave as the girl went on serving drinks to the *carabinieri*. Petrie sat sipping from his own glass, his eyes on the hard-faced peasant who was now standing up prior to moving towards the counter. The manoeuvre was obvious: Soldano had planned it to give the Sicilian a chance to get close to him while he whispered information in his ear. And the information would concern Petrie. Within a few minutes he would be under arrest. Several other peasants were also making their way towards the counter when Arturo whispered something to a man at a table behind him. The peasant stood up, bumped into Hard-Face, said a few words in Sicilian and grabbed the empty glass from his hand. He was on his way to the bar before Hard-Face could object. Reluctantly, the peasant sat down again and Petrie rubbed at his bristled chin to ease away the tension. A reprieve. But not for long, he guessed. A hand nudged him in the back, gestured over his shoulder to the bar where the girl was looking at him as she raised a bottle. What the hell were they up to?

Standing up, he eased his way between chattering soldiers, reaching the bar as Arturo's friend collected two full glasses and headed back for the tables. Soldano, slim and voluble, had turned round and was looking across the room, wondering why the Sicilian was still at his table. Keeping his folded jacket close to his body for fear he might bump someone and they would feel the hardness of the concealed gun, Petrie edged in towards the end of the counter where the girl directed him with a nod. This charade wasn't going to last much longer: Soldano was already wandering towards Hard-Face's table. If the mountain wouldn't come to Mahomet . . . Taking the glass from the girl, Petrie leaned against the wall near the phone and watched Arturo's friend handing Hard-Face the filled glass. The peasant was cautious – with a quick movement he took the other man's glass and raised it. *Salute!*

Sweat gathered on Petrie's back as he watched Soldano chatting to the grocer. It was going to be easy: the Italian had already spoken to several peasants, so when he stopped for a word with Hard-Face there would be no public display that he was an informer. The peasant who had brought back the grocer stood up, leaned over to pull at Hard-Face's sleeve, and the Sicilian turned nervously as the grocer spoke to him. Only a few words were exchanged but while Hard-Face was turned the other way Arturo emptied a phial into his glass. The sweat started to run down Petrie's back and when he glanced at the girl she jerked her head to indicate the door behind her. It only needed a violent distraction now, perhaps when Hard-Face swallowed his knock-out drops.

'You are still going out with Maria?' the girl asked

him brightly. Perhaps she thought it was too long since he had spoken to anyone, that it might soon be noticed.

'Of course!' Petrie drank more wine, watching Hard-Face. 'She is the loveliest girl in Puccio.'

'And you will be getting married – to Maria?'

'I suppose so.' Hard-Face was getting impatient or nervous. He had stood up, was edging his way towards Soldano with the glass in his hand. 'It's a little early to think of marriage,' Petrie replied.

'That's what you say about all of them!' the girl pouted. 'I don't think you're an honourable man at all.' She was polishing the same glass again and again, twisting the cloth tightly while she carefully didn't look in Arturo's direction. And it wasn't going to work; Hard-Face wasn't going to drink until he had spoken to Soldano. With the untouched glass in his hand he came out behind the tables to where Soldano was standing ten feet away from Petrie while he chatted with one of the peasants. A burly soldier with his rifle looped over his shoulder stood next to Petrie, lingering over his drink. A good try, Arturo, Petrie thought grimly, but it isn't going to come off. And he couldn't expect any help from the *mafiosi* if it came to a shooting match with all these *carabinieri* present. He asked the girl for brandy quickly, took the glass, held it ready to throw in the eyes of the soldier next to him as Hard-Face reached Soldano.

The Italian officer turned with his own glass in his hand as though to exchange a pleasantry with the new arrival. He raised his glass. *'Salute!'* Hard-Face automatically lifted his own glass, drank heavily from it. Then he was spluttering, screaming at the top of his voice, a scream which swiftly faded to a horrible gurgle as he clutched at his throat, lurched into Soldano, stumbled past him and crashed down on his back close to the bar. He lay still and his lips were purplish, had a burnt-out look. There was a moment's hush and then pandemonium broke out as the peasants stood up, started shouting, moving about. *'Dottore! Dottore!'* The grocer rushed to the door, pushed past the stunned sentries as the soldiers began shouting, trying to restore order as the confusion grew worse while the burly soldiers and Soldano bent over the Sicilian's lifeless body. Petrie slipped round the end of the counter, saw no one was looking in his direction, walked quickly past the girl and through the doorway at the back. Closing the door, he shut out the babble of sound, hurried along a narrow passage which was stone-paved and littered with straw. At the far end he opened another door slowly, saw sunlight on cobblestones, felt the heat on his face. He went out into a walled yard, shut the door behind him, ran to the end wall and scrambled over it. Beyond the village wall it was open country, a naked hill-side running down to a dried-up stream-bed, and in the distance he could see the rounded hilltop where he had told Johnson and Scelba to wait for him for one hour.

He ran awkwardly down the hill slope at first

because his muscles were taut with tension, but gradually he limbered up and moved faster, and when he first looked back the rooftops of Puccio were half a mile behind him and there was no one in sight. He kept on running, anxious to get under cover before any *carabinieri* appeared, and as he ran he couldn't force out of his mind the vivid picture of a Sicilian lying on his back with burnt-out lips. It wasn't knock-out drops Arturo had fed to the informer, it was prussic acid, hideous liquid which would have reduced the informer's innards to nothing in seconds. And the organization had been flawless. If this was what the mafia was capable of when it was outlawed, battered underground by the fascist police, what on earth would it be like if the monster was ever released from its cave?

The Wehrmacht armoured column was vanishing in a cloud of dust, disappearing westwards in the direction of Puccio as a grey Mercedes raced towards the Cefalù fork from the east. A hundred feet above the fork on a mound Petrie crouched with Scelba inside a shepherd's hut which was four stone walls open to the sky with an entrance at the back. The unsealed stones were loose and between gaps he had a clear view down to the road below, to the countryside beyond where precipices towered a mile back from the highway, and along the secondary road which forked off beneath them towards Cefalù and the sea.

Now that the German column had rolled past it was an ideal meeting place, Petrie was thinking – lonely, unobserved, except for the hilltop shelter where he waited with the *capo*. He took a tighter grip on the Schnellfeur as the car came closer and he tried to read the number plate, but the Mercedes was moving too fast, obviously wasn't stopping. 'This can't be Gambari,' he murmured to Scelba.

'Then he is late,' the *capo* observed, and there was something in his tone which suggested he was only too ready to criticize this Italian who worked for the Allies.

'He'll get here in due course. Gambari is very tough and very reliable – and while we're on the subject, Scelba, I don't want any trouble between you two. We're all on the same job, remember.'

'Trouble is our life,' the mafia boss replied cryptically.

Hunched down behind the wall, Petrie switched his gaze to another hole, and his disappointment was considerable as the car sped on. Passing the fork, it reduced speed, braked savagely, half-skidded on the edge of a chasm, then reversed rapidly as the sole occupant, the driver, twisted round in his seat to watch where he was going. Stopping at the junction, the driver leaned out, peered round, then settled back in his seat as he opened a map and studied it. The licence number was ML4820.

'You know this man, Gambari?' Scelba asked.

'Never met him in my life.'

'Then we had better be very careful.' Squatted on his haunches, the Sicilian checked his revolver, used the soiled handkerchief to wipe sweat off his forehead in case it ran into his eyes at the wrong moment. From his elevated position Petrie was looking straight down into the vehicle, was able to see that it was empty except for the driver, a bald-headed man wearing a dark business suit. Was this really Gambari? The car carried the correct number plate and there was only one man inside the vehicle, but the driver had given a most convincing performance of not knowing the district well, of being unsure where he was headed for. Or had he carried out a little charade in case the wrong people were waiting somewhere near the fork? 'We'll go down and have a look at him,' Petrie said. 'Keep well behind me and don't let him see you're armed.'

Returning the Mauser to the holster attached to his side, Petrie wriggled his way into his jacket, fastened it, and crawled out of the rear entrance. As he started scrambling down the steep slope towards the road below the driver reacted at once. Getting out of the car, he cupped his hands to stare upwards and then turned and opened the rear door for them. The easy acceptance alarmed Petrie: this man was careless – he had expected three people and only two men were coming down the slope. If he was as sloppy as this he could be sloppy about other things, about his departure from Scopana, for example. With growing anger, with the sun burning his back, Petrie stopped and looked along the road the way the driver had come, but it was still empty as far as the eye could see. He started scrambling down again, grabbing at boulders to keep his balance, then stopped. The driver had swung round, but this time his hands were no longer empty as he shouted the command in Italian. 'Stay exactly where you are – both of you!' The weapon aimed at them was a German machine-pistol.

'We hoped you could give us a lift,' Petrie called out quickly.

'Both of you – get your hands up! You in the front – come down by yourself!'

With his hands at shoulder level, Petrie edged his feet down the final section while Scelba halted higher up. The driver of the Mercedes was about five feet tall and broad across the chest; in his early forties, his smooth-skinned forehead was high and the wings of dark hair above each ear did not give him an angelic look. But there was vitality and intelligence – and a hint of ruthlessness – in his slightly curved nose and the quick-moving eyes which were heavy-lidded. A patch of dark moustache was neatly trimmed and his suit was well-pressed and expensive. It made Petrie feel like a tramp simply to look at him. The man smiled faintly as he aimed the machine-pistol point-blank at Petrie's chest.

'You have brought the consignment of oranges from Palermo?' he asked softly, repeating the recognition phrase.

'Yes, but the price cannot be high in season . . .'

'I am Angelo Gambari . . .'

'James Petrie . . .' He started to lower his hands but the gun muzzle jabbed at him and he lifted them again as Gambari went on speaking.

'Major Petrie, I have one problem, one doubt. I was expecting three people. Where is the other man?'

'Right behind you.' Petrie had raised his voice. 'And I'd be pretty careful if I were you, Angelo – he's been covering you ever since you arrived.'

From behind a boulder on the far side of the road Johnson stood up with his revolver levelled at the Italian's back. Gambari looked quickly over his shoulder, smiled again, then laid the machine-pistol on the Mercedes's running-board. 'So, you take precautions also? That is encouraging.' Mopping his bald head with a silk handkerchief, he stared up the hill slope where Scelba still waited with his hands hoisted. 'And that, I fear, will be Don Vito Scelba. I hope you don't regret using that mafia bastard on this operation.'

'We'd never have got here without him,' Petrie said tersely, then he introduced Johnson and waved for the *capo* to come down to the road. 'And we'll need him again to get us inside the docks at Messina,' he reminded Gambari.

'So long as you don't expect me to shake hands with him – and I want a private word with you.'

The shaking of hands proved to be no social problem. Scelba arrived on the road and when Petrie introduced him to Gambari he merely nodded and started cleaning his glasses. They had never met, these two, Petrie thought, and already they were showing by their attitudes that they hated each other's guts. Scelba undoubtedly feared that some of the credit he hoped to gain in the eyes of AFHQ might be diverted to Gambari; as for Gambari himself, Petrie had been warned by Parridge back in Tunis that the Italian had detested the mafia for years. So he'd better have a quick word with the man from Messina, let him get it off his chest. 'We're bloody short of time,' he warned Gambari as he accompanied him across a rough patch of ground between the highway and the road to Cefalù. Johnson and Scelba were climbing into the back of the Mercedes where the American had deposited the sack of explosives as Petrie halted in the open a dozen yards from the car. The Italian dropped the machine-pistol into a gulley at his feet. 'It might look strange if I was holding that if a car comes past,' he remarked. 'You had better hear about the disaster first.'

'What disaster?'

'We have lost all means of communicating with Africa: my transmitter – and agents – were seized by the Germans eight hours ago. You have brought your own?'

'No! I was relying on yours. What the hell happened?'

'I don't know. I was always careful to have people watching the approaches to the house for enemy detector vans when we were transmitting. I am wondering whether they are using some new method.' Gambari offered his pack of cigarettes. 'What worries me now is the fact that you have brought Scelba with you.'

'We need him.'

'I have a cousin who is a *mafioso*,' the Italian said vehemently, 'and I conceal my detestation of him because he is useful – but I know what scum these *mafioso* are . . .'

'We need Scelba,' Petrie repeated curtly.

'It is dangerous to use this mafia boss,' Angelo protested again. 'I have even heard that the Allies may offer him an official position when they occupy Sicily! That would be madness. Once in power he would . . .'

'Angelo!' Petrie's voice was ominously quiet. 'My job is to sink that bloody train-ferry. If it stays afloat it could cost thousands of lives by bringing in heavy reinforcements at the wrong moment. The only reason we've got as far as this is because Scelba was with us – and I'm convinced we're going to need him again to get us inside the Messina docks. I don't like the idea of using the mafia any more than you do, but Scelba is essential to the operation and he's coming with us, by God! From now on you'll live, breathe and think of only one thing – *sinking the Cariddi*! Do I make myself quite clear?'

'I am under your orders,' the Italian replied quietly.

'Do not walk towards the car yet – it will look suspicious. We will wait until this vehicle has passed us.'

'It's a Volkswagen.'

'I know. That is why I advised caution,' Angelo replied.

The Volkswagen continued towards them at speed as Angelo extracted a road map from his hip pocket, opened it out and pretended to study it. They had been standing in the full blaze of the afternoon sun and Petrie was feeling horribly fatigued as he watched the racing vehicle out of the corner of his eye while he looked at the map. The Italian's deeply-tanned forehead was coated with moisture, but otherwise he appeared unaffected by the high temperature as he glanced down at the machine-pistol lying in the gulley. The Volkswagen slowed down and Petrie guessed the thought running through Angelo's mind. 'If it stops,' he warned him, 'we don't want any trouble – our job is to get through without anyone knowing we've arrived.'

'That rather depends on the enemy, doesn't it?' Angelo inquired blandly. 'And this car is stopping. So please leave all the talking to me. The Germans have a contempt for peasants!'

Petrie glanced at his watch. Nearly 3.30 PM. Less than nine hours left to reach Messina and now another delay was coming up. The Volkswagen lost more speed, dawdled forward as a man in the front passenger seat peered out of the window, then it pulled up close behind the parked Mercedes. Petrie felt his heart thumping a little faster. Angelo had miscalculated badly. Two Germans in black uniform sat inside the car and the man sitting by the driver was an officer. Opening the door, he paused to say something over his shoulder to the driver, then he climbed out, stretched himself to his full height, hooked his thumbs inside his belt and stared at Angelo and Petrie. The SS had arrived.

Chapter Eight

Friday. 3.30 pm – 7.30 pm

The SS officer was tall and wide-shouldered and immaculately uniformed. His face and hands were almost white, which told Petrie that he could only have arrived on the island within the past few days, that he must recently have been stationed north of the Alps. But he was also an alert tactician: he had hardly got out of the car when the SS driver stepped out with a machine-pistol in his hands, a weapon identical to the gun Angelo had dropped into the gulley. He leaned casually against the bonnet with the weapon's muzzle aimed towards the rear of the parked Mercedes where Johnson and Scelba were still sitting with their backs to him. And the officer's holster flap was unbuttoned as he stood with one hand knuckled on his hip close to the butt of his pistol. 'What is your name?' he called out to Angelo in Italian.

'Who wants to know?' Angelo demanded.

The German stared for a moment, then reached a hand towards his trouser pocket. Taking out a pack of cigarettes he extracted one, placed it between his thin lips, returned the packet to his pocket. And then the pistol was in his fist, aimed at a point midway between the two men. A couple of deft squeezes and he'll have killed us both, Petrie thought grimly. The hand movement had been expert, as swift a manoeuvre as he had seen. 'Lieutenant Hauptmann of the Wehrmacht would like to know,' the SS officer replied softly. 'And you have exactly ten seconds in which to reply . . .'

'I am Angelo Gambari,' the Italian told him calmly. 'You are, of course, a stranger to Sicily . . .'

'Is this your car?' the German rasped.

Angelo was looking down at his map again as Hauptmann asked the question and he took his time before he raised his head and stared as though surprised that the SS officer was still there. He gazed back at the man steadily with an unpleasant expression which made Hauptmann turn his pistol a fraction so it was aimed point-blank at his adversary. For God's sake, watch it, Angelo, Petrie prayed, this young bastard is probably from Russia where they shoot first and inquire about your identity afterwards. He drew no comfort from Angelo's reply. 'Why?' the Italian inquired. Hauptmann had some difficulty maintaining his self-control. He looked over his shoulder where he could see Johnson staring at him through the rear window of the Mercedes while Scelba only showed the back of his thin neck. Then he turned his attention again to Angelo.

'I asked you a question.'

'And I asked you one!'

There was something compelling, almost arrogant

in the Italian's supreme self-confidence as he held the opened map and stared at Hauptmann as though he were interrogating a hostile witness in the box. The tension rose under the blazing sun, was close to breaking point as the German weighed up the opponent who was almost a foot shorter than himself, and Petrie knew they were only a whisker away from the squeeze of that white hand. What the hell was Angelo playing at?

'It is a German car,' Hauptmann pointed out.

'How observant of you . . .' Angelo's tone was mocking and without warning he had switched to speaking in fluent German. The surprise, the shadow of a doubt showed in Hauptmann's taut face.

'You speak German?' he interjected sharply.

'Again, how observant of you!' Angelo continued speaking in the officer's native language. 'Perhaps you have further observed that it carries Italian number plates?' Angelo let his map fall and it landed on top of the machine-pistol concealed in the gulley. He stooped as though to pick it up, changed his mind, and left it where it was for the moment. Petrie had no doubt that when the Italian next stooped to retrieve the map he would come up with the weapon in his hands. It wouldn't work, of course – Hauptmann could fire twice, kill two men before Angelo would be able to aim the machine-pistol. Then the driver would kill Johnson and Scelba before they were able to get out of the car. Angelo, who had spent over six months as a spy behind the enemy lines, had gone over the edge, had reached that shredded state of nerves when a man takes suicidal risks.

'What about the number plates?' Hauptmann demanded.

'Amazing as it may seem,' Angelo continued in German, 'we Italians do occasionally bend our national pride and buy another country's car. You should be pleased,' he went on, 'when I bought that car Germany needed the money!'

Hauptmann's white face showed a trace of colour as he began moving towards Petrie and Angelo. If he comes much closer, Petrie thought, he was bound to see the machine-pistol which was only half-concealed by the map. Angelo stared suddenly at the Mercedes and his quick glance worried the SS officer; swinging round, he looked at the vehicle where the two men sat placidly in the rear seat. 'What are you staring at?' he rapped out in German.

'A lizard,' Angelo explained innocently. 'It ran under the car – rather a rare variety. But you were saying?'

The brief diversion had worked: the German remained where he was as he studied Petrie carefully before he returned his attention to Angelo. 'I would remind you that this is wartime, that Sicily is a theatre of war. And two British spies are known to be in this area. Where are the car's papers?'

'They are in the pocket of the Mercedes . . .' Hauptmann turned his head to issue an order to the driver but Angelo stopped him. 'Wait a minute! I could show you the papers to prove my ownership but I have no intention of doing so. You have no authority! Furthermore . . .'

'No authority!' Hauptmann's rage was visible now and in the tenseness of the moment Petrie's fatigue vanished as the hand under his jacket touched the butt of the Mauser. He found himself noticing minute details: the slight flaring of Hauptmann's thin nostrils which quivered almost like a nervous horse's, the braced body of the German driver preparing to use his weapon, a red spot which could have been wine or blood on Hauptmann's collar-patch. 'Tell those two men in the Mercedes to get out and cover them with your weapon,' the German called out to his driver. 'Make them lie down on the ground and then search the car . . .'

Petrie calculated whether he could withdraw the Mauser from its holster and shoot the officer in time, then decided it was impossible as Hauptmann faced them again with his pistol levelled while the driver went to the Mercedes and spoke in German. The sack of explosives would be discovered within a minute: Ed had dumped it on the floor at his feet. Angelo spread out his hands regretfully as he spoke. 'Neither of those two men understands a word of German – and if your driver molests either of them I shall report the assault to General Guzzoni . . .' He waited as Hauptmann shouted a face-saving order.

'Hans! Leave them alone! They don't understand German.'

'That is better,' Angelo continued quietly. 'I fear that if I have to report your conduct you will be sent back to Russia within twenty-four hours . . .'

'You insolent swine!' Hauptmann levelled his pistol, aimed it direct at Angelo's chest, but the Italian still held his hands apart in a gesture of defencelessness as the German went on speaking. 'You realize you are threatening an officer of the Wehrmacht . . .'

'Merely warning him. The report would go via General Hubner.'

'You know him?'

'You asked my name – but you failed to ask me my profession. I am a lawyer and my services have more than once been called on by your own people. General Hubner is one of my clients – I have been handling a little legal matter concerning billeting for him and we have come to know each other quite well.' A change was coming over Hauptmann's attitude, a look of frustration and a hint of doubt in his expression as to whom this man, Gambari, might be. Changing his target, he glared at Petrie.

'You! What have you got in your hand?' he demanded in Italian.

'This!' Petrie withdrew the hand which was holding a pack of cigarettes. He let a foolish smile drift over his face. 'You would like a smoke, sir?' An Italian car passed along the highway at speed, followed by another. Neither of them seemed inclined to linger when they saw the German uniforms. Angelo addressed Petrie as though talking to a village idiot.

'Pietro! The officer doesn't smoke cigarettes made of dung! Keep quiet and let me deal with this!'

'Why does a man in your position travel with peasants?' Hauptmann inquired contemptuously.

'Because I need workers to help repair my offices in Messina which have been bombed by the bloody British!' Angelo snapped. 'You have only just arrived here so you know nothing of the situation and you are making blunder after blunder! The heavy bombing has made workers scarce in Messina, so we have to come to the country for them and pay outrageous wages.' His voice became vehement. 'Because you are new here you know nothing! Otherwise you would have seen nothing strange in an Italian owning a German car. And now I am going to remind you of the directive issued by Enna GHQ,' he stormed. 'The directive that the Wehrmacht must cooperate with their Italian allies in the most diplomatic manner! I do not think that holding me up at gunpoint qualifies for diplomatic manners . . .'

Hauptmann lowered the gun as he spoke, but he still held the weapon by his side. 'It seemed strange that in the heat of the day you should stand waiting in the sun. May I ask why you are waiting here?'

'To find my damned way, of course! What the devil do you think I was studying the map for? I am lost and there is no signpost.'

'You are going where?'

'To Scopana.'

'I have just come from there.' The German's manner

was stiff and watchful but less aggressive. 'It is in that direction. I still insist that when spies have been reported in the area we are entitled to check everyone.'

'There are ways of checking,' Angelo snapped. He stooped quickly, picked up his map and strode towards the Mercedes telling Petrie in Italian to hurry up. As they went towards the vehicle Petrie watched the German out of the corner of his eye. Hauptmann was still standing in the same position and he had only to walk a few yards farther to see the German gun lying in the gulley. Angelo got in behind the wheel with an impatient gesture as Petrie joined him in the front passenger seat. Closing the door, he picked up a toolkit which he placed in Petrie's lap. 'May need that,' he said briefly as he waited while a truckload of Italian troops sped past them towards Puccio. Petrie opened the toolkit flap, closed it: inside lay three German stick-grenades. 'They're still waiting there,' he murmured to the Italian as Angelo turned the Mercedes in the road until it faced the Scopana direction. 'The driver has got back into the Volkswagen . . .'

'Let us hope they drive over a precipice,' Angelo growled as he accelerated. 'Do not look back,' he warned the men in the rear of the vehicle.

Petrie glanced at his watch as Angelo built up speed and they began to move across a barren plain. It was 3.45 PM. Eight hours to the midnight deadline. 'Keep her moving,' he urged as another Italian truck sped past in the opposite direction. 'And this road's getting busy.'

'It is abnormal,' the Italian told him. 'Usually there is no traffic for miles in wartime along here. Those two cars which passed us while we were with Hauptmann both carried officers. Something is happening.'

'And something is happening behind us,' Johnson warned. 'Our friends are still with us.'

Petrie swung round in his seat, saw in the distance some way behind them a Volkswagen driving at speed. He shielded his eyes against the sun glare but still couldn't distinguish the occupants of the vehicle. 'Are you sure it's Hauptmann?' he asked.

'Positive. I saw them turning in the road. They're coming after us.'

They were a dozen miles east of the Cefalù fork, driving through country which was utterly flat, devoid of any human habitation, a land of dust which spread away on both sides of the endless road like an ochre sea. 'This,' Angelo informed them, 'is the dust bowl.' He glanced in the rear-view mirror. 'Once there were farms and fields here but the Sicilians are bad farmers – they plant no trees and the sun does the rest. Now this is nature's cemetery where the bones of old mules are bleached by the sun. They are still behind us, you know. What does Hauptmann intend, I wonder?'

'He couldn't be sure at the Cefalù fork,' Petrie said

grimly. 'Your bluff was powerful enough to worry him, but he's an intelligent bastard. He's new here so he decided to tread warily, to give himself a little more time. My guess is he's still suspicious so he's going to wait until we meet up with more of the Wehrmacht and then he'll pounce again – or maybe he'll just go on following us to see where we lead him.'

'Either would be a disaster,' Angelo observed thoughtfully as he shielded his eyes against sun glare from an oncoming vehicle. 'Christ, this road is busy today!' Another Italian truck flashed past them and then the road ahead was empty. 'I suppose he could keep on our tail all the way to Scopana?'

'He came from there,' Petrie pointed out, 'so his headquarters may be in the village. And he'll have more senior officers to back him up there.'

'We slow down, let him catch us up,' Scelba suggested from the back. 'Then we shoot Hauptmann and his driver.'

'No good,' Petrie replied. 'In any case, he's probably too bright for that one. And remember, our job is to get across the island without causing a general alert.'

'We just kill them and leave them,' Scelba persisted.

'What – out here in the open? So the first army vehicle which comes along finds them and raises the alarm? And in any case there's too much damned traffic on this road.'

'But when we reach Scopana Hauptmann is liable

to grab us,' Angelo objected. 'And he will have plenty of men there.'

'I know!' Petrie waved a hand out of the window at the desolation. 'Does it go on like this for much longer?' There was nowhere to hide a dead dog, let alone two fully-grown men, and when he looked back the blurred silhouette of the Volkswagen was still in view.

'For many miles,' Angelo replied.

'Reduce speed for a while. It's just possible they'll drive past us. They may simply be returning to Scopana.'

'Want to bet?' Johnson inquired.

The atmosphere inside the car driving through the heat of the afternoon was almost unbearable, but the temperature was temporarily forgotten as Angelo reduced speed and Petrie twisted round in his seat to watch the German vehicle. It was closing the gap fast as he stared through the rear window and he wondered if he had made a mistake, whether the SS men were going to overtake and stop them. He glanced ahead, saw that the road was still empty, then looked back. The Volkswagen had also reduced speed, was moving at the same pace as the Mercedes. 'They're following us all right,' Petrie said tersely, 'so you might as well speed up again. Our friends are coming all the way with us.'

'We are in a trap then,' the Italian observed. 'Because there is nowhere to hide them and because of the traffic we cannot deal with them on the highway, but if we keep driving on sooner or later we will run into more Germans. Then Herr Hauptmann will act.'

'A trap,' Petrie agreed, 'so somehow we have to get out of it. The problem's really damned simple,' he went on as Angelo built up more speed. 'We have to kill those two Germans quietly and without any risk of someone seeing us. But we have to do more than that – afterwards we have to hide two bodies and one car so they can't possibly be discovered for at least eight hours. They have to vanish into thin air. Any bright idea as to how it could be done?'

There was silence inside the car as they drove steadily on over the empty plain, drove on towards Scopana where the SS would be able to call up reinforcements, drove on with the Volkswagen always keeping the same distance between the two vehicles as solitary Italian trucks drove past them in the opposite direction at intervals, warning them that it would be impossible to tackle the enemy as the mileage between their present position and Scopana shrank with every revolution of the speeding wheels.

'There is this derelict farmhouse,' Scelba said quietly, 'and it is far enough from the road for us to do our work without being heard.'

'You're sure it's derelict?' Petrie queried.

'It is in the middle of all this – it has not been used for a generation. The buildings are in a state of collapse and no one ever goes there.'

'How far from the road?'

'A kilometre.'

'The road that leads to it – where does it go on to?'

'Nowhere. The track leads to the farm and stops. There is no way out.'

'No way out?' Angelo intervened. 'You mean you drive down this track into the wilderness and it's a dead end?'

'Yes. It will be a dead end for those Germans when they follow us. Literally.'

'It is too dangerous,' Angelo exploded. 'We would be driving into another trap. Supposing the SS simply wait by the highway until German troops come along? We would be hemmed in – it would be a death-trap . . .'

'The SS officer has clearly only just arrived on the island,' Scelba explained patiently. 'He will have little idea of the geography of this area. You yourself have been on the island a long time and you didn't know of the farmhouse's existence . . .'

'I do not like it,' Angelo flared, his enmity towards the *capo* bubbling to the surface. 'It is too great a risk to take . . .'

'Hold it!' Petrie snapped. 'We're supposed to be fighting the Germans, not each other. How soon do we reach the point where this track turns off, Scelba?'

'Pretty soon. Maybe in five minutes.'

'If the farm's derelict where do we hide the Volkswagen? We need at least eight hours before there's a chance it could be found.'

'There is an old barn where you could hide the vehicle.'

Johnson looked back, saw the Volkswagen still a quarter of a mile behind them. 'I suppose these guys couldn't be on a regular patrol of this road?'

'And if they are?' Scelba inquired.

'Then they'll be expected back at a certain time at their Scopana headquarters. When they don't arrive search parties will come looking for them, and along here there aren't so many places to search . . .'

'Ed's right,' Petrie said. 'Can you see this farm from the highway?'

'Yes,' Scelba replied. 'The country is completely flat for miles around, and since the farm is only one kilometre from the road . . .'

'First place they'll search then, I reckon,' Johnson said dryly. 'My vote goes with Angelo's. It's too damned risky.'

'Except that we're not putting it to any vote,' Petrie pointed out. 'We may be fighting for democracy, but here I take the decisions. Warn me, Scelba, when we get closer.'

'When we get closer you will see the place.'

So I've got about three minutes to make up my mind, Petrie thought. Three minutes in which to take a decision which could be fatal either way. Driving to the farm could lead them into a death-trap – if the SS men decided not to follow, to wait by the highway until a truckload of German troops came along. But as Scelba had pointed out, how could Hauptmann know that the track led to nowhere? Unless he had a detailed map of the area. Taking out his own map, Petrie spread it over his lap and checked it carefully, then passed it over his shoulder to Scelba. 'I can't see any track or any farm marked on this – check it for me.' A few moments later Scelba confirmed that the place wasn't shown. 'It is hardly surprising,' the *capo* remarked, 'since the farm has been abandoned for over thirty years. And you can see it now . . .'

The place was a blurred huddle to the south, a silhouette which might have been no more than a pile of stones amid the brown desolation, bleak and uninviting as a decrepit mausoleum. Through the heat dazzle Petrie watched it, watched for any signs of life as Angelo began to slow down and look for the track entrance while he waited for Petrie's decision. It would tell Hauptmann instantly that something was wrong if they turned on to the track, would confirm his suspicions because they would have left the main road to Scopana which Angelo had reported as his destination. How would Hauptmann react: wait cautiously on the highway or chase after them, confident now that he had been right to be suspicious? Petrie recalled the SS officer's attitude at the Cefalù fork and still couldn't be sure. Any decision could only be a guess and two out of the four men in the Mercedes believed it would be a fatal error to turn off the highway. Even at this late moment Petrie was in a neutral state when he saw another truck approaching from the other direction. If this were a German vehicle . . . 'I can see the entrance to the track,' Angelo said. 'Do I turn off or go on?'

'Slow down a little more. I want to see whether this is a Jerry vehicle.'

'That farm is too exposed,' Johnson said.

'We shall never reach Messina if we turn off,' Angelo pleaded.

Scelba said nothing as he stared at the farm. The truck roared towards them, Johnson reported that the Volkswagen had also reduced speed, the entrance to the track came close, a track almost buried under the dust of many years which had drifted over it. The truck sped past them, an Italian vehicle. 'Turn off!' Petrie snapped. 'We're going to chance it . . .'

'Hauptmann's pulled up on the highway! He's not coming after us,' Johnson shouted.

Angelo's lips tightened as he glanced at Petrie who said nothing. They were moving into the dust-bowl and conditions were appalling: the wheels of the Mercedes whipped up drifts of blinding dust which rose in a cloud like a smoke unit laying down a screen. The dust rose to the height of the car, plastered itself over the windscreen, filmed the bonnet, became so dense that the glare of the afternoon sun was blurred as the car bumped over the pot-holed track and shook so violently that the engine stalled. As Angelo tried to re-start it Petrie looked back and could see nothing through the dust, could gain no idea as to whether Hauptmann was still parked on the highway, confident that now he had them trapped. Then the motor fired and they were moving again, following a curve in the track which gave Petrie a clear view back along the fringe of the dust-cloud. Hauptmann was turning off the highway. The Volkswagen vanished inside the dust. They were coming.

'He's grabbed at the bait,' Petrie said tersely. 'Let's get it quite clear what we have to do. I don't want any shots fired – we're too close to that highway. We'll use knives and bare hands and I don't want anyone to get hurt . . .'

'Except the Krauts,' Johnson said quietly.

'Shut up, Ed, and listen! We have to do this job so no one hears us – and none of you is to take any risk that's avoidable. I don't want any heroics on this trip. So remember the driver has a machine-pistol and Hauptmann is quick with his gun – damned quick. I want to take them separately if possible – two of us to each man.'

'That will be difficult,' Scelba interjected. 'The farm is small . . .'

'The whole operation will be bloody difficult, and don't let anyone forget it. Now, I want to get to that farm well ahead of them . . .'

The Mercedes ground forward through the dust, lurching into a pothole, dragging itself out again, and then Petrie caught a glimpse of the buildings – a roof with half its tiles missing which gave it the look of a carcase picked clean of flesh by vultures, a crumbling wall over six feet high which surrounded the farm, the still intact roof of a long barn. Dust fogged the view and then they were coming in close as Johnson took out a knife and Scelba threw his dead cigar out of the open window. No one spoke as they crept through a gateway in the crumbling wall, entered a large yard in front of the farmhouse and saw the squat outline of a stone well in the centre of the yard. The place was more of a ruin than Petrie had anticipated and half the barn's wall had gone, exposing a framed view of the dust-bowl beyond. As a hiding-place for the Mercedes it was useless. 'Drive round to the back of the farmhouse,' he ordered. 'I want the car out of sight.' Angelo drove slowly past the barn and at the back the wall had crumbled into a scatter of stones. Only the farmhouse was still standing. 'This place is no good . . .' the Italian began.

'It will have to do!' Petrie snapped. 'Switch off and take the key with you. You come with me. Ed, you and Scelba get inside the barn . . .'

He ran round to the front of the farmhouse the way the Mercedes had been driven and glanced quickly round the yard. No hiding-places at all except behind the section of wall still standing – which was the first place Hauptmann would expect an ambush. As Angelo joined him Scelba ran into the yard. 'The well . . .' the *capo* began. 'Get to hell out of it back to the barn!' Petrie ordered. As the Sicilian disappeared Petrie ran over to the well, shone his torch down it briefly. A good thirty-foot drop down a cylindrical funnel with no reflection from the bottom. The well was dry as old bones and was useless for concealment because there were no projecting stones. He could hear the Volkswagen's motor now as the vehicle crawled along the evil track closer to the farm. Thank God for one thing: Hauptmann was still coming. 'The farmhouse, Angelo . . .' It was the only place where they could get under cover and he led the way, running light-footed over ancient cobbles half-submerged in dust. The door to the house was intact when he reached it, but when he touched it the structure fell inwards, leaving its rusted hinges and collapsing inside the house. Powder from the rotting wood sprayed the stone-paved floor beyond. He went inside, using his torch as the Volkswagen's motor coughed beyond the wall and then continued on course.

The house smelled of ancient decay and there was no furniture in the darkened interior; only the room walls were still standing and the doors had disappeared. The place was a shell. In a rear room he found the skeleton of a large bird lying on the stones and the back door was still standing; opening it he saw the empty Mercedes parked in the sun and he left the door wide open to keep an eye on the car: if the Germans disabled the vehicle they were finished. And now they could only wait, wait and hope that the

Germans came into the darkness of the farmhouse while their sight was still blinded by the sun's glare.

'Stop the car, Hans! I do not like the look of this.'

Hauptmann gave the order as the Volkswagen came close to the entrance in the wall. The driver pulled up, switched off his motor at a further command, and Hauptmann sat up with his head out of the window as he listened carefully. No sound of a car's engine. They must have stopped somewhere close to the farm. He opened the door quietly, stepped out with his pistol in his hand, motioned to Hans to follow him, to slide across the seat and get out of the same door. His eyes checked the wall for any sign of movement. The Italian had lied when he said his destination was Scopana; instead he was cutting across country to join some other road which would take him south instead of east. Or was this place some kind of rendezvous for spies?

'Shall I circle round this side of the wall, sir?' Hans whispered as he took a firmer grip on his machine-pistol.

'No! We stay together, you fool! Keep abreast of me five paces away. We will go up to that wall . . .'

They moved towards the entrance, placing their feet carefully. Hauptmann was suspicious of the blind side of the wall, the obvious place to lay a trap for anyone approaching it, and as they came close to it he picked up a stone and threw it. The stone ricocheted off the well at the moment the German peered round the wall. The cavernous hole in the barn, the empty doorway of the farmhouse gaped at him. 'They're not here, sir,' Hans whispered. For a moment Hauptmann was inclined to agree with him: the farm looked so damned deserted. Then he made a gesture and they began circling the outside of the crumbling wall. When they found that the track ended at the farm, when they saw the abandoned Mercedes, Hauptmann nodded. 'They panicked when they saw we were following them. Check that barn and then come over to the farmhouse – they will be shivering with fright in some corner . . .' Hauptmann examined the car to make sure it was empty, then went inside the house through the open rear door. Once inside he waited to accustom his eyes to the semi-darkness, then explored the downstairs rooms one by one. Empty. Except for a dead bird. But he was careful not to go upstairs alone: once the barn had been checked he could search the upper floor with Hans to back him up. Outside the house he began to have doubts; there had been no sound of anyone's presence since they had arrived, so perhaps they had panicked more than he had realized, were already making their way through the wilderness at the back to the farm. He walked slowly round the side of the house, his shadow preceding him as he made his way back to the Mercedes with his pistol held out in front and his eyes fixed on a window above him.

Pain like a stab of rheumatism caught him in the

back as he reached the rear corner. Petrie's gun-barrel smashed down on his right hand, grazed his knuckles brutally as he dropped the weapon and clubbed at his assailant with his left fist. Petrie saw the huge SS officer lurch towards him, felt hands grappling round his back as the German took him in a ferocious grip and tripped him behind the ankles with his boot, then he was falling with the full weight of the German on top of him. A fist clubbed his face for the second time as he took the shock of the fall on his shoulders and clawed for the German's neck. Hauptmann was still struggling with Petrie when Angelo bent over him, hauled out his stiletto knife, penetrated the German's back and rammed it home higher up. Hauptmann went limp but Petrie still had trouble disentangling himself from the body's weight, and when he staggered to his feet Angelo was staring down in surprise. 'He had my knife in his back . . .'

'Men have walked half a mile with a stiletto wound,' Petrie said breathlessly. 'Let's get over to the barn fast!'

When they entered the tottering structure they saw the German driver sprawled on the floor with a knife protruding from the back of his neck. 'We're up here,' Johnson called out. 'I was going to drop on him but Scelba got him first . . .' The two men were perched in a hay-loft reached by a ladder and the American was talking as he clambered down to join them. 'Scelba threw his knife – the range must have been a good fifteen feet but he got him in the neck.'

'He should have aimed for his back,' Petrie commented.

'I think he did, but we were lucky!'

'Hauptmann's dead, too,' Petrie went on quickly. 'Now we've got to hide these bodies . . .'

'The well! I tried to tell you earlier,' Scelba explained as he joined them at the bottom of the ladder. 'No one will ever find them there. I will deal with their carcases while you hide the car.'

'In here?' Johnson asked dubiously.

'No, I've got a better idea,' Petrie broke in. 'If search parties come looking for these two they mustn't find them or the car. Ed, the first thing is to drive that Volkswagen into the yard . . .'

Scelba attended to the disposal of the bodies without ceremony, dragging each one by the heels across the cobbles until he could loop the legs over the rim of the well. Hans went down the thirty-foot drop first, and because he was smaller the *capo* had no trouble with him, but Hauptmann proved more obstinate: his broad shoulders stuck in the neck of the well, refusing to budge as Scelba, sweating at his work in the heat of the sun, twisted and shoved at the crumpled form. Swearing at the difficulty, he padded over to the wall, helped himself to a large rock, went back to renew the onslaught. Raising the rock high above his head he hammered it down with great force. The rock struck the obstacle, leaving his hands as obstacle and rock dropped to the bottom of the deep funnel. He spent the next few minutes dropping more rocks into the well until he filled up the base so that anyone peering down would see nothing but stone. And when he had completed his grisly task the Volkswagen itself had disappeared.

The vehicle had been driven by Johnson into the yard and, under Petrie's instructions, parked close to the inside of the leaning wall. Angelo then used a tyre lever from the Mercedes as improvised crowbar, heaving at the instrument until the wall tottered and threw its great bulk with a crash over the vehicle parked beneath it. For ten minutes the four men worked furiously, piling up more rocks over the still exposed portions of the vehicle until it was totally buried under a wall which appeared to have collapsed naturally with the passage of time. 'We have spent too long on this,' the Italian observed as he wiped his filthy hands on a cloth and surveyed the result.

'You're wrong there,' Petrie told him. 'So far the only evidence that we're on the island is this car and those two dead Germans. If they were found an alert would go out over the whole of central Sicily, but somehow I don't think they're going to be found.'

The highway was deserted as they drove back along the track through another dust cloud, but Petrie only allowed himself to feel a sense of relief when they had reached it and were driving east again. As they sped along the road he looked back towards the blurred outline of the abandoned farm; they needed eight hours before the SS men were discovered, but it could be eight years before anyone unearthed the macabre secret of the dust-bowl.

Field-Marshal Kesselring was chewing a grape as he held the telephone in his hand and stared moodily out of the open window where brilliant sunlight lit the courtyard below. The clouds had gone from Naples so Allied reconnaissance machines would be active. The line crackled, he pressed the instrument closer to his ear, and the Luftwaffe base commander at the other end began speaking. 'You are inquiring again about the position of the 29th Panzer Division, sir?'

'Yes! There is some trouble with communications and I cannot reach Rheinhardt. Have any of your planes made contact?'

'Only half an hour ago, sir. One of our fighters saw a column of his tanks just south of Formio . . .'

'The cloud's cleared, you mean?' Kesselring asked anxiously.

'No, sir! It was only by a stroke of luck that my pilot saw them. There was a very brief gap in a heavy cloud bank and then it closed over. I doubt if any enemy planes will see him yet.'

'And the weather forecast for that area is?'

'Continuing heavy cloud until nightfall. Do you wish me to report if we see Rheinhardt again?'

'Yes, Honneger. Keep in touch. Formio, you said?'

'It is a small village in southern Calabria . . .'

'I know it! Goodbye!'

Replacing the receiver, Kesselring walked quickly to a side table and studied the map. Yes, Formio was exactly where he had thought it was, a hell of a long way south. The sabotaged bridge must have been replaced in record time and Klaus Rheinhardt was living up to his reputation as the fastest-moving divisional commander in the Wehrmacht. Surpassing that reputation, in fact: at this rate the 29th Panzer would reach the straits by eight o'clock in the evening. The decision now was whether to send Klaus straight across to Messina as soon as darkness fell.

Kesselring walked slowly round the huge room lost in thought. He was convinced that the next Allied objective was Sicily, whatever those fools at Supreme Headquarters in East Prussia might think, and he was tempted to send the order for the *Cariddi* to cross the straits at once from Messina and wait for Rheinhardt at Giovanni, the mainland port. But that might be dangerous: if the Gestapo saw what was happening they would inform Supreme Headquarters instantly. No, he would wait a few hours longer until Rheinhardt was closer to the straits. Until 7.30 PM.

'The target is still waiting for you at Messina,' Angelo said in answer to Petrie's question. 'All four thousand gross tons of her. As you know, your bombers sank five out of six of our train-ferries, but that was before the seven hundred guns were brought in to defend the straits. Now I think they will never get through.'

'So we will,' Petrie told him. It was an exhilarating feeling to be racing along the highway, speeding across a shimmering plain after the frustration of crawling along in the Fiat, after the back-breaking walk to Puccio. Fortunately there had been no further exchanges between Angelo and Scelba, and in the rear of the Mercedes the mafia boss sat quietly smoking his cigar while Johnson, tired and with nothing to keep him alert, had fallen into a semi-hypnotic trance as the car moved farther and farther east. The monotony of the endless plain also dulled the American's senses, but in the distance the scenery was changing where the big mountains of the Nebrodi loomed in the haze, jagged summits which seemed to float like islands in a vaporous sea.

'Major Petrie!' Scelba stirred and the overheated leather creaked under his bulk as Angelo's expression became wooden and Johnson, on the verge of falling asleep, forced his eyes to open. 'Somewhere along the way, perhaps when we reach Scopana, I have to make a telephone call.'

'No phone calls!' Angelo interjected firmly. 'We must have no more communication with anyone this side of Messina.'

'What about gas,' Johnson called out. 'We haven't enough in the tank to get us to Messina.'

'I know! When Major Petrie called me I left Scopana at once and there was no time for a refill. But that is no problem – I have a supply in Scopana and we fill up when we arrive there.'

'Then I can make my call while you attend to the petrol,' Scelba said equably.

'No phone calls! The *carabinieri* have been known to tap the wires. The call from Puccio was essential – but no more!'

Petrie listened to the argument without intervening: better to let them get a little of the spleen out of their systems so long as they didn't go too far. After a slanging match, the tension between the two men might relax a little. It was a slim hope, and Scelba's next words didn't do anything to reduce the psychological temperature building up. 'I see,' he said ironically, 'you are quite confident that you can get our friends inside the dock area all on your own?'

'Plans have been made.'

'On the basis that only the *carabinieri* will be guarding the gate to the *Cariddi* dock?'

'That is the situation,' Angelo snapped. 'The *Cariddi* is an Italian vessel and the authorities will not allow the Germans to interfere. Commandant Baade tried that once and was told to take a dive into the straits!'

'But the tension is rising now,' Scelba persisted. 'Soon a state of emergency may be proclaimed and then the Germans may reinforce dock security.'

'We shall know that when we get there,' Angelo replied obstinately. 'And now, perhaps, you will use your mouth to smoke that cigar while I concentrate on driving!'

'When we get there may be too late . . .'

'Major Petrie!' Angelo reverted to speaking in English so the *capo* wouldn't understand him. 'I do not think it is wise to let this man make any phone call.'

'Maybe we ought to see who he wants to phone and why,' Petrie suggested in Italian. 'Scelba, what had you in mind?'

'Getting you inside the *Cariddi* dock will be a very dangerous operation,' the *capo* began, stressing the enormity of the service he was rendering. 'You are already many hours behind your schedule, so when you arrive everything must be ready. There must be no delay. Is that correct?'

'Agreed,' Petrie said.

'Then it is essential that I phone a man in advance to make the arrangements . . .'

'What arrangements?'

'There are three possible methods which might be used . . .' Scelba trailed off vaguely. 'Only my men inside Messina will know what the present situation is, so I suggest we must leave it to them to decide . . .'

'You tell us nothing!' Angelo growled as he slowed a little to overtake a mule cart.

'Wait a minute!' Petrie's tone was sharp. 'I'll think about this before we get to Scopana, then I'll decide. Once we're inside Messina, Angelo, we can't afford any slip-up, any waste of time.' He let it go at that. It was obvious that Scelba was anxious to obtain all the credit he could out of helping them, but he didn't want to take any risk of losing the *capo*'s co-operation.

It was equally obvious that Angelo so mistrusted the mafia boss that he would happily have thrown him out of the moving car if he had his way. To compensate for his frustration, the Italian pressed his foot down farther. The speedometer needle climbed and in the back seat Johnson looked out of the window with wonderment as a stone wall shot past him in a long blur. Petrie dried his hands on the jacket rested in his lap; the way Angelo was driving they'd be wringing wet again within minutes. 'That cousin of yours you mentioned,' he said, phrasing it carefully so that Scelba wouldn't realize he was referring to a *mafioso*, 'he doesn't live in Scopana, does he?'

'Yes. He is the man who is supplying me with the extra petrol. It worries you?' he inquired shrewdly.

'Your cousin has other friends in Scopana?' Petrie asked.

'Yes, a number of them.' Angelo switched to speaking in English. 'The place is a headquarters for the mafia organization in the province. Does it matter?'

'Probably not.'

But it could matter. Petrie was thinking hard, trying to see round the next corner, to foresee the next danger point. It was this characteristic which Colonel Parridge had noticed long ago in Petrie, a characteristic which elevated him above the other officers in the Felucca Boat Squadron – the ability to keep one eye on the present and another on the immediate future. From what Scelba had told him in Palermo, Petrie reflected, the search for the mafia underground was intensifying, and since there was a mafia faction in Scopana the *carabinieri* might well turn their attention to that place. But they needed more petrol which could only be obtained there. Unfolding his silk map, he spread the coloured cloth out over his knees and studied it for a few minutes, then spoke to Angelo.

'What's this little railway which runs through the mountains beyond Scopana?'

'It is single-track, a very old railway even for Sicily.' Angelo frowned, stared through the windscreen at something in the distance. 'It goes through Sala past the big new German transport park I reported to Tunis about recently, then on to Enna where GHQ is.'

'We've bombed it, I imagine?'

'No, it is still functioning. They are using it night and day to shuttle troops from Enna to the Scopana area. I reported this also, but apparently your planes have been too busy to bother with it. This vehicle ahead is a German staff car . . .'

'With a motor-cycle escort.'

The atmosphere of soporific fatigue inside the Mercedes disappeared. Johnson checked his revolver, Petrie reached for the toolkit bag under his seat and extracted a stick-grenade, then passed the Mauser over his shoulder to the American. 'Keep this for the moment, Ed, in case you have to use it through the rear window. Motor-cyclists first, driver of the car next.' He swung round in his seat to emphasize his words. 'But don't forget this – at this stage we want to avoid trouble if we possibly can. Open up only if you have to!'

'Understood!' Johnson removed the magazine, checked the action, pushed the magazine home again. 'Maybe we should let him keep ahead of us?'

'Running out of time, Ed. We've got to maintain maximum speed while we can.' Turning to the front, he stared through the windscreen for a moment. 'Right, Angelo. Overtake!'

The German staff car, moving at speed less than a hundred yards ahead, was flanked by the motorcyclists and between them they occupied the whole highway. One of the cyclists, hearing the powerful car coming up behind them, turned his head, waved the Mercedes back. 'To hell with that!' Petrie snapped. 'Give them the horn.' Angelo reduced speed, pressed the horn continually with an on-off sound. The cyclist turned in his saddle again, pointed at the staff car, then waved them back viciously. 'Keep up the pressure,' Petrie said. 'They're going to have to shift!' Angelo glanced dubiously at Petrie as he kept the horn going, but Petrie ignored the glance. The last thing in the world an Allied sabotage team would be expected to do was to drive up behind an enemy staff car with a blaring horn – and they were late!

The cyclists and the staff car maintained their positions and Angelo kept his hand on the horn as the two vehicles swept along the highway. Petrie's eyes narrowed as the left-hand cyclist rode with one hand while he unfastened his holster flap, but a moment later a hand came out of the car and made an abrupt gesture. I wonder who the devil is inside this car? Petrie wondered, and then the left-hand cyclist, responding to the hand gesture, speeded up, turned in front of the staff car and the hand was waving again, waving them on. Wiping moisture from his forehead, Angelo swung the wheel, began pulling alongside the staff car, and as they drew level he glanced inside the other vehicle. Christ! The back of the car was empty. In the front beside the driver a uniformed German officer saluted them. Angelo returned the compliment automatically as Petrie spoke out of the corner of his mouth. 'What's the matter?'

'That's General Ganzl, German chief-of-staff at Enna! He's the brains behind the defence of Sicily.' The exchange took only seconds, the Mercedes was still level with the staff car, Petrie was gripping the grenade in his lap under his jacket. One quick toss out of the window . . . 'Get ahead!' he said instantly. The Mercedes pulled past the motor-cyclist, surged forward along the deserted highway. In the back Johnson's hand felt fixed to the butt of the Mauser, his whole body rigid with muscular tension. 'We'll never get another chance like that,' he said. Petrie didn't reply: for a split second when Angelo had spoken the name, Ganzl, his finger had tightened over the stick-grenade, but for a split second only. They had come to Sicily to sink a train-ferry, not to kill a general.

'Polite sort of chap,' he said as he looked behind and saw the staff car fading into the distance. 'And he must have read the Enna directive about showing courtesy to his allies.'

'We're in a German car,' Angelo reminded him.

'With Italian number plates. And Ganzl is good – he'd notice a little detail like that.'

They drove on a long distance until an army column brought them to a complete halt. They saw it coming, spread out over the full width of the highway, an endless line of tanks and trucks and guns, and they avoided it by Angelo's quick-wittedness. Dropping into a dip in the road, one hill crest away from the oncoming column, he swung the wheel savagely, took them off the highway, down a short slope and on to the dried-up bed of a river. They waited there for a long time, hidden from the column in the lee of the riverbank but fully exposed to the glare of the lowering sun, slowly melting as they sat in silence because no one had the energy to talk in the terrible heat of the late afternoon. Then the roar of the enemy's engines above them faded, Petrie went up to the highway, found it deserted, and within minutes they were driving east again at speed.

They were coming close to Scopana and Petrie was again studying his map as Angelo drove down a long valley with mountain slopes on either side; on the bare slopes tiny villages clung miraculously high up in the evening haze, so remote you wondered how they were ever reached, but Petrie ignored the scenery as he asked his question. 'That single-track railway which brings troops from Enna to Scopana – does the train take soldiers back to Enna?'

'No, it goes back empty.'

'You're sure?'

'Yes. They bring in troops from Enna, leave them, the train goes back empty. I was talking about the railway only a few hours ago with my cousin in Scopana.' The Mercedes sped past two goatherds with their flock trailing along the roadside in the blazing sun. As they overtook the little procession Petrie caught the faint tinkle of the animals' bells.

'So when it goes back towards Sala and Enna only the crew's aboard?'

'Only one man – the engine driver. In wartime he acts as fireman as well.' Angelo glanced at his companion. 'You are very interested in this railway?'

'How often does the train run?' Petrie asked, ignoring the Italian's question.

'About once each hour, I would say. As I told you earlier, it is a shuttle service and they keep it running through the night. There are two trains in use all the time – because the line is single-track the one from this direction waits on a side-loop about halfway to Enna until the other passes it. Why this great interest in the railway when we can get petrol in Scopana and drive all the way to Messina?'

'Just looking ahead,' Petrie replied noncommittally,

then he decided to explain a little more. 'For one thing there might be trouble in Scopana if the authorities go looking for your friends. For another, if one of your captured agents cracks under questioning he may tell them about you and this car. Pull up a minute, Angelo, I want to check something.'

When the car had stopped close to a withered tree, Petrie indicated a place on his map with his thumb. 'The petrol we have left would take us about there, wouldn't it?'

'You mean Scopana Halt? The railway terminus? But we have the transport and I still think . . .'

'Answer the question, Angelo! If we can stick with the Mercedes, we probably will. But I've got a feeling we may run out of luck soon.'

'With the petrol we have left, we could just about reach Scopana Halt. You are thinking about the German transport park at Sala?'

'Something like that had crossed my mind,' Petrie admitted as Johnson leaned over between them to study the map.

'You mean hijack a Kraut truck?' the American inquired.

'Look, Ed . . .' Petrie twisted round in his seat to face the two men in the back. 'We're so far behind schedule we may have to risk turning up to the coast road where we can make speed direct for Messina. For the moment, we'll keep moving for Scopana.'

'We shall be there in ten minutes,' Angelo told them as he started the car again. Five minutes later, at

Petrie's insistence, they stopped inside a little village called Pollazzo and Scelba made his phone call to Messina from a bar. During the waiting period Angelo drummed his knuckles savagely on the wheel. 'We are wasting precious time,' he complained eventually. 'You should have let me go with him to hear what he said.'

'And show Scelba we don't trust him?'

'I don't! He is the most powerful *mafioso* on the island . . .'

'Which is why I chose him to get us through,' Petrie replied mildly. 'Here he comes . . .' The *capo* climbed into the rear seat beside Johnson, deliberately not looking at the Italian as he told them that he had got through, that everything would be ready when they reached Messina. Angelo grunted, clashed the gears savagely and drove fast out of Pollazzo. The tension rose inside the vehicle as the Mercedes sped towards the end of the long valley and Scopana came into view, a large village perched halfway up a mountain slope, its huddled rooftops blurred in the evening haze. They were very close to their destination when Petrie leaned forward as Angelo reduced speed, his hands gripping the wheel tightly: the tail of a long *carabinieri* column was disappearing up the side-track which led off the highway to Scopana. Petrie reacted without hesitation. 'Drive straight on – for Scopana Halt!'

Chapter Nine

Friday. 7.30 pm – 8.30 pm

It was dusk, close to darkness, a warm purple-black darkness, and through the gloom the lights of the little train moved like an outsize glow-worm, its engine panting asthmatically as it belched clouds of dirty smoke into the air. They saw it coming from behind a pile of rocks beyond where they had abandoned the Mercedes, from the top of a slope which looked down into a gulch where the line ended, where an engine shed stood at the tip of a short spur track. A train comprising two small passenger coaches and a wagon which it pushed in front. The coaches which were lit up – a staggering breach of security – were crammed with *carabinieri,* and Petrie suspected that the large open metal wagon held more men, but he couldn't be sure in the fading light. The engine was hardly the latest model and the stack was a tall slim funnel; from the slope he caught glimpses of the engine-driver in the glow from the boiler as the train passed under them, then he stiffened as the little train slowed down and stopped close to the spur track with an impressive hiss of steam. 'First snag,' he whispered to Johnson. 'There *is* a fireman this time.' Doors were flung open, uniformed men left the coaches, scrambled down from inside the wagon and formed up with packs on their back as orders were shouted in the near-darkness. Within a few minutes a column of men on foot with their rifles slung was marching off towards a defile.

'That gorge leads through to a camp outside Scopana,' Angelo whispered. 'We'll wait till they've gone and then hope the engine-driver cooperates.'

'And the fireman – you've noticed there are two of them this time?'

'If they won't cooperate I might just be able to manage that little engine monster myself,' Johnson said quietly.

'You're joking, of course?' Petrie queried sharply.

'Not entirely. When I was with the Border Patrol I used to visit my opposite number on the other side in Mexico sometimes. They had a little train which went close to the border and I rode with the engine-driver a few times when we were checking the crossing-points. He showed me how the damned thing worked.' Johnson grinned in the darkness. 'But I never got any certificate for performance!'

They waited behind the rocks with growing anxiety while they listened to the fading steps of the retreating column as it passed inside the defile. Until the column was out of hearing it would be madness to make a move, and Petrie was praying that the train-crew wouldn't start back for Sala before they could emerge from their hiding-place. The fireman had disappeared inside the engine-shed, but the driver was standing below them, mopping his forehead with a handkerchief and then drying off his hands. He had not turned down the boiler and it was clear he was resting briefly before he began the return trip. By the glow from the engine's furnace they could see his every action thirty feet beneath them as he stamped his feet, blew his nose and stretched his arms. 'I'd better go down there and try and grab him,' Johnson suggested. 'He'll be going back any minute, I can feel it.'

'We'll go down together,' Petrie said. 'And whatever happens, no shooting. The sound of a shot would travel miles on an evening like this . . .'

'Better I go down,' Angelo interjected. 'You are dressed like peasants and the driver may not like that. It is lonely here and my clothes should reassure him.'

Scelba spoke abruptly, surprising them all. 'I will go with Gambari. Someone must watch out for the fireman and I speak the language.' Reaching inside his jacket pocket, he extracted a sheathed knife, removed the short-bladed weapon from its covering and tucked it up his sleeve.

'We will go together then,' Angelo said.

'What are you going to tell him?' Petrie asked.

'The truth – partly. It always sounds most convincing. I am a lawyer from Messina and my car ran out of petrol in Scopana. So I have walked here in the hope of finding a train to Enna where I have an urgent appointment. Could I borrow your revolver, Captain Johnson? It is smaller than my Luger which I will leave with you. Thank you.'

'We need that train-crew,' Petrie warned them, 'so handle it gently.'

'If we can,' Angelo replied. 'And I hope none of those soldiers remembers he has left something and comes back for it.'

'We'll cover you from up here. Good luck.'

The Italian shrugged. 'It is only two men.' With Scelba behind him, he made his way along the slope under the cover of more rocks, keeping an eye on the engine-driver below. The Sicilian was smoking a cigarette now as he walked up and down the single track and Angelo guessed that when he had finished his cigarette he would call to the fireman and they would start back for Sala. Coming to a place where the slope was negotiable, they started their descent through the vivid purple dusk, a light so unreal that the hills seemed to glow with banked-up fires. Remembering how far sound travelled at this time of evening, they placed their feet carefully as they went down while cicadas click-clicked in the warm darkness. At track level Scelba tugged at Angelo's sleeve and whispered, 'I will go to the other side of the train to the engine-shed and deal with the fireman.' Angelo nodded as the mafia boss disappeared. Now the tricky part was coming.

Foolishly, the driver had left on the coach lights, presumably switched on by the troops so they could play cards during their wearisome journey. Typical Sicilian carelessness, Angelo thought as he felt the Glisenti revolver in his pocket and walked quietly along the track. He was close to the driver before the man turned, saw him, dropped his cigarette and reached up a hand to climb into the cab. 'Wait a minute,' Angelo called out. The Sicilian paused, thrust his hand inside the cab and brought out a vicious-looking crowbar. Just beyond the glow from the furnace fireflies danced in the darkness as the Italian halted a few feet away from the driver. 'That is not necessary,' he said quickly. 'I need to get to Enna urgently – can you give me a ride? I will pay the fare, of course.' An inflated fare for the driver's pocket, he assumed. But the Sicilian, a stout man with an unpleasant face, shook his head as he took a firmer grip on the crowbar.

'This train has been commandeered by GHQ at Enna for military use only. And this time I stop at Sala.'

'Sala will do,' Angelo said easily. 'From there I can try and get other transport to Enna. It really is most urgent – my car broke down in Scopana and they said I might be lucky if I came here . . .'

'They told you wrong.'

'An empty train and only one passenger. Surely . . .' Angelo pulled out his wallet with his left hand.

'You can keep the money,' the driver said aggressively. 'You cannot ride on this train – it is for military use only. And now I must go.' He turned to climb into the cab and bawled across the footplate towards the engine-shed. 'Enrico!'

It was hopeless. Angelo realized that the man knew he was an Italian and many Sicilians detested the mainlanders. As the driver started to climb into the cab Angelo pulled out the revolver, but the Sicilian saw the action and jumped down, rushing at him with his crowbar. Angelo stepped back, swung the gun and the barrel caught the driver on the jawbone. Staggering, the Sicilian dropped the crowbar, stumbled, fell backwards, and in falling the rear of his capless head struck the footplate savagely. Too late, Angelo heard the scrape of a boot on metal, looked up, saw the fireman looming above him with a shovel upraised to smash down on his head. The fireman gave a horrible gulp, tottered as though uncertain whether to attack, then he crumpled on the platform and the shovel clattered harmlessly beside the track. Behind the collapsed form Scelba knelt down, used both hands to grasp the knife and ease it loose from the dead fireman's back, then he wiped the blade on Enrico's vest and returned it to its sheath. 'The engine-driver?' he asked. 'Is he all right?' Angelo stooped over the body lying by the track, checked the pulse, and shook his head. Standing up in front of the furnace glow he started to beckon to the others to come down but they were already descending the slope. 'I am sorry,' he said as he handed back the Glisenti to Johnson and took the Luger in exchange, 'but we have killed them both. They were stupid enough to rush me.'

'We saw it,' Petrie replied. 'The main thing is you were quiet about it.' He looked at Johnson. 'It's up to you now, Ed. At least the boiler's got steam up, so see what you can do with it. Scelba, could you give Angelo a hand to shift the bodies into that shed while I have a look at this train?' He left Johnson inside the cab, staring cautiously at the controls, and walked alongside the train. The two small coaches were incredibly ancient and had metal-railed observation platforms at either end. Climbing on to the rear platform of the second coach, he pushed open a door and went inside, where he felt horribly exposed by the lighting. But he resisted the impulse to switch off the lights in case they could still be seen by the marching column.

A small central corridor divided off the seats which were two to a side, and in the middle of the first-class coach nearest the engine he found a tiny lavatory compartment. As he went out on to the last observation platform facing the coal tender the train suddenly moved, went forward a few yards, and then jerked to a halt which almost hurled him from the platform. Promising, very promising: Ed was getting his hand in. Jumping down to the track, he went past the cab as the American called out to him, 'What the hell did you expect? Casey Jones?' The wagon in front of the engine was large with high sloping sides, and when he climbed up on to a buffer and looked inside he saw a mess of coal dust and something white which could have been cement powder. It probably explained why some of the troops had been brushing themselves off before they formed up to march away. As he dropped to the ground Angelo came back from the engine-shed followed by Scelba.

'I thought I heard the engine move,' the Italian called out.

'You did – in the wrong direction.'

Petrie climbed up to the footplate where Johnson was fiddling with the controls as he spoke. 'I hate to stick my neck out, Jim, but I think I might just manage this brute. That's the regulator – the cut-off's here. It seems pretty much like that old Mexican rattletrap I once drove.'

'Probably made by the same firm. Museum Pieces, Inc.' Using the shovel, Petrie dug out a place in the pile of coal spilt over the rear of the cab, secreted the sack of explosives, and piled coal back on top of it. Without the sack they might just as well have stayed at home. The toolkit containing Angelo's stick-grenades lay on the floor where Johnson had left them, and the Italian picked up his personal armoury as Petrie gave his order to the American. 'Ed, I'd like to get moving immediately!' He leaned out of the cab to shout down to the other two. 'Get aboard, gentlemen! The Santa Fé Special is just about to leave. And you have a choice – whichever you're used to. First or third class. Peasants go in the front coach!'

As he'd anticipated, conscious of his status, the mafia boss was not offended, but Angelo winked quickly as he looked up at him. 'I can only travel first – I am a professional man.'

The two men hurried aboard the coach behind the engine and then Angelo leaned out over the platform. 'What about the damned lights? We're lit up like a Christmas tree and a fighter plane could see us miles away.'

'Leave 'em on, Angelo, until Ed blows the whistle, then lights out – all of them. The *carabinieri* may have posted a guard above the defile and he might just get suspicious unless the train moves out as it came in. All right?'

'Let us hope so!' A door banged as Angelo went inside the train and Petrie looked at Johnson. 'You do realize we'll have to drive backwards, I take it? Can you do that?' Johnson stared at him without replying as he reached out for the controls. The train jerked backwards – towards Sala – fully ten yards, then stopped with a jarring halt which threw Petrie against the cab's side. Johnson tut-tutted amiably. 'Sorry about that! Just testing the brakes.' The train started moving backwards again and this time the engine didn't stop as it pushed the two coaches ahead of it and hauled the wagon behind. Leaning out of the cab, Petrie felt the warm night air on his face, saw the large shed which was now a temporary mortuary receding in the darkness, leaving behind Palermo, Puccio, Scopana, the whole bloody lot. He checked his watch. Exactly 7.30 PM. Four and a half hours to the deadline and they were only halfway to Messina.

*

At 7.30 PM the decoded signal from Field-Marshal Kesselring's Naples HQ was handed to Colonel Ernest Günther Baade, commandant of the Messina straits military zone. The high-sounding title meant that the German officer controlled all installations in the area with one exception – the *Cariddi* dock. It was this exception which made him frown as he read the signal in his office which overlooked the channel where night was falling as searchlights probed the sky. *Prepare* Cariddi *for instant departure for Giovanni immediately on receipt of next signal. If necessary invoke authority of Enna GHQ for this order. Confirm receipt of this signal. Kesselring.*

The hot glow of the furnace was on Petrie's back as he leaned from the cab and stared ahead. Darkness, the distorted shadows of the illuminated coaches flying over the ground, the chill clarity of the stars in the black vault above was all he could see. Soon the moon would rise, but that wouldn't solve the frightening problem which was insoluble. If there was anything in the train's path, if the line had been obstructed by a landslip, their first intimation of the hazard would be when the front coach smashed into the obstacle. Not knowing the track, taking the train blind through the night was fraught with risk, but at least they were moving as every revolution of the wheels took them farther east. The track was uneven, or the coaches badly in need of maintenance – whatever the cause, the train swayed unstably from side to side as Johnson built up the speed, the wheels hammered the track, the couplings rattled and the tall stack belched out furious bursts of smoke which lost itself in the dark. A good mile from the train-shed Petrie told Johnson to blow the whistle. It shrieked shrilly and then the drunken patterns of light sweeping over the earth vanished one by one as the men inside the coaches switched off; now the only light indicating the whereabouts of the racing train was the orange glow from the engine-cab, a glow which reflected off Johnson's face as he kept his balance with one hand and used the other for the controls.

To stay upright on the footplate was becoming a problem as the engine rushed forward, pushing its coaches, heaving at its wagon while the metal floor of the cab shuddered and vibrated under the rising speed and cool night air began streaming into the compartment, so they were alternately roasted by the furnace and chilled by the cold from outside. With a crisp gesture Johnson indicated to the fireman that more coal was needed for the boiler, so Petrie picked up the shovel and started feeding the furnace, an action which involved splaying his legs well apart midway between tender and furnace mouth where he could shovel up supplies and sweep them round into the redness. He went on digging out huge quantities of the dubious-coloured ore, sweeping them into the flames until Johnson, unsure of how much it would take to make the boiler burst, urged him to desist.

'We're not going all the way to Messina on this,' he shouted.

'Pity – I'd like to steam her straight on board the ferry!'

They had been travelling downhill for some distance but now the track started climbing and the train moved more slowly as they ascended into mountain country with massive slopes closing in on both sides while the engine panted with the effort, sending up wheezing smoke-bursts and shuddering irritably. The moon was visible now, a thin quarter-moon which began to illuminate peaks and saddles and ridges while the valleys and gorges below were lost in dense shadow, and as the track climbed and turned Petrie again leaned out and saw behind the pale curve of rails descending and then, beyond the coaches in front, another high curve disappearing round a mountain slope. Withdrawing his head, he took out the crumpled cloth map and looked at it by the light of the furnace with his feet well straddled. 'There's no station before Sala,' he said, 'and the Jerry transport park is just this side of the town.'

'Convenient.'

'It's about time something was, but they won't have what I'd ideally like.'

'Well we can't just keep going with old Bellow-and-Spit until we run into GHQ at Enna. I thought you were after a Kraut vehicle?'

'Frankly, an Italian truck would be better. The Italians own this island so they can stop anything, and from what I've heard of their relationship with the Wehrmacht they're liable to stop a Jerry truck just to show who's still boss over here. They're less likely to worry about their own transport. Yes,' he summed up, 'Italian would be better, but beggars can't be choosers.'

'And that's what we're beginning to look like.' Johnson had twisted round and was staring into the distance. 'We're coming up to a tunnel.'

'Where?' Petrie stuffed the map back into his pocket, hung on to the side of the cab and peered out. The tunnel entrance, no more than a quarter of a mile above them, had a sinister look. A squat archway at the base of an almost vertical wall climbing hundreds of feet, its dark aperture showed no sign of moonlight beyond. Petrie told Johnson to slow down and when the American protested that they were already at half-speed he repeated the order. 'I'm thinking about what could be waiting for us at the other end of the tunnel – there could be a whole mountain division camped alongside the track,' he explained. The train slowed down, the tunnel mouth came closer as the engine chugged backwards at crawling pace. 'When we get near the far end, stop,' Petrie said. 'I'll get down on the track and have a look before we go sailing out.' The track was levelling, the coaches jostling gently as the shadow of the mountain wall fell over them and the tunnel mouth loomed opaquely, more like a slab of dark wall than an entrance. Petrie was leaning well out of the cab as they trundled closer and he saw a head emerge from the coach in front, glance in both directions, then withdraw again. Angelo was wondering why they were moving so slowly. The engine shunted backwards, crawled inside the opening, and darkness enveloped them, a darkness relieved inside the cab by the glow from the furnace.

'We'll have to speed up when we get to the other side,' Johnson said irritably.

It was a long tunnel and it changed direction several times as the slow stamp of the pistons hammered their eardrums and the fumes accumulating under the low tunnel roof settled back into the cab. 'Exit coming up!' Petrie shouted. 'Keep her going until I drop my hand . . .' The train stopped almost without a jerk ten yards from the exit and as Petrie jumped down, hauling the Mauser out of its holster, Angelo appeared on the observation platform holding his Luger. 'Better come with me . . .' Petrie called up to him.

They walked past the darkened coaches and there was no sign of Scelba as Petrie asked about the mafia boss. 'He's on the other side,' Angelo explained. 'We are playing cards and I imagine he is stacking the deck against me for the next game!' Petrie grinned in the dark as his boots crunched over loose stones. An hour ago while they had the Mercedes Angelo had been prepared to ditch Scelba, but now he had the sense to realize that every man counted, especially a man of Scelba's brutal calibre. And it could have something to do with the fact that the mafia boss had saved the Italian's life when they tackled the train-crew. 'You'll end up being pals,' Petrie joked.

'Never with the mafia! But in wartime one must temporarily make use of people.'

'That's what I've been trying to tell you for the past few hours!'

They peered cautiously out of the tunnel and then walked out along the track. There was nothing in sight to indicate that human beings had ever lived here; only a slender thread of road far down the track where it passed over the railway via a level-crossing at least showed that people sometimes travelled through the terrible wilderness. The track dropped a great distance in a long curve almost immediately after leaving the tunnel, disappearing here and there inside a shadowed gulch before it reappeared again farther down, and at the distant bottom it crossed over a trestle bridge spanning a waterless river. From that height the trestle was tiny, no more than a toy bridge, but Petrie estimated that it was quite a long structure, curving in a considerable arc before it reached the far side where the track ascended again.

'We mustn't forget there'll be that other train heading towards us from Enna,' Petrie reminded the Italian. 'Have you any idea where the loop is where we wait until it's passed us?'

'My cousin mentioned that it was this side of Sala,' Angelo said vaguely. 'I wasn't taking too much notice at the time because it didn't seem important.'

'Well, it's damned important now if we're to avoid

a head-on collision,' Petrie snapped. 'Didn't he say anything else?'

'Something about a lake...' Angelo scraped a thumbnail over his dark-speckled chin where beard growth was showing. 'Yes, I remember now – the loop is next to the lake. There are very few lakes in Sicily so we should see it coming up.'

'You hope! We'd better get back on board now – and Ed will have to push the guts out of old Bellow-and-Spit until we reach that loop.'

The mention of the side-loop, the fear of a collision, had a sobering effect inside the cab as Johnson reacted to Petrie's instructions – although there was nothing sober about the way he began to drive the train. They came out of the tunnel at a sedate pace and then the American began manipulating the controls as they started the great descent. Soon the train was rocking, wobbling from side to side as the wheels revolved faster and faster while the coaches rattled and shook and shuddered under the increasing velocity. The gradient was steep and Petrie suspected that this was one of the many stretches where the regular driver would have taken it cautiously, but time was against them and they were reaching that inevitable stage in an operation he was so familiar with – the stage where you took more and more risks.

Moving to the other side of the cab, Petrie caught a glimpse of the structure, a high wooden trestle, much higher than he had realized earlier, then a flank of mountain shut it off from his view. He made his way along the cab, clinging to its side until he was close enough to the American to be sure he would be heard. 'Ed! I'll warn you later – but when we get near that bridge we'll have to slow down!' Johnson nodded, stared at the controls again as gauges flickered uncertainly. Moving at this speed they'd go straight off the bridge, no doubt about that. The train continued its headlong dash down the mountain, raced inside another gulch, a gulch so deep that again they were shut away from the moonlight and might have been inside a fresh tunnel as the reverberating clangour of the thudding wheels beat at their eardrums and made any kind of speech impossible. Seconds later they plunged out into the moonlight.

The bridge was clearly in view, a huge structure, far larger and longer than he had ever imagined, its straddled supports climbing high above the wide riverbed where rocks the size of small houses littered the watercourse floor, a floor which showed not even the track of a trickle. 'Slow it, Ed!' he shouted at the top of his voice. The bridge came closer and they were still descending too fast when Petrie caught a glimpse of something moving high up in the sky. Jerking his head back, he saw the blip-like silhouettes reflecting moonlight. One of the bombers dropped away from its friends, peeled off like a bird and then started diving steadily. It grew bigger very quickly, became identifiable as an American B17 as it came lower to pinpoint its target – the trestle bridge. Once again they were under attack not from the enemy but from the Allied air forces. Angelo's recent report was being acted on – to destroy the bridge, to stop the enemy troop movements. 'Stop the bloody engine, quick!' Petrie shouted. Johnson paused a fraction of a second, then applied the pressure. The train came to a bone-jarring halt, hauling back the still-moving coaches. Buffers collided, rebounded, collided again, but the train held the track as the first bomb came down.

They had stopped half-inside a gulch with the engine and wagon still protruding into the open as the whistle-shriek of the first bomb ripped at their nerve ends. The detonation was a dull thump, followed by the scream of the B17's motors as it climbed up again over the mountain slope, then for a brief time the only sound was the drone of the bombers high up. 'Get farther inside the gulch,' Petrie ordered and they dropped to the track as Angelo and Scelba appeared on the platform. Petrie led the way between train and rock wall and opposite the second coach he found alcoves cut in the wall where rusty track-laying tools lay on the ground. They pressed themselves into the alcoves and waited. 'If they get the engine they'll get the explosives,' Petrie said grimly.

'Christ! They'll get us too!' Johnson said in fear and indignation.

The comment was pretty valid, Petrie thought. A bomb landing on the engine would project the full force of its terrible blasting power straight down the gulch. The alcoves might save them but he doubted it. Angelo and Scelba shared the next alcove and Petrie could just see the toe of the mafia boss's large boot sticking out beyond the wall. Then the second whistle-shriek came, the horrible sound you never, never get used to no matter how many times you hear it, and as always, the bomb sounded to be heading straight for them, hurtling down to land dead centre inside the gulch. They instinctively stared upwards to where the noise was coming from. Its note grew shriller, hundreds of pounds of high-explosive confined inside its metal casing, falling briefly horizontally as it left the bomb-bay, then plummeting vertically downwards at incredible speed for the target. Muscles tensed, the bomb detonated, nerves jumped, relaxed limply. Not this time! 'It's your pals, this trip,' Petrie informed Johnson. 'B17s. Four of them!'

'Lovely!' Johnson swore colourfully. 'Not a single shot fired at us yet by the enemy . . .'

'Which is the way we planned it.'

'But this is the second time our own air force has come after us. We didn't bloody well plan that, did we!'

'It's the bridge they're after,' Petrie said calmly.

'But they'll have seen us!'

'Yes, they'll have done that. But they shouldn't make us the first priority . . .'

'Shouldn't!' The American was furious at being bombed by his own planes. 'I wish I had your touching faith,' he said savagely.

Johnson squeezed his body deeper inside the alcove as he heard the third bomb coming, pressing himself against the rock like a man trying to merge into it as the hellish sound was repeated. This time the detonation was deafening, a bursting roar which seemed to overwhelm them as a cloud of debris rained down over the coach-tops, and Petrie had to twist a finger inside his ear to clear the deafness. That one had been damned close. 'They're aiming for the train,' Johnson said as he clawed muck out of his hair. But Petrie didn't think so: they'd destroy the bridge first and only then, if they had any eggs left, would they try to lay them on the train. The last bomb had been an overshoot, but the four men were so close to the bridge that they were well within the bombing arc. It wasn't a pleasant thought as more bombs fell and a second plane soared up over the mountain. In all, he counted twenty bomb-bursts, and then a B17 roared over their heads. Petrie saw the five-pointed white star clearly on its fuselage, the plane vanished from sight, and suddenly it was strangely quiet. They listened for several minutes before Petrie eased his way out of the alcove and started walking alongside the track towards the bridge.

It gave them a shock when they saw how close the structure was; less than a hundred yards beyond the gulch the track wound its way out over the trestle. 'It's still standing!' Johnson said in amazement. 'Those buggers couldn't hit the White House if they were standing on it. Thank God!' he added a moment later.

'Wait here!' Petrie said. 'I'm going out over it a little way to see how it feels. Angelo! Get back to the engine-cab and guard it – the explosives are buried under the coal.'

'I'm coming with you,' Johnson said obstinately. 'Then if you get dizzy I can hold your hand.'

Walking along the trestle was a distinctly unnerving experience: the great drop so close on either side, allied with the moonlight, seemed to exert a magnetic pulling power, drawing him to the brink. Petrie looked ahead and that was no improvement: the continuing leftward curve of the trestle was equally unsettling. And he couldn't make up his mind whether or not the trestle trembled slightly as he went farther and farther out over the elevated span. 'I don't like the look of this one,' Johnson said and pointed downwards. A large crater had excavated the riverbed very close to one of the trestle legs, so close that Petrie couldn't understand why there was no apparent damage to the leg itself. It was chilly as he crouched to see more clearly, the chill of the night which drastically lowered the temperature in Sicily even in summer for a few hours, but his hands were moist with sweat as he tried to make up his mind and knew that it was impossible to be sure. Or half-sure. 'Let's get back to the train,' he said.

Scelba met them at the entrance to the gulch and

there was a strained look on the *capo*'s face as he asked the question. 'Will it support the train?'

'Can't tell until we've tried it,' Petrie replied noncommmittally.

No one said anything else as they quietly took their places aboard the train, and when they were inside the engine-cab the American wiped his hands carefully before he turned to the controls. 'Dead slow, I take it?' he asked rather unnecessarily. Petrie nodded as he took up his position close to the cab entrance. As though reluctant to proceed out on to the bridge, the engine made a false start, stopping as soon as it had moved a few feet. Johnson swore, took a deep breath to calm himself, then tried again. The train began moving, steamed slowly out of the gulch, each revolution of the wheels a deliberate turn. Gently, they descended the last hundred yards, and Johnson found himself looking at the firm ground with a pang of nostalgia as the train moved forward and they came close to the bridge. Perched in the cab entrance on the left-hand side where he could follow the span's curve, Petrie saw two heads leaning well out of the windows of the first-class coach as Angelo and Scelba peered out. Then the wheel sound changed, became a hollow echo. They were moving on to the trestle.

The two heads in front of him looked down, drawn by the awesome drop, then Scelba crossed himself quickly. It was the first time Petrie had ever seen the *capo* express fear outwardly, and he found himself experiencing an odd double sensation in his legs: the muscles felt tight and strained but the flesh felt like jelly. He stiffened himself as the hollow rumble went on and the whole train moved on to the trestle. At once the fragile-looking structure began trembling, a tremble which travelled up through the slowly-revolving wheels and into the footplate floor. He looked round quickly, caught Johnson's rigid glance, and looked away. The trembling seemed to increase as they steamed farther out along the span, following the gradual curve until they were approaching the place where Johnson had pointed out the large crater close to one of the legs. This, Petrie was convinced, was a critical moment. If one of the great bomb-blasts had been close enough it could have caused a structural failure which simply needed the weight of the train to expose it. The two heads peering out of the coach were staring fixedly downwards, hypnotized by the tremendous drop as the trembling went on and the train shuffled forward. The tremble might be natural, Petrie told himself firmly; once, before the war, he had crossed a trestle in Switzerland which also shivered as the train passed over it, but the Swiss were rather more highly respected than the Sicilians for engineering expertise.

'How's it . . .' Johnson coughed to kill the croak. 'How's it going?' he called out with exaggerated firmness.

'About a quarter of the way across.' He didn't have to look at Johnson's face to know that he was disappointed, that he'd hoped they'd be much farther along the span than this. The tremble increased as they passed over the place where Petrie estimated they had looked down at the outsize crater, and now the sensation of travelling aboard the train was different from anything Petrie had noticed earlier. Instead of shaking vigorously it was wobbling erratically as though its equilibrium were disturbed by no longer having firm earth under it, and as they moved out towards the middle of the trestle Petrie had a better view of the riverbed. It wasn't a view which enchanted him.

In the moonlight the distorted shadows of the trestle supports leaned ominously, had a crazy tilt as though the bridge were bending slowly under the train's weight prior to a total collapse. Then he saw something which brought instant sweat to his forehead, a moisture so copious that when he ran his hand over it the palm came away running. Midway between the centre of the bridge and the far side a portion of the trestle beyond the track had been sheered away, torn out as though some projectile had struck it. He knew exactly what had caused the gash – the projectile was lying on the riverbed close to the trestle's base. He had counted twenty bombs but there had been twenty-one – maybe twenty-five because if you started a count of falling bombs the fear often muddled you badly. But there had been at least one extra bomb – he was staring at it lying in the moonlight, still virgin in its sinister, cylinder-shaped casing. It could be a dud, but it could be a delayed-action job already close to zero. He licked his lips, turned, caught Johnson staring at him, winked and turned away without saying anything.

The bomb lying below them had fallen closer to the trestle than any of its fellows, and Petrie knew that if it decided to detonate within the next few seconds it would take away at least two of the supports, maybe four, slicing them clear out of existence with its fearful blasting power. Amazingly enough, neither Angelo nor Scelba seemed to have noticed the bomb; they were probably not seeing the riverbed any more, not seeing anything in their numbed minds as the train trundled patiently on while its fluted stack emitted short puffs of smoke. As they came close to the bomb Petrie stared at the obscene object hypnotically. It wasn't likely but it was technically possible: the vibration of the train's wheels might shiver the leg near the bomb. The vibrations might be transmitted through the hard rock surface of the riverbed, they might reach the casing and trigger off the hitherto defective mechanism – if it was a dud. With his elbow rested on the cab edge, Petrie watched the dark sausage-shape pass under him, then he glanced in front and saw two heads turning towards him. They *had* seen the bomb! Only Johnson had travelled in blissful ignorance of what lay under them. The train continued along the trestle, and hours later, so it seemed, the hollow thump of the wheels changed to a more solid sound and they were off the bridge.

Standing up straighter, Petrie had difficulty in

moving his elbow, which had stiffened with the tension. Taking a deep breath, he jerked his elbow, a bone creaked and it came loose. 'Build up a head of steam, Ed,' he called out. 'There's a big climb coming up and I want you to eat it. If we don't reach that side-loop before the other train we'll end up mashed.'

The train started the big climb up the mountain and Petrie watched for the lake which would locate the side-loop. It wouldn't be situated on the ascent, but he suspected that soon after they'd gone over the top they'd find it because beyond the summit of the long incline his map indicated a flattish area. The trouble was it didn't show either the loop or the lake. He was bothered about the timing now: they had waited in the gulch for the bombing to stop, a wait which more than compensated for the speed with which they had come down the incline beyond the tunnel. Which meant that if they didn't make up for the delay they were going to meet the train coming from Enna head-on.

The long ascent went on quietly under the moon, across wilds which seemed remote from war, so it was almost possible to believe that the bombing of the trestle must have been a bad dream. And it was getting colder as the evening wore on and they climbed to new altitudes, so chilly that the jackets they wore were hardly sufficient protection against the low temperature; the coats they had left behind in the Mercedes would have come in useful now, Petrie reflected, as he felt the gradient slacken and the engine move faster. They reached the top, left behind the sheer fall to their right, and because they were moving into flatter country it was difficult to realize they were still at high altitude. The train sped on over a rock-strewn plateau, and here Petrie was taking a calculated risk – their speed was taking them closer to the loop in minimum time, but it also increased the chances that they would fly past the vital point, missing lake and loop in their anxiety to reach them. The rocks gave way to an uncluttered area, an endless pancake of baked mud, and suddenly Petrie spotted the drooping reeds hanging over the mud. God! This was the lake! Evaporated by the sun to a desert. He called out to Johnson, 'Slow down!' Seconds later he saw the switch lever coming towards them. 'Full stop!' He was jumping from the footplate as the American jammed on the brake and as he ran towards the lever he heard a whistle blowing in the distance. The train heading from the other direction was almost on top of them. He heaved at the lever and it wouldn't budge. His hands were slippery, his muscles felt weak, and he heard the whistle again, louder this time, as he took a firmer grip, braced himself, and heaved with all his remaining strength. The lever moved, eased towards him as he went on pulling until it would move no farther.

'Get her moving, Ed!'

But the train was already moving, rattling gently

as the engine pushed the wagon and hauled the two coaches off the main track into the safety of the loop. The moment the second coach was off the main line Petrie pushed savagely at the lever and this time it worked at once, shifting the rails back into their original position. He ran along the track with the whistle again in his ears, ran to the front observation platform, dragged himself on board, almost falling inside the coach as he pushed the door shut behind him. Then, gasping for breath, he eased the door open a few inches.

From behind the almost closed door he saw the oncoming train racing into sight round a bend, moving far too fast as it sped towards the loop with smoke belching from its stack. Inside the engine-cab Johnson bent towards the furnace to avoid being seen clearly, but the precaution was hardly necessary as the train with four darkened coaches hurtled past them, its velocity momentarily shaking their own coaches. When he looked out of the cab all he could see was the receding rectangle of the last coach, and then Petrie was running back to the lever to operate it once more. When he climbed back on to the footplate Johnson offered him a cigarette, but Petrie shook his head as he held on to the side for support, his mind numbed by the nearness of their escape. 'Ed, you've got a clear line now,' he said. 'Full speed ahead for that transport park at Sala.'

Chapter Ten

Friday. 8.30 pm – 9 pm

The coaches jostled each other, a shudder passed through the train, and Johnson brought it to a halt as Petrie had instructed, brought it to a halt over the deserted level-crossing which carried the road leading to the transport park. They had waited for ten precious minutes aboard the train concealed in a nearby gulch, hoping for a lone German truck to drive down from the transport park a quarter of a mile away, but now something else was coming. From the front observation platform Petrie stared at a wrecked Wehrmacht truck with its nose crushed against a boulder close to the track. 'The poor devil must have skidded,' he told Johnson. 'The driver's gone clear through the windscreen. Now – if only this ambulance will keep on coming . . .'

The Italian army ambulance was driving down the hill towards the level-crossing at medium speed, the driver doubtless imagining that the train parked at the crossing would move on before he had to stop. The vehicle was still some distance away and the moonlight reflected dully off its white-painted surface. No siren going, Petrie noted, so it wasn't in too much of a hurry to get anywhere. He started giving quick directions, ordering Scelba to hide behind the stationary coaches, sending Angelo to hide behind a crag a little way up the road, telling Johnson to take up position behind the wrecked truck, but the American broke in with a protest. 'There could be casualties inside that ambulance – air raid casualties . . .'

'Ed, if there are, we'll have to let them drive on, but somehow I doubt it – the siren isn't going. If we find they have casualties aboard we'll pretend we're bandits after money and let them through. We certainly look the part.'

'And if there aren't any casualties inside?'

'We grab it!' He shook his head at Johnson's dubious expression. 'Ed, when we were on the train I worked out a simple specification of what we need to get through to Messina. We need a fast-moving vehicle which will take us clear through the checkpoints along that coastal highway.'

'It's against the rules of warfare . . .'

Petrie stiffened. 'So is the sinking of a hospital ship full of wounded troops – and that's what the Germans did in Greece with their Stukas. I know, I saw it happen. And we're only going to use this vehicle as transport to slip through the cordon the Wehrmacht has clamped round Messina. We're using this ambulance as a taxi . . .' He stared at Scelba. 'And unless it's absolutely vital there'll be no shooting . . .'

'They won't even be armed,' Johnson snapped.

'So there'll be no shooting,' Petrie repeated. 'But

watch it, Ed. This ambulance may not be as innocent as it seems.'

They waited out of sight and now the ambulance driver was becoming a little less confident that the obstacle blocking his way was going to move; three hundred yards from the crossing he saw the wreck of the army truck, slowed down, turned to drive over the ground towards the vehicle, then turned back on to the road. Petrie watched the change of direction with narrowed eyes as he glanced to his left where Scelba was crouched down behind the train, then towards the truck where Johnson was hidden. The site of the accident had an eerily deserted look, as though something inexplicable had happened between the stationary train and the wrecked vehicle, and he could imagine the bewilderment of the ambulance driver, but his reaction was odd. The ambulance was descending very slowly as its headlights splayed over the coaches, shining through the windows and out of the other side, showing up its emptiness. Twenty yards from the train the vehicle pulled up with its motor still running, which worried Petrie: if the driver swung his wheel, turned over the ground and drove back the way he had come there could be no question of opening fire. From where he crouched behind the platform he saw that the ambulance had a very large ventilator on the roof close to an aerial. Was there something odd about this vehicle?

The white-coated driver had his head twisted round now while he talked to someone in the back.

They had to wait until the driver got out to investigate – if he ever got out. The minutes ticked past and Petrie knew that something was seriously wrong: from his seat the driver would be able to see the condition of the truck and his normal reaction should have been to get out instantly to investigate the accident. The sense of something abnormal grew and Petrie blessed his caution in treating the hold-up as a military operation. Beside him Scelba placed his revolver on the ground, wiped his hand dry quickly on his trouser leg and picked up the weapon again. The Sicilian's face was impassive at this moment of tension, the impassiveness of a professional gunman who had experienced such situations many times before. Petrie stiffened as the ambulance driver opened his door, stepped out and walked cautiously towards the wreckage. As he walked he kept glancing over his shoulder at the apparently abandoned train, and when he reached a point where he could see inside the concertinaed cab he stopped. Again the wrong reaction: from where he stood he could clearly see the truck driver's body slumped over the wheel and an ordinary ambulance man would have run forward instinctively. But the short stocky man wearing the uniform of the Italian Medical Corps seemed more worried about the empty train as he looked back once more at the stationary coaches. Petrie stood up, walked to the end of the platform, stepped across the track with the Mauser aimed as the driver swung round, half-thrust his hand inside his tunic and then withdrew it when he saw the weapon.

'You have no money inside the ambulance?' Petrie rapped out quickly in German.

'Nein . . .' The driver stopped speaking, realizing he had been trapped into replying in German. Petrie was covering the driver with his gun when a rear door of the ambulance opened and a man dressed in civilian clothes, a belted coat, a soft hat, stepped into view with a machine-pistol grasped in both hands. The gun was firing, bullets were spattering on the ground a few feet to Petrie's left, when Scelba fired twice. The civilian collapsed, let his weapon fall as Angelo appeared running down the road, stooped, then pointed the machine-pistol inside the rear of the vehicle without firing. Johnson came up behind the ambulance driver, extracted a Luger pistol from inside his tunic, patted the man's clothes for other concealed weapons, and then spoke to Petrie. 'That's the lot. And this guy is the most lethal medic I've ever come across. What made you suspicious, Jim?'

'It came from the direction of the Jerry transport park – not that that proved anything. But this character certainly wasn't acting normally – and now I think we'll take a quick look at this so-called ambulance. Scelba, keep an eye on this medical gunman for a minute.'

The civilian lay dead in the road at Angelo's feet but Petrie ignored the body as the Italian gestured inside the vehicle with his gun muzzle. A brawny-looking youth was sitting at a small table between the couches, his hands high above his head while he stared at them sullenly. He was dressed in the uniform of the Italian Medical Corps but on the table was a pair of headphones and a rectangular object like a radio transmitter, which was hardly standard ambulance equipment. When Petrie spoke to him in German he shook his head and said he only understood Italian.

'I see,' Petrie went on in German, 'and that instrument in front of you is the latest blood-plasma machine, I suppose? Get out – or get shot!' The German scrambled out of the ambulance, suddenly familiar with the Teutonic tongue, and while Angelo watched him Petrie bent down and pulled out a wallet from the dead civilian's inner breast pocket. The identity card he extracted from the wallet didn't entirely surprise him and he handed it to Johnson without a word. The American stared at the document and then read aloud: 'Oscar Schliemann, Gestapo officer. What the hell's going on here?'

'Something AFHQ will be interested to hear about. Let's have a closer look at this latest version of an ambulance.' Stooping to clear the roof, he climbed inside, followed by Johnson. Against one wall, where it could easily be reached by a man sitting at the table, was a small control panel. The ambulance's motor was still running as he fiddled with switches and then Johnson stared upwards as they heard a noise of whirring machinery above them. A large metal box was attached to the underside of the roof and the whirring came from inside the box. Glancing up, Petrie pushed past the American and was stepping down out of the ambulance when Angelo reacted violently: reversing the machine-pistol, he struck his prisoner a savage blow on the back of the head with the weapon's butt, and then spoke with undisguised satisfaction as the German collapsed unconscious. 'The bastards!'

'What the devil's got into him?' Johnson demanded as he dropped to the road.

Petrie pointed upwards where the large roof ventilator had now expanded into a metal column supporting two metal wings like radar scanners. 'Diabolical, isn't it?' Petrie remarked pleasantly. 'This is a radio-detector van camouflaged to look like an Italian ambulance. And I'm pretty sure the Italians won't know anything about it. You see the point, don't you?'

'Not yet . . .' Johnson said slowly, but Angelo interrupted with a bitter look on his face.

'I see it only too clearly, Major. This is probably how the Germans detected my own transmitter, Orange One. A man who lived in the area where we hid it told me that the day before the transmitter was captured an Italian ambulance was parked in a yard nearby. Like a fool I thought nothing of it. And I also wonder whether the Italian Army would permit this . . .'

'If they didn't know, they wouldn't have any

option, would they?' Petrie commented. 'That thing on the table in there is a listening device. So I don't think we need worry overmuch about using this vehicle as a taxi.'

Going back inside the ambulance, he operated a switch and the machinery hummed again as the detector column was lowered inside the ventilator cap. He used his knife to cut the wires, then hid the headphones and the listening device inside a cupboard; the table he folded and put inside another cupboard. The ambulance had now returned to its normal function with the two leather couches fixed to each wall ready for casualties – and casualties were available. They worked with frantic energy under Petrie's prodding: uniforms were stripped from the two unconscious Germans, a task which made Angelo regret his burst of anger since undressing an inert man is far more difficult than making him strip himself; medical tape found in a drawer was used to bind up the two prisoners; and cottonwool from the same drawer was stuffed into their ears so they wouldn't overhear any conversation if they regained consciousness. These tasks were performed after they had hauled all three Germans inside the ambulance in case they had to make a swift departure, and while they were completing the jobs Johnson was inside the engine-cab, digging away furiously to rescue the sack of explosives Petrie had hidden beneath the coal. When he returned with the sack over his shoulder Petrie and Angelo were struggling into the Medical

Corps uniforms. Because they were of a similar build, the driver's outfit was the right size for the Italian, but Petrie had trouble forcing himself inside his own uniform; the tunic was a reasonable fit, the trousers were too short.

'If they made me do this for a living in peacetime I'd join the Army,' Johnson grumbled as he dumped the sack on the ambulance floor. He looked at the body of the Gestapo officer with distaste. 'Do we really need Herr Schliemann? I'm a bit fussy about who I travel with.'

'He stays with us for the moment, Ed,' Petrie snapped as he adjusted his tunic. 'When we've gone the only mystery will be the empty train – the truck obviously crashed and they may think the train-crew ran off in a panic.'

Johnson was regarding Petrie's appearance critically. 'Do ambulance drivers normally carry two days' growth of beard?' he inquired.

'They do in the British Army when they've been working eighteen hours non-stop, and I dare say the Italians have been known to work their drivers into the ground. In any case, it gives us a good excuse for not wanting to linger at any checkpoint – we're hell-bent back for our depot.'

'We dump the offal somewhere on the way?' Scelba asked, indicating the prisoners. 'Preferably with a bullet through their heads. Then they cannot talk.'

It wasn't a popular suggestion, and when Scelba saw the expression on the other men's faces he hastily dropped the subject as Petrie climbed behind the wheel and Angelo joined him in his neat uniform. The petrol tank was full, which was hardly surprising since the vehicle had probably been refilled inside the Wehrmacht transport park. 'I'll drive,' he told the Italian, 'and since you look so damned elegant you'd better be the chap who gets out – if anyone has to.'

'That will be logical,' Angelo agreed. 'You are the driver so you stay behind the wheel.'

'Unless we run into a real accident – in which case people are going to expect both of us to get out.'

Petrie re-started the engine he had switched off earlier. In front of them the little train stood abandoned over the level-crossing, and he had the odd feeling that it might stay there until the invading Allied troops found it – if they ever reached this point. All of which might depend a little on four men inside an Italian ambulance. He checked his watch. 9 PM. Thank God Parridge couldn't see him now: the colonel must be assuming he was already inside Messina. He swung the vehicle through a hundred and eighty degrees, straightened up and headed north. 'Theoretically we're already too late,' he said to Angelo. 'So when we hit the coast we'll go all out.'

The old duelling scar down the right-hand side of General Klaus Rheinhardt's face showed up clearly as he bent over the oil-lamp inside his tent to check the time. His wristwatch showed 8.30 PM. From the tent opening he could see clear across the moonlit channel of water to the mountains rising above Messina, to where he was going, to Sicily. Beyond the tent and under the olive groves of Calabria the enormous force under his command was already on the move. Two Panzer regiments comprising over three hundred Mark IV tanks; a rifle regiment of three motorized battalions and one motorcycle battalion; an artillery regiment of twenty-four guns; one anti-tank battalion; and an engineers' battalion. From where he sat on his camp-stool Rheinhardt could hear the clank of tanks' tracks moving away over the sun-baked ground, could hear the brusque shouts of NCOs issuing urgent orders. Thank God Kesselring had taken his advice and sent the command, *Move into Sicily at once!*

'What is it, Wengel?'

Colonel Wengel saluted from outside the tent. 'The ammunition train is just arriving at Giovanni, sir.'

'As soon as the ferry arrives from Messina, get it on board. I may travel with it to Sicily myself.'

Wengel saluted, went away, leaving the view through the tent opening clear again. It was this view which interested Rheinhardt because from this point, situated seven hundred feet above the straits, he would be able to see the *Cariddi* leaving Messina harbour on its way to the mainland. The moment he saw the train-ferry he would drive down to Giovanni.

Chapter Eleven

Friday. 9 pm – 10.30 pm

The headlights swept through the night as Petrie pressed his foot down, swept up over a pass and raced down the long slope beyond where the mountains soared up on both sides, majestic in the moonlight, their scarred ridges silvered and shadowed and without any sign of life. For a moment, at the pass's summit, they had caught a distant glimpse of sea like mercury, then they were plunging down the slope and a ridge blotted out the view. For a long way ahead the road was unnaturally straight where it ran between mountains which lay parallel to each other, and the surface was better than any they had encountered so far. It was still not good, would have counted as a lane in any other European country, but it was good enough for Petrie to risk a burst of speed as they tore down the deserted road towards the sea.

Beside him Angelo was sleeping, his chin sunk on his chest. Petrie glanced back through the small window into the interior of the ambulance where Johnson was sitting close to him while Scelba sprawled along the other couch, also fast asleep. They were the only occupants: the two German prisoners and the dead Gestapo officer had been left in a derelict barn close to the road a few miles back. 'Better get some kip in, Ed,' Petrie advised. 'There won't be much chance later.'

'What about yourself? You've been driving non-stop half the day and I could take over the wheel for a while – I may not be in medic's uniform but we're not meeting anything.'

'We will – if you take over the wheel,' Petrie assured him. 'And as you say, you're hardly dressed for the part. In any case, I'm geared up now and I'd sooner stay that way until the job's done.'

'You think we're going to make it? It's getting damned late.'

'We should do – so long as Kesselring hasn't started sending over the 29th Panzer already. And I don't think he will – he'll wait until he gets the report of the airborne lads dropping. Then he'll know.'

'And they'll drop when?'

'If they're coming tonight, my guess would be close to midnight – just before the moon fades. It will be an hour after that before the positive confirmations reach Kesselring.'

'And if we're lucky we'll reach Messina when?'

'A little this side of midnight would be my guess.'

'It's going to be pretty close then?'

'It could be pretty close, Ed,' Petrie agreed.

This sombre thought was occupying Petrie as he drove on down the long slope between tall hedges of prickly pear which reminded Johnson of New Mexico.

The American stretched out along his couch, listened to Scelba's snores, and then dropped off himself. Petrie had no inclination to sleep: he had got beyond it, and his nerves were so strung up that he doubted whether he could have slept if he tried. Sometime, after the job was done, he'd collapse, all reserves drained, and he'd probably sleep for thirty-six hours. After the job was done. Angelo woke up a few minutes later and Petrie began questioning him about the train-ferry to refresh his memory.

'. . . she was built in Genoa only eleven years ago,' the Italian went on. 'She has a gross displacement of over four thousand tons and is the largest train-ferry in western Europe still afloat. She measures about three hundred and fifty feet from stern to bows and is powered by three eight-cylinder diesel-electric Burmeister and Wain engines . . .'

'Speed?' Petrie queried.

'She can travel at seventeen knots, although her normal service speed is fifteen-and-a-half.'

'And how long does it take to make the crossing between here and Giovanni on the mainland? That's just in case we can't do the job while she's in harbour.'

'The distance is eighty kilometres. Allowing for leaving and entering harbour, she makes the crossing in twenty-five to thirty minutes.'

'Thirty minutes isn't very long,' Petrie said as he noticed the weather ahead; it looked to be changing, and not for the better. Heavy cloudbanks were coming in from the northwest and a breeze was starting to blow in the previously still night. 'Can we do the job while she's still in harbour?'

'Maybe.' Angelo shrugged his shoulders uncertainly. 'But there are many guards on the dockside and only a few on board while she is crossing the straits.'

'Then it may have to be done while she's at sea – that way she'd go down deep.' He swung the wheel to take the ambulance over an ancient bridge spanning a waterless riverbed, then straightened up as the road continued between the high prickly pear hedges. Silhouetted against the moonlight, the cactus extremities looked like crucified hands reaching up towards the starlit sky. Behind him boots hit the floor heavily as Scelba sat up, stretched, and then rested an elbow on the edge of the window at the back of the driving compartment. His sarcastic question showed that he had been listening to the conversation. 'And when you have finished the job you'll swim for it?' he demanded. 'There is a powerful current in the straits, Signor Gambari.'

'That has been taken care of,' Angelo snapped. 'One of my men – who is totally reliable – will take out his boat if the ferry sails with us on board. If necessary, he will keep pace with the ferry and then pick us up when we go overboard.'

'We'd have to have some means of signalling him,' Petrie pointed out.

'There is a Very pistol at my flat.'

'And this boat takes us where?'

'Down the straits towards Malta. We shall be very lucky if we manage it – the channel is infested with German E-boats.'

A match scraped behind them as Scelba lit a fresh cigar. He puffed to get it going and asked his next question casually.

'What colour will your signal light be?'

'Green.' Angelo twisted round in his seat to stare at the mafia boss. 'Why do you want to know a detail like that?'

'Because I also have made arrangements to see that the three of you get away safely after you have done the job,' Scelba explained blandly. 'At least, Giacomo is making arrangements for me . . .'

'Who is Giacomo?' Petrie interjected.

'The man I have instructed to prepare the way for you.'

'We may not need him,' Angelo said curtly. 'I have organized a complete plan – for getting inside the dock, for sinking the ferry and for getting away afterwards . . .'

'I'd still like to hear Scelba's plan, too,' Petrie intervened again. 'It gives us something to fall back on, Angelo, if anything has happened to your chap. Once a spy-ring's penetrated, they sometimes scoop in the lot.'

'That is true,' the Italian admitted. 'You mean, Scelba, that you could get us off the ferry even in mid-channel?'

'Certainly! By using a similar method to your own.

Giacomo is preparing a special vessel in case it should be needed – a swordfish boat.'

'What's that?' Petrie asked.

'The swordfish fishermen in the straits are my friends,' Scelba began. 'They use a peculiar type of vessel for their work and one of these is being adapted so it can travel at speed. One of the latest German outboard motors is being attached to it . . .'

'Where did you get that?'

'The Messina docks are packed with German equipment brought over from the mainland – largely by the *Cariddi*. Most of the men who work on the waterfront are my friends – so you see . . .' the mafia boss shrugged expressively. 'When the time comes I will ask Giacomo himself to take out the swordfish boat and he will carry a lamp at his masthead to identify himself in the darkness – a red lamp. Incidentally, the man in the swordfish boat who will try to take you to Malta, Giacomo, is deaf and dumb. I hope later that you will return him safely?'

'In one piece if possible,' Petrie said shortly. Deaf and dumb? The caution of the Sicilian was diabolical: it meant that there could be no question of interrogating Giacomo later to gain information about the mafia. This bastard doesn't miss a trick, he thought with reluctant admiration. 'There's one problem you haven't covered, Angelo,' he said. 'To do a real job on that train-ferry I need to get inside the engine-room, and I think one of our signals mentioned this. Can it be managed?'

'It is difficult but perhaps not impossible. To obtain detailed information about the *Cariddi* I have crossed and re-crossed the straits eight times within the past three weeks . . .'

'Hasn't that aroused suspicion?' Petrie asked sharply.

'Not at all! I am a lawyer. I have clients in Messina and clients on the mainland, so I tell them. Even in wartime people never stop fighting each other legally! During the crossings I made friends with the chief engineer, a dubious character called Volpe.'

'Dubious?' Petrie queried.

'Very! He is a great womanizer and loves to talk about his conquests – and Angelo Gambari can be a very good listener!' He grinned sardonically. 'Volpe has two passions in life – his women and his engines. Also he is very partial to good brandy, and by means I need not go into I have acquired several bottles of French cognac.'

'He lets you go down into the engine-room?'

'He lets my bottle go down – and since I hold on to it he lets me down, too, during the crossing!' Angelo rubbed his head as though stimulating a thought. 'Ah, I have it! A way to get the two of you down with me. You have wished all your lives to become engineers like Volpe, your families were too poor to pay for your training, but you are still fascinated by machinery. The larger the audience, the more Volpe loves to talk.'

They crossed another bridge, sped up a steep hill,

then slowed down as they came to a series of bends. So far they had not met another vehicle on the road which passed through some of the wildest country in Sicily, and soon they would be joined by the road Petrie had originally intended coming along direct from Scopana. It was a route he had chosen carefully after studying the reports from the aerial reconnaissance people which showed it was little used by traffic, probably because east and west of it there were more direct routes across the island. 'And how did you intend to get us into the *Cariddi* dock?' he asked.

'We walk through with the other peasants.'

'Walk through? Just like that? With the place ringed with troops?' Petrie stared at him critically.

Angelo showed annoyance and threw out a hand to emphasize his point. 'You do not understand the situation here! For years the ferries have been used like buses by people wishing to cross the straits – each time I crossed the ship carried ordinary people who work all their lives in the fields. They have to buy a ticket and they have identity papers, of course – but you have these.'

'And the Germans let them get away with this?'

'They have no option!' Angelo was becoming heated at Petrie's failure to grasp his explanation. 'The *Cariddi* is an *Italian* ship. Obviously you have no idea of the Italian feeling against German methods. It may seem strange to you, but this is the way Sicilians live and it will take more than the Germans to make them change their ways.'

'All right, Angelo,' Petrie said soothingly. 'I've got it. We go on board with the other peasants and all we have to worry about is the *carabinieri*.' They passed a signposted road turning off to their left which read *Scopana–Petralia*, and this was the way Petrie had planned to come when he was plotting out a route back at the Tunis base, so from now on he knew where he was going. At this point they were more than three-quarters of the way through the Nebrodi mountains and they had still met nothing on the moonlit road except a few mule carts, but Petrie was under no illusion that it would continue like this. Soon they would turn on to the strategic coastal highway linking Palermo with Messina, and soon they would meet the checkpoints – and the Germans.

He glanced over his shoulder as Johnson sat up, yawned and winked at him. All his three companions were showing grave signs of fatigue; short of sleep and food, their whiskered faces gaunt and haggard, they looked like men going on leave after a rough time in the front line. The trouble was the rough time lay ahead of them and they were going to arrive in Messina with most of their reserves drained away. It didn't exactly add up to a formula for success. 'I could do with a drink,' the American suggested tentatively. Petrie nodded and they shared what was left of the bottle of mineral water he had bought in Puccio. Later, he caught Angelo glancing at him, and from the Italian's expression he guessed that his own physical and mental state was being assessed. And I'm damned sure I don't look any better than the others, he thought grimly. Johnson had taken Scelba's place at the small window, gulping in air to help waken himself up. 'Looks like a storm coming up,' he remarked.

'It can happen without warning at this time of year,' Angelo told him. 'One moment the sea is calm, the next moment you wonder whether you will survive.'

'How much can the *Cariddi* transport in a single crossing?' the American inquired.

'A complete express train – ten coaches and the engine – or twenty-five large freight wagons. In one crossing it can carry fourteen hundred passengers.'

'Fourteen hundred?' Johnson whistled noiselessly. Double the number to allow for cramming troops aboard and that gave a figure of approximately three thousand troops per crossing. It would take only a few crossings to transport an entire division from the mainland to Sicily. No wonder AFHQ was in such a sweat about this huge train-ferry.

The ambulance sped on through the night and the mountains slid behind them as they drew closer and closer to the coast. The gathering storm arrived suddenly; one moment they were driving through a cool, calm night and then the breeze became a wind and they heard its howl above the motor-throb, heard the thump of its force against the vehicle's side while they saw the clouds massing overhead until the moon went out and they were driving into a forty-mile-an-hour gale. The landscape was transformed as shafts of moonlight reappeared, showing a cloud ceiling low and fast-moving as the wind strength increased and blew up scurries of dust which they saw eddying in the headlight beams. Through a break in the prickly pear hedge Johnson caught a glimpse of sheep hurrying for shelter followed by a man on horseback. If they're coming tonight, the American thought bleakly, the airborne boys will be in trouble, to say nothing of the landing-craft wallowing in the rising seas.

As they approached the critical highway the atmosphere inside the ambulance changed and the tension grew. They sat up straighter, checked their weapons unnecessarily, spent more time peering ahead where the headlights would show the first sign that they had reached the highway. Petrie himself sat up a little straighter and now he drove more slowly as he watched for any sign that would tell him they were close to the sea. Even without sight of the coast he knew they were coming near because the freshening gale battering the vehicle's sides carried a tang of salt air as it came blasting in from the Tyrrhenian Sea, and when he pulled up, turned off the engine and leaned out of the window the salt tang was strong. He stayed in this position for several minutes, listening for sounds of traffic on the nearby highway. The wind was cold, chilling his skin, but he welcomed the sensation after the heat of the day and the only sounds he heard were the hissing of pampas grasses, the whine of the wind and a surging noise which was the beat of heavy seas on the shore.

'Looks like we still have the world to ourselves,' Johnson said quietly.

'Maybe.' Petrie sounded doubtful. 'But we can expect trouble soon – this highway is a main communications route.'

'I protest!' Field-Marshal Kesselring burst out, unable to control his fury any longer. 'To hold back the 29th Panzer Division now would be a strategic blunder of the first order!' He gripped the telephone as though it were Colonel-General Jodl's neck as that august officer asked him to hold the line a minute.

The clock on his desk under the lamp registered 9.15 PM. The call from Supreme Headquarters in East Prussia could hardly have come through at a more awkward moment. The signal he was about to send to Colonel Baade in Messina ordering the *Cariddi* to cross the straits was on his desk, and Rheinhardt was at Giovanni with his division waiting to board the train-ferry. But he had been wise not to bring the vessel across sooner, Kesselring was thinking – that would really have taken some explaining now that Supreme HQ had grasped what was happening. It was, of course, the Gestapo who had tapped his line and relayed the information to the other end of Europe. Jodl came back on the line, his voice as thin and precise and emotionless as always. 'Rheinhardt must be kept where he is in southern Italy until we are sure where the enemy blow will fall . . .'

'It it fall on Sicily! Strickland always takes it step by step – and the next step is Sicily, *then* Italy! If we can smash them this time it will take them six months to reorganize another attempt . . .'

'We know all this.' Jodl's tone remained even. 'That is why we must first be sure where they are landing . . .'

'When you are sure in war it is too late!' Kesselring shouted, not caring any more. '*We* . . .' Jodl kept saying. The little man with the moustache was standing at the officer's elbow, probably even listening in on an extension, but the swine would never come to the phone himself. Kesselring took a deep breath. He was not going to give in this time. 'Before I accept that order I wish to speak to the Führer!'

'Wait a minute . . . there is a lot of noise at this end.' So the little man was there! But Jodl would never admit that he was no more than a messenger boy, passing on someone else's lunatic orders. While he waited, Kesselring's agile brain planned the next move. This time he mustn't fail. Rheinhardt *was* going to Sicily, whatever the madmen in East Prussia wanted. He heard Jodl cough on the phone, a sound he knew well: it meant that the colonel-general was embarrassed. 'Kesselring, the Führer is not available at the moment. And the order must stand. The *Cariddi* is still at Messina, I trust?'

'Yes. You mean that under no circumstances is

Rheinhardt to cross the straits?' Kesselring inquired craftily. 'Even if we have positive reports of airborne landings?'

There was another long pause. Stick that in your vegetarian soup and choke on it, Kesselring thought. He had them over a barrel now – the length of the pause showed that. Jodl coughed again when he came back on the line. 'If there are confirmed reports of *sea*borne landings in Sicily, then Rheinhardt can cross, but only then. You understand?'

'Positive reports of airborne landings . . .' Kesselring deliberately gabbled the words.

'*Sea*borne!' Jodl's tone was sharp. 'Seaborne, I said. You have understood me now, I hope?'

'Perfectly!' Kesselring was careful not to repeat the word himself. 'There was a lot of noise at this end,' he added maliciously, then he terminated the call. There was all the difference in the world between airborne and seaborne landings: the first enemy attack would be the airdrop, possibly just before midnight while the moon was still up. The seaborne landings would come hours later, so at least his manoeuvre meant he could send Rheinhardt across several hours earlier. If his guess was correct and reports of airborne drops came through near midnight the *Cariddi* could sail at once. He used the phone to order coffee as he began altering his signal to Messina. It was going to be a long night.

*

It was quite dark as Petrie re-started the engine and drove on slowly, knowing that their exit on to the coast road must be a critical moment. Turning a bend, he speeded up a little along a straight stretch and mounted a rise, then immediately reduced speed again. As the ambulance crested the brow of the hill it took the full force of the gale against its windscreen and the view opened out dramatically, spreading away in three directions as the moon came through the low-flying clouds and Petrie felt the wind-pressure tugging at his wheel. To the east the highway was a pale strip running in harness with the single-track railway from Palermo to Messina, but within a few hundred yards it disappeared temporarily behind a ridge and then reappeared in the direction of Milazzo. To the west it ran a long distance towards Palermo. Ahead of them to the north lay the open sea, a dark undulation of heaving waves surging shoreward, rolling in to crash on the deserted beach below with a heavy boom and a burst of surf. Their fears of army convoys, of tanks and troops, were only fears; there was no one, nothing in sight. And the raging sea was equally lonely and unused.

'We must be born lucky.'

Johnson said the words half to himself and then he noticed that Petrie was crouched over the wheel as the ambulance crawled downhill to where the side road joined the highway. What the devil was he worrying about now? At walking pace the ambulance came up to the intersection and Petrie was staring to his right, towards the portion of the highway concealed from view by the ridge. A level-crossing led over the rail track and down on to the main road; beyond that the beach ran out to a headland projecting into the sea with a fringe of shingle following its base. No wire on the beach to indicate minefields; only fishing-boats which were drawn up well back from the surf line.

Petrie drove on to the crossing, bumped over the track, came down on to the highway, was starting to turn his wheel when he saw the bottom of the shallow hill which had been concealed by the ridge. He took it in like a flash from a camera – the piled-up trucks, three or four of them which had been travelling too fast and too close together, the blocked road, the ambulance with its rear doors open . . . Then he drove straight across the highway down on to the beach and headed for the strip of shingle between cape and sea with the howl of the wind and the crash of the breakers echoing in his ears. Angelo stared at him but it was Johnson who spoke first. 'What the hell are you doing, Jim?'

'Heading away from trouble! There's an accident a few hundred yards down the highway – road's blocked and there's one ambulance there already. What chance do you think we'd have had of driving past that – in another ambulance? They were Jerry trucks, too.'

'We're waiting here?' Johnson sounded unhappy, became speechless in sheer disbelief as Petrie continued driving along the beach under the headland while to their left the sea surged in as though to overwhelm them.

'We're not waiting anywhere,' Petrie said tightly. 'There's no time left for waiting. We're now on the route I always expected to take – so I studied the aerial photos of this part of the coast before we left. I remember this headland – it goes out about half a mile and then goes back in again to hit the highway well beyond that truck smash . . .'

'You're not driving round this headland,' Johnson protested.

'That's exactly what I am going to do. The aerial photos showed a continuous strip of beach going the whole way round, so now, gentlemen, say your prayers and hope I have read the photos correctly.'

The car drove on. The storm was rising and the sea was rising with it as huge waves gathered up the waters and jostled in towards the cape with a dizzying motion. The strip of beach between headland and waterline was narrow, hardly wider than the girth of the ambulance, and in places large waves rolled in ahead of them and threw themselves close to the headland's base. Driving over the shingle was difficult: the wheels were inclined to slither among the unstable pebbles and the right front mudguard was moving along within a foot of the rock wall. If we arrive at a place where the sea comes right in, where we can't move forward any farther, Johnson was thinking, he'll never get us back to the highway. It was a thought which had not escaped Petrie, but now the time was so short that every risk had to be taken, because if they didn't reach Messina in time, if German reinforcements moved across the straits, they might as well never have come and all the risks taken so far would mean nothing. He was quite single-minded about what he was doing, determined to take the ambulance round the cape if it were humanly possible, but there was another hazard which aerial photos taken on a calm day would never show – the extent to which the sea came in when driven by the fury of a forty-mile-an-hour gale.

On the photographs the beach area had looked very narrow as it came up to the tip of the headland, and he suspected he might be driving with two wheels in the water for part of the way. The question he carefully hadn't raised in the minds of his passengers was whether at some point when he was driving through water the beach might not shelve suddenly, go down heaven knew how many fathoms. He drove on as the beach slowly narrowed; on his right the vertical rock wall was gleaming in the moonlight, its surface damp where windblown surf and spray had splashed it, while to his left where he looked straight out of the ambulance the sea was a turmoil of waves which seemed to be getting bigger, massive waves with leaping crests which rolled in as high as his head, broke, then sent a spume-discoloured carpet of water flooding in under the vehicle. The noise was nerve-rattling, a growing surge as millions of gallons of water swept in on the headland which barred their progress. Something slapped him lightly on the cheek and then ran down it. The surf was coming in much closer.

'Ed, keep an eye on the highway through the rear window, will you?'

This was an added anxiety – that some other vehicle would come along the highway from the west and see him apparently trying to commit suicide. But the highway had been deserted for a long distance when he drove over the level-crossing, so if he could only keep going they might make it. Frowning, he started the wipers to clear spray off the windscreen: in the distance the sea appeared to be surging right in to the cliff base, submerging the beach completely, but it could be an optical illusion in the bad light. He heard Scelba clear his throat, looked quickly at Angelo who had lit a cigarette and was watching the incoming sea with screwed up eyes as though estimating their chances of survival. Behind him Johnson's measured voice spoke quietly: 'Jim, I'd better get out and walk ahead of you. It may slow you down but we ought to know what's facing us before it's too late. And Scelba can keep an eye on the highway.'

'Agreed, Ed. And watch that shingle near the waterline – it may shelve suddenly.'

The American went out by the rear door and the wind took hold of him at once, nearly blew him into the cliff face. As he squeezed his way between the vehicle and the rock wall his feet were slithering over the wet treacherous shingle, and when he stumbled his way ahead of the ambulance the storm seemed to be worsening, buffeting his body as he struggled to retain his balance while the wind shrieked, the mighty waves roller-coastered towards him, spray doused his clothes and face, and above the surge of the sea and the hiss of the surf he heard from the direction of the headland's tip a more disturbing sound, the growling boom of rollers crashing against rock as though trying to shift the cape itself. Head down, he walked, slipped, forced himself forward, looking up frequently to see where the beach apparently narrowed even further. Soon Johnson was walking knee-deep in frothing surf as he deliberately moved along the edge of the sea, determined to make sure there was leeway for the passage of the vehicle, knowing that in places Petrie would be compelled to drive with his outer wheels in the water.

As he drew closer to the tip of the headland the character of the cape began to change; the cliff face receded deep into wide gulches which penetrated the rock, gulches of sand instead of shingle, gulches which were culs-de-sac and which always ended at a rock face. The boom from the headland tip was growing louder, developing into a low roar he heard above the wind's howl and the purr of the ambulance following twenty yards to his rear. Could this crazy gamble succeed, he kept asking himself over and over again. The moon was still out, shining down through a break in the ragged clouds scudding overhead, and by its light he could see great combers dashing themselves to pieces against immense rocks, hurling spray high in the air, spray which the wind blew back into the cliff face. He paused to wipe spray off his own face, looked back at the oncoming vehicle and saw the headlights blur as wind-blown surf fogged them. They would never get past the tip of the headland; he was sure of it. Petrie must have made some mistake in reading the aerial photo, in assuming the beach strip ran right round the headland. It seemed unlikely anyway; with a cape like this the beach always vanished when you reached its extremity. Waving his hand sideways to warn the ambulance to keep closer to the rock face, he turned and stumbled onwards.

The atmosphere inside the ambulance was claustrophobic and the passengers were developing a trapped feeling as Petrie drove slowly on after the walking American. It was cold, but the occupants were sweating with fear because the vehicle felt horribly unstable as the wheels ground forward over the shifting pebbles, the sea spread under them, scattered the stones with a loose rattle, withdrew and then came in again as the next wave broke and Petrie drove inches away from the cliff-face, holding the wheel tightly to counter the tendency of the ambulance to swerve seaward. He passed another of the sandy gulches and Angelo glanced longingly inside its walled sanctuary; at least in one of these coves they would be sheltered from the elements. Peering ahead, Petrie was trying to see the island, an island very close to the cape's tip as he remembered it from the aerial shot, but now they were coming near the end of the headland there was no island to be seen. Had he misinterpreted a shadow in the picture? In which case his theory of the feasibility of driving round the cape was exploded. He looked out of the open window to his left, the side of his jacket already soaked with spray, blinked when he saw what was coming.

A great roll of grey water was gathering up sea, inflating itself, furling at the mounting crest, sweeping up higher than the roof of the ambulance; it slammed forward, raced in without any sign of breaking as it climbed higher and higher and the crest lurched forward. Petrie stopped the vehicle, began winding up the window frantically as Angelo instinctively shrank against the other door. They were going to be overwhelmed, submerged, and the powerful backwash from such a comber could easily haul them over sideways, capsizing them into the sea. The wave broke, dropped to a third of its height as the water came on, waist-high, a foaming surge which lost more height just before it arrived and struck the ambulance's side. They felt its impact, felt the vehicle wobble, saw water all around them, then it was receding, battling with an incoming wave, colliding with it, sending spray from the collision high above the dancing waters. Petrie tried to start the engine. It failed. A moment later he saw that Johnson had vanished.

*

Johnson had seen the wave coming, had run inside the last of the gulches which penetrated the cliff face, a broad sandy channel which went in a hundred feet and then disappeared round a corner. The sea came in behind him, spread itself over the grey sand, stopped, went back. Sodden to the thighs, Johnson went back after it, came out of the exit and waved to the ambulance which was now stationary. The sound of the engine starting, failing, reached him, and a new coldness spread through him: the motor was waterlogged. The engine started again, failed, repeated the agonizing performance, then the third time it kept ticking over and the ambulance moved forward again as clouds began to blot out the moon and the headlights showed more sharply. Reluctantly, Johnson left the firmness of the sand and went on towards the headland's tip, his boots squelching over the slippery pebbles. Yes, Petrie had been wrong: he could see it positively where a mass of piled rocks like a breakwater were heaped against the cliff wall while their outer bastion took the tremendous shock of the sea. The beach had gone, ended by the huge rocks which blocked their way. He looked back and froze.

The ambulance had reached a point where the shingle strip was very narrow and Petrie was driving with half the depth of the outer wheels under water, but what scared Johnson was the angle of the ambulance – it was tilting sideways, tilting down towards the sea where the beach shelved steeply. It had only to tilt a few degrees farther, to slither a foot or two away from the rock wall, and it would somersault sideways. For long drawn-out seconds the booming of the breakers, the wind's howl, the realization that their way forward was blocked – all these things went out of his mind as he watched the horrible tilt and saw that Petrie was refusing to give up, was still forcing a passage over the treacherous shoal bank while the headlights wobbled alarmingly. The lights came closer, became parallel again as the ambulance resumed an even keel and approached the large gulch Johnson had fled inside when the wave came. Turning round, he walked on, hoping desperately that his eyesight had played him a trick, that there would be a continuous way round the headland. He came to the first of the great rocks and spray from the breakers showered over him, drenched him, and now the booming sound was deafening as he held up a hand to stop Petrie and then climbed the slippery face of damp rock to see whether they could continue forward on foot. He had climbed perhaps twenty feet when the view opened up to where he could see beyond the headland tip, could see the familiar shape of an Italian MAS boat coming round from the far side of the cape. Barely a quarter of a mile offshore, caught in the remaining moonlight, it turned to investigate their side of the headland.

He jumped back down the rocks, jumped dangerously from ledge to ledge, and when he hit the beach he nearly lost his footing on the pebbles. Recovering, he waved sideways frantically, waved to the ambulance to drive inside the gulch, but either they couldn't see him properly or they hadn't understood the gesture because they were still driving towards him and in seconds they would have driven past the sanctuary. He ran on, retaining his balance by a miracle, ran a dozen yards and then he stopped and waved again. The ambulance turned, slid behind the rock wall and was gone. Johnson resumed his lurching run, desperately trying to follow the vehicle inside the gulch before the MAS boat came round the rocks. He fell once, toppling to his knees which hammered the pebbles while his hands were scrabbling for balance, and during the few seconds he knelt there, half-winded, a wave broke and poured itself over him, soaking him afresh, so when he hauled himself to his feet and stumbled on he was bedraggled, his cap, jacket and trousers sodden, dripping with water as he staggered to the entrance, felt hard sand under his boots and forced himself into a run.

The ambulance had vanished beyond the curving rock wall, its tyre marks near the entrance obliterated by the water which had just washed over them. He ran forward, chilled, dripping, clammy, expecting at any second to hear the purr of the MAS boat's engine behind him. For some reason it had been playing a powerful light over the cliff's surface and he was scared the beam might come inside the gulch while he was still in sight. Were they checking for landing parties? He had no idea. He reached a point where the wall curved sharply, a point of safety, when Petrie came round the corner, grabbed his arm and pulled him behind the rock. 'You all right, Ed? What's the trouble?' Johnson couldn't get out a reply as he panted for breath and gestured towards the entrance. Petrie peered round the corner cautiously as the MAS boat came into view, tossing in the heaving sea while a signal lamp flashed from its deck. For one chilling moment Petrie thought it was signalling their discovery to someone on the coast road, when he realized it must be identifying itself to a coastguard station on the headland above them. 'It's all right, Ed,' he said. 'It can't see us and it's moving on . . .'

'MAS boat . . .' Johnson gulped for air. 'Flashing a light over the cliff . . . can't get any farther . . . rocks in the way.'

'Don't worry about it – and stop trying to talk. It was a routine signal – probably to the coastguard station above us. Take it easy, Ed, you saved our bacon there – and now you can get out of those wet things and wrap up in blankets for a while. There are loads of them in one of the cupboards.'

He helped Johnson back to the vehicle which was parked without any lights part way round the cliff. Scelba opened the rear doors, hauled the American inside and nodded to Petrie who went back to the driver's seat. As he settled behind the wheel darkness seeped into the gulch with the fading of the moon. Behind him the American was refusing to change until he had spoken to Petrie again through the dividing window. 'Jim, we can't go any farther round the cape – there are rocks in the way. The beach just gives up.' Angelo twisted round, offered him a cigarette, and by the match flare Johnson saw the Italian smiling, which was hardly the reaction he had expected.

'It's all right, Ed,' Petrie reassured him. 'I was damned sure I saw a small offshore island at the end of this cape in the aerial shot, but there didn't seem to be one. This is the island.' He pointed to his left out of the window. 'What we thought was the end of the cape is the island – it's cut off from the cape by this gulch which goes all the way through and out the other side. The exit links up with the beach and that will take us to the coast road.'

'You're joking,' Johnson said hoarsely.

'I checked it a moment ago. We go a few yards round this curve and we're at the other side of the headland. We'll give the MAS boat a few minutes to push off, I'll check the beach and road again, then we can get moving.'

'What about the coastguard station above us?'

'It's well back on the headland, about halfway between here and the road – I remember that now from the photo. We'll drive close in to the cliff as we did when we drove out here and I'm sure they'll never see us.'

They waited a few minutes; Petrie got out to make sure the coast road was still clear, then they were driving through the gulch and turning right out of its exit on to another shingle beach. Here the shore was wider, probably because the cape sheltered this side from the prevailing wind, and the sea close to the beach was calmer as they drove towards the deserted highway still visible in a shaft of moonlight. Reaching the main beach, Petrie pulled up and told the others to wait for him. He had to find the answer to a dangerous question: was the accident they had driven round the cape to avoid in sight? He climbed a sandy slope cautiously, wondering whether he should have risked driving straight on to the highway – if any vehicle came along now the ambulance parked on the beach was going to look pretty odd. Arriving at the verge, he stood up straight. The road to the west was empty, disappearing as it went down into the dip where the accident had occurred. He ran back to the ambulance, climbed in behind the wheel, drove up the slope on to the highway and checked his watch as he turned east. 10.25 PM. Ninety-five minutes to the deadline. He pressed his foot down.

Chapter Twelve

Friday. 10.30 pm – 11.30 pm

At eighty miles an hour the ambulance sped through the night along the hard-surface road which bordered the north Sicilian coastline, its headlights spearing through the darkness, the needle climbing up the speedometer, the air pressure whipping past them as the vehicle swayed round a gentle curve, as Scelba dug his fingernails into the leather couch to maintain his balance while Johnson braced his back against the rocking side. They were close to Messina; it was 11 PM; and they had already successfully passed through three different checkpoints. If Petrie kept up this speed of progress they would be inside the straits in fifteen minutes.

'Another checkpoint coming up,' Angelo said stiffly.

'We'll go through it the way we went through the others,' Petrie said confidently.

'One day this isn't going to work,' Johnson bawled through the window.

The red lights in the distance warned them they were racing towards another checkpoint, although as yet the headlight beams hadn't picked out the barrier or the men guarding it. Petrie operated the siren switch and an unearthly banshee-like scream cut through the night, warning the checkpoint control that this ambulance wasn't stopping, that it was coming straight through, so for God's sake get the barrier up before we drive clean through it. The headlights picked out the barrier, picked out men in *carabinieri* uniform scurrying madly as they moved the pole and got well out of the way. The ambulance streaked past. Angelo had a glimpse of white faces gaping in the night. Then the headlight beams were turned as they negotiated another curve, headlights which showed briefly a dual curve of steel track to their right, an empty meaningless track which might have led anywhere because the trains weren't running any more, while to their left and below them the troubled sea appeared as the moon came out again. The gale was still blowing, the clouds scudded like an urgent fleet through the sky above them, but moving at this speed the Tyrrhenian seemed to be no more than flurried, a jostle of moonlit waves trundling in to empty themselves on remote beaches. They passed inlets and headlands and bays, and often they saw dark shapes out at sea which were more patrol-boats watching for any sign of enemy intrusion while half a mile to the south of them the headlights of Petrie's ambulance sped east in its headlong rush for Messina.

'There are Germans at some of the checkpoints close to the city,' Angelo warned.

'They'll stop an Italian vehicle?' Petrie queried.

'Not often, but I have seen it happen.'

And at present, with the invasion pending, they'll be in a state of nerves, Petrie thought, as he took the ambulance up the road where it began its ascent into the Peloritanie mountains. The sea receded away from them to the north. The rail track moved over a bridge from right to left, headed east along its own separate route where it tunnelled through the mountains to Messina. The highway climbed and climbed and the temperature dropped a little more as, for the first time since they had landed, they passed wooded defiles and saw trees on the ridges. Then, ahead of them, they saw more lights. Another checkpoint. Petrie pressed the siren switch, accelerated. 'Be careful!' Angelo warned. In the moonlight the anti-tank gun showed clearly, its barrel aimed point-blank down the road towards them. German uniforms were also visible, about a dozen of them. On the other side of the road an Italian truck and two motor-cycles with riders on their saddles stood in a clearing under trees, and behind them were more Italian troops. And the barrier was down across the road. Petrie's expression tightened as he continued up the hill and then something happened which took everyone by surprise. It began to rain.

'I'm stopping,' Petrie said to warn the others as he lost speed rapidly and then skidded to a stop yards from the guard-pole. There was too much against them – the gun, the motor-cyclists to pursue them even if he'd attempted crashing the barrier. As the engine ticked over quietly the rain sound increased in fury, rattling down on the roof like miniature drills. Through the open side window he saw a German sergeant striding towards him with a machine-pistol pointed at the ambulance. The Wehrmacht NCO was soaked by the time he reached the window and behind him Italian soldiers were running out from under the trees as some natural water catchment began to flood the place where they had stood. 'Ah! You were not going to stop!' Petrie swore inwardly as he heard the German's fluent Italian, but his face wore a puzzled expression as he looked up at the NCO.

'We are on the way to the hospital with a patient. It's an emergency case.'

'That is no reason for not stopping when the pole is down! You see that gun over there?' The German, wiping the drips off his peaked cap, pointed with one hand while he kept his machine-pistol aimed with the other. 'Your patient could have been a dead man – and so could you.' Six foot tall and heavily-built, the NCO was a man in his late twenties, an arrogant bully, a typical product of the Nazi regime. 'Show me your papers,' he barked and the muzzle of the weapon prodded towards Petrie's face. The German was freshly-shaved, had obviously come on duty only recently, and his temper was not improved by the soaking he was receiving. Behind him several Italian soldiers stood at the edge of the road, keeping clear of the deluge of water cascading into the bowl under the trees they had just left, and the nearest man was a sergeant, a short determined-looking individual who was watching the scene curiously. 'Your papers!' the German rapped out again.

Something inside Petrie snapped. They had been on the move almost constantly for over twenty-four hours; they had survived a *mafioso* ambush, the Beaufighter attack, the terrible journey through the wilderness, the searching *carabinieri*, the B17 bombing raid, and now, almost within sight of Messina, they were being blocked by this bullying swine. He opened the door slowly, stepped out into the driving rain in his ill-fitting trousers, closed the door, and faced the German with his hands on his hips. 'You would have opened fire on an Italian ambulance?' he demanded. He had raised his voice deliberately, raised it so it carried above the sound of the rain to the Italians huddled by the roadside. Their sergeant took a step forward and then waited.

'This is a checkpoint!' the German shouted at him. 'You bloody well stop when you see a checkpoint!'

'And my fist bloody well curls when I meet someone like you! You think you've taken over the whole mucking island? You think we count for nothing any more, we Italians?'

The Italian sergeant behind the German came forward a few more steps and then waited again. A subtle but marked change in the atmosphere round the checkpoint was taking place; on one side of the road the Italian infantry with rifles in their hands stared beyond the ambulance to where the Germans on the far side were gathered round the anti-tank gun as they stared back. Then they transferred their gaze to the protagonists in the middle of the highway where the German NCO was looking at Petrie suspiciously. 'What is the matter with your uniform?' he snapped. 'And you haven't shaved for two days. You look like a peasant.'

Petrie waved his hand provocatively at the Wehrmacht uniform, calling out to the Italian soldiers as the rain poured down on him. 'So, because we haven't got a nice new uniform like Herr Bully-Boy we are peasants! Now we know what our charming allies think of us! Peasants! he said. I get blood all over one outfit, borrow another, and I'm improperly dressed! Twenty-two hours on duty without a break,' Petrie ranted on, 'and it's a crime because I haven't shaved! I should be so lucky as Herr General here whose chin is as smooth as a chorus boy's!' Very deliberately he spat close to the German's boot.

Inside the ambulance Angelo stiffened, sure that Petrie had gone too far. The German stiffened also, lost all self-control as he raised his weapon like a club to fell Petrie. The Italian sergeant jumped forward, grasped the weapon, and for several seconds the two NCOs struggled for possession of the gun as the rain beat down on them non-stop. On either side of the road the mood took an ugly turn. Seeing their sergeant struggling with the German, the Italian troops advanced with their rifles at the ready, aimed across the highway towards the group gathered round the anti-tank gun. A Wehrmacht corporal issued a sharp order and all but two men left the gun, spreading out along the roadside. Jesus, Angelo thought, we're going to be caught in a crossfire. It had happened once before near Catania, a fracas between the Italians and the Germans, and the incident had been carefully hushed up with units transferred to opposite ends of the island.

The Italian NCO rammed a boot down hard, scraped the German's instep, and when they broke apart it was the Italian who held the weapon as he carefully pointed the muzzle at the ground and shouted over his shoulder to his own troops: 'Lower those rifles, you fools!' Seeing his men obey the order, he swung round on the German. 'I shall report this incident the moment I go off duty!'

'Your men nearly opened fire on mine!' the German stormed.

'Look at your own men,' the Italian NCO said calmly. He was quite confident: he had done nothing except to prevent an assault on an ambulance driver and he had the offending weapon in his own hands, trailed harmlessly, as the German looked behind him and cursed. The Wehrmacht troops were lined up along the roadside in an obvious state of alert. He shouted an order in German and the men went back to the anti-tank gun, looking anywhere except in the direction of their allies across the highway. 'From now on,' the Italian sergeant continued, '*we* will check any Italian vehicles . . .'

'I shall make my own report,' the German retorted.

'That is your privilege – do not forget to include that you threatened to open fire on an Italian ambulance,' the NCO reminded him.

'That's a damned lie . . .'

'I distinctly heard you tell the driver that he could have been a dead man – and his patient.' The sergeant turned his back on the German to speak to Petrie who had carefully waited in the pouring rain because it established a state of mutual suffering. 'Your patient is seriously ill?' he inquired.

'He will be if I don't get him to Messina General shortly. He's a sergeant who was working on constructing a blockhouse when a concrete mixer fell on him. I think he'll pull through as long as he gets treatment quickly – that's why I was using the siren. And this is the second time in half an hour I've been held up by the *tedeschi* . . .' He deliberately used the Italian term of contempt for their Teutonic allies. 'They'll be the death of my patient if I'm stopped again before I get to Messina.' He glanced meaningfully in the direction of the two motor-cyclists who still sat astride their saddles in the downpour.

'You mean . . .?' The sergeant hesitated, and Petrie was careful not to push it. 'He is on the danger list?'

'You could say that. He needs an emergency operation and the only place he can have it done is at Messina. There's a surgeon standing by waiting for us now.'

'And you're worried you'll run into someone else like this?' the sergeant inquired in a low voice.

'Sicily is crawling with them.'

The sergeant, who looked not unlike a more benevolent Angelo, hesitated again as the rain thrashed down on to the highway with greater intensity and this new onset of the storm seemed to decide him. 'I will send the motor-cycle patrol with you,' he said quickly. 'They will get you through all the checkpoints without any hold-ups. You will be moving quickly so they should be back here soon . . .'

'Tell them to get us through the last checkpoint and then they can come straight back here. And the chap inside will be grateful – I'll tell him after the op.'

'I hope it is successful.' The sergeant went quickly across to the motor-cyclists as Petrie got back into the ambulance, and when he sat down his clothes squelched. While he waited for the barrier to be raised he used his handkerchief to dry his face and take some of the wet out of his hair. It suddenly seemed very quiet as they listened to the engine ticking over, the rain pattering on the roof and the wipers clicking backwards and forwards. 'The rain is stopping,' Angelo observed, 'and you almost had a real patient in here. Me! State of shock brought on by excessive terror!'

The barrier lifted, one of the motor-cyclists roared past it into the night, and the ambulance followed with the second motor-cyclist alongside. They drove steadily uphill at speed, moving up the Peloritanie slopes, and the escort took them easily through the remaining checkpoints. The cyclist who had gone ahead paved the way for them, ensuring that the barrier was always raised by the time the ambulance arrived, and as it stopped raining the clouds broke and the moon showed through again, illuminating dark tree-covered ridges. They reached the last checkpoint near the final crest; the motor-cyclists turned their machines round, saluted, sped off back the way they had come. Angelo took out a silk handkerchief and dabbed at his moist forehead. They were alone again. Johnson appeared at the window behind them for the first time in a while. 'God, you gave us the shakes there, Jim. We're through?'

'Last checkpoint behind us.'

Petrie said no more as he raced up the hill; his nerves were singing with the delayed action of the experience. While it had been going on he had felt ice-cold, observing every little detail which might be turned to their advantage, and the thing now was not to relax, not to let the sensation of relief affect him in any way – because worse, far worse, was still to come. They saw traffic ahead of them as they came up to the crest; German trucks coming towards them and branching off down a side road to the north, then another military convoy in front of them travelling in the same direction. A motor-cyclist raced past them heading for the west followed by a line of armoured cars. Almost before they realized what was happening they were surrounded by Wehrmacht vehicles travelling in both directions and the night was full of throbbing engines. It looked like a state of emergency.

Petrie could almost feel the tension in the way the Germans drove, shoulders hunched over the wheel, staring fixedly ahead. Christ, he thought, has the invasion already started? The convoys were travelling at high speed, a dangerously high speed for night-time driving, and he was praying there wouldn't be an accident – because if there was, an ambulance would be expected to stop and give a hand. He was sandwiched in the convoy now, a Wehrmacht truck ahead of him and an armoured car following close to his rear. It just needed something to stop without warning and there would be a multiple smash of the kind he had seen when they first emerged on to the highway, but a smash on a far greater scale. They went over the crest with the roar of Wehrmacht engines in their ears and it seemed as though every enemy division in Sicily was on the move.

'The harbour.'

That was all Angelo said as Petrie stared at the view where Messina could be seen far below by the light of the fading moon – the city itself, the sickle-shaped harbour, the silver-grey straits stretching away to north and south with the Calabrian mountains in the distance where the German reinforcements were waiting on the mainland. As they began the descent, hemmed in by the Wehrmacht, an air raid was in progress over the straits; flashes came from both sides of the channel and they heard clearly above the engine sounds the muted thunder of the ack-ack guns like the approach of a fresh storm. They had come through all the way from Palermo, the enemy still had no idea that they had landed, and it was exactly 11.30 PM as they entered the outskirts of Messina.

Chapter Thirteen

Friday. 11.30 pm – 11.55 pm

They drove on down an endless hill, still trapped inside the Wehrmacht convoy, and then Messina was closing round them, a city of substantial three-storey buildings. At the bottom of the hill they moved along a wide avenue with the thunder of the straits guns growing louder, hollow detonations with another kind of detonation mingling with the gunfire as bombs came down some distance away. The Allied air forces were pounding the waterfront non-stop. Petrie rubbed a hand over his damp forehead. 'Angelo, I want to get out of this traffic – if there's trouble we're locked in.'

'Prepare to turn right.'

Petrie slowed a little to increase the space between himself and the German truck in front, then signalled and swung right where Angelo indicated. Immediately they were alone, driving down a side street through the darkness with the massive buildings looming on both sides. No lights anywhere. It was late but the complete absence of lights made Petrie wonder whether the bombing had cut the power lines as he touched the accelerator. At Angelo's instruction he turned left and they drove down a broad avenue similar to the one they had just left, but this street was deserted, might never have been inhabited for all the signs of life they saw as they drove on between sombre buildings which reminded Petrie of municipal offices. Scelba, watching from the window, tapped Petrie gently on the shoulder. 'Stop when we get to the next intersection. I must leave you there.'

'You stay with us until we go to the dock!' It was Angelo who replied, his old suspicion flaring up like a festering sore as Petrie slowed down, then stopped. 'We must stay together,' the Italian protested. 'We only have to call at my flat for a few minutes and then we go straight to the dock, so why . . .'

'What's the idea, Scelba?' Petrie inquired as he looked carefully round. There was no one about. On the corner of the intersection was a shuttered café with a closed garage next to it. A pause in the gunfire allowed them to speak quietly and the ticking over of the motor sounded noisy in the novel silence. The *capo* stared impassively at Angelo and then spoke to Petrie.

'There is a car inside that garage. I must drive to the waterfront to warn Giacomo you are coming and to make sure everything is ready. Your flat is near here, Signor Gambari? Good.' He handed a folded street map to Petrie with some markings he had made on it. 'You come to this point on the waterfront – Gambari will know the way and it is only a short distance. I shall wait for you on this corner.'

Petrie took the map, handed it to the Italian. 'How long will it take us to get there, Angelo?'

'In the ambulance?'

'No – on foot. If we stay with this vehicle much longer we'll run out of luck. I can change into my old things at your flat.'

'Five minutes. I am close to the *Cariddi* dock.'

'We should see you about 11.50 then, Scelba,' Petrie said, checking his watch. They were talking in terms of minutes now, but he was careful not to show his impatience as Scelba went out by the rear door and walked quickly to the garage. As he drove forward Angelo told him to turn left; he completed the turn and was driving on when Angelo told him to stop. 'Why here?' Petrie pulled into the kerb as he asked the question. Angelo got out of the ambulance and ran back towards the intersection as Johnson's head appeared in the window. 'Kinda creepy round here. I suppose Angelo couldn't be right about Scelba?'

'No!' Petrie's tone was decisive as he looked at his watch a second time. 'He's forgetting that Scelba has come all the way across Sicily with us, so he's certainly not going to doublecross us now. What Angelo doesn't know is that we've promised the *capo* he'll be mayor of Palermo . . .'

'Why'd you let Angelo go check then – when we're so short of time?'

'Just to make absolutely sure . . .'

The sound of a car's engine came from behind them, crossed the intersection, then faded away as Angelo ran back to the ambulance and jumped inside as the vehicle began moving. 'Right down this next side street,' the Italian said breathlessly, 'then straight down almost to the bottom. I thought it was funny,' he said apologetically, 'but Scelba had the key to the garage door in his hand when he left us and it seemed a little too neat.'

'He's just well organized,' Petrie replied as he swung down inside a street so narrow that the sides of the ambulance almost scraped the walls. The familiar stench of rotting garbage drifted in through the window and the street ahead was a pitch-black canyon. 'He just came out and drove off, I take it?'

'Yes, he didn't waste a second. I also thought it funny that he had a car waiting for him,' he added, still reluctant to let go of his eternal suspicion of the mafia boss.

'He controls the waterfront labour,' Petrie pointed out, 'so he probably comes here fairly frequently.' He turned right at the Italian's instruction, and then left, which brought them out into the same wide avenue where they had dropped Scelba, but much lower down. 'I am keeping off the main streets as far as possible,' Angelo explained. He looked out of the window at the sound of distant gunfire and somewhere overhead he thought he could hear the drone of bombers. Behind them boots hit the floor and when Petrie glanced back he saw Johnson peer through the rear window and come back quickly to the front of the vehicle. 'Trouble, I think. A German scout-car's following us and it's keeping the same speed.'

'How many men inside it? Can you see?'

'Not clearly, but there could be four of them.'

'Angelo, how close are we to your flat?' Petrie asked quickly.

'We're almost there.'

Petrie swore. At the very last moment they'd been spotted. He adjusted his rear-view mirror and picked up the hooded headlights of the scout-car. He was coming up to an intersection and he had to find out whether this was simply a coincidence, which it might be if the car was patrolling Messina. Three turns in swift succession should confirm it – if the scout-car hung on their tail. His eyes narrowed as he saw the headlights coming up fast; they were no longer being followed – they were either about to be stopped or passed. He was starting to turn the wheel to move in from the centre of the road when the car nipped in alongside him to the right and kept alongside him as the man next to the driver flagged him down by waving his hands. Petrie pulled up a short distance from the intersection where there was a closed café on the corner and tables still littered the pavement. The driver of the scout-car called to him in German through Angelo's window. 'Please turn off the engine – we would like to see inside your ambulance.'

'We are going back to the hospital – I only speak Italian,' Petrie shouted back, but he realized it was useless – the demand to look inside the ambulance proved that. The men they had left tied up in the barn must have been discovered, must have circulated the ambulance's registration number. It was the only explanation for their being stopped by a German patrol. The scout-car's driver spoke again, but this time he issued the order in crude Italian. 'You will both get out of the ambulance – and I told you to switch off the engine!' Petrie nodded, released the brake, drove forward. As he expected, the scout-car also drove forward to keep alongside him but the ambulance had a few seconds' advantage and he was pressing his foot down as the bonnet of the German vehicle appeared beyond Angelo's window and Petrie swung the wheel viciously to the right in a wide sweep to take him round the intersection and block off the other vehicle. Angelo saw what happened: seeing the ambulance swinging broadside on to his light vehicle, the German driver swung his own wheel over much farther, mounted the kerb at the corner, drove against the empty tables and rammed the shop window. As they swept round the corner there was a sound of glass shattering and one table bounced past Petrie's front wheels as he straightened up and shot down the side street while Johnson peered out of the rear window and then shouted, 'He's backing into the street – he'll be coming after us!'

Without waiting for Angelo's instruction Petrie swung left again, turning out of the side street into another wide avenue as deserted as its predecessor. The guns were opening up again, the moon had gone, but in the distance the flashes briefly illuminated overhanging roof-lines, balconies, the silhouette of a great church, as the ambulance raced down the avenue and Johnson shouted a further warning. 'It's behind us now!' Petrie shouted over his shoulder for him to drop flat on the floor as he built up more speed, expecting any moment to hear the deadly rattle of the machine-pistol the man next to the German driver had carried looped over his shoulder. The gunfire was becoming a barrage which hammered at their eardrums above the high-pitched whine of the engine; the flashes were becoming more frequent and in the distance he saw flames flare suddenly where a bomb had detonated. They were heading straight into an inferno and by the light of the gun-flashes he saw ahead a line of trucks moving across his path so he swung to the left, headed down another side street in the direction of the avenue he had originally come into Messina along, reached the end of the street and swung left again, taking the corner with a scream of brakes and screeching tyres as Angelo cannoned into him and then straightened up as they entered a large square with trees in the centre. They were halfway round the square when the scout-car entered from the street across from them and as Petrie drove on, intending to circle the square and return the way they had come because at least it was deserted in that district, they heard the scream of the bomb coming down. The scream was awful, a head-splitting noise which clogged the mind with terror during the few brief seconds before it hit a building in the square, detonated with a deafening crack and threw a wall down bodily. The masonry tottered, heaved outwards, fell with avalanche force over the scout-car which had just completed its turn, and inside the anbulance they felt the tremor of the tremendous impact. Pulling up, Petrie stared at the cloud of dust, the enormous heap of debris under which the scout-car lay buried.

'How near the flat are we?' he rapped out.

Angelo was holding his head with shock, and Petrie had to repeat the question before he got an answer. 'Just the other side of this square – one minute, no more . . .'

'We'll take our old clothes with us then – change at your place. Ed! Don't forget the sack! Come on – we're ditching the ambulance here.'

Sitting at his desk at the Enna GHQ, General Guzzoni, the Italian commander-in-chief in Sicily, put his phone down quickly and looked up at Kesselring, who had just flown in from Naples. 'There are unconfirmed but reliable reports that enemy parachutists have landed in strength at Piano Lupo and near Syracuse.' He stood up, grabbed a pointer off his desk and tapped twice on the wall map. 'Here and here . . .'

'Send a signal to the *Cariddi* to sail at once for Giovanni! I'm bringing over Rheinhardt,' Kesselring ordered.

'You don't wish to wait for confirmation?'

'No! Just send that signal to Baade!'

As Guzzoni went back to his desk and picked up

the phone again Kesselring examined the wall map to discourage any more questions. He couldn't explain that as soon as he had learned that Strickland was commanding the British forces he knew it would be Sicily, but now he had his excuse for bringing over the 29th Panzer. Airborne forces had landed; the confirmation would come through later, and that would give him enough ammunition to talk down Supreme HQ. Not that he expected to have to: nothing was more calculated to silence the Supreme Command after the event than a correct decision taken before it. He glanced at the wall clock above the map. 11.52 PM.

Angelo's flat was on the first floor of a darkened building and they stumbled their way up an unlit staircase with the aid of Petrie's torch. The Italian had his key out when they reached the top, slid it into the lock and went inside. He checked the two rooms quickly, pulled the black-out curtains over the windows where gun-flashes lit the opposite wall, then ran back on to the landing where Petrie and Johnson waited with weapons in their hands. 'It is all right!'

They moved very quickly, but not so quickly that they wasted time. Angelo stripped off his uniform, collected a bottle of French cognac while Petrie changed into his peasant clothes. Then, because the electric light wasn't working, the Italian made his phone call to the man who would be ready with his boat by torchlight. 'Is Alfredo there?' he asked. Petrie saw his expression tighten as he slammed down the receiver. 'It was someone else – a man who spoke Italian with a German accent.'

'Then Scelba has to get us off that train-ferry or we go up with her,' Petrie snapped. 'Let's get out of this place.'

He was carrying the sack of explosives over his own shoulder as they hurried out of the building with Angelo leading the way through the bombardment, into a dark alley where the warmth of the day – and the backstreet smells of Sicily – still lingered. At the end of the alley Angelo stopped, peered out, and then beckoned to the men behind him to follow. Petrie came out into a large square and his mouth tightened as he saw several batteries of 88-mm guns sited inside a park in the middle of the square, saw Wehrmacht soldiers waiting close to the artillery by the light of distant gun-flashes. 'How far now?' he asked.

'We shall be there in less than a minute,' Angelo replied.

'You hope!' Johnson said under his breath. The gunfire had stopped suddenly and the three men could hear the quickening footsteps of a patrol coming up behind them. Less than a minute to the waterfront, Petrie thought grimly, and we're going to be stopped. Under his jacket his hand gripped the Mauser while the other hand supported the sack, but they couldn't afford a shooting-match here – not with those Wehrmacht troops only yards away to their left. The footsteps behind them came closer as Angelo, still leading the way, maintained an even pace.

The huge square was still intact, its stone buildings untouched by the bombing, and behind the stumps of trees, cut down to make way for the battery, uniformed figures of the Wehrmacht were watching them hurry past. They were almost clear of the square when they heard again the overhead droning of incoming bombers. An urgent order was barked out in German and the square erupted as three searchlights hovered, locked on to a plane, and the guns roared. 'Run!' Petrie shouted, seeing the perfect excuse for them to rush out of the square even though the patrol was behind them. Angelo ran into a side street, darted into an alley, ran a short distance, turned down another alley. With the others close behind him he ran out on to the waterfront and then stopped, panting for breath. 'That will have lost them – there are six different ways you can go inside that maze. And we're here!'

'And look what's waiting for us,' Petrie replied grimly.

The waterfront was a huge open space where dockside cranes towered against the flashes, where a queue led up to a gate, where a ship's slim funnel spired up behind a warehouse. The queue was made up of Sicilian peasants waiting to go on board, men in peaked caps and women in dark shawls who carried all their miserable possessions with them in their flight from the heavily-bombed city, people willing to brave the full fury of a major air raid in their anxiety to leave the island for the more peaceful mainland. 'That's the *Cariddi*?' Petrie asked. Angelo nodded. 'She must be leaving soon for Giovanni and somehow these people have heard. They always do.'

'Well, we're not just going to walk in through the main gate tonight.'

Unable to take over the *Cariddi* dock completely from their Italian allies, the Germans had reinforced the area with their own security forces. A file of Wehrmacht troops surrounded the queue and halfway along it three SS officers were checking papers. The Sicilian at the main gate was merely glancing at documents, more anxious to hurry people through, but the SS examination was painstakingly thorough. It was quite clear to Petrie that probably not everyone would get aboard before the ship sailed, but the SS didn't give a damn. Smoke was curling from the slim funnel as he spoke to Angelo. 'We've got to find Scelba – fast!'

'This way! If I'm not mistaken our villainous friend is waiting for us.'

They hurried along in front of the buildings facing the harbour and paused as they came close to an archway where a heavily-built man dodged under cover as bombs came down nearby. Overhead planes turned to evade searchlights, weaved, sideslipped in their desperate attempts to escape the tremendous firepower thundering up at them from both shores. As one battery paused to reload another would take its place, then another as the gunners spread a curtain of shells to prevent even one bomber breaking through. Scelba, tired and haggard, stepped out of the archway and spoke with his mouth close to Petrie's ear to make himself heard.

'You cannot get through the main gate – for some reason a special check is being made on everyone. Come this way . . .'

The mafia boss led them across to the waterfront about a hundred yards from the gate. Despite the intensity of the raid, one of the cranes was in operation, lifting great crates high up in the night and then swinging them sideways and lowering them to the deck of the waiting ship. Looking both ways, Scelba opened the left-hand side of two great double doors, stood holding the door while they slipped through, then closed and bolted the door. They were inside some kind of wharf and the place had a derelict look as Petrie shouted his question. 'That was damned easy – we're on the *Cariddi* dock?'

'Good God, no!' Scelba's tone was bad-tempered. 'This wharf isn't used any more – it's sealed off from the main dock.'

'Then why are we . . .'

'Come on! The ship is about to sail.'

The *capo* hurried through a long shed open to the wharf on his right, and then men began to appear, men dressed in working clothes and armed with shotguns. The smell of the decaying wharf filled their nostrils and the edge of the wharf was rotting away, the woodwork soggy and treacherous. 'Keep well back!' Scelba warned. Then they were out in the open again with a breeze off the straits in their faces as the gunfire died and was replaced by a weird silence. They heard water lapping at the wharf base, the murmur of the retreating planes. At the end of the wharf several Sicilians stood round two large crates and they stopped talking as the *capo* came up to them. He tilted his head back to stare upwards as he pulled a torch out of his pocket. 'You go aboard in these,' he said quickly. He was looking at the crane's cab which towered high above them from the next wharf. 'Are you ready? Two of you in the bigger crate, one man in the smaller. When you get aboard one of my men on the ship will rap three times on the lid and you will know it is safe to get out . . .'

'We just lift the lid?'

'No, you operate this catch which only works from the inside.' Scelba raised the lid, showed Petrie how the catch worked. 'And Giacomo is ready with the boat, ready to follow you into the straits. Remember – a red lamp is at his masthead. You fire a green light when you go overboard. Is that right?'

'Yes.' Like Scelba, caught by the man's urgency, Petrie was speaking quickly. 'But there will be civilian passengers aboard so I may have to set the charges to go on the return trip and we may still be on the ship – will Giacomo come back with it? In fact, he bloody well must – Angelo's man has been captured.'

'If necessary he will go backwards and forwards until you reach him!' Aiming his torch upwards, the *capo* flashed it four times as the cable of the crane started to ascend from the ship's hold. 'Now, you must get into the crates – who goes by himself?' Angelo took the single crate and while he was climbing into it and the lid was being lowered Scelba took Petrie aside. 'You will tell AFHQ about our arrangement?' he asked.

'Don't worry, I'll tell them. And thanks for getting us here.' He looked up as the whirring sound of the crane's machinery increased. Then there was a muffled explosion from somewhere beyond the high wall which separated the derelict wharf from the *Cariddi* dock. 'What the hell was that?' Petrie asked sharply.

'A little diversion to distract the attention of the guards over there.' Scelba gestured behind to where a Sicilian sat by a phone inside the shed. 'He called my people inside the *Cariddi* dock the moment I signalled to the man operating the crane.' The cable swung outwards high above their heads, crossed the derelict wharf, stopped and then came down. 'Get inside quickly,' Scelba snapped. 'Both of the crates will travel together . . .'

As Petrie climbed inside the larger crate with Johnson the huge hook suspended from the waiting cable swayed a few feet away from him and from beyond the *Cariddi* dock wall he heard a second detonation. My God, he thought as the lid closed on him and he huddled beside Johnson, these people are well organized. Outside he could hear the muffled clump of booted feet hurrying about on the wharf, the bark of the *capo*'s voice.

'Move faster!' Scelba ordered as he watched the operation, but the men were moving quickly without the injunction as they manhandled the crate containing Angelo closer to the cable. By this time the large hook suspended from the cable had already been inserted inside a ring attached to Petrie's temporary home. Scelba flashed his torch upwards, the cable hoisted the larger crate a few feet, stopped, and Angelo's crate was attached to another hook dangling beneath the larger container. Both crates were now linked to each other and both were suspended from the main cable as Scelba flashed his torch for the last time. The crane driver began winding up the cable, the two crates left the wharf, and the three men locked inside their cubes ascended into the darkness. The whole operation had taken less than two minutes.

The space inside the main container was very cramped for two men and Petrie was crouched double, sitting on his ankles with the lid pressing down on his neck as he heard the machinery whirring and felt himself being hauled into mid-air. Johnson was equally cramped with his knees pressed down on the sack of explosives, and already the heat of their bodies was lifting the temperature as the cable hoisted them higher and higher and the crate started swaying at the end of its hook, their only support as the endless ascent continued. 'I'm glad Scelba didn't tell us about this in advance,' Johnson muttered. Already he was streaming with sweat from his cramped position, from the gnawing fear of the experience itself, from the temperature inside the crate which was rapidly becoming intolerable as the swaying grew worse and he fought down growing nausea. Petrie was, if anything, in a worse state. Confined inside the tiny wooden cell he suddenly felt weary, unbearably tired, his eyes rimmed with fatigue as pain began pounding steadily behind his forehead. He knew he was going to faint. Ramming his fingernails hard into his whiskered skin he scraped them deep into the flesh and the sharpness of the pain pushed back the overwhelming fatigue, forcing a spark of alertness back into his brain as the cable stopped ascending and began to swing them sideways towards the invisible train-ferry. The movement had just started when they felt a horrible lurch. The crate dropped sideways, jerked, and they hung there, thirty degrees out of true, their weight now supported by the side with the floor tilted under them. The ring at the top of the crate was defective – or the hook was bending. Any second now and they would leave the cable, crashing down scores of feet, hitting the deck of the *Cariddi* or the wharfside – or plunge to the bottom of the straits . . .

Inside the crate the fear was naked and contained, contained within the six enclosing walls of the swaying cube, fear intense enough to stop a man's heart. 'The hook's giving way,' Johnson whispered between his teeth. The fear drove back the nausea, chilled his body like immersion in ice. 'Take it easy, Ed,' Petrie said, 'we'll be going down shortly. . .' The American felt suffocated as he interrupted, 'That's what bloody worries me.' Petrie's right arm was going dead but he let the sensation progress because he was scared that any movement on their part might topple the crate off the hook. 'We'll be down in one piece in thirty seconds,' he said. 'Start counting.' Johnson started counting as the cable began to lower them, and Petrie counted with him. Their bodies were so rigid now that they might have been in a state of muscular spasm – without saying a word both men knew that even the slightest movement could be fatal, so tilted sideways in the most awkward positions they held these positions as the cable went on lowering them. But the crane-driver had kept his nerve: he lowered them more slowly than usual and the hand which held the lever was as damp as the hands of the men inside the crates as the cargo slowly dropped and dropped and the train-deck of the *Cariddi* waited for them.

They had counted up to fifteen when the crate sagged a little farther, a slight jolt which sent a paralysing streak of fear through both men. The hook was giving way a little more – the hook or the ring. Petrie blotted out of his mind the futile attempt to diagnose the cause of the trouble and for a moment he couldn't remember where they'd got to. 'Sixteen . . .' he said through cracked lips, and Johnson joined him in the counting. Reciting the numbers gave them something for their sanity to hold on to, so they kept counting as the crates dropped lower and the air inside the tiny room became non-existent. The thud came at twenty-four, the thud when Angelo's crate hit the deck and their own toppled over it; when hands grappled with the crate and turned it upright and something hard struck the lid three times. Petrie released the security bolt and then had the devil of a job locating the catch, then the devil of a job getting it to work. When the lid was opened back and cold night air flooded in they lay inert, unable to move for several seconds until Petrie stirred himself, forced his legs to move again, forced his hands to get him upright, forced himself to climb out of the crate which was surrounded by other cargo which effectively hid them from anyone except the Sicilian who sat him down on a pile of sacks and then went to help Johnson as Angelo's head appeared out of the smaller crate. Petrie looked at his watch. The bloody thing must have stopped. It showed one minute to midnight.

Chapter Fourteen

Friday – Midnight

The wall of cargo which surrounded them had been dumped by the crane near the bows of the train-deck which rested against the dock, and above their heads was open air, moonlit sky. Glancing round the enclosed refuge they had been dropped inside, Petrie decided it was the perfect place to conceal the sackful of explosives while he got his bearings. 'Ed, hang on here a bit while Angelo and I take a look round . . .' Squeezing his way between cargo and bulkhead, he peered out and beckoned to the Italian to follow him. The massive bows of the vessel were open where the dockside link-span extended a single-track line up a ramp, connecting it with the train-ferry track, and the cavernous interior of the huge vessel was dimly lit with blue lights. But there were no coaches aboard for this trip where the single-track rail went inside and splayed out into three separate tracks, running the full length of the ship to the stern.

Petrie lit a cigarette as he leaned casually against the bulkhead, carefully shielding the match flame behind his cupped hand. 'You can get down into the engine-room from here?' he asked.

'No. We have to go up to the next deck . . .'

'In a minute. I'll look round here first.'

Even though time was so short he had to get some rough idea of the layout of the vessel: later, the knowledge could make all the difference between success and disaster. He looked up at the wheelhouse high above them, and behind it where the slim funnel was belching out smoke as the *Cariddi* made ready to sail. As he walked inside the train-deck he had the impression he was entering a great train-shed, a train-shed which floated, and under his feet the deck vibrated with the throbbing of the powerful engines. A little way in under the roof he waited for his eyes to get used to the gloom, then he saw that the interior was crowded with peasants sitting or sprawling over the three tracks, many of them asleep as though in the last stage of exhaustion. The huddled crowd of unsuspecting humanity decided him: the charges would have to be planted to detonate on the return trip, when these people were no longer on board. When he turned round to face the bows again he saw two civilians hurrying along the dock, but his pace didn't change as he walked back to where Angelo waited near the piled-up cargo. 'You see what's coming?' he said as he leaned close to the Italian.

'Gestapo!'

It was written all over the bastards. The standard uniform of belted topcoat and soft hat, one of them tall and thin, the other short and fat. 'Laurel and Hardy,' he murmured, then realized that Angelo wouldn't know what the hell he was talking about. The two men hurried up the link-span, stopped close to Petrie while they stared into the train-deck, then one of them produced a torch and switched it on as he came in under the roof. The torch-beam flashed over the haggard faces of the men and women sprawled on the deck, paused at each one, then moved on. As the torch-beam hit him, Petrie was smoking his cigarette, and blinked in the glare until the Gestapo man moved on to continue his examination. At the dock gate the SS had scrutinized everyone coming aboard, but now the Gestapo was conducting its own security check. 'Angelo,' Petrie said out of the corner of his mouth, 'tell Ed to get back inside the larger crate and stay there with the lid down until we come back. Four raps and he'll know it's us – two long and two short.' He waited while the torch beam brandished by Hardy proceeded along the train-deck. It was just going to make it that much more tricky – having those two characters on board. When the Italian came back he spoke again. 'More company joining us for the cruise – and you wouldn't ask them to dinner either.' Four SS men ran up the link-span on to the deck and then went immediately up the port staircase behind Petrie.

'This is most unusual,' Angelo whispered in a worried tone. 'Never before have I seen this on a previous trip.'

'So this could be a special trip. Now, where's the engine-room?'

They climbed the port staircase the SS men had ascended and reached the upper deck under the wheelhouse. The vessel was swaying ponderously as the wind rose and a heavy swell developed out in the straits. An open deck led along the port side where an enormous jetty wall curved northwards to the harbour exit. The Italian left the open deck, stepped over the coaming through a doorway under the wheelhouse into an internal companionway with cabins leading off to their left. The long corridor was deserted as he stopped, tried the door of Cabin Three, opened it into darkness and switched on the light. 'This is the deputy-engineer's cabin,' he explained. 'It would make a good base for us – I know from Volpe that his deputy is on leave so we shall not be disturbed here.' Petrie stepped inside and Angelo shut and bolted the door behind him. The single cabin was small and cramped with a bunk along one wall and a washbasin in a corner. Opening a cupboard, Petrie stared at the deputy-engineer's uniform suspended from a hanger, an ornate outfit with gold buttons. Cap, jacket, trousers. 'How big is he?' he asked.

'About my size and build. Why?'

'I just wondered. Is that the key to the door?'

Angelo took the key hanging from a hook over the wash basin. 'Yes. We can lock the place when we leave.'

'Funny he leaves it unlocked while he's away.'

'He is Sicilian.' Angelo shrugged expressively. 'Now I will show you the engine-room . . .'

'Just tell me how to get there.' Petrie's tone was urgent. 'You go back down to the train-deck and try and fetch Ed and the sack up here right away – before those Gestapo men nose around too much. If they come up here and find the door locked will they be suspicious?'

'Why should they be? I have never seen them on board before.'

They left the cabin quickly and Angelo showed Petrie a staircase farther along the companionway leading down to the deck below. 'At the bottom you turn right and halfway along you will find the entrance to the engine room. I can come with you . . .'

'No! Go and get Ed – I'll meet you back in the cabin. I'll rap four times – two long, two short . . .' He went down the staircase cautiously, pausing at the bottom to look round the corner to his right. Another long companionway extended into the distance, but this one wasn't quite deserted: an Italian sentry with a rifle was leaning against the wall farther along. Without hesitation Petrie went down the last step and started walking along the companionway which was closed off from the train-deck. The air was stuffier down here, the throb of the engines a more measured beat, and as he came closer to the soldier he saw he was leaning against a steel slab hooked back from an oval-shaped doorway. The thump of the machinery became very loud. The sentry glanced at Petrie as he passed, then looked away, bored stiff with being put on guard duty at this hour. The glimpse inside the oval-shaped doorway had been too brief to show much – a glimpse of heaving pistons as the engines built up power, of men working in soiled white vests and trousers beyond a metal platform just inside the doorway. Instead of walking the full length of the lower companionway, he turned right up a staircase, reached the upper companionway which was still deserted, turned left and hurried towards the stern.

The sway of the vessel seemed to have increased up here and he wondered whether another storm was on the way as he opened a door and stepped out on deck at the stern. Below him lay the roofs of trucks at the end of the train-deck and the wind whipped at his face as the ferry swayed again, but it was the view beyond the harbour wall which interested him. A solitary boat with a red lamp glowing at its masthead was moving steadily out into the channel: Giacomo was taking up station in the straits ready for the moment when they went overboard. He went back along the open deck on the starboard side and it was uncannily deserted. As Angelo had forecast, the ship was lightly guarded and the main defences were against air attack, a quadruple of 20-mm guns fore and aft with some singles behind the bridge. The comforting thought had just passed through his mind when a door opened and a *carabiniere* soldier stepped out. A flashlight blinded Petrie for several seconds and was then switched off. 'What are you doing up here?' the soldier demanded.

'I must have come up the wrong staircase – I'm trying to find my way back to the train-deck.'

'Straight along there, then down the stairs.' The soldier went inside, closed the cabin door, and a whiff of smoke and wine which had drifted out dispersed in the wind. Petrie hurried along the deck and then stopped at the head of the starboard staircase as Laurel and Hardy came up it. The short fat brute leading the way glanced at Petrie from under his hat brim. A rounded face with small eyes and a depressed nose flattened against the skin. He appeared to be walking past Petrie without taking any further interest in him when he stopped suddenly. 'Papers!' Against all wartime regulations the torch was flashed on open deck as the restless eyes wandered over Petrie's rags while the thin man stood with his arms folded. So Hardy was one of those, full of little tricks to catch a man off guard. Petrie used his left hand to pull the identity document from his breast pocket while he kept his right hand lower, inches away from the Mauser. As the squat Gestapo official took the papers and started examining them Petrie looked at the thin man who stood chewing while he stared out over the rail. His face had a bloodless look and the eyes were dead. This, Petrie guessed, was one of the trained executioners, one of the men sent on journeys to eliminate those whose continued existence was not healthy for the Third Reich: honest patriots, men who refused to collaborate, anyone who got in the way. A pretty pair to have on board as travelling companions. But it was the small man who worried him most, the man who would restlessly prowl the vessel checking – flashing his torch into people's faces, looking at papers, testing cabin doors.

Hardy returned his papers without a word, walked off along the deck with Laurel following. As Petrie ran down the staircase the *Cariddi* was on the verge of departure. Above him on the dockside a man was uncoiling a rope from a bollard as the deck swayed heavily and the engine vibrations increased. Crossing the train-deck, he went up the port staircase and then waited at the top to see if the enemy was sending any last-minute reinforcements on board. Ropes were cast loose, the uplifted bows of the ferry moved down, locked themselves in a small break between the rails. The ferry began to move. A gap of water appeared between its hull and the harbour wall as several Sicilians came out from the interior to watch the departure while smoke poured from the funnel and the vessel made for the harbour exit stern first. But there was one final point to check. Giacomo. Petrie spotted him again as the train-ferry steamed out backwards through the harbour exit where a tall monument on the jetty wall was a blurred shadow in the night. A red lamp at a masthead swaying drunkenly some distance ahead to starboard. He was back inside the cabin as the vessel turned, swinging its bows through an angle of a hundred and eighty degrees until they pointed northeast for Giovanni, then headed for Italy.

Three men inside the tiny cabin was one too many. 'It's like being back inside that blasted crate,' Johnson grumbled. 'When do we start?'

'Now,' Petrie said, emptying the contents of the sack on the bunk. Johnson and Angelo each took a Luger pistol and spare magazines while Petrie quickly examined the explosive. The charge was a floppy, putty-like substance, cylindrical in shape, and he put it back inside the sack to take up as little room as possible. The four timers he checked cursorily, then rewrapped them in newspaper and added them to the sack. 'I'll have this under my arm and it's damned heavy,' he told Angelo, 'so how do we explain it to Volpe when we get down into the engine-room?'

'You are a stone-mason, so those are your tools,' the Italian suggested promptly. 'With the present shortages it would be almost impossible to buy new ones – so he won't think it strange at all that you carry them everywhere. Probably he'll hardly even notice – he is a very egotistical man.' He picked up a large Very pistol from the bunk. 'This, of course, is vital for signalling to Giacomo, but it's too big to take with us. I suggest we leave it here for the moment.'

'Agreed,' Petrie said. 'This cabin is a perfect base – it's so close to the open deck when the time comes to jump for it. Angelo, how long does it normally take the train-ferry to disembark passengers and cargo and leave Giovanni?'

'Half an hour – but you can never be sure.'

'We'll play it as it comes then. I can't estimate how long it will take me to plant the charges.' He picked up the sack, tucked it carefully under his arm. 'Incidentally, there's an Italian sentry guarding the engine-room door . . .'

'That has never happened before!' Angelo was momentarily appalled. 'But my bottle of French cognac may do the trick!' He spoke of the spirit as though it were a weapon of war. 'If possible we must avoid trouble until you have planted your charges.'

'If humanly possible,' Petrie emphasized. 'Now, you'd better go out first – it might look odd if someone saw a couple of peasants leaving this cabin.' The Italian switched off the light, unlocked the door, stepped out into the companionway, froze as he saw the retreating back of an SS man in the distance. The German went out on deck at the stern, disappeared behind the closing door. Angelo waited a moment to make sure he wasn't returning, then beckoned. He locked the door when they had come out, then led the way. At the bottom of the staircase to the lower companionway he paused, looked up at Petrie in bewilderment. 'No sentry.' Petrie peered round the corner: the companionway was deserted, the engine-room door still folded back against the bulkhead. 'Hurry it up!' he snapped. 'Before he comes back.' The

into Angelo who shouted to make himself heard as he introduced them to a large fat man in his forties wearing dark trousers and a soiled vest. Chief Engineer Volpe was a fleshy-faced individual with a thin smear of dark moustache and greedy eyes. 'This is my cousin, Paolo,' Angelo said affably. 'He has wished to be an engineer all his life but when he was young there was not enough money . . .'

'Down here we run the ship,' Volpe began at once with an expansive gesture of his large hand. 'The bridge think they run the *Cariddi*, but the passage takes only thirty minutes so what can go wrong? Whereas down here we must watch everything. Now, you see this dial over here . . .'

'Pietro, also a cousin . . .' Angelo introduced as Petrie came round the corner and nodded, but Volpe hardly glanced at him as he went on expounding about the hazards facing a chief engineer. Johnson noticed immediately that Petrie was no longer carrying his sack, that he must already have hidden it in some convenient spot, and then Angelo was producing his bottle of French cognac and Volpe was drinking their health as Johnson gazed round with assumed wonderment. A few minutes later when the engineer's back was turned Petrie caught his eye and winked, and when Volpe swung round again he was holding a hand to his head as though the heat was getting too much for him. 'Pietro,' Johnson shouted quickly, 'suffers from seasickness, but it will soon pass off.' Volpe shrugged, his only comment on the weaklings of this world, and went on showing them his marvels, pausing only to shout an order to one of the crew occasionally. By moving round a little, the American observed there were six other men in the engine-room, and the presence of so many crew worried him: Petrie was going to have a hellish job planting the charges under these conditions. At least two men were close to the engine-shafts and Johnson knew that these were one of Petrie's prime objectives. A few moments later two things startled him: Petrie had vanished and the soldier with a rifle was standing on the platform above them while he peered down inside the room.

Johnson froze, then deliberately relaxed and folded his arms as he wandered after Volpe to another part of the engine-room with Angelo. Pressing back his worn cuff, he checked his watch. Christ! Eight minutes to Giovanni: Petrie could never plant the charges and get out of the engine-room before they docked now, and with the guard peering down from above he might be seen at any second. Johnson was sweating profusely in the steamy heat, but he suspected he would have been sweating in any case as he listened to the engineer's boastings and kept an eye on the soldier. For God's sake move, man, he prayed. Go away, get lost! 'Have some more cognac,' Angelo offered genially and Johnson hastily stared at some chomping machinery as Volpe upended the bottle for the third time. The chief engineer seemed to have deputized his duties to another member of the crew who stood watching a lot of gauges and issuing brief instructions. Johnson looked up at the platform again and his prayer had been answered: the soldier had gone. 'We have a very important cargo for our next trip, Angelo,' Volpe said grandly. 'And for the trip after that and the one after that. For hours, in fact. The Germans, you know!'

'Really?' Angelo seemed unimpressed as he raised his voice above the beating pistons. 'I thought Germans were crossing all the time?'

'But this is their big tank division . . .' Volpe belched loudly, stopped in mid-sentence as though he had said too much. 'I like your cognac,' he went on rather superfluously. 'Now this gauge tells you . . .' Johnson stood limply with his arms still folded and an interested look on his face which gave no indication of the shock he was experiencing. 'Their big tank division . . .' The 29th Panzer Grenadier Division was about to start its crucial crossing to Sicily. The airborne forces must have dropped and Kesselring had reacted instantly, ordering the 29th Panzer across the straits. And the *Cariddi* was still afloat, pushing her way through the swell to meet the waiting Germans on the Giovanni dockside. He could already feel the vessel slowing down and the clangour in the engine-room seemed louder as the engines slowed. Standing on the metal plates, surrounded by machinery thumping like a steam-hammer, fighting the dizziness which the clammy heat and the vessel's movements were bringing on, Johnson knew that Petrie had not yet managed to plant the charges. Volpe returned the half-empty bottle to Angelo who capped it and put the cognac back inside his pocket, knowing that the engineer wanted them to leave. 'If we can't get any transport out of Giovanni we may be coming back with you,' he said aimably and Volpe, remembering that the bottle was still not empty, looked disappointed as he scratched the back of his head.

'I am sorry, but no civilians will be allowed on board from now on . . .'

He broke off and started issuing instructions, bawling at the top of his voice. Angelo turned dubiously to Johnson as the engines churned more slowly and the American started back towards the ladder. He knew what Petrie was planning to do: since there was no chance of planting the explosives while the crew were driving the ship, he had hidden himself away in the hope that the engine-room would empty briefly before her next passage back to Messina. It was typical of Petrie to take this decision, knowing that he might be marooned in the bowels of the vessel, and Johnson was careful not to look for him as he went up the ladder followed by Angelo. And if the sentry was still waiting outside in the companionway there was another problem: he had seen three men go down into the engine-room, but only two would emerge. When he stepped over the coaming into the companionway the sentry was there, leaning against the wall with his eyes shut. The poor devil had gone to sleep standing up. As Angelo came out behind him the sentry stirred, blinked himself awake, then called out to them as they were walking away.

'Where is the other man?'

Johnson went back to him, stared at him closely. 'He came out ahead of us. You must have seen him.'

'Ah! I remember now,' the sentry lied quickly. 'Of course!'

They returned the way they had come; along the companionway, up the staircase, along the upper companionway. But when he reached Cabin Three Johnson walked past it and went out cautiously on to the open deck. It was again deserted and after the heat of the engine room the chill of the early morning wind cut through his shabby clothes as he kept inside the shadow of the wheelhouse and looked down. The view gave him a nasty shock.

On the train-deck below the passengers had moved near the bows, huddled closely together in their anxiety to leave the vessel which was now passing inside the harbour at Giovanni. Already the ferry was rocking less, gliding forward very slowly, and in the distance under hooded lamps which lined the dock-side the Wehrmacht was waiting. Trucks, petrol wagons, orderly rows of men seen only dimly in their soft-capped Panzer uniforms. And a train of many coaches, some kind of goods train. The spearhead of the 29th Panzer was ready to come aboard. A nerve-racking sight for the American. Perhaps he was looking at the death of an invasion, the Allied invasion.

As the vessel bumped the dockside, shuddering to a halt, ropes were thrown for mooring and the bows began to ascend. This was going to be a damned quick disembarkation, followed by an equally quick embarkation. 'It makes it more difficult, does it not?' Angelo said over his shoulder. Johnson turned and they went back to the cabin, closing and re-locking the door before they put on the light.

'Jim can't plant those charges while the crew's hanging around,' Johnson said savagely.

'They always come up,' Angelo told him. 'I have seen it happen when I stayed on board to give Volpe another drink. Can you imagine them staying down in that atmosphere for hours when they can come up for air while she's in port?'

'If he's not back here inside thirty minutes we'll be making another trip to that engine-room. And this time it won't be so easy.' Johnson put away the cigarette he had taken out from his crumpled pack; he was dying for a smoke but the atmosphere inside the tiny cabin was already suffocating. 'It won't be easy for several reasons,' he went on, staring hard at the Italian. 'The boat will be far more crowded. You heard Volpe say no civilians are being allowed on board, so we'll be spotted the moment anyone sees us. And tight German security will be in operation.'

'Anything else?' Angelo inquired ironically.

'I think that will be enough to occupy us.' Johnson pulled out the three stick-grenades they had hidden under the bunk's pillow and rolled them up neatly in a blanket. But there was something else he hadn't mentioned to Angelo. When Petrie had planted the explosive charges he would also set the timers and the whole fiendish mechanism would start ticking down to zero. And Johnson was pretty sure that the goods coaches waiting at the dockside to come aboard were an ammunition train. The Germans were about to convert the *Cariddi* into a floating powder house.

Forty minutes later they were still trapped inside the cabin by the constant procession of booted feet tramping along the companionway. They had sat in the darkness for what seemed hours, and while they had waited they had listened to the grinding of colliding buffers as an engine pushed the ammunition train up the link-span and inside the train-deck; to the shouting of German voices; to the endless tramp of the Panzer troops' footsteps marching past the cabin. The footsteps were becoming less frequent when, for the third time, an unknown hand grasped the door-handle from the outside and turned it, but the owner of this hand was more persistent. He rattled the door, then leaned against it with all his weight and pushed. The Italian, facing the door as he sat on the bunk alongside Johnson, held his knife pointed at the panel as his heart pumped faster in the darkness. The lock wasn't all that strong and it only needed sufficient pressure to burst it open. Johnson also held a knife ready for use – if shots were fired, if the alarm was raised at this stage with Petrie still imprisoned down in the engine-room, it would be a disaster. The handle was turned again, more pressure was applied. Some bastard who wants to travel first-class, the American thought. Well, first-class on this trip meant a knife in the belly. The assault on the door ceased abruptly. They sat in an odour of sweat and animal fear as they listened to footsteps retreating along the companionway. The ship's engines were beating faster when they heard the whirr of the mechanical bows descending, the sharp thud as it met the deck. Only seconds later the vessel started moving, backing stern first out of Giovanni harbour.

'We'll go get him now,' Johnson said hoarsely.

Angelo fumbled for the switch, pressed it, blinked in the unaccustomed light. 'In those clothes, it would be too dangerous for you to come with me, but no one will notice me in this uniform.' He stood up, studied himself quickly in the mirror over the washbasin. The deputy-engineer's uniform he had slipped on earlier fitted him well; in fact, he felt quite pleased with his appearance. He took the marine cap Johnson handed him and tried it on his head. 'A little too small, but it will do. It has to be this way,' he insisted. 'Ashore the postman is never noticed – people accept him. It is the same on board – a man in marine uniform is invisible. I must find out what the position is.'

'All right, but for God's sake be back in five minutes. We've got to get Jim out of the engine room before the charges detonate.' Johnson put down his knife and pulled out his handkerchief to mop his face and forehead as Angelo switched off the light and unlocked the door. The Italian looked both ways, saw the companionway was empty, stepped out and pulled the door shut behind him. A second later the squat Gestapo man Petrie called Hardy walked round the corner from under the wheelhouse. He stared and the Italian knew that he had seen him closing the door, and from the frown on the German's face he also knew it could only be a matter of seconds before he was recognized. The marine uniform was puzzling the Gestapo man for a moment, but he'd get there, Angelo had no doubt about that. Luckily, he seemed to be on his own. 'I have seen you earlier on board ship,' the German snapped. 'What is there inside that cabin?'

'Dirty vests and soiled linen,' Angelo told him insolently. 'None of your bloody business.' He raised his voice so Johnson could hear him and made his reply as provocative as he could. The Gestapo man stared at him again without positive recognition, muttered an oath and grabbed at the handle. Inside the cabin Johnson couldn't find his knife so he changed his tactics as the door opened, a rectangle of light flooded in, and the German entered. Johnson's hands grasped the Gestapo man by the throat, hauling him farther inside the cabin as Angelo lunged at his back with his shoulder, forcing him right inside the cabin. The Italian followed him, squeezed himself past the door and rammed it shut as he switched on the light. By now Johnson had toppled the German on to the bunk, was lying half on top of him as he maintained the pressure of both hands round the thick neck, jabbing his thumbs hard into the windpipe.

Temporarily caught off balance, the German began reacting violently, punching with his left hand at the American's face while he shoved his right hand inside his coat. Angelo grabbed at the right hand, forced it out, tore the Luger viciously from him, grabbed at the other hand. In the confined space of the cabin it was difficult and the Italian held on to the struggling hands, pulling them back behind the man's head as Johnson's slippery fingers tried to hold their grip. The German had his mouth open, attempting to shout, but the thumbs dug into his windpipe stopping him emitting anything more than a strangled gurgle as the fight went on. It can be surprisingly difficult to kill a man and the German had a lot of strength in his short body. Tearing his left hand free from Angelo's grip, he forked two fingers and aimed for Johnson's eyes. The American jerked his head back, still kept his grip on the German's throat as Angelo grabbed the man's wrist and forced the attacking arm down on the bunk. The German's heels hammered frantically and Johnson held on, tightening his grip, then the heels were thudding only spasmodically and suddenly they stopped, felt limp. Johnson waited a little longer before he released his throttling hold and wiped the back of his hand over his streaming forehead. The hand came away smeared with blood where the stabbing fingernails had gouged him. 'Christ! That was rough.'

'We must get him out of here,' Angelo urged, 'put him over the side – it isn't far . . .'

Johnson compelled himself to think, but it took only a few seconds to reject the idea. 'Too dangerous – we'd bump into someone. Leave him here and take a look round. But hurry! And leave the key so I can lock myself in – four raps when you come back, two long, two short . . .'

Angelo left the cabin, heard the lock turn in the door behind him, walked at a leisurely pace along the now deserted corridor despite Johnson's injunction to hurry: people who hurried drew attention to themselves. He went light-footed down the staircase to the lower companionway, pausing to look for a guard outside the engine-room. The Italian had gone – and in his place stood a German sentry with a machine-pistol looped over his shoulder. As Johnson had predicted, things were deteriorating. Still concealed behind the staircase wall, he took out his knife, fixed it inside the marine cap, then walked towards the sentry while he fluttered the cap as though the heat were becoming a bit much. He walked forward at the even pace a ship's officer would have adopted, knowing that within minutes the alarm would be sounded – after his encounter with the sentry. It had to be quick; it had to work the first time. The sentry watched him coming without interest; as Angelo had foreseen, the uniform was accepted without a trace of suspicion. But there might be another guard inside on the platform. As he came close to the engine-room door the sentry was so uninterested in the new arrival that he looked back through the open door, but then he looked back again as Angelo arrived, stopped not too close to him and spoke in Italian. 'I suppose Engineer Volpe is down there – there's some question about changed landing instructions when we reach Messina and I want to have a word with him.' He ran the words together in a gabble, but the German didn't understand a word of Italian. As he spread his hands to show his incomprehension Angelo let the cap fall, thrust his knife forward. The blade went in deep, the German gulped, and then he was falling. Angelo grabbed him as he fell, struggled to shift him back out of the companionway, but the weight was enormous and the soldier's limp feet caught the coaming. Angelo heaved him half over his shoulder, staggered on to the platform, dropped him and with an effort retrieved the knife, as he scanned the scene below. Volpe was standing with his back to him and the crew was concentrating on turning the vessel's bows through a hundred and eighty degrees to face Messina.

From behind a machine-cover Petrie stood up, ran to the foot of the ladder, came up it fast. 'Charges planted, whole bloody lot,' he said quickly as he reached the platform. 'The crew cleared out when the ship docked, but they came just as I'd finished . . .' Petrie looked gaunt, hollow-eyed, was streaming with sweat. Down in the engine-room Volpe turned, saw them, stared in astonishment, moved towards the voice-pipe, then stopped as Petrie aimed the Mauser and waggled it. Volpe moved away from the voice-pipe and now the rest of the crew were turning their heads. The moment we leave here Volpe will inform the bridge, Petrie thought grimly. 'Let him go,' he said to Angelo and the Italian released the body which rolled off the edge of its own volition and crashed to the deckplates twenty feet below. 'We'll have to move fast,' Petrie said as he went into the companionway. 'Where's Ed?'

'In the cabin . . .'

'You go first – you're in uniform. Any sign of trouble – take your cap off to warn me.'

Angelo put the cap he had retrieved from the companionway floor on his head, walked rapidly towards the staircase. With Petrie close behind him he ran lightly up the steps, paused at the top, took off his cap and instead of turning right along the upper companionway he went up the next staircase opposite. Petrie saw the warning signal, understood that there was someone in the companionway, and when he looked round the corner he saw an SS man close to Cabin Three. The German was kneeling on one knee, fastening his boot, a task which occupied his full attention as Petrie nipped across the companionway and followed up the staircase. Pushing open a door at the top, the Italian came out into the open on an upper deck. The chilling wind and the darkness hit him; moonset was at 12.30 PM and the blackness was total. He waited while Petrie followed him up, straining to get his eyes used to the night while the vessel completed its turn and the heavy swell splashed below him. 'We have to go along this deck,' he whispered, 'down a staircase, and then we're near the wheel-house.'

'Keep in front – and keep your eyes open!'

Angelo started walking towards the bows as the vessel headed for Messina. It was so dark that he didn't see the man in the open doorway until he had passed him. He took off his cap, hoping to God that Petrie could see the action. The figure waiting in the doorway was the tall Gestapo officer, presumably searching for Hardy, the man Petrie called Laurel. 'Just a minute! You there! Come back here!' The fluency of his Italian startled Angelo, but only for a moment. Swinging round on his heel, he took a long stride back to the German who was now standing on the deck, ramming his knife hard into the man's stomach. Petrie's knife entered his back as though the movements had been synchronized and the German sagged with only a gasp. 'Get him over the side!' Petrie snapped. 'We don't want anyone finding this yet.' Between them they hoisted the body up to the rail, shoved it over the edge, and the distant splash could have been a wave meeting the vessel as the *Cariddi* steamed forward and the body drifted back towards the thrashing twin screws at the stern. Angelo leaned over the rail, but there was nothing to see, only the shadowed heave of the sea. 'He'll be mincemeat for the fishes,' he said cold-bloodedly, and started walking again along the deck. The incident hadn't occupied more than twenty seconds.

Near the head of the staircase he slowed down, then stopped. From the deck below near the wheelhouse he could hear people talking in German. He tiptoed forward, looked over the rail, saw a blur of soft-capped heads below. There were anything up to half a dozen Panzer troops gathered under the wheelhouse while they killed time gossiping. He went back to where Petrie had halted. 'German troops just under the wheelhouse – so we can't get down that way. They must be pretty close to Cabin Three.'

'We'll go back the other way. You've seen Giacomo's out there, thank God.'

As they went back the way they had come a red light was bobbing in the night some distance away to their right as the *mafioso* took his craft on a course parallel to the *Cariddi*'s. There were other vessels' lights also in the straits so Giacomo's was conspicuous only by its colour. Leading the way with his cap on his head, Angelo turned down the staircase to the upper companionway. To his relief he found the corridor deserted. 'Run!' Petrie whispered behind him. They ran, pulled up before they reached Cabin Three which was close to the wheelhouse where the Panzer troops were chatting, then walked up to the door. Angelo rapped quietly with his knuckles, praying the Panzer troops wouldn't hear him, that Johnson would. The key turned at once and the American stood in the doorway with a knife in his hand. Pushing inside, the Italian grabbed the Very pistol from under the pillow on which Hardy's head rested. Johnson reached over him to pick up the blanket folded round the grenades as Petrie looked over his shoulder, saw the dead Gestapo officer and wasted no words on comment. 'The alarm will have been given, Ed, so expect trouble – a heap of it . . .'

In the short time since they had arrived at the cabin Petrie had released the wooden holster from round his waist, snapped the holster on to the Mauser butt, and now the weapon was ready for long-range use. Fast fire. Johnson thrust one of the stick-grenades in his hand and he pushed this down inside his belt, then he glanced out both ways and left the cabin, running along the companionway towards the stern. They had to get up that staircase again on to the upper deck where they would drop off the side after Angelo fired his Very pistol. Petrie was halfway to the staircase when two SS men came down it with pistols in their hands. He fired as he ran, one short burst, and the Germans had dropped when he reached the bottom of the staircase. He was on the first step when the door opened at the top and two more appeared. He fired upwards, stopped, fired again to discourage anyone else up there. A figure appeared, darted back out of sight as he raised the muzzle again and then didn't fire. 'No good!' he warned the others, then he jumped over the crumpled bodies of the two SS men and ran at top speed towards the stern. The situation was definitely getting difficult: they should have been off the ship before the alarm was raised. He reached the door at the end of the companionway, pushed it open with his gun muzzle and heard feet running along the upper deck towards him from his right. No chance of diving off that side – they'd be shot as they jumped. He went the only way he could – down a staircase leading to the train-deck.

Angelo followed behind him with Johnson bringing up the rear. As they came close to the door the American looked back and saw a soldier standing well back along the companionway, lifting his rifle. Aiming down the corridor would be like firing in a shooting-gallery: he couldn't miss. With the rolled blanket under one arm, Johnson swung round, aimed the Luger, fired one shot. He had taken prizes for shooting moving targets but this was the process in reverse: the marksman was moving, the target stationary. The soldier was falling as he turned and went through the doorway, and as the door swung shut behind him a bullet came through it. Johnson went down the steps to the train-deck three at a time and then he ran out of space. The three tracks were fully occupied by the ammunition train.

'This way!'

Petrie called out from behind a coach on the middle track and Johnson followed them down a narrow corridor dimly lit by the blue lights with his shoulders brushing the coaches on either side. It felt weird –

walking through what was apparently a goods yard with the floor under you heaving and falling while the couplings rattled gently with the motion and the coaches creaked. At the front Petrie walked with the Mauser gripped in both hands, a fresh magazine inside it while he watched for movement ahead. There had to be guards down here – this was the Wehrmacht for Christ's sake! His earlier fatigue had gone, his faculties were keen and sharp-edged, and his eyes were growing accustomed to the gloom as he walked forward at an even pace, not dawdling, not hurrying. There was shouting somewhere above them, but down here on the train-deck it was surprisingly quiet, so quiet he could hear the lapping of the water against the vessel's sides. They had one chance only of getting clear – they had come deeper into the vessel, which was probably the last place the search parties would expect them to run for. He was walking past another coach with the door half-open when a uniformed figure stepped out from between two coaches ahead of him and the man started addressing him in German. He hadn't expected any trouble and Petrie didn't want any noise, so while the soldier stared at him dull-wittedly Petrie raised his gun muzzle and brought it crashing down on the soft cap. The force of the blow jarred him up the arms and the German collapsed without a sound. Three more coaches brought him close to the bows and he slowed down as he heard a clatter of feet coming down a staircase, then a voice giving orders in German. 'Hans! You take a file of men between each line of coaches! Check carefully between each coach! Use your torches to check the roofs . . .'

Petrie pushed the other two further back the way they had come with his hands. When they reached the open coach he gestured upwards and they scrambled inside noiselessly, then he followed them. There wasn't much damned room – on this trip he seemed to be specializing in confined spaces like crates and one-man cabins. Now for the real tricky operation – closing the door. His heart was pounding so loud he felt the others must hear it as he eased the door sideways inch by inch, but the only sounds he heard were the shuffle of feet as the Panzer troops commenced their search of the train-deck. The door closed silently on its well-oiled runners. Wonderful German efficiency! When it was shut he used his torch to drop the handle into the locked position and then he flashed it on the piled-up boxes which three-parts filled the coach. On one box was stamped the legend 7.5 cm LK 70 PK 41. This was definitely an ammunition train. 'Wonder how long it will take?' Johnson whispered in the darkness. No one replied. No one knew as they waited and listened to the muffled sounds of the Germans searching, rattling at the handles as they checked each coach.

The search was quicker than Petrie had expected as the unseen men moved along the train-deck, and when he judged they had moved some distance away from the coach where they hid he unlocked the door, eased it open a few inches and listened. He heard faint sounds above the slap of the water against the ship's hull – voices, the clink of metal against metal – but he wasn't prepared to stay aboard any longer. The charges were timed to detonate any time from now on. Dropping to the deck, he looked both ways and saw nothing. He beckoned to the others and went towards the bows of the vessel. This area, at least, should be safe: it had just been searched.

The bows were a vague silhouette looming against a starlit night and here several petrol tankers, brought on board after the train, were parked close together. He climbed the port staircase slowly, step by step, and when he came under the wheelhouse he saw beyond the port rail a red lamp swaying in the distance. Giacomo was still there, still keeping a course parallel to the train-ferry as it drew closer and closer to Sicily. The others crowded up behind him as he reached the deck and peered along its darkness. Had a shadow moved there or was it simply strain – the nerves expecting something to be there? 'Send the signal,' he whispered. Angelo pushed past him, went to the rail, raised the Very pistol high above his head and fired it. High over the straits a green light exploded, flaring brilliantly. 'Get over the side!' Petrie rapped out. 'Both of you! Head for that red light fast!' A German soldier came round the corner from the companionway with a rifle grasped in both hands. He stopped, splayed his legs, aimed the weapon in one action. Petrie fired a short burst and the German sagged as Angelo went over the side. All hell was going to break loose now. The sound of a racing engine was coming closer from out at sea as Johnson dumped the blanket on the deck, unrolled it. 'Grenades!' Petrie swore at him. 'Get over the side!' Johnson was poised on the rail when bullets began spattering all round him and a wood splinter ripped across his forehead. As the American left the rail Petrie fired a long continuous burst straight down the upper deck where the shots had come from, arcing the gun slightly from side to side. He thought he heard thuds on the deck as he reloaded and the shots ceased. Then he picked up one of the grenades Johnson had left, went to the archway under the wheelhouse and threw the grenade blind as far as he could. That should clear the companionway for a moment.

The racing engine from the sea was a roar now. A searchlight came on, almost blinded him for a fraction of a second, then it dropped to sea-level. An E-boat was alongside, attracted by the strange Very signal. The craft was close to the train-ferry as it swivelled its light over the water, passed Angelo's head, then swung back to hold him in its glare as the manned machine-gun began to chatter. The Italian took a deep breath, dived under the water as Petrie ran to the rail, measured the distance, tossed the grenade and dropped flat on the deck close to the last grenade Johnson had left. He didn't see it happen, but the missile landed amidships, detonated before the crew knew what was happening. The explosion reached the fuel instantly, there was a dull boom and the E-boat disintegrated as flame flared and debris rained down on the deck of the *Cariddi*. Something hot seared the back of Petrie's neck and then it was quieter, quiet enough to hear the clatter of boots coming up the port staircase from the train-deck. Still sprawled on the deck, he saw a jostle of movement on the staircase as he grasped the last grenade and threw it. His face was buried in the deck when the crack came and when he looked up the staircase was empty and there was a strong smell of burning in his nostrils. He stood up with the Mauser and emptied the magazine along the upper deck which must be clear if he was to have any chance of survival when he went over the side. Hoisting himself up, he sat on the rail, pushed off, and the sea came up to meet him out of the darkness with a splash and a thump, then he was swimming furiously away from the ferry to get clear of the twin screws.

Hitting the sea was a shock; the water was horribly cold, probably felt colder than it was in his fatigued state, and swimming with his boots on was damned difficult. It was also incredibly dark, utterly black, and there was still a heavy swell as he swam forward with strokes growing in power. Once he thought he heard shots, but when he glanced back only the ferry's stern showed as it headed at top speed for Sicily, its own motion taking Petrie out of the firing line. The red lamp he could see but it seemed to be changing position and he hoped to God Giacomo wasn't puttering about trying to find them. All the Sicilian had to do was to stay put and they'd find him. With luck and the strength to reach him. The waves jostled his face, bounded under him, so it was like swimming on a sea of rubber as odd sensations began stirring inside his head. It was an illusion, of course, this dizzying whirling sensation as the waves gyrated round him, but it was no illusion that he was on the verge of fainting. The steady beat of the *Cariddi*'s engines was fading away and the only sound he could hear was the sloshing slap of waves as he forced his weary arms and legs to continue the rhythm, to continue swimming towards the swaying red lamp which he now believed was stationary. And he was becoming waterlogged: the weight of his sodden clothing was pressing his body lower in the water as the red lamp came closer with painful slowness. The dizziness became worse as he felt a powerful current pulling at him, sucking at his exhausted body to carry him away from the waiting red lamp. He had a moment of rebellion against this last enemy – the current – as he took an enormous breath of the cold night air and thrust out with all his remaining strength, trying to break free from the current's clutch. Then he felt something scrape his shoulder, hook deep inside his sodden clothes, graze the bare flesh under his shirt, a boat-hook which held him only because his clothes were so sodden since dry clothes would have torn apart under the pressure. The boat-hook held by

Giacomo hauled him steadily forward and then hands were grasping him, lifting him, hauling him aboard as Johnson and Angelo heaved him over the side and deposited him in the bottom of the boat.

'Are you all right?' the American asked anxiously.

'Fine . . .' Petrie gasped out as he flopped for a moment, staring up at their faces, at the red lamp beyond, at the brittle stars beyond that. The fainting feeling was coming back. 'Get me upright . . .' They sat him up with his back against the mast, a tall structure with wooden pegs like rungs projecting from the pole. Petrie had heard about these strange craft somewhere: the rungs were for the captain of the craft to climb to the masthead and direct operations from his elevated position when he saw the swordfish approaching. 'Thanks,' he said to Giacomo, then remembered that the man was a deaf mute. Short and squat, the Sicilian was large-bellied by the lamp's glow, and it was to the lamp he was pointing now as he picked up a shotgun and waved to them to keep their heads down. They waited with huddled heads while he aimed. The gun barked, the lamp shattered, showering glass into the boat. Giacomo had just used the most effective method available for putting out the lamp which could locate them.

'Those charges,' Johnson called out hoarsely from the stern near the outboard motor. 'You planted them where you wanted them?'

'Just where they ought to be – all of them,' Petrie assured him. 'Two ten-pounders in the propeller-shaft tunnels alongside the first bearing – and they're connected up, so both shafts should go at the same moment. The big job – the forty-pounder – I put inside a lubricating drum against the starboard side.'

'They'll all go together?'

'They're set to, but there'll probably be a thirty- or forty-second gap between them.'

'What will happen?' Johnson rested his bare feet on a rope coil as he dabbed at his blood-streaked forehead with a cloth the silent Giacomo had provided.

'At a guess the engine-room should flood inside thirty seconds, the next compartment inside a minute. I reckon the ferry will go down about five minutes after the first detonation.'

'The Germans will be searching the whole engine-room,' Johnson pointed out soberly.

'They will, and I expected the charges to detonate before now. But an engine-room is a complex place to search.'

Giacomo went to the stern, indicating with gestures that he wanted Johnson to move. Crouching low over the outboard, the Sicilian pulled at the starter cord and the motor growled into life as Petrie glanced anxiously around. There was no sign of other craft in the vicinity but the straits crawled with E-boats and he was counting on the expected detonations to distract them. The motor built up power, the boat began to move south down the channel towards distant Malta as four pairs of eyes stared in the direction where the train-ferry had vanished in the darkness.

They were staring in the same direction when the first detonation came, a gigantic hollow thump like a single blow against a giant drum. There was no flash with this detonation, no immediate smoke as the searchlights of three E-boats came on and roamed over her, only the hollow thump which seemed to make no difference to the ferry's progress until Petrie noticed a change in direction as the silhouette of funnel and high bridge and superstructure became foreshortened.

'She's altered course!' he shouted.

'She's heading for Paradiso Bay,' Angelo said.

'Her steering's smashed!' Petrie blinked to get a clearer view. 'The next charge will get her.'

The E-boats' searchlights remained focused on the train-ferry as she continued to turn, her steering mechanism smashed beyond repair while more E-boats scudded across the water towards the stricken vessel. The second detonation, the forty-pounder, made its predecessor sound like a tap on a door, and the straits seemed to shake as the detonation's thunder swept across the water and into the mountains so that in Messina and Giovanni it came to them like the crash of a whole battery of six-inch naval guns firing at the same moment. Seconds later there was a great flash, more illuminating than dawn, followed by another and then another. In the stern Johnson stared in awe. A whole ammunition train was starting to go. The explosive power confined inside the train-deck was unimaginable. Another detonation came and they felt its blast as it was followed by two more and the fire took hold, fire such as Johnson had never seen before, as enormous tongues of flame leapt over the crippled ferry and lit the straits with a glow which reflected redly in the grey waters. Then a fresh detonation of appalling violence, erupting like a minor Etna as flames soared and wavered in the wind and the smoke came, great belching black clouds so that soon the ferry was shattered from end to end, a floating furnace burning to the waterline as petrol flooded out, spread over the deck, engulfing men and materials as it ignited in a terrible combustion while the E-boats scurried about the doomed vessel like distracted ants, taking care not to speed in too close to the inferno. As the ammunition coaches jammed close together on the train-deck exploded with a continuous crackle they began to send debris in all directions. Part of the vessel's superstructure was already gone, exposing the train-deck beyond, outlining the ferry clearly in the flames – the silhouette of a petrol tanker, the crumbling bridge, the still-intact funnel, shadows against the red glare which itself was brilliant against the curtain of black smoke behind it. The petrol tanker burst, vanished, and now the funnel and the high bridge were going, heeling over as they were consumed by the flames and the vessel became a floating platform of burning petrol and exploding ammunition. Another detonation came, hurtling up white-hot debris which travelled a vast distance and showered down on patrolling E-boats which suddenly fled away from the disaster area in panic. Then the ship settled stern first, raising its bows briefly so they pointed skyward, their plates red-hot and glowing, and went down slowly. Despite the distance Petrie fancied he heard a hideous hiss as the water closed over the ferociously heated remnants.

No one spoke for a moment as they sat dazed by what they had witnessed, then Petrie stirred himself and went to the bows of the boat to keep watch. Johnson found him there an hour later as they proceeded steadily down the straits through the darkness, found him crumpled up, fast asleep. 'This I won't let him forget,' he told Angelo with a weary grin. 'Caught asleep on watch duty?'

In the early morning when the glowing disc of the sun climbed above the eastern horizon to roast Sicily afresh they were becalmed, out of petrol, out of sight of land as they floated on a gentle undulation of pale blue sea which caught the sun's reflections. Only Johnson and Giacomo were awake, and appropriately enough it was the American who had climbed to the top of the mast and hung there while he waved his shirt madly. Appropriately enough because the US flag was fluttering from the mast of the PT boat roaring towards them across the peaceful sea, the PT boat which was to take them southwest to Malta, away from the coast of Sicily where Allied troops were pouring on to the beaches prior to driving inland and conquering the island in thirty-three days.

Epilogue

Sometimes it is what happens later which is significant.

After the invasion Don Vito Scelba received his reward, largely on the strength of the bald but accurate report which Petrie felt obliged to submit to AFHQ. He did not become mayor of Palermo; instead he was given a more powerful post in the Allied administration which took over the conquered island. And while he used his position to increase his influence, Scelba was secretly organizing large-scale raids on Allied supply dumps, looting them systematically for the black market which plagued first Sicily and, later, Italy.

One thing led to another. The huge profits from the black market operation helped to build up his political power; by the end of the war he had linked up with the mafia in Naples, with the criminal underworld of Marseilles, and with the most powerful of the five families controlling the New York mafia. He had re-established an international mafia. Gradually it extended its operations over half the globe, operations involving prostitution, currency manipulation – and the drug traffic. It was this organization Scelba built up which years later directed the drug traffic which threatens the vitality of so many western nations – a system made possible because the Allies approached the Sicilian mafia for help in the middle of a war.

The ambush which eventually closed round half the western world was sprung in July 1943.

The death of Don Vito Scelba was ironic: he died of the dreaded *lupara* sickness. An ageing man, still travelling round Sicily in shirt-sleeves and braces, still peering at the world through his tortoiseshell glasses, he walked out of a Palermo hotel one hot July morning and found his car wasn't waiting for him. Ten years earlier he would have been instantly suspicious, but Scelba was no longer the *mafioso* who had stabbed a fireman to death one night at Scopana Halt. Instead, he lingered on the pavement edge while he wondered what had happened. Then a car came, a car driven very fast by four young men in dark glasses who, as they passed him, emptied their shotguns at point-blank range. When he fell on the pavement no one ran to help him. Don Vito Scelba had outlived his time.